Dorothy Simpson worked first as a French teacher and then for many years as a marriage guidance counsellor before turning to writing full time. She is married with three children and lives near Maidstone in Kent, the background to the Thanet series. *The Night She Died*, *Six Feet Under* and *Puppet for a Corpse* are the first three of the twelve novels in the series. The fifth, *Last Seen Alive*, won the Crime Writers' Association's Silver Dagger Award in 1985.

'Simpson can disinter the past with the best of them, and her portrait of a small community is matchless' *The Times*

'Dorothy Simpson is a contemporary Agatha Christie, renowned for weaving murder mysteries round credible characters in very English settings' *Annabel*

'Thrillers that are both well written and crisply plotted do not come along every day, so a Dorothy Simpson novel is a welcome and engrossing treat' *The Lady*

'All the traditional home comforts of English village murder, with a final twist' *Observer*

DOROTHY SIMPSON

INSPECTOR THANET OMNIBUS

THE NIGHT SHE DIED
SIX FEET UNDER
PUPPET FOR A CORPSE

WARNER BOOKS

A *Warner* Book

This edition first published in Great Britain in 1994 by Warner Books
Reprinted 1994 (twice), 1995 (twice), 1996, 1997, 1998 (twice), 2000

Inspector Thanet Omnibus Copyright © 1994 by Dorothy Simpson

Previously published separately:
The Night She Died first published in Great Britain in 1981
by Michael Joseph Ltd
Published in 1986 by Sphere Books Ltd
Reprinted 1990, 1991
Copyright © 1981 by Dorothy Simpson
Six Feet Under first published in Great Britain in 1982
by Michael Joseph Ltd
Published in 1990 by Sphere Books Ltd
Reprinted in 1992, 1993, 1995, 1996, 1999 by Warner
Copyright © 1982 Dorothy Simpson
Puppet for a Corpse first published in Great Britain in 1983
by Michael Joseph Ltd
Published in 1985 by Sphere Books Ltd
Reprinted 1986, 1988, 1989, 1990 (twice)
Reprinted in 1992, 1993, 1994, 1995 by Warner
Copyright © 1983 by Dorothy Simpson

The moral right of the author has been asserted.

A CIP catalogue record for this book
is available from the British Library.

ISBN 0 7515 0810 1

Printed in England by Clays Ltd, St Ives plc

Warner Books
A Division of
Little, Brown and Company (UK)
Brettenham House
Lancaster Place
London WC2E 7EN

THE NIGHT SHE DIED

For Keith

1

It was half past nine in the evening and Detective Inspector Luke Thanet was stretched out on the living-room carpet, staring at the ceiling. Despite the padding, the rolling-pin in the small of his back seemed to be cutting his spine in two. He cast an agonised glance at the clock. Only a minute had gone by since the last time he had looked. It seemed impossible that time could pass so slowly.

He heard Joan come downstairs and a moment later she put her head around the door. 'I think he's gone off at last,' she said. Ben, their one-year-old son, was teething. 'At least he didn't wake Bridget. I'll make some coffee. How much longer?'

Another glance at the clock. 'Ten minutes.'

She grimaced in sympathy. 'I shan't be long.' She went out and he could hear her moving about in the kitchen next door.

Coffee, he told himself. Concentrate on coffee, concentrate on anything but the discomfort.

Two weeks ago, injudiciously heaving the lawnmower out of the boot of his car, Thanet had joined the nation's army of back sufferers. His first reaction had been one of outrage. Why should this happen to him? Since then he had run the gamut of emotions, from anger with himself through frustration to despair. He had also suffered being massaged, pulled about, exercised and lectured by an astonishingly diminutive physiotherapist. How could someone so tiny have so much power in her hands, he had asked

5

himself incredulously. And when, when was his back going to get better? Never before had he realised the value of what he had until now taken so carelessly for granted – his health. And he swore that never again, if it were ever restored to him, would he fail to appreciate it to the full. Meanwhile, here he was, doing his daily fifteen minutes on the rack (the rolling-pin), an exercise designed to 'restore flexibility to the spine'.

Joan came in carrying a tray. 'Coffee,' she said. 'Shall I pour it now?'

Thanet shook his head, wincing at the stab of pain introduced by even that tiny movement. 'In a minute,' he said, between his teeth. Then, 'Talk, darling, for God's sake talk. What have you been up to today?'

They had scarcely seen each other this evening. Joan had eaten long before he arrived home and had spent most of the time since then upstairs, trying to get Ben off to sleep.

She poured out a cup of coffee for herself, sank down on to the settee with a sigh of relief. 'Nothing much, really.' She kicked her shoes off, tucked her feet up beneath her, sipped at her coffee. 'No, that's not true. I went to the last day of the Dacre Exhibition.'

'At the College of Art?'

'Yes. It's a pity you missed it. It was terrific. Her paintings are absolutely unique, like nothing I've ever seen before. They … '

The telephone rang.

Joan uncoiled herself wearily. 'I'll get it. I hope it's not for you.' But it was. 'Yes, he's here,' Thanet heard her say.

'Tell them to hold on. I'm coming,' he called out, shooting a triumphant glance at the clock. He was going to cheat it of two minutes. Impossible, though, to raise himself into a sitting position. With a groan he rolled over on to his stomach, tensing against the pain, raised himself slowly on to hands and knees and finally, moving very carefully, managed to stand up.

'Yes, yes,' he said irritably into the telephone. 'Of

6

course I'm fit.' He scowled at Joan who was raising her eyebrows in admonitory disbelief and turned his back on her. 'All right,' he said when he had replaced the receiver, 'but what do you expect me to say? That I've got one foot in the grave?'

She followed him to the cloackroom, laid her hand affectionately against his cheek and stretched up to kiss him. 'Don't wait up, love,' he said. 'I may be late.'

Already, she could see, his mind was moving ahead, away from her. 'Something serious?'

He shrugged into his coat, wincing, and nodded. 'Murder, they seem to think. A young housewife.'

Joan stepped back, relinquishing him. 'Take care, then,' she said.

It was too early for the pubs, cinemas and bingo-halls to have discharged their nightly crowds and the centre of the town was more or less deserted as Thanet headed for Gladstone Road. He found it without difficulty, a quiet cul-de-sac tucked away behind an area of densely packed terraced houses. As he turned into it his headlights briefly illuminated a stretch of rough grass and tangled trees on the other side of the road. This, he realised, must slope down to the railway line; as he drew up behind the other cars a train thundered by, invisible at the foot of the embankment.

As he eased himself out of his car he was glad to see that it was Detective Sergeant Mike Lineham who came forward to meet him. He enjoyed working with Lineham, who was both intelligent and thorough and would one day be a first-rate detective, if he could only overcome an irritating diffidence. His summing-up of the situation was typically concise.

'A young woman sir. Name of Julie Holmes. Body found by her husband when he got home from night school — accompanied by a friend. She's been stabbed in the chest. A kitchen knife, by the look of it.'

Becoming aware that Lineham's short, staccato sentences and air of urgency were having the effect of

7

hurrying him along, Thanet deliberately stopped and stood still. Lineham, taken unawares, found himself at the gate of the house alone. He turned, unconsciously subsiding into an attitude of resignation. He ought to have known better by now, he told himself as he watched Thanet's head turn slowly, questingly, from left to right.

Whereas many detectives would hurry straight to the side of the body, Thanet always liked to feel his way into a case. 'It's worth taking time to absorb first impressions properly,' he'd told Lineham once, when they were working on the first murder they'd ever tackled together. 'If I don't, they lose their impact. Time and again I've regretted rushing into things. Now I never do. A few minutes' delay at the start of a case will rarely hold things up and might save hours of work later on.'

Now, Thanet gazed about him at Gladstone Road. The place in which someone chooses to live can reveal a great deal about him, he believed, and this place was ... he groped for the word ... secretive, yes, that was it. Gladstone Road definitely had a secretive air about it. It was about two hundred yards long. Most of it, right from the corner where one turned into it up to the boundary of the Holmes's garden, was taken up by some sort of yard, a builder's yard by the look of it, silent and deserted now. Thanet took a few steps back along the road to peer at the black and white sign high up on the close-boarded fence which surrounded it, the street lamp in front of the Holme's house throwing just enough light to make it legible. *R. Dobson and Sons, Builders*, he read.

It looked as though at some point (the nineteen-thirties, probably, by the look of the Holmes's house) Dobson had decided to sacrifice part of his yard in order to make some ready cash, for the remainder of the short street had been divided up into two plots of equal size. Something however – the war? – had prevented him from building the second house;

beyond the Holmes house and separated from it by a similar high close-boarded fence was a patch of waste ground. Why, Thanet wondered, had it not been built upon since? Lack of funds, perhaps, followed by the dawning realisation that here was an appreciating asset?

Beyond the empty plot, closing off the end of the cul-de-sac, was a wire-mesh fence. Set into it, over to the right where the ground started to slope down for the railway embankment was what looked like a metal swing-gate. Beyond the fence stood a coppice of trees, their restless branches creating a shifting, irregular silhouette of denser darkness against the night sky.

Yes, Thanet thought, anyone choosing to live in Gladstone Road would value privacy above all. He took one last, comprehensive look around, gave an approving pat to the lamp-post beside him, then transferred his attention to Lineham who was shifting as unobtrusively as possible from one foot to another in an attempt to hide his impatience. 'Right,' he said, 'let's go inside.'

Lineham led the way with the alacrity of a retriever anxious to show his master a particularly juicy bone. Thanet followed more slowly, studying the house as he went. As he had already noted, it was of typical nineteen-thirties construction, with a front door to one side set back in a shallow, open porch, and bay windows on both floors.

'Round the back, sir. The body's just inside the front door.'

Thanet followed without comment.

Lineham led the way through a small, square kitchen furnished with a formica table and two matching, metal-legged chairs into a narrow hall where a photographer and two fingerprint men were already at work. Thanet nodded approvingly at Lineham, pleased to see that the sergeant had trusted his own judgement sufficiently to get things moving without waiting for Thanet's arrival. Seeing Thanet, the men retreated a few steps up the staircase to allow him access to the body.

And there she was.

Thanet always hated this moment. No matter how often he experienced it, no matter who the victim was, he could never quench his initial pang of pity, of regret for a life cut short. Almost at once he was able to become detached again, aware that emotional involvement could cripple his judgement, but this moment could never leave him unmoved and he was not sure that he would want it to. As he lowered himself gingerly to kneel beside the body, however, his face remained impassive. Many of his colleagues, he knew, would regard such feelings as weakness.

Julie Holmes had been young, not more than twenty-five, Thanet guessed. She lay sprawled on her back, her long hair a pool of spun gold on the uncarpeted floorboards, arms outflung and legs askew. She had, Thanet thought sadly, been a very pretty girl, perhaps even a beautiful one. Difficult to judge how animation would have affected that delicately modelled face, those deep-blue eyes. He glanced up at the photographer. 'Have you finished with her?'

'Yes, sir.'

Thanet closed her eyes. Let the others think what they would. Then he swiftly finished his examination. The girl was wearing a coat of brown herringbone tweed and had been stabbed right through it; the handle of the knife still protruded from her chest. There appeared to have been very little bleeding, but it was difficult to tell; the clothes she was wearing beneath the coat might well have absorbed a great deal. Pinned to the left lapel of the coat was a striking piece of jewellery, an enamelled brooch some three inches long in the design of a mermaid. Waist-length golden hair flowed modestly over the upper half of the mermaid's body, above the iridescent blue scales of the tail. Thanet could not decide whether he liked it or not. Mermaids had curious associations, an aura of paradoxically sexless nakedness ... He glanced around. 'Handbag?'

Lineham shook his head. 'No sign of it. I've had a quick look.'

Thanet struggled to his feet, wryly aware of the self-restraint Lineham was exercising in refraining from extending a hand to help. Thanet's touchiness on the subject of his back was well known. 'Where's the husband?'

'In there,' Lineham indicated the closed door beside them, 'with the friend who was present when he found the body. And Constable Bingham.'

'Right. Doc Mallard been yet? No? Well, let me know when he gets here. I'm going to have a word with Holmes. How many men have we got here?' Swiftly Thanet organised a search of the premises, the house-to-house enquiries, and then went into the living-room.

It was a room of curious contrasts. Like the hall, it was uncarpeted and there were no curtains at the windows. There was, however, a luxurious three-piece suite upholstered in gold and some expensive hi-fi equipment as well as a colour television set. In the bay window a gleaming sewing-machine stood on a long table on which were heaped swathes of cream and gold brocade.

The uniformed constable who had been standing just inside the door received Thanet's unspoken message and slipped out. Thanet turned his attention to the other two occupants of the room, only one of whom had looked up when he entered. This was a clearly angry young man in duffel coat and jeans who was standing in front of the empty fireplace, legs apart and hands thrust deep into his coat pockets. He was scowling at Thanet through a profusion of ginger hair. 'Look here,' he burst out, taking a step forward.

'Just one moment, sir,' Thanet said, turning to the other man, who was sitting on the edge of one of the

11

armchairs, leaning forward, head in hands. 'Mr Holmes?'

The man slowly lifted a dazed face.

'Detective Inspector Thanet, Sturrenden CID. I'm sorry to have to impose myself on you at a time like this ...'

'I should bloody well think so! I – ' cut in Holmes's friend.

'Just a moment, sir, please. But there are some questions I really must ask,' Thanet went on, turning back to Holmes.

'Questions! Where d'you think that'll get you? Why don't you leave this poor devil alone and – '

Thanet held up his hand. 'Look Mr ... ?'

'Byfleet. And I – '

'It's all right, Des,' Holmes said unexpectedly. He passed his hand wearily over eyes and forehead. 'I don't mind. The police have to do their job. Go on Inspector.'

'But he's told it all once,' persisted Byfleet. 'Does he have to go through it all over again?'

'It's all right, Des,' Holmes repeated. 'It's got to be done.'

His accent was definitely not Kentish, Thanet thought. A Londoner? He sat down opposite Holmes and said gently, 'If you could tell me exactly what happened this evening then, sir, right from the time you got home from work.'

Holmes, it seemed, was the manager of the local branch of Homeright Supermarkets. He had arrived home from work this evening at about twenty past six, as usual. His wife was there before him – she, too, worked locally, in the office of an estate agent – and they had supper together before Holmes left for his evening class at a quarter to seven. She had said that she was going to spend the evening working on the living-room curtains.

Holmes and Byfleet (who lived in a neighbouring village and had been on his way to the station) had walked back from the Technical College together, arriving in Gladstone Road at about twenty past nine. Byfleet had parted from Holmes at the gate but a few moments later had been called back by a frantic shout from Holmes, who had found Julie's body sprawled just inside the front door. They had telephoned the police and an ambulance at once, but it was obvious that she was already dead.

'Your wife was wearing a coat,' Thanet said. 'You're sure she said nothing about going out?'

'No. I told you, she said she was going to work on the curtains.' He nodded at the mounds of material on the long table.

'Have you any idea where she might have gone? To visit a friend, perhaps?'

Holmes shook his head. 'She didn't have any friends here yet. We only moved in six weeks ago. The only people she knew were the ones at work, and none of them live anywhere near.'

Holmes had apparently been offered a transfer to the Sturrenden branch of Homeright in October, six months ago. At that time he and his wife had been living in Brixton. They had at once started house-hunting, coming down to Sturrenden each weekend, but it had proved impossible to find the sort of house they wanted at a price they could afford. When the time came for Holmes to take up the appointment in early December he had had to go into lodgings, his wife staying on in London. Shortly afterwards they had found the house in Gladstone Road and had moved in as soon as completion took place, some twelve weeks later.

Thanet listened thoughtfully. So Holmes and his wife had been living apart for three months, long enough for either of them to have formed another attachment.

He transferred his attention to the belligerent Byfleet. 'Mr Byfleet, I wonder if you could tell me exactly what you remember of arriving here this evening? I take it you and Mr Holmes attend the same evening class?'

Byfleet scowled. 'Yes. And we was sitting next to each other all evening, if that's what you're getting at.'

'And you agree with Mr Holmes about the time of your arrival here?'

'Yeah, I'm sure, because I was keeping my eye on the time, because of my train at nine-thirty. It takes six minutes to get to the station from here, along the footpath. Bang on twenty past nine it was, when we got here.'

'The footpath?'

'The one at the end of the road. Cuts through that little wood, comes out near the station. Otherwise you have to go right round and over the bridge.'

Thanet made a mental note to check the topography of the place thoroughly. 'And you parted at the front gate?'

'Yeah. I'd gone, oh, fifteen, perhaps twenty yards along the road when John calls me back. Well, I ran. I mean, I could see straight away something was wrong. And there she was.' Byfleet stopped, glanced uneasily at Holmes.

'You didn't actually see Mr Holmes go into the house?'

'No.'

'The door wasn't locked,' Holmes said suddenly. 'I remember now, it was slightly ajar.'

'You didn't mention this before,' Thanet said sharply. 'You're sure?'

'I'm sure, all right,' Holmes said grimly. 'I ... I'd just forgotten. It ... the whole thing was ...'

Thanet waited, but Holmes did not go on.

'You didn't notice that the door was open, as you passed the house?' Thanet asked Byfleet.

'No. Why should I? We'd said good-bye, that was it, as far as I was concerned. I was thinking of my train.'

'You didn't glance back at all?' Thanet persisted.

'No. No bloody no. Like I said, why should I?'

He would have to leave it for the moment, important though the point was. Thanet sighed. 'All right, Mr Byfleet. So you would say that no more than fifteen or twenty seconds elapsed between the time you parted and the moment when you heard Mr Holmes shout?'

'Got it in one,' said Byfleet sarcastically, folding his arms.

Time enough for Holmes to have stabbed his wife? Thanet thought. Time enough for her to have died? He glanced at Holmes who, eyes glazed, hands lying limply along the arm of the chair, seemed to have withdrawn himself from the proceedings. Thanet lowered his voice as he said to Byfleet. 'Was there any sign of life when you first saw her?'

Byfleet shot a quick, concerned glance at Holmes and apparently reassured that his friend had not heard the question, shook his head. 'No.' He looked at Holmes again and then, as if making up his mind, came to sit beside Thanet on the settee. When he next spoke the belligerence had gone and he said quietly, 'Look, Inspector, John had nothing to do with it, honest he didn't. I was with him all evening, like I said and when we got here there just wouldn't have been time for him to ... She was dead before ever he opened the door, I'd swear to that.'

'Did either of you touch her?'

'No. John just stood there, like he'd been turned to stone. Well, I mean, you could tell just by looking at her with that bloody great knife sticking out of her.'

He would have to ask Doc Mallard exactly how long it would have taken Julie Holmes to die, Thanet thought. As if the thought had conjured up the police surgeon there was a knock on the door. Lineham put his head around it. 'Doc's here, sir.'

'Right, I'm coming.' Thanet stood up. 'Thank you Mr Byfleet. If you could bear with us just a little longer, I'll send someone in to take down your statement and then we'll get it typed out for you to sign tomorrow.' At the door he paused. 'Just one point, Mr

15

Holmes.' He waited, repeated the man's name twice before the dazed face turned towards him. 'Mr Holmes,' he said gently, 'did your wife usually carry a handbag?'

A moment's pause and then, 'Yes.'

'What was it like?'

Holmes's forehead creased as he tried to focus his mind on the question. 'Brown,' he said at last. 'Big. A shoulder thing.'

Fairly obtrusive, by the sound of it. And certainly nowhere in this room, Thanet thought, glancing about him again. They'd check properly later on, of course, but ... 'Thank you,' he said.

Constable Bingham moved unobtrusively back into the room as Thanet left.

In the narrow hall Mallard was bending over the body, his bald pate reflecting the light from the unshaded overhead bulb.

'I know, I know,' he said testily, glancing up at Thanet. 'Don't bother to say it. You can't imagine how boring it gets, hearing the same old questions every time.'

Thanet and Lineham exchanged amused glances and waited in silence while Mallard continued his examination.

'Well,' Mallard said, finally straightening up, 'We won't know for sure, of course, until after the P.M., but it looks as though she died instantly. And,' with a quelling glance as Thanet opened his mouth, 'sticking my neck out as you always press me to do, I'd say, provisionally, that she's been dead between one and two hours. That, of course, is unofficial.' He snapped his bag shut and stood up.

Thanet glanced at his watch. Half past ten. She must have died, if Mallard was right – and despite his caution he usually was – between eight-thirty and nine-thirty. No, between eight-thirty and nine-twenty, when her body had been found.

'Thanks Doc,' he said.

Mallard scowled at him. He had never learned to receive compliments or expressions of gratitude gracefully. 'How's that back of yours?'

'Improving.'

'Hmph. Teach you to go doing damnfool things like heaving lawn-mowers about,' growled Mallard, heading for the door.

'You can let them take her away now,' Thanet said to Lineham. 'And have another look around for her handbag – shoulder bag, actually. Brown, fairly big.' He hurried after Mallard. Thanet was always punctilious in observing the courtesies. The police owed a great deal to the surgeons who frequently turned out of bed in the early hours to come to the scene of a murder and in any case, despite Mallard's testiness, Thanet was fond of him.

'How's young Ben?' Mallard asked as he tossed his case on to the passenger seat and settled himself behind the wheel.

'Teething,' Thanet said tersely.

Mallard chuckled. 'Ah, the joys of parenthood,' he said. 'And I'm told it gets worse, not better. Give my love to Joan – and watch that back, now.' And with a smile and a wave, he was gone.

Thanet stood looking after him for a moment and then made his way thoughtfully back to the house, stepping back on to the lawn to avoid the ambulance men who were carrying a covered stretcher down the narrow front path. He watched as they slid their burden into the ambulance and closed the doors.

The end of a life, he thought. How inadequate were those few words to convey the aftermath of suffering always left by sudden death. And they marked, of course, only the beginning for him. Over the next days, weeks, months, perhaps, Julie Holmes would come alive for him in a unique way. Each of the people who had known her would have his own limited, individual view of her and Thanet would somehow have to reconcile all those views, assemble them into a composite whole.

17

It was possible, of course, that this might not happen, that the case might move to a swift conclusion. Most murders are committed by someone close to the victim and the most obvious person frequently turns out to be the murderer. Remembering that with good reason the police are always most suspicious of the person who finds the body, Thanet knew he must look long and hard at Holmes himself. Would there have been time for Holmes to have killed his wife, in the instant of opening the door? Impossible to say, as yet. Mallard's guess might be wrong. The girl might have been killed before her husband left for night school – analysis of her stomach contents would speak here. But if Mallard was right – as he usually was – and she had been killed between eight-thirty and nine-twenty, why had she been wearing her outdoor clothes? Had she just come in, or had she been about to go out? Thanet shook his head. There were too many imponderables as yet. It was pointless to speculate at this stage.

Lineham met him at the front door, visibly excited. 'No sign of her handbag, sir. They'd finished fingerprinting the kitchen, so I hope you don't mind, but I ... '

'Don't be so apologetic, Mike,' Thanet said testily. 'Of course you searched it, it's your job to use your initiative, isn't it? It's the knife, I suppose?' And felt ashamed of himself as Lineham visibly deflated. I really must not let his diffidence irritate me, he told himself. Apart from anything else it wasn't the best way to go about building up the sergeant's confidence. 'Come on,' he said, touching Lineham on the shoulder and heading for the kitchen, 'show me. It's an interesting bit of news.'

The kitchen knives were kept in a special board, in one of the drawers. They had probably, Thanet thought, been a wedding present. There should have been six, but one, the carving knife by the look of it, was missing. Looking at the largest knife of all, a gleaming small butcher's cleaver, Thanet thought that they ought to be grateful for small mercies. Holmes's ordeal (assuming he were not the murderer) would have been a great deal more unpleasant if that one had been used. They would check, of course, but it looked as though Julie Holmes had been killed with her own knife.

Suicide then? But by stabbing herself (a method rarely chosen by suicides) and in the hall, by the front door? And, what was more, dressed to go out? Highly unlikely, Thanet thought, but then people did sometimes behave in the most incredible, irrational ways. The possibility would have to be borne in mind, remote though it seemed.

But her handbag was missing.

A ring at the bell, then. Julie snatches up the carving knife(!), opens the door (why, if she was afraid?), mugger grabs handbag, seizes knife, stabs her, departs with the loot. Oh yes, he told himself sarcastically, very likely. He must stop all this nonsense and get on with the job. 'Find anything else?' he said.

'There's this.' Lineham pointed to the table on which sat a brown, simulated-leather box some three inches by two. A film of powder indicated that it had already been tested for prints. Nearby was a scrumple of tissue paper. 'I found it on the window sill. The paper was in the waste bin.'

'Have you opened it?'

Lineham shook his head. 'Johnson was still working on it when I went to tell you about the knife.'

Thanet picked up the box, pressed the catch. The lid flew open, revealing a white satin lining in which there was a shallow, curved depression. In the lid was printed in black: A. *Mallowby, Jeweller. High Street, Sturrenden.* Thanet glanced at Lineham. 'That mermaid brooch she was wearing, do you think?'

'That's what I thought,' Lineham said eagerly. 'Looks as though the box might have been wrapped in that tissue paper. In which case, he probably gave it to her tonight. The paper was right on top, in the waste bin.'

Thanet handed the box over. 'Find out. I'm just going to take a look around upstairs.'

Lineham nodded and disappeared into the living-room.

Thanet moved quietly up the uncarpeted stairs. There were, he discovered, three bedrooms, two good-sized rooms and one minute one. The tiny one and the bedroom at the back of the house were both stacked haphazardly with a jumble of furniture and unpacked cardboard boxes. Surely, Thanet thought, they ought to have made more progress than this in six weeks? Though Julie Holmes had been out at work all day, he reminded himself.

The third and biggest bedroom, however, showed where the time had been spent. Thanet switched on the light and stood looking about him with surprised interest. The room was carpeted in deep pink and had been freshly papered in a white wallpaper with a delicately pretty design of wild flowers in two shades of pink and a soft green. Curtains of exactly the same design hung at the big bay window.

'Well, well,' murmured Thanet, moving further out into the room. The bedspread was white lace over a deep pink backing which accentuated the pattern and along the whole of one wall was ranged a series of units of white furniture – good quality stuff too, Thanet thought, going to take a closer look – two wardrobes with a dressing-table built between them. There was an oval mirror fixed to the wall above the dressing-table. The overall effect of the room was fresh, pretty and strangely impersonal. It looked exactly like a magazine illustration, and was just as lifeless. There were the pretty ornaments, the carefully arranged posy of flowers on the bedside table, the tasteful prints. But there was a complete absence of clutter. The top of the dressing-table was bare, the surface of the twin bedside tables empty save for an alarm clock on one side (his, presumably) and the flowers (hers). There was absolutely nothing visible in the room to reveal the

20

personality of its owners.

The small drawers at the top of the bedside cupboards were slightly more fruitful. In Julie's was a bottle of sleeping tablets and a neatly folded clean handkerchief. In Holmes's was a well-thumbed stack of girlie magazines. Thanet pursed his lips over these, wondering how long the Holmeses had been married. Surely not long enough for him to turn to these, as a substitute for the real thing? Perhaps they were a legacy of Holmes's three months of relative celibacy, Thanet reflected as he carefully replaced them. Or perhaps not. Thanet looked around the room with new eyes. Holmes had, clearly, indulged all his wife's whims to get this room exactly as she wanted it. As a bribe? A distasteful thought, but one to be taken seriously.

Thanet moved across to the dressing-table. The top drawers contained neatly arranged cosmetics, the lower ones tights, underclothes, scarves, sweaters, all clean and carefully folded. The contents of the two wardrobes were much more revealing. Holmes's was almost empty, containing only one suit, two pairs of jeans, a pair of casual trousers, a denim jacket and, on the top shelf, a small pile of underclothes and two sweaters. On the floor were lined up two pairs of suede shoes, one pair of leather, a pair of slippers and some track shoes.

Julie's wardrobe was a very different matter. Thanet whistled softly as the doors slid back to reveal a full rack of dresses, coats, skirts, trousers, all of them good quality and many expensive. Thanet riffled through them, then stooped to examine a purple plastic carrier bag with TOPS in gold lettering on the side. Expensive indeed. Joan had bought an evening dress at TOPS for the first police ball after Thanet had been promoted to Inspector and the memory of the bill had made Thanet wince for months afterwards. It was a gorgeous dress, Joan had looked marvellous in it and he hadn't begrudged a penny of it, but still ...

21

He slid the door closed, thoughtfully, and took one last glance about him before making his way downstairs. Holmes, then, had been over-indulgent, uxorious. Remembering those magazines the word 'bribe' slid again into Thanet's mind. What had Holmes been trying to buy? Love? Sexual compliance? And if so, how would he have reacted if his wife had continued to reject him, if – remembering that she had evidently been out when she had said that she would be staying at home like a good little wife – he had been supplanted by a rival?

Thanet grimaced. It looked as though this case might be all too predictable.

2

Something was tickling his nose, tugging at his attention, dragging him up and away from the luxury of sleep. Thanet opened his eyes. Bridget was peering anxiously into his face.

'OK, Sprig,' he whispered. 'I'm awake. I'll be out in a minute.'

Satisfied, she trotted off towards the door.

Thanet, careful of his back, glanced over his shoulder to make sure that Joan was still asleep, then levered himself out of bed.

In the bathroom he splashed his face in cold water, to wake himself up properly before shaving. It had been half past three in the morning by the time he had finished his preliminary report, four by the time he got to bed, and shaving could be hazardous business when one was still three-quarters asleep. Joan had often tried to persuade him to use an electric razor but he didn't like them. Perhaps he ought to grow a beard? He peered at his narrow, unexceptional face beneath its thatch of thick brown hair, trying to visualise how he would look. Pointless speculation, really. Joan didn't like beards.

By the time he had finished shaving and had cleaned his teeth he was beginning to feel human again. He would shower later, before dressing. He opened the door on to the landing and with perfect timing three-year-old Bridget came out of her room, trailing dressing-gown and slippers. He helped her into them and then, unable to carry her as he usually did because

23

of his back, he took her hand and they tiptoed downstairs to the kitchen.

This was their special time. Making use of Bridget's inbuilt alarm clock which always woke her at half past six, Thanet had instigated this morning routine when Ben was born. It suited everybody. Joan could sleep on a little after night feeding and Thanet was able to spend some time with his daughter. The demands of his work were such that he frequently missed seeing Bridget in the evenings and all too often a week would go by without his having been able to spend more than a few fleeting moments with her. Bridget loved this early-morning time. At this hour Daddy was hers alone, his attention undivided and guaranteed.

Together they had evolved their own ritual, Bridget laying the table with extreme concentration while Thanet made tea and toast and dispensed cereal and fruit juice. After breakfast he would take Joan a cup of tea in bed before the day began in earnest.

'Bridget saw a baby horse yesterday,' she announced, when they were settled at the table.

'Oh? That was nice. A baby horse is called a foal. Where was that?'

Bridget's forehead creased while she thought about it. 'By the shops,' she said triumphantly at last.

Sounded most unlikely, Thanet thought. But why worry? It didn't matter what they talked about as long as they talked, enjoyed each other's company. As Bridget chattered on he watched her indulgently. She had inherited Joan's fair, clear skin and candid grey eyes, her honey-coloured hair. Whereas Joan's was short and curly, though, Bridget's was soft and fine, its silky tendrils brushing her shoulders. She would, Thanet thought, one day be a very beautiful girl.

At this time of day he tried never to think about his work but suddenly Julie Holmes's face was in his mind. She, too, had been a beautiful girl. If anything like that ever happened to Sprig ...

'Is your toast nasty, Daddy?'

Thanet realised that he was scowling, relaxed, shook his head. 'No, just something I was thinking of ... '

Sturrenden was a thriving market town of some 45,000 inhabitants. It lay deep in the Kent countryside, surrounded by some of the finest farmland in the South of England. Cattle and crops, fruit and hops all flourished, feeding the life of the town which was their heart.

In Thanet's opinion Sturrenden had everything: good shops, excellent schools, a plentiful supply of pubs, a number of churches, two cinemas and even, for the culturally minded, a small but first-rate theatre. It enjoyed all the benefits of country living, yet it was only an hour and a half by fast train to London and close enough to the coast to make summer picnics by the sea an attractive proposition.

As he drove to work on this fine May morning he looked about him with satisfaction. Not for him the dirt and grime of the metropolis, thank you very much. The police force in Sturrenden was well manned and, with very few exceptions, people worked smoothly together, which was good both for morale and efficiency.

There was a delay at the bridge and Thanet had time to notice that the flowering cherries along the tow-paths on either side of the river were just coming into bloom. In a couple of weeks he must remember to take Joan on one of their favourite outings, a drive through the orchards at blossom time.

By the time he arrived at the police station, however, his mind was focused firmly on work: first, a quick clearing away of any routine stuff which might have arrived on his desk this morning (fortunately there was nothing particularly time-consuming today), then he would go out to Gladstone Road to see how Lineham was getting on with directing the search of the area by daylight. After that he would return to the office to take a thorough look at the house-to-house reports,

25

which should be typed up by then. And then ... well, he'd decide later, when he'd seen what had come in.

He was in Gladstone Road by a quarter to nine. Lineham, Carson and Bentley were poking about in the patch of waste land next to the Holmes's house.

'Found anything?' Thanet asked.

Lineham shook his head. 'Not a sausage. Except for rubbish, rubbish and more rubbish, of course.'

'Have you seen Dobson, the builder, yet?'

'Yes. He came over to speak to us when he opened up the yard. Said we could search it whenever we liked, if we wanted to.'

'What's he like?'

'A bit gnome-like. About five two, with a bald head and lots of whiskers.'

'Age?'

'Sixty-five or so, I'd say.'

'Did he know anything useful?'

'No. The yard opens at eight and the men are sent off to their various jobs. Dobson glimpsed Mrs Holmes once or twice when she left for work, just before a quarter to nine, but he never actually spoke to her. The yard closes at four-thirty, so by the time she got home from work at a quarter to six it would all be shut up.'

'Have you seen Holmes this morning?'

'No. He's up, though. The bedroom curtains are drawn back now. Do you want to see him?'

'Not at the moment. I'm going to take a quick look around the other streets back there.'

It was a strange district, Thanet thought as he walked, a little world of its own, bounded on one side by the only road into the area, on the second by the railway line, on the third by the narrow band of trees behind the metal fence which Thanet had noticed the previous evening, and on the fourth by a row of shops.

Between Gladstone Road and the shops, and parallel to them, were three cul-de-sacs of mean little back-to-back Victorian terraced houses fronting directly on to the pavements, their back yards divided by narrow alleyways which Thanet certainly wouldn't have cared to use at night. They too, had been named after nineteenth-century politicians – Disraeli Terrace, Palmerston Row, Shaftesbury Road.

Thanet had no intention of visiting any of the houses as yet, so there did not seem to be much point in walking along one of the cul-de-sacs and back again. It was therefore not until he had returned to Gladstone Road and had gone to take a closer look at the swing gate and the footpath to the station that he made an interesting discovery: glancing to his left he found that the far ends of the cul-de-sacs were linked by a footpath which ran along between the metal fence and the blank sides of the last terraced house in each row.

Access to Gladstone Road was not then, as he had thought, limited to the road way in. The Holmes's house could also be reached by walking along any one of those cul-de-sacs and turning into the footpath which led to the railway station.

Thanet pushed open the swing gate and walked quickly through the narrow copse, emerging at the far end within sight of the station. The strip of trees, he now saw, separated the area of terraced houses from the grounds of a modern factory. He glanced at his watch. Those reports should be ready shortly. He must get back to the office.

He picked up Sergeant Lineham on the way and they both settled down to study the reports in a silence broken only by the little popping noises made by Thanet's pipe, the scrape of a match as he relit it from time to time.

Finally Thanet pushed the papers away from him, sat back. 'Television is the policeman's bane,' he said. The previous evening most people seemed to have been glued to their sets watching *The Pacemakers*, a new and very successful series which started at eight-thirty and finished at nine-thirty – unfortunately the very period which interested the police. 'The report on Mrs

Horrocks is interesting, though.'

Horrocks was a travelling salesman and the previous evening he had, according to his wife, been 'hopping mad'. The inhabitants of all those closely packed terraced houses had parking problems. There simply wasn't enough parking space, and some of the locals had to be content with leaving their cars in front of the row of shops, coming to regard certain spaces as theirs by right.

Horrocks, recently moved into the district, was one, and he had been incensed to find that on Tuesday evenings his parking space was frequently purloined by a green Triumph Stag. Last night had been no exception and every quarter of an hour or so he had gone out to see if he could catch the intruder and have it out with him. It had been especially irritating as he had been due to leave on one of his frequent selling trips up North – he preferred to do the long haul by night – and he had been angry at having to spend his last couple of hours at home in this way. What was more, he had again failed to catch the owner of the Triumph.

Unfortunately, by the time Thanet's man had called, Horrocks had already left and although his wife knew that the Triumph had been there when her husband had arrived home at a quarter past seven and had still been there when *The Pacemakers* started at eight-thirty, she did not know if it had gone by the time Horrocks left just before nine.

The presence of the Triumph was confirmed by a Mr Carne, who used the parking space next to Horrocks and who had noticed it when taking out his own car at eight o'clock to pick up his daughter from a music lesson. It had still been there at eight-twenty, when he returned.

'We'll have to try to trace Horrocks,' Thanet said. 'Send the same man – Bentley, wasn't it? – to go and find out Horrocks's schedule. And to see if he can get hold of Carne, find out if he can remember any details

28

of the Triumph's registration number ... Interesting, isn't it? Holmes's night-school evening.'

'You think the owner of the Triumph might have been visiting Mrs Holmes, sir?'

Thanet shrugged. 'Who knows? It's worth checking. Though if he was going to her house, why was she wearing outdoor clothes?'

'Perhaps they went out for a drink?'

'Possibly ... Then there are these two reports of "a tall dark man". No further details. How vague can you get? Seen passing the end of Disraeli Terrace in the direction of Gladstone Road at about a quarter to nine by the woman whose daughter had toothache. Also seen passing Shaftesbury Road in the direction of Gladstone Road by the man who'd been walking his dog, at about twenty to nine, he thinks. Where's that map?'

They bent over it together.

'As I thought,' Thanet said. 'Disraeli Terrace is nearer Gladstone Road than Shaftesbury Road is. The times should have been the other way around.'

'They both say they're not certain of the time. One of them must be a few minutes out.'

'Mmm. I think we'd better check on it all the same. And we want more details about our tall dark stranger. Better send Carson. He saw both these witnesses, didn't he? I know he says he pressed them, but they may have remembered something since.' Thanet paused, consulted his notes. 'And that's about it, isn't it?'

'Sir, what about ... ' Lineham stopped, swallowed.

'What about what?' Dammit, I must be more patient with him, thought Thanet. 'Go on,' he said, more gently.

'Well, the husband, sir. I know the evidence of his friend seems to let him out, but we don't know, do we? I mean, if he had stabbed her in the instant of opening the door, the friend wouldn't have been any the wiser, would he?'

29

'The thought had crossed my mind,' Thanet said drily, 'but at this stage I feel we ought to keep an open mind.' His pipe had gone out and he took time to relight it. 'For one thing, we ought to wait for the report on the knife, and for the path. report. If Holmes did kill her she would have to have died instantly for Byfleet to be so convinced Holmes didn't do it. If there'd been the least sign of life ... But of course, it's possible that Byfleet is lying to protect Holmes. And then, the whole set-up is peculiar. Stabbing, I always think, is more of an impulse crime. If Holmes had planned to use Byfleet as a witness to prove his innocence, he would not only have had to carry the knife with him to evening class but somehow have had to ensure that his wife was waiting for him at the door.'

'He could deliberately have left his key behind so that she would have had to open it.'

'Yes, but he couldn't count on her answering at once, could he? She might have been washing her hair or in the bath, then his witness would have been out of sight by the time she opened the door. That swing gate is only about a hundred yards away.'

'He could have tried it, then if it didn't work and she didn't answer the door before Byfleet was out of sight, he could have planned to put off killing her to another Tuesday.'

'He'd have to be a pretty cold-blooded character,' Thanet said grimly. 'And as I say, all this planning doesn't fit in with stabbing, to my mind, I could see him killing her in anger, or in a fit of jealousy – if he caught her with another man, for instance ... You saw their bedroom.'

'Yes. He was besotted with her, I'd say. All those expensive clothes, and his own wardrobe practically empty.'

'I know. So all right, he may have had a motive, there might have been another man ... She may have gone out to meet him, while Holmes was at night school ...

All the same, I'm not happy about the mechanics of the actual killing. I can't seem to visualise it, somehow. I just don't think we have enough to go on. So we'd better do some digging while we're waiting for the results of the lab tests and path. report. I want you to get along to Homerights, see what you can find out about Holmes, any gossip and so on. Did you manage to get that photograph of Mrs Holmes?'

Lineham took an envelope out of his pocket, extracted the print.

Julie Holmes was leaning against a five-barred gate, gazing solemnly into the camera.

'Holmes says it's a good likeness, sir.'

'Good. Get some copies made, then make sure it gets into tomorrow's papers – tonight's, if possible. If she was out last night, someone might have seen her.'

Thanet stood up and Lineham followed suit. Watching him, Thanet sensed a certain reluctance. Why ...? Suddenly it dawned on him. Lineham was dying to know what he, Thanet was going to do. Thanet remembered only too well how he'd liked to be kept informed, when he was in Lineham's position. 'I think I'll go along and have a sniff around the Estate Agents where Mrs Holmes worked. It's just possible there might be a man there who was interested in her. Or perhaps there'll be other girls who might have picked something up.'

He had been right. Lineham made for the door with alacrity now. Thanet was about to follow him when the phone rang.

'Thanet here.'

The fingerprints on the knife had been Julie's. Some were blurred but they were indisputably hers. The written report would follow.

Thanet relayed the information to Lineham, who was hovering at the door.

'Hers!' Lineham's forehead creased as he assimilated this interesting piece of information. 'Still, it's not really surprising, is it? It was her knife, after all. Do you think there's any chance it was suicide?'

31

'With her coat on? In the hall? I doubt it. I expect Doc Mallard's report will enlighten us. Meanwhile, let's get on. Don't forget to put those enquiries in hand before you go, will you?'

Lineham tapped his notebook. 'I've made a list.'

Yes, Thanet thought, Lineham would do. He would do very well indeed.

3

Jefferson and Parrish, Estate Agents, occupied choice premises in the High Street. Thanet parked without compunction in the small car park at the rear reserved for clients, noticing with interest a green Triumph Stag in the slot marked Mr J. Parrish. He made a note of the registration number before making his way around to the front of the building.

The clients of Jefferson and Parrish had generously supplied the firm with top-grade wall-to-wall carpeting, a spectacular rubber plant and a receptionist who could have stepped off the cover of a women's magazine. She was not without feeling however; when Thanet introduced himself and stated his errand the girl shivered, grimaced.

'I heard it on the news this morning. I couldn't believe it. Poor Julie ...'

'You knew her well?'

'Not really. She'd only been here four or five weeks. All the same, working with someone – '

The buzzer sounded on the girl's desk.

Thanet waited until she had finished with the phone. 'What was Mrs Holmes's job here, exactly?'

'She was Mr Parrish's secretary.' The girl's eyes swerved away from Thanet's.

'Then I'd like to see Mr Parrish, please. Perhaps I could have another word with you afterwards?'

Parrish was tall, dark, of athletic build and had the kind of good looks associated in television advertisements with masculine pursuits such as climbing, sailing, driving fast cars and smoking seductive cigars. He wore a beautifully cut, dark-brown hopsack suit, a cream shirt, a tie diagonally striped in chocolate, cream and coffee and a fawn waistcoat with a brown and red overcheck. The effect – no doubt carefully studied – was conservative with a dash of daring. He would, Thanet thought, be very attractive to women, with that studied charm and low, caressing voice. He also had two characteristics which Thanet disliked: a smile which switched on and off like a neon sign and never reached his eyes, and a habit of saying, 'mmm, mmm, mmm' all the while his companion was speaking – intending presumably to convey an impression of intense interest but succeeding only in making Thanet feel that he had to hurry through everything he said.

'A terrible thing,' said Parrish when they were seated. 'Terrible.' Thanet waited.

'I could hardly believe it, when I heard it on the radio this morning. I was shaving.' And he turned his head aside with a slight, rueful smile, to show Thanet the little cut on the side of the neck.

Thanet nodded, still saying nothing.

'Well, Inspector,' said Parrish, throwing himself back in his chair with an alert, eager movement and spreading both hands palm-downward on the desk before him, 'how can we help you?'

Thanet noted the first person plural, the implication that Parrish himself could do nothing of the kind.

'Mrs Holmes was new to the area. This was where she worked. We have to try to find out all we can about her and this seemed the obvious place to start.'

'But why? Surely ... look, didn't it say her body was discovered by her husband, when he got home from night school? Well, I mean, it must have been someone who thought the house was empty, broke in ... mustn't it?'

'At this stage we have to take every possibility into consideration. Now, I understand Mrs Holmes was your secretary. Could you tell me about her?'

34

'I'm not very good at describing people, I'm afraid,' said Parrish.

I bet you aren't, thought Thanet. He guessed that Parrish was too self-absorbed to take in much of other people.

'I get on well with them, of course, you have to, in this job, but ... well, Ju ... Mrs Holmes ... Oh, what the hell, I called her Julie, of course, this a small office and she was my secretary, after all. Well, she was very quiet, reserved. Didn't have much to say for herself. Efficient, though. I rarely had to explain anything twice, or had reason to complain. And that's about it, I suppose.'

'Did she get on well with the other girl?'

'Which one?'

'Is there more than one?'

'Yes. There's Maureen Waters – tall, brunette – and Joy Clark. She's a redhead. Wasn't she ...? Oh of course, I'd forgotten. Joy's popped along to the printers to pick up some brochures for a client who's coming in later this morning.'

'Well, did she? Get on well with them?'

'Oh yes – so far as I know, anyway. You'd better ask them.'

'Would you say that Julie Holmes was attractive to men?'

If this question alarmed him Parrish neatly concealed it by leaning across his desk to pick up a cigarette box. 'Cigarette, Inspector? No?' He took one himself.

Thanet detected no betraying tremor as Parrish lit up.

'Attractive to men,' Parrish repeated thoughtfully, as if the concept were new to him. 'Well, I don't know. Yes, I suppose she might have been. She was a very pretty girl, certainly, but of course, she was married ...'

'Are you?'

'Married? No, why?'

'Just wondered.'

35

'No, I ... well, I suppose I just haven't found the right girl yet. And of course, married women ... After all, there's plenty of the other sort around. Why risk getting involved with an enraged husband and so on if you don't have to ... '

'Quite. So there was no one special, as far as you know, paying attention to Mrs Holmes?'

'Not to my knowledge, no.'

'Mr Jefferson is the only other man here, I gather?'

Parrish gave a snort of genuine amusement. 'You're barking up the wrong tree there, Inspector. I don't suppose old Jeff'd notice if Simone Signoret walked stark naked through his office.' He sobered down. 'Sorry. Look, Inspector, it's a pity I can't help you, but really, there's nothing to tell. Julie Holmes was a nice, quiet, pleasant girl. She got on with the job, gave no trouble, scarcely caused a ripple. I'm sorry about what happened to her, very sorry, but I really don't see what more I can tell you.'

'Right.' Thanet rose. 'But there's just one other question.'

'Yes?'

'Last night. Could you tell me where you were between, say seven and nine-thirty pm?'

Parrish's eyebrows swooped into a frown. 'Now look here, Inspector, what are you implying?'

'Nothing, nothing at all. But you must see that, as a matter of course, we have to put that question to everyone who had anything at all to do with Mrs Holmes.'

Parrish was clearly sceptical. 'Well, I suppose there's no harm in telling you. I was at home all evening from about six o'clock. I was bushed, as a matter of fact – had a heavy day yesterday. So I thought I'd stay in, have an early night.'

'Is there anyone who can corroborate that?'

'I doubt it. We don't exactly live in each other's pockets.'

'We?'

'I've got a flat in Maddison House.'

The only block of luxury flats in the district. 'You're sure you saw no one, spoke to no one, all evening?'

'I don't think so. No, hang on. I saw Morrison, on my way in. He's the caretaker, lives in the basement with his wife.'

'And that would have been at ...?'

'About six, as I said.'

'Good. Fine.' Thanet closed his notebook with a snap. 'Well, I won't take up any more of your time, Mr Parrish. Thank you for being so helpful.'

'Not at all. Not at all.' Parrish accompanied him to the door, effusive now in his relief. 'Anything we can do to help. Any time.'

'You won't mind my having a word with your receptionist, then?'

'Er ... no. Not at all.' Parrish waved him into the outer office. 'Help yourself.'

Maureen Waters stopped typing as Thanet approached. She had been crying; her mascara was smudged. He perched on the corner of her desk and smiled down at her encouragingly.

'Tell me about Mrs ... about Julie,' he said.

'D'you think you could sit on a chair? You make me nervous, looming over me like that.' She gave an apologetic little laugh.

'Sure.' Thanet pulled up a chair, sat down and waited.

'She was very nice. Quiet ... Good to work with.'

'You got on well with her,' Thanet encouraged.

'Pretty well, yes. We both did – Joy and I, that is.' Maureen hesitated.

'But ...?'

She gave him an embarrassed, sideways glance. 'Oh, I don't know ... it seems so awful ...'

'What does?'

'Well, she's dead. I don't like to say anything that might give you the wrong impression ...'

'Look, Miss Waters, I can see you're not a gossip,'

37

Thanet said, meaning it. 'So if there's anything, anything at all which might help us to understand Mrs Holmes better ...'

Maureen sighed. 'Yes, of course.' Then she went on hesitatingly, picking her words with care, 'It's not that it's anything against Julie, not really. I mean, she seemed unconscious of it. Well, she had this attraction for men, you see. You only had to watch ... If a male client came into the office ... I don't want you to think I was jealous ... no,' she said painfully, 'that's not true. I was jealous, but only of that ... power she had, not of Julie herself, if you see what I mean. Well, any girl would be jealous. She didn't even have to make any effort, you see, it just happened. But you couldn't hold it against her because, well, how can I explain, it didn't mean anything to her. She just wasn't interested, really. But that didn't seem to make any difference, to the men, I mean.' She stopped, glancing uneasily at Thanet. 'It's so difficult to explain.'

'You're doing fine. Go on. Tell me a little more about this ... power she had.'

'Well, she was very quiet. Withdrawn. Dreamy. Very attractive, of course. And not shy, exactly, just ... reserved. She was perfectly fit, physically, so far as I knew, anyway, but she gave the impression of being frail, a bit helpless, I suppose. Anyway, men seemed to go for it – jumped to open doors for her, picked things up if she dropped them ... sort of hovered around her. I'm a woman and I honestly couldn't see what it was she had, but there was no doubt she had it.'

'There's something I must ask, and you might find it difficult to answer,' Thanet said. 'But please try. Was there anyone, either in the office here or amongst the clients, who showed her special attention?'

Maureen's eyes flickered to the door of Parrish's office and she shook her head, a tight little shake as though she were holding something back with difficulty.

He wouldn't put it past Parrish to have his ear glued to the keyhole, Thanet thought. He'd have to get

Maureen out of the office. He glanced at his watch in pretended surprise. 'I'm afraid I shall have to go,' he said. 'Could you walk as far as the car park with me, so that we could go on talking? It would save me time.'

'I suppose so.' She followed him reluctantly.

Outside he said, 'I thought it might be easier for you to talk out here. You didn't really answer my question just now, did you? *Do* you know of anyone who was interested in Julie?'

When she didn't reply he glanced at her. Her mouth was set in an obstinate line. He didn't press her but waited until they had reached the entrance to the car park. Then he stopped, turned to face her. 'Look Miss Waters, I'll be frank with you. I think I understand your problem. You have some information which you know I ought to have but something, loyalty I would guess, is holding you back. Am I right?'

She wouldn't look at him.

He tried again. 'Put it this way. If it turned out that the person you are reluctant to talk about had killed Julie, would you still want to protect him?'

That shocked her. 'No, of course not!'

'And if he didn't, how could anything you say harm him?' His point had gone home, he could tell. He waited a moment longer then went on softly, It's Mr Parrish, isn't it?'

She hesitated, then nodded miserably, biting her lip.

'Then you really must tell me.'

But still she stood silent.

'He was interested in Julie?'

Maureen nodded again then finally made up her mind. 'I suppose there's no reason why I shouldn't tell you really, there's nothing much to tell. In fact, that's about it. He was interested in her.'

'You mean she didn't respond?'

'No. Not at all, so far as we could tell. Of course, she was married, but Mr Parrish can be very ... persuasive, when he wants to be.'

'He likes women,' Thanet prompted.

39

'Yes. Oh dear, that makes him sound awful, and he's not. He's great fun to be with – yes, I've been out with him, in the past. So has Joy, for that matter. But it was never serious, not with either of us, and we both knew it. And it was ages ago, anyway, months before Julie came. I think he's had a girlfriend somewhere else, for some time, until Julie arrived. And then, well, I told you, she just had this terrific attraction for men, and I suppose working with her all day … It was obvious he'd fallen for her.'

'But she didn't respond, you say?'

'No. Not at all.'

'How did she react to him, then?'

Maureen shrugged. 'She just took no notice of him, when he tried to flirt with her. Just ignored it or, if it was very obvious, brushed it aside.'

'And how did he feel about that?'

'Well, he pretended to laugh it off, but he didn't like it, obviously. He's not used to that sort of treatment. He's usually the one who calls the tune.'

Maureen obviously had Parrish's measure, Thanet thought. It was interesting, though, that there was no bitterness. 'But you're quite sure there was nothing between them?'

'I'd swear to it, yes. And in any case, lately …'

'Yes?'

'I'm not sure if I should say this. I might have got quite the wrong impression.'

'Go on, please.'

'Well, it seemed to me that lately Julie had something else on her mind. Something that was upsetting her. I mean, she was always quiet, like I said, but for the last couple of weeks she's been acting strangely, sort of jumpy. And she's been looking unwell, pale, as if she hadn't had enough sleep.'

'But you've no idea what was bothering her, if there was something?'

'None, no.'

'Just one other thing. Did anyone here know that Mr

Holmes went to night school on Tuesdays?'

'Yes. We all knew. It came up over coffee one day.'

'Mr Parrish was there too?'

'Yes.'

'Thank you.'

Thanet gave a last, thoughtful look at Parrish's car as he drove off. Interesting that the man had pretended not even to have noticed Julie's charms. Guilt, or merely caution? In any case, unwise. He might have guessed the other girls in the office would have noticed his attempts to win her over.

So, some checking was now necessary. Someone would have to go out to Maddison House, to find out if anyone had seen Parrish go out last night. If Bentley had managed to track Carne down, he might perhaps have been able to find out the registration number of that green Triumph. If not, further enquiries would have to be made to find out if anyone else had noticed it. It certainly seemed too much of a coincidence, that Julie's boss should own one.

As he drove, Thanet mused on the possibility of Parrish's guilt, reproaching himself as he realised that he would be quite pleased if Parrish turned out to be the murderer. Really, just because he didn't like the man ... Where's that famous impartiality we're supposed to cultivate, he reprimanded himself. Not to mention the open-mindedness he was always advocating to Lineham.

The preliminary path. report was awaiting him and after despatching someone to Maddison House he skimmed through it eagerly, then read it again more slowly, twice. Julie had been stabbed in the heart, but in such a way that it was difficult to tell whether death had been instantaneous or whether she might have lived for some minutes afterwards. Why should there be any doubt on that point? Thanet wondered furiously. Surely they should have been able to tell? But in his experience Mallard was meticulous in his

41

work. Thanet would raise the question next time he saw the pathologist but meanwhile he would just have to accept his findings. So, Thanet thought ruefully, bang goes any neat elimination of Holmes.

The report went on to say that the entry to the wound was slightly ragged and the angle such that it could not have been self-inflicted. There was bruising on the back of both her hands, too.

Thanet laid the report on his desk, sat back and thought. Not suicide, then. Julie had been holding the knife, but had not killed herself. The bruising confirmed that there had been a struggle. Had she picked it up to attack someone, or to defend herself?

Try as he would, Thanet couldn't visualise the quiet Julie lying in wait for her husband with a carving knife. Nor, for that matter, could he see Holmes calmly taking the knife to night school with the intention of killing her when he got home. Yet if he were guilty, it couldn't have been any other way, there wouldn't have been time, with only those fifteen or twenty seconds to play with. In any case, it was Julie's prints that were on the knife – and not only on it, Thanet discovered, glancing at the written report which had now come in – but superimposed on many others in such a position as to indicate that she had been holding the knife as a dagger, not as a breadknife. Was it possible that Holmes could have killed her, that when she was dead he had simply taken her hand and pressed it around the dagger, holding it in the right position to give the impression she had been gripping it herself? He must ask Doc Mallard. But again, would there have been time? Thanet honestly could not see that there would. And in any case, his original objection still held: he could see Holmes driven into a stabbing, committing the crime on impulse in a fit of jealous rage, perhaps, but this way? Unconsciously he shook his head. It just didn't feel right.

Then, too, there was the question of why Julie had been dressed to go out.

No, he would guess that there must have been a quarrel. Not with Holmes, of course, but with someone else. He closed his eyes, tried to visualise the scene. Julie is either about to go out with someone or has just arrived home with him. In any case, she is wearing her brown tweed coat, the mermaid brooch on her lapel. They quarrel. Perhaps the atmosphere has been building up between them for some time. Finally it erupts into violence. He threatens her, she becomes frightened. They are in the kitchen and she snatches up the carving knife, runs into the hall. He follows, tries to take the knife away and in the ensuing struggle she is killed. She falls. He panics and runs, having enough presence of mind, however, to take her handbag in order to try to make it seem that she had been killed by an intruder. The struggle must have been brief, the murderer gloved; despite an exhaustive search nothing had been found that could lead to an identification of the killer.

Thanet gave a slow nod of satisfaction. Yes, this was a much more feasible reconstruction of what had happened. Gradually, now, he was feeling his way closer to the truth. Proving it, of course, was quite another matter. Thanet turned back to his desk.

During the next hour information began to trickle in. First, Lineham arrived to report on his visit to Homerights. Holmes had not gone into work this morning and Lineham had been able to question people without the embarrassment of having him around. Holmes, it seemed, was fairly popular at the supermarket. He was efficient, good at dealing with the staff and the only criticism seemed to be that he was somewhat over-ambitious. 'On his way up,' as they put it, Lineham said. 'Personally I think comments like that have arisen from jealousy. I gathered that at twenty-five Holmes is one of the youngest managers in the chain.' There were no whispers of any involvement with another woman and the consensus of opinion was that he was too fond of his wife for there to have been

43

any possibility of one.

Next the phone rang with the information that Julie's handbag had been found in the dustbin of the end house in Disraeli Terrace. Refuse was collected in that area on Wednesdays and a dustman who had heard the news of Julie's death on the radio that morning had recognised the importance of his find and had handed it in.

Thanet had the bag sent up and examined its contents; the wallet section of Julie's purse was empty. Holmes confirmed that it should have contained at least five pounds in notes, the remnants of the previous Friday's house-keeping money. The murderer, then, had had enough intelligence to carry through his plan of deflecting suspicion on to a house-breaker. Thanet was still not inclined to believe that she really had been killed by a thief; past experience had taught him otherwise. He could not yet, however, entirely dismiss the idea.

The next report came from the man who had been sent to check on Parrish. There was apparently nothing to prove or to disprove Parrish's claim that he had spent the previous evening in his flat. The caretaker confirmed that he had seen Parrish arrive home at about six, but he and his wife had gone out to visit a married daughter shortly afterwards, and no one else had seen Parrish all evening. His neighbours had been cooperative but unhelpful.

'Keep asking,' Thanet said.

Thanet and Lineham were still discussing Parrish when the phone rang again. Lineham could see the interest which sparked in Thanet's face as he listened. Thanet scribbled and put the phone down with an air of satisfaction. 'Bentley,' he said. 'Something positive at last. Carne remembered the letters of the registration number on that green Triumph – GKP – because of some personal association. They match the letters on Parrish's Triumph. It's not enough, of course, for a positive identification, but I think we can try a bit of bluff.' He looked at his watch. 'He's probably out at lunch at the moment. We'll have a sandwich at the pub, then go and see if he can wriggle out of this one.'

4

Parrish was clearly none too pleased to see Thanet back so soon. 'I was just leaving, to show a client over a property. It's an important sale, so I hope this won't take long.'

'I shouldn't think so, sir,' said Thanet pleasantly. 'There are just one or two small points ...'

Parrish did not invite them to sit down and remained standing himself, as if to emphasise that the interview would be brief.

'If we could sit down ...?' Thanet said.

'Help yourself,' said Parrish ungraciously and sat down behind his desk with an air of resignation.

'Now, about last night,' Thanet began, pretending to consult his notes, 'you say you were at home all evening?'

'I *was* at home all evening.'

'And you're quite sure that there is no one who can corroborate this? Please,' Thanet said, holding up a hand as Parrish opened his mouth, obviously to protest, 'do give the matter some thought. It really is very important.'

'No,' he said, 'there's no one. But then, why should there be? I live alone, as I told you, and unless I'm entertaining there rarely is anyone who could confirm that I'm there.'

'No phone calls from friends?'

Parrish thought again, shook his head.

Thanet sighed. 'Where do you keep your car, Mr Parrish?'

46

'In a lock-up garage at the back of the flats. There's a block of them, for residents.' Parrish shifted slightly in his chair. 'Look here, Inspector, what is all this about?'

'And last night your car was in your garage?'

'Of course.'

'Then perhaps you could explain,' Thanet said softly, 'how it is that we have two independent witnesses who swear that your car was parked last evening in front of the shops in Parnell Road?'

Parrish stared at him without expression for a few moments and then, lifting his hands in a gesture of submission, said with a rueful smile, 'All right, Inspector, it's a fair cop, as they say. I give in. Yes, I was out last evening, my car was parked in Parnell Road, and if you want to know why I didn't say so before, it's because there was a lady involved. She's married, and I didn't want to embarrass her.'

'I thought you made a point of avoiding married ladies, sir?'

'Fate occasionally pushes one in my direction. It's unfortunate, but it happens, and of course, when it does, discretion is called for.'

'But why not tell me this morning? Why bother to lie?'

Parrish shrugged. 'I suppose, because if one does have an affair with a married woman, one gets into the habit of trying to keep it quiet, even in these rather unusual circumstances. Also, I was trying to spare the lady. I knew that if I told you the truth, you would be bound to want to check with her.'

'So your lying had nothing to do with the fact that your car was parked only a few minutes walk from Mrs Holmes's house?'

Parrish sat up with a jerk. 'Only a few minutes from … My God. I had no idea.'

'You really didn't know that she lived quite close to Parnell Road?'

'Of course I bloody didn't. If I had, I'd have told you straight off where I was last night, instead of giving you reason to get suspicious of me!'

'So you won't mind, in the circumstances, giving us the name and address of this ... lady.'

'Certainly not. It's Phyllis Penge. 14, Palmerston Row. She'll confirm everything I told you.'

'And you arrived at her house at ...?'

'Not at her house, Inspector. At my flat. We might as well get it straight this time. I've got a flat over one of the shops in Parnell Road. I've had it for about three years now. It's very small, but quite useful.'

'Useful?'

'I use it to entertain my mistresses.'

'Why a second flat, when you have a perfectly good one already? It's not as if you were married.'

Parrish shrugged. 'Shall we say I find it easier not to get too, well involved, when they don't know where I live. Which is especially important when a jealous husband is involved.'

'I see.' Thanet was finding it difficult to hide his distaste. He was, however, not here to make moral judgements. 'So this flat is where, exactly?'

'Over the last shop in Parnell Road – the one at the far end of the row.'

Right next to that convenient footpath leading to Gladstone Road, Thanet thought with a lurch of excitement. His face, however, remained impassive. 'And you arrived there at what time?'

'About ten past seven.'

'And Mrs Penge?'

'A few minutes later.'

'Parnell Road and Palmerston Row are next to each other. 'Wasn't it a little ... difficult for Mrs Penge, living so close to your meeting place?'

'Not at all, Inspector. Quite the contrary in fact. It was very handy. Phyllis lives in the last but one house in Palmerston Row. An old lady who is deaf and near-blind lives in the last one. Phyllis just slips out, goes along that convenient footpath and into the entrance to my flat.'

So Parrish knew about that footpath. Would Parrish

have mentioned it, if he were guilty? If he were clever enough, possibly. 'You meet when, usually?'

'Always on Tuesday evenings. Phyllis's husband plays in a darts team on Tuesdays.'

'And you've known each other how long?'

Parrish thought. 'Three months or so. I bumped into her one evening when I was coming out of the flat. I was alone – I'd stayed behind to straighten things up a bit. I do from time to time.'

'After a previous rendezvous, you mean?'

'That's right, Inspector. As it happened, that affair was winding down anyway, so it was very convenient, walking into Phyllis like that.' Parrish was leaning back in his chair, thumbs hooked behind lapels, a reminiscent smile on his face. Clearly, he enjoyed his image of himself as The Great Lover.

'Does either of the girls here know about the flat?'

Parrish's smile disappeared. 'Good God no. I've taken them both out, but only casually. I've enough sense to keep my love life out of the office.'

'And you say you had no idea that Julie Holmes lived in the same area as your flat?'

'No. No idea at all. Why should I? I expect the address is on file, but I couldn't tell you where any of the staff live.'

'Gladstone Road was mentioned on the radio, this morning, when Julie Holmes's murder was reported.'

'Was it? I didn't notice. I was too shaken by the news to take in the details.'

'How long did you and Mrs Penge stay in the flat?'

'Until about half past nine. At least, she left at half past, I stayed on for a few minutes afterwards, to tidy up. In any case, as she lives so close we always leave separately. I don't suppose anyone's ever seen us together.'

'I see.' And he did, only too well. If Parrish's mistress confirmed these times, Parrish was well in the clear. Thanet's voice remained cheerful however as he said, 'Well, I think that's all for the moment, Mr Parrish.' He and Lineham stood up. 'I do wish, though, that you'd told me all this this morning. It would have saved us considerable time and trouble.'

'I do realise that.' Parrish was all contrition. 'I apologise, Inspector, I really do. Er ... You will be discreet, when you question Phyllis?' he went on anxiously, following them to the door. 'Her husband ... I wouldn't like him to ...'

'Find out that his wife is unfaithful? No, I can quite understand that, Mr Parrish.' Deliberately, however, Thanet withheld any such assurance. 'That'll give him a few nasty moments,' he said grimly as they walked to the car park, 'wondering if we're going to spill the beans. No question, was there, of protecting her once he realised his own neck was on the block?'

'Inspector!'

Thanet turned. A red-haired pocket Venus was running towards them, a somewhat hazardous undertaking in that tight skirt and those high heels, Thanet thought. He was right. Just as she reached them she stumbled and was caught by Lineham, who steadied her until she regained her balance. Lineham, Thanet noticed with amusement, was looking somewhat pink about the ears. He turned to the girl. 'Miss Clark, I presume?'

'Yes, that's right. Mrs Clark, actually.' She was out of breath. 'How did you know?'

'Mr Parrish described you to me this morning.'

'Oh.' Now it was Joy Clark's turn to blush. She quickly recovered herself, however. 'I'm Mr Jefferson's secretary and I was in his office when you came just now. Maureen told me I'd missed you. So I thought I'd better come after you.'

'There something you wanted to tell me?'

'Yes.' She glanced uneasily at Lineham, who took the hint.

'I'll go on to the car, sir ...'

She waited until the sergeant was some yards away, then said, 'It's about Julie, Inspector. I hope I'm not speaking out of turn, but, well, Maureen told me the sort of thing you were asking her about this morning, and when she said she'd told you she thought Julie'd been a bit jumpy lately, I suddenly realised I might know why.' She stopped.

'Yes? Do go on.'

'Well, I haven't told Maureen, because it's not something I'm very proud of, it's not the sort of thing you broadcast, but, well, Derek – that's my husband – and me, we haven't been getting on very well lately and in the end we decided to go to Marriage Guidance.' She had been gazing down at the ground, describing tiny arcs with the toe of one dainty shoe and now she glanced up at Thanet as if to gauge his reaction. Apparently reassured she went on, 'Well the long and the short of it is that one evening when we had an appointment, we saw another couple come out of the Marriage Guidance premises. It was Julie and her husband.'

'You've met him?'

'Yes, once.'

'And you're quite certain it was they.'

Joy's beautiful copper hair bounced as she nodded vigorously. 'Oh yes, absolutely.'

'Well thank you, Mrs Clark.'

'I didn't know if I ought to tell you or not ...'

'Every scrap of knowledge helps,' Thanet said, giving her the reassurance she obviously needed. 'Thank you again. And if you think of anything else ...'

In the car he relayed their conversation to Lineham.

'So there *was* something wrong between Holmes and his wife,' Lineham said.

'Looks like it. I don't see how it alters the situation as far as the murder's concerned – all the arguments against Holmes being guilty still hold. All the same, I think I'll go and have a word with him. You can drop me there and go and see Parrish's mistress. Pick me up when you've finished.'

'You think Parrish is in the clear, now?'

Thanet shrugged. 'Difficult to tell. If he's telling the

51

truth then obviously he must be. Question the girl closely. Make sure she has plenty of opportunity to trip herself up.' Thanet experienced a twinge of doubt. Ought he to go and question the girl himself? But he couldn't go back on his instructions now. His reason would be too obvious. In any case some work must be delegated and Lineham was a good man. He'd surely know if the girl was lying.

Thanet had to knock a second, then a third time before he heard shuffling footsteps in the hall and Holmes opened the door. The man was a mess. He was unshaven, the shadows beneath his eyes were so marked that they looked like bruises and he was wearing the same clothes as the previous evening. He probably hadn't taken them off, Thanet thought; he caught a sour whiff of stale sweat and unwashed flesh as Holmes stood back and without a word gestured to him to come in.

Holmes led the way through the hall, carefully walking around the chalk marks on the floor and almost kicking over a large, flat package leaning up against the wall. He stooped to steady it, then preceded Thanet into the living-room where an atmosphere thick with smoke and an ashtray piled high with cigarette stubs showed how he had spent the day. He collapsed rather than sat in one of the big armchairs, his body automatically assuming lines of hopelessness – head drooping, hands limply upturned on his lap, legs outstretched. He looked, Thanet thought, crushed, defeated.

Thanet came straight to the point. 'I understand that you and your wife had been consulting a Marriage Guidance Counsellor,' he said.

Holmes shook his head in disgust, reached for yet another cigarette. 'My God,' he said, 'you lot do enjoy digging up the dirt, don't you?' Then, when Thanet made no comment, 'Well, what of it?'

Thanet sighed. 'Look Mr Holmes, in circumstances like these it is our duty to try to find out everything, and I mean everything, about the people involved. Contrary to what you may believe, we don't enjoy this digging, as you call it, but it has to be done. And until we have found out who killed your wife we have to investigate every scrap of information that comes our way.'

The brief spark of belligerence had already died out of Holmes's eyes. His head sagged against the back of his chair. 'Oh, what the hell,' he said. 'What does it matter, now, anyway? Ask away, if you must.'

'I'd prefer you to tell me.'

Holmes shrugged. 'There isn't much to tell.' He sat up, lit another cigarette from the butt of the one he had been smoking. 'Yes, Julie and I went to see a counsellor – we were supposed to be going again tonight, as a matter of fact. She's – she's very kind, very understanding. You feel you can talk to her and she won't come all moral on you.'

'What's her name?'

'Mrs Thorpe.'

'Go on.'

Holmes frowned, looked thoughtfully at his cigarette. 'Well, we've been what, five times, altogether, I suppose.' He stopped.

Thanet sighed inwardly. It looked as though he was going to have to drag the information out of Holmes bit by bit. 'You went together each time?'

Holmes cast a quick, wary glance at Thanet as if trying to gauge how much he knew. 'We went four times together and Julie went once by herself, the time before last.'

'Why was that?'

'Why was what?'

'Why did she go by herself that time?'

Holmes's lips tightened. 'She wanted to.'

'Any particular reason?'

'Not to my knowledge.'

But he was lying, Thanet was certain of it. 'Was it prearranged?'

'What?'

'That she should go alone,' Thanet said patiently.

'No, she just decided.'

'When?'

'The day before we were due to go.'

'And you went how often?'

'Once a week.'

'Always on Wednesday?'

'Yes.'

'So that day, the day when she suddenly decided she wanted to go by herself, would have been a Tuesday, the Tuesday of the week before last, in fact.'

Holmes thought. 'I suppose so, yes.'

'And you really have no idea what made her want to go alone?'

'I told you, no.'

Thanet tried another tack. 'You must have started going soon after you moved here.'

Holmes made a sour face. 'That's right. I'd hoped … Oh, it was stupid of me, I can see that now, to think the move would make any difference. Places don't really matter, do they, people don't change? Anyway, I didn't realise that then, but when I saw things weren't any better I persuaded Julie to come to Marriage Guidance with me. She hated the idea at first, but once we'd been, she liked Mrs Thorpe and I began to hope we might get things sorted out.'

Poor beggar, Thanet thought, watching him. Suspect or no, the man was suffering, would go on suffering for a long time to come, by the look of it. He hated putting the next question. 'What, exactly, was wrong between you?' he asked.

Holmes shook his head, 'Sorry, it's no go. I'm not talking about my private affairs to anybody else. It was bad enough going to Marriage Guidance, to begin with, anyway, so no thank you. I don't care what you think. And I can't see that it matters much.'

'Would you have any objection to my going to see Mrs Thorpe?'

Holmes hesitated. 'I suppose not. Even if I said yes, I did object, you'd probably go anyway, and that'd put Mrs Thorpe in a fix. They won't discuss clients without their permission. And she's been very good to us ...'

Mrs Thorpe must be a very special person, Thanet thought, if at a time like this Holmes could set aside his own feeling out of consideration for her, 'Look Mr Holmes, I don't want to interfere, but I'm sure it's not good for you to be alone just now. Isn't there anyone around here you could go to, or who could come and stay with you?'

'I notice you don't suggest I get away for a while,' Holmes said bitterly. 'Not that there's anyone to go to. Julie's mother is dead and I never got on with my parents, so this is hardly the time to go running home to mum.'

'Oh I don't know. It might be the best possible time,' Thanet said. 'Parents often turn up trumps at a time like this. I've seen it happen.'

'Not my parents, believe me,' Holmes said.

Thanet stood up. 'What about going to a hotel for a few days?' But even as he spoke he knew that this was a fatuous suggestion. If he were in Holmes's position he would just want crawl away into a corner and lick his wounds for a while before he could feel ready to face the world again.

Holmes shook his head stubbornly. 'I'm all right here.'

Thanet hesitated a moment longer. But what could he do? 'I'll find my own way out,' he said.

Lineham was already waiting for him in the car. 'No joy,' he said. 'She was out at work. A neighbour said she won't be home until five-thirty. Apparently she works mornings on Mondays and Fridays, all day Tuesday, Wednesday and Thursday. I'll go back later.'

'What time does her husband get home?'

'A quarter past six on the dot, the neighbour said.'

'Try to make sure you leave before he arrives.' Thanet was feeling depressed after the interview with

Holmes. 'We don't want to make trouble for him unnecessarily.'

'Where now, sir?'

'Back to the office, I think. I'm going to try to get hold of the Holmes's Marriage Guidance Counsellor.'

This, however, proved impossible, as the only number in the book for the Marriage Guidance Council was switched into an Ansaphone service and Thanet had to be content with leaving a message.

'You don't look very cheerful.' It was Mallard, peering at Thanet over his half-moon spectacles. 'Back still bothering you?' he enquired gruffly.

'Oh hullo, Tom. Sit down. No,' said Thanet in surprise, 'as a matter of fact it's not. Today's the first day when I haven't been conscious of it more or less all the time.'

'So why the long face? Didn't you like my beautiful report?'

'It may have been beautiful to you, but it certainly wasn't beautiful to me.'

'What did you expect? Cast-iron evidence of who killed her?'

'Certainly.'

The two men grinned at each other.

'No, seriously, though,' Thanet said, 'it wasn't exactly helpful. Except that it does seem certain she didn't kill herself.'

'Right. Physically impossible, with the knife at that angle.'

'And it definitely was that knife, that killed her?'

'You're thinking it might have been substituted for the real murder weapon? No, no question of that. If there had been, it would have been in my report. That was the knife, all right.'

'But there was a slightly ragged entry wound. A struggle, you think?'

Mallard nodded. 'The bruises on the backs of her hands bear it out.'

'They couldn't have been made by the murderer

56

pressing her hands around the handle of the knife in the hope of making it appear suicide?'

'No.'

'The devil of it is,' Thanet said, getting up and moving across to the window, 'there's so little evidence. Nothing under her fingernails, for instance.' There was the hint of a question in the inflection of his voice and Mallard glanced up sharply.

'If there had been, it would have been in the report,' he said huffily.

'Of course, Tom,' Thanet hastened to reassure him. 'You are nothing if not thorough, I know that.'

'He was probably, wearing gloves,' Mallard said. 'And the struggle might have been very brief. The girl was no heavyweight, it wouldn't have taken much to overpower her.'

'Then there's this question of whether she died instantly,' Thanet said.

'Yes, unfortunate, that − that we can't be more definite. Mind, she wouldn't have lingered long. A few minutes, no more.'

Enough to clear Holmes, Thanet thought. 'But why the doubt?' he asked. 'I thought it was always possible to tell, after a post mortem.'

'Not necessarily. How the victim died, yes, but not how long it took. Let me explain. In this particular case the point of the knife pierced the pericardium − in layman's terms, the coating of the heart. Now if such a puncture is of sufficient dimensions, death is instantaneous. If, however, it is very small, only slight bleeding may occur at first. But the pressure of each successive pulsation of the heart increases the size of the wound until, bingo, suddenly the pericardium ruptures and there is a massive haemorrhage and death occurs. The point is that when this happens the pericardium tears and so in a post mortem it is impossible to tell whether or not the wound was sufficiently lethal to cause death at the moment of penetration, or whether its size was increased after a delay of some minutes.'

'I see.' Thanet thought for a while, absorbing the implications of this information. 'Some minutes, you say. The time could vary?'

'Oh yes. Depending on the size of the initial puncture and also on what the victim was doing. If he was lying down, the heart would not be labouring as much as if he were standing up, or doing something even more energetic.'

'Like struggling?'

'Yes, like struggling. So, yes, as you imply, in this case death would have been accelerated.'

'So it is still just possible that her husband could have done it?'

'Frankly, I doubt it, in view of various other factors — none of which, I freely admit, enters my province. And I certainly don't think you could ever take it to court unless you had some other pretty conclusive evidence. A good defence Counsel would make mincemeat of you on the medical evidence.'

'Quite,' Thanet said gloomily.

'Ah well, time I was on my way. Cheer up, Luke. At the moment you look as though you ought to be parading up the High Street with a sandwich board proclaiming *The End Of The World Is Nigh*.'

Thanet gave a shame-faced grin as he said, 'Thanks for the explanation, anyway,' and saw Mallard to the door.

Returning to his desk he skimmed quickly through the messages which he had pushed aside to ring the Marriage Guidance Council. The two witnesses who had seen the tall dark man walking in the direction of Gladstone Road had had nothing to add to their statements. Both said that their estimate of the time could have been out by a few minutes either way.

Bentley had been unable to get a detailed itinerary of Horrocks's sales trip either from the man's wife or from his firm; the former didn't know it, the latter said that they left such details entirely to their representatives. The best they could do was to provide a list of the towns which Horrocks would be visiting during the time he was away.

Negatives, negatives, negatives. There was nothing constructive, at the moment, that he could do. Thanet glanced at his watch. Six-fifteen. Lineham should soon be reporting on his visit to Parrish's mistress. But apart from that ... to hell with it, thought Thanet. What was the point in hanging about here beating his brains out for nothing? If he was needed, they knew where to find him. He'd just wait for Lineham's call, then he'd go home. He knew from past experience that this was probably the most constructive move he could make at the moment. Let things simmer for a while, try to put the case out of his mind, come back to it fresh tomorrow.

Lineham rang a few minutes later. Phyllis Penge had confirmed Parrish's account of their meeting in every detail.

'What's she like?' Thanet asked.

'Younger than I'd expected. Lush, sexy type.'

'Was she telling the truth, that's the point?' Thanet was aware of a feeling of unease, but couldn't put his finger on its source.

'Oh yes, I'm sure of that. She's not very bright. I don't think she could have been convincing enough if she'd been lying.'

'Good,' Thanet said, thinking that the news was anything but. 'Well, you get off home now, Mike. Get a good night's sleep. We could both do with it.'

He replaced the receiver thoughtfully. What was it, just now ...? But it was no use, it wouldn't come and he felt more depressed than ever. Parrish was out, then. Now what?

Home, he reminded himself.

It was healing to unlock his front door and hear the normality of splashing and squeals of delight from upstairs.

'Is that you, darling?' Joan appeared at the top of the stairs, face flushed from bending over the bath.

'Daddy!' Bridget appeared beside Joan, dressed only in pants and socks. She flew down the stairs to hurl herself at him.

Thanet grinned up at Joan. 'This one hasn't had her tub yet, I gather?'

'No. I'm just finishing Ben.'

'I'll do Sprig, then. Come on, young lady.' Thanet stooped to pick her up, just remembering his back in time. Better not risk it. He took her hand instead.

After supper Thanet helped Joan to wash up, then left her to make coffee while he selected a record. Bach's double violin concerto, he decided. It had a quality of certainty, of sureness and order which he needed tonight. When Joan came in she settled herself on the carpet at his feet, leaning back against his knees. Thanet stroked her hair, reminding himself thankfully that even if his work was going badly he always had this to come home to. He had a sudden, disconcerting picture of Holmes sunk in his armchair with the overflowing ashtray at his side, his house empty and silent, his much-loved wife dead and even his memories of her tainted by discord. By comparison he, Thanet, was rich beyond telling.

'Do you think ...?' he said softly.

Joan twisted her head to look up at him, smiling. 'Just what I was thinking,' she said.

He stood up, put out a hand to help her to her feet and softly, so as not to wake the children, they went upstairs together.

5

Julie Holmes's photograph appeared in the news-papers next morning and at once the usual flood of telephone calls began: she had been seen in places as far apart as Edinburgh and Penzance and engaged in every activity from roller-skating to prostitution. With their customary resignation Thanet and his team began checking the more likely sightings; one never knew when one might strike gold.

Thanet began ringing Sturrenden Marriage Guid-ance Council at regular intervals, but it was not until nine-thirty that the Ansaphone service was replaced by the secretary's voice and Thanet discovered that setting up an interview with Mrs Thorpe would not be as easy as he had expected.

It wasn't as though the secretary was rude or difficult, quite the contrary. She was polite, charming even, but adamant. She quite understood the circumstances, she said, and appreciated Thanet's need to see Mrs Thorpe, but she couldn't possibly release Mrs Thorpe's telephone number or make an appointment for Thanet to see her without clearance from Rugby.

'Rugby?' queried Thanet.

'Our headquarters.'

'Couldn't you get Mrs Thorpe to ring me, then?'

'I'm sorry. But in circumstances like this there is a certain procedure we have to follow, to protect the confidentiality we promise our clients.'

'But there's no question of breaking confidentiality

here. Mr Holmes has agreed to my talking to her.'

'Yes, I do understand. But I have to check, nevertheless. I'm sorry, Inspector, but I'm only doing my job. I do realise the urgency of your problem, though, and I promise that I will ring Rugby straight away and let you know the moment I have a decision.'

And with this Thanet had to be content. The girl, however, kept her word; at ten o'clock she rang back to say that Mrs Thorpe could see him at one, at the M.G.C. premises.

'No earlier?'

'I'm sorry. Mrs Thorpe is counselling this morning.'

'Right. One o'clock, then. Thank you.'

Frustratingly, it was just as he was leaving, at twenty to one, that the most interesting event of the morning occurred: a phone call from a man called Burt, landlord of the Dog and Whistle in Sturrenden, claiming that on the evening she died Julie Holmes had visited his pub with a man. They had, he said, been in several times before, and he was certain that it had been she.

'You're in luck, Mike. You can get a good pint at the Dog and Whistle. Get over there and we'll meet back here afterwards. I've a feeling this interview with Mrs Thorpe might take some time.'

As he drove through the lunch-hour traffic Thanet wondered if he was wasting his time. Wouldn't it have been more sensible to go to the Dog and Whistle with Lineham? The landlord's story certainly seemed the most promising lead they'd had so far. Having been so insistent over the need for the interview with Mrs Thorpe, however, he felt morally obliged to turn up. And, he had to admit it, he *wanted* to see her.

Why?

Well, partly because he genuinely felt that in a case like this, where there was a lack of material evidence, it was the job of the investigating officer to find out as much as he could about the character and life of the victim in the hope that his knowledge might lead him to the murderer, and also because, if he were honest with himself, Julie herself was beginning to intrigue him. He had now spoken to a number of people who had been close to her in her everyday life – her husband, her boss, the girls with whom she worked, and so far she still remained a shadowy figure to him, elusive. She must have trusted Mrs Thorpe, to have asked for an interview alone with her, and Thanet was hoping that she might have confided in her.

Thanet wondered what the counsellor would be like. What sort of a person would want to hear about other people's marriage problems? Thanet's own work was often depressing enough, but the thought of sitting listening to accounts of other people's misery day in, day out, made him shudder.

In the event, Mrs Thorpe was a surprise. She was in her early thirties, small – not much more than five feet – and very slim. She had a mop of dark, curly hair, wore an enormous pair of tinted spectacles and was dressed in faded jeans and a loose overblouse in some soft, blue material.

The counselling room, too, was a surprise. Thanet didn't know quite what he had expected, but it certainly wasn't this small, pleasant sitting-room furnished with comfortable armchairs.

'Do sit down, Inspector,' she said. Then she grinned. 'I'm not what you expected,' she said.

'Is it so obvious?'

'I'm used to it. I'm not quite sure what people expect when they come here, but I suspect it's someone rather staid, elderly and drab.' She shrugged. 'Still, it doesn't seem to matter what image they start off with. Once you've been with them a short while then you're "My counsellor" and that's it.' She looked at him expectantly and said, 'Now tell me how you think I can help you, Inspector. It was a dreadful shock to me, of course, to hear about Julie and anything I can do ... I'm sorry there was some delay in fixing this appointment, but we simply have to watch this confidentiality thing. If we didn't, people would never feel free to talk to us. D'you know, once a counsellor was called as a witness in a defended divorce case. Her client didn't want her to give evidence and she went to the court with her suitcase packed, ready to go to jail rather than break his confidence.'

'What happened?'

'Fortunately she wasn't called! Of course, that's an extreme case, but we really do regard it as a very important rule. So when you rang, naturally our secretary had to get clearance from the powers that be. And check with John Holmes, of course, that he had in fact given his permission for the interview.'

'But I told her he had.'

'We had to be sure.' She grinned again at the look on his face. 'I don't suppose you're used to people checking up on you!'

True, he'd experienced a momentary spurt of anger at the idea, but then he realised that this was unjustifiable. If it had been his marriage which was under threat of being exposed to a third party, he would have been glad to know it was protected so carefully. He said so.

'Good,' Mrs Thorpe said briskly. 'And now ...?'

There was silence as Thanet marshalled his thoughts. He felt he could trust this woman and decided to be frank with her. 'I'll give you the position first,' he said.

Briefly, he related the facts of the case and she listened carefully. She sat quite still, according him a quality of attention rare in his experience. People on the whole were far more interested in talking than in listening.

'... so you see, I'm here because I feel I have to try to find out all I can about Mrs Holmes, in the hope that this might lead me to finding out who killed her. There is one promising lead at the moment, but it might well just peter out, they often do.'

'Yes, I see. Well now, perhaps it would be best if I

give you a brief account of the Holmes's case and then you can ask questions if you wish. But first, how is John – Mr Holmes – taking it? Hard, I would guess.'

'Very hard. He's very depressed, I'd say … He told me he had an appointment with you last night. He didn't turn up, I gather?'

'No. Hardly surprising, in the circumstances … Perhaps I'll give him a ring. It's difficult, isn't it? But it might just help, to talk to someone about it. If he doesn't want to, fair enough.'

'At least it might make him feel someone cares. He had nobody, I gather, no one at all.'

'I'll do that then.' She paused, thinking. 'Well now, let me see. I've seen them five times in all. Four joint interviews and one, a fortnight ago with Julie alone. They've been married for three years and there was trouble right from the start. They came, ostensibly, with a sexual problem. Julie had no interest in sex, and although they made love from time to time there was no enjoyment in it for either of them. I think John hoped that when they moved here, started a new life in a different place, things would be different, but of course they just brought their problem with them and when he saw things weren't improving he persuaded her to come here. He'd been thinking about it for some time, I believe. Anyway, they'd only been in the area for a week or so when they first came.

'The trouble was, of course, that it wasn't just a sexual problem. As so often happens, their sexual difficulties were just a reflection of their day-to-day relationship. Julie … was a very reserved, withdrawn sort of girl and John quite a thrusting, aggressive, masculine type. That surprises you, I see. But you must remember you've seen him only in a state of acute depression.'

'True. And I can see that logically you are right. He'd scarcely be the youngest manager in the chain of Homerights' if he weren't pretty thrusting, as you put it.'

'Oh is he? I didn't know that. Yes, that is interesting. Anyway, these two types can go well together – the girl likes being dominated, acquiescent – but in this case Julie … well, it seems that she was incapable of any response. It was as if her feelings, her emotions were locked away somewhere inside her, inaccessible to anyone. And of course the trouble was that someone like John always responds to that sort of reaction by pressing harder, pushing for some kind of response, all the time. Then she withdraws more, like a snail retreating further into its shell, he redoubles the pressure, she withdraws even more and so on. It's a vicious downward spiral, in which the participants are helpless to prevent the situation from becoming progressively worse. In this particular case John's jealousy didn't help, either.'

'Was it justified, you think?'

'I can't be sure, of course, but no, I don't think so. I think Julie was as fond of John as she could be of any man. The trouble was, she was incapable of showing that affection in the way which would convince her husband that she did love him, and he therefore tended to suspect that she was as she was only because there was someone else.'

'And you're really pretty certain there wasn't? In your own mind, that is?'

'I told you, no.' Mrs Thorpe was silent for a moment, thinking, then she added, 'Not from Julie's point of view, anyway. I'm not saying there wouldn't have been someone hovering in the wings, ready to snap her up if her marriage went wrong. She was the sort of girl who would be very attractive to the same strong, masculine type as John. She appeared so soft, so gentle and feminine, that they would imagine conquest as inevitable and see resistance only as a challenge.'

'No one specific was ever mentioned?'

'No.' She sounded doubtful, though. 'There was someone in London before they moved down here. Someone who knew her before she was married and wouldn't leave her alone afterwards. John even had a fight with him once, but it didn't seem to put him off. I think it was the main reason why John was so keen to move down here when the opportunity arose.'

'It's surprising, in the circumstances, that he left her on her own in London while they were looking for a house down here.'

'Well, apparently this other man was abroad at the time, and this was the only reason why John agreed to the arrangement. And he used to ring her every evening, I gather, and go home at weekends, of course.'

'Do you remember this man's name?'

Mrs Thorpe thought for a moment. 'I'm not sure ... it was ... Kenny, I think. Yes, that's it. Kenny.'

'And his surname?'

'I don't think it was ever mentioned.'

'I'm sorry, we seem to have wandered somewhat. Do go on.'

'Yes, well let me see, what was I saying? Ah yes. They had become locked in this sort of impasse, then, with the situation becoming progressively worse, when they decided to come here. At first we got absolutely nowhere. It's absolutely essential, you see, to have your clients' complete confidence. And Julie, as I've explained, is the sort of person who finds it near-impossible to open up to anyone. She was just beginning to be less wary of me, I felt, when the situation suddenly began to deteriorate in a most unexpected way. Julie began to have nightmares of a particularly frightening kind. That was when she rang up and asked if she could come to see me alone. When she arrived she was in a terrible state – for the twenty minutes or so she just sat there, shaking. Eventually I managed to get out of her what was upsetting her.

'Apparently, the two nights previous to that interview – and regularly since, I might add – she had dreamt that she was in a cage. She was shut in, trying frantically to find a way out, and failing. And then she would become aware that whatever it was she was terrified of was in the cage with her, and that there was no way of escaping it. It was dark, but she knew that it was coming closer, and then, when it was so close that she could feel the heat of its breath on her cheek, she'd wake up. Just talking about it upset her so ... d'you know, when she'd finished, she rushed off to the cloakroom and was sick, really sick, poor girl. I went after her and I saw ...

'I did wonder if perhaps the cage represented how she felt about her marriage, but that seemed such a glib explanation and I felt there was more to it than that. I tried to find out what could have triggered off the nightmares, but we just didn't get anywhere. To her knowledge she'd never had this particular dream before, though she did admit to remembering creeping downstairs to look for her mother after bad dreams as a child. Later on, after she'd gone, there was one possible explanation which occurred to me. I already knew that Julie had been brought up by her mother – who died about a year ago – because her father had been killed in a car crash when Julie was very small, about three, I think. I wondered if, perhaps, she had been in the car at the time ... well, it would have been a terrifying experience for a small child, especially if her father died as a result of the accident. If she'd been trapped in the car, unable to get out ...'

'Quite a likely explanation, I should think.'

'But why should she suddenly start having night-mares twenty years later? I mean, what could cause the memories to be ... reactivated?'

'Did she have any memories of the crash?'

'Oh no, none. She talked about it as if she'd only heard about it from someone else – her mother, I assumed. She certainly showed no signs of distress when talking about it – though I suppose that's nothing to judge by. If the experience had been as traumatic as all that, then she might well have wiped it out of her mind completely.'

'Did you suggest this explanation to her?'

'There was no opportunity. The following time – last week – she and John came together, and she had asked for my assurance that I wouldn't tell him about the nightmares.'

'But he must have known she was having them, surely?'

'Yes, but not what they were about.'

'I wonder why she didn't want him to know?'

Mrs Thorpe shrugged. 'Who can tell? But she didn't, and of course, having promised, my hands were tied.' She hesitated, then went on, 'I was really worried about her. When they came last week … she looked awful. Very strained, desperate, almost, I'd say she was very near breaking point.'

'Breaking point?'

'Well, as I said, she found it very difficult to express her feelings – to talk about them or to show them. The only emotion I ever saw her show was distress, fear, if you like, over this nightmare. And John seemed incapable of understanding what I explained to you just now – that the harder he pressed the more she would withdraw from him, that what he needed to do was to ease up on that pressure, leave her alone, allow her some space in which she could have an opportunity to sort out her problems and perhaps begin to respond to him differently. Though frankly, I don't know if that could ever have happened.'

'So you felt that in a way circumstances were combining to push her towards this breaking point, as you call it?'

'Yes, I do. That was why I was very careful indeed not to put any pressure upon her myself. And she did seem to respond to the gentle approach.'

'But if there had perhaps been other pressures, about which we know nothing …?'

The counsellor lifted her hands in a gesture of helplessness. 'I just don't know.'

'Mrs Thorpe, I must ask you this, though I realise

69

that perhaps it is not a fair question. Do you think she was capable of turning on her husband with a knife?'

She shifted uneasily in her chair, considered. 'I'm sorry, I just don't know. Well, yes, I suppose it would have been possible, if he really had put intolerable pressure on her. It could have been some last, desperate defence of her privacy ... Once or twice I've seen what happens when people like Julie, people who seem incapable of showing their feelings, have been pushed too far. They lose control completely, become hysterical, incapable of rational behaviour.'

'But it would have to have been done in the heat of the moment.'

'Oh yes. I'm pretty sure about that. I simply can't see Julie planning a cold-blooded murder. Nor John, either, for that matter.'

'Thank you.' Thanet stood up. 'You really have been most helpful.'

As he left he glanced at his watch. Too late, now to get anything to eat in the canteen. On the way back to the car park he called in at a small pub for a beer and a sandwich. The place was almost empty after the lunch-time rush and he was able to settle down in a quiet corner and think in peace.

He felt he now had a much clearer picture of Julie. And he saw her, above all, as frightened. But, of what? Of her husband, of this boyfriend she had been meeting regularly, if the landlord's tale was to believed, of those nightmares ... or of herself? Had she sensed that she was being pushed towards that breaking point Mrs Thorpe had mentioned? And had she, the night she died, reached it?

The question, of course, was who had been with her at the time? The obvious choice (if the landlord's story was true) was the man in the pub. In any case, it looked as though her husband was in the clear, as Thanet had thought. For Julie to have cracked, as she did, there must have been some considerable build-up, a protracted quarrel. Holmes had been at night school

70

all evening, had walked home with Byfleet. Those fifteen or twenty seconds were simply not long enough for such a build-up, even assuming that the quarrel had begun before Holmes left at quarter to seven. No, there had to be someone else involved. Suddenly, Thanet could hardly wait to hear what Lineham had found out. He left his beer half drunk and hurried back to the car.

As soon as Thanet saw Lineham's face he could tell that the sergeant's trip had been fruitful.

'It was her,' Lineham said ungrammatically. 'That's definite. The barmaid saw her too and, being a woman, even described what she was wearing – a brown tweed coat with a mermaid brooch on the lapel. She particularly noticed the brooch because she fancied it, asked Mrs Holmes where she'd got it.'

'Good.' Thanet sat down, took out his pipe, began filling it. 'Go on then. Let's hear the details.'

It was, according to the landlord, the third or fourth time that Julie and her boyfriend had visited the Dog and Whistle, always on a Tuesday evening. The landlord was certain of this because Tuesday was Darts Match night and the couple always arrived, separately, soon after the match began at eight.

Last Tuesday had been no exception. The man arrived first, ordered drinks for both of them and waited, sitting at the bar because the pub was crowded and there were no tables empty. Julie arrived soon afterwards and shortly after that a table became vacant and they moved – the barmaid remembered this, because of her interest in Julie's brooch and because, practised at interpreting people's moods, she had seen at once that Julie was 'uptight', as she put it.

She had therefore kept an eye on them, interested to see what would happen. She was rewarded by signs of a developing quarrel, Julie shaking her head repeatedly and the man becoming more vehement, leaning forward and making angry gestures.

After about half an hour – the barmaid could be no more accurate than that – Julie had jumped up and run out of the pub 'in a real state, hardly knew what she was doing'. She had bumped into one of the darts team without apologising, earning herself some 'dirty looks'. Her companion had sat on for a few minutes, glowering into his glass and had then finished his drink and left.

'They didn't happen to see if he followed her?'

'No. They were very busy and anyway the windows in the Dog and Whistle are high up. The barmaid couldn't have seen without going outside to look and even if she hadn't been busy I don't think she'd have been interested enough to do that.'

'You didn't get the name?'

'No. The man wasn't a regular.'

'Pity. Still, things are looking up, aren't they? This all fits in beautifully with what I learned from Mrs Thorpe.' Thanet gave Lineham an account of his interview with her.

'Yes. I see what you mean, sir. You think this man might have followed Mrs Holmes back to Gladstone Road after the quarrel, started haranguing her again. She grabs the carving knife and in the struggle she gets killed.'

'Seems logical, don't you think, in view of what we now know? Fits all the known facts, too. Let me see. If they stayed at the pub for about half an hour, they must have left between, say, half past eight and twenty to nine. You didn't by any chance think to check how long it takes to walk from the Dog and Whistle to Gladstone Road?'

'Six minutes,' said Lineham, with justifiable smugness.

'And she died between eight-thirty and nine-thirty ... Did you manage to get a decent description of the man?'

Lineham opened his notebook but did not, Thanet noticed, do more than glance at it. He had the description off pat. 'About five eleven, good, athletic build, springy walk, hair thick, dark brown, cut to just

72

below his ears, eyes possibly brown. Wearing jeans and a brown suede jacket.'

'The barmaid?'

Lineham nodded.

'Wish there were more like her.'

Lineham grinned. 'She said she noticed him particularly because she fancied him. "Dishy", she said he was. I think that's why she kept an eye on him and Mrs Holmes. Hoped that if Mrs Holmes ditched him, he might drift in her direction ... He could be our "tall, dark man", sir.'

'He could indeed. Though neither of those two witnesses mentioned seeing Mrs Holmes.'

'Perhaps he stayed a little way behind her, to give her time to cool off before he approached her again.'

'Mmm. Possibly. Now, how to get hold of him ... I think we'll plump first for his being that former boyfriend of hers in London. Mrs Thorpe said he was a very persistent type. What did she say his name was? Kenny somebody, that's right. Let's go and see Holmes. No doubt he'll be only too delighted to supply us with the details.'

6

One of Dobson's lorries was backing out of the builder's yard. Thanet and Lineham had to wait until it had completed its manœuvres and driven off before they could pull in, in front of Holmes's house.

Holmes looked even worse than the previous day. Still unshaven, still wearing the same clothes, he said nothing when he saw the two policemen, simply turned and shuffled into the living-room, once again carefully avoiding the place where Julie's body had lain. He flopped down into his armchair, sinking at once into what had clearly become an habitual posture, eyes dulled and staring unseeingly at the floor. Thanet and Lineham might not have been in the room for all the awareness he showed of their presence.

Thanet grimaced at Lineham and without a word they cleared a space to sit down on the settee, which was littered with unopened newspapers and half-empty mugs, one of which had overturned, leaving a long brown stain on the golden velvet. Cups and mugs, interspersed with overflowing ashtrays, were scattered everywhere – on the mantelpiece, the floor, the transparent cover of the record-player, in the fireplace, even. There were, however, Thanet noted, no plates. Had Holmes not eaten since Tuesday evening? The air in the room was sour with more than a smell of stale sweat and cigarette smoke; the miasma of despair was so powerful as to be almost tangible.

There was one new feature, though. A painting, from the face of which the brown paper wrapping had been roughly torn away, stood on the floor, leaning up against one of the legs of the long work table in the bay window. Thanet remembered the flat, oblong parcel which Holmes had almost kicked over in the hall, the last time Thanet came. Shadowed by the table and with its back to the light it was only dimly illuminated, but Thanet thought it looked interesting. It was a painting of a cricket match, on a village green, by the look of it. There was something oddly familiar about the scene and Thanet would have liked to get up and examine it more closely. He refrained from doing so, however – he was not here to appreciate art.

'Mr Holmes?'

Thanet had to repeat the name three times before the dulled eyes swivelled slowly upwards to meet his.

'Mr Holmes, I'm sorry, but I'm afraid there are some more questions I must ask.'

No response.

'I know this is painful for you, but it really must be done,' Thanet persisted.

Something, the gentleness in his voice, perhaps, provoked a reaction. Holmes's eyes filled with pain and the muscles in his jaw contracted as he clenched his teeth. Then, 'It won't bring her back,' he said. His voice was rough, either from disuse or from too much smoking.

"No,' Thanet said. 'But it will, I hope, help us to find out who killed her.'

'Yes,' said Holmes dully. He made a tiny, helpless gesture with one hand. 'What the hell,' he said. 'Who cares?'

'I do,' said Thanet.

There was, he now saw, something to be done before he could hope to get anything out of the man. Holmes had sunk into this torpor because it was the least painful way of dealing with an intolerable situation. Somehow, he had to be brought out of it, not only because in this state he was useless to Thanet but for his own sake, because if he went on like this he would

75

surely, eventually, die. There was apparently no one to care whether he lived or not. Perhaps Thanet ought to try to get him into hospital? But he had a horror of interfering in people's lives to such an unwarranted degree, 'for their own good'. If the man did not wish to go on living, then ultimately the choice was his. Nevertheless, Thanet couldn't just stand by and let it happen.

'Mr Holmes, when did you last have anything to eat?'

'Eat?' A tiny furrow appeared between Holmes's brows, as if he had difficulty in understanding the question.

'Yes, to eat.' Thanet gestured at the room. 'It looks as though you've been living on coffee.'

The frown became more pronounced. 'I don't know.'

Thanet turned to Lineham. 'We won't get anything out of him while he's like this, poor beggar. Go out to the kitchen, see if you can rustle something up, will you? And take some of these mugs with you.'

They both got up, collected two fistfuls of mugs each and returned for more. Then Lineham began investigating the contents of the refrigerator and larder while Thanet emptied the ashtrays, finally moving to the bay window and throwing wide open two of the casement windows. Sweet, clean air rushed into the room and Holmes, who, during all this activity had remained motionless, turned his head towards the window as if its freshness had touched some chord in his memory.

'Here we are,' Lineham said cheerfully, carrying in a tray. 'Not very exciting, but the best I can do.' The aroma of freshly buttered toast filled the room, a wholesome, appetising smell. Lineham had scrambled some eggs, made a pot of tea.

Holmes ate reluctantly at first and then his appetite awakened, like a man who had just discovered the existence of food.

Lineham poured cups of tea for Thanet and himself.

'I'll recommend you for the staff canteen,' Thanet said, grinning, as he accepted his. 'Now then Mr Holmes, if you're feeling better ... '

'Much thanks.' Holmes had lit yet another cigarette, but he was, Thanet thought thankfully, at least looking alive again. The dullness had gone from his eyes, his movements were more positive.

'Good. But before we start, please try not to let yourself get into that state again.'

'Pull yourself together, you mean,' Holmes said bitterly. 'What for?'

'Very well,' Thanet said briskly. 'It's your choice and I'm not going to argue with you. But for God's sake make it a choice, not an abdication of responsibility. Now, these questions.'

Holmes blinked at Thanet's change of tone, but Thanet could see that he had at last given him cause to think. What more could he do? You can't make a man want to live. 'Now, I've been to see Mrs Thorpe and there are one or two points I want to clarify. First of all, I understand your wife's father was killed in a road accident. Can you tell me where they were living at the time?'

'London, so far as I know. Julie told me she'd lived in London all her life.'

'Which area?'

'Wimbledon, I think. That's where her mother lived, and Julie too, of course, before we got married.'

'Your wife had no memories of this crash?'

'No. Not to my knowledge anyway.'

'And you've no idea if she was involved in it herself?'

'No. Look here, what's all this about? How can it possibly matter?'

'I've no idea,' Thanet said. 'I'm trying to understand your wife's state of mind at the time of her death and Mrs Thorpe seemed to think that there might possibly be a connection between this accident and the nigthmares your wife had been having lately. Did your wife tell you about them?'

77

'No, she wouldn't. But they terrified her, all right. Me too, when she had them. She'd wake up screaming, and the first time it happened … It used to take ages to calm her down, afterwards.'

'She had them most nights?'

'Every night, since they started.'

'Have you any idea why they did start?'

'None at all.'

'She'd never had them before?'

'No, never.'

'Then something must have triggered them off. Now, I understand that the first one occurred on a Monday evening – that would be a fortnight ago last Monday.'

'Something like that, yes.'

'Try to think. I must know exactly when they started.'

Holmes frowned. 'I'm pretty sure – yes, it must have been that Monday, because it was the next day that she rang Mrs Thorpe and that was the day before we were due for an appointment. Yes, it was that Monday.'

'Now think very carefully. Can you remember what she did, that day?'

'Not offhand. She must have gone to work, I suppose.'

'You can't remember anything special about that Monday?'

Holmes passed a hand over his head and then pressed the thumb and forefinger into his eyes. 'I'm sorry. I just can't seem to think …'

'Do you think you could try to remember, when we've gone? Try really hard, I mean? And if you do, give me a ring?'

Holmes shrugged. 'If you like.'

'Good. Now wife's mother is dead, but if she and your wife lived in the same place all her life until you married, it's possible that your mother-in-law had some close friends living nearby. Do you know of any?'

'There's Mrs Lawton. Julie used to call her Auntie Rose.'

'Her address?'

'9 Wellington Road, Wimbledon.'

78

'Any others?'

'Not that I know of.'

'Right. There's just one other point.' Here it came. Thanet had deliberately left this till last. Now, he kept his tone as casual, as matter-of-fact as possible. 'I understand that while you were living in London there was a man who used to pester your wife. Could you give me his name, address and place of work?'

Holmes sat up abruptly. 'Kendon, you mean? What's he got to do with it? You don't think he – my God, wait till I get my hands on him!'

'Mr Holmes, calm down, please. We really have no idea. But we have to follow up every lead, however slight, and Mrs Thorpe just happened to mention his existence.' Thanet felt quite justified in pretending that there was no evidence to connect this man with Julie. For one thing, they were not yet certain that it was he who had apparently been meeting Julie on Tuesday evenings while her husband was out, and for another he didn't want a second murder on his hands; at the moment Holmes looked quite capable of committing one. 'Please,' he went on. 'There really is no need to get so worked up.'

'No? If I thought he'd followed her down here ... He never left her alone, even after we were married. Said she was his, by right – he introduced us, as a matter of fact. He knew her first, but that gave him no rights over her. I told him, it was her choice and that was that. And she chose me.' An expression of pride flitted briefly over Holmes's face.

'Anyway, as I said, it's just a matter of checking every lead. So if you could tell us where to find him ...?'

'Flat 4, Wallington Park Road, Putney.'

'And he worked?'

'At the BBC. He's Kenny Kendon, the disc jockey.'

Thanet was astonished, though he didn't show it. Kenny Kendon was one of the Radio 2 regular disc jockeys, with his own live programme each morning. 'Description?'

'A bit taller than me – five ten or eleven, I suppose. Brown hair.'

So, still in the running for the mysterious boyfriend, Thanet thought with satisfaction. He avoided looking at Lineham. 'Well, I think that's about all for the moment.' He stood up and Lineham followed suit. 'And if you take my advice, Mr Holmes, you'll get back to work as soon as possible. You won't do yourself any good hanging about here, brooding.' At the door he turned. 'Mrs Thorpe was very concerned about you, by the way. She said she'd give you a ring.'

This, he was pleased to see, meant something to Holmes. A spark of interest flared briefly in his eyes. He said nothing, however, as he let them out and watched them walk down the garden path.

'Well, what do you think of that, sir?' Lineham said excitedly, when they were in the car. 'Kenny Kendon!'

'Interesting.'

'You'll go and see him?'

'Tomorrow, I think. We'll both go, by car. You can visit this Auntie Rose while I'm seeing Kendon.'

'Where now, then?' Lineham asked.

Thanet looked at his watch. Four o'clock. 'Back to the office. I must get my reports up to date. I'm seeing the Super at five-thirty.' At least there were now some interesting developments to report. 'Remind me to ring the Met. will you? I'll have to let them know I'll be trespassing on their patch tomorrow.'

Nothing interesting awaited them at the office. Thanet managed to bring himself up to date on his paperwork, had a satisfactory interview with Superintendent Parker, then took himself home.

The children were already in bed but Bridget heard him arrive and came downstairs, begging for a story. Thanet obliged and then, protesting, did his stint on the rolling-pin while Joan was putting the finishing touches to supper.'

'Sylvia rang up,' she announced, when they were seated at the table.

Sylvia was an old school friend of Joan's who lived in Borden, a village some ten miles from Sturrenden. 'Said she hadn't seen us for far too long, and could we come to dinner on the fifteenth.'

'When's that?'

'End of next week.'

Thanet grimaced. 'It's so tricky.'

'I know, and so does she. But it is difficult, with dinner, letting people down at the last minute if you can't make it. Perhaps we'd better say no.'

Thanet smiled at her. 'Why don't you accept and then, if I can't come at the last minute, go by yourself?'

Joan frowned. 'I'd rather go with you.'

'I know, but it's hard on you, never having any social life because of my job. Why don't you? You know Sylvia well enough to turn up by youself if you have to.'

'I suppose so,' Joan said reluctantly. 'All right, I will. I'll say we'll both come if we can, if not I'll come alone.'

They ate in companionable silence for a while and then Joan said, 'How's the case going?'

Thanet told her. He'd seen so many policemen's marriages fall apart because their wives had been unable to cope with the irregular hours, the inconveniences, the broken promises, the loneliness and sense of isolation, that he had from the beginning vowed that this would never happen to him. He believed that if a wife felt involved in her husband's work she could more easily tolerate the demands it made upon her. Many of his colleagues, he knew, would disagree, would say that the only way to cope with pressures that were often near-intolerable was to keep their working and home lives completely separate, shut the former out of their minds the moment they stepped through the front door.

But for Thanet and Joan his way had worked, kept them close to each other. He trusted her completely, knew that she would never betray a confidence. What was more, talking to her often served to clarify his thoughts.

81

'Kenny Kendon!' she said, echoing Lineham, when he had finished. 'You're going to see him?'

'Tomorrow.'

'That'll be interesting. Seeing the inside of Broadcasting House and so on.' She laughed at his expression. 'All right, I know that's not what you're going for. All the same, it *will* be interesting. Out of the usual run.'

'True.' He could see that that was how it might seem to her. Her life at the moment was very much dictated by the demands of domesticity, above all the needs of the children. And, as anyone knows who has experienced it, the unremitting company of small children can be very wearing, however much one loves them. He leaned across, took her hand. 'Do you get very fed up with these four walls, love?'

She grimaced. 'Sometimes, I suppose, if I'm honest. But I tell myself it won't go on for ever. I'm glad you're not one of those Victorian types, though, who'd like to see his wife shut up in them for good. And you can stop looking so smug!'

Thanet grinned. 'Me, look smug? Nonsense!'

'All the same, it's nice to get some vicarious glimpse of the outside world, especially if there's a spot of glamour involved. Promise you'll be especially observant, tomorrow.'

'Cross my heart,' Thanet said.

7

Thanet and Lineham set off for London at half past seven the next morning. Thanet had checked the times of Kendon's daily programme in the *Radio Times*: seven thirty to ten o'clock. He hoped to arrive at Broadcasting House in comfortable time to catch Kendon when the programme ended.

On the way they tuned in to Radio 2 and listened with interest to Kendon's show, which proved to be the usual mixture of chat, jokes, phone-ins, record requests and pop music. It was comforting to know that their quarry was certain to be there, at the end of the trail. After a while Thanet switched off and they drove in silence.

'You know what strikes me as odd about this case, sir?' Lineham said eventually.

'What?' Thanet took out his pipe and started to fill it.

'The number of men who were interested in Mrs Holmes. I mean, the one thing that's obvious is that she was attractive to men. There's her husband, who was potty about her, Mr Parrish – according to Miss Waters, anyway – and now this man Kendon.'

'What's so strange about that? Some women are especially attractive to men.' Thanet lit up and waved his hands to disperse the clouds of smoke billowing around them.

'Yes, but this girl was different, wasn't she? I mean, often, when you get a woman who attracts men, it's because she's, well ...'

'Sexy?' supplied Thanet with a mischievous grin. He

never quite understood how Lineham had managed thus far to preserve a certain naivety in such matters. One would have imagined he'd have shed that long ago, in this job.

'Yes.' Lineham kept his eyes studiously on the road. 'And this girl wasn't … sexy, or at least, if she was she didn't seem conscious of it – even Miss Waters, who admits to being jealous of her, says that.'

'I know. But, for a start, I don't agree that girls who are attractive to men are necessarily sexy, even if they appear to be so. There's a certain type of girl, for instance, who is so unsure of her attractiveness – her femininity if you like – that she deliberately sets out to attract men, to appear sexy, to prove something to herself. Women like that are often cold underneath, frigid even, and frequently end up with the reputation of being heartless flirts. But Julie Holmes, I'm pretty sure, didn't fall into this category. As you say, even Maureen Waters, who admits to being jealous of her, says that Julie seemed unaware of her effect on men and certainly didn't set out deliberately to impress them.

'Anyway, the point is that because of the sort of person she was, Julie was under constant pressure from the men in her life, each of whom seems to have seen her as a unique challenge and was therefore not prepared to give up easily. Somehow, by her very nature, she invited it.'

'You mean she was a natural victim, sir?'

'In a way, yes, I suppose I do. But I think it was little more complicated than that. I think that under normal circumstances she could cope with pressure of the kind we've been talking about. The trouble started when something extra came along.'

'The nightmares, you mean?'

'It looks like it, from what we've been told.'

'But why should they have made that much difference? I mean, people often have nightmares, but they don't go to pieces because of them.'

84

'I don't think that these were just ordinary nightmares.' Thanet was gazing out of the window. They were now entering the outer suburbs and part of his mind was automatically mourning the rape of the countryside. 'They frightened her, of course, exhausted her probably because they disturbed her sleep, but I would guess they started because something deep in her mind had been stirred up, something that was best forgotten.'

'What sort of thing, sir?'

'Who knows? But,' Thanet said dreamily, still gazing at the monotonous pattern of houses, 'I would guess that it was something very nasty indeed. A veritable Kraken.'

'A what, sir?'

Thanet shot him an amused glance. 'A monster, Mike. A sleeping sea-monster which, suddenly awakened, stirs up an awful lot of mud. So that's one of the things I want you to do when talking to this Mrs Lawton, Julie's Auntie Rose. Keep an eye out for monsters.'

'You mean, try to find out if Mrs Holmes had any traumatic experiences as a child, sir?'

'Oh, for God's sake, man, stop being so pompous. But yes, that's exactly what I do mean.'

'Sir ...?'

'Yes?'

'No, it doesn't matter.'

Thanet suppressed his irritation and said softly, 'Look Mike, let me just tell you this. It's as good a time as any. I may be a bit impatient with you at times, but the only thing that really irritates me about you is your lack of self-confidence. It's such a waste, you see. The powers that be have had the wisdom to see that it doesn't stop you from being a first-rate copper, and no doubt hoped that early promotion would give your ego a boost. So give yourself a chance, will you? If you have a suggestion to make, make it.'

'It's not so much an idea as a question.' Lineham shot

a quick, assessing glance at Thanet. 'It's just that I can't see the point of digging into the girl's past. What does it matter to us, if she saw something nasty in the woodshed at the age of three?'

Now that Lineham had actually spoken out and had criticised him, Thanet irrationally felt angry – and then, almost at once, amused at himself. Typical, he thought. Encourage the man to express his ideas, then get mad because they're not the same as yours. 'I can quite see your point,' he said. 'But I can't agree with you, not at the moment. I have a feeling that her state of mind at the time was directly responsible for her death, and that it is therefore very important to know what was disturbing her. Anyway, until we actually have the murderer in our hands my policy is always to dig and go on digging, irrespective of what turns up.'

'I will duly dig,' said Lineham solemnly, then flashed a wicked, sideways glance at Thanet to see how he had taken the remark.

Thanet grinned and gave the sergeant a playful slap on the shoulder before turning to study his map. The traffic was thickening now and Lineham had to give his full attention to his driving. Thanet directed him. They crossed Blackfriars Bridge, found their way into the Strand, circled around Trafalgar Square, drove up to Piccadilly Circus. Thanet experienced the familiar surge of excitement which London always induced in him. The knowledge that he was at the hub of one of the greatest cities in the world never failed to affect him. They battled their way along Regent Street, negotiated Oxford Circus and experienced a sense of triumph as the greyish-white bulk of Broadcasting House loomed up ahead of them, dwarfing the delicate spire, slender columns and satisfying symmetry of All Souls Church. It was twenty to ten.

'Pick me up here at eleven-thirty,' Thanet said. 'You're sure you'll find your way?'

Lineham nodded. 'I took a good look at the maps last night.'

'Fine. See you then.'

Thanet watched Lineham out of sight around the one-way system, then turned to look up at the solid mass of Broadcasting House. Above the tall, golden doors was an impressive sculpture of an old man holding a young child. Thanet studied it for a moment, wondering what it symbolised, before going into the foyer. He crossed to the reception desk on his right and said that he wished to speak urgently to Mr Kendon. Deliberately he did not reveal that he was a policeman; he did not want to put Kendon on his guard.

The receptionist told him what he already knew, that Kendon was busy at the moment with his programme. She said that she would ring up to leave the message that someone was waiting to see him, and assured Thanet that Kendon would come down as soon as he was free. Thanet thanked her and sat down to wait on one of the red benches in the reception area, looking about him with interest.

The foyer was alive with movement. A constant stream of people flowed past the two security men behind the rope barrier. These, he noticed, were meticulously careful; during the next twenty minutes nobody entered the inner area without showing his pass. Remembering his promise to Joan, Thanet kept his eyes open for familiar faces but, disappointingly, there were none. Scarcely surprising, he reflected. If this had been the television centre, now …

It seemed no time at all before Kendon presented himself.

'Mr Thanet?'

Thanet rose as he acknowledged the greeting, studying Kendon with interest. The barmaid's description had been very accurate, he thought, and he could see why Kendon had made such an impression on her. Like Parrish, this man would be very attractive to women. He had rugged good looks, a fine physique, and considerable charm. He was wearing a white silk polo-necked shirt and tight dark green trousers in a fine, silky corduroy velvet. He looked disconcerted when Thanet produced his identification card, but soon appeared to recover his aplomb.

'We'll go across to the Langham,' he said. 'We'll be able to talk quietly there.'

As they pushed their way out through the tall swing doors and crossed the road, Kendon kept up a smooth monologue. They were, he said, going to the Club, a favourite haunt of those who worked for the BBC. The Langham used to be the Langham Hotel, and had been taken over by the BBC, famous ghost and all. Thanet stored it all up to tell Joan, wondering if this was Kendon's normal way of carrying on a conversation (if such it could be called) or whether the man was simply talking in order to forestall questions before he was ready to answer them.

More tall golden doors, green carpet, left along corridors to a high, spacious room furnished with small round tables, a bar on one side and a buffet on the other. Kendon insisted on paying for the coffee before leading the way to the far end of the room where a huge bay window overlooked the busy street below.

'It's just been redecorated,' Kendon said, looking about with a proprietorial air.

'Very nice,' Thanet said obediently. 'And now, Mr Kendon ...'

'Of course, of course,' Kendon said hurriedly. He sipped his coffee, set the cup down and sat back with an air of compliant readiness. 'How can I help you, Inspector?'

'I believe you knew Julie Holmes,' Thanet said. He caught the flash of real pain in Kendon's eyes before the man's features assembled themselves into an appropriate expression of solemnity.

'Yes, I did know her once, quite well, as a matter of fact. I read about her ... her death in the papers, of course.' He sipped at his coffee again. 'A terrible business.'

Thanet merely nodded, saying nothing. He frequently found silence a more effective weapon than questions. Few people could tolerate it for long. Kendon proved no exception. He took a further sip of coffee, put his cup down and looked uneasily at Thanet. Then he took out a cigarette case, offered it to the inspector and, when he refused, took a cigarette himself and lit up.

Thanet continued to sip his coffee and wait.

Kendon gesticulated with his cigarette, scattering ash into his coffee. He swore. 'What did you want to see me about?'

'I'm just waiting for you to tell me about Julie Holmes.'

'What d'you mean, tell you about her? Look here, Inspector, if you think I had anything to do with her murder ...'

'Did I say that?' Thanet said mildly. 'Just tell me about her. About your relationship with her.' He was satisfied, now, that Kendon was sufficiently on the defensive to be vulnerable. It seemed, however, that he had underestimated his man.

Kendon leaned forward. 'OK Inspector, I'll level with you. There's no point in doing anything else, I suppose. She was a drag. Wouldn't leave me alone. Even after she was married, even after she moved down to Kent.'

Thanet hid his astonishment at this unexpectedly mirror-image version of the relationship between Kendon and Julie as he had envisaged it. 'Go on,' he said.

Kendon stubbed out his cigarette. 'I thought I'd finally shaken her off when she married John – I introduced them, you know. I was always introducing her to men I hoped might get her off my back. And this time it seemed to work – for a while. For a couple of months I heard nothing from her and then it all started again. Letters, phone-calls ... it drove me mad. But I felt sorry for her, in a way, and I used to meet her from time to time, to keep her happy.'

'Even to the extent of going down to Kent once a week to see her?'

'Sure, why not?'

'Why, Mr Kendon?'

Kendon shrugged. 'I told you. I felt sorry for her. I had a soft spot for her. There was something, well, a bit pathetic about her. I was always afraid she might, well, you know, do something drastic.'

'Commit suicide, you mean?'

'Yeah.'

'If you didn't see her?'

'Right. Look Inspector, my job has, well, a certain glamour about it. Girls like that, they go for it. Julie was no different from any of the others.'

'And you put yourself out for all these lovesick maidens to the extent of sacrificing one evening a week to keep them happy?'

'Of course not. But I told you, I had a soft spot for Julie.'

'Go on.'

'With what?'

'Well, let's take last Tuesday for a start, shall we? The night she died.'

'Yeah, well,' Kendon ran his tongue over his lower lip, 'that was all a bit ... I suppose the people in the pub remembered us?'

'They did.'

'Not surprising, the way she took off. It was like this. I'd decided this was the last time I was trailing all the way down there to see her and told her so. She didn't like it, she begged, pleaded with me, but I told her I'd finally had enough and that was that. In the end she got very upset and ran off.'

None of this fitted in with the way the barmaid had described the quarrel but Thanet was ready to let this pass. It was the next bit that really interested him. 'Go on.'

Kendon leaned back in his chair, lifted his hands in a gesture of finality.

'That's it.'

Thanet looked at him in silence for a moment, considering which line would be most likely to produce the truth. Kendon's story was obviously going to be that after the quarrel he made his way back to the station and caught a train back to London. The question was, if he were allowed to produce this story, how would he react to being accused of lying? Would he cave in, or would he dig his heels in? Probably the latter, Thanet thought. Kendon's opinion of himself was such that he would always find it difficult to climb down. It would be better to make sure that the man did not find himself in that position.

'Not quite, I think, Mr Kendon. I must be frank and tell you that not only were you seen to follow Mrs Holmes when you left the pub, but that two independent witnesses saw you very close to Gladstone Road around twenty to nine.'

The man was cool, Thanet thought, watching him. He did not so much as blink, but merely gave a little shrug of submission, a wry grin.

'Ah well, it was worth a try ... All right, Inspector, I'll tell you the rest of it. As I said, I was absolutely fed up with the situation. I wanted Julie to understand that I had really meant what I said, that I didn't want her pestering me any more and that this was the last time I'd trail all the way down to Kent to calm her down. The way she left ... well, nothing had been resolved. She'd just run away from the situation, refused to face up to it and I could see it all going on exactly as it had before. So I finished my drink, gave her a few minutes to cool down, then followed her. Well, I say I followed her, but in fact she was out of sight all the way. There are a lot of turnings, in a very short distance, between that pub and where she lived. But I was sure she'd have gone home, so when I got to Gladstone Road I just marched up the path and knocked on the front door. She came to the bay window in the front room to see who it was – I just caught a glimpse of her before she disappeared. Anyway, she didn't come to the door straight away, so I knocked again.'

For the first time, now, Kendon's composure showed signs of slipping. 'I heard her steps in the hall and thought she was coming to let me in, but suddenly she shouted – well, screamed, really, – "Look through the letter box, Kenny." So I did.' Kendon leaned forward and his eyes flickered from side to side as if he were making sure that there was nobody within earshot, then he said softly, intensely, 'She was standing there holding a bloody great carving knife, Inspector! "Go away!" she was screaming, "Go away, or I'll stick this in you!" And she shook the thing at me!'

Kendon leaned sideways to extract a handkerchief from his trouser pocket and mopped at the sheen of perspiration on his forehead.

'And then?' said Thanet.

Kendon hesitated, ran his tongue over his lips. Clearly, he realised that this was the crucial point. Then he shrugged, leaned back, seemed to relax a little, as if he'd decided how to handle it. 'Oh come on, Inspector. Put yourself in my position. I'd played along with her for years, trailed down to Kent to see her regularly. It was a drag, I can tell you. And what happens when I finally decide I've got to make the break? She threatens me with a bloody great knife, for God's sake! When I saw her standing there like that I thought, that's it. I've bloody well had enough.'

'You were angry,' Thanet said softly.

'I bloody well was!' Kendon suddenly realised what he was saying and leaned forward earnestly in his chair. 'Oh, don't get me wrong, Inspector. I wasn't angry enough to kill her. Why should I risk my neck for her? No, like I said, I just thought she could go to hell as far as I was concerned. So I just walked away. I'd only got as far as the gate when I heard the front door open behind me. She was still waving the knife. "Don't ever come back," she was screaming. And, believe me, I didn't intend to.'

92

'So what did you do then?'

'Went to the station and caught a train home.'

'Which train did you catch?'

'The eight fifty-four.'

And Manson had said that it took six minutes to walk to the station from Holmes's house.

'Did you have to wait long, on the station?'

'Only a minute or two.'

Thanet was silent for a moment, thinking over what he had heard. 'Is there anyone who can corroborate what you have told me?'

The answer was a surprise. 'As a matter of fact, yes.' Kendon lit a fresh cigarette and inhaled deeply before going on. His self-possession had returned and there was even a hint of malicious satisfaction in his eyes. 'When Julie opened the front door and shouted at me I started off down the road towards the footpath, and there was this girl ahead of me, near the swing gate. I think she must have come along that footpath beside the wire fence, the one that links the ends of all those cul-de-sacs. Anyway, she obviously heard Julie because she stopped and glanced up the road towards us. Then she went on, through the swing gate and along the footpath. I caught her up and passed her just before we reached the station. She caught the same train as me. So you see, Inspector, I'm in the clear. Find that girl and she'll tell you that Julie was alive when I left her, and that I had no chance to slip back and kill her afterwards.'

'I see. Could you give us a description of this girl, to help us trace her?'

Kendon leaned back in his chair, narrowed his eyes in recollection. 'Mid-twenties, I should think. I'm afraid I didn't really notice her face, so she must have been pretty nondescript. After all, I didn't know I was going to need her, did I, or I'd have taken down her name and address, so to speak! Hair dark, I think. Yes, dark, straight, shoulder-length.'

'How tall?'

'Oh, medium. About five five, I should think.'

'What was she wearing?'

Kendon frowned in concentration. 'Nothing very striking, that's for sure. Something dark – yes, a dark coat, brown, I think. She was just as ordinary sort of girl.'

'Unfortunately.'

'Unfor ... oh, yes, I see.' Kendon looked anxious. 'You think she'll be difficult to trace?'

Thanet shrugged. 'Who knows? We'll have to wait and see.'

'And hope,' Kendon said drily.

'Yes, and hope. Did anyone else catch the train, by the way?'

'There were one or two other people on the platform, yes. But I honestly can't remember anything about them. To be frank, I was still very upset, after the scene with Julie. I kept on remembering how she looked, through that letter box ... Honestly, Inspector, she looked demented. Really demented. I couldn't seem to think of much else all the way back on the train ... Do you think I shouldn't have left her in that state?' he asked abruptly.

So the man was feeling guilty, asking for reassurance, Thanet thought. As well he might be. For his, after all, had been the hand which had given Julie the final push that sent her over the edge. On the other hand he had not been responsible for the forces which had gathered to drive her there. 'In a situation like that it's difficult to know what should be done for the best,' he said non-committally.

'Oh come on, Inspector,' Kendon burst out. 'What would you have done, tell me that?'

It was a cry from the heart and for the first time Thanet felt a twinge of genuine compassion for Kendon. Faced with the man and his smooth recital of his story Thanet had almost forgotten that if what he had previously learnt was true, Kendon had been in love with Julie for years. Now he had dropped his defences. Whatever Thanet thought of the man it would be inhuman to refuse to take his question seriously. 'I don't know,' he said. 'Called a doctor, perhaps?'

Kendon sat back. 'I feel so bloody guilty about it. If only I hadn't just left her like that, perhaps she'd still be alive ... There's something I haven't told you,' he added abruptly. 'I'm still not sure about it, you see. If I had been, I'd have contacted you before now, myself.'

So it could be important. Thanet thought. He made an encouraging noise. Kendon hesitated a moment longer before saying. 'It's just that when I reached the swing gate I turned back to glance at the house, see if Julie was still there.' He stopped.

'And was she?'

'No, but in the instant when I turned away again. I have the impression of movement, at the corner of the street ...'

Thanet experienced a sudden lurch of excitement in the pit of his stomach. It was as if he had just glimpsed the murderer, out of the corner of his eye. 'At the far end of Gladstone Road, you mean?'

'Yes. It was just an impression, as I say, but looking back I'm pretty certain that someone was just turning into Gladstone Road.

'A man or a woman?'

Kendon shook his head. 'It's no use. I've thought and thought and I still don't know. It really was no more than a flicker of movement on the very edge of my vision, before I turned away.'

'Well if you do remember, give me a ring at once, will you?' Thanet scribbled both his home and office numbers on a piece of paper, handed it over and stood up. 'I think that's about all for the moment, Mr Kendon.'

Kendon followed suit. 'I'm sorry I couldn't have been more helpful.'

He seemed to mean it and Thanet found that the last few minutes of their conversation had somewhat altered his feelings towards the man. They chatted amiably enough as they made their way back out on to the street. Kendon turned right and made his way off down Regent Street. Hands in pockets and head down, he looked thoroughly despondent. An act? Thanet wondered, as he watched him out of sight. He rather thought not.

'You think he was telling the truth?' Lineham asked when they had negotiated their way through the worst of the traffic and Thanet had given him an account of the interview.

'In his version of his relationship with Julie, no, I don't. It just doesn't fit in with what her husband and Mrs Thorpe told us. Or with the barmaid's account of their quarrel, for that matter. And I would say he just isn't the type to put himself out to that degree for a former girlfriend. No, I would guess he was just saving face, making it sound as if she was the one who was doing the chasing. But in the important thing, in his account of what actually happened on Tuesday night, then yes, I think perhaps I do, I'm inclined to, anyway. We'll have to do some checking – see if we can trace that girl he claims to have followed to the station. We'll put out an appeal, see what turns up. Or perhaps the ticket collector will be able to help us. If there weren't many people on that train it's just possible he might have some recollection of her, Kendon might have invented her, of course, and the same could be said of this mysterious person he claims to have seen turning into Gladstone Road. But if there really was somebody ...'

'It could be our murderer.'

'It's possible. I think we'd better go over all those house-to-house reports again and re-question everybody who was not stuck in front of *The Pacemakers*. What about you? How did you get on with Mrs Lawton?'

'Fine. I think I got everything we needed.'

Julie and her mother had apparently moved to

London from Kent when Julie was three, after her father's accident, buying a small terraced house in one of the respectable but less wealthy areas of Wimbledon. Julie had lived there until her marriage, her mother until her death a year ago.

For some time after the move from Kent Julie had suffered from nightmares but Mrs Lawton had no idea of their content and had at the time thought of them as normal under the circumstances, Julie having lost her father so suddenly. Julie had not been involved in the accident that killed him, Mrs Lawson had been positive about that, and Julie's mother had told her friend that she had moved because she wanted to get right away from the place which had so many associations with her husband. She had never remarried.

'Where did they live in Kent?' Thanet asked, when Lineham had finished.

'Little Sutton.'

'Little Sutton,' Thanet repeated slowly. He knew the village, of course, it wasn't far from where Sylvia, Joan's friend, lived. But in this particular context it struck some kind of chord. What was it? He frowned out of the window, trying to put his finger on it. He couldn't, and after a while he gave up. The feeling remained, however, and all the way home it remained lodged at the back of his mind, as uncomfortable as a grain of sand under an eyelid.

As soon as they got back to the office, Thanet sent for the file on the accident in which Julie's father had been killed while Lineham drafted the appeal for the witness Kendon claimed could clear him. It was still only half past two and with any luck they should catch the evening editions of the national newspapers.

They then worked together through the house-to-house reports, deciding which people should be interviewed again. At Lineham's suggestion one man would be detailed to knock on every door in the three streets with instructions to find out the names of all women between the ages of fifteen and thirty-five living there and their movements on the night of the murder. It was possible, of course that the woman Kendon claimed to have seen came from quite another area but, as Lineham pointed out, only someone with local knowledge would have known about that footpath. It was worth checking.

By now the file had arrived and while Lineham went off to make arrangements Thanet settled down to study it. He wasn't quite sure why he was doing this; on the face of it, the accident could have no relevance to the present enquiry. He simply felt that he should and experience had taught him that such feelings should be indulged. They were frequently based on connections made by his subconscious, connections which seemed obvious on looking back but which at the time seemed irrational or non-existent.

David Leonard Parr of Jasmine Cottage, The Green, Little Sutton, Kent, had died on November 18, 1960 in Sturrenden General Hospital at eight pm, five hours after his car had been in collision with a lorry in dense fog on the main Sturrenden to Maidstone road. The lorry driver had been unhurt and had later been cleared of any responsibility for the crash; Parr had been on the wrong side of the road and had skidded after going too fast into a bend which he had presumably been unable to see because of the fog. He had been twenty-nine years old and had been alone in the car.

Thanet read all the statements through twice, quickly, and then more slowly a third time. His instinct, he decided, had let him down. Try as he would he could not see that the accident to Julie's father had any bearing on her murder. Reading the report had been a waste of time. He closed the file and pushed it away with a gesture of disgust.

He stood up and moved to the window. Outside, the streets were crowded with people going home from work and traffic had come to a standstill at the pelican crossing a hundred yards or so away up the road to the

98

left. It had been a mistake to install one on such a busy road, Thanet thought. A constant stream of people pressing the crossing control-button could make it virtually impossible for traffic to keep moving. A conventional system of traffic lights would have been better, with an integrated pedestrian crossing control system. He really must remember to raise the matter with Traffic Control.

He felt as sluggish as the traffic below him. He hated this stage in a case, when the initial impetus seems to have slipped away and the possibility of failure rears its ugly head. Thanet privately thought of this time as the policeman's Slough of Despond. Not that such thoughts were put into words. On the contrary, there seemed to be a conspiracy of silence on the subject and Thanet sometimes wondered if many men superstitiously refused to acknowledge their doubts even to themselves, lest merely entertaining the possibility of failure should somehow blight their chances of success.

He knew that by now he ought to have had enough experience to be able to tell himself that his depression was normal, something to be expected at this stage of a case, but the trouble was that each time it happened came the fear that this time would be different, this time there would be no breakthrough, that he would have, eventually, to admit defeat.

The thought was enough to make him grit his teeth and turn back to his desk. There was only one way to deal with a mood like this and that was to immerse himself totally in work, to revert to patient, thorough, routine investigation. He must sit down, reread all the reports that had come in on the case so far, check, re-check and cross-check, discuss the matter exhaustively with Lineham and try and see what they had missed, what their next moves ought to be.

He pressed the buzzer on his desk. 'Find Lineham for me, will you?'

8

By the time Thanet arrived home at half past eight he felt as though his brain were stuffed with cotton wool. He and Lineham had gone over and over every scrap of information they had so far accumulated, had endlessly discussed the possible guilt of their three main suspects – Holmes, Parrish and Kendon, and had failed completely to reach any satisfactory conclusion or to see any way of breaking out of the impasse they seemed to have reached.

Joan took one look at his face and unobtrusively took charge. Thanet was shepherded into the living-room where Joan told him to sit down and relax, thrust a large drink into his hand and disappeared into the kitchen. Thanet sat gazing into space, sipping his whisky and thinking about absolutely nothing until she reappeared with a tray. He had thought he wasn't hungry but the sight and smell of one of his favourite dishes, steak and kidney pudding, revived his appetite and by the time he laid down his knife and fork he was beginning to feel human again.

Joan, sitting opposite him, watched in companionable silence. 'Better?' she said, finally, when he had finished, whisking away the tray.

Thanet stretched his legs out before him, loosened his belt one notch and patted his stomach ostentatiously. 'Much,' he said.

'Good. I'll fetch the coffee.'

Thanet waited, gazing absentmindedly at the painting which hung on the wall before him, above the

100

fireplace. It was an original oil which Joan had found unframed in a junk shop, shortly after they were married. She had managed to unearth an antique dealer who carried a stock of old picture frames, had persuaded him to cut one down to fit and had hung the finished product in pride of place. Thanet had always liked the painting, which was of a rural scene – cows grazing in the water meadows along the banks of a river. Such pictures, although not especially valuable had become increasingly difficult to find, Joan said. She'd always been interested in art and lately had been talking about taking a three-year course in the History of Painting at the College of Art when Ben was old enough to go to school.

'I forgot to tell you,' Thanet said when she returned with the coffee, 'I saw an interesting picture yesterday.'

'What was it? A portrait?'

'Landscape, I suppose. It was of a cricket match, on a village green. Very vivid colours and lots of tiny figures.'

'Really? It sounds like a Dacre. She specialised in village scenes, *Village Wedding, Church Fête, Shrove Tuesday* – that one was of a pancake race – and so on. As a matter of fact, I'm sure I remember the one you're talking about.' She rose, started rummaging through a pile of papers and leaflets on a low table in the angle of the chimney breast. 'I've got a catalogue here, somewhere. The style sounds typically hers, as I said – lots of tiny figures, brilliant colours. Ah,' she said triumphantly. 'Here it is.'

She sat down beside, Thanet, opened the catalogue and ran her finger down the list of exhibits. 'Yes, I thought so. Here we are. *The Cricket Match*. By courtesy of ... ' her voice slowed, wavered before going on, 'Mrs Julie Holmes.'

'Let me see!' Thanet started at the entry, his mind racing. The painting, then, had obviously just been returned from the exhibition – he remembered seeing the package in Holmes's hall on ... which day had it been? The day before yesterday? Yes, that was right. Wednesday, then.

'When did you go to the exhibition, darling?'

'On Tuesday.'

Surely it would have taken longer than that to dismantle the exhibits? Apparently not. Here was the evidence, in print, before him. A thought occurred to him. When had the exhibition started? He looked at the front page of the catalogue. It had been, apparently, a memorial exhibition to mark the twentieth anniversary of the death of Annabel Dacre, and had been open to the public from Tuesday, April 22 to May 6. The Private View had been held on the evening of Monday, April 21.

Thanet sat up with a jerk. 'Who would have attended the Private View?'

Joan shrugged. 'Local big-wigs, I suppose. Local artists, probably. And, of course, all the people who had loaned the paintings.'

Julie had loaned a painting. And on Monday, April 21 she had had that nightmare for the first time.

Thanet went to the telephone and rang Holmes. It sounded as though Holmes had pulled himself together for he was unusually forthcoming. He had forgotten about it but yes, now that Thanet mentioned it, he and Julie had both attended the Private View. They had received an invitation because Julie had loaned a painting. Holmes had found the occasion very boring. They knew nobody, and he wasn't interested in art anyway. Julie had wanted to go because she liked the idea of the privilege of attending a private view and because she'd thought it might be a chance to meet a few more local people. No, nothing, unusual had happened during the evening. Julie had been rather quiet on the way home, but he'd thought that was because she'd been a little disappointed that they hadn't enjoyed themselves as much as she had hoped. The painting had belonged to Julie's mother. Julie had found it tucked away in a box in the attic when she was clearing out the house in Wimbledon after her mother's death. Then, when she'd seen the advertisement in the *Sturrenden Gazette*, she was rather tickled at the idea of lending the picture and having 'By courtesy of Mrs Julie Holmes' in the catalogue. The advertisment had announced that a memorial exhibition of Annabel Dacre's work was to be arranged and requested the loan of examples of her work.

Thanet went back into the living-room, sat down and began to read the biography on the back of the catalogue. The first line brought him up short and he experienced that unique elation that comes when one suddenly understands something which has been puzzling one, that sudden fusing of apparently unrelated facts into a coherent whole so obvious that one wonders why on earth one hasn't seen it before.

'Darling, what on earth's the matter?' Joan had just come in with fresh coffee.

'Annabel Dacre was born and brought up in Little Sutton!'

'Yes, I know. What of it?'

Thanet jumped up, wincing as his back protested, and began to pace up and down. 'Well, it's just that there have been one or two things nagging away at the back of my mind, and I couldn't work out why. I knew, when I found out that the Parrs – Julie Holmes's parents – had lived in Little Sutton, that there was some reason why the name rang a bell – apart from the fact that I knew the place, that is. I'd seen that painting at Holmes's house, you see, and knew that there was something familiar about it. It was the background of course, the village green at Little Sutton. You know those two huge oaks, slightly off centre ... Why on earth didn't I see it before?'

'Darling, do stop pacing about like that. You're making me dizzy. Sit down, and explain why you're so excited about it.'

Thanet subsided on to the settee. 'Look. As a child Julie – Julie Parr, as she then was – lived in Little Sutton.

We found that out today. And it was in Little Sutton, presumably, that one of her parents bought the picture of the cricket match. Now when Julie is three her father is killed in a car crash and at once Mrs Parr, anxious to get away from painful memories, leaves the village and moves to London. She can't bring herself to destroy the picture – perhaps it had been a gift from her husband, but neither can she bear to look at it. So she tucks it away in the attic and for twenty years no one but she knows of its existence.

'Julie grows up, gets married, her mother dies and Julie finds the picture when clearing out the house. Then her husband's firm transfers him to Sturrenden. She moves with him, having no idea that she once lived in Kent, her mother for some reason having given her to understand they'd always lived in London. She is intrigued to read in the local paper that Sturrenden College of Art is appealing for the loan of paintings by Annabel Dacre for a special memorial exhibition. She offers to lend hers, is invited to the Private View, attends it with her husband – and that night she has the first in a series of nightmares which frighten her to such a degree that she asks her counsellor for a private interview and is sick after telling her about them. Even the people at work notice that she is looking ill – jumpy, nervous, was how one girl described it.'

'So you think something happened at that Private View to ... to what?'

'To, how shall I put it, reactivate something which had had a profound effect on Julie as a child.'

'But even if that is true, how can it possibly be relevant to her murder?'

'I don't know.' Thanet struck one clenched fist into the palm of the other. 'I just don't know. I just have this feeling ...' Thanet picked up the catalogue again and quickly read the rest of the biographical details on the back. 'What does it mean, "tragic early death"?'

'I've no idea. As it says, Annabel Dacre was twenty-five when she died. And it *was* tragic. I think the world lost a fine painter.'

'And that was twenty years ago. 1960. The same year Mrs Parr moved to London.'

'But that was because her husband was killed.'

'Yes, but it's a coincidence, and although coincidences do happen, I like to make sure that's what they really are.' Thanet tossed the catalogue on the table, turned to Joan, put his arm around her. 'I think a little visit to the College of Art is indicated, in the morning.'

Joan grinned. 'It's Saturday tomorrow.'

'Damn. So it is. Never mind, I expect we'll be able to dig someone up.'

He didn't doubt it. His mood of despondency had melted away and he felt buoyant, confident, on course again. He certainly wasn't going to be defeated by red tape.

He almost was, however. It took over an hour of telephone calls to get around the fact that the entire educational system of Kent closed down on Saturdays. In the end it was Lineham who, through a friend of a friend who was a student at the College of Art, managed to get hold of the man who was Head of Fine Arts at the College, and that only after working systematically through all the Johnsons in the local directory.

'At last,' Lineham said, triumphant but weary, handing the telephone over to Thanet.

Mr Johnson was not very pleased at having his weekend plans interrupted, but agreed, relucantly, to see Inspector Thanet.

'I'll be there in twenty minutes,' said Thanet. 'Thank you, sir.'

The Johnsons lived on a small, pleasant estate of individually designed modern houses which had been built in the grounds of a large country house in a village two miles out of Sturrenden. Each stood in a beautifully landscaped plot of about half an acre, generously endowed with mature trees which were

105

obviously a legacy from the original gardens of the stately home. Thanet wondered how on earth the builders had managed to get planning permission. 'Infilling'? he wondered.

From the outside the Johnsons' house was pleasant but unremarkable: large windows, random stonework, pleasantly mellow red brick. Inside, however, it was a very different kettle of fish. Only half the house had a first floor, the other half being one huge room open right up to the exposed roof rafters. It was divided into several clearly defined areas: a studio area with tall windows on the north side, an eating area and, fascinatingly, a sitting area which consisted of a kind of pit sunk into the floor, its edges defined by thickly padded bench seats, the whole close-carpeted in velvety peacock blue. Joan would have loved to see this, Thanet thought.

Johnson led the way down the three steps which descended into the pit and waved Thanet on to one of the benches. He was tall, stooping, half bald, with a tiny, wispy beard, sunken eyes and surprisingly luxuriant eyebrows. Thanet had clearly interrupted his work. He was wearing a paint-stained smock and scuffed moccasins.

'I must apologise for my reluctance on the telephone, Inspector,' he said with a rueful smile, 'but I'm afraid my free time is very limited and I always try to devote Saturdays to painting. I should have realised, however, that crime doesn't take the weekend off, so I hope you will forgive me.'

A girl of about seventeen, long-haired and barefoot, had silently approached with a tray. Thanet smiled his thanks as he accepted the coffee. The mug was of a striking design, pot-bellied and out-curving at the rim and thrown in satisfyingly heavy rough-surfaced stoneware.

'The work of one of our most promising young potters, a boy called Denzil Runyon,' Johnson said, noting Thanet's interest.

'Very attractive indeed,' Thanet said. 'No, I'm the one who should be apologising, Mr Johnson, for disturbing you at your work. But as you say, crime isn't a Monday-to-Friday business.'

'So how can I help?'

'I'd be grateful if you would tell me about the Dacre Exhibition – who suggested it, how it was set up and so on. I'm afraid I'm not at liberty to explain my interest, and indeed the information might prove to be irrelevant to the enquiry upon which I'm working. But we must follow up every lead, you understand.'

'So my curiosity will remain unsatisfied. What a pity. Well, never mind. I must grin and bear it, must I? Yes, well now, let me see. The Exhibition was suggested by Annabel Dacre's mother.'

Thanet was startled. He hadn't thought that Mrs Dacre would still be alive, but now, of course, he realised that it was quite feasible that she should be. If Annabel Dacre had been only twenty-five when she died, twenty years ago, and her mother had been, say, between forty-five and fifty-five at the time…

'She's in her early seventies now, and very frail. I've known her for many years and have long been aware of her hopes for a Silver Jubilee Exhibition of her daughter's work. Over the last year, however, Mrs Dacre's health has deteriorated to such a degree that I believe she came to think that she would not live to see it. So, when she came to me last autumn with the suggestion that the Exhibition should be held this year, I was quite ready to agree. Mrs Dacre has been most generous to our College. She has endowed five annual scholarships for further studies, which has meant that some of our most promising students have been able to go abroad after leaving us, when they would not normally have been able to afford to do so.'

'So what was the next step, after you had agreed?'

'Various bits of red tape – obtaining permission from the Education Authority, for example. It all took time. And then, in January, we started to run the advertisements in the local paper.'

'Requesting the loan of paintings?'

'Yes.'

'Why not in the national press?'

Johnson sighed, sat back and folded his arms. 'Unfortunately Annabel Dacre was not well known, though in the last year or two the value of her paintings has soared. But when she was alive most of her pictures were sold to local people – friends, neighbours. Many of them scattered, of course, moved away, and we did in fact insert two advertisements in the national dailies, but the bulk of her work is still hanging in houses locally. So we ran the advertisement in the *Gazette* fortnightly from the beginning of January to the end of March. By then the catalogues had to go to the printers, of course.'

'And you got a good response?'

'Very good. Twenty-four paintings, which was, I confess, more than I had hoped for. Some of them from quite interesting sources.'

'Do you remember a Mrs Holmes?'

'Ah yes, now that was a case in point – the painting had been bought by the girl's mother, stored away in an attic for ...' He stopped, abruptly. 'My God,' he said. 'I've only just made the connection ... Mrs Holmes ... that girl who was murdered ...'

'Yes,' Thanet said heavily. 'That's why I'm here. Though I would be grateful if you could keep this visit to yourself, at least until the case is solved.' One can sound confident even if one doesn't feel it, he thought wryly as Johnson hastened to assure him of his discretion.

'Did you have much contact with Mrs Holmes?' Thanet asked.

'No. I saw her twice, once when she brought the picture in for authentication – it was one of Dacre's best, by the way. *The Cricket Match.*'

'Yes, I've seen it.'

'And then of course I saw her briefly at the Private

View. With her husband. The place was very crowded and I soon lost sight of them.'

'You didn't notice anything unusual, out of the way, that evening?'

'No, I was terribly busy talking to people. I tried to get around everybody, but it was such a crush. There really was a gratifying amount of interest in this exhibition. So often one feels like a voice crying in the wilderness ...'

'I assume you have a list, of the people who were invited to the Private View?'

'Yes. In my office, at the College. No, wait a minute, I think my rough copy might still be in my briefcase. Would you like to see it?'

'I'd like to borrow it, if I may.'

Johnson seemed rather taken aback. 'Oh. Oh dear, I do hope there won't be any ... but still, I suppose we must try to ... very well. I'll go and see.'

He returned a few moments later, list in hand. 'I brought a catalogue, too, Inspector, in case you might find it useful.'

'Very kind of you. Thank you.' He took the proffered papers, glanced at them, then stowed them carefully away in his inside breast pocket. 'There's just one other point, Mr Johnson. Someone showed me one of the catalogues the other day, and the biographical notes on the back mention Annabel Dacre's "tragic death". What exactly does that mean? What did she die of?'

They were walking towards the door and now Johnson stopped dead. 'Dear oh dear, Inspector. You mean you really don't know?'

'Know what?' Thanet asked – and thought, later, that he should have foreseen, by the glint of amused malice in the man's eyes, what the answer was going to be.

'That Annabel Dacre was murdered. And what is more, Inspector, her murderer was never found.'

9

There had to be a connection between the two murders. Thanet told himself as he waited impatiently for the file on Annabel Dacre to be unearthed and brought to him. There just had to be. The link was too obvious for it to be otherwise. Somehow the events which led up to Julie's death had been triggered off at that Private View. But how?

Lineham had left a message saying that he had gone out to join the others in the second round of house-to-house enquiries. No witness had yet come forward in response to the radio and newspaper appeals put out in an attempt to confirm Kendon's story. Nor had there yet been any success in tracing the whereabouts of Horrocks, the salesman. So far they had not appealed for him by name. Thanet was always reluctant to advertise the names of witnesses except in cases of extreme urgency. The public always seemed ready to jump to unpleasant conclusions and it was all too easy for innocent people to suffer from such publicity. Besides, Horrocks was due back from his trip some time over the weekend and could be interviewed then. And now ... well, if Thanet's hunch was correct, most of the enquiries put in train so far could be irrelevant and all three suspects in the clear.

When the file arrived he had to restrain himself from snatching it from the man who brought it.

Annabel Dacre, he learnt, had been murdered on the evening of November 18, 1960. The same date, surely on which Julie's father had been killed? Thanet suppressed the urgue to check and read on. She had been found battered to death in her studio at the West Lodge, Champeney House, Little Sutton at 8.45 pm by Jennifer Parr, who had called the police. Julie's mother, Thanet thought excitedly. It was established that death had occurred between 7.45 and 8.45 pm, the vicar having spoken to Miss Dacre by telephone at the former time. Thanet paused at the name; the Reverend W. Manson. He took the catalogue and invitation list from his pocket, checked. Yes, as he had thought, it was on both lists.

As he read on carefully through the first pages of the bulky file the picture of what had happened on that foggy November day twenty years ago began to emerge.

Jennifer Parr and Annabel Dacre had been close friends. At three o'clock in the afternoon of November 18, Jennifer received a telephone call informing her that her husband had been seriously injured in a road accident and had been taken to Sturrenden General Hospital. He had been driving the Parrs' only car and as there would be no bus until half past four Jennifer had appealed to Annabel for help: could she run her into Sturrenden and look after Julie while Jennifer stayed at the hospital with her husband?

Annabel had agreed at once. She picked up Jennifer and Julie, drove them to the hospital and then took Julie home with her, having made Jennifer promise to ring her when she wanted to return home again. She would, she assured Jennifer, keep Julie for the night if necessary. She had done so on the odd occasion in the past and had installed her own old cot from the nursery at Champeney House in the corner of her studio, for this purpose.

At 7.45 pm David Parr died and shortly afterwards Jennifer began ringing Annabel. There was no reply. By ten past eight, knowing that Annabel should be at home looking after Julie, Jennifer, already in a state of shock over her husband's death, was beginning to feel panicky. She rang for a taxi which, owing to the fog, took twenty-five minutes to do the ten-minute journey, arriving at West Lodge at 8.45. The front door stood wide open and Jennifer, more uneasy than ever, asked the taxi driver to accompany her to the studio upstairs.

She found Annabel dead on the floor of the studio, the back of her skull smashed in, and Julie huddled in a corner of the cot which had, fortunately for the child, been placed in an alcove at the far end of the studio. Curtains had been partly drawn across in front of it, presumably to screen Julie from the light and enable her to go to sleep.

The police, however, were satisfied that although the murderer had presumably been unaware of Julie's presence, Julie would have been able to see what had happened. The theory that the child had actually witnessed the murder seemed to be confirmed by the fact that she was in a state of shock and unable to speak, a condition which lasted for several days. When she did recover she seemed to have no recollection whatsoever of what had happened.

Satisfied that Jennifer Parr had been under the eye of independent witnesses from three o'clock that afternoon until the discovery of the body and worried for the safety of the little girl, the police had advised Mrs Parr to leave the area at once. At no time, even at the inquest at which Jennifer Parr of course had to give evidence, had the fact of Julie's presence in Annabel's studio at the time of the murder been made public.

So. Thanet sat back and thought. Here, then, he was certain, was the source of Julie's nightmares. The cage was the cot in which Julie had been trapped during what must have been a terrifying experience.

Say, then, that the murderer had been someone known to Julie, say that, unable to cope with the memory of what she had seen, Julie had 'forgotten' it completely, wiped it out of her conscious mind. And then suppose that years later she sees the murderer again, but without conscious recognition? The experience might well reactivate those suppressed memories, bring them nearer the level of consciousness in dreams, nightmares in which Julie would experience once more the terror buried deep for so long.

There was an awful lot of supposing and speculation in all this, Thanet thought. Surely, for example, Julie would not have recognised the murderer, after all these years? But it wouldn't have been necessary, as he had already thought, for Julie actually to have recognised him. There would just have had to be something – a look, a gesture, an expression – which would activate the memories buried deep in her subconscious, causing them to work their way upwards, nearer to the surface of her mind and make their presence felt in those nightmares. Julie would have been bewildered, frightened, aware that something was disturbing her without having any idea of its real nature. Above all, she would have been off balance, vulnerable.

But what about the murderer? It was equally unlikely, surely, that he would have recognised, across a crowded room, a child he hadn't seen for twenty years? Thanet frowned, considering. Unless ... unless Julie looked very like her mother at the same age? Jennifer Parr had been twenty-five at the time of Annabel's murder and Julie had been twenty-three when she died. Mother and daughter resemblances are often striking. Perhaps it had been so in this case. Holmes would probably know.

Thanet picked up the telephone and dialled Holmes's number. No reply. Perhaps he had taken Thanet's advice and gone back to work? Thanet rang the supermarket. This time he was in luck. After a few minutes Holmes came on the line. His response to Thanet's question was puzzled but immediate. Julie had been the 'spitting image' of her mother. Holmes had seen photographs of Mrs Parr as a young woman and you would have thought they were photographs of Julie, if it hadn't been for the difference in the clothes.

Thanet replaced the receiver with satisfaction. So

113

far, so good. The next step would be to check which of the original suspects of Annabel's murder had attended the Private View. It would then be a matter of narrowing down the field by an examination of their movements on the night Julie had died. With the exhibition catalogue and the Private View invitation list spread out beside him he began to skim quickly through the reports of interviews with witnesses. Details could wait until later. First, he wanted to know how far his theory held up.

It was a relatively simple matter to pick out the names of the main suspects of the Dacre case. They had all been interviewed over and over again. It was, however, somewhat disconcerting to find that there were so many – five, in all. Thanet's excitement mounted as, one by one he checked them off on his lists and discovered that four out of the five had loaned paintings to the Exhibition and had therefore automatically received invitations to the Private View. It really was beginning to look as though he might be right. With any luck he might even be able to kill two birds with one stone and track down a double murderer!

His stomach gave a protesting rumble and he glanced at his watch. Half past one. He'd have a quick bite to eat, then settle down to study the file in detail. He frowned. For some time now he'd had a nagging feeling that there was something he'd forgotten to do. What could it be? Stiff from sitting so long in one position he flexed his back. The twinge of pain reminded him what it was. He'd had an appointment with the physiotherapist at twelve. He must ring and apolgise at once. Joan would be furious that he'd forgotten.

During lunch he brooded over what he had learnt. After that inital pang of pity and sorrow at his first sight of Julie's dead body his attitude to her murder had been intellectual. It was a puzzle to be solved, a jigsaw to be assembled, a challenge against which he

114

must pit his wits. Now he found that in the light of this new knowledge his feelings towards the case and above all towards Julie had changed.

To begin with, what sort of an effect would the witnessing of a brutal murder have had on a child of three? Thanet thought of Sprig, and shuddered. Would Julie have understood what she had seen? Probably not, he decided, but she must have sensed the violence in the air, have been terrified by the attack itself and by the sight of the bloody mess that had been the back of Annabel's head, frightened out of her wits by being left alone in relatively unfamiliar surroundings with only Annabel's body for company. She could have had to wait for anything up to an hour before her mother arrived, and to a frightened child even a minute must seem sixty seconds too long.

Small wonder, then, that Julie had unconsciously opted to 'forget' the whole affair, scarcely surprising that the police had deliberately suppressed any mention of her presence at the scene of the murder, and understandable that her mother had whisked her off to the anonymity of London, had given her to understand that they had never lived anywhere else and had hidden that painting away in the attic.

Mrs Parr must have thought that once those early nightmares ended – and Thanet had no doubt that they had been very similar in content to the ones Julie had recently experienced – that Julie had completely recovered from her horrific experience. But Thanet was beginning to believe that it had marked Julie for life, making her terrified of emotion and cutting her off from the prospect of ever making satisfying relationships. A part of her had, like Annabel, died that night and had never been able to come to life again. Fanciful? he asked himself. Perhaps. But he felt it explained so much about Julie that had hitherto puzzled him.

Julie hadn't really had a chance. Too late, now, to give her one, but not too late perhaps to fight back on her behalf, to track down the person who had crippled her mind and, if Thanet were right, had finally destroyed her body too.

He headed back to his office with a new sense of determination. Lineham was waiting for him. Thanet took one look at him and said, 'Bad morning?'

'Very frustrating. Nothing new at all. And no whisper yet of the girl Kendon claims to have seen. There were plenty of women between the ages of fifteen and thirty-five, of course, but none who fitted the bill. We asked about women who were visiting in the area that evening too, but with no luck. The girl could live anywhere in Sturrenden, of course, and if so, we'll just have to hope she comes forward in response to the appeals.'

'Any news of Horrocks yet?'

'Not so far. He's expected home some time tomorrow, though, so we should be able to get hold of him then.'

'Right. Well come on, sit down. There have been developments.'

Lineham listened attentively while Thanet outlined his discoveries of the morning.

'You can read it all up for yourself later, of course,' Thanet finished up, 'but what do you think?'

Lineham's pleasant face was troubled. 'Don't you think it's a bit, well, far-fetched, sir?'

Thanet was as taken aback, as if a pet mouse had bitten him and said sharply, 'Far-fetched? What do you mean, far-fetched?'

Lineham flushed and said defensively, 'You did tell me yesterday to say what I really thought.'

The pigeons were coming home to roost with a vengeance, Thanet thought. 'You're quite right, of course, I did,' he said, more gently. 'So go on, tell me what you mean.'

'Well, here we are with three perfectly good suspects, Holmes, Parrish and Kendon. I know we're not getting anywhere at the moment ...'

116

'Dead right, we aren't.'

'But that's always happening,' Lineham went on doggedly. 'Sooner or later, with any luck, we'll get a break. Kendon's witness will turn up, Horocks might come up with something new ... Whereas this theory, well yes, I admit it seems possible that Julie Holmes and Annabel Dacre were murdered by the same person, but isn't it much more likely that Julie was killed by someone who was involved with her now?'

'Why? If the motive is powerful enough ... It's common knowledge that when someone has killed once he will find it easier the second time. Just think, man. This killer has been safe for twenty years and suddenly, bang, his security is threatened. He sees the girl who witnessed the first murder, a girl he thought never to see again, he recognises her, is pretty certain she has recognised him. Isn't it logical that he'd try and get rid of her?'

'But sir, with respect, there's an awful lot of assumptions there. You're assuming he recognised her, assuming he thought she'd recognised him and, most important of all, assuming he knew she'd witnessed the murder. How could he have known that, why should he have thought that she was any danger to him at all. From what you say, Julie's presence in the Dacre woman's studio was a closely guarded secret. The police kept quiet about it, Mrs Parr took her away, right after the murder, and I should think everyone thought what they were supposed to think, that she'd gone away because the double shock of her husband's death and her friend's murder, both on the same day, had been too much for her. I really can't see why, even if the murderer did recognise Julie at the Private View, he should have thought she was any threat to him.'

'All right,' Thanet said, 'I admit there's a doubt there. But it could have happened. The murderer could have found out, afterwards, quite by chance, that Julie was in the studio that night. Someone could have seen Annabel Dacre with the child, going into West

Lodge, have mentioned it later, in casual conversation. She herself might even have mentioned that she was looking after Julie to the vicar, when he rang that evening to ask for news of Julie's father. News gets around in villages, almost as if it is carried on the wind from one house to another. The murderer might not have known at the time that Julie was there, but that doesn't mean he might not have found out later. Dammit, man, you must admit it's possible.'

'I can see that.' But Lineham was clearly not convinced. Thanet looked at him in exasperation for a moment or two and then said, 'In any case, what have we got to lose, by trying to find out? You admit yourself that we've come to a dead end at the moment.'

Grudgingly, Lineham agreed.

Thanet began to laugh. 'You certainly took my advice seriously, yesterday. No, don't apologise! All in all, I prefer it this way. Livens things up a bit.'

Lineham grinned.

'Good,' Thanet said briskly. He picked up his sheet of scribbled notes. 'Now then, I think the first thing is to find out exactly where these people are living now. Unfortunately their addresses are not on this rough list of Mr Johnson's, and I don't suppose for a moment they'll all still be living in Little Sutton.'

'No.' Lineham was clearly now giving the matter his full attention. 'Highly unlikely, I should think. A murder in a village, the murderer never found. People would have been bound to know who the main suspects were and life couldn't have been very comfortable for them, knowing that people were watching them, wondering if they were guilty. It's not easy to live down a thing like that.'

'No. So you'd better start digging. Try Johnson's secretary first, get her to go into the College today, if necessary. If you can't get hold of her, you'll have to ring Johnson again. He won't be very pleased, but it can't be helped. I don't really want to wait until Monday. If you can't get hold of either of them you'll have to use your own initia‿. e.'

'There were four names, you said?'

'Five suspects originally, three men and two women. Only four of them appear on both lists. The fifth, a man called Peake, isn't on either of them. But I'd like you to check on him just the same.'

'And the advertisement requesting the loan of paintings appeared in the national as well as the local press?'

'Yes. So you could find that these people are scattered all over the country. Some might still be around, though. One of them was the local doctor, a Doctor Plummer. It would have been difficult for him to give up his practice and start all over again – it was a family practice, too, so it's all the more likely he would have stayed. And two of the other suspects were a local builder and his wife, Roger and Edna Pocock. They might well still be in the area. Anyway, here's the list. I've written Johnson's number and his secretary's at the top. I'm going to spend the rest of the afternoon working through this file.'

Thanet took a few minutes after Lineham left to get his pipe drawing really well, then settled down to read. It was tedious, painstaking work, even for someone as experienced as he. The different threads of the case had to be teased out, woven together into a recognisable pattern, reports and statements read and reread until each slotted into its place in the design. Thanet worked his way steadily through the whole file, took a five-minute break and then went back to study in turn each batch of statements relating to the main suspects. These were a surprisingly disparate group of people, the link between them apparently being that they had all been members of the Little Sutton Dramatic Society.

The murder of Annabel Dacre, he reminded himself as he began, had taken place between 7.45 and 8.45 pm.

First, there was Dr Gerald Plummer, then aged

119

twenty-eight and unofficially engaged to Annabel. On the night of the murder he had taken evening surgery from 5 to 6 pm, had done some paperwork and had then had supper with his father who had recently had a serious illness and was in the process of withdrawing from the practice. They always ate early because the housekeeper left at seven thirty.

At seven forty-five there had been a phone call (confirmed) from the local midwife: one of Dr Plummer's patients had gone into labour and there were complications. He had set off at once but had had a puncture and had experienced difficulties in changing the wheel. He had therefore not arrived at the patient's home (normally some ten minutes drive away) until eight forty-five. The local garage confirmed that the next day Plummer had called in with a punctured tyre, but there was no telling, of course, when or how the puncture had occurred or how long, if at all, the doctor had really been delayed. Plummer had denied that Annabel had ever given him cause for jealousy and had expressed total bewilderment at the motive for such a brutal and senseless crime.

A bit of a stuffed shirt? Thanet wondered, reading through the statements again. The trouble was that it was difficult to gauge what the man was really like from the formal language of the official documents. Thanet sighed, relit his pipe and turned to the next suspect.

This was Edward Peake, aged twenty-five, also a bachelor, and an optician's assistant. He had lodgings in Rose Cottage, a breakfast- and evening-meal arrangement. He had had supper at seven. His landlady had recently had bronchitis and during her illness he had been in the habit of taking her dog for his evening walk. That evening he left at seven fifty, keeping the dog on the lead until he had reached the woods adjoining the grounds of Champeney House. He had then let it off the leash for a run and had, he claimed, lost it. He had blundered around calling and whistling, eventually giving up around eight twenty-five and arriving back home at eight forty. The dog had apparently been run over in the fog, its body being found in a ditch at the side of a road next morning.

The landlady was hot in Peake's defence. 'A nicer, kinder, more considerate young man you couldn't wish to find.'

But again, no alibi for the time of the murder.

The third male suspect was the builder, aged thirty and married. He was in much the same position as Plummer and Peake, the difference being that he should, if his arrangements had not gone awry, have had a comfortingly sound alibi. The Pococks had had supper at six thirty that evening because Pocock had an appointment with a client at seven thirty to discuss some alterations to a house which the client was buying some five miles away from Little Sutton. Pocock left just after seven, allowing plenty of time because of the fog. He claimed to have arrived at the house a few minutes early and waited in vain for the client to turn up. At nine he gave up, arriving home at nine twenty in a furious temper at his wasted evening. The client confirmed that the appointment had been made. Unfortunately he lived twenty miles away and, unfamiliar with the area, had lost his way in the fog in the maze of country lanes. Eventually he had given up, found his way back to the main road and returned home, ringing Pocock to apologise as soon as he got there, at ten.

Edna Pocock aged twenty-nine and the fourth suspect, was a different matter. Thanet was very interested to note that although she had at the time of the murder been confined to bed, having had a miscarriage three days before, the police had obviously not ruled her out as a suspect. Why? Thanet found himself becoming increasingly impatient with the bald facts presented by the statements. He read on.

Edna Pocock had had two days in bed and on Friday, the day of the murder, had got up for the first time in the late afternoon, going back to bed immediately after supper, when her husband left for his appointment. According to her doctor (Plummer) she had still been very weak at the time. In any event, she, too, had no alibi for the time of the murder.

Finally, there was Alice Giddy, aged twenty-five. She lived with her mother, Mrs Florence Giddy, and worked in Cooper's, a department store in Sturrenden which had had a reputation for high quality merchandise and which, Thanet remembered, had given up the ghost ten years or so ago, when Marks and Spencer had opened a branch in the town.

On the night of Annabel's murder Alice Giddy had arrived home from work at six to find that her mother had unwisely attempted to hang some curtains and had had a fall, twisting her ankle. Alice had decided that the sprain was not bad enough to warrant calling the doctor and had spent some time dealing with the matter herself, treating the ankle with cold compresses and binding it up. She had then cooked the supper which her mother had partially prepared earlier in the day and they had eaten at seven fifteen. Mrs Giddy had been due to do the Church Flowers next morning and had fussed and fussed over the fact that now she wouldn't be able to. Nor could Alice do them after work the following day, Saturday, as she had already made arrangements to go to the theatre in London with friends. So, after supper, Alice had set off for the church at around seven forty-five, had spent an hour doing the flowers and had arrived back home at eight fifty, having seen no one.

And that was it. Not one of the people whom the police had apparently suspected of having committed the murder had an alibi which would stand up, and no amount of patient digging had been able to confirm or to disprove any one of them. It had been a foggy November evening and people had not gone out unless they had to. Those who had had seen nothing of any significance.

Thanet pushed the file away and glanced at his watch. Five o'clock. He stood up and stretched. His back protested and, simultaneously, he experienced a twinge of guilt. Joan really would be furious, when she discovered that he had skipped his appointment.

He walked stiffly across to the filing cabinet, stretched out his arms to grasp two of the drawer handles at chest level, positioned his feet carefully and then, rising on tip-toe, arched himself over backwards as far as he could go, held the position for a count of three, returned to an upright position and relaxed. He repeated the exercise three times and then, feeling virtuous, returned to his desk and asked for some tea to be sent in.

Deliberately, while he sipped it, he kept his mind blank, giving his mental processes a necessary few minutes in which to recuperate. Then he swivelled his chair around, upturned the waste-paper basket, put his feet on it and leaning back, closed his eyes – a position strictly forbidden by his physiotherapist but most conducive to constructive thinking.

There had been no circumstantial evidence against any one of the suspects. Fingerprints of all of them had been found in the studio, but this information had proved worthless; rehearsals had often been held there. There had been no sign of a forced entry to the Lodge. Annabel had apparently let the murderer in herself and taken him up to the studio. The murder weapon had been a rough chunk of quartz which normally stood on one of the studio shelves. Either, then, the murderer had known of its being there and had counted on using it, or the murder had been unpremeditated and the rock seized as the nearest weapon to hand. There was no way of telling. For all the physical evidence Annabel, like Julie, could have been killed by a ghost.

Thanet could sympathise with the investigating officer. It was obvious from the file that the police had done their job with meticulous care. It must have been galling to fail. Thanet did not recognise the name of the man who had been in charge of the case – probably he had retired long ago. A pity, he thought. It would have been useful to discuss it with him.

On impulse he rang through to records, asked them to check. He was in luck. Sergeant West, to whom he spoke, was an older man and remembered Detective Chief Inspector Low. Low had retired about ten years ago, having transfered to Ashford some years previously.

'Could you get me his address?'

'Ashford might have it, sir, unless he moved right away when he retired. I'll check and ring you back.'

Thanet replaced the receiver. It would certainly help to talk to Low. Low would have known all the people involved in the Dacre case, would be able to put flesh on the bones of what Thanet had learnt.

Lineham came in and plumped down wearily in a chair.

Thanet grimaced in sympathy. 'Hard time?'

Lineham nodded. 'Johnson's secretary was out for the day, her daughter said. I couldn't get hold of Johnson, either. Anyway, I've got all of them but Alice Giddy. Two of them were easy – well, three, assuming the Pococks are still together. Their number and Dr Plummer's were in the telephone directory. He's still in Little Sutton, but they've moved to Sturrenden. Little Mole Avenue.'

'Ah yes. That's right on the edge of town, off the Canterbury Road, isn't it?'

'Yes. Both Peake and Giddy were much more difficult. Neither was in the directory. I rang Parry's, where Peake worked, and they confirmed that he'd left the area to go North, years ago. Well, to cut a long story short, he's dead, about five years ago, of a heart attack.'

'That's definite?'

'Yes. I spoke to his last employer.'

'Well at least that's one fewer to worry about. But you still haven't traced Alice Giddy?'

'Nope. She's probably moved away too. Short of going out to Little Sutton and asking questions, we'll just have to wait until we can get hold of Johnson's secretary.'

'I don't want to do that – go out to Little Sutton, I mean. I'd like to catch all these people completely unprepared. I should think the murderer believes himself to be absolutely safe.'

'If he is one of them.'

'Yes, of course,' Thanet was startled. He was so convinced by now that they were working on the right lines that he had forgotten Lineham's scepticism.

The telephone rang. Sergeant West had got hold of ex-D.C.I. Low's address and telephone number.

Thanet thanked him warmly. 'Low was in charge of the Dacre case,' he explained to Lineham. 'He's retired, lives out at Biddenden, apparently.' He dialled Low's number.

Low couldn't see Thanet that evening but readily agreed to an interview next morning. This suited Thanet very well. It had been a long day and he felt stale, semi-stupified by all the new information he had assimilated. He would prefer to be fresh and alert before interviewing any of these new suspects and as it would obviously be sensible to delay doing so until after he had seen Low, he now had the perfect excuse for going home. 'While I'm seeing Low you can get hold of Alice Giddy's address from Johnson's secretary,' he said to Lineham.

He shuffled together the loose papers from the Dacre file and pushed the folder across the desk. 'Here you are,' he said with a grin. 'Your book at bedtime.'

10

He was in a pit and he had to get out. Sprig was in danger, he knew it. He had to save her. He hurled himself frantically at the sides of his prison, seeking a toe-hold, finger-hold, anything by which he could lever himself upward, but there was nothing. The walls were soft, resilient, yielding beneath the pressure of his fingers. He looked up and saw suddenly that far, far above him there seemed to be some kind of ledge. Gathering together all his strength he sprang, the soft, furry surface receiving him suffocatingly into its embrace. And then he was free, the walls of the room soaring above him into darkness. They were hung with paintings and he knew at once where he was: Annabel's studio. And there, on the floor was Julie, long golden hair matted with blood. In the corner of the room stood a cot and he understood now his desperate sense of urgency. Sprig was in it and he had to get her away. He tried to hurry towards it but his legs were leaden. He could see Sprig now, clinging on to the bars of the cot, her eyes dilated with shock and terror. Just before he reached her he knew, without looking around, that the murderer was behind him. He spread his arms to protect her, but the murderer seized one of them, began to drag him away ...

He opened his eyes. Sprig's face floated before him, puckered with anxiety, and for a moment he hovered between nightmare and reality, uncertain which was which. Then she released his arm, at which she had been tugging, raised her eyebrows comically.

'OK, love,' he whispered. 'I'm awake now. I'll be out in a minute.'

Satisfied that their morning ritual was under way she trotted off towards the door.

Already the nightmare was fading, but the sense of distress still lingered and Thanet deliberately held on to his dream, forcing himself to remember, to try to interpret. That pit ... the pit in Johnson's studio, of course. And Sprig had been Julie, Julie Annabel ... He almost groaned aloud. What a mess.

But Sprig would be waiting. Silently, he slid out of bed.

'I forgot to ask,' Joan said suddenly, at breakfast. 'How did you get on with Mrs James yesterday?'

'I didn't. No,' Thanet held up a hand, 'please, darling, listen. I honestly didn't have time. But I did ring to apologise.' He didn't mention the fact that the apology had been made long after the appointment should have been kept, that he had clean forgotten about it.

'But you promised ...'

'I know. And I'm sorry, honestly. But so much happened yesterday.'

'Bridget hurt her knee,' Sprig announced, displaying the injury.

Thanet seized thankfully on the diversion. 'Oh dear. How did that happen?'

'Luke Thanet, you are trying to change the subject,' Joan said accusingly.

'So I am!' he said in mock astonishment.

'You did make a further appointment, I hope?'

'Well, as a matter of fact I was wondering if it was really necessary. My back's so much better now ...'

'Oh Luke, no! You can't sign off until she thinks you're ready.'

'Well ...'

'Darling, please!'

Thanet sighed. 'All right. I'll make one more appointment – just one, mind, and that'll be it.'

'See what she says,' Joan said vaguely. 'Come on now, Ben, one more spoonful.'

Ben obliged by scooping up some cereal and then, leaning over the side of his high chair, dropping it on the floor.

'Ben! Naughty boy!' Joan jumped up, fetched another spoon, closed Ben's cereal-covered fingers around it. 'Come on now, darling, just one more spoonful. In your mouth,' she added warningly. Then she fetched a piece of kitchen roll to mop up the mess.

'I shouldn't bother,' Thanet said, watching her, 'What's the point? He'll only do it again.'

Obligingly Ben did, the cereal this time narrowly missing the top of Joan's head. 'Ben!' she said and, catching Thanet's eye, began to laugh.

The little incident somehow succeeded in finally banishing the last of the shadow which had lingered as an aftermath of his nightmare and Thanet felt cheerful as he set off for the interview with Low. It was a glorious morning. A few fluffy white clouds enhanced the forget-me-not blue of the sky and the sun shone down upon a countryside clothed in the freshest and most delicate shades of green.

As soon as Thanet turned off the main road he found himself in narrow, winding lanes bordered on each side by a froth of Queen Anne's lace. He remembered the heady scent of it from earlier expeditions to the country and he wound down his window, inhaling the fragrance which drifted into the car. He found himself wishing that Joan were with him and remembering his resolution of a few days earlier to take her for a drive through the orchards. Here and there the apple blossom was already showing pink. Next Sunday, he promised himself, work or no work, they would have their expedition. If the weather were as good as this they might even take a picnic.

The prospect lifted his spirits still further and by the time he drew up in front of Low's bungalow he was feeling distinctly optimistic. It was, Thanet thought, rather an attractive bungalow. For himself, he preferred houses, but this one had some interesting features, being built entirely of stone in a style reminiscent of the Dordogne. He said so to Low, who had obviously been looking out for him; the front door opened before Thanet was half way up the path.

Low was delighted with Thanet's perception. 'We felt it was the next best thing to the genuine article. We'd have loved to retire to the Dordogne – a surprisingly large number of English people do, you know – but family ties kept us here and now, well, we've settled and don't want to change.' Low was a big man, a good sixteen stone, Thanet thought, and well over six feet. A luxuriant growth of white hair encircled a bald patch on the top of his head, and sprouted from his eye-brows. Although he must be now be well into his seventies his carriage was good, his flesh firm and well-muscled. Criminals, Thanet thought, must have found him a formidable opponent.

They chatted enthusiastically about the Dordogne (the Thanets had spent their honeymoon there) as Low led the way into a large, pleasantly furnished sitting room which overlooked the back garden. 'Would you like some coffee, Inspector? I was just about to make some.'

The coffee was good: hot and strong. How would it be, he wondered, when he and Joan were old? How would he feel about retirement? Would he simply feel that he had outgrown his usefulness, or would he be relieved that he could at last do all the things he never now had time for? He smiled to himself. He could just imagine Joan's reaction if he were saying all this to her. 'We've got another thirty-odd years to get through first,' she'd say. And of course she'd be right. It must be something about the atmosphere of this place …

'Right,' Low said, seating himself opposite Thanet. 'Now, it's the Dacre case you're interested in, you said?'

Thanet nodded. 'Yes, I'll explain.' Briefly he described the progress of the Holmes case to date. Low listened with complete attention, but it was not until Thanet came to the link with the murder of Annabel Dacre that he interrupted for the first time.

'Little Julie Parr!' he said.

Thanet could see from Low's face that he had added two and two together and come up with the same answer as Thanet. 'Exactly,' he said.

'I see,' Low said slowly. 'But what ...? No, I won't ask any questions until you've finished. Go on, please.'

'I almost have. We've traced all the suspects but Alice Giddy, and my sergeant's working on that now. Peake is dead, by the way – five years ago, of a heart attack. He moved up north soon after the murder.'

'So now you'll be questioning them all about the night of Julie's murder. Well, I wish you luck. She was a sweet kid. To think he got her in the end ...'

'He?'

Low shook his head. 'A manner of speaking.' He stood up and walked restlessly across to the window. 'I never forgot the Dacre case.' He looked back at Thanet over his shoulder and gave a wry grin. 'For one thing it ruined my track record. We put everything we had into that damned case, and all for nothing. So, if there's anything I can do to help, anything at all ...' he returned to his chair, lifting his hands in a gesture of largesse, 'just ask.'

'What I want from you really is the background to the case – relationships, personalities, the sort of stuff you can only guess at from reading the formal statements. Together with your own feelings about the case. You were there, you knew these people at the time. You'd be bound to have a much better grasp of what was going on between them than I could ever hope to attain now, twenty years later.'

'I don't know about that,' Low said modestly, 'but I'll have a go.' He leaned back in his chair, thrust his hands hard down into the capacious pockets of the thick knitted woollen jacket he was wearing, as if digging deep into the past.

130

Then he relaxed, his eyes glazing with concentration. 'It's a long time, of course, but since you rang last night I've been thinking, and it's all been coming back to me. The five suspects and Annabel Dacre were, as you've no doubt gathered by now, all members of the Little Sutton Dramatic Society, where they were on equal terms in a way they couldn't have been in everyday life. They came from very different classes. Annabel Dacre, of course, was the squire's daughter, from "the big house" and as such one of the social queens of the district. Alice Giddy was closest to her, socially. Her mother was a wealthy widow and Annabel and Alice more or less grew up together – went to the same prep and boarding schools and shared an interest in art. Their paths divided when they left school. Annabel went on to study art in London and Paris while Alice had to stay at home. Her mother's health was deteriorating and she was insistent that Alice should live at home. They engaged a day companion for Mrs Giddy and Alice found herself a job.'

'In Cooper's.'

'That's right, in the fashion department. I can see you're wondering why she needed to work. The answer is that financially she didn't. I've no doubt at all that she took the job to get out of the house during the daytime. Mrs Giddy was an impossible woman, demanding, capricious ...'

'I thought she was hanging curtains on the day Annabel died. She sprained her ankle, didn't she? If she was sick ...?'

'Typical,' said Low. 'She'd do something like that – hang the curtains – just to make Alice feel guilty. She was furious that her daughter had refused to stay at home all the time and look after her. So she'd manoeuvre situations to make unpleasantness for Alice, even if it meant inconvenience for herself.'

'You're not saying she'd actually go so far as to sprain her ankle ...?'

'No,' though Low didn't sound too sure, 'but she

certainly had no need to be climbing ladders, I assure you. She had a daily help as well as a companion.'

'It's a wonder Alice didn't go to the Sturrenden College of Art,' Thanet said, 'if she was that keen.'

'She did consider it, I believe, but rejected the idea – said she wasn't going to settle for the second-rate. She wanted to study dress design – had real talent, I believe.'

'I don't suppose the Principal of the College of Art would be very flattered by that point of view!' Thanet said, with a grin.

Low returned the smile. 'No. Anyway, the one bright spot in Alice's life, so far as I could see, was her fiancé, Gerald Plummer.'

'Plummer! But I thought ...'

'That he was engaged to Annabel? He was, at the time of her death, or so he claimed. Perhaps I should explain that Annabel Dacre was a very beautiful woman. Before she came back to Little Sutton and set up her studio in West Lodge after her years of study abroad, Alice Giddy and Plummer were always together. There was no formal engagement, you understand, but every last person in Little Sutton was convinced they'd marry and saw Mrs Giddy as the only obstacle to the union. Then Annabel came back and all of a sudden Alice was out in the cold. And make no mistake about it, she would care, would Alice. She might hide it, but she'd care all right.'

'What was she like?'

'Tall, dark, elegant. Good-looking in an odd kind of way, but too intense for my taste.'

'So Alice would have had motive, means and opportunity,' Thanet said. 'If she'd been awaiting her chance to take her revenge on Annabel – or perhaps merely to tackle her in private about Plummer – her mother's insistence on her doing the church flowers would have been a tremendous stroke of luck. A foggy night, an excuse to be out ... She would have known about the chunk of quartz and no doubt Annabel would have let her in without hesitation ...'

'Certainly. But unfortunately it's not quite as simple

132

as that. The same could have been said of every other one of the four suspects.'

'Every one?'

'Every single one,' Low repeated firmly. 'Plummer included. Let me explain: Annabel, as I said, was a very beautiful woman and very attractive to men.'

'Didn't do her or Julie much good, did it? Almost makes me hope my daughter will grow up plain but worthy.'

'Yes. Well, it seems to me that the main difference between them, from what you say, was that whereas Julie seemed unconscious of her power over men, Annabel positively revelled in hers. She had them all eating out of her hand, believe me, and the thing was, she was totally undiscriminating in the bestowal of her favours. One week it would be Plummer, the next Peake, the next Pocock. And so on, in various alternations. They couldn't have known where they were with her, any of them, and that's enough to drive any man mad, especially with a woman as beautiful as she was.'

'Pocock was married, though.'

'Didn't seem to make any difference. Annabel wasn't the first, as far as he was concerned, but way out of his class, really, and I don't think he'd have enjoyed being strung along. No, whoever did it, I think it may well have been Annabel's blow-hot, blow-cold technique which brought about her death.'

'What about Pocock's wife? Why was she suspected? Surely, if she was used to her husband's affairs, one more wouldn't have made much difference?'

'This one might have been the proverbial straw that broke the camel's back. And in any case, Edna Pocock was in an unusually fragile state of mind. She'd just had a miscarriage – not the first, either.'

'And that's another thing. Wouldn't she have been too weak, to get out of bed, walk to West Lodge in the fog – how far away was it, by the way?'

'About ten minutes walk from the village.'

'... walk to the West Lodge, kill Annabel, walk back, get rid of any evidence – blood stains, mud-stained shoes and so on – and be comfortably back in bed by the time her husband got home?'

'I agree it's unlikely,' Low said, 'but possible all the same. She had plenty of time. If I remember rightly, Pocock left home at about seven that evening and didn't get home until about half past nine.'

'I only wish I had a memory like yours!' Thanet said. 'To be able to remember a detail like that after twenty years ...'

'Believe me, the facts of this case were burned on to my brain,' Low said.

'What was she like, Edna Pocock? How long had they been married?'

'Ten years. Oh, she was small, plump, a motherly-looking type. Not terribly bright – not stupid, but just not very intelligent. I always hoped she might have managed to have children later, she seemed to me to be the sort of woman who would have made an excellent mother – warm, kind, comforting, you know?'

'What about Peake? I know he's out of it, but I'd still like to know.'

'An entirely different type from Plummer. Now Plummer was tall, solid, a good family-doctor type, but Peake was thin, nervous, intense, the sort who would worship from afar, I should think.'

'But Plummer? How would he have reacted to cavalier treatment?'

'Not well. I think there was a streak of vanity there. I think he rather enjoyed being a big fish in a little pond.'

'Hmm. Well, here comes the sixty-thousand-dollar question. Who do *you* think did it?'

Low sat back in his chair, steepled his hands beneath his chin and looked back into the past. 'Who do I think did it?' he murmured. He lifted his hands in a gesture of helplessness before letting them come to rest on the arms of his chair. 'Well, for my money, Alice Giddy. But there is nothing, absolutely nothing to substantiate that suspicion.'

'I realise that. I shouldn't have asked, I suppose,' Thanet said. He tapped the burning ash from his pipe into the big ashtray, made sure it was safe before stowing it away in his pocket. 'Well, I think that's about it for the moment, Chief Inspector.'

'Mr,' said Low, with a rueful smile, 'and it's been a pleasure. I hope you get him. He's had twenty years' grace already.'

The burly figure, hand raised, remained reflected in Thanet's driving mirror until he turned the corner at the end of the road.

11

It was now ten-thirty and it occurred to Thanet that Little Sutton was only three or four miles out of his way. Suddenly he wanted to see it. He'd been there before, of course, in passing, but on those occasions it had been a village like any other, with no particular significance for him. Now he wanted to look at it in a different light, as the place where the Holmes case had really begun. And he'd like to see West Lodge, where Annabel had lived and died ...

He pulled up at the next telephone box.

'Mike? Thanet here. Any luck with tracing Alice Giddy?'

'Just got it.' Lineham's voice was faint. 'Hang on a minute.'

'Can you speak up? This is a terrible line.'

'I got Johnson's secretary to go in to the College and open up her files.' Lineham's voice was faint and Thanet pressed the receiver hard against his ear.

'She – Alice Giddy, that is – now lives in ...' His voice faded out.

'Can you repeat that? Speak up, can't you? I can hardly hear you. Oh, Maddison House, you say. Where Parrish lives! That's interesting.' Any connection there? he wondered.

Lineham's next words were unintelligible. It occurred to Thanet that there was no interference on the line, and that Lineham seemed perfectly to understand everything he said. 'Mike, are you all right.'

'Yes, of course.' The answer was clearer this time, as if Lineham had made an effort.

'Who else is in, this morning?'

'D.C. Bennet, D.C. Stout, D.S. Parkin ...'

'Put Parkin on, will you? Parkin? What's the matter with Lineham. He sounds odd. Is he ill or something?'

'He won't thank me for telling you, sir, but we think he's got 'flu. He looks like death warmed up, and ...'

The connection was cut. Thanet swore, dug out some more coins, dialled again. 'Parkin? Now look here, I'm going to tell Lineham to go home. You make sure he does just that, will you? Now put him on.'

The matter was soon settled. The token resistance Lineham put up showed Thanet just how ill his sergeant must be feeling. He knew himself how frustrating it was to have to pull out of a case just when things were getting really interesting. Thanet checked that nothing else of note had come in that morning and rang off.

He found Little Sutton without difficulty, but did not stop in the centre of the village. Hoping that his memory was serving him correctly he drove around the Green and out by a different road. Half a mile out of the village he smiled with satisfaction as a tall, crumbling red-brick wall came into view on his left. As he had thought, these were the grounds of Champeney House.

A hundred yards further on he pulled up in front of a pair of tall wrought iron gates. The drive beyond them, curling away into the distance and disappearing into an avenue of tall, dead elms, was obviously never used. Couch grass and other weeds had thrust their way up through the old tarmac which was visible only in crumbling patches. A small, stone-built lodge, solidly built but undoubtedly empty and neglected stood within the gates, to the right.

Thanet got out of his car, locked it and approached the gates. The words WEST LODGE were cut into the stone of the right-hand pillar. The gates, however,

Thanet saw to his disappointment, were padlocked. Flakes of rust came off on his hands as he gripped them to peer through at the little house.

Weeds and overgrown shrubs grew right up to the walls, half covering the windows, and ivy climbed the walls unchecked, thrusting destructive fingers through rotten window frames, entwining gutters and drainpipes in a stranglehold which must surely soon bring them down. Broken window panes gaped everywhere, hastening no doubt the process of decay by letting in the wind and rain. Thanet gave the gates one last, frustrated rattle and was about to turn away when he hesitated, stooped to examine more closely the tangled chain which had been loosely wound several times around the inmost bars of the gates. Surely that link should not be projecting like that? He began to fumble with the rusted links and almost at once saw with satisfaction that at some point long ago – for the ends had rusted over – someone had cut through the links and then twisted them around each other so that to a casual inspection they still appeared unbroken. It took him a few minutes to disentangle them, then he was through, pushing the gates roughly together behind him.

His hands were covered in rust and he bent to rub them impatiently on a clump of rough grass before pushing open the little wicket gate which led into the overgrown garden. Here and there a few flowers still survived: a sprawling, woody tangle of forsythia, a single peony thrusting its way up through a tangle of last season's dead foliage, a drift of bluebells carpeting the ground beneath an old apple tree at the far side of the garden.

Thanet approached the front door and pushed. It was, of course, locked. He picked his way around to the back of the house, pausing to peer into one of the front windows as he went. Here a surprise awaited him: the room was furnished – sketchily, true, but furnished nevertheless. For a moment he was afraid that the place was, despite all the signs, inhabited after all, but a second glance reassured him. That room had not been lived in for years. Annabel's mother, then, had presumably not bothered to clear the house after her daughter's death. Would Annabel's studio, like Miss Havisham's wedding feast, have been preserved intact over the years? The thought excited him.

At the back of the house he had better luck. As he had hoped, someone – children or courting couples perhaps – had been unable to resist the temptation of breaking in. When he put his shoulder to the door it yielded to him, its sagging timbers scraping protestingly over the stone threshold.

The dank, musty smell of a long-uninhabited house filled his nostrils as he stepped into a large, square kitchen with generous windows on two walls. Attempts had been made to modernise it, presumably when Annabel had come to live here: there was a stainless-steel sink, dull and dusty from disuse, and units with formica work surfaces along two walls. Out of curiosity Thanet opened one of the cupboards. Yes, as he had thought, the house had never been cleared. The decayed remains of cardboard packets mingled with liberal sprinklings of mouse droppings. A quick glance into some of the other cupboards told him that, predictably, everything of any value had long since been stolen.

It was the same story everywhere else on the ground floor. Even now, after all this time, lighter patches on the wallpaper showed where prints or pictures had once hung, and the only items of furniture which remained were those which would have been too cumbersome to move. Carpets and rugs had been taken, but curtains still hung at the windows, presumably to give the impression that nothing within had been disturbed. Empty coca-cola bottles and crumpled crisp packets showed that children had played here, no doubt relishing the atmosphere of strangeness and decay in games of mystery and adventure.

Treading gingerly for fear of rotting floorboards, Thanet began to move softly up the short, straight flight of stairs, his footsteps muffled by the rotting remnants of the stair carpet. Somewhere above him was Annabel's studio and his curious, irrational need to see it, his hope that it might have survived the depredations of the thieves who had more or less stripped the ground floor, caused his heart to beat faster, his breathing to become ragged.

And so his first, reaction as he stepped into the long, narrow room which took up one half of the entire first floor and ran through from the front of the house to the back, was one of disappointment. Here, too, little had been left. A bulky button-backed settee, its linen covering discoloured and rotting, still stood beneath the front windows and a long deal table, its top liberally stained with faded splotches of paint, had obviously been dismissed as having no commercial value.

Thanet walked to the centre of the room, his footsteps sounding hollow on the bare floorboards, and then stood looking about him. The windows in the rear wall – the north wall, presumably – had been enlarged and the light was excellent. To the right of them was a deep alcove, the alcove in which Julie's cot must have stood. Thanet walked across to look at it. At one time it must, he decided, have been a dressing-room leading off the back bedroom. The dividing wall had been removed and then, perhaps at a later date, a ceiling curtain track installed. This was, no doubt, the very curtain which had saved Julie's life. Thanet fingered the rotting material and then grimaced, rubbing his hands on the seat of his trousers.

He turned away. There was nothing to be learnt here. If the ghosts of the past still lingered, they had nothing to say to him. He had done what he had wanted to do, however. He had seen the place where it all began, and some need in him was satisfied. He made his way softly down the stairs, shut the back door firmly behind him.

Back in the village people were just coming out of church. Thanet pulled into the kerb and watched them disperse, some by car and some on foot. Many of them no doubt would clearly remember the murder of Annabel Dacre, some might even still mourn her. He waited until the last car had driven away, then he got out of his own, locked it and strolled across to the lych gate at the entrance to the churchyard. The sun was warm on his back as he turned to study the peaceful scene.

Little Sutton was a typical English village. There was a large, roughly triangular area of somewhat ragged grass, surrounded by a hotch-potch of houses, some large, some small, reflecting the development of English architecture from Tudor times to the present day. Tiny black and white timber-frame cottages rubbed shoulders with Georgian aristocrats in mellow red brick and the occasional Victorian upstart with its usual quota of stained glass and dank evergreen shrubs. The only modern house, a chalet bungalow with picture windows and a green-tiled roof had obviously been built in the former garden of one such monster.

To one side of the Green were the two huge oak trees which Thanet had recognised in *The Cricket Match*, their massive trunks ringed with white wooden benches – no doubt a favourite place for the older men of the village to congregate on summer afternoons, thought Thanet. But today, despite the sunshine, it was still too chilly for anyone to be sitting about in the shade, and the green was deserted except for a boy of about twelve who was throwing sticks for his dog.

In a little while he would try to find Sutton House and interview Dr Plummer, Thanet thought. Meanwhile the sleepy calm of the place had infected him and without any conscious purpose he turned and strolled into the churchyard, admiring the satisfying simplicity of the Norman church tower, the mellowness of the stone. A pity, he thought, that its setting was so unkempt. The churchyard was large, many of its graves overgrown with grass. An attempt had been made to tend a wide swathe of ground on either side of the path, however, and there was an area with well-tended graves and modern headstones which was trim and neat.

Thanet left the path and began to wander about amongst the older graves, pausing now and then to try to read an inscription; many were quite illegible, worn away by centuries of wind and rain.

He had not yet admitted to himself what he was doing and it was not until he came across it that he knew. The grave cried out to be noticed, an island of order in the surrounding chaos.

ANNABEL DACRE
1935–1960
'Snatched away in beauty's bloom'

The grass was close-cut, the edges neatly trimmed, and in the centre of the rectangle was a perfect circle of miniature rose bushes, strong new shoots giving a promise of the flowers to come. Someone, even after twenty years, was still taking a good deal of trouble over Annabel's grave.

Who? Thanet wondered. Her mother? Remembering the Memorial Exhibition for a daughter twenty years dead, the pain which had caused Mrs Dacre to seal up Annabel's house and let it fall down rather than allow anyone else to live in it, Thanet could well imagine Annabel's mother making a regular pilgrimage to tend her daughter's grave.

'Beautifully kept, isn't it?' The voice behind him made him jump.

The woman was tall, almost as tall as Thanet, and thin, painfully so. The brown knitted suit she was wearing hung loosely on her, and her cream straw hat topped a face from which the flesh had melted away.

Skin the colour of parchment accentuated the shockingly skull-like effect. Her eyes, however, were beautiful, a deep, delphinium blue and alert – disconcertingly assessing, Thanet felt, the effect her physical appearance was having upon him.

'Theodora Manson,' she said, putting out her hand. 'My husband is vicar here.' Her hand in his felt as dry as a dead twig, as insubstantial as a dead leaf.

'Luke Thanet,' he responded. He gestured at the grave. 'It's a long time for someone to have kept on coming, year after year, to keep it looking like this.'

'Her mother does it' Mrs Manson said. 'She's getting old now and she's had a lot of ill-health lately, but she still manages it somehow.' She looked down at the grave. 'Annabel was a lovely girl – beautiful, that is. And a very talented painter. Such a waste.'

'I think I've seen one of her paintings,' Thanet said. 'A village cricket match.' He nodded over his shoulder. 'On the Green.'

'Ah yes, I know the one you mean. I saw it at the recent exhibition of her work. You didn't go, I gather?'

'No, I'm afraid not. I didn't see the painting until after the exhibition was over, or I would have. I liked it very much.'

'Would you like to see another of her paintings?'

Thanet concealed his surprise at the invitation. 'Yes, I would. Very much.'

'Come along, I'll show it to you. We're very proud of it. It's called *The Church Fête*, which was why I especially wanted it for my husband. I bought it for his birthday, the year before Annabel ... died. It seemed a wicked extravagance at the time, but I've never regretted it. Apart from anything else, it has proved to be an excellent investment, though we don't think of it that way. We simply enjoy looking at it.'

They turned on to a footpath which crossed the churchyard towards the high stone boundary wall. Mrs Manson led him through a rickety wooden gate into

143

the vicarage garden. Thanet exclaimed in delight and Mrs Manson smiled with undisguised pleasure at his reaction.

'It's my hobby,' she said.

Smooth green lawns stretched away on either side, bordered by curved flower beds packed with a profusion of shrubs and flowers. Thanet knew very little about gardening, but he could recognise the hand of an artist when he saw one, could appreciate the hard work and expertise behind an apparently casual yet perfect effect like this.

'It's beautiful,' he said. 'Really beautiful.'

'I've worked on it for thirty years. I don't do the lawns, now, of course, but I still managed the rest somehow. Fortunately it doesn't need much maintenance. It's so stuffed with plants there's no room for weeds. We'll go in through the french windows,' she said, setting off across the lawn towards the house.

The long windows stood open to the warmth of the midday sun and the scents of the garden. Thanet followed the tall, gaunt figure through a faded sitting-room into what was obviously the vicar's study. Mrs Manson gestured towards the painting. 'We hung it where it gets the best light,' she said.

Thanet stepped forward eagerly. This was the first of Annabel's paintings that he had seen properly. It was small, perhaps ten inches wide by eight inches high, and glowed on the pale wall like a jewel. Thanet leaned forward to examine it more closely. In brilliant, primary colours, Annabel had painted the village fête on the Green. There were the two tall oaks, the circular white-slatted benches, the scatter of houses set around the vivid emerald of the grass. The painting was crammed with detail – stalls, sideshows, red and white striped fortune-teller's tent complete with turbaned head protruding from between the flaps. And everywhere were people – buying, selling, talking, laughing, walking, gesticulating – tiny, stylised figures yet each uniquely individual.

144

'It's marvellous,' Thanet said, meaning it. 'Fascinating.'

'That's me.' said Mrs Manson with a smile, pointing to the turbaned head. 'I used to be rather good at fortune-telling. Not particularly appropriate for a vicar's wife,' she added with a gleam of amusement in her eyes, 'but there we are. We have to use the talents God gives us, don't we? Especially when they bring in money to repair the church tower.'

'She put real people into her paintings?' Thanet said with interest. 'I didn't realise that.'

'Oh yes, we're all there. That's my husband.'

Mr Manson, sober in black suit and clerical collar, was bending over to comfort a sobbing child.

'Remarkable perception, Annabel had, for one so young.'

The last words came out in a gasp and Thanet, turning sharply, found Mrs Manson supporting herself on the back of a chair, her lower lip drawn in and clamped between her teeth, her forehead beaded with sweat. He exclaimed in concern, helped her to a chair and lowered her gently into it.

'Can I get you something?'

She shook her head feebly. 'No thank you. I'm sorry. I'll be all right in a few minutes.'

'A glass of water?' he persisted.

'No, really.' She leaned back, closed her eyes, seemed to withdraw into herself, somewhere far away from him. Thanet stood awkwardly in front of her for a moment or two and then tiptoed softly to the door. It seemed rude, ungrateful to go without a word of thanks, but he felt that he had no right to intrude any longer. At the door he paused. Had she said something? He turned, found that she had rolled her head towards him, was looking at him.

'I'm sorry.' The words were scarcely more than a whisper.

He was suddenly angry, at the pain she must be suffering and at her need to apologise. 'Don't,' he said fiercely and then, modifying his tone, 'Thank you for showing me your picture. Are you sure there's nothing I can do for you?'

Her head moved slightly in a gesture of gratitude. 'I'll be all right in a little while.'

He raised his hand in farewell and then left, walking swiftly through the garden without seeing it, his mind a confused jumble of emotion – pity for Mrs Manson, whom he had liked, anger at his own helplessness, admiration for her stoicism, guilt at his deception. He was back at the lych gate before he realised that there was something else, too – frustration that their discussion of the painting had been interrupted. He would have liked to identify more of those tiny figures. Amongst them, quite possibly, had been the murderer.

The thought made him feel even more angry with himself. 'Heartless pig,' he muttered as he crossed the road towards his car. He had unlocked it before he realised that he had not yet finished his work here. He still wanted to see Dr Plummer.

He relocked the car and looked about. The boy and his dog had gone and the Green was deserted. Somewhere not too far away, though, someone was using a motor-mower. Thanet stood quite still, trying to detect the source of the sound. Then he set off across the Green.

In the garden of one of the little black and white cottages a young man, stripped to the waist, was cutting the grass. He switched off the machine, came to the gate. 'Doctor Plummer?' He walked across the pavement and pointed. 'That house. The big one with the white windows.'

Thanet thanked him and walked on.

Sutton House was one of the classic Georgian ones. The man who opened the door was in his late twenties. 'Doctor Plummer? I'm sorry, he's not here.'

'I'm really very anxious to get in touch with him.' Deliberately, Thanet did not yet identify himself. If he could get what he wanted without doing so, he would.

No point in giving Plummer prior warning. 'Will he be back, later?'

'I'm sorry, no. Actually, he's in hospital – went in just over a week ago. I'm standing in for him. Can I help you?'

'Thank you, but it's a personal matter,' Thanet said. 'Could you tell me which hospital?'

'Sturrenden General.'

So, when Julie was murdered last Tuesday evening, Plummer had been in hospital. Easy enough to check, Thanet thought as he went back to his car. That left Alice Giddy and the two Pococks, out of the original five suspects. In the car he began to sing.

Things were definitely looking up.

12

A treat, Sunday lunch at home: roast beef, meltingly tender; roast potatoes, crispy on the outside, white and fluffy inside; white cabbage cooked in its own juices with chopped bacon and onions; individual batter puddings, as light as soufflés; thick, rich gravy and finally, apple pie and cream. Thanet appreciated every mouthful. In the present economic situation this was a tradition which was becoming increasingly difficult to maintain, but he and Joan had agreed that however much they had to tighten their belts during the week they would keep it up as long as they possibly could.

Afterwards he was tempted to linger. The thought of a long lazy afternoon reading the Sunday papers, chatting to Joan, playing with the children, beckoned to him. He knew, however, that if he gave in to temptation the reality would not be like that. He would be restless, unable to settle down all the while he knew that there was work he should be doing. So when he had topped off the meal with a refreshing cup of tea he kissed Joan a reluctant good-bye and set off for Maddison House.

How the builders had ever managed to obtain planning permission to build the place was a mystery to him. There must, he thought, have been some palm-greasing somewhere. It was a single, ten-storey block of luxury flats which had been built in a wooded area about half a mile from the edge of Sturrenden. Clearly visible above the trees from some distance away, it looked as out of place as a beached whale.

148

Thanet looked about with interest as he emerged from the approach road through the wood into the extensive, cleared space around the building.

Neatly tended lawns and rose-beds, and well-placed urns of velvety, wine-red wallflowers indicated that the tenants of Maddison House employed a gardener who was industrious if not inspired. Thanet bent to look more closely at one of the elaborate lead urns, then tapped it with his knuckles. He straightened up with a grimace. Fibreglass, without a doubt. He didn't like the spurious.

Wide glass doors led into a spacious hall floored with black and white marble tiles. Against one wall was a long oak table and on it a huge bowl of scarlet tulips. Thanet remembered the caretaker (possibly cum-gardener) that Parrish had mentioned. No doubt it was his job and possibly his wife's, to give the place this groomed, carefully-tended air and to keep it running smoothly and efficiently.

Thanet consulted the wall indicator and discovered that Flat 26 was on the seventh floor. He took the lift, stepping out into a red-carpeted lobby some twelve feet square with four front doors in it. He rang the bell of Flat 26 and waited, conscious of the silence. There must be dozens of people living in this place and yet so far he had not seen or heard a single sign of life. What did they all do on Sunday afternoons? Sleep?

As soon as the door of 26 opened, however, he realised that the flats were extremely well sound-proofed; waves of sound assailed his eardrums. He recognised Beethoven's Pastoral Symphony. Alice Giddy obviously had an efficient stereo system.

'Miss Giddy?' He looked at the woman before him with interest. Tall, dark, elegant, Low had said. Good-looking in an odd kind of way, but too intense for his taste. Alice Giddy had not changed much, it seemed. Almost as tall as Thanet, she was wearing a striking dress – robe was perhaps a better word, Thanet thought – in peacock blue, with a swirling, abstract design in black from shoulder to hem. Her hair was short and straight, glossy as a blackbird's wing and beautifully cut to the shape of her neat head. Cool green eyes surveyed Thanet from a face which reminded him of a Siamese cat's in more than shape; it had the same quality of independence, of indifference to the opinions of others.

'Yes?' she said, lifting her eyebrows in polite enquiry.

He introduced himself, showed his identification at her request. After a moment's hesitation she turned. 'You'd better come in.'

The room into which she led the way was as strikingly individual as Johnson's studio-cum-sitting-room. The walls were chocolate brown and decorated with a series of huge murals in swooping whorls of orange, gold, purple and green. The carpet was thick, white, shaggy and there was little furniture: a low glass-topped table and two long, white leather sofas heaped with tiny cushions in many colours, fabrics and shapes.

She crossed to the elaborate stereo system against one wall and stopped the record on it before waving him to one of the sofas. 'Do sit down.' She seated herself opposite him, crossed her legs, folded her hands neatly in her lap and waited. Her very lack of curiosity or interest intrigued Thanet and warned him that he would have to be very careful if he were not to lose control of this interview. Certainly there would be no question, with this woman, of setting her at her ease and catching her off her guard or, for that matter, of fobbing her off with evasions and half-truths. He decided to be as impersonal, as business-like as she.

'I'm here in connection with the murder of a girl called Julie Holmes,' he said, and watched carefully for her reaction. As he had expected, she showed nothing but faint bewilderment. One eyebrow arched.

'I'm sorry, Inspector, I really fail to see ...'

'It will no doubt become apparent to you,' he said crisply. 'Perhaps you would begin by telling me of your movements last Tuesday evening.'

150

She shifted her body slightly, a movement of impatience. 'Oh really, Inspector!'

'Please,' he cut in again. 'I can assure you I have a reason for asking.' He was beginning to enjoy himself.

She raised one hand slightly, in a gesture of concession. 'Very well. I'll go and fetch my diary.'

She disappeared into an adjoining room, returned a few moments later with a large green leather-bound desk diary. She sat down, leafed through its pages in silence. 'I'm afraid there's nothing of any use here. You can see for yourself.' And she handed him the diary, open, with an 'I've-nothing-to-hide' gesture.

Tuesday May 6 was blank. Thanet nodded acknow-ledgement and handed it back to her. 'You really have no recollection? It is, after all, only five days ago.'

She shrugged, impatient again. 'As there's nothing in my diary, I assume that it must have been a perfectly ordinary day.'

'Which means?'

'That I would have worked in the shop until five-thirty, then come home and spent the evening here.'

'The shop?'

'My boutique in Sturrenden. TOPS.'

Thanet had a quick mental image of the bag he had found in Julie Holme's wardrobe. Purple, with TOPS in gold lettering on the side. Another connection ... A thought struck him. Could he have been wrong? Could Julie have come face to face with the murderer not at the Private View, but in Alice Giddy's boutique? If so he must now tread warily indeed.

'Which is why I'm here,' he said, with a flash of inspiration. 'Mrs Holmes was a customer of yours. We found one of the carrier bags from your shop in her wardrobe.'

'Really?' Alice Giddy said, with indifference. 'Is that so surprising? I should think there'd be one of our carrier bags in the wardrobe of many of the women in

Sturrenden – or at any rate in the wardrobes of those who can afford us.' And, for the first time, a glint of wry amusement showed briefly in her eyes. 'I must say I'm surprised that an inspector, no less, should turn up on my doorstep to follow up so tenuous a link.'

'You don't remember the girl?'

'What was she like?'

Thanet told her, but at the end of his description Alice Giddy shook her head. 'I'm sorry. We have so many customers ... and in any case I might well have been working in the office above the shop when she came in, in which case my assistant would have served her.'

'Perhaps I could have your assistant's address,' Thanet said, keeping up the fiction.

'By all means, though I really can't see much point.' She dictated it to him and then leaned forward, preparatory to rising. 'And now, if that's all, Inspector ...'

'Not quite, I'm afraid. You still haven't told me how you spent last Tuesday evening.' Even at the risk of looking ridiculous he had to persist.

She did not sit back again, but remained poised on the very edge of the settee. 'I told you, I can't remember. I assume I spent the evening here, as usual.'

'Alone?'

'Alone.'

Thanet gave up. Clearly, there was no point in continuing. He stood up. 'Very well.'

Her eyes, looking up at him, mocked him, dared him to go on, to thank her for her help in the conventional way.

'If you remember later on, perhaps you could contact me.' He took out his card and laid it on the glass-topped table.

'By all means,' she said, uncurling herself. They stood for a brief moment facing each other across the low table, both of them paying tribute to a worthy

152

adversary, before she turned, led the way to the door and showed him out.

In the car Thanet was thoughtful. Had he been right to switch his strategy like that when he had learnt that Alice was the owner of TOPS? He wasn't sure if it had been good tactics or a simple loss of nerve. It had suddenly seemed so much more likely that Alice Giddy was the murderer and if so he wanted not only more time to think but to keep as many cards up his sleeve as possible. As it was she was free to think that the police, at a loss how to proceed, were simply casting their net wildly in the hope of coming up with a useful lead. But she was no fool and if she were guilty and he had so much as mentioned the Dacre Exhibition she would have realised at once that he was on to the past link between Julie and herself.

Thanet began to feel depressed. Alice Giddy had impressed him. She would be a tricky adversary indeed. If she were guilty he could not imagine her admitting it even if the evidence were incontrovertible.

And, when it came down to it, what evidence was there, at the moment?

None. None whatsoever.

13

Fortunately there was no time for the depression to take too firm a hold upon him. The journey back into town took only ten minutes and he had to put the interview with Alice Giddy firmly behind him and free his mind for his intended visit to the Pococks.

Little Mole Avenue was on the far side of Sturrenden and he decided to call in at the hospital on the way, to check up on Dr Plummer. The doctor's stand-in had, he found, been telling the truth. Gerald Plummer had been admitted to the hospital on May 2, four days before the murder. On May 5, after two days of tests, he had undergone an operation, and was now convalescent. He had, moreover, been under constant supervision, having refused to go into a private room on the grounds that what was good enough for his patients ought to be good enough for him. It was out of the question that on May 6 he had been either fit enough or free to have been in Gladstone Road, committing a murder.

Thanet left, satisfied.

As he swung out of the hospital car park and into the Sunday quiet of the streets he reviewed what he knew of the Pococks. They had been slightly older than the rest of their little group at the time of Annabel's murder, Pocock being thirty and his wife a year younger, and they had been the only married couple involved. Pocock at that time had, according to Low, been a philanderer and Edna the complaisant (or ignorant) wife. She had also been that eternally tragic figure, the motherly woman who is denied children. What would they be like now? How would the years have treated them? Was Pocock now an ageing Don Juan, and would his wife at last have found fulfilment in motherhood?

The answer to this last question was obvious the moment Thanet pulled up outside the Pococks' house. This was in a sedate neighbourhood of large Victorian houses set in sizable gardens. Most of them, Thanet thought, would probably now be divided up into flats, having proved too expensive to run. The Laurels stood out from its neighbours by virtue of its cluttered garden and the noise which emanated from it. Thanet, standing at the gate, counted five children of varying ages. A teenage boy was working on an upturned bicycle in front of the garage, two little girls of about ten were sitting on the front doorstep with dolls on their laps and a scatter of tiny dolls' clothes spread around them, a boy of around seven was riding about on a tricycle and a toddler of indeterminate sex was sitting in a sandpit, banging an upturned bucket with a spade. It looked as though Edna Pocock had more than made up for her earlier misfortunes.

The little girls, absorbed in their game, did not notice him until he was almost upon them and then they looked up. They were so close in age that they must either be friends or non-identical twins, Thanet thought. One was as fair as the other was dark. The dark one looked up unsmilingly at him as the fair one jumped up, beaming.

'Hullo,' he said. 'Are your parents in?'

They exchanged a solemn look before the fair girl nodded. 'They're round the back,' she said. 'I'll show you.'

Thanet felt himself to be the focus of many eyes as he followed his guide. The teenager had straightened up, spanner in hand and the other boy had brought his tricycle to a halt. Only the toddler remained oblivious of the visitor, completely absorbed in his sand pies.

There was, Thanet felt, something wary, almost hostile in this silent scrutiny. He smiled at the seven-year-old, raised his hand in a salute to the teenager, but neither responded. Thanet shrugged inwardly. If they didn't want to be friendly there was nothing he could do about it. He turned his attention to the girl beside him. As if aware of his discomfort she gave him an encouraging smile.

'What's your name?' he asked.

'Melanie. Melly for short.'

Thanet did not believe in talking down to children. 'What did I do wrong?' he said.

She glanced back over her shoulder, shrugged. 'Nothing. It's not you, really. They're always like that.'

Following her glance Thanet was slightly surprised to see that all four other children had now left what they were doing and were trailing behind, at a distance. Curiosity? He didn't know, but once again he had that curious impression of wariness, mistrust.

They were now about to turn the corner of the house into the back garden and Melly put up her hand. 'Could you wait here a minute?' she said.

Thanet stopped, glanced back again. The other children had stopped too. Their solemn, watchful gaze reminded him very much of natives scrutinising the first white man to come their way. Of course, he thought, that was it. They were afraid. But why?

Before he could begin to think about this, however, Melly returned. 'It's all right,' she said. 'Come on.'

By now Thanet was intensely curious and he approached the small, sheltered terrace in the angle of the house with interest. After this build-up the two people who advanced to meet him seemed disappointingly nondescript. The man was of medium height with crinkled, greying hair, a drooping moustache and a solid, well-muscled frame. The woman was shorter than he and plump, with the tiny hands and feet of the type. She was wearing a shapeless dress in indeterminate colours and her plain features were not

156

enhanced by untidy brown hair pulled back into a straggling bun. Not a woman who cared for appearances, Thanet thought. Then, as she smiled in welcome he realised that she was not nondescript at all. The warmth of her personality was something very special indeed.

As he introduced himself the smile faded, however, and her eyes went beyond him to where the children stood silently watching, some yards away.

'It's ... it's not anything to do with the kids? she said anxiously.

Thanet was puzzled. 'No, of course not. Why should it be?'

She sighed then, a tiny exhalation of relief, and raised her hand. 'It's OK kids, nothing to do with you,' she called to them, and Thanet watched astonished as the little group erupted into noisy relief and ran, whooping and calling, back around the corner of the house.

Roger Pocock was setting up another folding deckchair and his wife waved Thanet into it. 'They're not ours,' she explained. 'They're all foster kids and they're always scared stiff of being taken away. When anyone turns up unexpectedly they always think the worst. They've all had a bad time and they're used to being moved around from pillar to post at the drop of a hat.'

'I see,' Thanet said, and he did. He looked at Edna Pocock with new respect. 'It must be very difficult work.'

She smiled, that warm, transforming smile again. 'Oh it is. But we enjoy it, don't we, Rodge?'

Her husband nodded and both men followed her gaze to the corner of the house, where the younger boy had just come into sight on his tricycle. 'You wouldn't believe the difference it makes to them, once they settle down and begin to feel part of the family,' she said. 'Anyway,' and she settled herself more comfortably in her chair, 'you haven't come here to talk about them, so ...?'

They both looked at him with mild curiosity, the embodiment of people with easy consciences.

Thanet was feeling distinctly uncomfortable. The generosity of this couple made his enquiries seem almost obscene. How many people, he wondered, would be willing to fill their lives with the battered survivors of other people's tragic mistakes? Certainly no one could do so who did not genuinely love children and have their welfare at heart. No wonder those poor kids had treated his appearance with such suspicion. Nevertheless he was on a murder enquiry and questions had to be asked. He decided to be honest about how he felt.

'Look,' he said, 'I came here to ask some very unpleasant questions. Now that I've seen you, seen the children ... well, frankly I find it difficult to put them.'

'No need to feel like that,' Edna Pocock said reassuringly. 'It's nothing to do with the kids, you say, and I really can't think Rodge and me have done anything criminal, so go ahead. Ask away.'

A crash, a scream, a rising crescendo of sobs interrupted the conversation. In a flash she was out of her chair, hurrying towards the corner of the house. There was a babble of raised voices and she returned, carrying the younger boy whose knee was bleeding badly. The other children trooped behind her, Melly leading the toddler by the hand.

'I'm sorry,' Edna Pocock said. 'I'll have to go in and see to this.'

Thanet nodded his understanding and she went into the house, the other children following. If one of their number was threatened, it seemed, they habitually closed ranks, drawing comfort from proximity.

Roger Pocock caught Thanet's eye, shrugged. 'They're good kids,' he said. 'Can we get your questions over while my wife's inside?'

If they did, Thanet guessed, Pocock would tell some white lies when she came back, to reassure her. And why not? he asked himself. Wouldn't he try to protect

Joan in the same way, in similar circumstances? He made up his mind. 'It's about last Tuesday evening,' he said. 'I'm afraid I can't explain, but I would be grateful if you could tell me what you and your wife were doing.'

Pocock frowned. 'You're asking us for alibis?'

'In a way. It's just that there are some loose ends in a case I'm working on, and they've got to be tidied away. You and your wife might be able to help.' It was lame, and he knew it. Pocock, he could tell, knew it too. He hoped the man wouldn't press for details.

Pocock looked at him in silence for a few moments, clearly debating whether or not to do so. Then he shrugged. 'Well, I can't see that either of us was doing anything we shouldn't have been. My wife always goes to evening classes on Tuesday, and I babysit for her.'

'And this was what happened last Tuesday?'

'Yes, I'm sure of it. She's never missed a class yet, unless she's ill or one of the children can't be left. She's doing pottery.'

Thanet steeled himself and said, 'Is there anyone who can vouch for either of you?'

Pocock's expression hardened. 'My wife's classmates, I suppose. And the kids for me, if they have to. But I don't want them dragged into this if I can help it.'

'No,' Thanet said. And then, feeling a heel, 'Is there any way we could do it without upsetting them?'

Pocock scowled. 'I don't know. If we have to, I suppose.'

The sound of voices announced that the others were returning.

'Leave it to me,' Pocock said hurriedly.

The children all crowded around as the boy exhibited his bandaged knee. Edna Pocock sat down and flapped her hand at them. 'Go on now,' she said. 'Off you go.' She turned to Thanet as they began reluctantly to drift away. 'This one hour on Sunday afternoons is the only time we keep for ourselves. It does them good, makes them think of someone else for a change.'

Pocock had been watching the children thoughtfully

159

and now he suddenly called after them. 'Hey kids, come back a minute, will you?' He waited until they had come flocking back and then said, 'Mr Thanet here and me have been having an argument. He says no one can ever remember properly what they were doing five days ago. Now I say you can. So let's see if we can prove him wrong, shall we?'

Four pairs of eyes swivelled to Thanet, one of them wary. Pocock's ploy had clearly not fooled the older boy. The toddler, of course, had not understood either the question or its significance. Seeing his opportunity for an unexpected cuddle he simply climbed up on to Edna's lap and burrowed his face into her ample breasts.

"Course we can,' said Melly scornfully. Then, turning hesitantly to Pocock, 'What day was that, Dad?"

'Tuesday,' said Pocock. 'Say Tuesday evening.'

Edna Pocock glanced questioningly at her husband and he shook his head slightly in warning. Leave it, the gesture said.

The children were silent, thinking back.

'Aw, this is stupid,' said the older boy suddenly. He took a pack of chewing gum from his pocket and distributed sticks as if they were reassurance. Then he leaned against the wall of the house, nonchalantly. "Course we can remember,' he said deliberately, watching Thanet, challenging him. 'Mum was at evening class and we were all here. Dad, Melly, Sally and me watched *The Pacemakers*.'

'That's right, Dad, we did,' It was Melly's turn now, her face alight with triumph. 'Don't you remember, Dad? You said Sally and me could watch till nine so long as we promised that if we came to a bit you didn't think we ought to see we'd close our eyes. And there was that bit about the operation and you said don't look, and we didn't.'

'I should hope not!' said Edna Pocock. 'So that's what you get up to while I'm out, is it?' But she was not really

160

angry, only pretending to be, as Thanet and the children could tell by her affectionate glance at Pocock. 'All right, kids, that's enough now. I think we've proved your Dad's point. Off you go.'

They went noisily this time, pleased at their triumphant refutal of Thanet's so-called theory.

Then she turned to Thanet. 'And now,' she said quietly, 'perhaps you'd tell me what all this is about.'

She listened in silence as Thanet explained in much the same terms as he had to her husband, then said, 'Well, I was at evening class, like Rodge says. I left here about a quarter to seven, left the class as soon as it ended at nine and got back here about a quarter past.'

'How did you go? By car? Bus?'

'By car.'

So, Thanet thought with sinking heart, Edna Pocock could still be his quarry. 'You can confirm that your wife arrived home around nine-fifteen?' he said.

Pocock nodded. 'Around then. It was well before *The Pacemakers* ended, anyway.'

And that was at nine-thirty. 'You can't be more precise?'

'No I bloody well can't. And if you ...' He glanced down at the restraining hand Edna put on his sleeve, took a deep breath and continued in a tight, hard voice, 'If Edna says a quarter past nine, a quarter past nine it was.'

He'd have to leave it there. Thanet heaved himself awkwardly out of his deck chair, apologised for disturbing their Sunday afternoon and left.

The interview had made him feel uncomfortable, guilty almost, and angry with himself for feeling so. At the traffic lights in the High Street he stalled his engine, grated a gear change. He swore.

There were times when he hated being a policeman.

14

By the time Thanet had finished the reports on the day's interviews he had had enough. He tidied his desk and headed for home, feeling in need of the comfort Joan's company would bring him.

Tomorrow there was much to be done. First he would send a team to make enquiries at Maddison House, to see if anyone could be found to confirm or disprove Alice Giddy's claim that she had spent Tuesday evening at home. Also, enquiries would have to be made at the Technical College. He would have to contact Edna Pocock's pottery teacher, check that she had indeed attended her class that evening and, if necessary, get a complete list of the members of the class and question them all, find out if any of them saw where she went when the session ended.

It certainly seemed that his five suspects had been reduced to two. Peake dead, Plummer in hospital, Pocock alibied by the children. Thanet believed them. He wouldn't have put it past the elder boy to lie on behalf of his foster father, but he certainly couldn't believe that Melly had done so. He was pretty certain she had been unaware of the significance of her contribution. No, when Julie was killed, Pocock had been sitting at home in front of the television set. Thanet only wished that the same could be said of his wife.

Was it possible that that kind, motherly woman could have killed twice? Reluctantly, he had to admit that it was. It was common knowledge that in defence of her children even the mildest of women could become a tigress and in Edna Pocock maternal love was stronger than in most. If she had thought that Julie could destroy the secure world that Edna and her husband had so painstakingly built up for those children ... yes, Edna Pocock was still very much in the running.

As indeed was Alice Giddy. Now there was someone whom he could very well imagine a murderess. Unlike Edna, who would kill from passion, Alice would set about it in a cool and calculated manner, making sure that the risks she took were minimal. There was no doubt about it, of the two he very much hoped that she would prove to be the guilty one.

It was quite wrong of him, of course, to hope anything of the sort. His job was to see that justice was done and if he didn't very much like what his investigations turned up, that was just too bad. For that matter, even if he did find out which one of them was guilty, he couldn't at the moment see how he was going to prove it.

Thanet grimaced and pulled up behind an ice-cream van parked at the side of the road. He'd buy some choc ices to take home.

'Oh, lovely,' said Joan, receiving the newspaper-wrapped parcel with a kiss. 'In the kitchen to eat these, don't you think?'

Thanet watched Ben and Bridget as they ate the ices. Most of Ben's seemed to end up on chin, hands or bib, whereas Bridget approached hers fastidiously, taking neat, incisive bites and holding it carefully by the wrapper. Thanet thought of the Pocock children earlier in the afternoon, of their wariness and fear when a stranger arrived. Sprig might feel shy, but never threatened. She and Ben were secure in their little world and please God they would stay that way. Once, Julie Holmes must have felt just as safe in hers and then, without warning, it had disintegrated. She had lost father, home and confidence in other people in one fell swoop. Thanet was convinced that, whoever the murderer was, Julie had known her as a friend of her mother's. It was scarcely surprising that she had grown up wary, unable to commit herself to others for fear of being hurt. A wave of protective passion swept through him and he picked Sprig up, choc ice and all, and hugged her.

'Darling, look at your jacket!' Joan rinsed a cloth in cold water and began to sponge at the smear on his lapel. 'What's the matter?' she said softly.

He shook his head, pulled a face. 'Just this damned case.' But he knew that he was telling only half the truth, that what was really upsetting him was the thought of the Pocock children. Damaged as they already were, how much more so would they be if Mrs Pocock proved to be the murderer? Was the case, which had begun so many years ago with another damaged child, Julie, to end by ruining more young lives? And was he to be the instrument of destruction?

Joan was chatting on now about something that had happened earlier in the day. He tried to concentrate. Someone, he gathered, had asked her to do something and she hadn't been able to say yes because of the children. And then this someone had made Joan feel thoroughly guilty, had implied that Joan had refused simply because she couldn't be bothered to help.

'Wretched woman!' Thanet said, indignant on Joan's behalf.

'But she made me feel so awful ... honestly, people who haven't got children just don't seem to take them into account, don't realise how one has to arrange things around them, especially when they're little like ... What's the matter?'

'What you said, just then. Say it again.'

Joan repeated her complaint.

Thanet stared at her, frowning. There was something in what she had said that was important for him, but he couldn't put his finger on it. What *was* it?

'Did I say something wrong?' Joan was looking

puzzled. 'Don't you agree with what I was saying?'

'What? Oh yes. Yes, of course, love. It's just that I ...' he shook his head. 'It's no good. It won't come. Something you said rang a bell, but I can't think why.'

Joan picked Ben up and began to wipe away the smears of chocolate. 'You know what's the matter with your daddy?' she said to the baby. 'He's been working too hard. There.' She set Ben down on the floor again, handing him his favourite toy, a very noisy rattle, and came across to put her arm around Thanet's shoulders and drop a kiss on his forehead. 'And you know my remedy for overwork? A nice quiet evening doing nothing. Watch television, listen to music, let your mind go blank, recuperate.'

Thanet leaned his head against her breasts. 'That's easier said than done, love.'

'I know that, of course I do. But we can at least try.'

So they did. But all through the evening Thanet was aware of a steadily increasing pressure at the back of his mind. Deliberately he held it at bay, wanting Joan to believe that her therapy was working, and it was not until they were in bed and her steady breathing told him that she was asleep, that he allowed himself at last to return to the question that had been niggling away at him all evening. What was it, in what Joan had said, that had been significant for him? He tried to recall her exact words. 'People who haven't got children just don't seem to take them into account.'

And then, seemingly out of nowhere, he heard Lineham's voice saying, 'Why should anyone start to wonder whether the child had witnessed the murder?'

Only someone who did take children into account would have done so.

Thanet lay rigid, staring at the ceiling, willing himself not to disturb Joan by jumping out of bed and beginning to pace restlessly about the room.

There was only one person who, twenty years ago, would have taken little Julie Parr into account, and that was Edna Pocock. She knew the Parrs, might well have babysat for them. Even then she had been, Inspector Low had said, a woman who loved children.

Thanet thought back, trying to project himself into her mind at the time of Annabel's murder. Edna Pocock had been expecting a child. She had already had more than one miscarriage and must have been hoping, passionately, that this time her pregnancy would go smoothly. Then she discovers that her husband is chasing Annabel. What if she had taken him to task about it? Suppose they had quarrelled, that Edna had become hysterical, that she had even flown at him and he, in defending himself had struck back, causing her miscarriage? How would she have felt lying there in bed, her hopes shattered once again, full of bitterness and anger against her husband and against the woman who had been the cause of it all? Might she not have decided to confront Annabel, to tell her what she had done, to make her realise her responsibility for the death of Edna's unborn child?

Thanet could see it all: Edna, unhinged by grief, laying her plans, seizing the opportunity when it came; hurrying through the foggy night to Annabel's house, being admitted by the unsuspecting girl, following her up to the studio. Then would come the accusation. Annabel must have said or done something which snapped the last thread of Edna's control. Edna seizes the piece of quartz, strikes Annabel in a frenzy and then departs, unaware that all the time, in the half-curtained alcove at the far end of the room, Julie, rigid and silent with terror, has been watching.

Then would come the aftermath of the murder, the news of David Parr's death, of Jennifer having been the one to find Annabel's body. It would not have taken Edna long, with her child-orientated mind, to begin to wonder where Julie had been while her mother was at the hospital. Discreet enquiries might have led her to the inescapable conclusion that Jennifer had gone to the studio that night because Annabel had been looking after Julie, and Jennifer's hasty departure from the village would have confirmed what by now Edna might have suspected, that Julie might well have witnessed the murder.

She must have waited in terror at first for Julie to identify her. When it hadn't happened she must slowly have begun to recover her confidence, to think that even if Julie had been in Annabel's house, she couldn't have seen what had happened.

Years later, abandoning hope of having children of her own she must have conceived the plan of being a foster mother. Her husband, perhaps shocked out of his infidelities by the consequences of his pursuit of Annabel and anxious to make amends, must have fallen in with her plans. All had gone smoothly until the evening of the Private View. There Edna sees Julie, her mother's double, and wonders if Julie might have recognised her. She had to find out: did Julie witness the murder and if so, has she now recognised Edna as the murderer? All the old terrors of discovery are reawakened. Now she has far more to lose and she cannot afford to induge in foolish optimism. She must find out for sure.

So as not to arouse her husband's suspicions Edna decides to go and see Julie on her pottery class evening, Tuesday. But first she has to find out Julie's address. This might not have been easy and would perhaps account for the lapse of a fortnight between the evening of the Private View and Julie's murder. She goes to Gladstone Road, finds Julie hysterical after the quarrel with Kendon. There is a struggle and Julie is stabbed. Edna runs, the pattern having repeated itself. On neither occasion did she set out with murder in mind, on each circumstances combined to cause her to commit it.

A lot of this was speculation again, of course, nevertheless it fitted, in its broad outline, with all the known facts.

Except ... Thanet scowled up at the ceiling, shifted restlessly. Joan turned over, murmured something in

167

her sleep and he froze, keeping quite still until the even pattern of her breathing had been re-established.

Except that the time element did not fit.

If his story was true, Kendon had left Julie between eight-forty and eight-forty-five. If night school had not ended until nine, it would have been at least ten or a quarter past by the time Edna arrived, having parked her car somewhere out of sight (two points to check up on: what make of car did she drive, had anyone in the Gladstone Road area seen it that night?). By then Julie would surely have calmed down, have taken her coat off and put that carving knife away?

Unless Edna had left her class early? A pottery class was not like an academic session. People would be moving about all the time, working to different schedules. If Edna had made sure that she finished early on Tuesday, had left before the class ended ...? More checking.

And, at the end of it, no real satisfaction, if he were proved right. Those children ...

Thanet spent a restless night.

168

15

Thanet arived at the office next day with none of the eager anticipation he usually felt at this stage of an enquiry. His quarry might be in sight, but the hunt had lost its savour. He saw no joy whatsoever in the prospect of tracking down Edna Pocock.

First, however, he had to determine whether or not Alice Giddy could definitely be eliminated as a suspect and he turned to the batch of reports which Baker had written on his enquiries at Maddison House in connection with Parrish. In the hours before dawn Thanet had had a faint recollection of something that he had read in one of them ...

At this point Lineham walked in.

'What the hell are you doing here?' said Thanet.

Lineham looked terrible, like a rag doll whose stuffing had gone limp.

'Home,' said Thanet, crossing the room, taking him by the shoulders and propelling him firmly towards the door. 'Bed. And I don't want to see you again until you're properly fit.'

'But sir ...'

'Home,' repeated Thanet. 'What are you trying to do, start a flu epidemic? In any case, what use do you think you'd be here, in that state?' Seeing Lineham's face, Thanet relented. 'Oh look, Mike, I know how you feel, having to duck out at this stage, but you really have no choice, have you? Have you seen a doctor?'

'Not yet, no.'

'In case he told you not to come back to work, I

169

suppose. Well, call him. You'll be back all the sooner if you get proper treatment.'

When Lineham had made his reluctant exit Thanet returned to the sheaf of reports on Maddison House. Of course, when Baker had been sent out there he had simply been concerned to find out whether or not anyone had seen Parrish either entering or leaving the building on the evening of the murder. All the same, Thanet was sure ... Ah yes, here it was.

Mrs Barret of Flat 27 had not seen or heard anything relevant to Baker's enquiry as she had spent the evening watching television first of all at home and then in the flat of a neighbour.

There had been four doors on Alice Giddy's landing, Thanet remembered. Hers, Flat 26, had been the second from the left. She should, then, be Mrs Barret's next-door neighbour. Baker reported that the occupants of Flats 26 and 28 had been out when he called. Presumably he had not returned to them later because he had been called off the enquiry before he could do so; when Phyllis Penge, Parrish's mistress, had confirmed Parrish's alibi, Thanet had not considered further enquiries necessary.

So, which neighbour had Mrs Barret spent the evening with? Alice Giddy or the occupant of Flat 28?

Thanet picked up the telephone. 'D.C.Baker in?'

Baker, he learned, had just gone out, would not be back until late morning.

Thanet swore under his breath. 'Send him up the minute he gets back, will you?'

He could either ring or go to see Mrs Barret himself, but he would prefer to talk to Baker first. He didn't want to risk alerting Alice Giddy any further until he was more sure of his ground. He would wait.

Glancing at his watch he saw that by now the Administrative Staff should have arrived at the Technical College. He checked the telephone number and dialled.

Edna Pocock's pottery teacher, a Mrs Caroly,

apparently worked at the College on only two evenings a week. The secretary had no idea whether Mrs Caroly had a day-time job. There was an address and telephone number, however, and she gave them to Thanet. She could supply a list of the names and addresses of the class members and Thanet arranged that someone would call around to pick it up within the next half an hour.

He sent Carson off on this errand, then tried Mrs Caroly's number. There was no reply. Another man was despatched to find out where she was and when she would be available.

Now what? Thanet rang through for some coffee, stood up and moved restlessly across to the window. Outside lay the promise of another beautiful spring day. A breeze had sprung up and fluffy white clouds promenaded across the sky. The traffic had thinned now that the morning rush was over, and the people on the streets were moving in a more leisurely manner: young mothers with a pram and a toddler in tow, old men with no object but to find somewhere warm and quiet where they might pass the dragging hours. Watching one of them Thanet was invaded by melancholy. Is that where life led? Was that how he would end up, thirty years from now?

A young constable arrived bearing Thanet's coffee.

Thanet turned away from the window, sat down again. The coffee was lukewarm and he grimaced in disgust.

A knock at the door and Mallard came in. 'My,' he said, 'aren't we cheerful this morning!'

'Hullo Doc,' Thanet said. 'Want some coffee?'

'If that's a specimen of what'll be produced if I say yes,' said Mallard peering into Thanet's cup, 'then no, thank you. I have too much respect for my digestive system.'

'I think we can do better than this,' Thanet said, picking up the telephone.

'How's the back?' Mallard asked, while they waited

171

for fresh coffee.

'Oh, much better, thanks. I hardly think of it now.'

'Good.'

The coffee, when it came, was hot and strong. As they sipped in silence Thanet became increasingly uncomfortable under Mallard's scrutiny. Consciously he avoided meeting his eye.

'Well,' Mallard said at last, putting his cup down with gesture of finality, 'if you won't tell me, I'll have to ask, though I'm damned if I see why I should. If your back's all right, what's the matter? Case going badly?'

Thanet shrugged. 'It's going,' he said. 'Which is more than could be said a few days ago.'

'Then why the long face?'

Thanet looked away, out of the window. High up an aeroplane glinted silver. Some lucky devils off somewhere, he thought irrelevantly. 'I just don't like the way it's going, that's all.'

Mallard studied him in silence for moment or two longer, then leaned forward. 'Correct me if I'm wrong, but do I understand you to say that although you're making progress in the investigation, you are unhappy about it?'

'That's right.'

'Why? Because you think you are investigating along the wrong lines, or because you don't like what you're finding out?'

'The latter, I suppose.'

'Well well. So you don't like what you're finding out,' Mallard said sarcastically. 'How d'you think I'd go on working at all, if I allowed myself to feel like that?' He heaved himself out of his chair, stumped across to the window. 'I'll tell you this, Luke. If I allowed all those corpses to be anything more than specimens to me, I'd go mad at the sheer bloody waste of it all.' He spun around, pointed a finger at Thanet. 'And as you know perfectly well, that's how it should be with you. The minute you let yourself get involved, you're sunk,

172

finished, kaput.' He returned to his chair, plumped down in it. 'So don't you forget it,' he said.

He was right, of course, Thanet thought. And yet ... it was so much easier for Mallard. He dealt only with the dead.

'Oh, I know what you're thinking,' Mallard said disconcertingly. 'You're thinking it's easier to switch off when you're dealing with corpses. And you're right, of course. It is to a certain extent, anyway. But just remember this: you are not here to judge, just to investigate. So don't try taking over the Almighty's job. He's much better at it than you could ever be.' He glanced at his watch. 'I'll have to go now.' He stood up. 'It is the Holmes case we've been talking about?'

Thanet nodded.

'I don't know what right I have to go sounding off at you like this. If it'll make you feel any better, the truth of the matter is that it's myself I'm angry with, really, for being in the same boat. I've just been doing a P.M. on a child. She was only five ... It's a hell of a life sometimes, isn't it?'

He and Thanet exchanged a rueful grin before Mallard went out, closing the door behind him with uncharacteristic gentleness.

Thanet looked after him, thoughtfully, and then picked up the telephone. Mallard was right. He had been becoming positively maudlin. 'If Carson's back, send him in.'

Thanet took the proffered list of Edna Pocock's classmates and studied it. There were twelve names in all. Quickly he ran his finger down them, noting the addresses, then returned to the second name on the page. Mrs A. Bligh, 14 Upper Mole Road. He reached for his town map and checked. Yes, as he thought, this was the next turning off the Canterbury Road beyond Little Mole Road. If Mrs Bligh travelled by car, she would no doubt take the same route home as Edna Pocock ...

He made up his mind. Not a telephone call this time. He would go and visit Mrs Bligh himself.

Mrs Bligh was short, plump and thirtyish with a frizz of tightly permed blond hair. She was wearing a flowing smock dress in shrieking greens and orange which merely served to accentuate her generous curves. Her reaction, like that of most people who are unexpectedly faced with a CID man on the doorstep, was puzzled, apprehensive and somewhat wary. She studied his warrant card carefully before inviting him in.

'We'll have to go into the kitchen, Inspector. My little girl's in there.'

In this house Monday was still washing day, Thanet saw as he followed her into a large, light kitchen, well-equipped with mod. cons. A long central table was covered with piles of washing, some dry, some wet, and an automatic washing machine was making an infernal row in one corner.

'Just a minute, I'll switch it off,' shouted Mrs Bligh.

The resulting silence was almost deafening. 'It makes an awful din.' she said apologetically, as if she were personally responsible for the machine's noisiness, 'but it saves so much work I try not to notice it. Sandra, this is Mr Thanet.'

Sandra was about the same age as Bridget. She was standing on a chair at the kitchen sink, arms plunged into a froth of bubbles.

'Hullo, Sandra,' Thanet said. 'My little girl likes doing that, too.'

Mrs Bligh, apparently reassured by this evidence of Thanet's humanity, gave a timid smile. 'Sit down, Inspector, won't you?' She pulled out a chair at the long table, pushed aside a pile of clothes. 'Sorry about the mess,' she murmured, seating herself opposite him.

'That's quite all right,' Thanet said dismissively. 'Now then, I expect you're wondering why I've called.

174

There's nothing to worry about, I assure you. There was an incident last Tuesday evening and we're trying to trace witnesses.'

'What sort of incident?' Mrs Bligh said nervously.

'Don't worry,' Thanet said gently. 'There really is no need. Now I understand that on Tuesday evenings you attend a pottery class at the Technical College.'

'Yes. But how did you ...?'

'I'm sorry, but I really can't give you any more information. Please, Mrs Bligh, just relax. If you can't help us, I'll go away and we'll forget all about it.'

She did relax a little now, sat back in her chair.

'You attended the class last Tuesday?'

'Yes.'

'And stayed the full length of time?'

'Yes.'

'So you left at nine, as usual?'

'That's right.'

'And you came home by your usual route – I'm sorry, I forgot to ask. Do you go by car?'

'Yes I do. And yes, I came home by the same route as usual last week.'

'That would be right at the entrance to the Technical College, left into Wallace Way ...?'

'Yes. Then let me see ...' she gave a nervous laugh. 'I do it so often it's automatic. Yes, then left into Park Road, left again into Canterbury Road, then straight on all the way until I turn into this road.'

'Good. Now, I want you to think very carefully. On your way along Canterbury Road last Tuesday evening, did you see anything unusual?' The question, of course, was misleading. To his knowledge Canterbury Road had been as peaceful and well-ordered as Sunday Morning Service last Tuesday, but he wanted to divert Mrs Bligh's attention from the real purpose of his visit.

'No, I don't think so. Let me think.' Her eyes narrowed in concentration as she searched her memory. 'No, I'm sure I didn't.'

'Right, thank you.' Thanet stood up. 'You don't happen to know of anyone else who regularly travels by that route on Tuesday evenings, do you?'

'Well, there's Mrs Pocock, she lives in Little Mole Road. She comes to the same class as me.'

'You travel together, you mean?'

'Oh no. My husband works in London, you see, and I'm never quite sure what time he's going to get home, so it's awkward to travel with anyone else. I mean, it's bad enough having to be late yourself, but if you make other people late as well ...'

'Yes, of course. But Mrs Pocock? She attended the class last Tuesday?'

'Yes. She works next to me, as a matter of fact. We're both learning the same technique at the moment, and we tend to compare notes a lot.'

'And she comes home by the same route as you?' Thanet's palms were beginning to sweat as he approached the crucial question.

'Yes. It's the most direct way, of course.'

'And last Tuesday. Do you happen to remember if she left before you?'

'No, we left together. In fact, I followed her car all the way home from the Tech. I remember thinking how clean hers was, in comparison with ours, and deciding I really must get my husband to wash it at the weekend.'

'You followed her all the way home,' echoed Thanet flatly.

She misread his incredulity as disappointment. 'Yes, I'm sorry. So that means she wouldn't have seen anything either – not unless it's just that I'm completely unobservant and missed noticing something she might have seen.'

'You're absolutely certain you were behind her all the way?'

'Yes, I told you, her car ...'

'I see,' said Thanet with finality. 'Well, thank you very much Mrs Bligh. I'm sorry to have taken up so much of your time.' At the front door he paused. 'I forgot to ask. What time do you usually get home on Tuesday evenings?'

'At about a quarter past nine, give or take a minute or two.'

'And last Tuesday?'

She shrugged. 'Same as usual, I suppose. I didn't really notice. But I wasn't held up at all, so it must have been about then.'

Thanet reiterated his thanks and left.

He drove around the corner and parked. He felt dazed, disorientated. So, he had been wrong about Edna Pocock. That was a relief, but a frustration too. That moment of illumination last night had been a sham, the hours of agonising over her foster children a total waste of time and emotional energy. What a fool he had been!

He put the car savagely into gear and was half way back to the office before fear began to niggle away at him. Out of the original five suspects only Alice Giddy was now left. If her alibi for the night of Julie's murder proved as watertight as Edna Pocock's, if she too were innocent – Thanet shook his head, a tight, angry little shake. No, it wasn't possible. For in that case his whole beautiful theory would collapse around him like a house of cards. There would be no double murderer and the Dacre painting, the Private View, the fact that Julie had witnessed a murder as a child, none of this would have any relevance to his case.

He would be back where he started, days ago.

Back at the station the constable on duty raised a startled face at Thanet's snapped 'Baker back yet?' Thanet was not usually so peremptory.

'Yes sir. Gone up to the canteen, sir.'

'Find him,' Thanet said. 'Now. And send him up to my office.'

The man was already reaching for the phone. 'Right away, sir.'

Thanet paced restlessly up and down while he

177

waited. No, he couldn't, wouldn't believe it. All that patient, painstaking unravelling of past and present, the beautiful logic, the *rightness* of it all ...

'Sir?'

News of Thanet's mood must have travelled. Baker looked distinctly apprehensive. Thanet experienced a pang of compunction. Why should Baker be put through the mill just because he, Thanet, was furious with himself?

'It's all right, Baker,' he said, with an attempt at a smile. 'You haven't done anything wrong. I just need your help, that's all.' He sat down, shuffled through the papers on his desk, selected the one he wanted. 'It's to do with those enquiries you made at Maddison House, in connection with Parrish's alibi for the night of the Holmes murder. Now, in your report you state that a Mrs Barret of Flat 27 spent part of the evening watching television with a neighbour. Do you happen to know which neighbour?'

Baker had already taken out his notebook and was leafing through it. 'Ah yes, I remember her,' he said, as he searched. 'Couldn't stop talking. Her set broke down just after *The Pacemakers* started, and her son's a fan, wouldn't give her any peace until she went to ask if they could watch next door. Ah, here it is. They went to Flat 26, occupied by Alice Giddy. I didn't actually interview Miss Giddy, sir. She ...'

'Was out, I know. Then you were pulled off the enquiries because they were no longer considered necessary.' Thanet was doing his best to ignore the sinking feeling in the pit of his stomach. 'They stayed until the end of the programme?'

'Yes, sir.'

'Did she by any chance say anything to indicate that Miss Giddy was actually there with them all the time, watching the programme?'

Baker consulted his notes, considered. 'Not specifically, no, sir. But by implication, yes. I mean, like I said, the woman went on and on and on. I mean, I

178

heard all about Miss Giddy, how stand-offish she is and how she – Mrs Barret, I mean – wouldn't have plucked up the courage to ask if it hadn't been for her son going on and on about it. And how Miss Giddy was a *Pacemakers* fan herself and that Mrs Barret had therefore felt that it might be all right to ask her after all as Miss Giddy would know how she would have felt if her set had gone wrong just after the programme started. I really think she would have mentioned it if after all this Miss Giddy had gone out at all during this programme.'

'So you really don't think she could have slipped out for say, twenty minutes or so?' The absolute minimum time necessary to get from Maddison House to Gladstone Road and back again, Thanet considered.

'No, sir, I don't. Honestly, if you'd heard the way she goes on … she just isn't the sort to keep anything back.'

'Intelligent?'

'Not particularly'

'Do you think you could find out from her whether Miss Giddy did in fact go out at all during *The Pacemakers* without arousing her suspicions?'

'I should think so, sir.'

'Good. Do it now. Oh Baker …'

'Yes sir?' Baker, already on his way to the door, turned back.

'I suppose there's no doubt in your mind that the woman's story was genuine?'

'About the set breaking down and going next door to watch? No, no doubt at all sir. Her son was home when I called – he was off school for a dental appointment and from time to time she dragged him into the conversation – you know the sort of thing, 'Didn't we, Desmond, wasn't it, Desmond,' that sort of thing. I honestly don't think he was lying, just rather bored with the way she was going on and a bit embarrassed, as kids are at that age. He's about thirteen, I'd say. And apart from that, the repair engineer had just finished working on the set when I arrived. He was leaving as I came in.'

'Which firm, did you notice?'

Baker screwed up his face in concentration. 'I'm not sure. He was wearing an orange overall, I do remember that.'

'White lettering?'

'I think so.'

'Rentaset,' Thanet said. He used the firm himself. 'All right, thanks. Go and check now with Mrs Barret.'

When Baker had gone, Thanet consulted the telephone directory. Until all this was confirmed he wouldn't allow himself to think ...

It took only a few minutes for Rentaset to check their records and come back with the information that Mrs Barret had left a message on the Ansaphone at 8.35 pm on Tuesday May 6, and that the set had been repaired the following morning.

A few minutes later Baker returned. Alice Giddy had watched the entire programme with Mrs Barret and her son. So that really was the end of that particular road. Thanet thanked Baker, sent him off and then began to pace restlessly about the room.

He was a fool, a blind, self-opinionated fool.

After a while the confusion of anger and self-disgust in his mind settled down into a steady ache of disillusionment. Where had he gone wrong?

He sat down again, leaned back in his chair and, staring into space, began to work it out. Eventually, after a great deal of heart-searching, he came to the conclusion that he had been led astray by two factors: curiosity and vanity. Julie Holmes had intrigued him. He had wanted to understand her, to know what made her tick. The trail had led back into the past and he had followed it like a hound on the scent of the fox, deaf and blind to all else.

And vanity ... oh yes, there was that, too. Hadn't he been delighted with his own cleverness in working out this elaborate double murder theory? The truth of the matter was that he was just plain incompetent. Even Lineham had seen it. What had he called Thanet's idea? Far-fetched, that was it. Far-fetched.

Thanet made a little *moue* of self-disgust as he remembered how outraged he had felt at Lineham's attitude, how he had pretended to take Lineham's objections seriously when all the while he was mentally discounting them.

There was something else that Lineham had said, too. What was it? 'Isn't it much more likely that Julie Holmes was killed by someone involved with her now, in the present?'

But of course he, Thanet, in love with his theory, had refused to listen. Well he would eat humble pie. He at least owed Lineham that.

Meanwhile ... meanwhile he would have to begin all over again.

16

This time, Thanet swore, he would do things the right way around: facts first, theories afterwards. He began yet again to work systematically through every single report or statement which had been made or taken since the beginning of the case. Anger and self-disgust, he discovered, were wonderful aids to concentration but did not necessarily produce results. He found nothing significant which he had missed before, came across nothing which in any way shed new light on the problem.

What he did realise was that since setting off like a crazy, blind fool to prove his own cleverness, he had neglected to tie up one or two loose ends which now dangled reproachfully at him. Take the girl Kendon claimed to have seen, for example. Further efforts must be made to trace her. So far house-to-house enquiries had produced nothing, and there had been no response to the radio, television and newspaper appeals. Why?

There seemed to be three possible explanations: one, the girl did not listen to the radio, never watched television or read a newspaper – unlikely unless she had been out of the country or on holiday, perhaps. Thanet made a note: if necessary the appeals would be repeated at weekly intervals for the next three weeks.

Two, the girl did not exist. If she did not turn up in the next three weeks Thanet would presume that this was why, and devise a line of attack on Kendon.

Three, the girl existed, was aware that the police

wished to see her, but did not want to come forward for some reason of her own – perhaps she didn't like the idea of her husband or family knowing where she was that night. Thanet made another note: make sure that the wording of the appeal be altered to make it clear that the police would treat information received from this witness as confidential as far as possible.

Meanwhile he would arrange that tomorrow evening, Tuesday, exactly one week from the murder, someone would be on duty at the railway station to question regular travellers. The ticket clerk had proved useless, a surly little man so uninterested in his customers that he didn't even bother to look up as he pushed the tickets across. Yet another note: question Kendon again about other people on the station that evening.

As far as Parrish was concerned there was one really glaring omission ...

Thanet picked up the telephone again. 'Send Bentley in, will you?'

News of Thanet's mood had clearly travelled. Bentley stood stiffly correct, avoiding Thanet's eye.

'It's all right,' Thanet said, able now to be amused. 'You can relax. I'm not going to bite this time.'

Bentley's mouth twitched at one corner and his shoulders visibly relaxed.

'This man Horrocks, the salesman. I believe you questioned his wife, is that right?'

'Yes, sir.'

'And I understand he was due back from his sales trip last night?'

'So she said, sir.'

'Right. I want you to find out where he is and go and see him. Let's hope he hasn't flitted off again.'

'His firm said he'd be in this area for three weeks after coming back, sir.'

'Good. Now this really is very important. Horrocks first noticed Parrish's car parked in front of the shop at seven-fifteen. We know from Carne – that's the chap

183

who was picking up his daughter from a music lesson – that it was still there at eight-twenty. Mrs Horrocks says that her husband left on his business trip just before nine, but that she doesn't know whether or not the Triumph was gone by then. 'The point is that Parrish claims that he was with his mistress from about ten past seven to nine-thirty. She confirms this and if it's true, of course, he's in the clear. But she may well be lying to protect him and I want to go and see her again. But first I want you to find out from Horrocks whether or not the Triumph was still there when he left just before nine.'

'Right, sir.'

I must be missing Lineham, Thanet thought as Bentley left. He didn't usually give long explanations when sending his men out on such simple errands. He stretched, then stood up. Suddenly he felt lethargic, stupefied, almost. The atmosphere in the room, he realised, was so thick with pipe smoke one could almost cut it into cubes. From his favourite position at the window the world outside beckoned to him, fresh and enticing. He glanced at his watch. He had completely missed his lunch-hour and could with justification take some time off. He had promised Joan that he would at some point try to get out to buy the Snoopy for which Sprig was yearning as a birthday present. In any case, his brain felt so addled that if he didn't have a break he might as well go home, for all the work he would be able to do.

He left his window open to freshen the room and set off down the High Street. It was good to feel part of the normal world again, to be an ordinary person going shopping for a birthday present for his small daughter. The purchase did not take long. Sprig's needs had been clearly defined. Thanet accepted the large, squashy parcel and wandered around the toy shop for a while before leaving. What a marvellous selection of toys there was for children these days! Surely toy shops had never been like this when he was young? He hung yearningly for some time over a complex model railway lay-out. Perhaps when Ben was older ...

By the time he left he felt refreshed, with a pleasant sense of duty done. The office smelt sweeter now and Thanet balanced his large parcel on top of the coat rack, so that he would see it without fail when he went home, and sat down at his desk.

What now?

He tried without success to get hold of Kendon. He would have to ring again this evening. Then he sat staring at the pile of papers before him, drumming impatient fingers on his desk. Surely Bentley should be back soon? And if Horrocks confirmed that Parrish's car had still been there at nine? More house-to-house enquiries, he supposed, this time directed exclusively towards finding out if anyone else had seen the Triumph that night, noticed when it left.

Meanwhile there didn't seem to be a single thing he could do.

What about Holmes? Should he perhaps try a reconstruction of the crime, aimed at discovering whether or not Holmes could have committed the murder in those fifteen or twenty seconds that had elapsed between the moment when he and Byfleet parted at the front gate and the moment when Holmes had called Byfleet back?

But all Thanet's original objections to the idea that Holmes was the murderer still held. No, a reconstruction would be time-consuming and pointless.

It was possible, of course, that both Parrish and Kendon were innocent too, that some casual caller or potential burglar had been unlucky enough to have happened to approach the house in Gladstone Road just after Kendon's departure. Thanet groaned at the thought. If that were so, unless some new evidence turned up of its own accord, it looked as though the chances of catching the murderer were very slim indeed, if not non-existent. And to have to admit failure, particularly in view of his own misguided behaviour …

A knock at the door, and Bentley entered. Thanet could see at once that he had found something. Could it be a break, at last?

It was. Horrocks, leaving his house at just before nine o'clock and having to walk to his car, parked two streets away, had been infuriated to find that he was just in time to see the tail lights of the Triumph disappearing up the road.

'He's certain?' Thanet asked eagerly.

'Absolutely, sir. He'd been out every quarter of an hour or so all evening, as you know, so he really was mad just to have missed him like that.'

'Good. Excellent. Well done, Bentley.'

So Parrish had lied again. Thanet's immediate impulse was to confront the man, but instinct told him to go carefully indeed. Parrish was a very smooth customer. He would no doubt have prepared some tale in case of this very eventuality. Besides, Thanet would like to have some further confirmation of Horrock's story. If Parrish had lied, so had his mistress.

Yes, a visit to Phyllis Penge was definitely the next priority.

Palmerston Row was noisy with the sound of children playing and Thanet prudently drove past, parked his car in front of Dobson's yard in Gladstone Road and walked back. The girl who answered the door of number 14 was younger than Thanet had expected, not much more than nineteen, he guessed. She had long, elaborately curled blonde hair, heavy eye make-up and wore a pink satin blouse and a tight black skirt slit to the knee on one side. Her welcoming smile slipped a little as Thanet introduced himself, and her eyes slid past him as if assessing the effect of his visit upon the neighbours.

'You'd better come in,' she said, standing back.

Thanet had to squeeze past her in the narrow hall,

and he was aware of the slither of satin against his sleeve, of a whiff of surprisingly good perfume before she pointed at a half-open door.

'In there,' she said.

The room was comfortable, if claustrophobically full. Thanet's eyes skimmed over a three-piece suite, three strategically-placed coffee tables, a large glass-fronted drinks cabinet well stocked with bottles, an imposing stereo system, an elaborate radio-cassette, a long rack of records and another of cassettes, and one of the largest colour television sets Thanet had ever seen. There was not a book or newspaper in sight.

She waved him into a chair and perched on the edge of the settee, tugging her skirt down over the knees as if conscious that too much exposed flesh was not appropriate to the occasion.

Thanet wondered if a formal approach might work best. The girl was obviously nervous – as well she might be, having lied to the police – and, he judged, ready to talk. If she had only told the truth when questioned last time Thanet might, he realised ruefully, have been saved from making a fool of himself. He couldn't feel angry with Lineham, though. Looking at the girl he now understood why Lineham had slipped up. Astute though the sergeant was, girls, especially sexually attractive girls like this, tended to throw him. Thanet found the thought comforting. After his own fiasco it was good to know that Lineham, too, had his Achilles heel.

'Now then, Mrs Penge,' he said, taking a notebook from his pocket, flipping it open and pretending to consult it, 'on Wednesday May 7 you made a statement to my sergeant regarding your movements on the evening of Tuesday May 6. Have you anything to add to that statement?'

She passed her tongue nervously over her lips. 'What do you mean?'

'Would you like to alter or amend that statement in any way?'

187

A slight shake of the head. 'I don't think so.'

'Perhaps you'd just like me to remind you of what you said in it? You state that on Tuesday May 6 you left this house at seven pm, walked along the footpath at the end of the cul-de-sac and entered the side door of a flat which is situated over the Greengrocer's shop in Jubilee Street. This flat belongs to Mr Jeremy Parrish. He was waiting for you and you stayed with him until nine-thirty when you left. You then returned home.'

He glanced at her. She was staring at him as if mesmerised, gnawing at the quick of her little finger.

'Well, Mrs Penge?'

She lowered her hand from her mouth, tugged again at the hem of her skirt, a jerky, nervous movement. 'Well what?' she said, with an attempt at a coquettish smile.

'Your statement.' Thanet tapped his notebook. 'We just want to check that it is correct. So often, you see, people get flustered when they are asked to make a statement, and can't think straight. And then later on, when they've had a chance to think it over, they realise they got something wrong. Now I have a feeling that this happened in your case. Am I right?' There, he had given her a way to back down without losing face or being too afraid to admit it. Would she take it?

She shook her head slightly, a nervous, ambiguous movement.

He leaned forward, spoke very gently, reassuringly. 'Please, Mrs Penge, it really is very important that we should know.' And then, as she still said nothing, 'Murder is a very serious business.'

Her eyes dilated. 'You're not saying ... You don't mean Jeremy ...?'

'I'm not accusing anybody, Mrs Penge. But we have to know the truth, not just from some people but from everybody. That way we can slowly build up a picture of what happened on the night Mrs Holmes was killed. Did you know her?'

A quick, tight shake of the head.

Somehow he had to break through the barrier of her loyalty to Parrish. 'She wasn't much older than you, you know. Just a young girl, with all her life before her.' That was laying it on a bit thick, he knew, but it worked. Phyllis's identification with Julie lasted just long enough for her to burst out, 'He said he'd tell ...' and stop, knuckles pressed hard against her mouth, as if to hold the words in by force.

Thanet understood at once. 'Mr Parrish said he'd tell your husband about his relationship with you, if you didn't back him up?' So it hadn't been loyalty which had held her back, but fear. The bastard. The out and out bastard.

She nodded and, burying her face in her hands, began to cry. It was a near-silent weeping, almost a mourning, Thanet thought as he thrust a clean handkerchief into her hand. For the death of love? he wondered, for illusions destroyed? Or was her reaction one of simple fear that now her husband would find out that she had been unfaithful?

'Now, I think you'd better tell me all about it, don't you? Mr Parrish said he'd tell your husband about your affair if you didn't back him up. Back him up over what? He knew the answer, of course, but it was sweet to hear her say it.

'Over the time he said we'd stayed together until, that Tuesday evening,' she said ungrammatically.

'Half past nine, you mean?' Then, as she nodded, he said softly, 'So what time did you part?'

'Twenty-five to,' she said, almost inaudibly.

'Twenty-five to nine?'

She nodded.

'You left together?'

'No. I always leave first. Jeremy stays behind to lock up and that.'

'And you're sure about the time?'

'Certain sure.' Her voice was stronger now. 'There was something I specially wanted to see on the telly at nine so when I got down to the street I looked at my

189

watch to see if there was time to nip along and pick up some chips before going home. I was hungry.'

Thanet's stomach contracted with excitement. 'The fish and chip shop in Jubilee Road?'

'Yes.'

'And did you go?'

She nodded. 'There was bags of time.' Her eyes flickered away from his.

'You saw something, didn't you?' he said softly. 'While you were in the shop?'

That startled her. 'How did you ...?' She broke off, twisting his handkerchief nervously, looking miserably down at it as if it could give her guidance.

'How did I know that you saw Mr Parrish go by?' Her silence confirmed that he had guessed correctly. 'Did he notice you?'

An almost imperceptible shake of the head.

'You were in the shop ...' he encouraged.

She relinquished the handkerchief as she came to her decision. 'I saw him in the mirror,' she said. 'It's a big one, on the wall behind the counter. Ted – that's the chap what serves there – he bent down to pick something up and in the mirror, in the space where he'd been standing, like, I saw Jeremy go by. At first I thought, he's going to his car. But then I knew he couldn't be. It was parked between the flat and the chip shop, so he'd already passed it.'

Thanet hazarded another guess. 'So you went to the door, to see where he was going?'

She nodded.

'And?'

'He walked to the end of the road and turned ... and turned left.'

In the direction of Gladstone Road. 'You're sure?'

'Yeah.' She leaned her head against the back of the settee. The strain of the last few minutes was telling on her now.

'Thank you.' He tucked his notebook in his pocket. 'Just one other point, Mrs Penge. When, exactly, did

Mr Parrish contact you and ask you to back up his false statement about the time he left?'

She thought for a moment. 'In the afternoon, before your sergeant came to see me. He rang me at work.'

After the second visit to Parrish, Thanet thought. He must have been on the phone to Phyllis the minute they left.

'Good,' he said briskly. He rose. 'Well now, if you'll come along with me to make a statement ...'

She shrank back against the settee. 'You're arresting me?' she whispered.

Thanet laughed. 'No. No, of course not. All I want is a statement.' And the certainty that as soon as he had left she wouldn't be on the phone to Parrish to warn him that the game was up. He didn't think she would but he had no intention of risking it. 'All you have to do is tell one of my men exactly what you've been telling me, then he'll type it all for you, you'll read through what he's written to check that he's got it right, and you'll sign it. And that will be that, you'll be able to come home.'

'Does ... Will my husband have to know?'

'I'm sorry. I really can't say at the moment. It depends on what happens.'

She looked so miserable that Thanet couldn't help feeling sorry for her. She was, after all very young.

'Come on,' he said gently. 'We'd better be on our way.'

17

It was five o'clock by the time Thanet arrived back at the police station. He handed Phyllis Penge over to Carson and told him to take her statement.

'Spin it out, will you? Don't let her make any phone calls and don't let her go until I say so. I've got to go out again.'

Then he ran upstairs to his office, taking the steps two at a time. All the way back from Palmerston Row he had been trying to work out the best way to approach Parrish. It could now be proved that Parrish had been lying, but Thanet was well aware that there was still no shred of evidence to tie him in with the murder. Parrish could simply say that he had wanted a breath of fresh air after leaving the flat, had gone for a short stroll before returning to his car and driving off just before nine. He could claim that he had not dared tell the police this before, because he had been afraid that they wouldn't believe him.

And let's face it, Thanet thought, it might well be true. Parrish might yet be innocent – as innocent as Edna Pocock had proved to be. Thanet found himself reserving judgement. Once bitten, twice shy.

Just as he was parking his car, however, Thanet had had a stroke of inspiration, had suddenly seen a way in which he might, if he were very lucky, trap Parrish into an admission, if he were guilty. It might not work of course, such ploys frequently did not, but in this case there was just a chance and he was determined to take it. For it to work, however, his interview with Parrish –

and he would take Bentley as a witness – would have to take place in Parrish's office, and preferably today. Thanet grabbed the telephone.

'Bentley? Bring Julie Holmes's effects up, will you? And fast, man.'

Bentley arrived minutes later, out of breath. Thanet ignored the polythene bag in which Julie's clothes were shrouded and seized the large brown envelope in which smaller items had been placed. He emptied it over the desk, exclaiming with satisfaction as his fingers closed over the object he sought. He slipped the thing into his pocket. 'Right. Let's go.'

'But the effects. Shouldn't we return them, sir?'

'Later, man, later.' Thanet almost pushed Bentley out of the office in his impatience to be gone. 'If we don't hurry, we'll miss him.'

Outside the building Bentley automatically turned towards the car park. Thanet grabbed his sleeve. 'It'll be quicker to walk. Too much traffic.'

Bentley said nothing, merely swung after Thanet who was setting off at a half-run in the direction of the High Street. The pavements were filling up rapidly with people on their way home from work and already the traffic in the High Street was at a standstill.

By the time they reached Parrish's office it was almost half past five and Thanet was steeling himself for disappointment. If Parrish wasn't there …

But he was. Just. Thanet and Bentley reached him as he turned away from locking the door.

'Could we have a word, do you think, Mr Parrish?'

Parrish turned. 'Oh, for God's sake! This is a bit much. I was just on my way home.'

'Could we go back inside for a few minutes, sir?'

Parrish hesitated, frowning. 'Won't tomorrow do?'

'I'm sorry. There's just a small point to clear up. It shouldn't take too long.'

With an ill grace Parrish turned back to the door, set his elegant black executive briefcase down with a thump and fished the keys out of his pocket. He unlocked the door, pushed it open and stalked across the reception area to his own room. Thanet, who had been afraid that Parrish might have stayed in the outer office for the interview, followed him with satisfaction. Parrish's office suited his purpose marginally better.

Parrish put his briefcase on the desk, turned and, folding his arms, half-sat on the front edge of his desk facing them. 'Well, Inspector?'

'Could we sit down, Mr Parrish?' Thanet asked. He wasn't going to let Parrish take charge of this session.

Parrish gestured towards two chairs and sat down behind his desk. As if to underline the proposed brevity of the meeting, however, he kept his coat on.

Thanet picked up one of the wooden armchairs which stood against the wall and set it down in front of his desk, facing Parrish squarely. Bentley sat down a little distance away and took out his notebook. Parrish opened his mouth to speak, but Thanet quickly took the initiative.

'It's simply a matter of checking certain facts, Mr Parrish.'

'What facts?' Parrish made a show of pretending to relax, sat back in his chair with his hands thrust casually into his pockets. Thanet was sorry about the hands. They were always a give-away. He would be willing to bet that they were tightly clenched, knuckles white.

'Such facts as the precise time at which you left Mrs Penge on the evening Julie Holmes died.'

The muscles around Parrish's jaw tightened. 'At half past nine. I told you.'

'Yes, you did, didn't you. The second time we interviewed you. The first time you told us you'd stayed at home all evening.'

'I explained that. I was trying to protect the lady.'

Thanet shrugged. 'For whatever reason. The point is, that when someone has lied to us once we tend to be, how shall I put it, a little suspicious of him? And, of course, to check what he says very thoroughly. As we did with your story.'

Parrish raised his eyebrows. 'And?'

'And we discovered that you had lied to us again.'

Parrish shrugged. 'I don't know what you mean.'

Despite his casual tone, however, his eyes had become wary.

'Oh, I'm sure you do,' Thanet said. 'Unfortunately for you, Mr Parrish, you happen to have been parking your car, on Tuesday evenings, in the space which custom allots to a certain local resident. And he's been getting rather angry about it. Now last Tuesday evening, your car was again in his parking space, and as he didn't know where to find you he kept a very close eye on it, hoping to catch you when you drove away. So close an eye, to be precise, that he went out every quarter of an hour. Your car was still parked in Jubilee Road at eight-forty-five, but when he came out just before nine he saw you driving it away. Needless to say, he was very angry to have missed you.'

'Damned cheek,' Parrish growled. 'I've as much right to that parking space as he has. I'm a householder there, aren't I? I pay good rent for that flat.'

'That, as you well know, is not the point. The point is, why did you tell us you didn't leave Mrs Penge until nine-thirty?'

'You're wrong,' Parrish said calmly. 'You've only his word against mine. And you yourself admit he's got a grudge against me. He must be laughing his head off, thinking of the jam he's got me into, lying about the time he saw me leave.'

'Oh no, Mr Parrish. Not only his word.' Thanet paused. 'Mrs Penge confirms that you and she parted before nine-thirty. In fact, she says she left you at twenty-five to nine.'

Parrish looked at Thanet in disbelief for a moment, his eyes narrowed into slits. Then, 'The bitch,' he said. 'The lying bitch.'

'I think not, sir. As you well know, Mrs Penge has everything to lose by making this statement.'

The barb had gone home. 'She won't get away with this!'

'Charming,' said Thanet. 'Can I believe my ears? A lady to protect, I believe you said?'

'No lady would behave like that. A lady would've stood by me.'

'Stood by you in what?' Thanet said softly.

Parrish stared at him for a moment or two and then, astonishingly, began to laugh. 'Oh no, Inspector, you're not going to catch me like that. OK, so I told you a second lie. The very fact that you're here now proves that my reason for doing so was justified. When you came here the second time and told me that my car had been seen parked in the area, I could see that I had to come clean about Phyllis. So I did. But I made a mistake. A genuine mistake. I got the time wrong. Usually, you see, we do split up about nine-thirty, but that Tuesday I was feeling a bit under the weather. Things didn't go with their usual bounce, so I decided to call it a day earlier than usual. Then, when I thought back, after you'd gone, I realised that I'd made a mistake in time. Now, Inspector, what would you have done? You told me yourself, a few minutes ago, that when someone has been caught out in a lie once, the next time you're even less inclined to believe him. So I thought it would be more sensible to ask Phyllis to stick to our usual time of nine-thirty, if she was questioned.'

'You didn't think of ringing me up, to tell us of your "mistakes"?'

'No thank you, Inspector. So far as I knew you were off my back, and I wanted it to stay that way.'

'So what, exactly, did you do, after she had left that evening?' Please God, thought Thanet, he'll say he stayed in the flat for a little while, got straight into his car and drove away. To be caught out a third time in one interview might just rattle him.

Parrish narrowed his eyes, apparently in recollection. 'Phyllis left at about twenty-five to nine. I tidied up, made sure that everything was secure and left a few minutes later – at about twenty to nine, I suppose. Then I went for a little stroll.'

196

'In which direction?'

Parrish shrugged. 'I really can't remember. Does it matter?'

It might. Did you see anyone?'

Parrish shook his head. 'Not a soul, so far as I can remember.'

'At a quarter to nine on a fine May evening?' Thanet leant back casually in his chair, put his hands in his pockets.

Parrish lifted his shoulders, spread his hands. 'It was getting dusk. No doubt there was the odd person about.' He gave a pseudo-charming smile. 'It'll be your job to find them, won't it, Inspector?'

It would if his ploy didn't work, Thanet thought grimly. He took his hands out of his pockets and stood up. 'Right, Mr Parrish. I'm sorry to have delayed you.' Thanet stooped. 'There's something on the floor under your desk,' he said. He straightened up, held out his hand.

Parrish stared at the enamelled mermaid, his face set. 'That's not mine, it's Julie's.'

'It belonged to Mrs Holmes?'

'Yes. Damned office cleaners. Can't trust them to do anything properly these days. It must have been lying there all this time.'

'Yes,' said Thanet heavily. 'Almost a week, if it was hers. You're sure it didn't belong to one of the other girls?'

'Of course I'm sure,' Parrish said testily. 'She was my personal secretary, remember. She must have dropped it one day, without realising it. She used to take dictation sitting almost where you were, in that chair. I saw her wear it.'

'When, Mr Parrish?' Thanet said softly. 'When did you see her wear it?'

Parrish shrugged again. 'Does it really matter, Inspector? It's hers, that's all I can tell you. It's a very distinctive thing, the sort of thing you don't forget easily, isn't it?'

197

'It certainly is,' Thanet said. 'Which is precisely why I picked it for my purpose.'

'Your purpose?' Now, for the first time, Parrish looked rattled.

'Yes. I'm afraid, Mr Parrish, that there is no way in which you could have seen Mrs Holmes wear that brooch in this office. Her husband bought it for her on the way home from work the night she died, gave it to her after supper that evening. She was wearing it when she was killed ...'

Now at last Parrish understood the trap into which he had fallen and Thanet watched with satisfaction as the confident lines of the man's face began to blur, to disintegrate.

As Parrish dropped his head into his hands Thanet nodded to Bentley.

The words of the charge were music in his ears.

18

'So then what happened?' Lineham asked eagerly.

It was later the same evening and Lineham was sitting up in bed, looking absurdly young in blue and white striped pyjamas.

Thanet grimaced. 'Oh, it was rather disgusting really. He broke down, grovelled. It hadn't been his fault, he hadn't intended to kill her and so on and so on. Says he went there on impulse. Since Julie appeared on the scene he'd been getting more and more tired of Phyllis Penge. Julie was a much more attractive proposition and the resistance she was putting up to his advances had merely served to whet his appetite. I think he genuinely believes himself irresistible and thought Julie's apparent rejection of him was a token resistance, put up for the sake of form. He was also convinced that if only he could get her alone, away from the office, he'd win her over. The trouble was that she refused all his invitations to lunch, drinks and so on and he was getting more and more desperate. The more she held off, the more he wanted her.

'The night she died he'd found Phyllis Penge less interesting than ever and he decided to cut their time together short. He says that when she'd gone and he'd tidied up he looked at his watch, found that it was only twenty to nine and remembered that Julie's husband always went to night school on Tuesdays. Personally I think he'd been building up to this for weeks. He was well aware that Julie lived only a few minutes away

199

from his little love nest. And in view of the night school, Tuesday was the obvious day for him to try to get her on her own. On the other hand he didn't want to lose his present mistress until Julie showed signs of being more forthcoming .

'Anyway, whether the decision was made on the spur of the moment or not, he waited until he thought Phyllis was safely out of the way, then set off briskly for Julie's house. He arrived there just a minute or two after Kendon had left – though he didn't know that, of course. It seems highly likely that Parrish was the person Kendon glimpsed turning into Gladstone Road as he entered the wood to take the footpath to the station. And Parrish remembers seeing a man just going through the swing gate as he turned into the road.

'Anyway he claims that he put up his hand to knock at the front door, but before he could do so Julie flung it open and came at him with a knife, screaming at him. Instinctively he put up his hands to defend himself, grabbed for the hand with the knife, they struggled and she was killed.'

'But why attack Parrish?'

'My guess is that she thought he was Kendon. Just think. The door of that house is half-glazed and Kendon and Parrish are much the same height and build. Now Kendon had been at the door just a minute or so before, trying to get Julie to let him in. Through the glass panel it might well have looked as though he'd come back for one more try, and even when the door was open Parrish would have had the light – which was fading anyway – behind him. And I think that she was in such a state by then that she was incapable of thinking rationally. I doubt if she stopped to look at him, she just launched at him.'

'She'd reached the point of no return, so to speak.'

'Breaking point, as Mrs Thorpe put it. Yes.'

Lineham was silent for a while, thinking it over. Eventually, 'You said he *claims* that this was what happened. Don't you believe him?'

'Oh come on, Mike. I believe the bit about Julie coming at him with a knife and so on, yes, because it is entirely consistent with everything else we know, but the rest of it ... No, he's just trying to save his skin. Can you see him being so frightened by Julie's attack, so little in control of the struggle that he has to kill her to defend himself? Julie was small, slight. She wouldn't have had a chance against someone his size.'

'They do say that people who have gone over the edge have an abnormal strength,' Lineham offered diffidently.

'Maybe, but not to that degree. I just can't believe it. Anyway, it's not for us to decide, thank God. We can leave that to the powers that be. But I have a feeling that a good prosecuting counsel will make mincement of the self-defence idea. No, I think it was deliberate all right. Not premeditated, no, but I would guess that the attack was the last straw for our Jeremy, as far as Julie was concerned. I think he genuinely believes himself to be God's gift to women and thought that Julie was just playing hard-to-get. I expect he thought that if only he had a little while alone with her she'd melt like snow in summer. I bet he set off for her house as jaunty as a peacock and what happens? She comes at him with a knife, for God's sake! It must have been a shattering blow to his ego, his vanity. He couldn't possibly have known, of course, that she wasn't really seeing *him* at all, or why she was in that state. So I would guess that his instinctive reaction was anger. 'The little bitch. Leading me up the garden path ...' Something like that. And of course, he had to act fast because there she was, coming for him with a knife. He didn't have time for second thoughts. So he turned her own knife against her.'

'Deliberately.'

'Sure. Deliberately. Incidentally, Mike, something occurred to me. You remember those two reports we had, of a tall, dark man walking towards Gladstone Road and how we thought the witnesses must have got the times wrong?'

'Of course! You mean it wasn't one man but two. First Kendon, passing Disraeli Terrace, then Parrish passing Shaftesbury Road – which explains why the sighting further away was five minutes later.'

'Exactly.'

There was silence for a few minutes while both men thought back over the case.

'Of course,' Thanet said eventually, 'we're still no nearer knowing who killed Annabel Dacre.'

'You're going on with that?'

'No. Oh no, not likely. After all, there's no new evidence, is there? And Low did as thorough a job as you'd hope to find. No, I'm afraid Annabel's murderer is safe.'

'But I thought you said you were pretty well convinced that it was Mrs Pocock who killed her?'

'I still am, yes. But being convinced is one thing. Proving it, as you well know, is another.'

'It goes against the grain, though, to know that a murderer has gone free.'

'Yes,' Thanet agreed automatically. But he was thinking of the Pocock children and knew that they were getting on to dangerous ground. If there had been even the remotest chance of proving Edna Pocock's guilt he would, he knew, have had to take action. As it was, he didn't want to examine his own feelings too closely. If one started feeling sympathetic towards murderers there was no telling where one would end up. And there was something that had to be said. He braced himself. 'So you see, Mike, you were right.' The effort it had cost him to make the admission made his voice sound harsh, almost aggressive.

Lineham looked startled, as well he might. 'What about?'

'About it being much more likely that Julie was killed because of what was happening in the present, rather than because of something that had happened in the distant past.'

With the temperature Lineham was running Thanet

wouldn't have thought a blush would be visible, but it was. It spread slowly up Lineham's neck, into cheeks and forehead.

'My goodness,' said his mother, coming into the room with a cup of coffee for Thanet and a jug of lemonade neatly covered with a snowy white linen napkin for her son. 'Just look at you!' She handed the coffee to Thanet, set the jug down on the bedside table and laid the back of her hand against Lineham's forehead.

'I'm all right, mother,' he said irritably, with an embarrassed glance at Thanet.

She stood back, looked at him consideringly, her head tilted to one side. 'I could have sworn ... Here,' she took the thermometer from the little glass of disinfectant on the table beside the bed, 'just let me ...'

Lineham waved it away. 'Not now, mother, *please*. Later, when Inspector Thanet has gone.'

Thanet could see why Lineham was finding it difficult to spread his wings.

Mrs Lineham's lips set in a disapproving line. 'Very well, dear.' She poured a glass of lemonade, thrust it into his hand. 'Anyway, try to keep drinking now, won't you. It'll bring your temperature down quicker than anything.'

Lineham took the glass without protest, waited until she had left the room, then set it down on the bedside table with a rebellious thump. He caught Thanet's eye.

'Women!' Thanet said, and was relieved to see Lineham grin. 'Anyway,' he went on, draining the last of his coffee, 'I knew you'd want to hear how it all ended.' He set the cup down, stood up. 'Well, I suppose I'd better be getting home.'

'Just a minute,' Lineham said quickly.

Thanet sat down again.

'I wanted ... I wanted to apologise.'

Now it was Thanet's turn to look startled. 'Whatever for?'

'For wasting your time, sir.' Lineham hesitated, then

went on. 'If I hadn't slipped up over Mrs Penge, if I'd managed to get the truth out of her the first time, then you wouldn't have wasted your time following up the Dacre case.'

Undeniably true, but Thanet somehow couldn't bring himself to feel even slightly angry with Lineham. Despite his own bruised pride, he suddenly realised he didn't regret any of it. Dammit, he had *enjoyed* it. That delving back into the past had rounded off his understanding of Julie, had satisfied his need to know.

'We all make mistakes,' he said, 'thank God. If we didn't we'd be insufferable. I think we've both learned something from this case. So let's leave it there, shall we?' He stood up again.

'Yes, sir. And, sir … thank you.'

Thanet raised his hand in a half-salute of farewell, and left.

19

On a fine summer evening some three months later Thanet and Joan were strolling hand in hand towards the main car park in the centre of Sturrenden. It was Joan's birthday and Thanet had taken her out to dinner to mark the occasion. They were in a mellow mood, full of good food and wine, at peace with the world.

'Darling, look!' Joan was pointing across the road at a small art gallery which had recently opened. On an easel in the centre of the window, spot-lit from above, was a painting. 'Surely that's *The Cricket Match*?'

They crossed the road to see.

'I thought so. Mr Holmes must have sold it,' Joan said. 'I'd have recognised it anywhere.'

They studied the painting in silence. It was the first time that Thanet had had the opportunity to examine one of Annabel Dacre's paintings at leisure. And there was no doubt about it, he thought, she had been good. The painting drew the eye like a magnet, its jewel-like colours, distinctive style and crowded canvas a source of never-ending fascination.

'Did I tell you she put people she knew in them?' he murmured.

'Really?'

'Mmm. Mrs Manson told me. Look. I bet that's her, with her husband. He's wearing his dog-collar.'

They leaned forward, pressing their noses against the glass of the shop window. The Reverend and Mrs Manson were holding cups of tea, standing near the long table which had been set up beneath one of the two huge oaks on the Green at Little Sutton, its white cloth gleaming in the shade. Yes, he would swear that that was Mrs Manson, Thanet thought, a younger, more vital version of the sick woman she had become. Extraordinary how, in such tiny figures, Annabel had managed to capture some essence of the person's individuality, so that they were immediately recognisable.

And there, he saw with a sense of shock, was Julie – no, not Julie of course, but her mother, Jennifer Parr, Julie's 'spitting image' as Holmes had put it. The man beside her was presumably David Parr, Julie's father, whose tragic accident had triggered off the train of events which had culminated in Julie's death. If Jennifer had not left Julie with Annabel while she was at the hospital Julie would not have witnessed the murder which had had such a profound and far-reaching effect upon her. At Mrs Parr's feet, her yellow dress vivid against the green of the grass, caught in the act of picking a daisy, was a child of about eighteen months who could only be Julie herself.

He pointed her out to Joan, who grimaced. 'Poor kid,' she murmured. And then, 'You mean they're all in this, all the people you've told me about?'

'More than likely, according to Mrs Manson. I wouldn't mind betting that that's Alice Giddy, for example.'

Alice was walking across the Green towards the other spectators, supporting a woman who was clearly leaning heavily upon her – Alice's mother, Thanet supposed. Alice's glossy black hair was caught back in a chignon, accentuating the cat-like slant of the eyes, the high, prominent cheek-bones. Her strongly individual dress sense was even then apparent. She was wearing a sky-blue tube which narrowed to the hem, a complete contrast to the rather nondescript summer dresses of the other women.

Thanet looked for the Pococks, but found them less

206

easy to identify. Was that Roger, at the wicket, and that Edna, bending over the pram of a neighbour's baby? Peake and Plummer, of course, he had never met. He straightened up with a sigh.

'Three hundred guineas,' Joan said thoughtfully. 'Worth every penny, and a good investment, I should think.'

'No!' Thanet said vehemently. 'I couldn't bear it. Even if we had the money to spare, which we haven't, I really could not bear to have that hanging on our living room wall. D'you realise it was this painting which was really responsible for sending me off on that wild goose chase?'

'Poor darling. You still feel sore about it, don't you?'

'Less now than I did.' He grinned. 'I don't know. Perhaps it would be a good idea to buy it after all – hang it up where I could see it every day as an Awful Warning.'

'Not on your life! Home is not the place for Awful Warnings.' Joan tugged at his arm and with one last reluctant look at the painting, he yielded.

'There's no doubt that it is Holmes's painting, I suppose?' he said as they walked on.

Joan shook her head. 'None. I remember reading somewhere that it was Annabel Dacre's policy never to do more than one painting of the same subject.'

'Poor devil. I wonder if he's still in Gladstone Road. If he has any sense he'll have moved by now. Anyway, I'm glad to know he sold that picture.'

'Why?'

Thanet shrugged. 'Because it's rather macabre, I suppose, to think of him having it hanging in his house unaware of its significance.'

'You mean, he didn't know that all those people were in it? Julie, her parents, Annabel's murderer ...?'

'He didn't strike me as being the type to be interested in painting. The figures are so tiny, I doubt that he ever studied *The Cricket Match* sufficiently closely to have spotted Julie in her mother's likeness.

And he knew nothing of Annabel's murder. I did wonder whether to tell him, but I thought it would probably make him even more unhappy, give him a whole new set of circumstances to brood over, just when he was beginning to take up normal life again. I don't know. Perhaps I should have told him. Perhaps he had a right to know. What do you think?'

A heavy lorry swung around the corner just as they were about to cross the road and Thanet seized Joan's elbow. They watched it go by and then he piloted her across to the car park entrance.

'Mmm?' he said, making it clear that he was still awaiting an answer.

'I don't know,' she said. 'I honestly don't think I know enough about it to be able to judge. But, why worry about it now? It's all past, done with. You did what you thought right at the time, surely that's what matters? What are you grinning at?'

Thanet's smile broadened. 'Something Doc Mallard said to me once. "Don't try taking over the Almighty's job," he said. "He's much better at it than you could ever be."

Joan's eyes sparkled with pleasure. 'Typical,' she said. 'But he's right, you know.'

'He usually is,' Thanet said. 'Whereas I ...'

'And so are you,' she cut in. She gave him a wicked little grin. 'Well, most of the time, anyway.'

They were still smiling when they reached the car.

SIX FEET UNDER

For Mark, Ian and Emma

Cruelty has a Human Heart,
And Jealousy a Human Face;
Terror the Human Form Divine,
And Secrecy the Human Dress.

The Human Dress is forged Iron,
The Human Form a fiery Forge,
The Human Face a Furnace seal'd,
The Human Heart its hungry Gorge.
                    William Blake

Author's Note

People often ask me where my ideas come from. Often I don't
know.
But not in this instance.
In December 1975 the newspapers were full of a story which
fascinated me. I followed it, filed it and forgot it – or so I
thought. Then, when I was thinking about this book, the idea
popped up: why not use that story as a basis for a murder
mystery? The characters and setting would of course be my
own creation.
The result was SIX FEET UNDER.

1

Detective Inspector Luke Thanet was a happy man. He had an interesting job, no pressing financial worries, two healthy lively children and, perhaps best of all, a wife who was all that any man could wish for. And so it was that on this blustery March evening, blissfully unaware of the nasty little shock that Fate was preparing for him, he stretched out his toes to the fire, settled back into his armchair and reflected that he wouldn't change places with any man in the world.

Reaching for his pipe he tapped it out, scraped it, inspected it, blew through it, then filled it with loving care.

"It's nine o'clock," Joan said. "D'you want the news?"

"I don't think so. Do you?"

"Not particularly."

She went back to her book. Thanet lit his pipe and picked up the newspaper. He hadn't been reading for more than a few minutes, however, when he realised that Joan was unusually restless. Normally, when she was reading, she plunged at once into total absorption. One one occasion Thanet had counted up to a hundred from the time he asked her a question to the moment when she looked up, eyes unfocused, and said, "What did you say?"

Now she fidgeted, crossed and re-crossed her legs, fiddled with her hair, chewed the tip of her thumb.

Eventually, "Book no good?" Thanet enquired.

She looked up at once. "Mmm? Oh, it's all right. Very interesting, in fact."

"What's the matter, then?"

She hesitated, gave him a speculative look.

He laid down his newspaper. "Come on, love. Out with it."

To his surprise she still did not respond. "Joan?" He was

7

beginning to feel the first faint stirrings of alarm.

She shook her head then, a fierce little shake. "Oh, it's all right. There's nothing wrong, not really. It's just that I've a nasty feeling you aren't going to like what I'm trying to pluck up the courage to say."

"Oh?" he said, warily.

She looked at him with something approaching desperation. "It's just that . . . oh, dear. . . . Look, you know we've said all along that when Ben starts school I'll go back to work? Well, that's only six months away now. So I really ought to start thinking about what I want to do."

"I see," Thanet said slowly.

"There you are. I knew you wouldn't like it."

"Darling, don't be silly. It's just that, well, the idea will take a bit of getting used to after all this time, that's all."

"Don't pretend," she said. "You're dead against it really, aren't you? I can tell."

And she was right, of course, he was. They had been married for eight years now and for all that time Joan had been the good little wife who stayed at home, ran the house efficiently and without fuss, coped with two children and made sure that everything was geared to Thanet's convenience. Unlike the wives of so many of his colleagues, Joan had never complained or nagged over the demands of his job, the irregular hours. Now, in a flash, he saw everything changed. Uncomfortable adjustments would have to be made, there would be inconvenience, irritation, arguments. Theory and practice, he now realised, were very different matters. All very well, in the past, to contemplate with equanimity the prospect of Joan returning to work one day, but to accept that that day was almost here . . . No, she was right. He didn't like it at all.

"Nonsense," he said. "We've always said you would, when the children were old enough."

"Oh, I know you've always *said* you wouldn't mind. But that's very different from not minding when it actually happens."

"I thought you'd more or less made up your mind to do an art course."

8

"No. Oh, I did think so, at one time. I'm very interested, as you know. But . . . I don't know, I'd like to feel I was doing something, well, less self-indulgent, more useful. Oh, dear, does that sound horribly priggish?"

He grinned. "To be honest, yes. But I know what you mean."

"Do you?" she said eagerly. "You don't think I'm being stupid?"

"Not in the least. What sort of thing did you have in mind?"

"Well, that's the trouble. I'm just not qualified for anything. That's why I feel I ought to start thinking about it now, so that if I have to do a course, or any special training, I can get myself organised for September."

"Yes. I can see that. You haven't gone into it yet, then?"

"I wanted to speak to you about it first. Oh, darling," and she came to kneel before him, took his hands, "you're sure you don't mind?"

"No," he lied valiantly. "I knew, of course, that the time would come, sooner or later . . ."

Very much later, he told himself, as he drove to work next morning. And preferably not at all. He had awoken still feeling thoroughly disgruntled and the weather matched his mood: grey, lowering skies and a chilly wind.

In his office he scowled at the pile of reports awaiting his attention, riffled through them impatiently. It wasn't even as though there was anything particularly interesting on at the moment . . . With a sigh he opened the top folder, began reading.

A moment later he was on the phone.

"Where's Lineham?"

"Gone out to Nettleton, sir."

"What for?"

"Some woman making a fuss, sir. Name of . . . Pitman, sir. Marion Pitman. Apparently there's this old girl who's an invalid, a neighbour of Miss Pitman, and her daughter's disappeared."

"What d'you mean, disappeared?"

"Didn't come home last night, sir. The old woman . . .",

9

the sound of papers being rustled came clearly over the phone, "Mrs Birch, didn't find out until this morning."

"Probably out on the tiles," Thanet said. "What the devil did Lineham have to go out there himself for?"

"Miss Pitman was most insistent, sir. Apparently the daughter, Miss Birch, just isn't the type to . . . er . . . stay out all night. A middle-aged spinster, sir."

"Well, as soon as Lineham gets back, tell him I want to see him."

But Lineham did not return and half an hour later Carson rang through.

"Sir, DS Lineham's just been on the radio. That woman he was looking for, they've found her. Dead, sir, in an outside toilet . . ."

"Lavatory," growled Thanet, who didn't like euphemisms. Poor old girl, what a way to go . . .

"Murder, sir, he thinks," Carson finished eagerly.

In a matter of minutes Thanet was on his way. As he passed the desk he paused to say, "Manage to get hold of Doc Mallard yet?"

"Yes, sir. We're having to send a car for him. His has broken down."

"Don't bother. I'll pick him up. I have to pass his house anyway."

Mallard came hurrying down the path as Thanet drew up in front of the trim little bungalow into which Mallard had moved after his wife's death some years ago. Thanet had known him since childhood and was fond of the older man, patient with his moods, aware that Mallard's testiness was the result of his inability to come to terms with the loss of his wife. "It's as if half of me has been amputated," Mallard had once said to Thanet in a rare moment of intimacy. "And the half that's left never stops aching."

Thanet greeted him warmly, told him the little he knew of the reported murder.

"Lineham's already out there, you said?"

"Yes."

"Think he'll make it to the altar this time?"

10

Lineham was supposed to be getting married on Saturday. Thanet grimaced. "Don't know. I hope so, for his sake. He'll go berserk if it has to be put off again."

Detective Sergeant Michael Lineham was an only child. His father had died when Mike was six and Mrs Lineham had never remarried, had lavished all her love, care and attention on her son. Lineham had fought the first great battle of his life over his decision to enter the police force; the second was still in progress. Twice already the wedding had had to be postponed. On both occasions Mrs Lineham had had a mild heart attack the day before.

"Those attacks," Thanet said now. "They are genuine, I suppose?"

"Oh yes. No doubt of that. Brought on, I would guess, partly by distress over losing her son and partly by the subconscious desire to delay the wedding."

"So there might well be another one, this time?"

"Quite likely, I should think."

Thanet sighed. "I do hope not, for Mike's sake. And for Louise's, of course. She's a nice girl, but I can't see her putting up with these delays indefinitely. And who would blame her? Ah, this is where we turn off."

Nettleton was a small Kentish village of around a thousand inhabitants, a couple of miles from the centre of the ever-expanding town of Sturrenden, where Thanet was based. At one time it had been a completely separate community but over the last ten years the advancing tide of houses had crept inexorably over field and orchard until Nettleton had become little more than a suburb on the very edge of Sturrenden.

"At this rate the English village will be a thing of the past by the end of the century," muttered Mallard.

Nettleton, however, had still managed to retain something of its individuality, perhaps because the main Sturrenden to Maidstone road did not run through the centre of it. Mallard and Thanet looked around approvingly at the picturesque scatter of cottages on either side of the road, the black-and-white timbered building which housed the general shop and post office.

"Village school's gone, I see," said Mallard, gesturing out of the window.

It had shared the fate of so many of its kind and had been converted into a private house.

"One of the biggest mistakes they ever made," the doctor went on. "And now, of course, they're howling over the cost of transporting the kids so far to school. Typical."

"Here we are," Thanet said. "Lineham said to park in front of the church."

There were already several police cars in the small parking area. Thanet got out of the car, locked it and then stood frowning at a small crowd of sightseers clustered on the opposite side of the road around the entrance to a footpath which ran along the back of a row of terraced cottages.

"Ghouls," he muttered — aware, however, that the sudden tension in him, the flutter of unease in the pit of his stomach, had nothing to do with the onlookers. The moment he always dreaded was approaching. He had never admitted it to anyone, even to Joan, but he hated his first sight of a corpse, could never dissociate the dead flesh that he would have to handle from the living person it had so recently clothed. Other men, he knew, evolved their own method of dealing with the situation, erecting barriers of callousness, indifference or even, as in the case of Mallard, macabre levity, but he had never been able to do so. Somehow, for him, that moment of suffering was necessary, a vital spur to his efforts to find the killer. Without it his investigation would lack that extra impetus which usually brought him success.

He and Mallard crossed the road together.

"Move these people away," Thanet snapped at the constable on duty at the footpath entrance.

Preoccupied as he was with the coming ordeal, he and Mallard had walked on a few paces before it registered: in the knot of sightseers one face had been familiar. Whose was it? Thanet stopped, turned to look back, but the little crowd was already dispersing, drifting away reluctantly with their backs towards him.

Thanet shrugged, followed Mallard to the spot where a

12

second constable stood guard, at an open doorway in the ramshackle fence on their right. He peered in at a long narrow garden crammed with mounds of sand and ballast, planks, bricks, paving stones and bags of cement, then picked his way through the clutter to the little brick building tucked away in a corner, behind the fence.

Here Lineham was watching the photographers, who were already at work. They all moved back as Mallard and Thanet approached.

Thanet steeled himself, looked.

The bundle of old clothes, crammed into the confined space between the wooden lavatory seat and the door, resolved itself into the body of a woman, head slumped forward on to raised knees, face invisible. There was dried blood in her sparse brown hair.

Thanet took a deep, unobtrusive breath.

"Which shots have you taken?" he asked.

The photographers had been thorough.

"Better get her out, then," Mallard said. "It's impossible to examine her properly in there."

They spread a plastic sheet upon the ground and Lineham summoned the constable at the gate to help him. Together they stooped to ease the body out of its hiding place. It was not an easy task. Rigor had stiffened her and Lineham had to struggle to lift the upper half of the body sufficiently to enable the other man to manoeuvre the feet through the narrow doorway. Gently, they lowered her on to the plastic.

"Turn her on her side, for God's sake," said Mallard. "Looks like a bloody oven-ready chicken."

The bent head, knees tucked up to the chest and splayed feet did indeed look grotesque and the two men stooped hurriedly to obey the police surgeon's command.

Perhaps Mallard, too, resented the fact that the woman had been denied any dignity in death, Thanet thought, moving closer as the doctor squatted down beside the body.

The woman was, as he had been told, middle-aged — in her early fifties, perhaps? She was small, slight, and her clothes were drab: brown woollen skirt, fawn hand-knitted jumper, brown cardigan, sensible black lace-up shoes, worn and scuffed. Thanet's limited view of the side of her face gave him a glimpse of sparse eyebrows, muddy skin. There was a large mole sprouting hairs just above the jaw-line.

An unobtrusive little woman, Thanet decided. Unassuming and probably undemanding. And, above all, a most unlikely corpse. Women like this were not usually the victims of deliberate violence. Of a casual attack, a mugging perhaps, yes: that might, of course, be the answer here. If so, it would be the first crime of its kind in a village community in this area. There had been several cases in Sturrenden itself of late, but so far the villages had remained immune.

Thanet grimaced at the thought. Brutality against the old was a particularly repellent manifestation of violence. But in any case this explanation somehow didn't feel right. The victims of muggings were usually struck down and left to lie. Here, trouble had been taken to hide the body.

"This lavatory in use?" Thanet said to Lineham.

"No, sir. The house is empty. It's being done up by a builder, but in any case it has an indoor loo, has had for years."

"Any sign of the weapon?"

"Not yet, sir, no."

"What was her name? Birch?"

"Yes, sir. Carrie Birch."

"Carrie Birch," murmured Thanet. Insignificant though she may have been, Carrie Birch had been a person with her own hopes, fears and daydreams and she had had as much right as anyone to live to enjoy them.

I'll get him if I can, Thanet promised her silently.

14

2

Thanet shifted his buttocks into a marginally more comfortable position and resumed his contemplation of Nettleton. From his perch on the five-barred gate he had a clear view of the area which interested him, the area around the church.

At the beginning of a case he always liked to establish in his mind the geography of the place in which the crime had been committed. After that came the people and then . . . ah, then the part which really interested him, the relationships between them. Always, somewhere in that intricate web of attitude, emotion and interaction, would lie the truth of the murder. Who and where and how and why would slowly become evident as his understanding grew, as would the unique position of the victim in that web, murder the inevitable outcome of its weaving.

The row of terraced cottages in which Carrie Birch had lived lay at right angles to the road and almost opposite the church. They looked out upon open fields and in front of them a narrow lane wound its way to a cluster of farm buildings. The gate upon which Thanet was sitting was a hundred yards or so further on along that lane.

Behind the cottages ran a footpath which, according to Lineham, provided a short cut to the church from the far side of Nettleton. On the other side of that footpath and immediately opposite the church was the vicarage, an attractive modern house, brick and tile-hung in traditional Kentish style. The Old Vicarage on the other side of the road was a much larger and presumably therefore uneconomic building, and was the last house in the village. Between it and the church, in what must once have been its extensive grounds, had been built two relatively new modern houses, one a wooden Colt bungalow, the other a much larger and more opulent construction of brick, plastic "weatherboard" and generous expanses of glass.

Thanet already knew that Carrie Birch had lived in number four, Church Cottages, with her mother. Number one, next to the road, was occupied by a young couple and their baby; number two was being renovated, number three housed a family of four and number five an elderly woman. Not, Thanet thought, a particularly promising bunch of suspects. Perhaps someone more interesting might turn up. . . .

Suddenly aware that his buttocks had gone numb, Thanet slid down off the gate and began to rub them, grimacing at the discomfort. He began to walk back down the lane towards the cottages.

According to Doc Mallard, Carrie Birch had been killed between 9 pm and 11 pm the previous evening. She had been struck on the head with the traditional blunt instrument, but in his opinion it might not have been this blow which had caused her death. He was unwilling to commit himself before the post mortem, of course, but there seemed to be indications that she might have been suffocated. After the twelve or thirteen hours which had elapsed since her death the blueness of the features normally associated with suffocation had worn off, but some unpronounceable condition of the tiny blood vessels under the skin of her cheeks was apparently sufficiently marked to give him cause for suspicion.

It seemed possible then that the murder, even if not premeditated, had been deliberate; a blow on the head could be struck in anger, but subsequent suffocation was a very different matter.

An increasingly deafening roar from behind him made Thanet press himself back against the fence as a red tractor came trundling around the bend. Its driver grinned and raised a hand in salute as he rattled by. Thanet waved back.

The tractor turned left on to the main road and almost at once an ambulance entered the lane, pulled up in front of number four. Behind it came Lineham, walking swiftly. Thanet moved forward to meet him.

16

"That'll be for Mrs Birch, sir," Lineham said, gesturing at the ambulance. "There's no one to look after her now, so the social services have arranged for her to go into hospital. Do you want a word with her, before she goes?"

"Not at the moment, I don't think."

"Don't blame you."

Thanet looked at Lineham sharply. "What do you mean?"

Lineham shrugged. "I had a word with her earlier. Couldn't stand her, myself."

"Why not?"

"Oh, I don't know. I'd guess she ran that poor little woman off her feet and never once said thank you for it. All she can think of now is herself — what's going to happen to her. Why did Carrie have to go and get herself murdered, that's her attitude. Makes me sick."

It was unlike Lineham to be so vehement. Thanet made no comment, however, and the two men strolled on past number four as the ambulance men went up to the door and knocked.

"She last saw her daughter at just before nine o'clock last night, you said?"

"That's right," said Lineham. "Apparently Miss Birch had arranged with a neighbour, the Miss Pitman who rang the station this morning, to go and look in on Miss Pitman's father, who is also an invalid, while Miss Pitman was at the Parochial Church Council meeting. Apparently this was a regular arrangement whenever Miss Pitman was out in the evening. Miss Birch worked for the Pitmans in the mornings, too, cleaning and generally looking after the old man's needs. Anyway, Miss Birch settled her mother for the night before leaving and that was the last Mrs Birch saw of her. She went to sleep and when her daughter still hadn't brought her morning tea at half past eight this morning — she used to bring it at eight, regular as clockwork — Mrs Birch panicked. She tried shouting, ringing the little handbell she has in case she needed her daughter in the night, but there was no answer and in the end she managed to get help by banging on the wall between her bedroom, which is on the ground floor, and number three."

"Who lives there? A family of four, you said?"

"That's right. Name of Gamble. He's a fitter at Brachey's, on night shift at the moment. He was in bed and sound asleep by then and his wife and son had already left for work. His daughter Jenny was still at home, though, and she heard Mrs Birch banging on the wall."

"How did she get in?"

"The Gambles have a key to number four, in case of emergency."

"Is the daughter usually at home in the daytime?"

"No, she works in Boots in Sturrenden."

"Funny, leaving the spare key there, then, if there's usually no one except the father home during the daytime, and he's in bed. Why not leave the key with the other neighbour, the woman in number five?"

Lineham shrugged. "She's a bit of a recluse, I gather. Not the sort of person you leave keys with."

"What's her name?"

"Cox."

"Miss?"

"So far as I know."

They had reached the end of the lane now and turned to watch as a small procession wound its way out of number four: the two ambulance men, a bulky woman in a wheelchair and a second woman carrying suitcase and carrier bag.

"Who's that?" asked Thanet.

"Miss Pitman. She's been sitting with Mrs Birch until the ambulance came. When Jenny Gamble found that there was no sign of Miss Birch and that her bed hadn't even been slept in, she ran across to the Pitmans'. The Gambles haven't got a phone."

The two men stepped back against the fence as the ambulance edged its way past them and drove off in the direction of Sturrenden. Thanet looked with interest at the woman who was hurrying along the lane towards them.

"Miss Pitman?"

"Yes?"

Thanet introduced himself. "I'd like a word with you, if I may."

18

She was in her early forties, he guessed, a tall woman with untidy brown hair and a harassed expression.

She put a hand up to her forehead. "Yes, of course Inspector. It's just that . . . oh, dear, everything is haywire this morning. Poor Carrie, and then Mrs Birch. . . . And I really must see to my father, he's an invalid. Do you think you could possibly come over to the house with me? I must check that he's all right."

Her eyes, Thanet noted, were beautiful, large, velvet-brown and expressive. He took pity on her.

"Of course, Miss Pitman. But there's no desperate urgency. There are one or two things I must see to here. Why don't you go on and attend to your father and I'll be across later? The bungalow, isn't it?"

"That's right. Oh, thank you, Inspector. That's very kind. Do you want this? It's the key to the Birchs' cottage."

Thanet took the key with a murmur of thanks and watched her go. He firmly believed in the value of courtesy to the public. There were, of course, occasions when it was a complete waste of time, but on the whole he had always found that polite consideration elicited the highest degree of cooperation from witnesses.

"Come on," he said to Lineham. "I want to have a look around number four."

As they passed number two, however, a man erupted from the open doorway, hammer in hand. For a split second Thanet wondered wildly if Fate had decided to hurl the murderer into his arms, blunt instrument and all.

"'Ere," said the newcomer. "You in charge of this lot?" Tall and muscular, wearing tee-shirt and jeans, he was an impressive figure. Bright blue eyes glowered at Thanet from a face barely visible behind its luxuriant growth of hair.

"I'm in charge of the murder enquiry, yes," said Thanet calmly.

"Well, when am I going to be able to get at my stuff?"

"Stuff?"

"Been held up all morning, haven't I? While your lot's been poking around in the back garden. Bill and me wanted to get

19

on with them new partitions on the first floor this morning, and so far we haven't been able to do a bleeding thing.''

"I'm sorry that you've been inconvenienced," said Thanet, keeping his anger at the man's manner well under control, "but a woman has been killed, you know, Mr . . .?''

"Arnold," said the man, Thanet's mild tone having its desired effect. He looked suitably abashed. "Jack Arnold. Yeah, well, I know you've got to do your job, but I got to do mine, haven't I? I mean, time's money, isn't it? And there's little enough profit in these sort of jobs nowadays as it is.''

"I'm sure we can come to some arrangement," Thanet said. He turned to Lineham. "How are the men getting on in the garden of number two?''

"They should be almost finished by now. I'd have to check." Lineham's face was wooden and Thanet knew by experience that the sergeant was hiding his amusement with difficulty.

"If you tell Sergeant Lineham what you want, I'm sure he'll be able to arrange for you to have it.''

"Twelve eight-foots of three by two and two twelve-foots of three by two, and them big sheets of plasterboard," Arnold said promptly. "Thanks, Guv.''

"Perhaps you'd better go with the sergeant, Mr Arnold, and make sure you get what you want," Thanet suggested, seeing Lineham's eyes glaze. "When you've finished, Lineham, come along to number four, will you?''

"We can go through the house," Arnold said, turning away with alacrity.

"Just one or two small points," Thanet said quickly. "That outside lavatory. Was it ever used?''

Arnold turned back reluctantly, impatience in every line of his body. "No. There's a toilet in the house, see. The landlord had toilets and bathrooms built on to the back of all these cottages a few years back, before he decided to sell them off as they come vacant.''

"Are you working here alone, except for . . . er . . . Bill?''

"Most of the time, yes. But we sub-contract the special jobs like wiring and plumbing.''

"What time do you arrive for work in the mornings?"

"Eight o'clock."

"And you get into the house which way, front or back?"

"Front, always."

"Did either of you go into the back garden before the alarm was raised over Miss Birch's disappearance?"

"Naw. No reason to, see. We was finishing off taking out that old partition wall — the one we're wanting to get on with."

Thanet ignored the hint. "Did you know her?"

"The old . . . Miss Birch, you mean? Not really. Passed the time of day, that's all, when she went past in the mornings."

"What was she like?"

Arnold shrugged his massive shoulders. "Dunno. Quiet. Mousy type. Couldn't say, really."

"All right. Thank you." Thanet turned away.

At the gate of number four he hesitated, then walked back the few paces which took him to the other side of the narrow lane. He stood looking at the row of cottages. It was obvious, from here, which of them were in private ownership and which were still rented out.

They were Victorian, he guessed, built of ugly yellow brick with slated roofs. Except for the two end cottages which, he had noticed earlier, both had attic windows in the gable end, each had one window and a front door at ground level and two windows on the first floor. Number one, where the young couple lived, was spick and span, with gleaming white paintwork and a yellow front door. The downstairs sash window had been replaced by a curved bow window with small square panes, one or two of which were bottle-glass. A similar bow window had already been installed in number two, which Arnold was renovating, and in number three, where the Gambles lived. This house, too, looked well maintained. The other two, numbers four and five, looked dingy and neglected by comparison, the paintwork peeling, the roofs in poor condition.

It was interesting, Thanet thought, just how much could be learned about the occupants of houses just by looking at the curtains. Young Mrs Davies sported frilly net curtains, looped

21

back, the Gambles bright modern prints, the Birches traditional half-net curtains flanked by drab florals and the last house in the row, where old Miss Cox lived, full-length nets. Thanet looked thoughtfully at the latter before crossing the road again to let himself into number four.

The front door, he discovered, led directly into a small living room which was spotlessly clean but depressingly furnished in indeterminate shades of brown and beige. It was dominated by a large colour television set and in the most comfortable corner of the room, away from draughts and next to the gas fire, stood an upright armchair with padded seat and back and wooden arms, flanked by all the impedimenta of an invalid's day: footstool with neatly folded rug, round table cluttered with pill bottles, women's magazines, water jug covered with a folded tissue, jar of boiled sweets.

Behind the living room was old Mrs Birch's bedroom. An ancient iron range and built-in dresser testified to the fact that this had once been the kitchen. Now, the cooker, kitchen sink and cupboards were crammed into what was little more than a narrow passage leading to the new bathroom which had been built on behind.

Thanet did little more than glance at all this. What he was really interested in was Carrie's bedroom. The staircase, he discovered, was hidden away behind a door beside the head of the bed in the former kitchen. The stairs were steep and narrow and led to a minute landing with two doors. Thanet pushed open the one on his left. This bedroom was at the back of the house and had no doubt once belonged to Mrs Birch. A dressing table still stood under the window, its mirror spotted with age and clouded by neglect. The overflow from the cramped scullery appeared to have crept up here; vacuum cleaner, aluminium stepladder, sweeping brush and mop stood against the wall just inside the door.

The front bedroom, then, must have been Carrie's. Thanet opened the door with keen anticipation. What had she been like, that little mouse of a woman? Disappointingly, her room appeared to offer little enlightenment. It was clean and neat, drably furnished with brown linoleum and a threadbare rug

22

beside the bed. The green candlewick bedspread was bald in places, neatly darned in others.

Thanet crossed to the bedside table. The alarm clock had stopped at twelve fifteen, presumably because its owner had not returned to wind it last night. There was also a small round biscuit tin painted blue, a pair of spectacles and a paperback book. Thanet inspected the latter. *Victory For Love*, it was called, and the cover depicted an extravagantly beautiful girl gazing up adoringly into the face of a suitably square-jawed hero. So he had been right. Little Miss Birch had indeed had her daydreams, her escape-hatch from the narrow confines of her life. There was a small cupboard in the bedside table and Thanet opened it, peered in. It was crammed to the top with similar books.

The only incongruous feature of the room was a full-length mirror composed of mirror tiles stuck on to the wall beside the window. Thanet frowned, crossed to run his fingers over the satin-smooth surface. Why should Carrie Birch have taken the trouble to put up such a thing? She certainly hadn't struck him as being the sort of person to spend much time gazing at her own reflection.

Beside the fireplace there was a curtained alcove which presumably served as a wardrobe and Thanet went now to examine it. Yes, here hung Carrie's clothes, a much-mended and indescribably dreary collection. Just looking at them made Thanet feel depressed. What a miserable life the woman must have had, with only her paperback romances to relieve its tedium. What, then, could have singled her out for murder? Pure chance? No, he still couldn't believe that.

So, there must have been something.

He glanced again around the comfortless little room, his gaze lingering on the mirror. If Carrie had had a secret, it was not hidden here, it seemed. Unless . . .

He went back to the bed, lifted the mattress and ran his hand along the springs. His fingers encountered something hard and flat. With a surge of excitement he pulled it out. It was an oblong packet wrapped in brown paper and secured with an elastic band.

23

Fumbling in his eagerness he removed the band, unfolded the wrapping. Then he stared in disbelief at its contents.

It was a bundle of pound notes. Fifty at least, at a guess.

Carrie's savings, hoarded for a rainy day . . . or for some long-desired treat?

He put the bundle on the floor, grasped the edge of the mattress and heaved it aside.

Neatly arranged in a row right down the centre of the bed were many more similar packets. A swift examination confirmed that their contents were identical to those of the first and a rapid calculation produced an astonishing answer.

Little Carrie Birch had had almost a thousand pounds hidden under her mattress.

3

"Where the hell did she get it from?" Lineham's language, like his face, proclaimed his amazement; his mother did not approve of swearing.

"Your guess is as good as mine. Interesting, though, isn't it?"

"I'll say." Lineham grinned. "I bet her mother didn't know about this little lot." The idea obviously gave him pleasure.

"No. But the point, as you say, is, where did she get it?"

"Saved it?"

"It would have taken her years," said Thanet. "Cleaning isn't exactly the most lucrative occupation in the world. Besides, I should think her mother would have known what she earned down to the last penny, from what you say of her."

"She won it, then."

"How?"

"Football pools, sweepstake, lottery, premium bonds?"

"She'd have had to have some sort of written notification of a win on any of those. I can't see her keeping it from her mother."

"Stole it?" suggested Lineham.

"From whom? It's a sizeable sum not to have been missed. If she did, its loss would surely have been reported. You'd better check, I suppose. The only other possibility, it seems to me, is. . . ."

"Blackmail!" said Lineham, triumphantly.

Thanet nodded. "And in that case, of course, the question is, who was the victim?" Thanet walked across to the window and looked out across the fields. The red tractor was working in the distance and over to the left he could just catch a glimpse of the farm buildings, half hidden behind a clump of tall trees.

25

"Who owns the farm?"

"Man called Martin."

"Do these cottages belong to him?"

"I don't know. I could find out."

"Do that." Thanet turned away from the window. "Well, we'd better get on with it. You go and see what the neighbours have got to tell you about last night, if you can find any of them at home. And find out all you can about Miss Birch — what she was like, where she went, who she talked to, the usual sort of thing. Not a word about the money at the moment, though. I'll go across and have a word with Miss Pitman. She should have finished seeing to her father by now."

"What shall we do with all this?" Lineham nodded at the packages of pound notes.

"Leave it where we found it for the moment. We don't really want to cart it around with us all day and I should think it's most unlikely that the place'll be burgled, with the area crawling with coppers."

The two men replaced the mattress and left the house, Thanet locking the door behind him and pocketing the key.

"What happened to the key Jenny Gamble let herself in with this morning?" he said.

"That's it, I think. Miss Pitman kept it."

The two men looked at each other. "My God," Thanet said. "I'm slipping. Miss Birch's bag! Where is it? She wasn't wearing a coat, so I didn't think . . . For that matter, where *is* her coat, if she'd been out?"

"Perhaps she came back?" said Lineham.

"Better check," Thanet said. The two men went back into the house and made a quick but thorough search. Lineham found two empty handbags on the floor of Carrie's makeshift wardrobe, but there was no sign of one in use. A worn brown coat hung on the back of the scullery door.

"Looks as though this was the one she used most," said Thanet. He would have to ask Miss Pitman. "I'd give a lot to know where that bag is now," he said.

Outside again, "I'll start with Mrs Davies," Lineham said. "I'm pretty certain she's in."

As they set off down the lane Thanet experienced a prickle of unease between his shoulder blades. He turned around, expecting to see that there was someone coming along the road behind them, but the lane was deserted. He frowned, scanned the windows of number five. Had he seen one of the net curtains move? He couldn't be sure. The movement, if there had been one, had been very slight, glimpsed only on the very periphery of his vision. It would not, of course, be surprising if old Miss Cox was watching them. She must be aware that they would want to see her, would probably be looking out for their visit. Well, Lineham would be along shortly.

"What's the matter?" said Lineham.

"Nothing," Thanet said, walking on.

He and Lineham parted and Thanet crossed the road to the Pitmans' house, which was uncompromisingly called The Bungalow. Miss Pitman had obviously been looking out for him; the front door opened as he walked up the path.

"Do come in, Inspector. I'm sorry I was in a bit of a state, earlier." She stood back to let him pass. She had tidied her hair, put on a little discreet make-up and looked altogether more composed.

"Not at all. It must have been a very distressing morning for you."

The room into which she led the way overlooked the garden at the back and was light and airy, with large windows on both outside walls. The colours echoed the view outside. There was a grass-green carpet, a settee and armchair with loose covers in an attractive design of sprays of green leaves on an off-white background. The floor-length curtains were made of the same material and there were a couple of Victorian button-back chairs, one covered in cream, the other in a deep, muted blue. The large stone fireplace was flanked by ceiling-high book-shelves and the general effect was comfortable, attractive and unpretentious. Thanet felt immediately at home.

"Your father's all right?" he said politely.

"Oh yes, fine. He's eighty-two, you know, and needs quite a lot of care. He is badly crippled with arthritis and can do very little for himself now. I don't know what I'm going to do

27

without Carrie, I really don't. Oh, I'm sorry, that sounds so selfish. . . ."

"Understandable, though, if you relied on her." Briefly, Thanet verified the information Lineham had given him: Marion Pitman had arranged for Carrie to come in at about nine the previous evening to check that all was well with her father. He also learned that Carrie had never bothered to put on a coat to cross the road unless it was bitterly cold or pouring with rain, and that she had invariably carried an old black handbag. Marion herself had attended the PCC meeting at the vicarage, leaving the house at seven twenty-five and returning at ten fifteen.

"That was when the meeting ended?"

"No. It ended at ten, but I stayed on for a few minutes to discuss something with the vicar. I'm treasurer, you see."

"So most people would have left at ten?"

"That's right."

"And on your way home, did you see or hear anything suspicious?"

"I'm sorry, no. Since . . . since Carrie was found, I've thought and thought about it, just in case there could be anything relevant. But there was nothing."

"A pity. Miss Birch worked here every morning, I believe?"

"That's right. I teach part-time, you see, in a school for handicapped children in Sturrenden. Carrie's coming made that possible. It's not that my father needs constant attention, it's just that she was here if he needed anything. I don't like leaving him alone for long periods."

"Had she worked for you long?"

"Oh yes, for years. She first came when I was teaching full-time, it must be, oh, fifteen years ago now. She cleaned the house for me, two mornings a week. Then, as my father's health deteriorated, she came more often until eventually it was every morning. As I say, I don't know what I shall do without her."

"You got on well with her?"

"Oh yes. Of course."

Thanet detected some slight reservation in her voice.

28

"But . . .?" he said.

"Nothing." She gave a little, nervous laugh. "Really. I didn't see very much of her, of course, I was always out when she was here."

"Except in the school holidays."

"Well, yes."

Her reluctance intrigued him. "What was she like?"

"Carrie?" Miss Pitman looked away, out of the window, as if trying to catch a distant glimpse of the dead woman. "Quiet. Unobtrusive. Got on with the job. Undemanding. She didn't say very much, really."

"What did you talk about? On the odd occasion when you must have had a cup of coffee together, for example?"

"Nothing much. The weather. Village affairs."

"Nothing personal?"

"Not that I can remember."

"She never, for example, said anything about her relationships with other people?"

Miss Pitman looked startled. "Who, for example?"

"I don't know. I'm hoping you'll tell me."

"I don't think she knew many people, other than very casually. She worked for the Selbys two afternoons a week. They live in the Old Vicarage."

"Had she been with them long?"

"Ever since the Selbys came to live here, about five years ago. Irene Selby asked me if I could recommend a cleaning woman and although . . . I suggested she approach Carrie."

"Although?"

Miss Pitman shook her head. "Nothing."

"The Selbys are a big family?"

"No, just the three of them. Susan, their daughter, is seventeen and still at school. But it's a big, rambling house to manage alone."

"And Mr Selby?"

"Major. He's managing director of Stavely's."

Stavely's was a thriving timber yard in Sturrenden.

"He's standing for the County Council elections next month," she added.

29

"And how did Mrs Selby get on with Miss Birch?"

"All right, I believe. I'm afraid I couldn't really say. We've never discussed the matter."

"Can you tell me anything else about what Miss Birch used to do with her time?"

"She used to clean the church. But apart from that, nothing much. Her mother was very demanding."

"Did she ever complain about her mother?"

"No, never. But no one could help noticing how Mrs Birch treated her."

"Didn't she belong to any village organisations? WI for example?"

"No."

"You make her sound a pathetic little creature."

"Well I suppose she was, rather,"

"And yet," Thanet said softly, "I have the feeling that you had reservations about her."

"Reservations?"

Thanet said nothing, simply waited. But Miss Pitman merely gave that nervous little laugh again and shook her head.

"I can't imagine what you mean, Inspector."

Thanet could see that it was pointless to pursue the subject at the moment.

"Do you think I could have a word with your father now?"

Her laugh was a little too loud, explosive with relief. But there was genuine amusement in it. "You don't think I'd get away with keeping you from him, do you? He'd be furious. He may be frail but believe me he has all his wits about him and he's been looking forward to your visit all morning!"

Thanet grinned, stood up. "Then we'd better not keep him waiting any longer, had we?"

Old Mr Pitman was sitting up in bed, looking expectantly towards the door. This, too, was an invalid's room, but very different from Mrs Birch's. There was colour, light and evidence of much activity. The bedspread was scattered with books and newspapers and beside the bed there was a large Victorian mahogany tea-trolley, its three tiers laden with many more books, a radio, tape-recorder and rack of cassettes, boxes of slides, viewer, stamp catalogues and albums, magnifying glass, tweezers, scissors and a jar of felt-tipped pens.

The owner of all this ordered clutter looked alarmingly frail, the skin stretched taut over nose and cheekbones, hanging in loose folds about the neck. He had once, Thanet guessed, been a tall, strong man but now he was merely gaunt, shrunken and twisted sideways against the mound of pillows, as though it was impossible for him to sit upright. His hands, resting one on top of the other on the neatly folded counterpane, were blotched with the brown spots of old age, swollen and mis-shapen with his disease. The eyes which twinkled out at Thanet beneath the quiff of white hair, however, were piercingly alive and brilliant, a clear periwinkle blue. It was as though all the old man's life and energy were now concentrated in his mind, visible only through those penetrating blue orbs.

"Come in, come in," he said. "Sit down." And he nodded at an armchair set beside the bed. "Where I can see you properly."

"This is Inspector Thanet, father." Marion Pitman approached the bed and, in a ritual that was clearly so familiar as to be second nature to them, she put her arm around his shoulders and helped him to lean forward, plumped up his pillows and eased him back against them.

"Thank you, my dear," he said. "Now, off you go. The Inspector and I will do very well without you." But there was no sting to the words and he watched her fondly as she left the room. "She's a good girl, Marion," he said, when the door had closed behind her. "I don't know where I'd be without her. Well, I do, of course. In hospital. Though I sometimes think it would be much better for her if I could persuade her to let me go. It's not much of a life for her, you know, looking after an old wreck like me. However," he said briskly, "you haven't come here to talk about us. How can I help you?"

"I believe Miss Birch came here last night?" Thanet said. "Do you by any chance remember exactly what time she arrived and left?"

"Certainly. I've had plenty of time to lie here and think

about it this morning," said the old man. "She came in bang on nine o'clock — I'm sure of that because the news was starting." He nodded at a portable television set on a table pushed against the wall. "And she left a few minutes after it ended, say at nine thirty. I know that's so because I always like to listen to the news and it used to annoy me that she came just then — she always did, when Marion was out."

"Couldn't you have asked her to come earlier, or later?"

"I did hint, but to no avail. It was her mother, I believe. Like an alarm clock, that woman was. Though heaven knows, I shouldn't complain about that. When one's in this sort of situation it's all too easy to be thrown when one's little routine is disturbed. You wouldn't believe how easy it is to sin lying here in bed! The temptations are endless — to bad temper, self-pity, lack of consideration . . . It's so easy to justify one's lapses, you see, to think you have every right to indulge in them . . .' He grinned wickedly at Thanet. "Confidentially, I do allow myself the occasional self-indulgence, just for the pleasure of feeling guilty afterwards. It convinces me I'm still alive!"

Thanet laughed out loud. "I must remember that, the next time I'm tempted."

"But I mustn't waste your time, Inspector, must I? It's just that it's such a pleasure to see a new face, have a new audience. . . . You see how easy it is to slip? I'm doing it now! Please, do go on with your questions."

"I'd be very interested to know what you thought of Miss Birch."

"What did I think of her," said the old man ruminatively. Like his daughter, he looked away, out of the window, as if to recapture an image already blurred by the passage of time. Or was he simply trying to gain time while he thought up a suitable answer? Thanet waited with interest.

The reply, when it came, was a disappointment, echoing Marion Pitman's.

"Quiet. Unobtrusive. A good worker, and reliable. I don't know what we'll do without her."

And Mr Pitman had the same reservations as his daughter,

Thanet noted. He tried again. "But . . .?"

The old man did not evade the question nor did he answer it satisfactorily. "But I never really warmed to her. Mind, she had a very bad time with that mother of hers, so it's not surprising that she was so . . . reserved."

"What did you talk about, when she was here?"

"We didn't talk, not really. She had work to do, but apart from that our conversation was strictly about practicalities — what I wanted, needed and so on."

"Did she have any close friends, do you know?"

"Not to my knowledge. She led a very circumscribed life, you know. Whenever she wasn't working she was dancing attendance on her mother. I shouldn't think she'd ever been further away from Nettleton than Sturrenden in her whole life."

Thanet was being distracted and he knew it. But he didn't want to alienate Mr Pitman. An old man like this, with a lively, enquiring mind and considerable local knowledge might be a valuable ally. There were already questions crowding into Thanet's mind, but he wasn't ready to ask them yet. He wasn't certain that they were the right ones. Those, he knew, would emerge as the case progressed and then he would enlist Mr Pitman's help openly. He was sure that the old man would be delighted to cooperate. There was just one point, though . . .

"Was she honest?" he said, suddenly.

Mr Pitman looked startled. "Did she steal, you mean? Not to my knowledge. If she did, I've never heard a whisper of it."

There was something about that reply that was interestingly off-key, but Thanet decided not to query it. He rose. "Well I think that's all for the moment, Mr Pitman. May I come and see you again, if I think of anything else I want to ask you?"

The old man grinned. "I didn't think you'd need my permission. But in any case, I'd be delighted. I'll be keeping my eye on you all, of course."

Now it was Thanet's turn to look startled.

Mr Pitman nodded at the wall behind Thanet. On it there was a large convex mirror which reflected the road outside. Thanet half squatted until his head was on a level with

Mr Pitman's and alongside it, then looked at the mirror. The area which it reflected was surprisingly extensive, stretching from the new vicarage gate on the left to well past the entrance to Church Lane on the right. As Thanet looked, a familiar figure, slightly distorted by the curvature of the mirror but readily recognisable, emerged from the front gate of number five and started to walk down the lane towards the road: Lineham, his interview with Miss Cox over.

"So I see," Thanet said, straightening up.

A pity, he thought as he took his leave, that it had been dark last night when Carrie left the Pitmans' house. Mr Pitman would not only have seen where she had gone, he might even have seen the murderer.

4

The exterior of the Plough and Harrow in Nettleton was unprepossessing, its car park almost empty.

"Just our luck," said Thanet to Lineham. "The food'll be terrible, the beer unspeakable, by the look of it. Still, at least it should be quiet." He pushed open the door and they went in.

The two men had left their cars parked in front of the church and had walked down to the pub, which was at the other end of Nettleton on the main Sturrenden to Maidstone road. Thanet had enjoyed the short stroll. The temperature had risen several degrees and the sun was doing its best to break through the dense bank of cloud which earlier had so depressed him. His mood had lightened considerably now that he had something on which to focus his energies.

On the way he had filled Lineham in on the interviews with the Pitmans. Now he was eager to hear how Lineham had got on.

They bought pints of beer and the soggy tomato sandwiches which were all that the pub had to offer in the way of sustenance and settled themselves in a corner of the bar. The only other two customers were a middle-aged executive type in a dark blue suit, striped shirt and floral tie, and a pretty girl of about twenty. One thing about a place like this, Thanet thought — if you wanted to conduct a clandestine love affair, there wasn't much danger of being spotted.

He put his paper plate down on the red formica table and took a long swig of beer. Just as he had expected. Tasteless. He should have stuck to bottled.

"Well," he said. "What about you? How did you get on?"

"Nothing," said Lineham with a grimace. The Davieses had watched television all evening apparently, and had heard nothing, seen nothing, outside the walls of their living room.

Lineham had been unable to rouse anyone at number three. "If Gamble was there, he must sleep like the dead," he said sourly.

"I believe they do. Nightworkers, I mean. The seasoned ones, anyway. They just switch off. What about the old girl next door on the other side?"

"Mmmm?" Lineham's eyes were on the electric clock behind the bar and it seemed an effort for him to re-focus on Thanet. "Oh, Miss Cox. Nothing there, either." Lineham's eyes wandered back to the clock. It was twenty past one.

"Mike," said Thanet, "do you think you could keep your mind on the job, if it's not too much effort?"

Lineham started, flushed. "Sorry, sir. Look, would you mind if I just slipped out and made a quick phone call? There's a phone box outside, I noticed as we came in."

"Go on," said Thanet with resignation. "But be quick about it." Perhaps then he would have Lineham's full attention. He refrained from saying so with difficulty, watched the younger man as he half ran towards the door. Then he smiled, indulgently. Lineham probably wanted to give Louise a ring. Thanet well remembered how vital it had once seemed, when they were courting, to hear Joan's voice just for a few seconds, how the need would obsess him to the exclusion of all else. The thought of her, however, reminded him of his present dilemma and he frowned, took another swig of the flat beer. He would have to let her go, of course, but he didn't like the idea one little bit.

"All right?" he asked when Lineham came back, transformed.

"Yes, thanks. It's mother," Lineham went on, clearly feeling that some sort of explanation was necessary. "She wasn't feeling too well this morning and I just wanted to catch her before she goes up for her rest at half past one, to see how she is."

So his guess had been wrong. Nevertheless, Thanet could sympathise. With the wedding on Saturday and two fiascos already clocked up, Lineham must be watching his mother as if she were a time-bomb about to explode.

"You were saying, about Miss Cox," Thanet said.

This time Lineham gave his mind to the matter. "Ah yes. Funny old bird. Pathetic, really. She was in a real state when she opened the door. Shaking, all over."

"Perhaps she thought you'd come to arrest her," said Thanet jokingly.

"No," said Lineham, apparently taking him seriously. "I think she was just upset about Miss Birch and alarmed by all the activity. And I expect she's worried about how she's going to manage — she's got one leg in plaster and I gather that Miss Birch had been doing her shopping for her."

"If I know Marion Pitman," Thanet said, "she'll be making arrangements for someone to take that job over. Do you want another of those?" He nodded at Lineham's glass.

"No thanks. Do you?"

"Not on your life," said Thanet. "Let's go, shall we? No," he went on as they left the pub and began to walk back through the village, "I expect Miss Cox is just scared stiff, poor old thing. If you live alone and you've got one leg in plaster and the woman next door gets murdered, you're bound to wonder if you're going to be next, I should think. Anyway, she couldn't tell you anything useful?"

"Not a thing. She was in all evening, but she was listening to the radio — wireless, she called it. Would you believe, she hasn't got a television? And she had her machine going last night too, she said."

"Machine?"

"Sewing machine. That's how she makes her living, I gather. Making loose covers for Barret's."

Barret's was the largest department store in Sturrenden.

"Surely someone, at some point, must have seen or heard *some*thing,' said Thanet in exasperation.

"I don't know. It's not like a town out here. I get the impression everything closes down when it gets dark."

"Except the pubs, of course." Thanet stopped dead. "That's an idea. It's just possible that someone going either to or from the pub might have seen something. Send someone back down to the Plough and Harrow this afternoon to find out if any of last night's customers came from this end of the village. The landlord'd be sure to know the locals by name.

37

What do you think, Mike, d'you think our man — or woman, of course — is a local?"

"Oh, definitely," said Lineham at once.

"You sound very sure about it."

"Only a local would have known about that disused toilet," said Lineham with conviction.

"But if he was a local, why bother to hide the body at all? He must have known that Carrie would be missed by her mother within a very short time, and have realised that any sort of search would find her."

Lineham frowned. "A need to get her out of sight, fast, for some reason? Or panic, perhaps, because if he'd left her where she was the place would have given away his identity."

"Not so much *cherchez la femme* as *cherchez l'endroit*," said Thanet, who rather prided himself on his French.

"Er . . . yes," said Lineham, who had abandoned French after O level with a sigh of relief. "You mean, if we could find out where, we'd find out who . . .?"

"Precisely."

"Of course, it could have been a straightforward mugging."

"But in that case, why hide the body at all? Besides, if it had been muggers, they might have hit her on the head but I can't see why they would have bothered to finish her off afterwards, as Doc Mallard thinks likely."

"Unless she had recognised them. Which she probably would have done, in a small place like this, if they'd been locals."

Thanet shook his head. "I can't see it. It just doesn't feel right, somehow. Though I suppose we'll have to keep it in mind. You'd better get some of the men to check up on the whereabouts of the local talent last night."

"Right."

"She looked such an inoffensive little thing," mused Thanet. "And yet, there was all that money . . . I think we'll go and take a look at the other people she worked for, the Selbys. Though I imagine he'll be out at work at the moment. He's a local big-wig. He's standing in the County Council elections next month. Now *he*'d be a good subject for blackmail. He'd have a lot to lose — prestige, position . . ."

"What about the Pitmans, sir?"

"Most unlikely blackmail victims, I would have thought. Though I did feel that they were both holding something back, as I told you. Perhaps Marion Pitman had her fingers into Church funds . . . we'll just have to keep an open mind at present."

They were passing the Pitmans' bungalow now and Thanet raised his hand.

"Who're you waving at?" said Lineham, puzzled. No one was visible at any of the windows.

"Old Mr Pitman." Thanet explained about the mirror. "He's as sharp as a needle, doesn't miss a thing. I've a feeling he may be very useful to us, when I've a better idea of where we're going. Ah, here we are. Let's hope someone's in."

Neatly tacked up on a wooden notice board beside the front gate of the Old Vicarage was a blue-and-white Conservative election poster exhorting the population of Nettleton to vote for Henry Selby. Thanet and Lineham paused to study it. Selby had thinning hair, a toothbrush moustache and gimlet eyes. Only the eyebrows defied discipline, sprouting luxuriantly forward as if to compensate for the lack of hair on the top of the head and giving Selby the air of an aggressive Jack Russell.

Lineham voiced Thanet's thought. "He looks an awkward customer."

Was this the face of his adversary? Thanet wondered as they moved on.

Well screened from the road by densely planted trees and shrubs, the house stood at the end of a short but immaculately kept gravel drive which curved away around the side of the house, presumably in the direction of the garage. It was typical of the many vicarages which have been abandoned by England's clergy in favour of smaller, more convenient dwellings — big, rambling, not particularly attractive and no doubt very expensive to heat. Not, by the look of it, that the latter consideration would much concern the Selbys, Thanet thought. The place had the unmistakable aura of money: well-manicured lawns, weedless flower beds, shining windows, gleaming paintwork and a general air of well-fed smugness.

Thanet rang the bell and the succeeding silence was broken by the crunching sound of wheels on gravel. After a few moments around the corner of the house came a man pushing a loaded wheelbarrow. He was small and bent and had what Thanet felt was a distinctly appropriate resemblance to one of the gnomes beloved of suburban gardeners.

"You'll have to go round the back," he said, jerking his thumb and peering up at the two men from beneath the rim of a cap which looked as though it had been bought third-hand at a jumble sale many years ago. "Bell's out of order and She won't have heard you."

Interesting, thought Thanet, how he had managed to invest the pronoun with a capital letter.

Thanet thanked him and they made their way around the corner of the house to a door at the far end of the side wall. Thanet knocked once, twice and then, when there was still no response, put his head into the kitchen and called, "Mrs Selby?"

Here again there was evidence of money: streamlined units built of solid wood, ceramic hob, battery of electrical gadgets, ceramic tiles on walls and floor. The place, however, was in a mess, littered with dirty saucepans and unwashed dishes.

Thanet took a step inside and called again.

This time there was a response and a few moments later footsteps could be heard. A woman came into the kitchen, frowning.

"Mrs Selby?", Thanet said quickly. "Detective Inspector Thanet, Sturrenden CID."

"Oh," she said. "I thought I heard someone."

Thanet studied her as he introduced Lineham. She was small and fair, with a face in which middle age was definitely winning the battle against youth. The skin beneath the eyes was slack and puffy and the frown which Thanet had thought directed at himself and Lineham was a permanent feature, deep vertical creases scored between her eyebrows. And yet, he thought, she must once have been a pretty woman and she certainly hadn't given up on her appearance; her hair had clearly been freshly set and her clothes, a well-cut tweed skirt and matching cashmere sweater, were casually elegant. He shook the surprisingly large, strong hand she proffered and followed her along a wide corridor, through a spacious drawing room dominated by a grand piano and into a glass conservatory which had been built along one side of the house.

"Do sit down, Inspector." She waved a hand at the cane armchairs and began to transfer coffee cups and glasses from the low bamboo table on to a wicker tray. "If you'll excuse me, I'll just get rid of these. I shan't be a moment."

She disappeared through the door by which they had entered and the two men examined their surroundings. Joan would love this room, Thanet thought. It was all light and air and growing things. Against the house wall was a wide, raised flower bed edged with brick and overflowing with plants. Above them was trained an exotic climbing plant with variegated foliage and apricot-coloured, bell-shaped flowers.

"What a delightful room, Mrs Selby," he said, when she returned.

"Yes, isn't it? It's my favourite room in all the house. My husband says he thinks I would be quite happy to live in it all the time." She seated herself opposite him. "Now, what can I do for you, Inspector?"

Now that he had a chance to study her closely, Thanet could detect signs of tension. The knuckles of the hands clasped in her lap were white and there was a tiny, uncontrollable tic in her left eyelid. As he spoke she put up her hand as if to brush it away.

"We are investigating the murder of Miss Birch, of course," he said. "And naturally we are asking everybody in the neighbourhood if they noticed anything suspicious last night."

"You mean lurking strangers, that sort of thing," she said, with an attempt at a smile.

"Anything at all unusual," Thanet said.

She was shaking her head, a curiously regular, clockwork motion. "I'm sorry, I can't help you, Inspector. I didn't go out last night and as you will have seen when you came in, we are well screened from the road."

"Miss Pitman had to go to a PCC meeting last night and she arranged for Miss Birch to look in on Mr Pitman during the evening. Some of your upstairs windows overlook the

41

Pitmans' garden and there is a street lamp outside their house. Did you by any chance see her arrive or leave?"

"I'm afraid not. I was in here, watching television." She nodded at a small portable colour set which stood on a low table in one corner.

"Alone?"

"Yes. My husband arrived home just after ten — he'd been away on a business trip since last Thursday — and my daughter a few minutes before that." The eyelid twitched. "She spent the evening with a friend, in Sturrenden."

"And neither of them mentioned having seen anything out of the ordinary?"

"No. Certainly not."

"Is your husband at home now, by any chance?" Thanet was remembering the coffee cups.

"No. Though you've only just missed him, as a matter of fact. He came home for lunch, today."

"I should like to have a word with him, just in case he did notice anything unusual last night," Thanet said. "Will he be at home this evening, do you know?"

"I think so, yes."

"Good. Now, about Miss Birch. She worked for you two afternoons a week, I believe?"

"That's right. She should have come today, as a matter of fact. Hence the mess you will no doubt have noticed in the kitchen. Usually she sees to that."

"What was she like?" asked Thanet softly.

"Like?" Something moved in the depths of the blue eyes and was quenched. Mrs Selby made a vague gesture. "Oh, mousy. Insignificant. A good enough worker. She was a bit heavy-handed, but with a place this size one's grateful for any help one can get."

"Did you like her?"

She shrugged. "Well enough, I suppose. I can't say I ever gave much thought to the subject."

"You had no reservations about her, then?"

"Reservations? Well no, of course not. Why should I?"

But like Marion Pitman, Mrs Selby was lying, Thanet was certain of it.

"Oh, no reason," he said. "No reason at all. I'll call again this evening, if I may, to see your husband. Say, nine o'clock?" He rose and Lineham followed suit.

"By all means." Her air of relief was unmistakable and she stood up with alacrity. "I'll see you out."

"Well, what did you think of that?" said Thanet as he and Lineham walked away down the drive.

"Like a cat on hot bricks, wasn't she? Couldn't wait to get rid of us."

"I wonder why," said Thanet thoughtfully.

People on the whole do not enjoy being caught up in a murder investigation, and a certain degree of tension is understandable. Nevertheless, he thought . . .

"You think the Selbys are involved, sir?"

Thanet shrugged. "Too early to tell, yet. What puzzles me is that I have this feeling that they're all holding back about Carrie Birch, for some reason. And I just can't get a clear picture of her. She's like a negative that's too thin for printing." He made up his mind. "Look, I think I'll just nip down to Sturrenden General and have a word with the mother. You stay here. Send someone down to the pub, as I suggested, and get some enquiries organised about the local yobs, just in case it's a simple case of mugging after all. Try the Gambles again and then see if anyone's at home there." He nodded at the large modern house between the Pitmans' bungalow and the church. "I shan't be long, an hour at the most, I should think."

Perhaps, he thought as he drove towards Sturrenden, Mrs Birch might be able to enlighten him about Carrie. Or perhaps he was looking for something that simply wasn't there. Perhaps Carrie really had been as uncomplicated as people seemed to want him to think. He shook his head, a fierce, involuntary movement. No — muggers apart, simple uncomplicated people just didn't get themselves knocked on the head and then suffocated.

And then, there was the money. . . .

No, there was something about her that they were all covering up, he was sure of it. And he was going to find out what it was if it was the last thing he did.

5

"I'm afraid she's a bit disorientated," said the nurse as she led Thanet into the ward.

"What, exactly, is the matter with her? Medically, I mean?" he asked.

"A combination of things. Weak heart, diabetes . . . She had to have a foot amputated a few years ago. She really is not capable of looking after herself. As soon as there's a place at The Willows, she'll go there."

This was the first time Thanet had ever been in a geriatric ward. His father had died a mercifully swift death from a heart attack and his mother, at the age of sixty-five, was as sprightly as ever. He had seen much of the stuff of human tragedy in his work, but this place shocked him. These old people were sick, of course, any natural liveliness they might possess quenched by illness, but even those who were sitting out in armchairs beside their beds looked but half alive. Only their eyes moved, following Thanet and the nurse as they walked down the ward, and he felt that even this degree of interest arose only from the fact that they were moving objects in an otherwise stationary world.

It was unnerving, and he was relieved to reach his destination. Mrs Birch was seated in a wheelchair with a rug over her knees and Thanet's first reaction as he looked at her was one of astonishment. He had seen her before, of course, from a distance, when she had been wheeled out to the ambulance, but it had not been obvious then just how monstrously fat she was. Little piggy eyes sunk in deep folds of flesh peered out venomously at him as the nurse introduced him, and although he could feel pity for the woman's physical state it nevertheless aroused an unexpected revulsion in him; he could not help remembering Carrie's thin, bird-like body and he suppressed with difficulty the macabre thought that in some way Mrs Birch's bloated flesh had fed upon the dessicated body of her daughter, draining it of life and vitality. Certainly, unlike the other old women in the ward, Mrs Birch was very much alive.

" 'Ave you found 'im yet then?" she demanded, when he was settled upon the stool which the nurse pulled from under the bed.

"Not yet, no," he said, consciously gentle. He reminded himself that personal dislike was irrelevant, could only get in the way, warp his judgement and cloud his ability to think clearly. Besides, there was genuine cause for compassion in the woman's physical condition. Nevertheless, he found it difficult to believe what he was hearing.

"Trust Carrie to go and get 'erself killed like that," she said. "Typical. Born useless, that girl was." The bright little eyes dared him to disagree.

It was pointless to waste time arguing. He plunged straight in.

"Could you tell me what time she went out, last night?"

"Five to nine, wasn't it, same as usual when she goes to visit the old man."

"You're sure?"

The eyes sparked malevolence at his daring to challenge her.

" 'Course I am. Always like to be settled in me bed by five to nine, don't I? Light out at nine, on the dot."

"Did you hear her come back?"

Her eyes told him that she considered this a stupid question. "Asleep, wasn't I? Took me tablets, as usual. Asleep, always, by half past."

"So when your daughter went across to the Pitmans' house in the evenings, you never heard her come in?"

"No." A glint of satisfaction. "Trained her to be quiet, didn't I? Don't like me sleep to be disturbed."

Thanet subdued with difficulty the spurt of anger he felt on Carrie's behalf. Trained her, indeed! As if she were an animal! He had a brief, unpleasing vision of the dead woman creeping through the silent house, easing open the staircase door beside the head of her mother's bed, terrified to make a sound, while this monstrous woman lay snoring soundly only inches away from her.

"So you had no idea that she was missing until she didn't appear this morning?"

"S'right. Eight on the dot she used to come down to make me tea. Well, by half past I was wondering what was up. Rang me bell, shouted, not a sound. Thought she'd overslept, didn't I? In the end I banged on the wall with me stick and that Jenny from next door come over. Took long enough about it, too. Dead loss that lot are, noisy, you wouldn't believe. Telly going till all hours, pop music blaring . . ."

"You don't like them?"

"They're all right, I s'pose, apart from the noise. Keep themselves to themselves, that's all."

Scarcely surprising that the Gambles hadn't been exactly eager to be on close terms with a woman like this, Thanet thought. Who would?

"Noisy last night?" he said hopefully.

"Not too bad. Told you. Went to sleep. No, it was the other one who woke me up last night."

"Other one?" said Thanet, suddenly alert.

"Old maid next door."

Miss Cox, presumably.

"Calling that blasted cat of 'ers, fit to wake the dead."

Not the happiest of analogies in the circumstances, Thanet thought. "What time was that?"

" 'Ow should I know? Woke me up, that's all. And if I'm woke out of me first sleep I 'ave terrible trouble getting off again."

"Did you do anything about it?"

"What, f'r instance?" She gave him a withering glare. "What d'you expect me to do, like this?" And a pudgy hand reminded him of that overweight, diseased mountain of flesh.

"Call your daughter?" he suggested.

"Well I tried, of course I did. But she didn't answer. Stands to reason, don't it? She wasn't there. Thought she was asleep. Always did sleep soundly."

Or, thought Thanet, had developed a necessary deafness to her mother's night-time demands.

"So you really have no idea what time it was, when you heard Miss Cox calling her cat?"

"Told you. No. Didn't put the light on — thought it would wake me up even more."

A thought struck him. "Where was the calling coming from?"

She looked at him as though he were out of his mind. "Next door, of course."

"Was Miss Cox inside or outside?"

"Outside."

"You're sure?"

Again that withering glance. "Dead certain. That's why she woke me up, see. Must've been going down the garden path after 'im. Mad about that cat, she is. Went on and on and on."

"She can get about with that leg of hers, then?"

"When she wants to," said Mrs Birch darkly. "Of course, that didn't stop 'er getting Carrie to do 'er shopping. And ungrateful!" Mrs Birch leaned forward. "D'you know, with all that Carrie did for 'er since she broke 'er leg, she still didn't let 'er over the threshold!"

"Really?" Thanet was genuinely interested.

Mrs Birch shook her head ponderously, so that her jowls wobbled, "Typical, that is. Real old 'ermit, that woman is."

"Has she always been like that?"

"Far back as I can remember. Ever since that kid brother of 'ers was killed in the war. Doted on 'im, she did. Still, you gotta go on living, 'aven't you, no matter what happens." Mrs Birch scowled around at the ward, as if to say, Look at me, I'm surviving, aren't I? "But I did think when she got Carrie to do 'er shopping that she'd at least ask 'er in for a cuppa tea or something. I mean to say, it's only common politeness, isn't it?"

It was a real grievance, Thanet could see. No doubt Mrs Birch had been longing to know all the ins and outs of her neighbour's life.

"As if Carrie didn't 'ave enough to do, what with me to look

47

after and all 'er other jobs and all.''

"Other jobs?''

"Pitmans every morning. Selbys two afternoons, church two evenings. Peanuts she got paid for that, too.''

"For cleaning the church, you mean?''

"Yer.''

"Which evenings did she go there?''

"Tuesday and Thursday. But them Pitmans was worst of all. Thought that just because 'e'd been 'er old 'eadmaster, she could always be at 'is beck and call.''

"Mr Pitman?''

"Yer. 'ead of the village school 'e was, until 'e retired.''

In that case, Thanet thought, as well as Carrie herself Mr Pitman would have known some of the other people involved, way back. . . . "Well,'' he said, rising, "thank you very much, Mrs Birch. You've been most helpful.''

The currant eyes looked vaguely affronted, as though his thanks were anything but gratifying. What did I tell him that was so interesting? she seemed to be asking herself as she gave an ungracious nod and said goodbye.

Disorientated was a charitable way of describing her condition, Thanet thought.

The many eyes watched him dully all the way back down the ward and it was with a sense of relief that he left the hospital and took deep breaths of fresh air again. In the car he did not start the engine immediately but sat staring sightlessly out across the hospital car park which was now filling up. Visiting time was approaching, he supposed.

That woman! What a miserable life poor Carrie must have had, always dancing attendance on her mother. It must have been one long round of cleaning, running to and fro for her mother and more cleaning. No wonder she had needed that little pile of paperback romances to provide her with a temporary escape from the unremitting grimness of it all. But would that have been enough? Could Carrie, in some as yet undiscovered way, have needed to seek further excitement?

Thanet thought again about the money, and wondered.

He realised that he hadn't had a pipe since early morning

and began to fill one, absently, as his mind ranged back over the people he had met so far. Would any one of them be a good candidate for blackmail? He wouldn't have thought that the Pitmans were sufficiently well off to be suitable subjects, but of course the money could have been paid over quite a long period. The Selbys seemed much more promising. As he had said to Lineham, Major Selby had more to lose and, on the face of it, more money available. Thanet was looking forward to meeting him.

Meanwhile, there was work to do. He set off again for Nettleton. He wanted to see Miss Cox, partly because his curiosity had been aroused, partly because he wanted to check the time at which she had made her sortie into the back garden to look for her cat. She might very well have seen or heard something of which she did not realise the significance.

First, however, Thanet wanted to talk again to old Mr Pitman, fill in a little background information on all these people. Why hadn't the old man mentioned that he had been Carrie's headmaster, that he had known her since childhood?

This was the first question he put to Mr Pitman when he had settled himself in the armchair beside the bed. He tried not to sound too accusing but he needn't have bothered; the old man was quite unabashed.

"Because I knew you'd find out soon enough, Inspector," he said, a wicked glint in his eye. "And that then, of course, you'd have to come and see me again. Why should I deny myself the pleasure of a second visit by telling you everything I know at our first meeting? Just as a matter of interest, who told you? No," he added quickly, "let me guess." He was silent for a moment. "Could it have been the ravishing Hilda? Carrie's mother," he explained. "Ah, I thought so. What did you think of her, Inspector?" But it was clear that he didn't expect an answer.

"So you've known Carrie ever since she was a child? What was she like?"

"Plain, I'm afraid. Plain and not very bright. A most unprepossessing combination. And, of course, completely under her mother's thumb, as always." Mr Pitman sighed. "Poor

49

Carrie, the dice were loaded against her right from the beginning.''

"What happened to her father?''

"A rather nasty accident with some machinery at the farm — he worked for Mr Martin. Did you know that there is an exceptionally high risk factor in working as a farm labourer? Strange, isn't it?''

"No, I didn't. That's interesting. You'd think that a peaceful, rural existence would guarantee a long and healthy life, wouldn't you? How old was Carrie at the time?''

"Oh, quite young. Seven or eight, I suppose.''

"How did she get on with the other children at school?''

"She didn't. They just didn't like her. She was always the one who would be standing on the sidelines, watching. Pathetic little thing, really. And, as I said, so unprepossessing. Scrawny, unattractively dressed, hair in two little plaits so thin I'm afraid they always made me think of rats' tails. Not surprising, really, that the other children didn't take to her. And the situation was made worse by her attitude. Somehow you felt that she expected to be ignored, left out of things. It was that mother of hers, I'm sure of it. I expect Carrie was so used to being belittled at home that she didn't expect anything different at school.''

"You really do paint a pathetic picture of her, don't you? Strange, you know, earlier on I wouldn't have said you were, how shall I put it, quite so sympathetic to her.''

"Oh?''

"No.''

A brief silence. Then Thanet went on, "In fact, I felt that you had distinct reservations about her.''

"Did you now?''

"I did.''

Another silence. The old man obviously wasn't going to relent, Thanet decided. He sighed, tried a different tack.

"I suppose you knew the Coxes, too. I gather they've lived here all their lives as well.''

Mr Pitman pounced upon the change of subject with a relief he couldn't quite conceal. "The Coxes. Ah, yes. Now there's another unhappy case. Mrs Birch told you about it, I suppose?''

"Only the barest outline," said Thanet. "I'd be very interested to hear more."

"Yes, well, Matilda Cox — Matty as we always call her — was ten when her brother Joseph was born, and her mother died giving birth. It must have been a very bad time for her, poor kid. This was back in nineteen twenty-five, you understand, a couple of years after I came to Nettleton as Assistant Teacher."

A swift calculation told Thanet that Miss Cox must now be sixty-six.

"Anyway," Mr Pitman went on, "she seemed to compensate for her mother's death by turning all her capacity for love on to the baby. Her father was not a particularly affectionate man and God knows what he would have done with the baby if Matty hadn't been around. Anyway, she took the child over. Even brought the baby to school with her! There were several neighbours who offered to have him during the day, but she wouldn't agree and we all felt so sorry for her that the Headmaster agreed, providing that the child wasn't a nuisance."

"Extraordinary," said Thanet. "It could never happen today."

"System's so much more impersonal," agreed the old man. "Anyway, it seemed to work out very well. Matty looked after the house and the baby, left school at the earliest possible moment and devoted herself to bringing Joseph up. Inevitably, of course, she was over-protective and he had a hard time of it when he started school. Kids always know when one of their number is weak and it seems to bring out the worst in them. I'm afraid poor Joseph suffered badly from their teasing — and worse than teasing on occasion, too. It didn't do him any good, just made him retreat more and more into himself and that's how he grew up — shy, nervous, withdrawn. Disaster struck, of course, when he was called up in 1943." Mr Pitman broke off. "I'm sorry, perhaps I'm boring you. Is this the sort of thing you wanted me to tell you?"

"Exactly the sort of thing. Do go on, please."

"I was away at the time, in North Africa, but my wife told me about it. Matty's father was out in Africa too, but he was less fortunate than me. He was killed that year, and it was only a couple of months afterwards that Joseph got his papers. As you can imagine, Matty nearly went mad trying to get him exempted but she failed and off Joseph went. Into the RAF. And you can guess what happened next."

"Shot down?"

"Yes. In the Berlin raids, just before Christmas. Missing, believed killed. Everyone thought that Matty would go berserk, but she took it very calmly. Said she didn't believe he was dead. My wife said it was heartbreaking. Matty lived in daily expectation of his coming home. His room was kept ready at all times and week after week, month after month Matty would do her best on her miserable rations to keep up a supply of Joseph's favourite food in preparation for his homecoming."

Thanet pulled a sympathetic face. "I expect there were a lot of women who behaved like that."

"No doubt. And in some cases, of course, their patience was rewarded. But not in Matty's. And with her it was an obsession. Anyway, in the end she stopped, quite suddenly, about a year later. Mary, my wife, was surprised, thought that she would have kept it up until all the men had finished trickling back from the prisoner-of-war camps, but Matty didn't. Mary thought that perhaps it was some sort of defence against disappointment — better to hope for nothing and be overjoyed than to live on a knife-edge all the time and be doomed to perpetual disillusion. But it changed her — Matty, I mean. She just withdrew into her shell and she has scarcely emerged from it since. Never goes out, except to do her shopping, never, ever asks anyone in. Not that she ever was a particularly sociable type but now, well, she's a total recluse. I just don't know how anyone can live like that."

"My sergeant says she's very shaken, over the murder."

"She would be. Not that she was on close terms with Carrie or with anyone else, for that matter. But an event like that, happening right next door, must have a pretty cataclysmic

52

effect on a life like hers, withdrawn as she has been from reality for, oh, it must be nearly thirty years now."

"Have you any ideas about who might have killed Carrie?"

The old man shook his head. "But then, you see, if it was someone local — and I think it must have been, don't you? — I wouldn't, would I? After all, one is bound to find it near-impossible to suspect people one has known for years."

"What makes you say it must have been someone local?"

The old man sighed, then listed all the arguments which Thanet had already worked out for himself.

"But you really have no suspicions?"

Mr Pitman folded his lips in a stubborn line.

"You said you found it near-impossible to suspect people you had known for years. Who were you referring to?"

The old man described a tight circle in the air with one of his misshapen hands. "Carrie's life was very circumscribed, you know."

"Yes. So you're talking in particular about . . .?"

A shake of the head. "It's no good, Inspector. This is where I dry up. Facts, past history I will give you, yes. But gossip, speculation about my neighbours, no."

"But if you do think of any relevant facts . . . you will let me know?"

"I won't lie to you, Inspector. But I can't guarantee to volunteer information if I am not sure of its relevance."

"But if you are sure?" Thanet said, quickly.

"Then I'd have to think about it. I do realise that this is a murder investigation, that it is my duty to help you in any way I can."

And with this assurance Thanet had to be content.

6

Thanet watched appreciatively as the driving door of the scarlet MGB opened and a pair of long, slim legs appeared. Not many women could extricate themselves as gracefully as this from a car like that, he thought with admiration.

The rest of the woman matched his first glimpse. She was, he thought, a real stunner: curves in all the right places, long, very dark hair which curled with disciplined abandon about the pale oval of her face, delicately modelled nose, really beautiful dark eyes and white, even teeth which were now revealed in the tentative half-smile she gave Thanet as he advanced upon her.

As he had reached the gate of the Pitmans' bungalow, the MGB had turned into the driveway of Latchetts, the modern house next door, and he had followed it up the drive. If the woman had been out, Lineham might well have missed her when he called earlier.

"Detective Inspector Thanet, Sturrenden CID," he said. "Did my sergeant call to see you, this afternoon?"

"Joy Ingram," she responded, the smile a shade more positive now. "I'm afraid I've been out since mid-morning."

Now that he was closer he could see that her beauty was marred by the frown lines on her forehead and that she was considerably older than he had originally thought: in her late thirties, probably, he decided.

"You will have heard about the murder?" he said.

"Yes," she said, and the frown lines deepened. "Poor Miss Birch. What a terrible thing. Who on earth could have wanted to kill an inoffensive little creature like that?"

"Naturally we are asking everybody in the area if they saw her at all last evening."

She shook her head, slowly. "I'm afraid not."

"She must have passed your house, you see, twice. Once at about nine, on her way to the Pitmans' next door, and again when she left there, at nine-thirty. You're sure . . .?"

"No." Her voice was firmer now. "We didn't see her, I'm sure of that."

"Your husband was at home?"

"Yes. Yes, of course. Why do you ask?" It was as if her concentration had suddenly sharpened by several degrees.

"You said, 'We'."

"Oh . . . oh, I see. Yes." She turned, stooped to reach for her handbag which lay on the passenger seat. Then she slammed the car door with an air of finality. "Well, if that's all, Inspector . . ."

"What about your husband?" he persisted.

"What about him?"

"Could he have seen anything?"

"I'm sure he didn't." She slung the bag over her shoulder, half turned, as if to walk towards the house.

"You're certain he didn't look out? Either then or later?"

"Inspector." She swung back to face him squarely. "My husband and I were in all evening. Together. The curtains were drawn and after dinner we watched television. Then we went to bed. I'll leave the rest to your imagination. Now, if you'll excuse me. . . ." And without waiting for an answer she marched towards the front door, did not look back as she took the key from her handbag, let herself in.

After the door had closed Thanet stood gazing thoughtfully after her for a moment or two before crossing the road to Church Cottages. Her reaction at the mention of her husband had been distinctly interesting. He was content to let the matter rest for the moment, but he thought that a visit to the Ingrams this evening might perhaps be fruitful. He had to come out to Nettleton anyway, to see Major Selby; he could kill two birds with one stone — no, three, he corrected himself. If the Gambles were out all day, he would probably have to see them this evening too.

He walked up the front path to number five with a certain degree of anticipation. Matty Cox was an eccentric and he enjoyed eccentrics. Obviously she couldn't care less about appearances. All the other gardens of Church Cottages were trim and well kept but this one had long been neglected. The bricks in the path were green with algae and many were broken, clumps of grass thrusting their way up through crumbling mortar. A few sad daffodils almost obscured by long grass still struggled vainly to brighten the sour little plot but otherwise nothing flourished but grass and weeds.

Nor did Miss Cox bother with the exterior of the house; the paintwork couldn't have been washed in years and the windowpanes were thick with the winter's grime.

There was no immediate response to his knock and he waited several minutes before knocking again. Matty Cox, after all, had a leg in plaster and he must allow her time to get to the door. There was still no sound within, however, and this time his knock was more peremptory. Come on, my beauty, he thought, I know you're in there.

With a roar the red tractor turned into the lane from the main road and rattled past on its way back to the farm, the driver lifting a friendly hand. Thanet waved back, then turned to knock again, only to find that the noise made by the tractor had drowned the sound of the door opening.

Miss Cox did not fit his image of her. He had expected someone small, plump, motherly; a shy, retiring little woman with a disillusioned, embittered face. But this woman was tall, almost as tall as he. And very unfeminine. Her face was square, her jaw heavy and her coarse grey hair was short and straight, held back on one side by a hairgrip. She probably cut it herself, he decided, noting its uneven length, rather than expose herself to the cheerful chattiness of a hairdressing salon. She wore no make-up and her clothes heightened the masculine effect — baggy brown corduroy trousers and checked shirt. Only the heavy, drooping breasts straining against the buttons of the shapeless cardigan betrayed her sex.

"Miss Cox?"

The woman did not reply, merely waited, leaning heavily on a walking stick held in her left hand. Her right gripped the edge of the door, effectively barring any move he might have made

56

to enter the house. Intentional or not? he wondered, his curiosity whetted. To think that no one had entered this house for almost thirty years . . .

"Detective Inspector Thanet, Sturrenden CID," he said. "I believe my sergeant came to see you this morning."

She nodded, opened her mouth. Thanet waited but still she did not speak and after a moment he said, "I'm sorry to trouble you again, but there is one small thing . . . I went to see Mrs Birch at the hospital this afternoon, and she tells me that she heard you calling your cat last night. She thought the sound came from outside the house . . . Were you outside last night, looking for him?"

Her hand on the door slipped an inch or two and the stick wobbled as she shifted her position slightly. She cleared her throat.

"It was the wind," she said. Her voice was hoarse. From disuse, he wondered?

"The wind?" he repeated blankly.

"It blew the door to, shut Tiger in the shed."

As if on cue a large tabby cat emerged from the house, sat down at Miss Cox's feet and fixed Thanet with an unwinking stare.

It was almost, thought Thanet fancifully, as if it had decided that its mistress needed some moral support.

"I see," he said. "What time was this?"

"Ten o'clock."

"It was ten o'clock when you put him out?"

A little, impatient shake of the head. She seemed to be more at ease now. "Ten o'clock when I missed him. I always puts him out at five to ten, see. He's out five minutes, then I opens the door and he comes back in. Last night he didn't." For her, it was a long speech.

"So what did you do?"

"I calls for another minute or two, then I puts on me coat and goes to look for him."

"And you found him in the shed?"

"S'right."

"Where is this shed?"

"Bottom of the garden."

"You managed all right, with your leg?"

"I got me stick. I managed."

"And it would have taken you how long, to go down the garden, find him and get back to the house?"

The effort of standing was clearly beginning to tell upon her. The knuckles of the hand gripping the stick were white with strain. She frowned. "Dunno."

"Try to think, please. It could be very important."

She looked at him sharply, then down at the cat. Tiger appeared to have lost interest in the proceedings. He was now washing himself, one leg stuck up in the air in a position which looked anatomically impossible. "Ten minutes?" she said, at last.

"Now," he said, "I want you to think very carefully indeed. While you were out in the garden, did you hear anything? Anything at all, I mean?"

It was a long shot, of course. Carrie had been killed between half past nine, when she had left the Pitmans' house, and eleven — give or take a little. It was too much to hope for, that the murder should have taken place during the only few minutes when someone in the neighbourhood was actually outside the house, not glued to the television set. Still . . . he awaited her answer eagerly.

"What sort of thing?"

"Anything. Anything at all."

She frowned. "It was too windy. I told you, it was blowing hard."

Damn that wind, he thought, remembering how blustery it had been last night.

"You're sure?"

She nodded, clearly hoping that the interview was at an end. Thanet sighed inwardly. Another blank. "Well, thank you very much, Miss Cox. If you do remember anything you might have heard, though, please let me know. My men'll be about all day and would be glad to take a message."

Already Tiger had whisked inside and the door was closing. Thanet turned away. So even that slender hope was now gone.

He really seemed to be getting absolutely nowhere. It was all vague suspicions, feelings. . . . What he needed was some satisfyingly positive lead, something he could really get his teeth into.

He scowled, looking about him for a focus for his irritation. Where were all those men he had mentioned to Miss Cox, anyway? There wasn't a policeman in sight. Thanet set off down the lane, at a brisk pace. At the corner he almost collided with Lineham.

"Where the devil have you been?" he snapped. "And where are all the others?"

"Sorry, sir," said Lineham defensively. "But we've only been carrying out your instructions. Bentley and Carson are checking up on the local yobs and the others are split between doing a house to house and searching the back gardens of Church Cottages."

"No sign of the weapon yet?"

"None, sir, so far. Nor of the handbag. I've been up to Church Farm to see Mr Martin — you wanted to know if he owned the Cottages."

"And does he?"

"Yes, sir. But it looks as though he's in the clear for last night. He was at a charity dinner in Sturrenden and we can easily check on that."

"Ah well," Thanet said. "It was a very long shot anyway. I can't really see a prosperous farmer bumping off the daughter of a crippled tenant just to gain vacant possession, can you? Look, let's go and sit in the car for a few minutes."

They waited while a laden articulated lorry went grinding past them.

"Ridiculous allowing monsters like that on roads like these," said Thanet. "The truth is, Mike," he went on as they crossed the road towards the church, "I just don't feel we're getting anywhere. It's all bits and bobs of useless information." Quickly, he gave Lineham a summary of what he had learned from Mrs Birch and old Robert Pitman.

"Miss Cox didn't say anything to me about going out last night to look for her cat," Lineham said, when Thanet had finished.

"I suppose she didn't think it sufficiently important. Anyway, she swears she didn't see or hear anything unusual while she was in the garden and I really can't see that there's any reason to disbelieve her. Did you go down to the pub, by the way?"

"Yes. The landlord says that the only person he remembers coming in from this end of the village was Mr Ingram. He . . ."

"Ingram?"

"Yes." Lineham raised his eyebrows at the surprise in Thanet's voice. "He lives in that . . ."

"Yes, yes, I know where he lives. It's just that I saw his wife just now — I gather she was out when you called earlier — and she swears that they were both in all evening."

"Does she, now?"

"The landlord's sure of this?"

"Certain. Apparently the pub was fairly empty last night — the weather wasn't good, if you remember. It was very windy. He says Ingram came in at around ten — he couldn't be more precise — and stayed for about half an hour. He was in a pretty grim mood apparently. Had four double whiskies and was very unsociable."

"More and more interesting," mused Thanet. "I think I'll pay Mr Ingram a little call this evening."

"Will you need me, sir?"

"I should think I could just about manage without you holding my hand," Thanet said with a grin. "Why?"

'Well I had promised Louise to give her a hand with a bit of decorating we wanted to finish off before Saturday, but of course if you want me . . ."

"So long as I know where to find you," said Thanet. "You go ahead with your plans. You only get married once." If you manage to get married at all, he added silently. "How are the others getting on with checking the whereabouts of the local talent last night?"

"They're waiting for them to get home from school," Lineham said. "There are four possibles, apparently, and they all go to Littlestone Comprehensive and come home on the school bus. It gets to Nettleton about four, so Carson and Bentley should be finished some time in the next hour."

"Good. Well I think I'll go back and get started on reports. There's not much more I can do here at the moment. You hang on until you've heard what they've got to report. If there's anything interesting, I'll come back out. If not, you can get off home."

"Right," said Lineham, getting out of the car. "Thank you, sir."

Thanet was still hard at work on his reports when Lineham rang an hour later to say that it looked as though all four youths were in the clear. They had, they claimed, been to a disco in the next village where they were all well known. Their story would be checked, of course, but it didn't look too hopeful.

The news didn't surprise him, thought Thanet as he put the phone down. For local youngsters, Carrie Birch would scarcely have seemed a fruitful target. Unless there had been any rumours about money in the house? But no attempt had been made to break in. No, Carrie's death had been no random killing, he was sure of it, and sooner or later the real reason for her murder would become clear.

He hoped.

7

Bridget and Ben were already in bed but the sound of Thanet's key in the front door brought them both thundering down the stairs with demands for a story and in the resulting confusion any constraint between Thanet and Joan passed unnoticed.

"Go back up to bed this minute!" said Joan, emerging flushed from the kitchen.

"Up you go," said Thanet, with a playful slap on each small bottom. "I'll be up in a minute." He gave Joan a kiss. "Hullo, love."

"Better go straight away," said Joan, disappearing into the kitchen. "Supper's nearly ready."

After an instalment of *Paddington* for Bridget and one of *Mister Clumsy* for Ben, Thanet returned downstairs.

Supper, as usual, was first-rate: chicken fricassee with savoury rice and french beans, followed by home-made blackberry ice-cream. How long would it be, Thanet wondered gloomily, before such delights were a thing of the past?

They talked, as usual, about their day's activities. Thanet had always been careful not to exclude Joan from his work. His theory was that the resentment and bitterness felt by many police wives over the demands of their husbands' work could be avoided if they felt that they were not being excluded from it. For Joan and himself this approach had always seemed to work but now he found himself questioning its value. Clearly, it left her unsatisfied. She listened as eagerly as ever to his account of the day's progress, asked pertinent questions, as usual, but underneath Thanet was aware of new reservations in her. Or were they in himself? He wasn't sure. The fact was, they were there.

"What about you?" he said at last. "What have you been up to?"

"Oh, nothing much." Her mouth tugged down at the corners. "Ironing, cleaning. Took Ben to the playgroup this morning, fetched him home again." She shrugged. "Just the usual."

Not a very inspiring list of activities, he thought guiltily, assessing them in the light of Joan's projected foray into the world of work. Especially when one considered that they were repeated over and over again, day after day, week after week, year after year. Many of them, naturally, were centred around the children, especially Ben, and for the first time he really thought about how it would be for her when Ben went to school.

Boring, he decided guiltily. Condemned to such an existence himself he would have gone quietly mad.

"Look, love," he said. "I've been thinking about what you said last night . . ."

The eagerness in her face as she looked up heightened his guilt.

"Yes?" she said.

"I meant it, you know. You go ahead, sound out the position. Make enquiries, find out the sort of thing you'd enjoy." But the false heartiness in his tone did not deceive her and she bit her lip, glanced away from him.

She shook her head. "It's no good, Luke. I can see you don't like the idea."

He could not bring himself to lie again, knowing that in any case he could not do it with conviction. "Look," he said, leaning across the table to take her hand, "all right, it's true, I can't say I'm keen. At the same time I know it's unreasonable to expect you to stay cooped up in the house for the rest of your life. So I mean it. You go ahead."

But her hand beneath his lay lifeless, unresponsive and again she shook her head. "What's the point, if you're so much against it?"

"But I'm not so much against it, as you put it," he said, withdrawing his hand in exasperation. "I just like things the way they are, that's all. Is that so wrong of me?"

"No of course not," she said quickly, "but — oh, darling,

63

don't you see? I just don't want to do it if you're not whole-heartedly behind me.''

"So what do you want me to say?'' he cried. "You want me to lie, is that it? To say, Yes, go ahead, marvellous, I'd love to have a working wife, to come home to an empty house and have latch-key children. Is that what you want? Well, I can't and that's that. Go ahead if you wish, and I'll back you to the hilt, you know that. But don't expect my approval because in all honesty I can't give it.''

She stared at him for a moment, eyes dilated and then, with a little choking sound of distress, she got up and ran from the room.

Thanet half rose to follow her and then sat down again. What was the point? He'd been honest with her, hadn't he? Told her how he felt? And told her to go ahead when it was the last thing in the world he wanted. What more did she expect?

Scowling he rose, began to clear the table. He carried some of the dishes into the kitchen, put them down on the table and then, with a sigh, started up the stairs.

As he had expected, she was lying face down on the bed, still in tears. Suppressing a sigh of exasperation he sat down beside her, put his arm across her shoulders. "Joan,'' he said. "Come on, love, cheer up. It's not the end of the world, you know. I'm sure we'll work something out.'' He thrust a handkerchief into her clenched fist. "Here, blow,'' he said.

Obediently she raised herself on her elbows, mopped at the tears, blew her nose. Then she rolled over on to her back. She avoided looking at him, however, covering her swollen eyes with the back of one hand.

"That's better,'' he said, smiling.

"It doesn't solve anything, though,'' she muttered.

"But honey, what do you want me to do? I can't change my feelings, can I?''

"Nor can I,'' she said, with a touch of defiance.

"I know.''

"There you are,'' she said.

"What?''

"It's going to be a barrier between us.'' And to his dismay, the tears began again.

"Darling," he said, putting his arms around her and lifting her up to hold her close against him. "Don't. It'll only be a barrier if we let it."

"But how can we prevent it?" she murmured into his shoulder.

"There'll be a way," he said, with a confidence he did not feel. "You'll see."

She pulled away from him then, tried to smile. "I only hope you're right," she said. She swung her legs over the side of the bed, stood up and walked to the dressing table. "What a mess!" she said, peering into the mirror. She picked up her hairbrush, began to tug it through her mass of fair curls. "What time do you have to go?"

"Now, I'm afraid," he said, glancing at his watch. It was almost half past seven. "I've got three calls to make this evening." He crossed the room to stand behind her, put his arms around her. "Feeling better?" he said, dropping a kiss on the nape of her neck where the hair curled softly into a little point.

She put down the brush, turned. "Yes," she said. "Sorry."

They kissed with the ardour of a sincere desire for reconciliation, but Thanet was aware that underneath nothing was resolved. The problem would rear its ugly head again and again until . . . what? Mentally he shrugged. Time would no doubt bring some sort of resolution, some compromise equally unacceptable to both. Shocked at his own cynicism he released her. "I'd better be off, then," he said. "I shan't be too late, I hope."

It was equally shocking to experience a sense of relief as he shut the front door behind him. Usually, if he had to go out in the evening, he left Joan with reluctance. As he drove back to Nettleton, however, he managed, with an effort, to slough off his domestic problems and focus his mind on the evening ahead. He found that he was looking forward to it, and particularly to the interview with the Ingrams. True, there was no reason whatsoever to show that either of them had been involved with the murder, but Mrs Ingram's lie had somehow

65

made him feel fractionally more optimistic. It was only a tiny lever, but if he could wield it correctly, he might just manage to open up a crack in the wall of silence which he felt these people were building around Carrie Birch.

There were already several cars parked in front of the church and the lights were on in the building itself. It was a clear but moonless night and after locking the car Thanet stood quite still for a few minutes, adjusting to the darkness. There was a dim light on in the lychgate and a little street lamp in front of the Pitmans' bungalow, but to Thanet's town-orientated gaze it was practically pitch dark. Across the road the footpath at the rear of Church Cottages was in total darkness. Had there been a moon last night? He ought to check.

Pausing only to note with satisfaction that the lights were on in number three, where he hoped later to see the Gambles, Thanet picked his way carefully up the drive of Latchetts. He wanted to tackle the Ingrams first.

The curtains were drawn across the huge front windows but as Thanet approached the front door he could hear the sound of angry voices. He soon traced their source: a tiny window set into the wall at eye level in the shallow portion of wall which projected forward at right angles to the front door. It was obviously used for ventilation and someone had forgotten to close it. Thankful now for the concealing darkness Thanet pressed himself against the house wall and listened.

". . . bloody stupid!" That must be Ingram. And furious, by the sound of it.

His wife's response was only a murmur, her words, muffled probably by thick curtains, indistinguishable. By her tone of voice, though, she was on the defensive.

"Well of course they're bound to find out," said Ingram angrily. "This is a murder investigation, isn't it? And in a murder investigation everyone but everyone even remotely connected with the victim is put under the microscope."

Mrs Ingram obviously protested, for her husband went on, "*I* know there wasn't any bloody connection, *you* know there wasn't, but *they* don't, do they? And you can be damned sure they'll try to find out. And if anyone's caught lying — don't

66

you see? Even if they're innocent, it looks bad. Why the hell couldn't you simply have told him the truth?"

"How could I, when I didn't know what it was?" This time Mrs Ingram's voice was audible. She, too, was getting angry.

"And just what the hell do you mean by that?"

"What I said!" she snapped. "That I didn't know what the truth was. All I know is that we had a row, you stamped out of here at about a quarter to ten and you didn't come back until about half past. Oh, I know you *said* you'd been to the pub . . ."

"And what the devil do you think I'd been doing? Bumping off that poor little woman across the way?"

Her reply was inaudible, but he was obviously dissatisfied with it.

"No, come on, tell me. Just tell me, will you? Precisely what do you think I was doing in that three quarters of an hour?" His anger had reached its zenith now and inevitably his wife's flared up to match it.

"How should I know?" she screamed at him. "Having it off with that cow Marion Pitman, probably!"

From the dead silence which followed Thanet deduced that Ingram's astonishment matched his own.

Then, unexpectedly, came laughter. "Marion Pitman . . ." Ingram spluttered. "Marion Pitman . . ."

"I've been watching the pair of you for months," Mrs Ingram went on, her voice still raised to make herself heard over his continuing laughter. "Don't think I didn't know what you were up to!"

The laughter stopped abruptly. "Look, Joy," said Ingram, his voice suddenly very cold, "you'd better stop this nonsense at once. There never has been, is not and never will be anything between Marion Pitman and myself."

"Amen," mocked his wife. "You expect me to believe that?"

"Believe it or not," he said. "It's true. I like Marion well enough, she's a very nice woman, but that's as far as it goes."

"What about all the little trips next door?"

"What little trips?"

Thanet had heard enough. He wasn't interested in a purely domestic quarrel and it was all too obvious now where it was leading. By the sound of it Mrs Ingram, despite her beauty, suffered badly from the disease of jealousy.

He rang the bell. At once the voices stopped and a moment or two later the light went on in the hall and Ingram opened the door.

"Yes?" He had himself well under control, Thanet was interested to note. A cool customer, then. He was tall, well built and as fair as his wife was dark. One lock of hair flopped boyishly over his forehead and he brushed it away with what was clearly an habitual gesture as he absorbed Thanet's self-introduction. At once he was all affability.

"Derek Ingram," he said, holding out his hand and shaking Thanet's vigorously. "Come in, come in, Inspector. This way."

The room into which he shepherded his visitor was all glass and stainless steel, angles and geometric patterns in pale, bleached shades of cream, off-white and beige. Mrs Ingram, intentionally no doubt, was a stunning contrast in a flame-coloured floor-length dress in some soft, clinging fabric which moulded itself to her beautiful body as she stood up and held out her hand. Her smile was dazzling.

"Inspector," she said, with an emphasis on the second syllable, as if he were the one person in the world above all others that she wanted to see. "What a surprise! Do sit down."

Having overheard their earlier conversation it was easy for Thanet to interpret the looks which flashed between them. What do we do now? said hers. Leave it to me, his responded.

Mrs Ingram subsided gracefully on to the long, low couch of blond leather and Ingram sat down beside her. The curious-looking contraption of tubular steel and strapped leather into which Thanet gingerly lowered himself was, he found, surprisingly comfortable.

"I'm afraid," said Ingram, taking the initiative with a deprecating little laugh, "that first of all I must clear up a slight misunderstanding. When you saw my wife this morning she rather misguidedly, perhaps, but understandably, I'm sure

68

you will agree, misled you."

"So I gathered," said Thanet dryly. "The window's open," he went on, inwardly amused at their blank faces. "And I'm afraid you were talking rather loudly. . . ." There was a moment's silence while they assimilated this and he could see that they were frantically trying to recall exactly what had been said.

"I gather you went down to the pub last night?"

Ingram nodded eagerly, clearly relieved, now that the initial shock was over, to be saved the trouble of explaining. "That's right."

"And — correct me if I'm wrong — you left here at about a quarter to ten, returned at about half past."

"Yes."

"So, I would be most grateful if you could cast your mind back and try to recall if you saw anyone or heard anything on the way there, or on the way back."

"Inspector," broke in Mrs Ingram. "May I just ask a question?"

"By all means."

"What . . . do you know what time Miss Birch was . . . killed?"

"I'm afraid I can't tell you precisely, but the period in which we are particularly interested is between nine thirty and eleven o'clock last night. I really must stress how vital it is that people should be frank with us. If you have nothing to hide, you have nothing to fear."

The rebuke was gentle but she bit her lip, flushed, glanced at her husband.

He, however, ignored her. Clearly, he was thinking. Eventually, "I'm sorry, Inspector, but I simply don't remember seeing anybody either on the way down or on the way back. It wasn't a very nice night, if you remember, blustery and rather chilly. Needless to say, I wish I had seen somebody, if only because they would presumably be able to vouch for me."

"Quite," said Thanet. "But you're sure?"

Ingram shook his head slowly. "I'm sorry."

"Can you by any chance remember if there was a moon?"

"Intermittently, yes. At times it was quite bright, then the clouds would blot it out completely."

"Any cars parked in front of the church?"

"Oh yes, a number. I assumed there was a meeting at the vicarage."

"The PCC, I believe," said Thanet. "What about when you came back?"

"None. I remember thinking that the meeting must be over."

A sudden clamour of bells made Thanet start. Joy Ingram rose and reached behind the curtain to shut the little window and at once the sound receded to a distant tintinnabulation.

"Bellringing night," she said with a grimace.

Thanet rather liked it but refrained from saying so. Perhaps, if he lived next door to the church and had to put up with it once a week as the Ingrams did, he would feel the same as she.

"Well," he said, rising, "I think that's all for the moment. I'd be grateful though, Mr Ingram, if you would try very hard to think back to last night, see if you can remember anything which might be useful to us."

"Certainly," said Ingram, leading the way to the door.

Outside the air vibrated with the clangour of the bells pealing out into the night. Thanet walked down the path to the Ingrams' front gate and then stood listening, his face turned up to the stars which out here in the country shone with an unfamiliar clarity. He felt strangely uplifted, exhilarated by the cascades of sound rippling through the darkness. The bellringers, whoever they were, were very good indeed.

Enjoyable though the experience was, however, it would not advance him in his task and reluctantly he dragged his attention back to the matter in hand. Could there be any truth in Mrs Ingram's astonishing accusation? Could her husband be having an affair with Marion Pitman? Thanet tried to visualise the two together, but somehow they didn't match up. In any case, it was a pointless exercise. The attraction of one person for another is frequently, to the outsider, a mystery. But if it was true . . .

Could Carrie Birch have found out, have threatened either

Marion or Ingram with exposure? Say, for instance, that she had approached Marion first and that Marion had given her money to keep quiet, but had said nothing to Ingram for fear that he would react violently. And that Carrie had become greedy, that Marion had been unable to step up the payments, that Carrie had then decided to approach Ingram. Say that she had done so last night, had perhaps lurked outside the Ingrams' house in the hope that he might come out. Ingram had a temper, as Thanet had heard for himself this evening. He might well have lashed out at the blackmailer and then have been forced to finish her off in order to prevent exposure. . . .

There was a streak of brightness across the sky, so swiftly gone as to have been almost invisible. A shooting star! Thanet had never seen one before and he blinked, his concentration broken, trying to recall the superstitions attached to seeing one. If he made a wish, would it be granted? Or had it marked someone's death?

He shook his head impatiently. What on earth was he doing, mooning over church bells and shooting stars! He must find some way, he told himself briskly as he set off across the road towards the Gambles' cottage, to check this story about Ingram and Marion Pitman. But how, without starting a rumour which might be completely false? He needed someone with absolute discretion.

It was at this moment, as if Fate had for once decided to give him exactly what he needed at the precise moment he needed it, that he became aware that someone was crossing the road parallel to him some ten yards away to his left. Dim though the light was Thanet could see that this person was wearing some sort of long dress which flapped about its ankles. The figure marched purposefully up to the vicarage gate and pushed it open and at once Thanet realised: not a dress, but a cassock.

"Excuse me. . . ."

The figure turned, waited as Thanet approached.

"Yes?"

"We've not met before, Mr . . ."

"Ennerby."

". . . Mr Ennerby. Inspector Thanet of Sturrenden CID."

"Of course. Poor Miss Birch. A terrible thing. . . ."

Thanet found himself shaking the warm, strong hand which was extended to him.

"There is a rather delicate point on which I would very much appreciate your help, Mr Ennerby."

"By all means. Come along in, won't you?"

Thanet followed the tall figure with its billowing robe to the front door. A light had been left on in the shallow, open porch and as they reached it Mr Ennerby stooped, picked something up. The front door, the policeman in Thanet noted disapprovingly, was not locked — was not even latched, for the vicar pushed it open with his foot before leading the way inside.

"We'll go into the kitchen," Ennerby said. "It's warmer in there."

He was right. The room was bright, modern, well-equipped, with a Raeburn cooker which gave forth a comforting heat. Thanet had not realised just how chilled he had become standing out there by the Ingrams' gate and he moved towards the stove, extending his hands to the warmth.

"My parishioners are convinced that if I'm left to my own devices I shall starve," Ennerby said, carefully setting down on the table the object which he had collected from the porch. It was, Thanet now saw, a large earthenware casserole. Ennerby, then, must be either a bachelor or a widower. An unmarried parson was no doubt the object of much solicitude, particularly from the unattached women of the parish, a perfect focus for the attentions of romantic and maternal alike.

"Do sit down, Inspector," Ennerby said, removing his cassock and flinging it over the back of a chair.

The two men seated themselves on opposite sides of the formica table.

"Now,' said the vicar. "How can I help?"

Thanet looked at him carefully before broaching the subject, for vicars after all are only human and although confidentiality is supposed to be their strong point he would like to be sure of this one's discretion before continuing.

He liked what he saw. Ennerby was not good-looking in the conventional sense but there was strength in the lines of face and jaw and his steady grey eyes evoked a sense of confidence. Here, one felt, was a man who would listen and understand without judging, one who looked as though he himself had suffered. He was, Thanet guessed, in his early fifties.

"As I said, it's rather a delicate matter. That is why I wanted to approach someone who would respect a confidence."

"Don't worry, Inspector, I can keep my mouth shut, I assure you." The man's grin showed that he had appreciated the hint.

"As you can imagine, in an investigation of this kind one turns up all sorts of rumours and naturally one has to look into them. The one I am concerned with at the moment concerns Miss Pitman and Mr Ingram."

The vicar's reaction was interesting. He was clearly astounded and a faint colour crept up into his cheeks. His voice, however, was level enough as he said, "Are you suggesting that there is some kind of attachment between them?"

"I had heard something of that kind, yes."

Ennerby gave a little laugh. "Absolute nonsense, I can assure you, Inspector."

"You're sure of that?"

"Quite, quite sure. You can take my word for it. I can't imagine who . . ."

"It doesn't really matter," Thanet said. "So long as you're certain. And I don't think the person concerned is going to spread the rumour any further, so . . ."

"I do hope not. If there had been any truth in it I would have heard, I'm sure of it. It is a sad fact that people are always only too anxious to let me know if one of the church members is suspected of backsliding."

"Fine," said Thanet. "I'm quite happy to accept that. Now, while I'm here . . . I understand that there was a PCC meeting here last night. Could you let me have a list of those who attended it?"

"By all means." Ennerby rose, left the room and came back a few moments later with a sheet of paper. "Here you are. This is a complete list of PCC members, so I've crossed out the names of those who weren't able to attend the meeting last night."

Thanet glanced at it. Selby's name was there, he noted, duly crossed out.

"Thank you," he said, rising.

"I must confess," Ennerby said, opening the door and leading the way into the hall, "I'm at a complete loss to imagine who on earth could have wished to kill an inoffensive person like Miss Birch."

"You knew her well?"

"Not well, no. She wasn't a church-goer. But she's always been about and I'd occasionally see her in the church on the evening she cleaned it, have a little chat with her, you know . . ."

"The *evening* she cleaned it, did you say?" Thanet stopped with his hand on the front door jamb.

"Yes. She always came on Tuesdays."

"Only on Tuesdays?" Thanet wanted to be quite sure.

"Yes, why?"

"I had been given to understand," Thanet said carefully, "that she cleaned the church on two evenings a week."

"At one time she did," Ennerby said. "But about, let me see, three years ago we had to have an economy drive and we cut it down to one."

Interesting, Thanet thought as he headed once more for the Gambles' house. Mrs Birch had been very positive about it. What could Carrie have been up to on Thursday evenings, if she had not been innocently engaged in scrubbing the church floor?

Whatever it was, she obviously hadn't wanted her mother to know about it.

8

Thanet's knock at the door of number three was answered by a girl of about twenty. Her jeans and baggy mohair sweater suited her rather gamine good looks — neat features, pointed chin and shining cap of short, dark hair.

She led the way into a sitting room which was all warmth, colour and noise; a gas fire was heating the room to suffocation point, a bright green carpet patterned in yellow fought with an orange three-piece suite and the television was turned up several decibels too high for comfort. There were two other people in the room, a plump middle-aged woman toasting her toes in front of the fire and a good-looking young man a little older than the girl who had answered the door.

"The Inspector, Mum." The girl had to shout to make herself heard above the noise of the television.

"Eh?" The woman turned a puzzled, tired face towards Thanet.

"About . . . you know," said the girl. "Her. Miss Birch."

Comprehension flooded into the woman's face and at once she began to struggle to her feet. "Chris, turn that thing off, for goodness sake," she said to the young man, flapping her hand at the television set. "We can hardly hear ourselves think. Take a seat, Inspector, do."

Welsh, decided Thanet. And now, looking at her more carefully, he could see the Celtic strain: small stature, sallow skin, dark hair and eyes, all reproduced in her daughter. The son, though, was of a different type; stocky, yes, but with much lighter hair and hazel eyes. Took after his father, no doubt. Thanet was not concerned that Gamble was not here. Lineham had checked with the factory this afternoon and had been satisfied that last night Gamble had been working right through the period during which Carrie had met her death.

"A terrible thing," went on Mrs Gamble. "Terrible. I could hardly believe my ears when I heard about it."

"When was that?"

"On the bus. On the way home from work. Full of it, they were. Strangled, they said, and in her own back garden."

Although they lived next door to the Birches, the Gambles knew very little about the tragedy, Thanet realised. Mrs Gamble and her son had already left for work when the alarm was raised, Mr Gamble had slept right through the commotion and even Jenny Gamble, who had gone to Mrs Birch's aid, was unaware of the details of what had happened later; as soon as she had handed over responsibility to Marion Pitman she had had to leave for work.

"It wasn't quite like that," he said. "You can't believe all you hear, in a case like this." And then, because the details would become public soon enough and these people, after all, had as much right as anyone to know the facts, living next door to the victim as they did, he went on, "As a matter of fact someone hit her on the head and then hid the body in the outside privy of number two."

"Duw," breathed Mrs Gamble. "D'you hear that Jen, Chris? There's terrible."

She was genuinely shocked, no doubt about that, Thanet thought.

"What time did it happen?" she said.

He told her.

"Between half past nine and eleven," repeated Mrs Gamble. "But . . . but we was *here*, wasn't we, Jen? And to think that right next door . . ." She shuddered and reached for her daughter's hand.

"You were in, you say. All of you?"

"Well my hubby was at work, of course. He left about a quarter to eight. He's on the night shift, you see. And Chris was out, at the pictures. What time did you go, Chris?"

"Caught the quarter to seven," said her son, speaking for the first time.

"And you came back . . .?" asked Thanet.

"On the twenty-five to ten."

"Rather early, surely, if you'd been to the cinema?"

"No choice, is there?" Chris Gamble scowled. "Twenty-five to ten's the last bus out from Sturrenden, unless you want to walk." It was obviously a sore point.

"He's saving up for a car," said Mrs Gamble fondly. "They're looking out for one for him, at the garage."

"The garage?"

"Where he works. He's a mechanic, aren't you, love? But he doesn't want any old rubbish, do you? He's waiting till he sees a really good bargain."

"Oh mum," growled the boy, looking embarrassed. "The Inspector don't want to hear about cars."

"I'd have thought a lad like you would've got himself a motor bike," said Thanet.

"That's his dad," said Mrs Gamble quickly, as the boy opened his mouth to speak. "Don't hold with them. Dangerous things, they are."

"Still . . ." said Thanet. Boys of twenty-one didn't usually refrain from doing things they wanted to do just because their fathers didn't approve.

"Didn't have much choice, did I?" said Chris bitterly. "Not if I wanted to go on living at home. And how much would I have had left from me pay packet, if I'd had to pay for digs?"

Thanet saw that he had unwittingly touched on a long-standing bone of contention. "Anyway," he said hurriedly, before Chris and his mother launched into a full-scale argument, "you say you caught the twenty-five to ten home last night?"

"Yeah."

"What time does it get into Nettleton?"

"Between ten and five to ten."

"Good," said Thanet. "Now look, Chris, the murder was, as I said, committed between nine thirty and eleven last night, so it's just possible you might have seen or heard something useful. Could you think back very carefully and tell me exactly who you saw and what you heard on the way back from the bus stop — where is it, by the way?"

"Opposite the post office," said Mrs Gamble. "You all right, Chris?"

He ignored her. Thanet doubted that he had even heard her. His eyes had glazed and he was frowning a little in concentration. They all watched him expectantly.

"It's no good," he said. "I just can't remember."

"Start from further back," suggested Thanet. "Were there many other Nettleton people on the bus?"

"A few."

"Anyone else from this end of the village?"

Chris hesitated and his sister, who was sitting on the arm of Mrs Gamble's chair, stirred uneasily.

"I don't think so," he said.

"But you're not sure?" Thanet was convinced that Chris was lying. But why?

"I told you, I'm not sure." But he avoided Thanet's eye.

Mrs Gamble opened her mouth, then closed it again as Thanet looked at her expectantly.

"But if there were only a few Nettleton people on the bus," Thanet said, "surely you can remember whether or not any of them were from this end of the village?"

"I wasn't really paying much attention," mumbled Chris.

Thanet decided not to press the point any further at the moment. Perhaps it would be a good idea to try to get hold of the boy's mother or sister at a time when he was not there. By the look of it, they both knew what he was holding back. Whatever it was, Thanet had a feeling that it was irrelevant to his enquiry — or at least, that all three Gambles considered it to be so.

"Did you see anyone on the way home?"

Chris considered. "There was several cars parked in front of the church," he volunteered.

"Did you recognise any of them?"

"Mr Waley's Rover three thousand five hundred, Mr Martin's new Range Rover, Mrs Dobson's Mini, Mr Parson's old Cortina . . . I think that's the lot."

Predictably, Thanet thought with resignation, a young mechanic would notice cars rather than people.

"There was a PCC meeting at the vicarage," he said. "Did you see any of the people coming out?"

Chris shook his head. "There was lights on in the vicarage, I noticed. But I didn't see nobody."

"Which way do you come in, front or back?"

"Back in the day, front at night. Back door's locked at night and I got a front door key of me own."

Pity, Thanet thought. "Now think very carefully. As you passed the entrance to the footpath last night, did you see or hear anything, anything at all?"

It was obvious that all three members of the family were aware of the importance of this question. Chris frowned fiercely, his mother clamped her teeth over her lower lip and watched him tensely and his sister raised her free hand to her mouth and began to gnaw at the quick of her first finger.

"I dunno," he said at last. He ran one hand through his hair. "I've just got this feeling there was something, but . . ."

His audience of three watched him with total concentration. Suddenly he snapped his fingers, making them all jump.

"Got it!" he said. "It was Miss Cox from number five, calling her cat."

The sense of anticlimax in the room was almost tangible.

"You saw her?" Thanet asked.

Chris shook his head. "Heard her, that's all. Must've been in her back garden."

"Nothing else?"

"Nope. Sorry."

Thanet switched his attention. "What about you, Mrs Gamble? And Jenny?"

The two women looked at each other, but there was no complicity in the glance they exchanged.

"In all evening, wasn't we, Mum?" said Jenny, entering into the conversation for the first time.

"Had the telly on, I'm afraid," said Mrs Gamble.

"The entire evening?"

They nodded in unison, like two clockwork dolls.

"Good film on," said Jenny.

"Oldie," said her mother. "*For Whom The Bell Tolls.*

79

Didn't finish till eleven. Chris watched it too, after he come in."

"Neither of you went upstairs for any reason, looked out of the window?" Stupid question anyway, Thanet thought. It had been pitch dark at the relevant time.

"Toilet's downstairs," said Mrs Gamble primly.

"Well, thank you," Thanet said. "I think that's about it, for the moment. No need for me to tell you to be careful about locking up. . . ."

The television blared behind him as he stepped out into the night. The church bells were silent now but only temporarily; before Thanet reached the road they began to ring again.

Who else, from this end of the village, had been on that bus, Thanet wondered, and why should Chris Gamble wish to protect him — or her, of course? Thanet's pace faltered as a possible answer came to him. The Selby girl! Mrs Selby had said that her daughter had spent the evening in Sturrenden with a school friend and had arrived home just before ten. So, unless she had used her mother's car — assuming that Mrs Selby had one, and that her daughter could drive — she must have come home on the same bus as Chris Gamble. And if so, Chris's lie aroused interesting possibilities. Suppose that he and the Selby girl were going out together . . . a man of Major Selby's position and status might well not approve.

Thanet clicked his tongue in exasperation. That was the trouble with police work. People lied, evaded, prevaricated for the most irrelevant of reasons, afraid, presumably, that their little secrets would be made public. The problem was, trying to sort out which lies or evasions were relevant and which were not — always a frustrating waste of time.

The light from the little street lamp in front of the Pitmans' house did not penetrate the dense shrubbery which fronted the Selbys' garden and the first section of the curving drive was very dark. Ahead, however, was some kind of illumination and when he rounded the bend Thanet could see that a lamp outside the front door had been switched on, perhaps in expectation of his visit. The door opened almost at once in answer to his knock.

"Inspector . . .?"

"Thanet. That's right. Miss Selby?"

She nodded, stepping back. "Come in."

A real honey of a girl, this one, thought Thanet: tall and slim, her unconscious elegance lifting her outfit of tight jeans and ruffled blouse into the eye-catching class. Her colouring was pure English Rose — fair complexion, eyes the colour of a summer sky, long, silky blonde hair.

"This way," she said. "Daddy's expecting you."

Major Selby was planted squarely in front of the hearth in the drawing room with his hands clasped behind his back, feet slightly apart. Behind him, a cheerful fire crackled. He was shorter than Thanet and of slender build, but he gave the impression of a whip-cord strength. He was expensively dressed in a well-cut tweed suit of lovat green, tattersal check shirt and shoes which shone like ripe chestnuts. Perhaps the poster had made him look more aggressive than he really was. Certainly his greeting was affable enough.

"Ah, Inspector . . .?"

"Thanet."

"Inspector Thanet. Of course, of course. Sit down, won't you?"

The two men shook hands and Thanet complied, irritated to find, however, that Selby did not follow suit but returned to his original position in front of the fire, thereby giving himself a slight psychological advantage.

"Drink, Inspector? It would have to be something soft, I'm afraid. We're teetotal. Or we could offer you coffee, or tea . . .?"

"Thank you, no."

Selby's daughter had been hovering at the door and he now gave her a dismissive nod.

"Just one moment, Miss Selby, if you don't mind," said Thanet quickly.

She hesitated, clearly torn between responding to Thanet's request and obeying her father's unspoken command. Selby was frowning.

"I don't see . . ." he began.

"I understand Miss Selby came home on the twenty-five to

ten bus from Sturrenden last night," said Thanet.

"So I believe," said Selby. "But quite what . . ."

Thanet sighed inwardly. Clearly he was going to have to fight for any scraps of information she could give 'him. "Please, Major," he said politely, and turned to the girl.

She hesitated a moment and then, as her father did not intervene, said, "That's right, yes."

Thanet had already decided not to risk compromising her in front of her father. If she and young Chris Gamble had indeed been out together the previous evening, 'it was none of his affair. So he merely said, "Could you tell me, do you think, whether or not you saw or heard anything suspicious on the way home from the bus stop? Particularly in the region of Church Cottages?"

He thought he detected a flicker of relief in her eyes before she replied, "I've already thought about that. Mummy thought you'd want to know. And no, I'm afraid I didn't. There were some cars parked in front of the church, that's all."

"PCC last night," said Major Selby testily. "And now, if you've finished with Susan . . . She has some prep to do, I believe."

Thanet had no choice but to let her go. Privately, however, he made a resolution to try and catch her on her own. She looked a bright, intelligent girl but it was pointless to try to get her to talk freely with her father present. He turned his full attention to the man before him.

The Major seemed to relax a little now that his daughter had left. He turned, picked up the poker and prodded the fire into a brighter glow.

"Mrs Selby well?" Thanet surprised himself by saying. He had no intention of putting questions to a man's back, but even so. . . . Unwittingly, he seemed to have touched some kind of tender spot. Unmistakably the Major's hand hesitated and his back stiffened slightly before he stooped to replace the poker.

"A little tired, that's all," he said as he turned back to face Thanet. "Naturally, today has been rather a strain for her. She knew Miss Birch — Carrie, as we called her — quite well, of course."

"She had been working for you long?"

"Ever since we came here, about five years ago." And now, at last, Selby relaxed sufficiently to sit down.

"And they got on well together?"

The Major stared. "I presume so." The woman, his gaze said, had not been here to "get on" with his wife, but to work.

"What did you think of her?"

Selby considered. "Never had much to do with her really. She was usually here only when I was out, of course, during the day."

"But you must, over the years, have seen something of Miss Birch, have formed some opinion of her."

The Major waved his hand. "She was a little mouse of a thing. Did what she was paid to do well enough, I suppose, but she never had much to say for herself."

"You arrived home just after ten last night, I believe," said Thanet, giving up.

"As I'm sure my wife will have told you. Yes."

"And did you by any chance . . ."

"See or hear anything suspicious? No. Come, Inspector, I was tired after a long trip, thankful to get home. I merely drove into the garage, parked the car and came indoors. The road is invisible from the house, as you will no doubt have noticed and in any case I used the kitchen door, which is closer to the garage."

It was pointless to go on, Thanet thought. He thanked the Major and left.

Half way back to Sturrenden he suddenly remembered the money under Carrie's mattress. He really ought not to leave it there all night. He'd look an absolute idiot if by any chance it were stolen. Cursing, he did a three-point turn on the deserted road and headed back once more to Nettleton.

It was now a quarter to ten and lights were still on downstairs in numbers one, three and five. Thanet fumbled the unfamiliar key into the lock of number four and stepped into the small living room, closing the front door behind him and groping along

83

the wall for a light switch. He found none. Perhaps it was on the far side of the room, near the kitchen door. The room smelt musty, as if its occupants were already long departed and it had been shut up for some time. There was, too, the unmistakable odour of sickness and old age, overlaid with a faintly medicinal smell reminiscent of hospital corridors.

The room's dreariness struck him anew as he found the switch and clicked the light on. The overhead bulb encased in its dreary shade was of too low a wattage and drained out of the room the little colour it possessed. Thanet did not feel inclined to linger and he pushed open the door into the old woman's bedroom, using the light filtering through from the front room to locate the switch for the staircase.

Upstairs in Carrie's room he heaved the mattress aside once more and quickly counted up the packets of pound notes. There were twenty. He began to stow them away in his raincoat pockets, his movements slowing as he became aware of a feeling that there was something he had left undone. When he had finished he lingered, looking around the room, trying to pin down the source of his unease, but it was no good, his mind remained obstinately blank.

And God, he was tired. It had been a long day, not as long as many he had known but long enough, nevertheless. At the beginning of a case there was always so much to absorb and there was work yet to be done before he would be free to go home. He still had to get this money counted and checked into the office safe and write up his reports on tonight's interviews. He had found from past experience that if he procrastinated on these they would pile up into unmanageable proportions with unbelievable speed. Besides, irritating though it was to have to spend so much time on paperwork, it frequently helped to have to get it down in black and white, the act of writing it down forcing him to reassess what he had learned, to clarify his impressions and try to be objective about them.

He looked about him once more at the cheerless little room and shook his head. Perhaps, if he stopped thinking about it, the elusive reason for that nagging doubt would surface of its own accord.

Stubbornly, however, it refused to do so. It was one o'clock by the time he got to bed and he was still no nearer understanding it.

Consciously, he tried to relax, to empty his mind of the crowded impressions of the day. But for a long time this proved impossible and endlessly, obssessively, he retraced his steps, relived jumbled snatches of conversation.

Just before he slept the first two lines of Blake's poem floated irrelevantly through his mind.

"Tyger! Tyger! burning bright
In the forests of the night . . ."

9

When Thanet arrived at the office next morning Lineham was already at work.

"Finish your decorating?" said Thanet, giving his raincoat a shake before hanging it up. Overnight the sky had clouded over and it was a grey, cheerless morning with intermittent showers borne on a blustery March wind.

"Yes, thanks. Most of it, anyway."

"Interesting?" Thanet nodded at the report Lineham was studying.

"The path. report," said Lineham, handing it over. "Doc Mallard was right, as usual. She was hit on the head and then suffocated."

Thanet scanned the report quickly and then read it again, brooding over certain passages. "Yes, he's quite definite about it isn't he? 'Cause of death: asphyxia.' So the blow on the head — there was only one, I see — would just have knocked her out."

"That's right," said Mallard, who had entered the room as Thanet was speaking. "It certainly wouldn't have killed her."

"And our old friend the blunt instrument was used."

"Yes. Poker, stick, length of piping . . ."

"Arnold — the builder — would be using copper piping for the plumbing work on number two," Lineham said.

"I shouldn't think he'd leave it lying around," Thanet said. "It's valuable stuff these days. But check, anyway. So," he went on thoughtfully, "she was knocked out by a not-very-hard blow on the head, and then suffocated."

"By something handy, I should guess," Mallard said. "Pillow, cushion . . ."

"Indoors, then?" Lineham said eagerly.

". . . coat, blanket, travelling rug," intoned Mallard.
Thanet and Lineham grimaced.

"Could have been anywhere," Thanet said.

"Well, mustn't sit about here doing nothing." Mallard
stood up. "Should have started a clinic half an hour ago." At
the door he paused, peered over his half-moon spectacles at
Lineham. "You look as though you could do with a good
night's sleep. Build up your strength for Saturday." And with
a wicked grin he was gone, leaving Lineham pink about the
ears.

Thanet glanced sharply at Lineham. Mallard was right. The
sergeant was looking distinctly drawn. The skin beneath his
eyes was shadowed and the rounded lines of cheek and jaw
seemed to have sharpened, adding years to his appearance.

Thanet opened his mouth to speak but Lineham said
hurriedly, "Did you find out anything interesting last night?"

If Lineham didn't want to talk about his private life, that
was his affair, Thanet thought.

"There were one or two intriguing suggestions. That Marion
Pitman is having an affair with Derek Ingram, for instance."

"Any truth in it, you think?"

Thanet shrugged. "The vicar doesn't seem to think so."

"He would know, surely, living smack across the road like
that."

"Quite. All the same, I don't think we ought to dismiss the
idea out of hand."

"Who suggested it?"

"Mrs Ingram herself. Oh, not to me directly. When I went to
see them last night I happened to overhear a conversation
between her and her husband. There was a window open. . . .
Odd, how often the jealous ones are absolute knockouts. Have
you seen her?"

"Mrs Ingram?" Lineham shook his head.

"She really is something. Nobody'd ever think, looking at
her, that she could possibly be jealous of anyone. But she is
. . . which is very interesting from our point of view."

"I don't see what you mean, sir."

"Well, what happens when his wife accuses an innocent

man of having an affair with another woman?"

"He denies it, I suppose."

"Yes, but does she believe him?"

"If she's the jealous type, presumably not."

"Then what? Put yourself in his position. Year after year you are falsely accused. At first you love your wife, protest your innocence, but you get tired of all the suspicion, the arguments, the tears, the rows, the fact that you can't even look at a woman let alone speak to one without your wife thinking you're ready to hop into bed with the poor girl. . . ."

"I don't know," Lineham said. "I suppose if it went on long enough and I got fed up enough, I might think, well, I'll give her something to complain about. . . ."

"Exactly," Thanet said. "And we have one unfaithful husband who, if he'd been left in peace might never have strayed at all. She drives him to it, don't you see, and in the end she herself brings about the very situation she has been afraid of all along. Now, suppose that at just this stage a third person intervenes . . ."

Sudden understanding dawned in Lineham's eyes. "You mean . . ."

"Carrie. Yes."

"If she'd found out," Lineham said excitedly, "threatened to tell Mrs Ingram . . ."

"We'd have a neat explanation for all those nice little piles of pound notes."

"Yes . . .!" breathed Lineham.

The two men sat in silence for a while, contemplating this theory which did at least have the merit of fitting all the known facts. Ingram had left the house at a quarter to ten on the night of the murder. Suppose that Carrie had been blackmailing him, and had arranged to meet him that evening, that the quarrel with his wife had been manipulated by Ingram in order to give him an excuse for stamping out of the house at the appropriate time. . . . Suppose that Carrie had then stepped up the pressure, had demanded more money. . . . There would just have been time for Ingram to kill her and dump her in that convenient little outhouse before hurrying down to the Plough and Harrow. The landlord had said that Ingram had arrived around ten.

"It could fit, sir," Lineham said.

"I agree. But 'could' is the operative word, I think. We'll keep an open mind at present. One thing I would like you to do is to try to find out if Ingram had a girlfriend in Sturrenden."

"You don't think he is having an affair with Miss Pitman, then?"

"I don't think he's her type. Nor she his, for that matter. I could be wrong, but I'd guess that he would go a little further away from home for consolation. Carrie could still have found out about it."

"But how, if the girlfriend lives in Sturrenden? So far as we can gather, Carrie never seems to have left the village, not even to go shopping. Though I suppose she must have, occasionally."

"I think there was more to Carrie than meets the eye. I forgot to tell you that there was another interesting little fact I gleaned last night." And Thanet told Lineham what the vicar had said about Carrie and the church cleaning. "So you see, there was one evening a week when nobody, not even her mother, knew what she was up to. She may have spent it somewhere in the village, of course, and if so, no doubt the fact will emerge eventually, but she might well have gone into Sturrenden. Make enquiries about Thursday evening buses, see if you can get hold of the drivers."

"Well, well, well," Lineham said, grinning. "Good for her. I'm glad she managed to put one over on that horrible old woman." Then, abruptly his smile vanished and his eyes grew bleak.

Thanet hesitated and then said gently, "What's the matter, Mike?" He could guess, of course. Mention of Carrie's mother had made Lineham think of his own. "Look," he went on, as Lineham pursed his lips and shook his head, "I know I've no business to interfere, but . . . it's your mother, isn't it?"

"Yes," Lineham admitted miserably. "She's not well again this morning and . . ."

"You're afraid the wedding'll have to be called off again. Right?"

Lineham nodded.

Thanet stood up abruptly and walked to the window, looked down into the street. It was pouring with rain and there were few people about. It wouldn't be very pleasant out at Nettleton this morning.

"Look," he said, turning, "perhaps I've no right to say this, but you're going to have to make up your mind what to do, if she is taken ill again."

"I won't have any choice, really, will I?" said Lineham grimly. He had been fiddling with a ball-point pen and now he stabbed viciously at the blotting paper in front of him before throwing the pen down in disgust.

"Won't you?" Thanet said softly.

Lineham's head came up with a jerk. "What do you mean?"

"Well," Thanet said carefully, "there *is* a choice, isn't there?" He would have to be very tactful.

"You mean, I should go ahead with the wedding regardless?"

Thanet returned to his desk, sat down again. "Look, Mike, I don't like to interfere, as I said, but you can't go on like this. If you have to put up with much more of it you'll be a nervous wreck. What does Louise feel about it?"

Lineham grimaced. "She's fed up, naturally. But she says I have to make up my own mind."

"Very sensible of her. If she put pressure on you, you'd only resent it later, if anything went wrong."

"That's what she says."

"So what are you going to do?"

"I don't know. What do *you* think I ought to do?"

Thanet considered. He was treading on dangerous ground and he knew it. If he told Lineham to go ahead and Mrs Lineham had a fatal attack, he, Thanet, would feel responsible for her death. On the other hand, in Thanet's experience, people only took advice if it was what they really wanted to do anyway. Perhaps Lineham simply needed some moral support in order to go through with what amounted to outright rebellion against his mother.

"If you really want to know, I think you should plan to go ahead."

"Regardless?"

"Regardless. But as Louise so rightly says, you are the only one who can really decide. And it's a miserable position to be in, really miserable, I know that. But try to look at it objectively. Twice, already, you've had to postpone the wedding. Now this can't go on indefinitely. From what I know of her, Louise isn't the sort of girl, however much she loves you, to be prepared to play second fiddle to your mother for ever. I know it's hard, but it seems to me that sooner or later you'll have to choose between them. And the longer you put off that decision, the more likelihood there is that you're going to lose Louise in the process. How much does she matter to you? That's what you have to ask yourself."

Lineham was obviously thinking hard and Thanet waited for a minute or more before going on.

"And if that happened," he said eventually, "how would you feel about your mother? My guess is that you'd be bitterly resentful and you'd end up by being on bad terms with her too. So what I would suggest is this — and remember, it is only a suggestion — that you go to her, tell her that although you are naturally worried about her health, you feel that you have no right to keep Louise dangling like this. Say that you therefore feel that whatever happens you have to go ahead with the wedding arrangements this time. And see how she reacts. You never know, if she sees that you really have decided, she might just accept it. . . ."

"You think so?" said Lineham bitterly.

Thanet shrugged. "I wish I could say yes, Mike, but I can't. I just don't know."

Lineham looked away, out of the window. "We've even thought of slipping off quietly to the registry office, without saying anything to anyone, even to mother. That way, we thought she might not have time to get worked up about it and if she knew it was done, over, she might get used to the idea in time."

"But?"

"We just didn't like the idea of being so underhand about it. And Louise especially wants a church wedding — oh, not for the fuss and bridesmaids and so on but because she goes to church regularly and won't feel properly married, she says, if it's just a civil ceremony. So it just wouldn't do." He looked thoughtfully at Thanet. "I might just try what you suggest, sir."

"Well, as I said, it's your choice. But if you do tell her you're going to go ahead regardless, make sure you do just that. Otherwise . . ."

"Yes," Lineham said. "There'd be no end to it, would there? Well, thank you sir," he added stiffly. "I'm sorry to bring my problems to work with me."

"We all do," Thanet said, "from time to time."

Twenty minutes later, after briefing the others, he and Lineham made a dash across the car park to their respective cars, heads lowered against the driving rain. Thanet had handed over to Lineham the list of PCC members which the vicar had given him, with instructions to cross-check their stories and also find out if any of them had seen anything of interest when leaving the vicarage on Monday evening.

The sudden flurry of movement, the sting of rain on his face, exhilarated him and as he swung out of the car park and headed for Nettleton he found himself looking forward eagerly to the challenge of the day ahead. Whom should he see first?

He wanted to check up on his hunch about Susan Selby and Chris Gamble and he also wanted to dig a little further into that rumour about Marion Pitman and Ingram just in case his instinct was wrong; but most of all he wanted to try to deepen his understanding of Carrie herself. In a case like this it was essential to get to know the victim and it was extraordinary, really, how little he felt he knew about her. He had now talked to all the people in her claustrophobic little world and she herself still remained shadowy, elusive, a pathetic ghost hovering in the wings. Perhaps she would stay that way. Perhaps she really had been such a nonentity, had had so negative a personality, that there was nothing of real interest to be discovered.

And yet, he thought once more, there was that money. . . .

Perhaps it was time for a change of tactics. Perhaps he ought to stop pussy-footing around and try a little bull-dozing instead. But he'd never found that that sort of approach worked for him. He had always found patience and subtlety infinitely more effective. Perhaps he had just been too *busy*, had not given himself sufficient time to absorb, think, weigh. . . . A leisurely talk with old Pitman was what he needed. The man was no fool and Thanet was convinced that there was a great deal yet to be learned from him about his unlovable former pupil. Poor Carrie. After such a life, to have met such an end . . .

Thanet frowned, remembering his certainty, the previous evening in her bedroom, that there was something he had failed to do. What *was* it? He still hadn't pinned it down but it was very near the surface now. He could feel it hovering there, on the very fringe of his awareness.

As he turned into Nettleton he made up his mind. Before seeing Robert Pitman he would go and take one more look at Carrie's room.

He was suddenly convinced that it had not yet yielded up all its secrets.

10

There were no chairs in Carrie's room so Thanet took off his dripping raincoat, hung it on the end of the curtain rail, and perched on the bed. The wan, grey light filtering through the half-net curtains did nothing to enhance the dismal little room. The hands of the old alarm clock still stood at twelve fifteen and indeed time itself seemed to have stopped here. The very air of the place seemed as devoid of life as its former occupant.

Thanet sat with shoulders slumped and hands clasped between parted knees and gazed aimlessly about him. The sense of urgency which he had experienced in the car, the impetus which had sent him hurrying up the narrow staircase, had dissipated the moment he had stepped into the room. He must have been crazy to expect otherwise. He and Lineham had searched the place thoroughly enough the first time, after all. And yet . . . this had been Carrie's own domain, the one tiny corner of the whole world in which she could have been assured of complete privacy. Even her mother had not been able to penetrate up here: those steep, narrow stairs had been as effective as a drawbridge. Once up here, had Carrie really been satisfied with nothing more than a cupboard full of cheap romantic fiction?

And why not? he asked himself impatiently. Having so little in her life outside this room, why should she not have been contented with very little more inside it?

Thanet stood up and began to pace restlessly about in the narrow corridor of space between the bed and the window. The point was, Carrie had got herself murdered. He didn't, couldn't believe that hooligans had killed her and therefore there must have been something about her, something in her character, knowledge, habits, behaviour, that set her apart, something that had ultimately provoked that final act of violence.

Surely it was therefore not unreasonable to expect to find traces of that something here, in the only place which had been truly hers?

Unnoticed by Thanet his cracked and slightly distorted reflection advanced and receded in the mirror of tiles as he passed to and fro, scowling down at the worn brown linoleum with its herringbone pattern of imitation wood blocks. Absorbed in his thoughts as he was it took some time for him to register that one small area of this shabby flooring seemed more scuffed than the rest of it. At once he stopped. Why should that be? Enlightenment came swiftly. The spot was about eight feet from the tile mirror. Here Carrie must have stood whenever she wished to study her full-length reflection.

Thanet frowned. A Carrie who lingered to admire herself in the mirror did not fit the image of the Carrie he had seen. She had looked to be the sort of woman who would use a mirror only in the most cursory fashion, to check quickly on over-all neatness.

A Thanet neatly divided into squares advanced to meet him as he approached the mirror. He had seen these tiles in the shops. Six inches square, with a self-adhesive backing, they were a quick and easy way for an amateur to achieve the effect of a full-length mirror. Also, of course, they were both small and portable. If Carrie had wanted to install a long mirror up here without her mother knowing, then they would have provided her with the perfect solution. Smuggling them up a few at a time would have presented no difficulty. She had made a good job of sticking them up, too, Thanet conceded. He ran his fingers over the satin-smooth surface. If only mirrors could talk, he thought fancifully, what tales they would have to tell. . . .

He swung away, impatient with himself. The question was, why should it have been important to dessicated little Carrie Birch to have a full-length mirror on the wall of her bedroom? Thanet squatted to look more closely at the worn patch on the linoleum. It was roughly circular, and within there were a number of tiny indentations. Thanet's eyes opened wide in astonishment as understanding came.

Carrie Birch in high heels?

A sudden, vivid image of Carrie's feet in their sensible black lace-up shoes flashed into Thanet's mind and sent him hurrying across to the curtain behind which Carrie had kept her clothes. He drew it aside, stared down at the floor, where Carrie's shoes were lined up neatly: cheap, sensible and low-heeled, every one.

Perhaps the marks on the floor dated from long ago? Perhaps Carrie had once been young and glamorous, high heels her normal foot-wear? Thanet shook his head. It was possible, of course, but he couldn't somehow believe it — though it was certainly more credible than that Carrie should have worn them recently. He went back to the worn patch, squatted once more and ran his fingers over the crescent-shaped depressions like a blind man reading Braille. He pursed his lips. Comparatively recent, he would say.

Thanet stood up abruptly, wincing as he did so. At incautious moments like this the spectre of his former back trouble tended to raise its ugly head. Testingly he eased his pelvis this way and that, gave a sigh of relief. No harm done this time, it seemed. He looked about him once more. How could he and Lineham have missed something as distinctive as a pair of high-heeled shoes? Perhaps Carrie had got rid of them?

His gaze travelled methodically around the room, lingering on each of the few items of furniture before quartering the walls. Then he turned his attention to the ceiling.

His stomach gave a great lurch of excitement. There it was, so normal a feature of at least one room in every house that until now its presence had not registered: an oblong trapdoor set into the ceiling to provide access to the roof space.

Surely he remembered seeing a step ladder leaning against the wall just inside the door of the back bedroom? Castigating himself for not having thought of the loft before, Thanet hurried across the landing and into the other bedroom. Yes, there was the ladder. He seized it, hastened back to Carrie's room and set it up beneath the trapdoor. Climbing on to the third step he raised both arms and pushed. The door swung back easily. It was hinged on one side and Carrie — for who else could it have been? — had kept the hinges well oiled. Eagerly, he climbed two more steps.

The bedroom ceiling was low and his head and shoulders were now projecting up into the roof space. Despite the gloom he saw at once the row of carrier bags ranged around the sides of the opening. Treasure trove indeed! One by one he seized them, eased them through the opening and lowered them to the floor. Behind the furthest one he found a tiny suitcase. Like a small boy prolonging the anticipation of a treat, he waited until he had removed them all before descending the ladder and carrying the first across to the bed.

Each bag had been encased in a larger, plastic one, presumably as a protection against dust — though there was very little of that, he noted. He slid the inner bag clear of the outer one and peered inside. On top was something soft, black and silky and he pulled it out, his eyebrows climbing his forehead as he realised what it was.

A woman's slip made of black satin, trimmed with lace. . . .

A matching pair of panties followed and then bra, suspender belt, sheer black stockings. Beneath this complete set of lingerie was another, in pale blue silk and then a third, in peach-coloured satin. Thanet laid them all out neatly on the bed and stood staring at them for a moment before arranging them in three neat little piles and turning to the next bag.

Dresses, this time. Day dresses, he supposed they would be called, all of them expensive, made of the highest-quality materials — wool, cashmere, crêpe and silk.

Bag after bag yielded up its treasure: sweaters, blouses, skirts, evening dresses, suits, nightdresses and negligees, cocktail dresses. Finally, there was a bag of shoes, all of them made of the finest leather, shoes for every occasion: high-heeled sandals and court shoes, walking shoes (but how different from those in Carrie's official wardrobe!) and even a pair of calf-length boots in soft grey suede.

By now the bed was heaped with finery. Thanet stood looking at it, struggling to relate such luxurious elegance to the insignificant, unpretentious little woman who had been the public Carrie. He couldn't ever recall feeling so truly astonished.

He stepped back, as if distance could give him a better

perspective on his discovery and almost tripped over the little suitcase, which he had left to last. Carrying it to the end of the bed, he cleared a small space in which to sit. Then he laid it across his knees and clicked open the locks.

Make-up this time, the lot. This was a vanity case, with fitted compartments for everything. Thanet picked up one of the bottles: Elizabeth Arden.

But the most interesting discovery was still to come. As he removed the tray Thanet saw human hair. He plunged his hand into its silkiness and lifted it out. A wig, blonde, short and softly curling. He shook his head in amazement, trying — and failing — to visualise Carrie wearing it.

So she had had a complete disguise, an entire transformation kit for her fantasy persona. Had she been satisfied with dressing up behind closed doors, he wondered — or could she have, *had* she ventured forth into the outside world? Truly, the imagination boggled.

Thanet tucked the wig back beneath the tray, snapped shut the lid and set the little case gently on the floor. He stood up and contemplated Carrie's secret wardrobe once more. There must be hundreds of pounds' worth of stuff on that bed — thousands, perhaps. He couldn't wait to see Lineham's face when he saw it.

Well, Thanet thought as he made his way reflectively down the stairs and let himself out of the house, he had been looking for another dimension to Carrie's character and he had certainly found one. The question was, how did it affect his thinking about the case? And where — where, and *how* — had she come by all that money?

Engrossed in speculation, he was at the gate before he realised that old Miss Cox had, for once, emerged from her self-imposed isolation. She was sweeping the front path, or trying to; crutches under armpits, with the cat Tiger weaving around her feet. If she wasn't careful, she'd end up breaking the other leg, thought Thanet as he said good morning, offered to complete the job for her.

"I've just finished, thank you," she croaked in that rusty voice of hers. Then she just stood, not looking at him, not speaking, the cat rubbing against her legs, the steady rain slicking down her hair and dripping into the upturned collar of the old raincoat she was wearing. Clearly, she was expecting something.

Thanet realised that she had probably been lying in wait for him, that she must have seen him go into the Birchs' house and, despite the rain, had decided to sweep the path so that she should not miss him when he came out. No doubt she was longing to know what progress he had made. Her chosen isolation must be cold comfort at the moment, with an empty house next door, her leg in plaster and a murderer at large.

But what reassurance could he give her? He certainly felt no nearer at the moment to discovering the identity of Carrie's killer and even if he had he could not have divulged the information. However, the degree of pressure which her unspoken demand was making upon him was extraordinary. He could feel her willing him to speak and the intensity of her need both aroused his pity and stiffened his resistance. It was all too easy in a situation like this for compassion to lead to indiscretion.

"You're getting very wet, Miss Cox," he said gently. "I should go in now, if I were you."

She gave him a quick, puzzled glance as if he had been speaking a foreign language and then, as he turned to leave she said, "Please . . ."

He paused, reluctant yet unable to ignore her plea, raising his eyebrows in hypocritically polite incomprehension.

"Please," she said again. "Have you found out yet . . .?"

He shook his head. "Not yet, no."

She stood staring at him, her eyes dark with fear, her lips working as if she were trying to bring herself to ask him some further question.

Thanet waited and when she did not speak said firmly, "We shall, though, I promise you."

She let him go then, abruptly turning back towards the house, the cat running ahead of her and disappearing through the half-open door.

Thanet hunched deeper into his raincoat and set off down the lane. So certain was he that she must be watching from her doorstep that in front of the Gambles' house he turned, half-raised his hand in a farewell salute. But her door was shut. Perhaps she was standing at the window, invisible behind the net curtains.

He shrugged and was about to continue on his way when he caught a flicker of movement in the front room of the Gambles' house. Now who could that be? Mr Gamble, unable to sleep? Or one of the others, home from work for some reason?

He set off up the path to the front door.

It was Jenny Gamble who answered his knock, eyes watering and with a handkerchief to her nose.

"Don't come too close," she said. "I've got a shocking cold."

"If I had a penny for every cold germ I'd met in the course of my work," Thanet said with a grin, "I'd be a billionaire."

She opened the door wider. "Suit yourself," she said.

Once again the sitting room was suffocatingly hot. Jenny plumped down into the armchair next to the gas fire, which was on full blast, and blew her nose. "It came out overnight," she grumbled.

"It's a streamer all right," said Thanet. It made his eyes water just to look at her. All the same, he wasn't going to allow sympathy to deflect him from his purpose. "Why didn't you tell me your brother was going out with Susan Selby?" he said casually.

She fell right into the trap. Her eyes flicked open wide with shock and she became very still. After a moment, "How d'you find out?" she said. "Did . . . it wasn't Major Selby, was it?"

Thanet shook his head.

"Thank God for that," she breathed. "Chris would've done his nut."

"Is that why you didn't tell me last night? Because you were afraid Major Selby would find out?"

She nodded. "It's supposed to be a deadly secret." Her eyes narrowed. "How *did* you find out? Susan didn't tell you, surely?"

"No. Never mind how, I just did. But that's not the point. The point is, it's dangerous not to be frank in a murder investigation. It could give us all sorts of odd ideas."

"Such as?" she said, warily.

"That you didn't want us to know because there was some connection with the murder."

"But that's stupid!" she burst out. "How could Chris and Susan going out together have anything to do with . . . what happened?"

"Well now, let me see," said Thanet thoughtfully. "Say your brother was determined that at all costs Major Selby shouldn't find out about him and Susan. Then say Miss Birch saw them together somewhere, threatened to tell . . ."

He saw at once that she had remembered something which frightened her. She was staring at him aghast. "No," she breathed and then, more vehemently, "No! You can't believe that, surely! Chris just isn't. . . . He'd never hurt a fly, let alone an old woman like Miss Birch. He *couldn't*. . . ."

"You'd be astounded if you knew how often we hear the families of young offenders say that."

"I don't care what other people say! I know Chris and I just don't believe he could ever do a thing like that, no matter how desperate he was. Anyway," she went on, as Thanet remained silent, "I'm not sure they'd mind all that much if Major Selby did find out."

"That wasn't what you said two minutes ago," Thanet said gently.

Jenny sneezed rapidly four or five times in succession before blowing her nose and mopping at her streaming eyes. "I know," she said at last. "But that's because that's what they *say*. They both *act* as though it'd be the end of the world, too, but I'm not sure."

"What do you mean?"

"Well, Chris hates all this hole-in-the-corner business. He just falls in with it to please Susan, I know that. But Susan . . . I can't really make her out. . . ." She stopped.

Thanet waited in what he hoped was an encouraging silence.

"I'd go mad if my dad carried on like hers," Jenny said. "He's a real pig. She mustn't have any boyfriends, she's not allowed to go to discos, she's always got to be in by ten o'clock at night, and she always, always has to let her parents know exactly where she is at all times. I mean, you can understand her going behind their backs, can't you? After all, she is seventeen! But I've sometimes wondered . . . I mean, she's really something, Susan, isn't she? Have you seen her?''

Thanet nodded.

"Then you'll know what I mean. So, what I wonder is, why Chris? He's my brother and I'm fond of him but let's face it, he's no oil painting and he's not all that brilliant, either.''

"I'm not quite sure what you're getting at.''

"Well, just lately I've been wondering if she's after some kind of show-down with her father. And she's kind of using Chris. The way I see it is, if she does something awful — awful in her father's eyes, like having a boyfriend who's a motor mechanic — and her dad finds out, she might be able to wangle herself a bit more freedom.''

"You mean she'd say, 'I'll give him up if you let me go to discos with my girlfriends', that sort of thing, so he'll feel he's choosing the lesser of two evils?''

She nodded.

"It's possible, I suppose,'' Thanet said. Though even if that were so, he reflected, and Susan really wouldn't have minded too much if her father found out, Chris wouldn't have been aware of the fact. If Carrie had tried a spot of blackmail he might well have felt it his duty to protect Susan. But, to the extent of killing for her? Frankly, Thanet doubted it. And as far as long-term blackmail was concerned, a young motor mechanic certainly wouldn't have been able to come up with the kind of sums Carrie had been amassing. Perhaps — perish the thought! — she had had more than one victim?

"Where did Miss Birch see Susan and your brother together?'' he asked softly.

Jenny shook her head, a fierce little shake as if repudiating both the question and the necessity of answering it.

"Oh come on,'' Thanet said. "She did, didn't she?'' And then, when Jenny still said nothing, "Remember what I said just now,'' he said gently, "about being frank with us? And just remember this, too: to solve a crime like this we need every scrap of information we can collect, every bit of help we can get. If your brother is innocent, you may be helping to clear him by telling us everything you know, even if on the face of it the information seems to incriminate him. Now, where *did* Miss Birch see them together?"

She hesitated a moment longer and then, with an air of resignation, said, "In Sturrenden."

"Exactly where? Do you know?"

"Catching the last bus home."

"This happened more than once?"

"Every week."

"On Thursday evenings, I presume?"

"Yes, but how did you . . .?"

"It figures," Thanet said.

So, he thought, as he thanked Jenny for her help and left, while Mrs Birch thought that her daughter was innocently engaged in cleaning the church, Carrie had been living it up in Sturrenden.

It was still raining hard. Turning up his collar against the relentless downpour, Thanet hurried down the lane and crossed the road towards the Pitmans' bungalow. With his hand on the gate, however, he hesitated. He didn't feel quite ready to talk to old Mr Pitman yet. He'd like a few minutes in which to assimilate what he had learned this morning. There was only one place to go: the car.

What could Carrie have been doing in Sturrenden every Thursday evening? he wondered, staring through the streaming windscreen at the blurred outline of the church. Briefly, he had a wild fantasy of Carrie dressed up in some of those glamorous clothes, blonde wig gleaming, soliciting on the pavements of Sturrenden or besporting herself on the floor of the town's one and only dancehall. Don't be ridiculous, he told himself. You're letting your imagination run away with you. But was he? If anyone had told him what he would find in Carrie's attic he would have laughed at him. And wouldn't prostitution explain away that hoard of cash?

He caught a glimpse of himself in the car mirror. He was grinning like an idiot. Just wait till Lineham hears this one, he thought. He'll think I've flipped!

All the same, could it be possible? Carrie would only have

had to put her gear into an old carrier bag and change her clothes in a ladies' lavatory somewhere in the town and she'd be all set. He'd heard Joan say that nowadays any woman could be attractive if she took enough trouble over her appearance, and miracles could be achieved with make-up. The old, conventional ideas of prettiness were gone forever. Nevertheless, it required a superhuman leap of the imagination to transform poor duck-like Carrie into the swan appropriate to those glamorous clothes.

Nonetheless, it had happened — if not in public, then at least in the privacy of Carrie's bedroom. Thanet was convinced of that. He pictured her waiting until she was certain that her mother's sleeping pill had taken effect and then stealthily setting up the step-ladder, taking the carrier bags down from the loft and emptying them of their contents, gloating over the quality and texture of satin, silk and lace, cashmere and lawn, standing in front of the mirror and holding the dresses up against her body one by one, selecting, discarding, making her final choice and then, finally, dressing up, preening in front of her transformed image. . . .

Suppose that for a while this secret satisfaction had been enough for her, but that there had come a time when she wanted to test out this other, glamorous self in the world outside, emerge from her chrysalis as the butterfly she might have felt herself truly to be. . . .

A knocking at the car window aroused him from his reverie. Lineham was peering in, his face distorted like that of a drowned man under water by the rain-washed glass.

Thanet wound down the window.

"You all right, sir?" Lineham was frowning anxiously.

"Think somebody'd bumped me off?" said Thanet with a grin. "No such luck, I'm afraid. I was merely engaging in the noblest activity known to man. Thought," he explained to Lineham's blank look. "Stand back, will you, I'm coming out."

He leaned across to take his torch from the glove compartment, then wound up the window and got out of the car.

"Come on," he said, anticipation filling him with boyish glee, "I've got something to show you."

104

11

"I've come to throw myself on your mercy," Thanet said.

"Really?" Old Robert Pitman's eyes sparkled. "You give me an agreeable sense of power, Inspector, an unfamiliar sensation for me these days, needless to say. Sit down and tell me more."

Thanet sat. He and Lineham had spent the lunch hour chewing over Thanet's find. Lineham's reaction to Carrie's cache had been most gratifying. Together he and Thanet had climbed up into the loft and searched it thoroughly; it had occured to Thanet that if Carrie had indeed been indulging in a spot of blackmail she might possibly have hidden away evidence of some kind up there. But they had found only dust and cobwebs. Now, he was determined to tap the reservoir of Robert Pitman's knowledge. He settled back comfortably into his chair.

"A murder investigation is a fascinating affair," he said discursively. "I'm not talking about gang warfare or terrorist activity, of course, or about the random killing for gain. Domestic murder is something quite different."

The old man's attention was fully engaged, Thanet was pleased to see. Robert Pitman was sitting quite still, his eyes fixed unwaveringly upon his visitor's face.

"So often," Thanet continued, "we find that it has been committed by the victim's nearest and dearest — husband, wife, son, brother and so on. But sometimes, as in this case, the victim's closest relation could not possibly be responsible. Quite apart from the fact that Mrs Birch had everything to lose in terms of physical comfort by her daughter's death, as you know she had to have a foot amputated some years ago and it would have been quite impossible for her to have dragged her daughter's body as far as that privy.

"So then, of course, we have to look a little further afield, widen the area of investigation. And I always find that it helps enormously to understand the victim himself — or, as in this case, herself. Somewhere in his or her character there always seems to be some quality which has — how shall I put it? — interacted with the character of the murderer in such a way as to provoke him to violence. It may be something which other people would find merely irritating. We all vary so much in our reactions to other people's quirks. But the murderer, on one particular occasion, finds that quality truly intolerable, so intolerable that he cannot endure its continued existence. So he destroys it." Thanet glanced at the old man, who was still listening with rapt attention. "I'm sure you can see where I'm going," he said.

"Fascinating," said the old man. He settled back deeper into his pillows and folded his swollen hands together gently, as if every tiny movement was painful. "So you want to pick my brains about Carrie," he said.

"Who better?" Thanet said. "You've known her nearly all her life."

Robert Pitman nodded gently, then his eyes went out of focus and he seemed to withdraw into himself, gazing away perhaps down the long corridor of time which led to himself as a vigorous young schoolmaster, and Carrie as the scrawny, unprepossessing child he had described the last time Thanet had come to see him.

Thanet sat still, relaxed, legs stretched out before him, hands clasped loosely in his lap, prepared to wait as long as was necessary.

Finally the old man stirred and his gaze returned to Thanet.

"Bowed but not broken," he said.

Thanet raised his eyebrows.

"That's how I'd describe Carrie." Mr Pitman hesitated. "I told you before, she was a little mouse of a creature, unobtrusive, always creeping about so you'd hardly notice she was there. And yet, somehow, you always did."

"What do you mean?"

The old man sighed. "I don't like talking like this, you know. There's always that 'mustn't speak ill of the dead' feeling. Which is perhaps why I was less than frank with you last time. But I do see that such an attitude can be highly obstructive. Someone, after all, has been killed, and you have to try to find out who did it. All the same, that doesn't alter my feelings."

"I can understand that," said Thanet.

"I know," Mr Pitman said. "Otherwise I wouldn't be talking to you like this." He sighed again, looked down at his hands. "The truth of the matter, I suppose, is that I couldn't stand the woman." He cast a quick, shamefaced glance at Thanet.

Thanet's immediate feeling was one of profound relief. At last a crack had opened up in that wall of silence. But he said nothing.

"There was something disconcerting about her," Mr Pitman went on. "I've been thinking about her a lot since it happened, of course, trying to work out what it was. And I've come to the conclusion that she had, as it were, gone underground. It's very difficult to explain what I mean, exactly. You see, there she was, the quiet, cowed little woman I've described to you and yet underneath you felt that she was, well, not exactly laughing at you, but gloating in some way. And although up *here*," the old man painfully lifted his hand to point at his forehead, "you knew you ought to feel sorry for her because of what she had to put up with from that awful mother of hers, down *here*," and the hand crept down to lie gently against the old man's heart, "you felt quite differently about her. Perhaps I'm not putting this very clearly, but you seemed to react to her on two different levels simultaneously, and the result was that you felt very confused about her. Or at least, I did." He stopped, his eyes begging Thanet for understanding.

"Yes. Yes, I see," Thanet said slowly. "I do see, exactly what you mean." He paused, thinking. "So when you said, 'bowed but not broken', you meant that although on the surface she had apparently given in completely to her mother's, what shall I call it, tyranny, underneath there was something rebellious that had never quite been subdued."

"Yes. That's exactly right. That's what I meant by 'gone underground'." The old man appeared more relaxed now. "Occasionally you'd catch a glimpse of it in her eyes, just as one might catch sight fleetingly of a wild animal in the jungle. One second it's there, the next it's gone, and you're left wondering if you really saw it at all."

"But you really do feel that as far as Carrie was concerned, it was there?"

"Oh yes. It was there all right."

"And was it ever more than a feeling on your part? I mean, did you ever see any evidence that this hidden self of Carrie's ever surfaced?"

"Ah, there speaks the policeman! Give me evidence, sir, he says. Oh, I'm sorry, Inspector, I suppose that wasn't really fair. After all, you are a policeman, and evidence you must have."

"Evidence would be useful," Thanet said with a grin. "It always is. But make no mistake about it, Mr Pitman, what you have just told me is immensely valuable to my understanding of the case."

"Good." The old man beamed. "Excellent, in fact. I can feel I haven't bared my soul in vain."

"But it *would* be useful . . ."

". . . if I could also produce something a little more concrete. Yes. Well, I suppose I might as well go the whole hog and tell you the worst. To put it bluntly, Carrie was a snooper of the first water."

"Ahhh . . ." It was a long exhalation of satisfaction. So that was why everybody had been so reticent about Carrie. Together with the effect that she had had on people, which Mr Pitman had just described . . . Yes. Thanet was experiencing a steady beat of excitement. "You caught her at it?"

"Hardly." Mr Pitman grimaced down at the inert body beneath the neatly folded sheets. "Though always, when she was dusting in here, I had the feeling she didn't miss a thing. But Marion was sure of it. Oh, it was only little things — a letter replaced the wrong way around in an envelope, things slightly displaced in drawers, that sort of thing — but after a while Marion got into the habit of making sure she never left lying around anything she wouldn't want Carrie to know about."

"But why go on employing her, if you were so sure that she was snooping?"

The old man lifted his hands in a hopeless gesture. "What alternative did we have, with me like this? It's not easy to find someone reliable, to do Carrie's job. And she was at least that. Marion often talked of giving up her work, staying at home permanently to look after me. And if it had just been the money, well that wouldn't have mattered so much. It's nice to have it, of course, but we don't have expensive tastes and we could easily have retrenched a bit. But I was dead against it. It's bad enough for me to know what sort of limitations I put on Marion's life as it is, without having to feel I'd cut her off completely from any personal satisfaction. She loves her work, you know, she's really devoted to those children. So we decided we'd grin and bear it." The old man gave Thanet a rueful grin. "Not the ideal situation, but there we are."

"I can see that," Thanet said with sympathy. "Do you think," he went on, carefully, "that she would ever have been tempted to use anything she might have learned in that way?"

The old man's eyes narrowed. "Blackmail, you mean? Now there's a thought. . . ." He considered. "I just don't know," he said at last. "But if so . . ."

"Exactly," Thanet said. "And I don't need to ask you to keep that idea under your hat."

"No, but . . . I've often asked myself what she got out of it, why she did it. And I came to the conclusion that it was the sense of power it gave her. To know people's secrets, and think they didn't know she knew."

"Nasty."

"Quite." The old man's tone was dry.

"I don't suppose you happen to know where she went on Thursday evenings?" Thanet asked casually.

"To clean the church I think. Why?"

"Just wondered." So old Mr Pitman didn't know everything that went on in the neighbourhood.

"Well," Thanet said, standing up and walking to the window, "it looks as though it's stopped raining at last." The unbroken mass of grey cloud which had earlier obscured the sun was beginning to break up, and a little wind was teasing the shrubs in the front garden. As Thanet watched, some forsythia blossom drifted down on to the bare brown earth in the border against the low front wall.

He turned away from the window, went to pick up his raincoat. He still had to ask the most delicate question of all. He liked the old man, didn't want to upset him, but it had to be put. If Mr Pitman thought him insensitive, it couldn't be helped.

"Your daughter never wanted to marry?" he inquired, in as casual a tone as possible.

He could see at once that he had underestimated the old boy. The blue eyes sharpened at once.

"Come now Inspector," the old man said. "I know you better than that. What are you getting at?"

Thanet gave a rueful smile. "Just a rather unpleasant rumour I heard, that's all," he confessed. "I didn't want to mention it, but I have to check up, you understand."

"Stop pussy-footing," said the old man testily. "What was it?"

"That your daughter is having an affair with Mr Ingram next door."

Mr Pitman's reaction took Thanet completely by surprise. The old man threw back his head and laughed. Thanet's eyes narrowed. Did he hear the unmistakable timbre of relief there?

"With that jackass? Credit her with more sense, Inspector, for heaven's sake!"

"I should think he could be very attractive to women," Thanet said stiffly.

"To some women, maybe. But not, I'm afraid, to Marion. And I can guess where the rumour came from. The delectable Joy has been at it again. Don't look so surprised, Inspector.

110

We do live next door to them, you know. And in the summer you'd be surprised what floats in through my open windows. I'm afraid, to put it crudely, she gives him hell.''

"Jealous," Thanet said.

"That poor fellow", Pitman continued, "has been accused of having affairs with just about every woman under the age of fifty in this village. And with a lot more besides.''

"I'll be off then," Thanet said. "Thank you for your help. And don't forget."

"I know," said the old man, laying one misshapen forefinger against his lips. "Mum's the word. Oh, Inspector," he added as Thanet turned towards the door, "there is just one thing.''

Thanet waited, one hand on the doorknob.

"Have you talked to Marion since yesterday morning?"

"Not properly, no."

"Only, she said that you'd been asking about Carrie's routine and that she'd forgotten to mention that whenever Major Selby was away, Carrie used to pop in to the Selbys' house morning and evening.''

"What for, do you know?"

The old man shook his head. "No idea. To be frank, I've often wondered, myself. All I know is that the length of time she stayed there used to vary enormously. Sometimes it would be a matter of minutes, sometimes as much as an hour.''

"Really?" Thanet was intrigued.

"And that she had a key to let herself in on such occasions.''

"You mean, she didn't normally have a key when she went there to work during the day?''

"No. I only know this because on one occasion when Carrie came in here in the evening before going on to the Selbys' she got into a terrible tizz because she'd lost the key. She found it, in the end. It had fallen out of her handbag when she'd dropped the bag in the hall on the way in. Anyway, I happened to mention this to Marion, later, and she was very surprised — said that she knew Carrie didn't usually have a key to the Selbys'. It's the sort of thing next-door neighbours get to know

111

about, especially in a small village. I remember we thought it quite a little mystery."

"One to which you never found the answer?"

"I'm afraid not." The old man's eyes were twinkling. "So if you do uncover it, don't forget to let me know, will you, Inspector? It's not good for me, in my condition, to be prey to unsatisfied curiosity."

Thanet grinned. "So on Monday evening, after leaving you, Carrie would have gone around to the Selbys'?" Why hadn't the Selbys said so, he wondered.

But Robert Pitman was shaking his head. "No. She never used to go on the evening Major Selby was expected back."

More and more interesting, Thanet thought.

Marion saw him to the front door. He realised that he had forgotten to mention Miss Cox's plight to her, and did so. He needn't have bothered, however. Marion had already arranged for someone to do her shopping for her.

"I only wish it was as easy to find a replacement for Carrie," she said, with a worried frown.

"Try Mrs Gamble," Thanet said, with a sudden stroke of inspiration.

"But she's already got a job, in Sturrenden."

"When I saw her last night she looked dead tired," Thanet said. "It might be worth a try."

"It'd be marvellous if she could," Marion said wistfully. "But I couldn't pay her anything like what she'd earn in a full-time job."

"You never know. She wouldn't have bus fares and lunches to offset against her earnings You'd have nothing to lose by asking."

"Perhaps I will," she said "Thank you, Inspector. You're very kind."

Social-worker Thanet at your service, he said to himself wryly as he left. It was the old, old problem: how to tread the tightrope between entering too fully into the lives and minds of the people he came across in the course of his work, and remaining too detached from them. He had constantly to be on his guard against the emotional involvement which would, he knew, cripple his judgement.

Outside, he stood for a moment breathing in the smell of wet earth, the faint fragrance of rain-washed flowers and then he walked thoughtfully down the path, turning at the gate to wave to Mr Pitman who would, he was sure, be watching him in the mirror. Had he imagined the note of relief in the old man's laughter at the suggested liaison between Ingram and Marion? And if not, what was the reason for it? Had he come close to a truth which Mr Pitman had not wanted him to discover? If so, the implication was that Marion might not be involved with Ingram, but she was with someone else.

Who?

Outside the gate Thanet hesitated, unable to give his attention to the question of where he wanted to go next. Perhaps he shouldn't have talked so freely to the old man. If Carrie had discovered that Marion had a lover, had threatened her with exposure. . . . Thanet shook his head impatiently. He couldn't believe that the Pitmans would have been able to find the sort of money Carrie had been raking in. All the same, it was extraordinary the lengths that people would go to, to scrape blackmail money together. Perhaps Marion had come to the end of her resources and, unable to meet Carrie's demands, had decided to kill her?

It was no good, he couldn't believe it. He just didn't see Marion as a murderer. Nevertheless the annals of crime are well stocked with murderers whose guilt astounded those who knew them best. He would not entirely rule out the possibility. Who might the man be? Someone at the school where she taught, perhaps? Lineham would have to do a little discreet checking.

Thanet glanced at his watch. Half past two. He had already decided to try to catch Susan Selby as she came out of school at ten to four. So, he had another hour or so in hand. Perhaps he would pay another call on Mrs Selby.

Those twice-daily visits of Carrie's, whenever Major Selby was away, intrigued him. He walked briskly along the road and up the Selby's drive.

113

12

There was no sign of the little gnome of a gardener today, but someone — Mrs Selby, he presumed — was in. Music floated down the drive to meet him. A piano recital on Radio Three, he decided as he approached the front door, listening with pleasure to the great arching ripples of sound. Then, with his hand on the knocker, he became quite still. Had that been a wrong note? Could it possibly be Mrs Selby who was playing? Almost at once there was a crashing discord, as if someone had brought his hands down with despairing anger upon the keyboard. Thanet stood motionless, listening. Silence.

Eventually he knocked at the door and waited, knocked again and then a third time. If she didn't answer, he decided, he would go around and try the back door. Just as he was about to turn away, however, he heard footsteps and Mrs Selby opened the door, blinking at him as though she had never seen him before. Her clothes were just as expensively elegant as yesterday — a pale green woollen dress with softly draped skirt and long full sleeves — but there was an indefinable difference in her. Thanet studied her closely as he spoke, trying in vain to pinpoint it.

She was clearly reluctant to let him in but she did, standing back and setting off down the hall without a word. Once again she led the way to the conservatory. In the big drawing room the grand piano stood open and there were sheets of music scattered around on the floor. The grate had not been cleared and the room looked untidy, neglected. Clearly, Carrie's absence was making itself felt.

Warmth and the damp, slightly musty odour of plants growing in a confined space enfolded them as they stepped into the conservatory.

"Sit down, won't you," said Mrs Selby, waving him into one of the cane armchairs. "Will you excuse me for a moment?"

Without waiting for a reply she left, crossing the drawing room towards the hall with a purposeful yet curiously hesitant stride. Thanet watched her out of sight, frowning, then strolled around the conservatory while he waited, thinking once again how Joan would have loved it. The plants which climbed the walls and scrambled along the roof, filtering the light, imparted to the little room an air of natural grace, and created an atmosphere of restfulness which soothed the spirit. Thanet had never been in a room quite like it before yesterday and he felt that he could now understand the Victorian addiction to such places. A green oasis such as this would provide its owner with a unique solace.

The plants in this one were many and varied in shape, size and habit, but all of them had one thing in common: beautiful foliage. Gold and silver, plain and variegated, delicate, feathery or heavily sculptural, they stood stiffly upright, arched or scrambled according to their nature. It was early in the season and there were as yet few flowers, but there was one plant in bloom and Thanet strolled towards it.

He had noticed it the other day. It was trained against the wall and had now reached head height. Its foliage was graceful, trilobate and stippled in random patterns and speckles of yellow on green. The flowers which adorned it were unlike any Thanet had seen before: bell-like, their petals were of palest apricot, fragile as tissue paper. Delicately, Thanet put up a finger, tilted one to look inside and was astonished to see that depending from one of the petals was a tear-drop. He touched it with a fingertip and it rolled on to his skin, but sluggishly. Not water, then? He bent his head, cautiously put out his tongue. Honey! No, he corrected himself. Not honey, nectar. He licked again. This, then, was the food of the Gods.

He stooped once more, to see if all the flowers had this extra-ordinary quality and it was at this point that he caught the glint of glass in amongst the dense foliage at the base of the shrub. He bent down and parted the leaves. It was a bottle, three-quarters empty. He picked it up, looked at the label: gin.

Beside it, planted in the moist, warm earth, was a glass. *We're teetotal, I'm afraid*, Major Selby had said.

It was one of those moments when the tumblers whirr and everything clicks into place. If Mrs Selby was a secret drinker, perhaps even an alcoholic . . .

Hearing the tap of her heels in the hall he wheeled around, sat down hastily in the chair she had indicated. He observed her closely as she entered the room, watching with new eyes that careful pacing, the tic beneath her eye, the beginnings of disintegration in her face.

"Forgive me for asking," he said as she sat down, "but was that you, playing the piano as I came up the drive?"

He had thought to put her at her ease by introducing a neutral topic and was astonished at her reaction. Those surprisingly large, capable hands — pianist's hands, he could see it now — curled involuntarily into fists and she closed her eyes briefly, as if in pain. Her smile, as she replied, was little more than a grimace. "I'm afraid so, yes."

"Afraid so? But you play wonderfully well," Thanet said, sincerely.

"You should have heard me when . . ." Abruptly she stopped. "But you obviously haven't come to talk about my prowess as a musician, Inspector. What did you want to see me about?"

On the alert, now, Thanet could detect the meticulous enunciation of the secret drinker. She was holding herself under a tight rein, every muscle stiff with tension. He had no doubt, however, that her self-control would hold. She had a long way to go before she reached the stage when she would fall apart. He might as well come straight to the point.

"I understand that when Major Selby was away, Miss Birch used to call here morning and evening."

Once again, her reaction surprised him. Almost at once she rose, her movements curiously stiff, as though she were a marionette. She walked jerkily to the windows overlooking the garden and stood looking out, her back to Thanet. Was it that she didn't trust herself to look at him, for fear of what he might read in her face?

116

"Yes, that is so," she said, and her voice had a waiting quality. He could hear the dread in it.

"Major Selby was away on Monday," he said. "I wondered if Miss Birch had called in here on the way home from the Pitmans'?"

"Oh," she said, turning around, lightness in her voice now, face transformed. "I see. Oh . . . no, of course not. We knew that my husband was expected home that evening, so there was no need."

"No need?" he said, seizing the opening he had hoped for.

Had he imagined the flash of panic in her eyes? She crossed the room in a sudden, unsteady flurry, sitting down in her chair and gripping the armrests as if she were clinging on to them for safety. Then suddenly, bewilderingly, her manner changed. She looked coyly down at her lap, positively fluttered her eyelashes at him.

"It's my husband," she said confidingly. "He fusses so. When he's away. . . . He just likes to be sure that someone is keeping an eye on us . . . on our safety, that is. Susan's and mine. A house like this, you know, such a temptation to burglars . . ."

Thanet listened incredulously. A more unlikely watchdog than Carrie he could not conceive of.

"Oh, I can see what you're thinking," Mrs Selby went on. "You're thinking Carrie wouldn't have been much protection. And it's true, of course, she wouldn't. But my husband had given her instructions to ring him immediately if she suspected that there was anything wrong. He always made sure she knew where to contact him. As long as there's an outside person keeping an eye on the place he can go away with an easy mind, he says." She stopped, looked at him hopefully and he could almost hear her thinking, *Does he believe me?*

And of course, he didn't. He could see, of course, that there was some kind of sense in what she was saying, but it wouldn't have been necessary for Carrie occasionally to stay up to an hour if she had only been checking to see that Mrs Selby and Susan were safe. A knock at the door and a moment's conversation would have told her that. No, Thanet now had a much more credible explanation of Carrie's visits. But one thing was certain: if his theory was correct, Mrs Selby was never going to admit it.

"Yes, I see,' he said, watching the relief in her face with compassion. Irene Selby would never have made an actress. "And you're certain she didn't call in last Monday?"

"No, she didn't. I told you, Henry was due back on Monday evening. There would have been no point."

"Thank you then, Mrs Selby," Thanet said, rising. "I'm sorry to have troubled you again."

Relief made her almost gay. "That's quite all right, Inspector. I know you have to get to the bottom of this awful business and anything we can do to help . . . any time . . ."

Through the dusty drawing room, down the hall to the front door her voice flowed on, babbling platitudes. Thanet left her with relief. It was now almost half past three; time to be on his way, if he wanted to catch Susan on her way home from school.

En route he thought about the Selbys. Major Selby must be worried sick about his wife's problem. He was the kind of man to whom position, status in the community, would matter very much indeed. So, where did Carrie come in? Working in the house as she did it was more than likely that she had long ago discovered Mrs Selby's secret. The point was, how had she used that knowledge? From what he knew of her and of Major Selby, Thanet could not imagine the subject ever having been directly broached between them; but he could see how, by hints and sly glances, Carrie could have communicated her understanding of the situation to her employer.

And then?

A meek request for higher wages, perhaps, granted by a secretly fuming Major Selby. How he would have hated being in the power of a nonentity like Carrie Birch.

And those visits while he was away? Thanet could see the situation having arisen in which, much as he would have loathed being beholden to Carrie, Major Selby could have decided to turn Carrie's knowledge of his wife's secret to his own advantage. Those business trips must have been a source of tremendous anxiety to him, for how could he keep his eye on his wife from a distance? Carrie must have seemed the perfect watchdog.

Thanet grimaced in distaste as he imagined Carrie, with licence to search, ferreting about for undetected bottles. In such a situation, Irene Selby could have swung violently between humiliation and anger; nothing infuriates an alcoholic as much as having his supplies taken away from him.

Suppose, then, that after leaving Robert Pitman on the night she died, Carrie had for some reason — misunderstood instructions, perhaps? — gone to the Selbys' despite Major Selby's return? Suppose that she had found Mrs Selby belligerently drunk and had tried to remove her store of alcohol . . . Here, indeed, was a potentially explosive situation. Thanet could imagine the whole distasteful scene, picture only too well Carrie's sly satisfaction, her sense of power as her employer pleaded with her. Driven by desperate need, Irene Selby might well have attempted to seize the bottle by force; might have struggled with Carrie, knocking her over perhaps and causing her to bang her head as she fell. And then, aghast at what had happened she might have panicked . . .

And this was where the theory foundered, thought Thanet. He could visualise everything up to this point, but he could not then imagine Irene Selby picking up the nearest cushion and cold-bloodedly finishing Carrie off. Why should she? She would have achieved her object, retrieved her bottle. . . . Unless, of course, her hatred of Carrie had by then been such that the opportunity to get rid of her for ever had been irresistible?

He was now driving past the tall hedge which marked the boundary of Sturrenden High School. In a moment he would come into sight of the main entrance. Rounding the bend in the road he was relieved to see that he was in good time. A long line of parked cars stretched down the drive and out on to the road: mothers, waiting to ferry their daughters home. Sturrenden High was a single-sex school, fee-paying and with an excellent academic reputation. Some of its pupils boarded but most came daily, travelling sometimes quite considerable distances from outlying villages. Thanet parked on the opposite side of the road, on the bus-station side of the school. From here he had a good view of the school gates and a reasonable chance of catching Susan as she went by.

A bell rang somewhere inside the building and almost at once the tranquil scene became one of swarming activity. The trickle of girls issuing from the building became a stream, then a flood. The cars crept steadily forward, picking up their passengers and then sweeping around the curve of the one-way drive to emerge on to the road some fifty yards away. Thanet began to worry in case Susan had had a lift or was perhaps staying on for some after-school activity. It was stupid of him, perhaps, not to have come earlier and asked for her to be brought out of lessons for an interview. But he hadn't wanted either to alarm her or to cause gossip. For the nth time in his career he told himself that he was too soft, that he would have to toughen up, stop being so ridiculously considerate of other people's feelings.

Then he saw her. By now the flood had dwindled to a trickle again. She was with two other girls, but even from this distance she was unmistakable. That silken curtain of blonde hair, the eye-catching figure and elegant, swaying walk — she would stand out anywhere. Susan Selby, Thanet reflected, would be able to earn a living as a model any day. As soon as the girls turned out of the gates he started the engine, pulled across the road and into the kerb a little way ahead of them. Then he got out of the car and stood waiting.

She recognised him at once and her step faltered. Then she said something to the other girls and they smiled, nodded, flicked their fingers in economical gestures of farewell and walked on without her, casting inquisitive glances at Thanet as they passed.

"I wondered if you might like a lift home," he said, smiling at her as she came up to him.

"The third degree in comfort?" she said, arching her eyebrows. She gave a slight shrug. "OK."

She waited until they had pulled out in the traffic and then half turned to face him, resting one arm on the back of her seat so that her fingers were brushing his shoulder

"Fire away," she said

13

Thanet did not immediately respond to her challenge. The afternoon traffic was building up and he waited until they were clear of the worst of the congestion and out on the Nettleton Road. Once they started to talk he wanted to be able to give her most of his attention. Meanwhile, he thought about what he was going to say. Some of it could be distinctly tricky.

He began blandly enough.

"I just wanted to talk to you about Monday night."

"Surprise, surprise! But I really haven't anything to tell you, Inspector."

"You were out that evening, though."

"Yes."

"In Sturrenden?"

"Right!"

"At the cinema, with Chris Gamble."

Silence. Then, "If you damn well know it all, why bother to ask?"

She didn't deny it, though. He wondered what she was trying to hide behind that flippant, half-cynical manner. Thinking of her parents, it wasn't difficult to guess: a rampant insecurity, a bitterness which could poison her life if she weren't careful. He would have to be gentle with her.

After a moment she said sulkily, "Who told you, anyway?" And then, "I suppose you're going to tell my father?"

He ignored the first question. "Why should you assume that?" he said.

She shrugged. "Isn't that your job? Stir us all up and see what crawls out?"

"That's not how I see it. There's no virtue in causing unnecessary distress. I simply want to catch a murderer."

121

A quick, sideways glance showed that she didn't believe him; she was staring out of the window, lips set in a stubborn line, arms folded defiantly. He sighed inwardly. This was going to be difficult.

There was a lay-by ahead and he signalled, pulled into it, switched off the ignition. Then he turned to face her. She really was a beautiful girl, he thought, with the kind of good looks that would improve with age: a smooth oval of a face and a classic bone-structure.

"Did either of you see or hear anything unusual on your way back from the bus stop?"

She lifted her shoulders. "I don't know about Chris. I didn't."

"You're sure?"

"I told you, no."

No point in pursuing the subject. "What did you think of Miss Birch?"

'Oh, *her*." Her mouth twisted and she looked away, out of the side window.

"You didn't like her." It was a statement, not a question.

"She was a creep, a real creep."

"In what way?"

She looked at him then, a long, considering look. He could hear her thinking, *How much shall I tell him?*, almost as clearly as if she had spoken the words aloud. At last, "She snooped," she said. "Poked her nose into everything." Indignation made her expansive. "I'd get home and find she'd even been through my underwear drawer, for God's sake!" Her nose wrinkled in distaste. "I didn't fancy wearing it, I can tell you, when I knew she'd been pawing it. She thought I didn't know, of course, but she never put things back in exactly the right way. You wouldn't believe how tidy I got, laying little traps for her. And she fell into them every time. If I could have locked up everything I owned, I would have."

"You never tackled her about it?"

"What was the point?" Susan said scornfully. "She would simply have denied it. There was never any proof, you see. And she never actually took anything."

122

"To know that you knew might have been enough to stop her."

"Not on your life. She loved it, you see. Poking and prying. I bet that's what finished her off in the end."

"You mean, she found out something. . . .?"

"That someone couldn't afford to let her know."

"Who, for example?"

"Mr Casanova Ingram, perhaps, and his fancy woman. I bet he wouldn't want his wife finding out about her."

"You know who she is?"

"The girlfriend? Sure. Works in that glam hairdressing salon in Turtle Street. Blonde and very painted."

Useful information, if true. As it probably was, for it could easily be checked. But why was Susan being so free with it? Diversionary tactics?

"I heard your mother playing the piano this afternoon," he said. "She's very good, isn't she?"

She looked at him warily. "Very." She hadn't been fooled by the apparent inconsequence of his remark, he could see.

He would have to come out into the open, do it as gently as he could. She was painfully vulnerable and he didn't want to hurt her, but he had to find out exactly what part Carrie had played in the Selby household.

"Susan," he said gently. "I'm sorry, but I know . . . about your mother."

She didn't pretend to misunderstand him, just stared at him for a moment, eyes stretched wide.

"My God," she said, "you're despicable, d'you know that? You're as bad as *her*, aren't you, poking about in other people's lives, turning over the stones and gloating over the nasties that crawl out. How can you do it? What sort of satisfaction do you get out of it?" She was shouting at him now, her face distorted with anger.

He bowed his head, waiting for the storm to pass, recognising the pain that lay beneath. He was only too familiar with the agonies of distress and humiliation experienced by the families of alcoholics and Susan was, despite her veneer of sophistication, only a child.

Her anger suddenly fragmented and she began to cry, arms folded across her body, hugging herself as if to try to contain her distress. Thanet pushed a handkerchief into her hand and waited in silence.

When, finally, her sobs had abated she blew her nose and whispered, "You don't know what it's like. You can't imagine."

He said nothing.

"It's him, you see. My father." She blew her nose again. "He's. . . . You're right, you know. Mum *is* a fine pianist, but she's nothing now to what she was. I've read her press cuttings. She could have been really first-rate — world-famous, even, perhaps. And *he* stopped her. Wanted a meek little wife to cook his meals, warm his carpet slippers and generally run around him in circles. God knows why she was prepared to do it. I suppose she was in love with him, wanted to please him, and before she knew where she was it was too late to change things. He's a tyrant, d'you know that? A real tyrant. D'you realise, he won't even let me go out in the evenings unless he knows exactly where I'm going, who I'm going with. . . . No boyfriends. . . . I haven't been to a party since I was thirteen. . . . So I'm not making any excuses about deceiving him over Chris. And, believe me, once I'm eighteen, he won't see me for dust."

She glanced at Thanet, looking at him properly for the first time since her anger erupted.

"Oh, I know what you're thinking," she said. "You're wondering what'll happen to Mum then, if I do go. You're thinking I'm a selfish bitch. Well, maybe I am, but if so, then it's him that's made me so. As for Mum. . . ." Her face crumpled and for a moment Thanet thought she was about to start crying again. She regained control, however, and looked down at her hands, twisting his handkerchief into a long, tight spiral. "I've just got to save myself, you see. It's too late for her, he's ruined her, so I've just got to get away. It's the only way I can survive. . . ."

She looked at him again then, a surprised, assessing look. "No," she said. "You weren't thinking that at all, were you?"

124

Thanet shook his head gently.

The compassion in his eyes made hers fill with tears. "What am I going to do?" she said. "Oh, what am I going to do?"

Thanet reached out to take her hand, squeezed it briefly before releasing it, and laid it back in her lap. It would need far more time than he could give, to help her. "Isn't there anyone you could talk to, in confidence?"

Her mouth twisted. "Who, for example?"

"One of the teachers at school, perhaps?"

"Not really. Well, perhaps there is one . . ."

"Why not think about it? Or there's a youth counselling service in Sturrenden."

She gave a quick, vehement shake of the head. "I couldn't talk to a stranger."

"I'm a stranger, and you're talking to me," he said. "People say it's often easier, to talk to strangers. They're not part of your life, you see. You don't have to face them, afterwards."

"I hadn't thought of it like that." She was much more composed now and she pulled a rueful face. "Wow, look at the mess I've made of your handkerchief. I'll have to buy you a new one."

"Forget it," he said. "Losing handkerchiefs is an occupational hazard."

She smiled, then, for the first time and Thanet caught his breath at the transformation. "Susan," he said, "before we get back to what we were discussing, let me just say this. Try not to let your relationship with your father poison your life. After all, if you think about it, that really would be letting him win, wouldn't it?"

She bit her lip, frowned, looked away.

"And now, back to business," he said.

It was much easier, this time. And he had been right, he discovered. It had been impossible to hide Mrs Selby's sickness from Carrie and Major Selby had decided to use the fact to his own advantage, to employ her as a watchdog during his frequent absences on business. Her job during those morning and evening visits had been to hunt out Mrs Selby's hidden reserves of alcohol and pour away the contents of any bottles she found.

"Can you imagine what it was like" Susan said bitterly, "knowing that she knew, feeling that she had Mum at her mercy, so to speak? And what was the point anyway? Mum always managed to hide it away somewhere . . ." She stopped, clearly torn between loyalty to her mother and dislike of the cleaning woman. "It's an illness, you know," she said, defensively. "Mum just can't help herself. I've read up about it. And it can be treated, there are places. . . . But Dad could never look at it like that. He sees it as a simple matter of will-power. . . . *Simple*!" She gave a bitter little laugh. "I tried to persuade him to get her some proper treatment, but he would never listen. He's too afraid it'll get out, that his precious social standing would be smirched, if people knew. He'd rather sacrifice his own wife. . . ." She gave Thanet a shame-faced little glance. "I did try to help her, but he wouldn't have it. I wanted to give up school after my O Levels, stay at home with her, but he wouldn't allow me to. He preferred to use that woman, instead."

"He wasn't afraid she'd talk?"

"Oh, he paid her well, believe me. No, she knew which side her bread was buttered."

How well? Thanet wondered, remembering the bundles of notes, the carrier bags of expensive clothes. And had Carrie become greedy, put pressure on him? Major Selby wouldn't have liked that. Nor, for that matter, would he have enjoyed being beholden to her. Perhaps he had begun by finding it the lesser of two evils, ended by finding it intolerable.

"You arrived home before your father on Monday evening, I believe," he said.

She looked at him with quick understanding. "Yes, I did. And if you're thinking what I think you're thinking, you can forget it. Carrie had left even before I got home."

"She was there on Monday night?"

"She must have been. She always came when Dad was away."

"But not on the evening he was due home, surely?"

126

"No. But he came home early this time. He wasn't really due until Tuesday. He got through his business more quickly than he had expected, I gathered."

"Would he have let your mother know that he was coming home early?"

"Probably."

"In that case, she would surely have got a message to Carrie, saying that it was unnecessary for her to come?"

"I suppose so. You'd have to ask her."

Thanet didn't say that he already had, that Mrs Selby had lied over her husband's expected time of arrival. And why should she have done so? Because she didn't want Thanet to know that there had ever been a possibility of Carrie having been in the house on Monday evening? Could she suspect her husband of the murder?

"Where was your mother, when you got home?"

"In bed." Susan grimaced. "Well, not exactly. She was, to be precise, lying on top of it. . . . And if you're thinking she could possibly have had anything to do with Carrie's death, you can forget it. Mum was out for the count. Had been for some time, by the look of it. I went straight up to her room when I got in and I'd just managed to get her under the covers when Dad arrived. So I could just pretend she was in bed and asleep, thank God."

But, thought Thanet, what if Major Selby was at that point arriving home for the second time? What if he'd come home earlier, while Carrie was there, and found his wife in a drunken stupor? Might he not then have accused Carrie of incompetence, have lost his temper? Thanet could just imagine the scene: the Major purple in the face, Carrie meek, submissive yet all-powerful — just the sort of situation to provoke a man like Selby beyond endurance.

"You heard your father's car come into the drive?"

"No, just the back door shutting."

So it was possible. Selby's car could already have been in the garage at the back of the house when Susan arrived home. Perhaps it would be possible to trace someone who had actually seen the Major's car turning into the drive?

Thanet had learned as much as he could from Susan for the moment so he thanked her, started the car and drove her back to Nettleton in thoughtful silence. Just as she was getting out, however, he thought of something he had forgotten to ask.

"I believe that on several occasions you saw Miss Birch on the last bus back from Sturrenden? Always on Thursday evening, I understand?"

Susan turned back, stooping to talk to him through the open door. "That's right, yes. I wondered if she'd tell Dad about Chris and me, but she never did. She'd just give me that sly, knowing look of hers. It seemed enough for her, to know that you knew she knew, if you see what I mean."

"Can you remember how she was dressed on those occasions?"

Susan's eyebrows rose. "Sure. Same as usual. Drab old this and that. As if she'd just walked into a jumble sale and grabbed the first dreary things that came to hand."

"Did you happen to notice if she was carrying anything?"

Susan considered. "Just a handbag I think. Nothing very bulky, anyway."

'Did you ever run into her earlier in the evening, in the town?"

"No, never."

"And she never gave you any indication of where she had been, on those Thursday evenings?"

" 'Fraid not." Susan's attention had strayed now and she was looking over her shoulder at the house, wondering no doubt what sort of state she would find her mother in today.

It was with compassion that Thanet said goodbye and watched her walk away up the drive towards her expensive home and her daily purgatory.

14

"What the hell has it got to do with you?" snarled Ingram.

Dennis Ingram was the owner of the largest employment agency in Sturrenden and his office was as modern and expensive as his house: thick carpets, chrome and leather chairs, smoked glass tables and paintings to which Thanet wouldn't have given house room. Its one enviable feature in his opinion was the view of the river, framed in a window the length of Thanet's living room.

"Nice view you've got here, sir." Thanet said, crossing the room to look out at the broad expanse of water, shimmering in the late afternoon sun. The inconsequence of the remark was, he knew, deliberately provocative. When people were angry they were often indiscreet. And he was comfortably sure of his ground. After dropping Susan he had called in at the hairdressing salon in Turtle Street before coming here. Ingram's "blonde, very painted" had freely admitted her involvement with him — which was evidently more than Ingram was prepared to do, the other way around.

"Never mind the bloody view. I don't see what right you have to come poking about in my private life." Head down, colour high in cheeks, Ingram looked like an angry bull about to charge. There was no doubt about it, he was over-reacting. Because he was afraid that his wife would now find out about his girlfriend, or because he had been involved in the murder? Thanet was determined to find out.

"Mr Ingram," Thanet said in a world-weary tone, "your private life is, I can assure you, of no interest to me except insofar as it touches upon the murder I am investigating. No," he said, holding up a hand as Ingram opened his mouth to interrupt, "please, let me finish. The young lady in question has already admitted her involvement with you. I am merely asking you to confirm it. If that involvement has no bearing on the case, I can assure you that my interest in the matter will cease forthwith.''

Ingram stared at him, eyes narrowed. ''You mean,'' he said at last, ''that my wife doesn't necessarily have to know about this?''

''What would be the point in my telling her? Assuming, of course, as I said, that there is no connection with the murder.''

''But what possible connection could there be?'' said Ingram. He had relaxed a little now and was sitting back in his chair. He picked up a pencil and began to slide it through his fingers from one hand to the other in a smooth, rhythmic movement that Thanet guessed was habitual.

Thanet found this reaction interesting. Hands were often a give-away, less easily controlled than facial muscles. It really began to look as though Ingram's main concern was his wife.

Thanet shrugged. ''At this stage I'm casting around amongst Miss Birch's acquaintance, seeing what turns up. Seeming irrelevancies can often prove to be of vital significance.''

''Well, this one won't,'' Ingram said. ''It's true that I have been . . . involved . . . with Miss Parker, but I really do fail to see how that fact could have even the remotest connection with the death of Miss Birch.''

''You knew Miss Birch, and. . . .''

''So did the postman and the dustman,'' Ingram cut in with a little laugh. ''And are you investigating them? Seriously, Inspector, my acquaintance with Miss Birch was no closer than theirs. I passed the time of day with her when I saw her and that was as far as it went.''

Ingram was still slightly on the defensive but that could be perfectly natural. Thanet knew that even innocent people feel obscurely threatened when being questioned by the police. He was becoming more and more convinced that Ingram was telling the truth.

On the other hand, he reflected as he drove back to the office for the daily stint of reports, Ingram might simply be a superb actor. He must, after all, have had plenty of practice in lying to his wife and, if he was guilty, the fear of being found out could be enough to inspire the finest performance of his life. If so, Thanet could only hope that sooner or later some kind of clinching evidence would surface. It was surprising how long it sometimes took for this to happen. People hesitated, forgot, did not realise the significance of some piece of information and it could be days or even weeks before they came forward.

Meanwhile, he began to hope that Lineham or one of the others might have turned up something interesting today.

No such luck, however. Lineham was just completing his reports when Thanet arrived and he shook his head gloomily in response to Thanet's question.

"More or less a blank, I'm afraid," he said. "It's all here," and he tapped the little stack of papers beside him, "but briefly, there's still no sign of the weapon or the handbag, no news of Ingram's girlfriend, if he had one, and none of the PCC members saw or heard anything of interest on the night of the murder. They all left the vicarage together at ten, except for Miss Pitman. She's the treasurer and stayed behind to have a word with the vicar about something."

"Yes, she told me. She didn't see anything either, I'm afraid."

"The only interesting fact we've gleaned all day," said Lineham, "is that Miss Birch used to catch the last bus home from Sturrenden on Thursdays."

In view of all the unfruitful work the others had put in today, Thanet felt a twinge of guilt that he had already learnt this for himself, but he told himself not to be so sensitive. That was, after all, police work: hours, days, weeks, sometimes months of dreary slog, only to find when you finally turned up something interesting, that the other chap had beaten you to it. "So I heard," he said. "Jenny Gamble told me, and Susan Selby confirmed it. Tomorrow you'd better get the men on to trying to find out where she went in Sturrenden. Incidentally, Susan also put me on to Ingram's girl friend." And briefly, Thanet gave Lineham an account of his afternoon's activities.

Lineham left shortly afterwards and Thanet settled down to his own reports. By the time he had finished it was eight o'clock and his brain felt as though it were stuffed with cotton wool. He rubbed his eyes, stretched, then relaxed, consciously trying to empty his mind. What he needed now was a peaceful evening and a good night's sleep.

A peaceful evening! Inwardly, he groaned. Not much prospect of that. In his absorption in his work he had temporarily forgotten about Joan's back-to-work campaign. As he drove home he hoped devoutly that she would not broach the subject again that evening. He really didn't have the mental energy left to discuss it. Today he had seen so many people, assimilated and assessed so much information that he didn't think he could manage anything more taxing than an evening sunk in stupor in front of the television set.

For once it was a relief to find that the children were in bed and asleep. Thanet sniffed appreciatively as he stepped into the hall: some sort of savoury casserole, he decided. With herb dumplings, perhaps? Mouth watering, he made his way into the kitchen and gave Joan an enthusiastic kiss. As he did so, he felt a pang of regret. Would this kind of welcome soon be a thing of the past?

Joan must have sensed the sudden reservation in him. "What's the matter?" she said.

"Nothing," he lied. "Wearing day, that's all."

She wasn't sure whether to believe him or not, he could see. Always sensitive to his moods, she was probably interpreting his behaviour towards her at the moment solely in the light of his attitude to her problem. Correctly, as it happened.

"Supper's all ready," she said. "I'll dish up. Why don't you go and have a drink, while you're waiting?"

The stiff whisky helped and by the time they sat down at the table he was a little more relaxed. Even so, he found himself on his guard, waiting for her to bring the subject up again. She did not do so until they were seated peacefully by the fire, drinking coffee.

"Darling . . ." she said diffidently. Here it comes, he thought.

". . . what you said last night . . ." She was still hesitating.

"Mmmm?" he said, head resting against the back of the

settee, eyes closed. Even this non-committal response managed to sound irritated, long-suffering, he realised.

". . . about me going ahead," she finished. "Did you mean it — really?"

"Honey," he said wearily, "can't we leave it, just for tonight? I'm whacked."

She said nothing and he opened his eyes to look at her.

She was staring into the fire, her lips set in a mutinous line. Guilt and anger warred within him, the latter flaring up as she said tightly, "Luke, we have to get this sorted out."

"But why now, for God's sake?"

She turned her face towards him and he caught his breath a little at the unhappiness in it. "But that's the trouble, don't you see?" she said. "It never is the right time. That first evening, when we started to talk about it, I told you I'd hesitated to broach the subject because I didn't know how you'd react. But I didn't tell you just how long I'd been hesitating, did I? Almost a year, d'you know that? And do you know why? Because it's never the right time. Because you're always too busy, too tired or too late, too *some* damn thing!"

The unfamiliar, mounting anger in her voice suddenly faded and she turned away, staring miserably into the fire again. "Oh, I'm sorry . . . I didn't want to say all that. I hoped it wouldn't be necessary, that you'd just say whole-heartedly, 'Go ahead.' But don't you see, Luke, it's time now for me to have something of my own to work for. All these years . . . I've tried hard to be the sort of wife you want, and I've even hoped that would turn out to be enough for me. But it isn't, and there's no point in pretending otherwise. So, don't you see, we can't just go on shelving the problem, hoping that it'll go away. It won't. And I can't go ahead without your approval, I just can't. I'm not that sort of woman. It's not simply that, if I do get an interesting job, I'll need you to be pretty easy-going in all sorts of practical ways — it's that I want you behind me, morally speaking, interested in what I do. Can't you see that?" And she looked at him pleadingly.

Thanet was torn. Half of him acknowledged that what she said was true, that she had been a good wife, put his well-being

133

and comfort first, always. But the other half was rebellious. Couldn't she see that what she was asking was unreasonable? He'd told her last night to go ahead. What more could she ask? He couldn't be expected to change his feelings, could he?

"Of course I see all that," he said, and was relieved that the irritation wasn't showing in his voice. "And I told you last night, go ahead. Investigate the possibilities. Find something you'll really enjoy and I'll back you all the way." But the words lacked conviction and he knew it.

So did Joan. She looked at him dubiously. "You really mean that?"

"Darling, how many times d'you want me to tell you?"

A million times would not be enough, he realised, so long as he felt this way. Joan knew him well enough to sense that he was lying, however convincing he tried to be. He told himself that it couldn't be helped, that he couldn't change the way he felt, that she would just have to be satisfied with what she'd got. He felt aggrieved. Surely he had done all that could be expected of him, and more? Not many men would have done as much, he was sure.

Perhaps she had acknowledged this, for she smiled at him now, gave him a thank-you kiss. And, reluctant as he had been to enter into the discussion, he realised that it was after all better to have talked; now at least they could relax.

Thanet meditated, not for the first time, on the way people function on two different levels simultaneously. On the public one they speak, gesture, apparently react; but it is on the other, the private one, that they are truly themselves. Here lie their secret thoughts, fears, hopes, fantasies; shared but occasionally, and only with those they really trust, those with whom they can allow themselves to be vulnerable.

He had always thought that he and Joan were lucky. They were able to be themselves with each other — or so he had always imagined. Now he was learning that he had been wrong; all this time, Joan had been hiding away from him the side of herself that dreamed, aspired. As he, now, was hiding from her his true feelings on this subject. Perhaps their relationship was going to go the way of so many he had seen;

134

perhaps their best and closest years together were over. It was a depressing thought and something that he was determined to prevent, if it was in his power to do so. But it seemed that if he was to succeed, somehow he was going to have to change his attitude towards this job business. And how could he do that?

How could one change the way one felt?

In bed later he lay listening to Joan's even breathing and thought back over his day. In the darkness and the silence he gradually became aware of something hovering on the edge of his consciousness. He had no idea of its nature, but there it was, on the very periphery of his awareness. What could it be? The significance of some fact, so far dismissed as unimportant? Or some insight, vital to his understanding of the case? But it wouldn't come. Perhaps, while he was asleep, his subconscious would give it a shove and in the morning there it would be, waiting for him when he awoke. It had often happened that way in the past. It was as if that submerged level of the mind was able to operate better when the surface ones were not functioning. From which level, he wondered, did the impulse to murder come?

This meaty question occupied him until he fell asleep.

15

"Inspector Thanet?"

"Speaking."

"Paul Ennerby here, vicar of Nettleton. Do you think you might be coming out to Nettleton this morning?"

"Yes, I'll be along shortly, as a matter of fact."

"Only, I've got something to tell you. Do you think you could call in at the vicarage?"

Words to gladden any policeman's heart, thought Thanet. Perhaps they would compensate for the fact that his subconscious had let him down; no dazzling revelation had awaited him this morning. "By all means," he said. "What time would suit you?"

"Fairly early? I've got a Mothers' Union coffee morning at ten thirty. I'll be working at home till then."

"Nine thirty, then?"

"Fine. Thank you. Goodbye."

Lineham had just come in.

"The vicar of Nettleton is about to Reveal All, by the sound of it," Thanet said. Then, "You're looking remarkably cheerful this morning, Mike."

"I told her," said Lineham, beaming.

Evidently he had plucked up the courage to tackle his mother.

"You said you'd go ahead regardless?"

Lineham nodded. "Not quite as bluntly as that, though. I . . . er . . . wrapped it up a bit."

"Naturally," Thanet said. "And there's no need to ask how she took it, by the look of you."

Lineham was going to tell him anyway. He was positively bubbling over with it. "To be honest, sir, I was scared stiff.

Well, I thought, perhaps she'll have a heart attack here and now, and she wouldn't have if I hadn't told her, if you see what I mean, and then I'd wish I'd kept quiet." He stopped, looked hopefully at Thanet, as if wondering whether Thanet was following him.

"Quite," said Thanet encouragingly, pleased at the success of Lineham's stand (and relieved, too, for if Mrs Lineham *had* had another heart attack it was he, Thanet, who would truly have been responsible, no doubt about that) but impatient to get out to Nettleton to see the vicar. It must surely be important, or Mr Ennerby would not have bothered to phone. Perhaps someone had confessed to him? No, it couldn't be that. The secrets of the confessional were sacrosanct.

"So she said . . ." Lineham was saying. He was obviously determined to give a blow-by-blow account of the conversation and Thanet didn't have the heart to discourage him. Thanet couldn't help rejoicing for his sergeant. He looked as though the troubles of the world had suddenly been lifted from his shoulders. Mrs Lineham had apparently been a little tearful to begin with, but when she realised that her son really meant what he was saying, she had given in gracefully. "D'you think I could just give Louise a ring, sir?" Lineham finished up. "I can't wait to tell her and I didn't like to ring from home . . ."

"Go ahead," said Thanet resignedly, thinking for the umpteenth time that he would be glad when all these traumas were over and Lineham was comfortably settled into married bliss. "You can follow me out to Nettleton. I'm going to see the vicar first, but then I want you with me when I see first Mrs Selby, then her husband. We really must find out whether or not Carrie went to the Selbys' after leaving the Pitmans'. Susan says she must have, because Major Selby was not expected home until Tuesday, but it's only an assumption on her part. I'll see you in the church car park around ten."

The uncertain weather of the last few days had vanished overnight and it was a sparkling March morning. A frisky wind propelled fluffy white clouds briskly across the sky and tree branches dipped and swayed in the gardens as Thanet sped past.

When he got out of the car in Nettleton he stood quite still

137

for a moment or two, taking deep breaths of country air. There was a builder's lorry parked opposite the end of the footpath which ran along the back of Church Cottages and two men were unloading sacks on to the narrow pavement. One of them set off along the footpath as Thanet passed on his way to the vicarage gate. He was trundling two of the sacks in a wheelbarrow.

The other man was Arnold, the builder. He was systematically marking each thick paper sack with a wide-tipped black felt pen. Thanet stopped, intrigued.

"Morning," he said.

Arnold glanced up, returned the greeting. "Bloody waste of time," he muttered. "If you lot did your job properly, I wouldn't have to be doing this."

Thanet came closer, peered down at the marks Arnold was making: a circle approximately six inches in diameter, with a capital A inside it. "What do you mean?" he said.

"Some perisher's been nicking my stuff, hasn't he? Bag after bag of cement, sand, ballast . . . You name it, he's had it."

"All in one go?"

"Naw. Bit at a time. But it all adds up. Lost nearly fifty quid's worth of stuff, I have, in the last month. And your lot have done damn all about it."

"You've reported it, then?"

Arnold stood up, glanced impatiently along the footpath. "You bet. And a fat lot of good it's done me. Where the devil's Bill got to? Bill!" he yelled.

"So you decided to mark it. Good idea."

"Only if we spot any of the stuff after. But believe me, if I do, I'll knock the bleeder into the middle of next week."

"Much more sensible to let us know, first," Thanet said mildly. "You wouldn't want to end up on a charge of assault, would you?"

"Justice!" muttered Arnold. He took one or two steps away from Thanet and peered along the footpath. "*Bill*!" he bellowed.

The sound of the wheelbarrow heralded Bill's appearance.

"Where the hell've you been?" said Arnold. "We haven't got all day, you know."

"I . . ."

"Don't give me any of your guff," Arnold said. "Been chatting up that bird from next door again, haven't you?"

Bill did not deny the accusation, merely bent to lift another sack into the wheelbarrow.

"Mr Arnold . . ." Thanet said, when Bill had set off once more.

"Yeah?" Arnold was reaching across to ease a large sheet of plasterboard off the lorry. It, too, had been marked, Thanet noticed.

"The night of the murder," Thanet said. "Was anything taken?"

Arnold slid the plasterboard into a vertical position and leaned it against the side of the lorry. Then he shook his head. "Nothing's been nicked since the weekend. Saturday night it was, the last time. A yard of ballast! Makes you think, don't it? I mean, it must be someone local. The bleeder must have carted it off in a wheelbarrow. Well he ain't building Buckingham Palace at my expense, I can tell you. If anything else goes missing I'll camp out in the house at night until I get him. I'm hoping this murder might've scared him off. It's an ill wind, they say. . . . Now, if you'll excuse me." He lifted the sheet of plasterboard and set off down the footpath, crabwise.

Pity, thought Thanet, watching him go. If the thief had been at work on the night of the murder he might possibly have seen or heard something and it would have been worth making an all-out effort to catch him.

All the same, he thought as he pushed open the vicarage gate and walked up the path, the fact that nothing had been stolen on the night of the murder did not necessarily mean that the thief had not been in the garden of number two that evening. He might have gone along to steal something and been disturbed. Say that he had heard someone coming. . . . He would have hidden — there was plenty of cover. He might even have seen or heard the murderer as he dumped Carrie's body in the privy.

The vicarage door stood ajar and Thanet knocked absently, his mind far away. It could even be, he realised, that the thief himself was the killer. Say that on her way home Carrie had

139

seen or heard something suspicious — someone carting something away in a wheelbarrow, for instance. Arnold might well have complained to her about the pilfering, told her that he suspected a local. He might even have asked her to keep her eyes open. Suppose, then, that she had recognised the thief. . . . This might be the reason why, after the initial blow on the head, the murderer had decided to finish her off: he could not afford her to recover consciousness and reveal his identity.

Surely, though, this would have been rather a thin motive for murder? But people had been killed for far less, he reminded himself. In any case, if the thief had killed her, or even if he had simply seen the murderer, he would surely have gone away empty-handed, if he had any common sense at all. He would not have risked drawing attention to himself.

At this point Thanet had a strong feeling that there was something he should be remembering. Not that elusive fact or insight which had been floating around last night, no, but something which had been triggered off by this most recent train of thought. What *was* it? He shook his head, scowled. He was losing his grip.

And where was the vicar?

Lurid thoughts flashed through his mind, born of detective novels in which those with interesting information to impart invariably met a sticky end before they could disclose it. He pushed the door wider, stepped into the hall.

"Mr Ennerby?" he called.

No reply.

He went to the foot of the stairs, called again.

A door banged at the back of the house, making him start.

"Is that you, Inspector?" The vicar appeared in the kitchen doorway. "Sorry, have you been here long? I just popped out to the greenhouse while I was waiting." He extended grubby hands. "I'll just wash these. Come on in, won't you?"

The kitchen was just as hospitable by day as by night. Sunshine streamed in through the window and a kettle was hissing on the Raeburn.

"Cup of coffee, Inspector? Do sit down."

Thanet shook his head and took one of the chairs at the formica table. The room was neat and tidy, breakfast dishes cleared away, work surfaces uncluttered. The Reverend Paul Ennerby obviously coped very well without a wife.

"I hope you didn't mind my asking you to call," the vicar began, seating himself opposite Thanet.

"Not at all."

"It's just that . . . oh, dear, I really do find it extraordinarily difficult to. . . ." He was gazing fixedly at his hands, which were clasped on the table in front of him, and now he glanced up at Thanet. The grey eyes were — what were they? thought Thanet. Embarrassed? Shamefaced? Pleading? He began to wonder what was coming.

"You might think," said the vicar, having apparently decided on an approach to the subject, "that I am a bachelor, or a widower, perhaps." And he glanced around the kitchen, as if to underline the absence of a wife in this most feminine of provinces.

'Well I had . . ." began Thanet.

"Well you'd be wrong. I am married, but my wife isn't here. She's . . . she's in a mental hospital. I won't go into the details, but she's been there now for ten years or more, and they say there's no hope of a recovery."

Ennerby paused, but he wasn't asking for sympathy. He was simply sketching in the background of what he had to say. Thanet simply sat and waited. It was evident that the difficult part was coming next. The vicar's knuckles were now white with tension, and he moistened his lips before managing to summon up the resolution to continue.

"Forgive me, Inspector," he said, with a nervous little laugh, "but as you will see. . . . The fact of the matter is," he went on, his voice suddenly much stronger, "that after you came to me the night before last with that absurd rumour about Miss Pitman and Mr Ingram, I . . . Well, I know that in a murder investigation all sorts of things turn up, are uncovered, so to speak, that have no relevance to it. And I am well aware that those who have something to hide can quite easily fall under suspicion even though what they are hiding might have no connection whatever with the case. . . . In short, for Miss Pitman's sake, I felt I had to explain to you that if you feel she is holding anything back she is, in fact, trying to protect . . . me." His voice tailed away and he bowed his head.

Thanet still wasn't sure what the vicar was trying to tell him, but the man's embarrassment seemed to point to only one explanation. He remembered the note of relief in old Mr Pitman's laughter at the suggestion of a liaison between Marion and Ingram. "You mean," he said slowly, hoping that he hadn't got it wrong, "that you and Miss Pitman . . ."

"Yes," said Mr Ennerby. And then, quickly, "Oh, not in the conventional sense, Inspector. I mean, we haven't . . . it hasn't been an *affair*, so to speak. But we are in love, yes, although we know that the situation is hopeless. My wife . . . although her mind has gone, she is physically healthy and is expected to live for very many years."

What a miserable, miserable situation, Thanet thought. No doubt, for a vicar, divorce and remarriage would be out of the question. He would probably have to leave the church. All very well if his religion was hollow, but if it was not. . . . He looked at the Reverend Paul Ennerby's fine, strong face and knew that his was not.

"The point is, you see, that no one knows about this. Even though we have nothing to hide in the conventional sense, if it came out there would be a great deal of talk and inevitably Miss Pitman would suffer. She has a difficult enough life as it is, though she never complains. And I know that out of a sense of loyalty to me, she would say nothing to you about our . . . relationship. Vicars, as you no doubt realise, are especially vulnerable to gossip. I felt I must explain all this to you myself so that you wouldn't misinterpret any evasiveness on Miss Pitman's part. I hope you don't feel that I am insulting you when I add that all this really is in the strictest confidence."

"It won't leak out in the parish through me, I can assure you," Thanet said. "Unless, of course, it has some bearing on the case."

"It hasn't," said the vicar eagerly. "The very fact of my having been frank with you shows how confident I am that it hasn't."

Thanet hoped that he was right. "Did Miss Birch have any inkling of this?"

"No, certainly not. I told you, I'm one-hundred-per-cent

certain that nobody has. Except Miss Pitman's father, of course, and he is absolutely to be trusted. If they had, there would have been whispers, glances, innuendoes — you know the sort of thing — and I would have been bound to be aware of it. I just felt that it would be better to get in first with the truth than have you suspicious of Miss Pitman for the wrong reasons.''

"I can see that," Thanet said, rising and holding out his hand, "and I appreciate your confidence."

"There was one other thing," Ennerby said quickly.

Thanet sat down again.

"I should have remembered before, I suppose, but it wasn't until last night that it came back to me. My study is at the front of the house and when I have phone calls at night I tend not to bother to switch the light on. I know the study like the back of my hand and in any case I usually leave the study door open so that the light from the hall shines in. I never draw the curtains. It wasn't until last night, when I answered the phone about nine thirty, that I remembered having had a phone call towards the end of the PCC meeting on Monday night. I think it was because the circumstances were exactly reproduced — I was standing there, gazing absentmindedly out of the window into the darkness and it suddenly came back to me. Just before that call ended, the one on Monday night I mean, I saw Miss Birch coming along the pavement on the other side of the road."

Thanet's stomach clenched with excitement. It was almost as though he had caught a glimpse of her himself.

"Where was she, exactly?"

"On the far side of the Pitmans' bungalow, walking this way. I assumed she'd been to the Selbys', but I may be quite wrong."

But he probably wasn't, thought Thanet. The old vicarage was the last house in the village. Where else would Carrie have been coming from, at that time of night? Here was confirmation that Mrs Selby had lied. "You're sure it was she?"

"Absolutely. I know it's some distance along the road, but when I saw her she was just coming into the light of that street lamp which is outside the Pitmans' gate. I saw her pretty clearly, and besides, she was a very individual figure, you know."

143

"And you're sure she was on the far side of the Pitmans' house?"

"Certain."

"She couldn't simply have been letting herself out of the Pitmans' drive?"

"No. Absolutely not."

"And this was just before the end of the PCC meeting, you say?"

"Yes, at about, let me see, say ten to ten?"

"Did you see where she went?"

"I'm sorry. I just caught this glimpse of her at the very moment when I was putting the phone down. And of course, I didn't think anything of it at the time. The next second I'd turned away. I was anxious to get back to the meeting."

A pity, but it couldn't be helped. Ennerby could be lying, of course, but Thanet didn't think so.

"Thank you for suggesting Mrs Gamble as a substitute for Miss Birch, by the way," the vicar said as he preceded Thanet to the front door. "Miss Pitman spoke to her about it and she's agreed. Miss Pitman's over the moon about it."

Thanet made self-deprecatory noises but couldn't help feeling distinctly smug.

Lineham was sitting on the churchyard wall. When he saw Thanet emerge from the vicarage he jumped down and crossed the road to meet him.

"Anything interesting?" he said.

"Could be." Thanet gave him a brief summary of the interview.

"So Mrs Selby was lying," said Lineham.

"If we believe Mr Ennerby's story, yes."

"Don't you believe him?"

"I don't think he's lying," Thanet said, "but he could be mistaken. There's only a few yards in it, and it was some distance away, and in the dark. I've been here at night, and that lamp outside the Pitmans' isn't all that bright."

They had walked rather aimlessly a few paces along the road while they were talking and were now at the entrance to Church Lane. As they waited to cross to the old vicarage a blue van

144

with BARRET'S on it in bold white lettering turned into the lane and pulled up in front of old Miss Cox's cottage.

"Just a minute," Thanet said, putting a hand on Lineham's arm to restrain him from setting off across the road, and the two men watched as the driver jumped out of the van, went up to the door of number five and knocked.

Barret's, Thanet remembered, was the store for which Miss Cox made loose covers, a skill presumably learned years ago before she became a recluse. Aware that he was wasting time, but driven by sheer curiosity to see how she handled this sole contact with the outside world, Thanet began to stroll along the lane. With a puzzled glance Lineham fell into step beside him.

"I forgot to tell you," Thanet said, as they passed number two, where sounds of vigorous hammering could be heard. And he recounted Arnold's information about the sneak thief. "After we've seen the Selbys, scrape together as many men as you can and put them all on to going through the village with a fine-toothed comb. We'll see if we can find any of Arnold's marked materials, flush this character out."

Miss Cox's door had opened and she and the driver exchanged a few words. Then Miss Cox went back into the house, leaving the man standing on the doorstep. As Thanet and Lineham approached the cottage Miss Cox reappeared, slowly backing towards the front door in a half-stooped position. The van driver said something, bent to touch her on the shoulder and she stood aside for him. He leant forward, swung the large, plastic-wrapped bundle she had been dragging on to his shoulder and set off briskly down the path to the van. Thanet caught a glimpse of swathes of floral material through the plastic covering before the driver closed the double doors of the van. Miss Cox, he was aware, had seen himself and Lineham approaching.

"Morning, Miss Cox," he said, raising a hand in salute. "Lovely day, isn't it?"

She croaked something, presumably a greeting, then began to hobble down towards the front gate. She was using her stick again today. The crutches, yesterday, had presumably steadied her for sweeping the path.

Thanet and Lineham pressed themselves back against the picket fence as the van reversed down the lane. Then they turned to the old woman. There was something infinitely pathetic about that combination of masculine garb and vulnerability, Thanet thought.

"Have you made any progress?" she said in that rusty voice of hers.

"Oh yes, we're coming on, aren't we?" said Thanet, looking to Lineham for confirmation. "Definitely."

"Definitely," echoed Lineham, nodding like a mechanical toy.

"How much longer?" she asked. Her face was screwed up with anxiety.

"Oh, it'll be soon now, I hope," Thanet said, with what he hoped was hearty reassurance. "Very soon."

She peered into his face and then, apparently satisfied, gave a tight little nod, turned and lurched awkwardly back towards the house.

"Extraordinary, the unspoken pressure that woman puts on one, have you noticed?" Thanet remarked as they returned to the main road.

Lineham nodded. "You really think it will be soon?"

Thanet shrugged. "I repeat: I *hope*. But strangely, in a way, yes. I feel that the pattern's begining to emerge, that any minute now I'll see it. All last night I felt that it was there, waiting to be understood. . . . " He shook his head. "D'you know what I mean?"

"Not really. It all seems a mess to me, a jumble of people and motives, little mysteries that don't seem to have any relevance . . ."

"Yes, but don't you see?" said Thanet. "The fact of the matter is, that there *is* a pattern, there *is* an explanation, it's simply a matter of uncovering it. And we're getting closer all the time, if only we could see it. It's like a view that's just around the bend in the lane. You know it's there, it's just a question of waiting until you've turned the corner."

Lineham said nothing. It was obvious that he did not share Thanet's optimism.

16

It was again necessary to knock several times before Irene Selby opened the door. When she saw who it was she stood back without speaking, then led the way once more to the conservatory.

Now that he was aware of the nature of her sickness, Thanet wondered how he could have failed to recognise its symptoms, so obvious were they to the enlightened observer. His attitude towards her had, he found, changed considerably since his conversation with Susan yesterday afternoon. Mrs Selby was no longer a middle-class housewife with a drink problem but a frustrated concert pianist denied the natural expression of her gift by a repressive husband.

Nevertheless this was a murder enquiry and Irene Selby had lied. The effort which Thanet had to make to suppress his newly-awakened feelings of compassion for her made him sound unusually brusque and he was aware that when he spoke Lineham glanced at him in some surprise.

"Mrs Selby, when I came to see you yesterday I asked you if Miss Birch had called here after leaving Mr Pitman on Monday evening. You told me that she hadn't, because your husband was expected back that evening and a visit was therefore unnecessary."

"That's right, yes."

"I have since learned that he was not due back until Tuesday."

Silence for a moment, while Irene Selby stared down at her tightly clasped hands. Thanet could almost feel her willing herself not to look at the bottle, which she had hidden in the same place as yesterday; he could just see the tip of it projecting above its screen of leaves.

Mrs Selby put up her hand to brush away that tic again. "Originally that was so. But he got through his business much more quickly than he expected, so he rang me early on Monday evening to say that he would be arriving home around ten o'clock that night, instead of next day. He asked me to let Carrie know that it wouldn't be necessary for her to call in."

"So you went across to see her?"

"No. I knew that there was a PCC meeting that evening and that she would be looking in on Mr Pitman during Miss Pitman's absence, so I went out to the front gate at a few minutes before nine and caught her as she went in. She was always as regular as clockwork. It was easy enough to time it exactly."

What a pity it wasn't summer time, Thanet thought. Old Mr Pitman's mirror would no doubt have reflected this encounter, if it had taken place. "Why didn't you tell me this before?"

She shrugged. "You didn't ask. And it didn't seem important."

"What time did your husband ring?"

"I'm not sure. Between six and seven, I think."

And if this story had not already been agreed between them, there was no doubt that Irene Selby would be ringing her husband the moment Thanet and Lineham left, to make sure that Major Selby knew of this phone call he was supposed to have made.

Had made?

Could Susan's assumption that Carrie had called to see Mrs Selby that evening be wrong? Could the vicar have been mistaken? Or lying?

No, Thanet thought, as he and Lineham returned to the car and set off for Major Selby's place of work, he was convinced that it was Irene Selby who had been lying. He said so, to Lineham. "What do you think, Mike?"

Lineham didn't hesitate. "I agree, sir."

"So, why?"

Lineham considered. "Protecting her husband, I should think. He could have got back earlier than he says he did. Like you said, when Susan heard him he could have been coming

148

back into the house for the second time. Say he got home first between nine thirty and nine fifty, when Carrie was still there — and found his wife dead drunk. He could have lost his temper with Carrie, lashed out at her . . . he looks just the type to have a nasty temper, don't you think?"

"He does, I agree."

"Or," said Lineham eagerly, getting into his stride, "Mrs Selby herself could have killed her. Say Carrie tried to take her last bottle of drink away and Mrs Selby tried to get it back, struggled with her. They could have toppled over and Carrie could have hit her head as they fell."

"But why finish her off? I can see Mrs Selby trying to get her bottle back, but even if she was drunk I honestly can't see her smothering an unconscious woman, can you?"

"I suppose not," said Lineham reluctantly. "And then, of course, she'd have had to get the body across the road and into the garden of number two, somehow. I shouldn't think she'd be strong enough."

"And she'd still have had to drink herself into a stupor before Susan got home. There just wouldn't have been time. Unless Susan is lying too, which I don't think she is."

"She could have disposed of the body later?"

"Then where was it in the meantime? No, it just doesn't feel right."

"But none of this applies to Major Selby, does it, sir? I mean, I shouldn't think he'd have had any scruples about finishing Carrie off, would he, not from what you say of him? If she'd been blackmailing him, he might have thought it the ideal opportunity to get rid of her."

"He could have hidden the body in the stables," Thanet said. "Then he could have waited until everyone was asleep, carried her across the road . . ."

". . . and dumped her in the privy at his own convenience," Lineham finished eagerly. "Do you think that's how it could have happened?"

"Let's not get carried away," Thanet said. "Or committed to any one idea yet. There are too many other possibilities. Carrie *could* have got knocked out in a struggle with Mrs

Selby, but my guess is that Mrs Selby would then have departed in triumph with her bottle and proceeded to drink herself into oblivion. Then when Major Selby arrived home he could have found Carrie unconscious and seized the chance to put an end to what must have been a pretty intolerable situation for a man like him. Anyway, let's see what he has to say for himself.''

They had arrived at Stavely's and were quickly ushered into Major Selby's office. The Major was standing behind his desk. He gave his secretary a terse nod and the second she had left the room exploded into outraged speech.

"This is intolerable!'' he said. "Absolutely intolerable!''

"What is, Major Selby?'' said Thanet innocently.

"This . . . this invasion of my office,'' spluttered Selby. He strode fiercely across to the window and back again. "I have a position to maintain here, you know and I really cannot see, in any case, why you should be . . . harassing me at all. My connection with Miss Birch was of the most tenuous nature.''

"Perhaps you wouldn't mind telling us, Major, exactly what that connection was?'' Thanet said.

Selby stopped his pacing and lowered his head, glowering at Thanet from beneath those luxuriant eyebrows. "What, exactly, are you insinuating, Inspector?''

"Not insinuating, Major, merely enquiring. May we sit down?''

Selby waved a hand in impatient permission, then went to sit behind his desk.

Perhaps, Thanet thought, he hoped by this move to establish his control of the interview, underline his authority as managing director of a thriving business. Certainly the office lent weight to the image. It was luxuriously appointed, with a thick, fitted carpet, antique furniture and an impressive array of up-to-date telecommunications equipment on the highly polished desk. A moment later it became apparent that Major Selby, Captain of Industry, had decided to change his tactics.

"I'm sorry, Inspector,'' he said, with an attempt at a smile. "You've caught me at a bad moment, I'm afraid. A minor crisis . . . Would you and your sergeant take some coffee? Or a pre-lunch drink, perhaps?''

150

Thanet preferred the man when he was fighting. What was more, the sudden switch was patently out of character. If I hadn't been suspicious before, he thought, I would be now.

"Thank you, no," he said. "I simply wanted to ask you one or two more questions about Monday night. Now," he went on smoothly, as Selby opened his mouth, no doubt to protest that he had already told him all there was to tell, "I understand that you were not due back from your business trip until Tuesday?"

"That's right, but . . ."

"And that when you were away, Miss Birch used to call at your house morning and evening?"

"Certainly, but what on earth . . ."

"So that, in the normal way of things, not expecting you home until Tuesday, she would have called in on Monday evening. Yet, she apparently did not do so. Could you tell us why that was, Major?"

"Because," said Major Selby, leaning forward across the desk and more or less spitting out his words, "I rang my wife on Monday evening, told her that I would be home at about ten and asked her to let Miss Birch know that it wouldn't be necessary to call. And now, Inspector," he said, rising, "I really am a very busy man, so if you'd excuse me . . ."

Thanet did not move. "I haven't quite finished yet, I'm afraid," he said.

Selby's face flamed. It was obvious that he was quite unused to having his authority challenged. "Very well," he said, controlling himself with a visible effort. "But I wish to make it clear that I consider this intrusion into my private life absolutely inexcusable."

"You don't consider murder sufficient excuse?" Thanet said quietly. "Look Major," he went on, "I think it only fair to tell you that we know why you employed Miss Birch to keep an eye on your wife."

Silence. Thanet could almost have felt sorry for the man. The high colour seeped slowly out of Selby's face and in ten seconds he seemed to age as many years.

"I don't know what you mean, Inspector," he said, but his

eyes avoided Thanet's and there was no conviction in his voice.

"I think you do, Major. So could we please cut out the skirmishing and stick to plain facts?"

Selby said nothing.

"You didn't really ring your wife on Monday evening, did you?"

Selby looked up. "Certainly I did." There was a note of — what? — defiance in his voice now. Clearly he had decided to stick to his story. A predictable reaction, Thanet thought. Selby was the sort of man who, more than most, would find it difficult to admit to having lied. A pity. For a moment there Thanet had thought the man's defences sufficiently breached to make him acknowledge defeat. "At what time do you claim to have made this phone call?"

Selby did not react to the implication. "About six thirty."

"From where?"

"A call box at a motorway service station."

Untraceable, of course. "And you arrived home at what time?"

"Just after ten, as I told you."

It was obvious that Selby was not going to budge.

"Thank you, Major," Thanet said briskly, and stood up.

Selby looked up at him with a slightly dazed expression, as if he could not quite believe that the interview was at an end.

"We'll see ourselves out."

He and Lineham were almost at the door before Selby reacted. "Wait!" he said urgently, and came hurrying after them. "Just a minute. Er . . . look, Inspector," and he swallowed, as if the words he was about to say were stuck in his gullet, "I apologise for over-reacting just now. As I said, we're in the middle of a minor crisis here and of course my wife is very upset about this business. . . . The County Council Elections are coming up next month. . . . A man in my position has to be seen to be above reproach. . . . What I'm trying to say is, what you said just now, about knowing the reason why Miss Birch used to . . . er . . . keep an eye on things for me while I'm away . . ."

Thanet couldn't stand it any longer. Selby trying to be

152

ingratiating was a nauseating sight. "Don't worry, Major," he said, "we're not in the habit of broadcasting people's secrets unless it's absolutely necessary."

"Yuk!" said Lineham, when they were safely out of earshot.

"My sentiment exactly," Thanet said.

Despite his earlier conviction that they were drawing close to a solution to the case, Thanet suddenly felt depressed, partly because of the abortive interview with Major Selby, which he felt he had perhaps mishandled, partly because he knew that they had now reached the stage in the case that he always loathed: it was time to sit down at his desk and work systematically through every single report that had been made since the beginning of it. It was astonishing just how fruitful this task could be. It gave one an overall picture, enabled one to see the wood instead of just the trees, and at the same time refreshed the memory. Facts, remarks, comments, observations which earlier, in isolation, had appeared to have little or no significance, took on new meaning when they were linked with others which had surfaced or been made subsequently.

"Desk time, I think," he said to Lineham, with a rueful grin.

Back at the office, Lineham organised a thorough search of Nettleton for any trace of Arnold's pilfered building materials while Thanet made sure that all the reports were up to date and at hand. Lineham ordered coffee and sandwiches for a working lunch, then they settled down to it.

For the next three hours the atmosphere of concentration in the room was almost palpable. The telephone rang from time to time and occasionally one of the two men would query some point or comment upon something of significance. Otherwise the silence was unbroken save by the scrape of a match and the little popping noises made by Thanet as he puffed at his pipe.

At five o'clock Mallard poked his head around the door.

"Good grief," he said disgustedly, fanning away the coils of tobacco smoke which by now were as dense as one of the celebrated old London smogs. "Look at you!" he said as Thanet and Lineham raised dazed faces from the heaped papers on their desks. Then, striding across the room, he flung up both sash windows. Sweet, fresh air poured into the room. "It's a miracle your brains are functioning at all." he said. "Next time I'll bring an oxygen mask with me."

"Nonsense," said Thanet with a grin, laying down the report he had been studying. "Ideal working conditions, aren't they, Mike?"

"Well . . ." said Lineham, who didn't smoke.

"There you are," Mallard said. "If you're not careful, Luke, you'll be up on a charge of poisoning off your subordinates." He propped himself against the window ledge. "How's it going, anyway? Still with the delectable Miss Birch, are you?"

"So so," said Thanet. "Nothing definite yet, I'm afraid. Though there've been one or two surprises." And he told Mallard about the money and the clothes.

"Not really so surprising, I suppose," said Mallard. "Fairly typical pattern. Domineering mother, repressed spinster daughter. It's got to come out somehow."

"Ah yes," said Thanet. "But that's just the point. How, exactly, did it come out? I agree, the clothes are understandable enough, but where did she get the money? Did she earn it, win it, steal it, or did she get it by blackmail? I forgot to tell you that she was a snooper. There's a very interesting old man, used to be her headmaster years ago. He knows her pretty well, she used to clean house for him. Anyway, he thinks that her real passion was the sense of power it gave her to know other people's secrets. He thinks that just to know was enough for her — but of course, there's always the possibility that it didn't remain enough, that sooner or later she was tempted to use what she'd learned."

"And was there anything — anything she could have used for blackmail, I mean?"

"Nothing earth-shattering. But then, the things which matter most to ordinary people are not usually sensational, are they? Just grubby little secrets which they'd rather nobody else knew about. And we've turned up a number of those, haven't we Mike?"

Mallard wrinkled his nose in disgust, heaved himself off the window ledge. "Rather you than me. Give me a nice healthy corpse any time. Well, let me know when you come up with something definite." He looked at his watch. "Got to be off. I'll leave you to your dirty washing."

"And that's the trouble, isn't it, Mike," Thanet said when Mallard had gone. "That's all it appears to be, dirty washing." He waved his hand at the mounds of papers. "All this, and no real evidence of any kind."

"Oh I don't know. If Miss Birch had known about Ingram's affair with the hairdresser . . ."

"If. That's the point. If. There's not a shred of proof anywhere that his relationship with Carrie — if such it can be called — was anything but what he claims it was, absolutely superficial. In all the stuff the men have dug up there's not one reference to any significant connection between them."

"She would have been pretty careful not to be seen talking to him though, surely."

"Why? Who would have suspected that the innocuous Miss Birch was indulging in a spot of blackmail? And in any case, if there's no evidence, Ingram's in the clear as far as we're concerned, isn't he?"

"What about Major Selby?" said Lineham. "He's much more promising."

"True. But again, there's no evidence. I admit he's got a lot to lose, especially with the elections next week . . ."

"Don't you think it's pretty peculiar that he should employ someone like Miss Birch as a sort of watchdog for his wife, sir?"

"I do. But then, it was Hobson's choice, wasn't it? His daughter is at school all day and you know what alcoholics are like about hiding their supplies. Carrie would have been bound to be aware that Mrs Selby drank, cleaning the house as she did, and I suppose Selby thought he might as well cash in on the fact that she knew and pay her well enough to make sure she kept her mouth shut."

"Perhaps that's where all the money came from."

"I very much doubt it. There was just too much of it, for that."

"Perhaps she got greedy, sir?"

"Possibly. Who can tell? And that's the trouble with this case. There's too much speculation, and speculation just isn't enough. Sooner or later we've got to have something more concrete."

The two men sat in silence for a while, thinking.

"Mike," said Thanet eventually. "Major Selby . . ."

"Yes?"

"How did he strike you?"

"Not my cup of tea."

"I know that, but what did you think of him?"

"Typical army type."

"Too typical?"

Lineham frowned. "What do you mean?"

"Well, just think about him for a minute. I mean, he's almost a caricature, isn't he? Clothes, appearance, manner, the lot. You don't think it's just a bit too much?"

"You mean, he's an imposter? But he's managing director of Stavely's!"

"I'm not talking about that," said Thanet with an impatient wave of the hand. "I'm talking about the army bit. These titles, Major and so on, they carry social weight, don't they? And that's something Selby is rather fond of, I should think."

"You'd like me to check? Where should I begin?"

"You'd need to know his regiment first. I'll ring Mr Pitman now. He'll be sure to know. Then you'll have to check in the Army lists. They're in the Public Record Office at Kew. They'll be shut now. Get on to it first thing in the morning."

Thanet had been dialling the Pitmans' number as he spoke and now a brief conversation with Marion Pitman produced the information he needed. "He was in the North Kents," he said, replacing the receiver. "If he was a fraud and Carrie found out, while she was poking through his desk, perhaps, then that really would have given him good reason to want to get rid of her."

Thanet surveyed his untidy desk, groaned and began to shuffle papers together, stopping now and again to glance once more through a report. He felt discouraged. The afternoon's work had been a waste of time after all.

"What about the vicar?" said Lineham, who was doing the same thing. "Or Miss Pitman?"

"Shouldn't think so," said Thanet. "I really cannot see him killing someone to preserve his secret. Oh, I know it would be unpleasant for both of them if it came out, but they'd weather it all right. It's surprising how people rally to the support of their vicar when things go wrong."

"Chris Gamble, then?" suggested Lineham.

"Another dead duck," said Thanet. "Theoretically, Susan doesn't want her father to know, but I have a feeling she wouldn't be exactly heartbroken if he did. Young Jenny Gamble said something of the sort, and I think she was pretty near the mark."

"Chris Gamble might not know that, though."

"Even so," said Thanet with an air of finality. He thumped the last report down on the pile. "Let's face it, practically everyone connected with the woman has some sort of motive. I bet we could even find one for poor old Miss Cox, if we tried hard enough."

"What, for example?"

"Well, let me see. What does Miss Cox value most? Her privacy. Carrie could have threatened that, in some way."

"How?" said Lineham. "Miss Cox wouldn't let her over the doorstep, we know that."

"She could have sneaked in somehow," retorted Thanet. "Let me see. Yes. If you remember, the cat got shut in the shed that night. Perhaps Carrie heard Miss Cox down the garden, calling it, and realised that this was her chance to have a quick snoop around. After all, just think what a frustration it must have been to someone like her to live next door to a hermit. She must have been dying to take a peek. So she grabs her chance and then Miss Cox comes back and finds her."

"Surely she would have made sure she was out of the house by the time Miss Cox got back?" objected Lineham.

"Perhaps she got carried away, didn't realise how quickly the time had gone. Miss Cox was only away about ten minutes."

"So Miss Cox finds her snooping, takes a swipe at her . . ."

". . . with her walking stick!" said Thanet. "The ideal weapon, literally to hand."

"And then puts a cushion over her head and finishes her off?"

The two men grinned at each other. "All right," said Thanet, lifting his hands in a mock gesture of defeat. "It was a nice little exercise in fantasy, I agree. The rest I can see: Carrie grabbing her chance, Miss Cox being angry, hitting out at her — though even that is straining the imagination a bit. But then deliberately to finish her off . . ."

"And manage to drag her all the way to the privy in the garden of number two with that broken leg . . ."

"Well, it was a nice idea," said Thanet. "And it proves my point. Look hard enough and there's a motive under every bush. What we need are some nice hard facts. Perhaps the men will have turned up something about that pilferer. . . . Oh, to hell with it. I'm going home to sleep on it and you can do the same." He grinned. "Only one more day before Saturday, now. Then you'll be a staid old married man."

Lineham blushed.

"All being well," he said.

17

The streets of Sturrenden were quiet, almost deserted, as Thanet drove home. Darkness was coming swiftly now and light from illuminated shop windows spilled softly on to the empty pavements. Only outside the old Embassy Cinema was there any sign of activity; this had been converted to a bingo hall some years ago and a steady trickle of women was flowing towards its brightly illuminated façade.

The pace of Thanet's driving reflected his state of mind. He felt sluggish, as if every last ounce of mental energy had been sucked out of him by the sustained effort of the afternoon. And all for nothing, he thought dully as he left the shops behind and turned into the Ashford Road. So lethargic did he feel, however, that even this dispiriting reflection aroused no more than the faintest flicker of disappointment in him.

He was not allowed to remain in this state for long. The second he opened the door two small bodies supercharged with energy came flying towards him.

"Hey," he said, reeling under the impact and squatting to gather both of them into his arms at once, "what're you two doing up at this time of night?"

"It was Peter's party, Daddy. We *told* you." Bridget's eyes were shining, her face flushed.

Ben had already wriggled out of Thanet's grasp and disappeared into the kitchen. Now he came running back with a red balloon bobbing at the end of a piece of string, a paper bag in his hand. "Look what Mrs Darwin gave me, Daddy," he said, opening the bag and peering inside as if to reassure himself that his treasures had not disappeared, before thrusting it under Thanet's nose.

Thanet duly inspected the contents (an apple, an orange and

a bar of half-melted chocolate before making impressed noises and handing it back to Ben.

"They're terribly over-excited," said Joan, as Thanet and the children entered the kitchen. She was obviously trying to get supper going before putting the children to bed.

How was she going to cope with this sort of situation if she started a full-time job, Thanet wondered, as he said, "It's all right. I'll get them bathed. And there's no hurry for supper. I shouldn't have to go out again this evening."

"I'm afraid it'll be a job getting them calmed down," she said, stopping what she was doing to come and give him a grateful kiss. "We might well have tears before long, I should think."

"Don't worry, I'll cope," said Thanet. "Right, you two! Off we go."

It was a rare treat for their father to be home in time to bath them and put them to bed and Thanet managed to tone down their almost frenzied state of excitement by the simple expedient of telling them that if they didn't quieten down he would go downstairs again and they could put themselves to bed bathless and storyless. He couldn't help feeling pleased with himself when, half an hour later, he was able to say to Joan, "No problems. They'll be asleep in two minutes, I shouldn't wonder. Looking as though butter wouldn't melt in their mouths, of course, as usual."

Joan had been busy in the meantime. There was an appetising smell in the kitchen and a welcoming fire in the living room. Thanet sank down in front of it with a sigh and picked up the newspaper. Strangely, he felt much less tired than when he had arrived home. The interlude with the children had refreshed him; for a whole half an hour he had been able to put his work out of his mind entirely.

Now, however, he found himself unable to concentrate on the lines of newsprint. Snippets of information and conversation relating to the Birch case kept floating into his mind and distracting him.

"What's the matter?" Joan said as she came in to lay the table.

"Nothing. Why?"

"You were frowning."

"Was I?"

"Positively scowling, in fact." She was briskly unloading table mats, cutlery and glasses from the tray she was carrying. "Supper's just about ready now," she said.

Abstracted as he was it was not until they were eating dessert (lemon meringue pie, one of his favourites) that Thanet became aware that Joan was secretly excited about something. He had seen that look before. It was in the lightness of her movements, in the lift at the corners of her mouth, the extra sparkle in her eyes when she smiled.

For the first time in their marriage his immediate reaction to it was a sudden sinking of the spirits. *She's found a job*, he thought, and was tempted to pretend he hadn't noticed. But this would have been quite out of character for him. He would have to pretend that nothing was amiss.

"Well," he said, laying down his spoon and looking at her expectantly. "When are you going to tell me?"

"Tell you what?"

"Come on, darling," he said. "No point in pretending with me. I can read you like an open book."

"What it's like," she said, gathering up the dishes and marching off towards the kitchen, "being married to a policeman!"

He couldn't help grinning and his spirits rose a notch. Perhaps he was wrong, perhaps Joan's news would be perfectly innocuous after all.

She waited until they had settled down with their coffee and then she said, "You were asking just now . . ."

"Mmm?" he said, pretending abstraction.

"What I had to tell you."

"Ah, yes. I thought you said there wasn't anything."

"One of these days, my darling, you'll get a cup of coffee poured over your head, if you're not careful! Now, do you want to hear it or not?"

He shrugged. "If you insist," he said, then put up his arm in mock self-defence as she raised her cup in the air. "Just as you

161

like, dear," he said, with exaggerated meekness.

But she couldn't waste time playing games any longer. "Well," she said, wriggling herself into a more comfortable position, "I went along to the probation service this morning."

"Oh?"

His wariness must have shown in his voice, for she glanced at him doubtfully before continuing.

"I thought, well, I've always been interested in probation work and although I didn't think that there was the slightest chance that they would be interested in me, as I have no qualifications whatsoever, I thought it might just be worth enquiring. . . . Well, anyway, it seems I was wrong. Apparently there's more than one way of becoming a probation officer, and the fact that I've done regular voluntary work with the mentally handicapped over the last couple of years while Ben's been at playgroup means that they might be prepared to take me on either as an unpaid volunteer or, what's even more exciting, as an assistant probation officer, with a view to seeing whether I suit the work. Then, if all went well and they were satisfied with me, they might sponsor me through a proper training. That means they'd actually pay me, while I was doing the training! Isn't it exciting!"

"I don't quite see what working with mentally handicapped children has to do with the probation service," Thanet said carefully.

"The fact that it happens in my case to be handicapped children has nothing to do with it, really," Joan said. "What matters, apparently, is that I've worked for the community in what they called a caring capacity."

"A caring capacity indeed! You're picking up the jargon already."

"It was their expression, not mine. And what else would you call it?" Joan said rebelliously. "You know perfectly well what I mean and you're deliberately ignoring the point."

"Which is what?"

"That they may be prepared to take me on despite my lack of formal qualifications."

"I must say that piece of information does not exactly

162

inspire confidence in the probation service."

"Now you're being ridiculous! I've just explained that of course I'd have to do a proper training, but not until they were satisfied that I'm suited to the work."

She was right, of course. He was being petty and mean-spirited and his attitude could lead only to disaster. He took a deep, calming breath.

"Sorry, love. Look, I accept that you need to find something interesting to do. But does it have to be this?"

"It doesn't *have* to be, I suppose, but why not? It's a fascinating job, and the running-in period would give me a chance to see if it would really suit me, before I start the proper training course. Oh darling, why not? It would be ideal, don't you see?"

"Ideal for whom?"

She stared at him. "Well for me, of course. What do you mean?"

"Have you thought how it could affect us?"

"Us? In what way?"

"You haven't thought that there could be a certain, well, clash of interests?"

"No. Why should there be?" She had drawn away from him and was sitting rigidly upright against the arm of the settee. She looked wary, hostile.

He sighed. "Look, the probation service and the police, they're often poles apart in their attitudes to criminals."

"But they're both on the same side really, surely? They're both concerned to maintain peace and order in society?"

He shook his head. "Maybe. But that doesn't stop them frequently being in conflict. I don't suppose you've had much to do with probation officers, but I have. And I grant you they do very fine work, many of them. But that's not the point. The point is, as I say, that their attitudes to criminals are different. Don't you see that it's impossible to shed one's working attitudes in one's private life? They become an integral part of one, as basic as breathing. I can see all sorts of situations in which this thing could become a barrier between us."

"How, for example?"

He shrugged. "Well, for one thing, I've always shared my work with you, haven't I? Told you everything, without reserve, knowing that I could trust you not to talk about it."

"But I still wouldn't," she cried. "You know that, surely?"

"Maybe you wouldn't talk about it, but your attitude to what I tell you would be bound to be different, don't you see? It's inevitable that you'd be looking at the whole question of crime from a different point of view, from the side of the criminal, his guilt, his rehabilitation, whatever. . . . Darling, don't you see that? You must, surely."

"Not necessarily. Probation officers have to be detached, they can't afford to identify with their clients or they couldn't work properly."

"And what if it turned out that we were both working on the same case? That I had arrested someone for a crime and you had to do a social enquiry on him? And suppose then that it was your evidence in court that got him off even though I strongly felt that he should have had a sharp sentence to bring him to his senses?"

"I would think that the chances of that happening would be very slight. And if it did happen, couldn't one or the other of us request that we should be taken off the case?"

"And that would create a barrier between us, too. Joan, you must see it. It would limit us, put restrictions on our work. We'd be bound to resent it. And there would be other barriers — just in ordinary life, in casual conversation, we'd have to be guarding our tongues, watching what we say to each other . . ."

"I think the truth of the matter," she said tightly, "is that you don't want me to work at all."

"It's not that . . ."

"Isn't it?" she cut in. "Are you sure? Oh," she went on miserably, "I was so excited about it. To think that I could have a really interesting, challenging job despite my hideous lack of qualifications . . ."

She was near to tears now and she stood up abruptly, pulling away from his restraining hand. "It's all right for you," she said. "You really love your work, don't you? Well, why shouldn't I be able to do something I enjoy, too?"

"Darling," he said, in what he hoped was an eminently reasonable tone, "I'm not saying you shouldn't. I'm just saying, does it have to be this?"

"Well I'm still not convinced that that is all you're saying. Oh, what's the point in talking about it any longer. I'm going to have a bath." And she swung away and walked quickly out of the room before he could stop her.

Thanet looked gloomily after her. The situation seemed to be deteriorating by the day. And this idea of hers . . . It was crazy, absolutely crazy. Not that he couldn't see that she would enjoy the work, probably be very good at it . . . Oh, to hell with the whole business, he thought. He glanced at his watch. Nine o'clock. He would watch the news.

He switched on the television then sat back on the settee, tried to relax. At first it was impossible, but when the news ended there was an interesting documentary on behavioural patterns in the criminal and he gradually became absorbed in the programme.

When it ended he switched off the television, unplugged it and listened to the silence of the house. Joan must have gone to bed long ago. He fixed the spark guard firmly in position in front of the fire, checked that both front and back doors were securely locked and went upstairs.

In the bedroom the little lamp on his bedside table was still burning and Joan was merely a humped shape, turned on to her side away from the light. Presumably she was asleep, or pretending to be. She did not stir as he entered the room, came and went to the bathroom, undressed and got into bed.

Thanet switched out the light and composed himself for sleep. But the darkness, the silence (broken only by Joan's soft, even breathing) and the absence of any form of distraction combined to create the perfect conditions for his mind immediately to start working again in top gear. Unable to prevent it functioning, and unwilling to discipline it to logical thought, he let it go free. Like a dog newly released from the lead it ran about with abandon, briefly following one train of thought then switching abruptly, for no apparent reason, to another.

165

At first he brooded over his recent argument with Joan and then he meandered off into disjointed thoughts about the case: fleeting images of the people involved, snatches of conversation, fragments of the reports he had read that afternoon. Lineham appeared briefly from time to time, commenting on the case or expressing anxiety about the wedding. And in and out of it all, a pathetic, elusive and really rather unpleasant little wraith, floated Carrie Birch.

Despite what he had learned about her, Thanet found to his surprise that he still felt sorry for her. Who knows what she would have been like, if the circumstances of her life had been different? Shaped and moulded by that monstrously self-centred and domineering mother, Carrie had been forced to find her secret satisfactions or perish as a person. Who could really blame her if those satisfactions had taken a form distasteful to those fortunate enough not to have been warped by their upbringing? God forbid that he and Joan should ever cripple Bridget and Ben in that way, he thought.

In a philosophical mood by now, Thanet reflected on the damage caused by possessiveness. Convinced as he was that it was in ferreting out some secret that Carrie had brought about her own death, he thought now that in all justice the true murderer was Carrie's mother, Mrs Birch. Although it was a fate that he would not wish upon any one, perhaps in a way it was only poetic justice that she should have ended up alone, unwanted and abandoned — for can love not flourish only and above all where it is freely given?

Look at Marion Pitman and her father, he thought, warming to his theme. The old man asked nothing and in response was loved without reserve, to the point of self-sacrifice on Marion's part; whereas so many of the other people in the case seemed to have been crippled in one way or another by possessiveness.

Take the Ingrams, for example. Thanet was willing to bet that if Joy Ingram had not been so fiercely and unremittingly jealous of her husband he would never have been driven to find consolation elsewhere.

And then there were the Selbys. Susan, panting to get away,

seething with bitter resentment against her father; and poor, pathetic Irene Selby, her fine talent gone to waste, driven to the bottle for the comfort which her life with that pompous, posing little monster of a husband could never give her.

And there was poor old Miss Cox, self-condemned to a life of loneliness, shying away from any kind of personal contact simply because many years ago she had invested all her loving in a boy who died.

Nearer home there was Lineham's mother, in danger of losing her son altogether because she had sought to bind him too closely to her.

How strange it was that these people, the ones who demanded the service, allegiance and obedience of their nearest and dearest as a right, could never see that in the long run it was they themselves who were the losers.

At this point in the catalogue Thanet stopped. For the last few minutes he had been aware of a feeling of pressure inside his head, a sensation of — what? — restlessness in his limbs. The atmosphere of the room seemed suddenly to have become oppressive and he felt stifled, found that he was sweating slightly.

Could he be ill? Perhaps he was going to have a heart attack. He had heard that these frequently occurred in the small hours, though he had never understood why. It really was suffocating in here. He had to have some air.

The absence of pain in his chest decided him that it was quite safe to get up. Taking care not to wake Joan he slid out of bed and crossed to the window. It was slightly ajar, but easing up the catch he opened it wide and leaned out to breathe in great gulps of the chill night air.

After a moment or two he felt calmer but still uneasy and very wide awake. He decided that he would go down and make himself a pot of tea.

Downstairs it was chilly. The central heating was always switched off at night and the kitchen had no other form of heat. He unearthed an electric fire from the cupboard under the stairs and plugged it in while the kettle boiled. Soon, with the tea made and a comforting glow emanating from the bars

167

of the fire he was sitting at the kitchen table.

With nothing to do but think.

And this, he discovered, he was reluctant to do.

Why?

Cautiously, like someone gently testing an aching tooth with the tip of his tongue, he groped his way back into his previous train of thought.

He had been thinking about Mrs Birch.

And about Joy Ingram.

And Henry Selby.

And old Miss Cox.

And Lineham's mother.

And there it was again, the same sense of pressure within his brain, the same need to get up and move about, as if his body were telling him, run, run like hell.

He stayed where he was, putting his head down between his hands and pressing his fingers to his temples.

What was the matter with him?

And then, suddenly, he knew. The moment of revelation was sudden, blinding and exquisitely painful. He closed his eyes as if to blot it out, but of course the knowledge remained, once perceived never again to be denied, ignored or hidden away from his consciousness.

Just as all these people had in one way or another crippled their relationship with those they would claim to love the most, *so was he crippling his relationship with Joan*. By seeking to hold her he would most surely lose her.

He found that he was staring fixedly at the wall, sitting rigidly upright with hands clenched into tight fists. He stayed that way for a minute or so longer, braced against further pain. Then, slowly, he began to relax, to hold this revolutionary new idea up for scrutiny.

He was exaggerating, he told himself. How could his relationship with Joan possibly be compared with these others? Had he not always been a faithful, appreciative husband? But, he admitted with painful honesty, that wasn't the point. Relationships do not remain static and what might have been satisfying to them both in the past sufficed no longer. From

168

what Joan said it was clear that her dissatisfaction had been growing for some time.

What a fool he had been, he thought, remembering the arguments of the last few days, the widening rift between them — what a blind, selfish fool! After all, what right had he to expect that Joan should sacrifice herself to his needs, deny herself a fuller life simply because it would bring inconvenience, discomfort to his? What was the point of forcing her to remain in a role which was preventing her from developing her abilities to the full, if by so doing he would be stultifying, perhaps destroying the relationship which he had always counted one of the most precious things in his life?

He stood up abruptly. He couldn't wait to tell her, to apologise, to ask her forgiveness and explain the reasons for his change of heart. Upstairs in the bedroom, however, his newly-awakened guilt and contrition made him hesitate. Why wake her up, just to satisfy his own need for expiation? Quietly, stealthily, he slid into bed and, contemplating pleasurably the prospect of her delight in the morning when she heard what he had to say, composed himself at last for sleep.

But it still wouldn't come.

Stimulated by his new insight he felt as alert as ever and returned to thinking about the case. Once again the principal characters marched across the stage, parading themselves for his inspection. One by one he contemplated them, thinking back over facts, conversations, snippets of information picked up disjointedly here and there, trying to penetrate the secret places of their hearts.

And then there came to him an idea so monstrous, so bizarre that his eyes snapped open and he sat bolt upright in bed.

Was it possible?

Joan stirred, mumbled and he froze, scarcely daring to breathe. His desire to talk to her had evaporated, ousted by his need to think. She settled back into sleep and, careful not to disturb her again, he lay down. Was it possible? he thought again. Could it be true?

It was a fact that the person he had in mind had once behaved in a totally uncharacteristic manner, but surely this was not sufficient ground upon which to base a theory so outlandish, so truly extraordinary?

He began to think back over the case in the light of this new idea and found that it had radically changed his thinking. Behaviour which at the time he had interpreted in one way he now saw could equally well be interpreted in another. It began to seem that his theory could hold water. Above all it provided him with a motive, a motive so powerful that he now understood at last why it had been essential for Carrie to be silenced.

Yes, it all made sense at last.

18

"But where are we going, sir?" Lineham sounded positively plaintive, as well he might. No sooner had he arrived at the office than he had been scooped up by an impatient Thanet and whisked downstairs to the car.

"To see an old friend of mine."

Thanet had awoken with a name in his mind: Harry Pack.

"You see," he explained to Lineham, "yesterday, after Arnold had been talking about his sneak thief, there was something nagging away at the back of my mind. You know how it is, when you just can't put your finger on it. Anyway, this morning I realised what it was. The first time I arrived in Nettleton, with Doc Mallard, there was a crowd of onlookers at the entrance to the footpath behind Church Cottages. I had them sent packing, of course, but just as they were all drifting off I realised that I'd recognised somebody in the crowd. You know what I mean. I'd seen him, without it registering properly, and I just had this vague feeling that I'd glimpsed a familiar face. I didn't bother to follow it up at the time. I didn't think it could be important and anyway I wanted to get on with the job."

"You mean, it was someone with a record?"

"Yes. A man called Harry Pack. He's a petty thief, a pathetic specimen — you know the type, in and out of job after job, spends most of his time living on social security, has swarms of kids and a wife who can't cope and is so useless he can't help getting himself caught every time he puts a toe outside the law. I happened to be in court on another case the last time he came up. He was put on probation for what they assured him was the very last time. If he was caught again he'd be inside quicker than he could pick a lock."

"You think he might have been in the garden of number two, the night of the murder?"

Thanet shrugged. "It's a bit much to hope for, but you never know. The point is, if he was, he'd never have dared to come forward because if he did he'd have to say what he was doing there and he'd be virtually sending himself to prison."

"In that case, he'll never admit it anyway, surely?"

"I don't know. We might just be lucky. Harry's so dim that if he's the pilferer he's bound to have left some evidence lying around. Even if I hadn't remembered seeing him that first morning, the men would have turned him up in the end, I'm sure. I checked their reports this morning and they haven't got as far as Harry's council estate yet. I could be wrong, of course. He might be in the clear. But I don't think so. It all fits, somehow. It's just typical of Harry to set out to pinch a bag of cement and find himself involved in a murder."

"But . . ." said Lineham, and stopped.

"But what?"

Lineham shook his head. "Nothing."

"Oh come on, man. It's obvious there's something. How's your mother, by the way?"

"Fine, so far."

"Excellent. Well?"

Lineham still hesitated. "Well, sir, I don't quite see why all the rush. OK, Harry Pack may be the thief and he may have been there that night, but, well, it's very much a routine enquiry, isn't it? And you're not usually so . . . keyed up as this."

Thanet grinned. "On the ball, aren't you, Mike? You're quite right, of course. Certainly I'm interested in what Harry'll have to say, but there's something else I'm far more interested in checking. But just in case Harry *was* there and did see something, well, I want to see him first. So I'm in a rush to get him over with, so to speak, because I want to get on with the other thing."

"I gather I don't get to hear what that is, yet?"

"No need to huff," Thanet said. "No, I'm not telling you at the moment, but not because I don't trust you. It's just that

I'm afraid of looking a fool."

"You mean you think you know who the murderer is?"

"I might. Now look, Mike, stop fishing. I'm not telling yet, and that's that."

"But you're pretty sure, aren't you?"

"What makes you say that?"

"Well, because you're looking so . . ."

"Smug?" Thanet laughed out loud. "Well, I may be, but that's nothing to do with the case." He remembered with satisfaction Joan's reaction this morning when he had told her of his change of heart.

"I really mean it, darling," he'd said, smiling at her. "Go ahead. With whatever you want to do. And I'll back you all the way."

She had naturally been reluctant to believe him, had thought at first that once again he was only seeking to placate her, but he had managed to convince her at last and their reconciliation had been sweet.

What a relief it was, Thanet thought now, to know that everything was all right between them once more.

Nevertheless his euphoria was tinged with sadness. Examining his theory about the murder in the cold light of morning, he still thought that it might well hold water; but his initial elation at having solved the mystery had faded as its implications sank in.

It was at times like this that he felt that he was perhaps not cut out to be a policeman after all. There was a softness at the core of his nature, a lack of single-mindedness, perhaps, which so often prevented him from experiencing undiluted pleasure in the apprehension of a criminal such as this one.

Many of his colleagues, he knew, had no such qualms. For them, right and wrong were white and black; whereas for Thanet there were many shades of grey between. It was ironic that the very qualities which made him so successful in the solving of such cases as the present one — his intuitive understanding of people, his ability to grasp the subtleties of their motivation and their relationships — were the very qualities which in the end robbed him of unqualified satisfaction in his success. Having entered into the mind of the criminal, he found it all too easy to understand the crime — and even (and he found it very difficult to admit this, even to himself) to excuse it. It was only because murder was truly abhorrent to him, because he passionately believed that no one had the right to take the life of another human being, that he was able at times like this to go on functioning as an instrument of justice.

And so it was that this morning he found himself divided. Part of him was anxious, as he had told Lineham, to forge ahead, prove his theory correct; while the other part held back, shrank from inflicting the pain which would be inevitable. There was never any doubt in his mind which part would win. He just wished that it could be a more comfortable process.

He shifted uneasily in his seat as Lineham made the now-familiar left turn into Nettleton.

"Pack lives in the little group of council houses on the right, half way through the village," he said. "Number nine."

Number nine stood out from its neighbours by virtue of its squalor. Most of the other gardens were trim and neat, bright with daffodils and forsythia, but Harry's was a square of balding grass and weeds, strewn from end to end with broken plastic toys, rusting tricycles, bits of rope, empty coca-cola cans and crisp and sweet packets.

Two toddlers were scratching in the dirt with bits of stick and broken china, both of them dressed in grubby clothes much too big for them. Neither of them looked as though he had seen soap and water for some time. As Thanet and Lineham pushed open the gate they glanced up with slack faces and eyes devoid of interest or curiosity. Poor little devils, thought Thanet, smiling at them. He couldn't help contrasting their appearance and behaviour with that of his own alert and lively children. What chance did they have, with a home like this? They reminded him unnervingly of the old people he had seen in the geriatric ward when he had visited Mrs Birch.

Lineham had to knock several times before the door was finally opened. The woman who answered it was carrying a baby's feeding bottle and the child's thin, protesting wail rose from somewhere at the back of the house.

The woman herself, though probably in her early thirties, looked a good fifteen years older, Thanet thought. Her sagging breasts, protruding stomach, blue-veined legs and lank, greasy hair proclaimed that continuous child-bearing and the inability to meet the demands of a large family had long ago destroyed her will to do anything more than survive with the minimum of effort. Families such as these were the eternal despair of the social workers.

" 'E's still in bed," she said, in response to Thanet's request.

"Could you tell him we'd like a word with him? We'll wait outside, in the garden," Thanet added.

If such it could be called, he thought, as he and Lineham strolled around to the back of the house. Here, too, was the same neglect, the same detritus of living. There was, however, one interesting feature. He and Lineham exchanged significant glances at the sight of the straggling, uneven concrete path which stretched two thirds of the way beneath the washing line. It was clearly still under construction; broken planks shored up its sides.

"Got him, I think," said Thanet with satisfaction, making for a pile of rubbish against the fence. He stooped to pick up an empty cement sack. On its side, clearly visible, was the sign with which Arnold had been marking his property. He folded the sack up and whipped it behind his back as the rear door of the house opened and Harry appeared, bleary-eyed and unshaven. He was a small man with a whippet-like face and cringing manner.

"Sorry to interrupt your beauty sleep, Harry," Thanet said. "Just one or two little questions we wanted to ask you."

Pack stood aside as Thanet and Lineham approached, and led the way through a urine-smelling kitchen to a grubby living room.

"You know why we're here, of course," Thanet said, declining the invitation to sit down. He smiled benignly at Harry, who darted a nervous glance at the notebook and pencil which Lineham had ostentatiously taken from his pocket.

"Don't know what you mean, guv'," Harry mumbled.

175

"This, Harry," said Thanet. And, careful to keep the marked side away from Harry he produced the sack, unfolded it and displayed it like a magician who has just conjured a white rabbit out of thin air. "This."

Harry licked his lips, said nothing.

"You know what it is, of course."

Harry glowered.

"Precisely. It's a sack. And we both know what was in it, don't we? *Don't we*, Harry?" he said more fiercely, when there was still no response.

"How should I know what was bleedin' in it?" said the little man sullenly.

"Oh, come on," Thanet said wearily. He gave the sack a little shake and a fine powdering of cement dust drifted down to coat the accumulated layers of dirt upon the floor. "That's a very fine path you've been laying out there, isn't it, Harry?"

"It was the wife," said Harry defensively. "On and on about it, she was, the mess what got carried in after she'd been hanging out the washing . . ."

"Never mind the excuses, Harry. Just give us the facts. No don't bother, or we'll be here all day. I'll give them to you instead. This sack contained cement and you stole it from the garden of number two, Church Cottages, didn't you, Harry?"

"That's a bleedin' lie," Harry burst out.

"Is it?" Thanet shook his head, clicked his tongue. "Poor old Harry, you do have bad luck, don't you? Trust you to nick something that's marked." And indeed, he couldn't help feeling sorry for the man. He was one of life's natural victims. It showed, now, in the look of resigned despair in Pack's eyes, as if he had been half expecting something like this to happen.

"Marked?" Harry's voice was little more than a croak.

"I'm afraid so, yes." Thanet turned the sack about, to display the circle with the A in it. "A for Arnold. Mr Arnold — that's the builder who's renovating number two, Church Cottages — got a bit tired of someone walking off with his building materials and decided to lay a little trap."

"I've never seen that sack before," Pack said desperately.

"Blew over the fence, did it? What a shame. Let's hope the

magistrates believe you. What was the suspended sentence? A year? But, let's face it, you'll be inside a lot longer than that. Murder's a very different matter from pinching a few tea spoons, isn't it?''

The unhealthy pallor of Pack's skin became suffused with a pink which faded as quickly as it had come, leaving him ashen. He opened his mouth, but no sound emerged.

"Did you say something, Harry?" Thanet said.

Pack tried again. "Murder?" he croaked. "What d'yer mean?''

"Oh come on, Pack," Thanet snapped. "Stop playing games. You bumped into her that night, didn't you? Miss Birch? She caught you in the act, didn't she? So you had to shut her up, make sure she didn't talk because if she did, as we both know, don't we, Harry, you'd have been inside before you could have said, 'probation'. So you bashed her on the head with a handy bit of wood and then . . .''

"*No! No, I never*," said Harry desperately. He had been watching Thanet like a rabbit mesmerised by a stoat, but now he could contain himself no longer. "It wasn't like that, I swear it wasn't . . .''

"Then what was it like, Harry?" Thanet said softly. "You tell us.''

Pack looked at Thanet's face, then at the marked sack in his hand. His thought processes were almost audible. What's the point in not coming clean? he was asking himself. They've got me anyway. Then his eyes narrowed as a new idea occurred to him and he stiffened, gave Thanet a calculating look. "What if I did see something . . . something that could be useful to you, like . . .?''

Thanet said nothing.

"Well, I mean to say, if I help you . . .''

"You scratch my back and I'll scratch yours, eh, Harry?" said Thanet. He folded his arms across his chest and gazed at Pack sternly. "Come on, now. You know I can't make bargains like that. All the same . . .''

"Yes?" said Pack, pathetically eager.

"Well, it's nothing to do with me, mind, but the authorities

177

do tend to look more favourably upon those who've given us a helping hand . . ."

"You'd put in a word for me?"

"Let's hear what you've got to say, first. And, mind you, I want the strict truth. No frills. My sergeant here'll be taking it all down, word for word."

"Well it was like this," said Pack.

"Just a moment. I think we'd all better sit down," said Thanet.

Pack took the sagging armchair by the empty fireplace and Thanet and Lineham chose two upright wooden chairs which appeared to be reasonably clean.

"Right," said Thanet when they were settled. "Let's hear it."

Thanet listened to Pack's story without surprise. It had all happened exactly as he had envisaged it. Lineham, however, had difficulty in concealing his amazement and kept glancing at Thanet as if expecting him to challenge the truth of Pack's tale.

Thanet, however, was convinced. Pack had been there. Every detail of his story tallied with what they already knew. When he had finished Thanet took him back over it, querying, probing, questioning, but he could not shake the man. His evidence would convince any jury. Carrie's murderer was in the bag and Thanet only wished that the thought gave him more satisfaction.

But there was something else worrying him now and a growing sense of urgency was making him restless. For the last ten or fifteen minutes his mind had been working on two different levels simultaneously: the surface part had been applying itself to an examination of Harry's evidence, but the subterranean part had been questing back yet again over his last encounter with the murderer. What was it that was causing this pricking unease, this itching impatience to be gone?

Suddenly, he had it: it was not so much what had been said that was worrying him, but how it might have been interpreted — or rather, misinterpreted, in the light of what he now knew or could guess of the murderer's character and motive. And if he was right. . . . He stood up abruptly, cutting Pack off in mid-sentence.

Both Pack and Lineham glanced up at him, surprised.

"Let's go," he said, terse in his anxiety.

The other two came to their feet, still looking puzzled.

"We'll have to hurry," he said. "Get your coat, Harry, quickly." By the time Pack and Lineham joined him at the front door he was practically dancing with impatience.

"What's the hurry all of a sudden?" asked Lineham as they bundled Harry into the back seat.

"Later," said Thanet. "I'll drive."

They took off in a cloud of dust, paused to scoop up Bentley who was coming out of one of the council houses as they went by, and turned the corner into the main street of Nettleton with a squeal of tyres. The sense of urgency was overwhelming now and Thanet cursed himself for not having been more percipient before. Perhaps it was already too late.

They skidded to a halt in front of number five, Church Cottages. With a hurried word to Bentley to stay with Pack, Thanet and Lineham flung themselves out of the car and ran up the path to the peeling front door. The curtains were still drawn and the house had a forlorn, abandoned look. There was no response to their repeated knocking.

"Gone?" said Lineham.

Thanet shook his head tightly, compressed his lips. "We'll break in," he said. They had no warrant, but his degree of certainty was such that he brushed the thought aside.

The Yale lock on the door presented no problem and in a matter of seconds they were inside. The darkened sitting room within was deserted. But not completely. Lineham cannoned into Thanet from behind as he came to a dead stop.

"Look at this, Mike."

It was Tiger, stretched out stiff and cold in their path. The sight convinced Thanet, as nothing else could have done, that he had been right to be afraid. No doubt, now, of what they would find upstairs. Nevertheless it was just possible that they were not too late and they pounded up the narrow staircase one behind the other. The doors to all the bedrooms stood open

179

and a quick glance inside showed that they were empty.

"The attic," said Thanet, remembering the window he had noticed in the gable end of this house, the last in the terrace.

A cupboard-like door in the corner of the landing revealed the even steeper flight of stairs leading to the roof space. There was no door at the top and the room itself was in pitch darkness. Thanet fumbled for a light switch on the wall nearby and as Lineham came up behind him, found it. The room sprang to life in the sickly yellow glow of artificial light in daytime.

Both men froze.

It was as if they were seeing double: twin beds, twin bodies, each with cropped grey hair, faces overlaid with the unnatural pallor of death, both dressed in identical garb of corduroy trousers, men's shirts.

It was only on closer inspection that the mirror-image impression splintered and resolved itself into male and female.

"Her brother Joseph," said Thanet heavily, gazing down upon the weak, unshaven face of the slighter of the two bodies. "The only person she ever cared about in her whole life."

"But how did you know?" Lineham's face was a study in amazement.

"Something old Mr Pitman told me. He said. . . ."

"*Sir*?" The voice reverberated through the empty house, reaching them only faintly. Its note of urgency, however, was even at this distance clearly audible.

Both men made for the head of the stairs. "Up here," Thanet called. "In the attic."

Bentley appeared at the bottom of the staircase, puffing slightly. "Sir, message on the car radio . . ."

"Well? Get on with it, man," Thanet snapped.

"It's Mike's . . . DS Lineham's mother, sir. She . . . she's had a heart attack, been taken to Sturrenden General." Bentley peered miserably up the stairs at Lineham's frozen face.

"Sorry, Mike," he said.

19

"Now then," said Joan, settling herself into the passenger seat with a sigh of relief, "tell me all."

It was half past one the following afternoon. Ben and Bridget were safely parked with friends and Joan and Thanet were setting off for the little country church where Louise and Lineham were to be married. It was wedding weather — bright sunshine, cloudless blue sky and a little breeze which set the daffodils nodding in the gardens as Joan and Thanet went by.

This was their first opportunity to talk. When the news of Mrs Lineham's heart attack had come through, Thanet had insisted that Lineham leave at once for the hospital. Fortunately the attack had once again proved to be mild and although the hospital insisted on keeping her in bed and under observation for a few days Lineham had been able, after some qualms of conscience, to stick to his ultimatum and go ahead with plans for the wedding. On Louise's suggestion, the newly married couple would visit Mrs Lineham in hospital in their wedding finery and present her with the bridal bouquet before changing to leave on their honeymoon.

Meanwhile, of course, Thanet had found his workload doubled. In the aftermath of the deaths of Matty and Joseph Cox there had been much to do. Joan had been in bed and asleep by the time Thanet had finally crawled home last night, and this morning he had had to return to the office to try to clear away the accumulation of paperwork which was the inevitable accompaniment to the end of a case. Until now there had been no time to give Joan anything but the bare details.

"It's difficult to know where to begin," he said.

"Start with how you guessed. However did you? What

181

made you suspect Miss Cox in the first place?''

Thanet frowned, thinking back. ''It's difficult to tell, really. It wasn't so much that at one particular point I said, ah, there's something fishy about that. It was more an accumulation of things which in themselves didn't seem to have any special significance but when added together pointed to only one conclusion.''

''What sort of things?''

''Well, in a case like this you have to try to get inside the skins of those involved. The sort of people who lived in Carrie Birch's world don't go around killing each other for nothing. The trouble was that, as so often happens, once we began investigating all sorts of unpleasant secrets began to surface.''

''Like poor Mrs Selby's drinking, you mean?''

''Yes. That's a typical example. And there's no doubt about it, they do confuse the issue for us. Mrs Selby had no idea we knew about her drink problem and her main concern was to prevent us finding out. Looking back, I think that the real reason why she lied to us about Carrie having been there that evening was because she was so drunk that she didn't remember anything about the visit and thought it would be simpler to lie than to risk being questioned about it.''

''You think Carrie did go to the Selbys' that night, then?''

''I think she must have, because of the timing of what happened later, in Miss Cox's house.''

''And Major Selby lied because his wife had asked him to?''

''Yes. All of which, of course, made us highly suspicious.''

''I suppose that if you look hard enough, most people would have something in their lives that they're ashamed of, either in the past or in the present.''

''That certainly applied to the people in this case,'' Thanet said. ''Which gave us plenty of grounds for suspicion when we discovered that Carrie was a snooper.''

Joan wrinkled her nose. ''Nasty.''

''Yes. But, be fair, in her case it was understandable. If you'd met that mother of hers. . . . Poor Carrie. Her secret indulgences just weren't enough to satisfy her. I would guess they were too inward-turning, too . . . sterile. She wanted something real, involving other people. But she was incapable of making good relationships with them so she settled for finding out about them instead."

"And you think that was enough for her?"

"I do, yes. I don't think it ever entered her head to use that knowledge in blackmail. Certainly there's no shred of evidence that she did. Prying is a nasty, shabby business and perhaps she deserved some kind of punishment. But to pay with her life . . . it does seem altogether out of proportion to her crime, if crime it can be called."

"But if she didn't get the money from blackmail, where did she get it from?"

Thanet grinned sheepishly. "Would you believe it? From bingo."

"Bingo? Oh darling, no! I just don't believe it!" Joan began to laugh. "What a let-down, after all those dramatic explanations you thought up — blackmail, theft, gambling. . . ."

"Well bingo is a form of gambling, of course . . . But it just shows that it doesn't pay to let your imagination run away with you. It's a sad and rather dreary fact of life that the obvious explanation is often the true one. And in this case, well, it really should have been obvious to me that she was a bingo sort of person. I must admit I felt a bit of a fool when we found out."

"How did you find out?"

"As so often happens, when we were following quite another line of enquiry. The men were on house-to-house, trying to track down the sneak thief, and Bentley came across this woman who was also a bingo addict and regularly used to see Carrie on bingo night at the Embassy. Carrie had quite a reputation for being lucky, I gather. . . . Where was I?"

"Talking about Carrie's snooping."

"Ah yes. Well anyway, when I began to understand just how nosey Carrie was, I started to think about Miss Cox. Just imagine how frustrating it must have been for a woman like Carrie to live next door to someone who is a complete enigma. For years she must have longed to get her foot inside Miss Cox's front door. I expect that when Miss Cox broke her leg and accepted Carrie's offer of help with the shopping, Carrie thought that she was going to make it inside number five at last — but no, she never got over the threshold. And I could imagine her planning all sorts of stratagems to worm her way in. It might well have become an obsession with her. Burning curiosity and the determination to satisfy it . . . in certain circumstances they can be a pretty fatal combination, as Carrie found out.''

"I see!" said Joan. "So you think that's what happened. She managed somehow to get inside Miss Cox's house and either saw brother Joseph or something which betrayed his presence . . .''

"And Miss Cox came back and found her. Yes, that's how it was, I'm certain of it. I'd guess Miss Cox lashed out in anger at first, with the walking stick she was using — forensic have confirmed that that was the weapon used to knock Carrie out — and then, realising that if Carrie were allowed to live the secret would be out, decided that there was only one safe place for her from now on and that was in a wooden box, six feet under.''

"Poor Carrie. I suppose that the second she put her foot over the threshold of number five she had, in effect, signed her own death warrant. But I still don't really understand why. Why was it so important to keep Joseph's presence a secret?''

"He was a deserter,'' Thanet said. "After being shot down in the Berlin raids he must somehow have made his way back to England and headed for home instead of reporting to the authorities. He was a quiet, timid lad and I should think he would have found his war experience more shattering than most. And then, well, once she had him safely home again I bet his sister persuaded him to stay. Even at that stage I expect they would both have been afraid that if the truth came out he would be arrested.''

"What was the penalty for desertion?''

"Well, that's the point. I expect they thought he would be shot. Deserters were, during the first world war, and during the second the myth persisted that they still would be. In fact, it would probably simply have meant a term of imprisonment.''

"I suppose one could understand them feeling like that while the war was still on, then, but afterwards . . . Surely there was an amnesty for war-time deserters?"

"That's the tragedy of it, there was. I checked. In February 1953. After that he could safely have come out of hiding at any time. If only they'd known. But they were very simple people, living such circumscribed lives. If they hadn't actually come across the information by chance, either on the radio or in the newspapers, I'm sure they'd never have thought of enquiring. For that matter, I'm not sure they would have known what an amnesty was if they had heard about one."

"So how d'you think Carrie did manage to get in, in the end?"

"On the night of the murder, Tiger — Miss Cox's cat — went missing. She was very attached to it and when it didn't come to her call she went out to look for it. It had got shut in the shed at the bottom of the garden, she said, and she blamed the wind for banging the door closed. It may have done, of course, but I've wondered since if Carrie might not have shut the cat in the shed on purpose, knowing that Miss Cox would go out to look for it. Miss Cox, like Carrie herself, was very much a creature of habit and Carrie would have been able to anticipate her movements exactly. Miss Cox still had a leg in plaster and Carrie would know that it would take her some time to get down the garden path, locate the cat and get back again, long enough for Carrie to slip into the house and have a quick snoop around."

"But if Miss Cox had a leg in plaster how on earth would she have been able to move the body from her house to where it was found? It was some distance away, wasn't it?"

"A hundred yards or so, I'd guess. Yes, that leg was one of the things which threw us off the scent and made us tend to discount her. But it is extraordinary what one can achieve with sufficient incentive and determination. I think she must have rolled the body — and Carrie was a small woman, remember — on to one of the big plastic sheets which she used for wrapping up those loose covers she made for a living. Then, when all the lights were out in Church Cottages and everything was quiet, she dragged the body down the garden path, along the footpath and into the back garden of number two — where, unluckily for her, Harry Pack had gone to pinch another sack of cement for his wife's concrete path. He told us he'd left home at midnight, so it must have been about twenty past when he had the fright of his life and almost bumped into her as he was coming back out on to the footpath. Although he couldn't see exactly what she was doing, he didn't wait to find out. He was terrified of being caught red-handed, knowing that it would mean prison this time, so he dodged back into the garden and hid behind the privy."

"Where she hid the body!"

"Exactly. When she'd gone, curiosity made him peep inside. You can imagine how he felt when he saw what was there."

"And he's quite sure it was Miss Cox?"

"Certain. He knows her well by sight. There was a fitful moon that night and enough light for him to identify her beyond any shadow of doubt. There was that leg in plaster, too. He must have had a very nasty half an hour or so while she laboured to cram Carrie's body into the privy only feet away from him."

"But surely, the fact that Miss Cox hid the body doesn't necessarily mean that she was the murderer?"

"You mean, Joseph might have done it?"

"Why not? It would have been natural for her to cover up for him, wouldn't it? And everything you've said about the murder could equally apply to him. Carrie could have come upon him, startled him, and he could have killed her in the shock of discovery."

But Thanet was shaking his head. "No, I can't agree. It's all wrong. Just think about that relationship, Joan. When Matty Cox lost her mother she invested all her loving in that baby. It wasn't so much that he needed her — I'm sure that if she hadn't looked after him, somebody else would have — but that she needed him, emotionally speaking. He was her life-line and the intensity of her love for him increased rather than diminished with the years. He became, if you like, her raison

186

d'être. Think how she must have felt when he was called up, how she would have grabbed with both hands at the chance of keeping him at home, when he eventually turned up after making his way back from Germany. I'd guess she would have done anything, anything at all, to prevent his being snatched away from her again — well, she did, didn't she? She killed for just that reason.''

"But did she? I agree with all you're saying, and yes, I can see she might well have done the killing, but I still think it could equally well have been Joseph.''

"Well, look at it this way. Think of the effect that that kind of obsessive love would have had upon him. She cocooned him in it so thoroughly that, over the years, I should think his will-power would have been completely destroyed. I'd guess that by now he would have been incapable of any sudden act of aggression, let alone one as violent, as extreme as murder. Faced unexpectedly by Carrie, I should think that his instinctive reaction would have been to turn to his sister for rescue, just as hers was to strike out in his defence. No, I'm as certain as I can be that he couldn't have done it.''

"Yes," Joan said slowly, turning it over in her mind. "I see what you mean. Yes, I suppose you're right." She shivered. "It's frightening, isn't it, to think what one person can do to another, in the name of love?''

"Yes," said Thanet, remembering grimly how he himself had so narrowly escaped that particular trap. "It certainly is.''

Joan was silent for a while, thinking.

"But I still don't understand how you cottoned on to the idea that Joseph was still alive and living with his sister," she said at last.

"It was something old Mr Pitman said. You see, peculiar as people can be, they are usually consistent in the things which really matter to them.

"We're both too young to remember it, but I understand that many, many women whose men were reported 'missing, believed killed' in the last war refused to accept that they were dead, preferring to think that they were really stuck behind barbed-wire fences in some prisoner-of-war camp. And, of course, a lot of them were. Usually news filtered back from the camps before the war ended, but there were plenty of cases when men turned up unexpectedly some considerable time later. After hearing about young Matty Cox and her single-minded devotion to her brother Joseph, I was surprised that she hadn't gone on hoping that this was what had happened to him long, long after most women would have given up. But she didn't. Mr Pitman told me that she stopped expecting him to come home about a year after he went missing, towards the end of 1944 — *long before the end of the war.*

"The Pitmans apparently thought that this was because it was too painful for Matty to go on living in perpetual disappointment, that the only way she could cope was to accept that he was dead — but I bet that was the moment when he finally arrived back home. It was also at that point that she abruptly became a recluse. People accepted this, of course, thought that the shock of losing her brother had unhinged her. And I don't know, but I would guess that it was then that she gradually began to adopt a mannish appearance."

"You mean, so that if by chance anyone should catch a glimpse of Joseph, they would think it was her?"

"That's right. And they did indeed look very similar, dressed alike and with the same hairstyles — cut by Miss Cox herself, I imagine."

"But just think," said Joan with awe, "to live like that for more than thirty years, shut up in one room . . ."

"Not necessarily in one room. At night, with the curtains drawn, I should think he would have been able to have the run of the house." Thanet remembered his recurring feeling of being watched by someone in number five, and for the first time he wondered: could that have been Joseph, not his sister? It was possible.

"What was it like, the attic?"

"It takes up the entire roof space. The partition wall between number five and number four had been heavily insulated, presumably so that he wouldn't have to worry too much about keeping quiet all the time — and the room itself . . . you should have seen it. He had everything he wanted up

188

there, I imagine, and yet it was so pathetic, somehow, a substitute for life. There was a vast model railway layout on a properly constructed base, books on bird-watching and on almost every aspect of country and wild-life, and some very fine binoculars. There was a carpenter's bench with a splendid set of tools — most of the furniture in the house had been made by him, by the look of it. Games, records, you name it, he had it. I should think Miss Cox spent every penny she could spare on keeping him happy.

"And yet, it was almost as if Joseph had never become a man at all, as if he was a small boy whose hobbies had to be indulged. . . . I suppose he'd grown used to it. I expect he'd lost the will to live in any other way and would have found the modern world a bewildering and perhaps frightening place. No, I think that the most astounding aspect of the whole affair is that he could have lived in a terraced house in an English village for that length of time without anyone once suspecting that he was there. I suppose if he'd ever been seriously ill the game would have been up."

"It's no good. I *still* don't see how you guessed. I wouldn't have, in a million years."

Thanet laughed. "Flattery will get you everywhere," he said. "Did I tell you how gorgeous you're looking today, by the way?"

Joan was wearing a new spring suit in a deep hyacinth blue which suited her fair colouring to perfection. On her head was perched a minute straw hat decorated with tiny blue and white flowers.

"That," he went on, "is the most ridiculous and adorable hat I have ever seen in my life."

Joan looked pleased and a faint flush of pleasure bloomed in her cheeks. "I'm glad you like it," she said demurely, "but you're not wriggling out of it like that. You still haven't explained to me . . ."

"My word, you certainly deserve full marks for persistence," Thanet said with a grin. "Well, I admit there was something else . . . something apparently quite irrelevant. By itself it would have had no significance, but linked to Carrie's love of snooping and Miss Cox's inconsistent behaviour over her brother's reported death . . . You see, at one point I began to suspect that Major Selby was a fraud.''.

Joan looked blank. "I'm not with you at all," she said. "What's the connection?"

"It just seemed to me that he was too much of a good thing. As I said to Lineham, he was almost a caricature of what an ex-regular Major should be.''

"I still don't see the point. Was he?"

"Was he what?"

"Genuine?"

"No idea. We never got around to checking. Patience, darling," he said, as Joan made an exasperated sound. "Patience, and all will be revealed. I know it's a bit tortuous, but you did ask. . . . You see, the point is that once I'd started thinking along those lines — about the army and the war in general — I side-slipped on to Joseph Cox. I remembered thinking how strange it was that Miss Cox had suddenly given up hope of his return, when there was really still quite a strong possibility that he hadn't been killed at all, but picked up and put into a POW camp. And then I thought, what if he hadn't been killed *and he hadn't been picked up, either*. What if he'd lain low for a time and then managed to find his own way back to England, as many men did. . . . You see? Once I'd reached that point, my whole thinking about the case altered. I saw that I could have been misinterpreting Miss Cox's behaviour all along.''

"What do you mean?"

"Well, I had thought she was afraid. And I was right, of course, she was — but *not*, as I had imagined, because the murderer was still at large. What she was really frightened of was that I should learn the truth. The tragedy was that in trying to reassure her, by telling her that the end of the case was in sight, I achieved precisely the opposite effect and pushed her into action. If I hadn't done so she wouldn't have panicked and both she and her brother would still be alive. I can't help feeling guilty about that.''

"You mustn't blame yourself. How could you have known?"

"That's beside the point."

"No, it isn't!" Joan cried passionately. "You were simply trying to be kind. And anyway, how much better off do you think they would have been if they were still alive? You said yourself that Joseph would have been lost if he'd had to cope with present-day living. What do you think it would have been like if he had had to do so without his sister to help him? And how absolutely miserable she would have been, if she'd had to go to prison and not only have to live without him but know that he was hopelessly ill-equipped to fend for himself?"

Thanet was silent for a few moments and then he gave Joan a shamefaced grin. "I hadn't thought of it quite like that," he said.

"That's because you're always too ready to blame yourself for everything that goes wrong. But when it comes to taking the credit . . ."

"Here's the church," interrupted Thanet with a smile. "Just at the psychological moment, before you get well and truly launched on that one."

Joan released an exaggerated sigh of mock exasperation. "Sometimes, my darling, you are well and truly impossible!" she said. But her curiosity had been satisfied now and she was leaning forward to look eagerly out of the window, eyes shining in anticipation. "I am glad they've got such a lovely day," she said. "Oh look, the bridesmaids are arriving."

And there they were, one girl in her early twenties and two tiny ones, all of them looking like spring flowers themselves in their pretty pastel dresses.

"It's a shame Mrs Lineham couldn't have been here," said Joan, as she and Thanet walked along the ancient flagstones to the church porch.

"I don't want to sound hard," Thanet said, "but in a way she has brought this on herself, you know. All the same, I do agree. It is a pity. But I think Mike made the right decision in going ahead regardless. If he hadn't . . ."

"True. He'd never have got away, then. I don't think Louise could have borne a third postponement."

Thanet and Joan took their places on the bridegroom's side of the church. Half the police force of Sturrenden seemed to be

191

present, unfamiliar in their Sunday best. Thanet thought how glad he was that with the Birch case solved Lineham would be able to go off on his honeymoon with a clear conscience.

Briefly, his mind skimmed back over the case, pausing to rest for a moment on each of the main characters. For a very little while he had impinged upon their lives and they upon his. Some of them would stick in his memory, he knew: old Robert Pitman, for example, with his unquenchable fortitude and zest for life — and, yes, Carrie Birch herself with her pathetic daydreams, her thirst for vicarious living. She would never know it, but he would remember her with gratitude. For did he not, after all, in some strange way, owe her Joan? He shivered involuntarily to think how close he had been to losing his wife.

"Cold?" she whispered.

He shook his head, smiled at her.

Lineham and his best man were rising now, moving to take their places for the ceremony. The bride must have arrived. Heads turned, seeking a first glimpse of her, as the congregation came to its feet.

Then the organ burst forth into the gloriously triumphant opening chords of the Wedding March and Louise began to move serenely down the aisle on her father's arm.

Thanet felt for Joan's hand and pressed it, savouring the quick response. They exchanged affectionate glances.

Yes, he was whole-heartedly in favour of marriage, himself.

PUPPET FOR A CORPSE

Praise for PUPPET FOR A CORPSE

'A whodunnit in the fine tradition of the puzzle game'
The Times

'The sort of book you curl up in bed with on wet days
. . . good, lazy reading' *Literary Review*

'Riddle after riddle and clever plotting' *Standard*

'Neatly constructed plot' *Times Literary Supplement*

'A thriller with a twist in the tale' *Manchester Evening
News*

'Dorothy Simpson is expert at manipulating her readers,
and in *Puppet for a Corpse* we, no less than Inspector
Thanet, are surprised at the tragic answer to the riddle'
The Lady

For my mother

The regimen I adopt shall be for the benefit of my patients according to my ability and judgement, and not for their hurt or for any wrong. I will give no deadly drug to any, though it be asked of me, nor will I counsel such, and especially I will not aid a woman to procure abortion. Whatsoever house I enter, there will I go for the benefit of the sick, refraining from all wrongdoing or corruption, and especially from any act of seduction, of male or female, of bond or free. Whatsoever things I see or hear concerning the life of men, in my attendance on the sick or even apart therefrom, which ought not to be noised abroad, I will keep silence thereon, counting such things to be as sacred secrets.

Extract from the Hippocratic Oath

1

The smell of burning toast drifted upstairs to the bathroom, where Detective Inspector Luke Thanet was shaving. He grimaced at his foam-bedecked reflection, laid his razor down on the wash-basin and went out on to the landing.

The smell was stronger here and a faint bluish haze was issuing from the half-open door of the kitchen, like ectoplasm. The sound of a one-octave major scale, haltingly played, indicated that Bridget was dutifully doing her early-morning piano practice. Thanet was loath to disturb her.

"Ben!" he bellowed. "Toast!"

A small figure clutching a comic shot out of the sitting room and into the kitchen and Thanet heard the clunk as the defective release mechanism on the toaster was operated.

"Put some more in, will you, Ben?" he called. "And watch it, this time."

He went back into the bathroom, took up his razor, frowning slightly. Joan was presumably next door again, administering an early-morning dose of comfort to their neighbour, Mrs Markham. It was about time he put his foot down. This had gone on long enough.

Joan had been working for eighteen months now as an Assistant Probation Officer, prior to launching into her formal training. She loved the job but it was very demanding and, although Thanet tried to help as much as he could, Bridget and Ben still needed a good deal of attention. And at the moment they weren't getting it, he reflected grimly as he rinsed and dried his face. There was a limit to what one woman could do. It was unreasonable of Mrs Markham still to be making such powerful bids for Joan's time and attention. Mr Markham had been dead for a year and, although Thanet had

7

initially been full of sympathy for his widow, it annoyed him that she was now exacting from Joan the same degree of attention and service that she had expected from her husband.

When Thanet had dressed he went downstairs firmly resolved to speak to Joan about it. It was disconcerting to find that she still wasn't back.

"I can't find my leotard, Daddy," Bridget said, the moment he entered the kitchen.

She and Ben were munching their way through plates of Rice Crispies.

"I don't suppose it's far away." Thanet poured himself a cup of coffee and sat down. "When did you have it last?"

"Mummy was going to mend it for me. Daddy, I *must* have it for today. It's dance club and they're doing auditions for the Christmas pantomime." Bridget's grey eyes were beginning to glisten like pearls.

"Don't worry, Sprig." Thanet gave a reassuring smile, reached across to pat her hand. "I'll just eat this piece of toast and we'll go and look for it. Ben, how many times have I told you not to read your comic at the table! Anyone know if Mummy's had any breakfast yet?"

That was another thing, he thought grimly as they shook their heads. More often than not Joan was going off to work without even a cup of coffee these days.

Fifteen minutes later his decision to have it out with her had become full-blown determination. An exhaustive search had failed to turn up Bridget's leotard.

"Where can it *be*?" The tears were beginning to flow freely now.

He squatted to put his arms around her. "Hush, sweetheart, don't cry. It's bound to be here somewhere. Ben, run next door quickly and ask Mummy where she's put Sprig's leotard. Say she has to have it to take to school today. We really must go soon, or we'll be late." He hated to see the children go off to school distressed. His head was full of all the angry things he'd say to Joan when he had the opportunity. He had no intention of making a fuss in front of the children this morning though. He didn't want to upset Sprig further by having her witness an angry scene between her parents.

Joan came in with a rush, followed by Ben. "Sorry, darling," she said. "I just couldn't get away."

She avoided looking at him, he noticed.

"Don't worry, Sprig," she went on. "I know exactly where your leotard is. I've just got to put a stitch in it and . . ."

"You mean, you've still got to *repair* it?" Thanet could feel the anger building, fuelled by Bridget's distress and by the knowledge that they were already late, would now be delayed even further.

"It won't take a second," Joan said, disappearing into the sitting room. "I'll have it ready by the time you drive the car out of the garage," she called.

"Right, come on then, kids," said Thanet. Just as well it was his turn to take the children this morning. "Coats and scarves on, quickly now. We're late already."

True to her word Joan came running out with the leotard as Thanet was backing out of the garage. Thanet wound down his window to take it from her, handed it to Bridget.

Joan leant in to give him a quick peck on the cheek, blew kisses to the children. " 'Bye darlings," she said. "See you this afternoon." One of Joan's friends earned pin-money by collecting Bridget and Ben from school with her own children. She would give them tea and keep them until Joan was free to pick them up.

Joan waved until the car was out of sight. Thanet watched her diminishing figure in the car mirror until he turned the corner. At the school he waited until Bridget and Ben were safely inside the playground and under the eye of a teacher before driving off.

"Beautiful day!" called another father, similarly engaged.

And it was, Thanet realised, noticing it properly for the first time, a perfect autumn day: unclouded sky and a sun whose strength was already dissipating that early-morning crispness which is a foretaste of frosts to come. His spirits began to rise, his mind to move forward to meet the day ahead. His undischarged anger was still there, underneath; but now, by some strange process, it was becoming translated into energy. By the

9

time he reached the office he was brimming over with it and he began to hope that something really challenging would come in today. One of the things he liked about being a policeman was never knowing what would come along next.

It was a disappointment to find that his In tray held nothing of interest and after a cursory inspection he rose and crossed to the window. Down below in the street people and cars hurried by, intent on their destinations, seemingly imbued with a powerful sense of purpose. Thanet shifted restlessly from one foot to the other, envying them. He ached to be out there *doing* something.

Unfortunately, he told himself as he settled down at his desk, life is not in the habit of producing just what we want when we want it and for every exciting, challenging task there are usually a hundred dull ones to be tackled. He opened the first of the files awaiting his attention.

At once, as though Fate were giving him a pat on the head for Cultivating Correct Attitudes, the phone rang.

"Thanet here."

"DS Lineham, sir." Thanet grinned. Trust Mike already to be out on the job. "I'm at the house of a suicide, reported this morning. A Doctor Pettifer."

"It's Dr Pettifer *himself* who's committed suicide?" Thanet's tone betrayed something of the sense of shock, betrayal almost, which he experienced whenever he heard of a member of the medical profession killing himself.

"Yes, sir."

There was, Thanet thought, something almost obscene about the suicide of any man who had taken the Hippocratic Oath and dedicated himself to the saving of life. Unfortunately, the stress experienced these days by overworked, over-burdened doctors took a heavy toll; the suicide rate in the profession, like alcoholism, was high.

"Apparently," added Lineham.

"What d'you mean, apparently?"

"Well, it all *looks* straightforward enough — an overdose helped on by alcohol, by the look of it. There's even a suicide note. But his wife's away and his housekeeper, well, she's hysterical, been with him since the year dot and swears he had no reason to do it . . ."

"That's what they all say," said Thanet. He knew only too well that the disbelief initially experienced by those closest to a suicide frequently equals and sometimes even exceeds their grief.

"Anyway, I thought I'd better give you a ring."

"I'll come along. I was just hoping for an excuse to get out of the office. It's that big Victorian house at the end of Brompton Lane, isn't it?"

"That's right. Pine Lodge. The one with the entrance pillars painted white."

"I'll be with you in ten minutes. Have you called a doctor?"

"The housekeeper says she doesn't know who his personal doctor was."

"Even though she's been with him for years?"

"I know it sounds odd, sir, but that's what she said. He was very healthy, apparently and I suppose doctors tend to treat themselves for minor ailments . . . Anyway, I didn't feel it would be right to ring one of his partners. I thought we might give Doc Mallard a ring." Mallard was the local police surgeon.

"It's not usual, with a suicide," said Thanet. "But in the circumstances, yes, it's the best thing to do. I'll see if I can get hold of him. If not, I'll arrange something else from this end. See you shortly."

Mallard was soon contacted and Thanet arranged to meet him at Pine Lodge. Brompton Lane was in the prime residential area on the far side of Sturrenden, which was a thriving market town in the heart of Kent. Thanet had been born and brought up here, so naturally he knew most of the prominent people by sight. In the car he tried to recall what he knew of Pettifer, who was — had been — a striking figure: tall, thin, with a beaky nose and jutting chin, a distinctive, bony face. He hadn't looked an approachable man and had had the reputation of being a first-rate doctor whose patients were for that reason prepared to overlook his lack of a bedside manner.

And of course, Thanet thought, with a spurt of interest

11

— he had been married to the actress, Gemma Shade! She was his second wife and much younger than he. Their marriage had been the talk of Sturrenden last year — or was it the year before? Thanet wasn't sure. Miss Shade's reputation as a serious actress was high and everyone had been astounded when she had chosen to marry a country GP. It had not fitted her somewhat exotic public image. Thanet wondered where she was this morning.

He was now nearing Brompton Lane and was aware of the growing knot of tension in his stomach; aware, too, that he was deliberately making his mind work in order to prevent himself thinking of the ordeal ahead. Not one of Thanet's colleagues knew how he dreaded the first sight of a corpse. There was something about that initial glimpse of the recently dead which moved him unbearably, especially when the death had been unnatural. Perhaps it was regret at the waste, perhaps a sense of being closer at this time than at any other to that central mystery of life, the moment when a living being loses his individuality, his identity, and becomes no more than a collection of discarded bones and flesh. At one time Thanet had been ashamed of such feelings, seeing them as unmanly, inappropriate to his calling; but slowly he had come to recognise that, paradoxically, they were one of his strengths, acting as a spur to his subsequent efforts. Acknowledging the value of what had been destroyed, he replenished his own sense of purpose.

There were the gateposts which Lineham had mentioned, painted white no doubt to act as landmarks for a tired GP trying to find his driveway in the dark after a night call.

Well, there would be no more night calls for Pettifer, Thanet reflected as he swung into the drive of neatly-raked gravel and parked beside Lineham's Renault 5.

Pettifer's sleep would never be disturbed again.

2

The Pettifer house was typical of so many Victorian family homes built towards the end of the nineteenth century. Constructed of rather ugly red brick it boasted large, square bay windows on either side of a shallow entrance porch and radiated an air of solidity and respectability. The figure of the uniformed constable planted outside the front door struck an incongruous note.

"Morning, Andrews," said Thanet. "DS Lineham inside?"

"In the kitchen I believe, sir, with the housekeeper." He stood aside for Thanet to pass.

Thanet nodded and stepped into the house, closing the door behind him. The hall was wide, with doors to right and left and a broad staircase straight ahead rising to a half-landing illuminated by a stained-glass window similar to the panels on either side of the front door. A corridor alongside the staircase led presumably to the kitchen. The floor was patterned in black and white ceramic tiles and adorned by a truly magnificent Persian rug whose reds and blues gleamed in the dim light like semi-precious stones. On a carved antique oak blanket chest against the right-hand wall stood a deep pink bowl filled with Michaelmas daisies of all hues from pink to dark red, pale blue to indigo, echoing the rich colours of the carpet. The walls were hung with oil paintings, each with its own individual spotlight.

Thanet stood quite still, absorbing the atmosphere of the house. The place was well-ordered, no doubt about that, and there was both taste and money. Whose taste and whose money, he wondered. GPs didn't exactly starve, but neither did their incomes run to furnishings of this quality. And although Mrs Pettifer was well known, Thanet wouldn't have

13

thought she was enough of a show-biz personality to be earning huge sums.

A door at the back of the house opened and closed and Detective Sergeant Lineham appeared, advancing along the narrow corridor beside the staircase.

"Ah, there you are, Mike," said Thanet. "Where is he?"

"In his bedroom. Are you ready to go up?" Lineham had worked with Thanet for several years now and was accustomed to Thanet's slow initial approach to a case, had even come to agree that those vital first impressions could be lost for ever if there was too much haste.

"Lead the way," said Thanet, standing back to allow Lineham to precede him.

As he climbed the stairs he was aware of that knot in his stomach again, of the dryness in his mouth, his quickened breathing. He braced himself.

Lineham led the way not into one of the principal bedrooms but into a small room above the front door. It was simply furnished, spartan even, with a single bed, a bedside table and one small upright chair over the back of which Pettifer's dressing gown was neatly folded. There were no ornaments, no pictures, no concessions to luxury apart from one meagre bedside rug on the polished floorboards. Later, Thanet was to realise that this had originally been a dressing room for one of the principal bedrooms; one wall consisted entirely of built-in cupboards and there was a communicating door. For the moment, however, his attention was entirely focused on the occupant of the bed.

Doctor Pettifer had died peacefully — indeed it was difficult to believe that he was not simply asleep. He lay comfortably curled on his right side, chin resting on right hand, only his stillness and the unnatural pallor of his skin betraying his true condition.

"No doubt that he's dead?" Thanet murmured.

"None, sir. He's been gone for some hours. He's cooling fast."

Thanet laid his hand against Pettifer's cheek and found that is was cold, clammy to the touch. Lineham was right. Some time last night, then. He stepped back, clasping his hands

14

behind his back. Better to be safe than sorry, touch nothing, just in case. Though he had to admit, everything looked innocuous enough, if suicide can ever be so described. Already his own tension was beginning to ease and he noted the empty pill container on the bedside table, the stained tumbler, the half-empty wine bottle. He stooped to peer at the label: Taylor's 1908 Vintage Port.

"Looks as though he went out in style," he said. "There was a note, you said?"

Lineham reached into his breast pocket, passed Thanet an envelope, handling it with care. "Addressed to his wife. Seems clear enough."

On the envelope was one word, *Gemma*. The letter was brief and to the point.

Darling,

Forgive me for letting you down like this. Please, try and make it up to Andy for me, will you?

Ever yours,
Arnold

Thanet stared at the piece of paper. It seemed so ... inadequate a message. But then no letter, no matter how long and tender, could possibly console a wife for being left in this way. The act of suicide was in itself explicit enough, the message inescapable: You don't matter enough to me to make my life worth living.

"Who's Andy?"

"Doctor Pettifer's son by his first marriage. He's away at boarding school."

Thanet frowned. "Poor kid. He'll have to be told, of course. Where is Mrs Pettifer?"

"In London, apparently. She's due back any minute, according to the housekeeper. Went up last evening, to have dinner with her agent and discuss a new play. She's Gemma Shade, the actress."

"Yes, I know. She stayed the night, then?"

"That was the arrangement."

15

"What time did she leave?"

"Mrs Price — the housekeeper — doesn't know. She was away last night too. It was her day off yesterday and she left soon after breakfast, to spend it with her sister out at Merrisham. When she came back this morning she found the curtains still drawn everywhere, no sign of Dr Pettifer having had breakfast, so she came up to investigate and found him like this. She's very upset. As I said, she's been with him for years."

"Bit odd, wasn't it, being away overnight? I'd have thought she'd have had to be back in time to prepare his breakfast, especially if Mrs Pettifer was away."

"In the normal way of things, she would have been. But she had special permission to spend the night at her sister's. There was something on in the village that they both particularly wanted to go to."

"Pity."

A car crunched on the gravel outside.

"That'll be Doc Mallard," said Thanet, crossing to the window. "Yes, there he is. Go down and meet him, will you?"

While Lineham was out of the room Thanet glanced around once more, noting for the first time the little pile of personal possessions on the seat of the upright chair. He moved across and glanced through them: wallet, thermometer, two bunches of keys, a couple of pens, some loose change and a diary. Thanet picked the latter up, found yesterday's date. *G London*, he read. *Mrs P to sister*. These were the only entries for this week. He flicked quickly through the rest of the diary but found nothing of interest. Most of the pages were blank, the few entries consisting chiefly of social engagements and Andy's beginning- and end-of-term dates.

Thanet put the diary back on the chair thoughtfully. It was interesting that Mrs Price's visit to her sister had been entered. Would a man normally note down the fact that his house-keeper was going to be away for the night? Surely not, unless he had a special reason for doing so — wanting the house to himself, for example. No, this had been no dramatic gesture carefully staged so that the suicide attempt would be discovered in time, Pettifer hauled back from the brink of death. Pettifer had meant to die, had timed the whole thing carefully. With both wife and housekeeper away until morning there would have been little chance of an unwelcome last-minute reprieve.

What a waste, Thanet thought, moving back to gaze down on the peaceful face of the dead man, what a waste. What could drive a man like Pettifer to kill himself? Despair, presumably, but over what? Thanet had met despair in many guises and in the most unexpected places, but suicide was something he had always found difficult to accept with equanimity. Was it not, after all, a form of murder — self-murder — surely no less heinous a crime than murder itself, if more understandable. And in one way, far more damaging to others: the murder victim is less likely to leave behind such a burden of guilt and self-reproach on his nearest and dearest. How close had Pettifer been to his wife, Thanet wondered. How significant was the fact that they had had separate bedrooms?

Mallard and Lineham entered the room, breaking into Thanet's train of thought. Mallard brushed his hand uneasily across his bald head as they greeted each other. He looked unusually grim. That was understandable. If Thanet found it hard to accept that a doctor had killed himself, how much more difficult it must be for a colleague. And, for all Thanet knew, the two men might have been friends. A tactful withdrawal was indicated.

"We'll wait downstairs," Thanet said. "There's not much room in here."

Mrs Price was huddled at the kitchen table, both hands clasped around a mug of steaming liquid, seeking comfort. The room was large, high-ceilinged and had an old-fashioned air, with a tall built-in dresser, a row of servants' bells labelled with the names of the different rooms and glass-fronted wall-cupboards painted institution green. Mrs Price matched her kingdom both in her ample proportions and in her slight dowdiness; her patterned crimplene dress and neatly waved brown hair would have passed unnoticed anywhere. She was,

17

Thanet guessed, in her early sixties. As the two men entered the room she turned a dazed, tear-stained face towards them.

Thanet advanced, introduced himself, apologised for having to ask more questions. Courtesy paid off with all but the very few, he found. Mrs Price clearly found it reassuring. Thanet quickly learned that she had left the house at nine-thirty the previous morning and had travelled to her sister's by bus, arriving just before eleven-thirty. They had spent the afternoon at home and in the evening had attended a meeting in the village. This morning she had caught the workmen's bus at six-twenty in order to be back in time to clear up the breakfast dishes.

"I gather you don't usually spend the night away, on your day off?"

"No, but I specially wanted to go to this meeting and Doctor Pettifer said I could. If only I'd stayed at home . . ."

"When did you ask him?"

"About three months ago." Mrs Price's cheeks were pink. "I didn't often ask," she said defensively. "The last time was when . . ."

"Nobody's questioning your right to the occasional night off," Thanet said soothingly. "How did Dr Pettifer seem before you left, yesterday morning?"

"Fine. Real cheerful, he was," the housekeeper said promptly. "That's why I can't believe . . ." Her lips began to quiver and she dabbed at her eyes, blew her nose. "I *don't* believe it," she said vehemently, recovering herself. "The doctor would never've done it, never. Happy as a sandboy he was, yesterday. Well, I suppose that's putting it a bit strong. He never is . . . was . . . one to wear his heart on his sleeve, but I knew him and I could tell."

"How long have you been with him, Mrs Price?"

"Fifteen years," she said proudly. "Ever since Andy — that's his son — was a baby. And very happy I've been."

But there was a hint of reservation in that last statement. "So you must have run the house alone after the first Mrs Pettifer's death," he said, hazarding a guess as to where the trouble lay.

18

"That's right. For five years. Managed fine I did, too."

So he was right. Mrs Price had resented having to hand over the reins to a second Mrs Pettifer.

"Did you know that Mrs Pettifer was going up to London yesterday?"

"Yes, because of the meals. 'We'll both be out to lunch, and dinner'll just be for one,' she says to me, after breakfast yesterday morning. 'I'm going up to town this evening to see my agent and I shan't be back till tomorrow.' Well, I was a bit annoyed. I mean, I'd had this trip to my sister's arranged for months, like I said. 'But I'm going to be away tonight too,' I says. 'What about the doctor's breakfast tomorrow morning?' 'I expect he'll survive,' she says, as cool as you please. And now . . ." Mrs Price's eyes filled with tears.

"Oh come, Mrs Price," Thanet said gently. "You surely can't be saying that the doctor did what he did because you weren't here to cook his breakfast?"

The deliberate absurdity of the question made her smile. "No, but if I hadn't stayed away . . ."

"Mrs Price," Thanet said firmly. "Even if you had been here, what could you have done? I don't suppose that in the normal way of things you would see Dr Pettifer after he retired for the night?" He waited for her shake of the head. "There you are, then. And besides, you must remember this. If someone is really determined to kill himself, nothing will stop him. If anyone prevents him, he'll just try again. And from the way in which Dr Pettifer selected a night when he knew that both you and Mrs Pettifer would be away . . ." He paused to allow the point to sink in.

"It's no good, I still can't believe it," she said stubbornly. "He just wasn't the sort to give up, no matter what it was. When the first Mrs Pettifer was dying — she had cancer, and you know what that's like, she was ill for two years before she died — well, he never gave up hope, never gave up trying to save her. And just now, what with Mrs Pettifer being pregnant and all . . ."

"Mrs Pettifer is pregnant?"

"Six months gone, she is. The baby's due in the new year.

He was that thrilled about it . . . And then there's Andy . . . Oh, who's going to tell Andy? Doted on his father, he did." And she dissolved into tears again.

"I think I can hear Doc Mallard coming down," said Lineham softly.

Thanet nodded, patted Mrs Price on the shoulder and went out into the hall, followed by Lineham. They met Mallard at the foot of the stairs. The police surgeon shook his head, his mouth tucked down at the corners.

"Doesn't seem much doubt about it, does there? The post mortem will verify it, of course, but that combination of alcohol and drugs . . . pretty typical of how a doctor would choose to go, if he wanted to. By far the most comfortable way to kill yourself, if you're set on it. Was there a note?"

Thanet nodded.

"That clinches it then, I should think. Why was I called in, by the way?"

"The housekeeper didn't know who his own doctor was and Mrs Pettifer is away. She's due back shortly."

"What a mess. She's pregnant, I believe."

"So the housekeeper said. Did you know him well?"

"Pettifer?" Mallard pursed his lips, shook his head. "Not really. I knew him, of course. Most doctors in a place the size of Sturrenden run into each other from time to time, at meetings and so on."

"What was he like?"

"Medically, his reputation was excellent. As a man, well, you'd have to ask his wife, or his partners. They operate from the Health Centre on the Maidstone Road."

So Mallard hadn't liked Pettifer, or at least had had reservations about him. Interesting, Thanet thought. "Have you heard of any reason why he might have done this? Rumours of depression, poor health, marital troubles, financial worries?"

"None. Truly, not a whisper. I won't say it's incomprehensible, because no one ever knows just what's going on inside someone else's mind, but in this case . . . Anyway," Mallard said, more briskly, "that's it, for the moment, as far as I'm concerned. I must get on."

20

"What time do you think he must have taken the overdose?" Thanet asked as he escorted Mallard to the car.

"Difficult to estimate exactly. Death would probably have been pretty swift. He would have known the appropriate dosage of whatever drug he used, of course, and the alcohol would have speeded things up enormously. He'd probably be dead within an hour or two. But there are various factors which would have delayed the cooling of the body — the fact that he was warmly tucked up in bed, that it was a mild night anyway . . . I'd guess he took it between ten and twelve last night."

Mallard's guess was good enough for him, Thanet thought as he watched the police surgeon drive away. Mallard's integrity and acumen were widely respected in the force. Thanet was fond of the older man, had known him since childhood. Pettifer's death had shaken Mallard, Thanet reflected as he returned to the house. The doctor's usual dry humour and testiness had been conspicuous by their absence.

Back in the kitchen he accepted the mug of coffee which Mrs Price had made while he was away. She looked calmer now, had perhaps found the tiny chore therapeutic.

"Well now, Mrs Price," Thanet said carefully, "the police surgeon has examined Dr Pettifer and I'm afraid it really does look as though he committed suicide. He even left a note, for Mrs Pettifer. Are you absolutely certain that you can't think of any reason why he should have done this?"

Mrs Price shook her head, her lips compressed in a stubborn line.

"No money worries?"

A vehement shake of the head this time. "There's never been any shortage of money in this house. Doctor Pettifer had a good practice and I've always understood that the first Mrs Pettifer left him everything when she died. And I believe she wasn't short of a penny."

"No . . . difficulties in his second marriage?"

Mrs Price folded her arms and glared at him. "No. Not that I'd tell you if there had been, I'm not one to gossip, but you can take it from me there weren't. I'd have been the first to know, living in the house. No, he worshipped the ground she walked on."

"And Mrs Pettifer?"

"She treated him well, I can't say different."

And, thought Thanet, it was clear that she would have liked to. It sounded as though there had been no problem there. All the same . . . "I did notice," he said delicately, "that Dr and Mrs Pettifer did not share a bedroom . . ."

"That," said Mrs Price, with an air of putting someone in his place, "was simply out of consideration for Mrs Pettifer. He didn't like her being disturbed at night. He was often called out, you know. So, ever since he knew she was expecting he's insisted on sleeping in the dressing room. So polite and considerate, he always was . . ."

Tears were imminent again and Thanet intervened quickly. "What about health? Did he have any problems there?"

"As strong as a horse, he was. Never a day's illness as long as I've been here. That's why I don't know who his doctor is, or if he's got one, even. Perhaps it's one of his partners. Oh, I'm not saying he didn't have the odd cold, that sort of thing, but he used to dose himself and there was never anything serious. I can't recall him ever being off work for more than a day or two in the last fifteen years. No, I tell a lie. He was laid up for a few days last year. He tripped over something and tore a muscle in his leg. But he didn't make a fuss about it. He put a lot of store by keeping fit. Didn't smoke, didn't drink — except at a dinner party, perhaps — and took regular exercise."

Dr Pettifer, Thanet thought, sounded dauntingly self-disciplined. "Any family worries? Parents? Son?"

"His parents are dead and Andy's as nice a boy as you'd hope to find, specially these days with all the tales you hear about youngsters. No," and Mrs Price sat down suddenly, her eyes filling with tears yet again, "there's no reason, no reason at all, I tell you. It must have been an accident."

Thanet and Lineham said nothing. Who better qualified or more aware than a doctor, of the dangers of taking drugs and alcohol together? And there was the note. But there seemed

22

little point in saying so. Mrs Price would have to come to terms with the tragedy in her own time.

"What time is Mrs Pettifer due back?" Thanet said.

"Around a quarter to ten. She's got an ante-natal appointment at ten-thirty this morning."

They all looked at the clock. Ten to ten. And, as if she had timed this entrance as carefully as one of her appearances on stage, the front door slammed and a woman's voice could be heard in the hall. Thanet and Lineham rose in unison.

It sounded as though Gemma Pettifer was home.

3

Thanet turned hurriedly to Mrs Price. "What is the name of Mrs Pettifer's doctor?" *Six months pregnant, I should have thought of this before.*

"Dr Barson."

"Get in touch with him right away," Thanet said to Lineham. "Mrs Pettifer will need him."

"There's a phone on the wall over there," said Mrs Price. "And if there's anything I can do . . ."

"Make some tea," Thanet said on his way to the door. "I expect she could do with some." Tea, he thought. The English panacea for all ills. What would this nation do without it?

Mrs Pettifer — or Gemma Shade, as her many fans would call her — was standing in the entrance hall facing an uncomfortable Constable Andrews.

"Accident?" she was saying. "What sort of an accident?"

"Ah, Inspector Thanet," Andrews said with relief. "This is . . ."

"Ins*pect*or?" she said, turning.

Thanet wondered if he had caught a hint of wariness in the questioning look she gave him. He had never seen her off-stage or at close quarters before and his immediate reaction was one of surprise that she should look so ordinary. She was small and slight, with long brown hair caught back in an elastic band, and she was wearing a flowing Indian cotton dress which effectively concealed her fairly advanced state of pregnancy. He managed to manoeuvre her into a chair in the drawing room before breaking the news to her.

"Dead?" she said, staring up at him. "Of an overdose? *Arnold*?"

She was, he now saw, older than he had thought, in her

24

mid-thirties, perhaps, but still a good ten years or so younger than her husband. Her one outstanding feature was her eyes, which were a clear willow green with very distinct irises. Thanet was conscious of an unusually strong surge of compassion.

"I'm afraid so," he said.

Her eyes slid away from his and she folded her hands protectively across her swollen belly, as if to reassure the child within that she at least had no intention of abandoning it. He could almost feel her trying to assimilate the facts of her husband's death and the significance of the word "overdose" — Pettifer's medical knowledge, the near-impossibility of its having been an accident . . .

"Suicide, you mean, then," she said at last.

"Yes. I'm sorry. There'll have to be an inquest, I'm afraid." He took out the note. "Your husband left a letter for you."

She stared at the proffered envelope for a moment before reaching out to take it between the tips of two fingers, warily. Then she glanced up at him, the green eyes accusing. "It's been opened," she said.

"Yes, I'm sorry. It's what one might call standard procedure in these circumstances."

"Standard procedure," she breathed scornfully as she took out the single sheet of paper. Her eyes took in the brief message in one single sweep. "And this is . . . all?" she said.

Thanet understood at once what she meant. She was echoing what he had felt when he first read it and she was right. Those pitifully few words did seem a totally inadequate valediction. "I'm afraid so. And I shall have to ask for it back, temporarily."

She returned it to him, then shook her head. "It's no good. I still can't believe it."

"Why not?" said Thanet gently.

She frowned and stared down at her hands as if they held the answer. "All sorts of reasons," she said slowly. "As far as I knew he had no health problems — and surely I would have known, if there had been anything sufficiently serious for him to . . . And then, he was so looking forward to the baby's arrival." She bit her lip. "Only yesterday, at breakfast, we were discussing names . . ."

25

"Was that when you last saw him? At breakfast?"

The door opened and Lineham entered, bearing a cup of tea. Dr Barson, he announced, would be here shortly. Thanet repeated his question.

"No, that was at about six o'clock last night," she said, accepting the tea with a grateful nod, "when I tucked him up in bed, so to speak, with a hot drink and a couple of paracetamol. He said he thought he had a cold coming on . . . and whenever that happened, which was rarely, he'd always have a hot bath, take a couple of paracetamol and put himself to bed."

She was still calm, remarkably calm really, Thanet thought. But he had seen this kind of reaction before. He guessed that at the moment she was being cushioned by a sense of unreality. Later on, when it hit her . . . He sat down and said gently, "Do you feel up to telling me briefly about yesterday?"

"What do you want to know, exactly?"

"If you could run through the day, so that I could have some idea of your husband's movements . . ."

Yesterday, it seemed, had been a day like any other, with no hint of the tragedy to come. Dr Pettifer had left for the Health Centre immediately after breakfast. After taking surgery he had done his usual round of late-morning visits before returning home to lunch, when he had behaved just as usual.

"He didn't seem at all depressed?"

"Not in the least, no."

"You really wouldn't say that there was anything out of the ordinary in his behaviour or his attitude?"

"No, nothing."

"And after lunch?"

After lunch Mrs Pettifer had gone up to her room for the afternoon rest upon which her husband had insisted during her pregnancy. Pettifer had returned from his second round of visits at around five-thirty. This was when he had first said that he thought he had an incipient cold. As his wife was going to be out for the evening he had decided to take a hot bath right away and go to bed early. Mrs Pettifer had waited until he was in bed and had then taken up the hot drink and paracetamol.

26

"And that was at about six o'clock, you say?"

"Yes, just before I left. My taxi was due at ten past six. I was supposed to be catching the six twenty-seven and when I went up I asked if he'd like me to cancel my engagement and stay at home. But he said no, that was quite unnecessary, that in any case it would be silly for me to keep him company in case I caught his cold. I suppose he knew I'd be disappointed if I didn't go. You see, I stopped work a couple of months ago, because of the baby, and he knew I'd found it difficult to adjust. I was so excited when my agent sent me this new part to consider, but then I simply couldn't make up my mind whether to accept it or not. That's why I was meeting him, to discuss it with him. So my husband . . ." She stopped.

"Yes?"

She shrugged. "Nothing. As I say, he just said it was unnecessary for me to stay, that no doubt he'd be right as rain by morning."

This wasn't what she had been going to say, Thanet was certain of it, but he didn't feel he could press her at the moment. He let it pass. "You gave him a hot drink, you say?"

"Yes. Cocoa." Her eyes widened. "He didn't . . . it wasn't in the cocoa that he took the . . ."

"No. You left the drink with him, then?"

"Yes. It was very hot and he was still sipping it when I left."

"And you also gave him some paracetamol, you said?"

"That's right. Two tablets. That's all he'd ever take."

"And you left the container on the bedside table?"

"No. The paracetamol are kept in the cabinet, in the bathroom. I took two out, put the container back."

"And you're sure they were paracetamol?"

"Certain."

"It's labelled, the container?"

"Of course. But there couldn't have been any mistake anyway. Both of us have . . . had a bit of a thing about drugs. Neither of us ever used anything but paracetamol, unless it was absolutely essential to take an antibiotic, perhaps, and we never keep any other drugs in that cabinet."

"Could you tell me if your husband would ever take a drink

27

before he went to bed, to help him sleep, perhaps?"

"Alcohol d'you mean? Good heavens, no! Never!"

Her astonishment was genuine, Thanet was sure of it. But remember, she's an actress, and a first-rate one at that, whispered the voice of caution. All the same, he could see no reason to disbelieve her. Mrs Price had said much the same thing. By now he thought he had a clear picture of what had happened. Pettifer had waited until he was certain that there was no possibility of his wife returning and had then disposed of the cocoa mug. (But why bother? And where was it now?) Then he had fetched the bottle of port, the glass and the necessary quantity of drugs and had returned to bed to seek eternal oblivion.

But why?

He must have had his reasons and they must have been cogent, powerful indeed — and yet, both wife and house-keeper had been blissfully unaware of their existence. What was more, Pettifer had played into that ignorance, had fostered and encouraged it, had kept the charade up right to the end. And why the fuss about something as trivial as a cold, if he had intended suicide? To enjoy, one last time, the luxury of being cosseted by his wife? Surely, someone who intended committing suicide would be past caring about such things?

"Oh, I don't understand it," Mrs Pettifer burst out. "I just don't understand it. He was so cheerful yesterday. How can he have . . . I know that by evening he thought he was getting a cold, but that was nothing, such a . . . trivial thing. He insisted that I should still go to London . . . I simply can't believe that all the time he was planning to . . ." She was becoming more and more agitated and now she stopped abruptly, blinked.

Here it comes, Thanet thought.

She struggled clumsily to her feet. "No!" she said, her voice rising. "It's not possible! Not Arnold. He'd never do such a thing. Never. He'd never leave me all alone, like this . . ." She sounded near panic now and with one brief gesture at her belly somehow managed to evoke all the bleak and lonely years ahead, bringing up the child alone.

Thanet rose as Lineham jumped up and took one or two

uncertain steps towards her. The front door banged and voices could be heard outside in the hall. Lineham swung around and made for the door with evident relief. "That's probably the doctor."

Barson was tall, balding and wore pebble-lensed spectacles. One sweeping glance told him the situation. "Gemma," he said, hurrying across the room to take both her hands. "I am so very sorry."

His use of Mrs Pettifer's Christian name surprised Thanet a little, but he realised at once that it was only to be expected. Pettifer had no doubt known Barson well — he would, after all, scarcely have entrusted the health of his wife and coming child to a mere acquaintance.

"I think Mrs Pettifer should rest," Barson said, with a hostile glance at Thanet. "She can't afford to take risks at this stage. So if you don't mind . . ."

"By all means." Thanet watched them go, Barson solicitously supporting her. The doctor's arrival had been fortuitously well-timed, coming as it had just at the moment when Mrs Pettifer's self-control had begun to crack.

The thought slid insidiously into his mind: too fortuitous? Had Mrs Pettifer heard the doctor's car, in the drive?

Somehow, with her going, Thanet felt a curious shift in his attitude towards her. Compassion for her plight was natural in the circumstances, but now, thinking back over the interview, it occured to him that the strength of his reaction had been surprising. One of the hall-marks of a first-rate actor is the degree of response he is able to arouse in his audience. Had he, Thanet, just witnessed a truly superb performance, so carefully calculated, so understated that at no point had it crossed his mind that it could be anything other than genuine? Or was he being less than fair to Gemma Pettifer?

"Poor woman," said Lineham, as the door closed behind them.

"You think so?"

Lineham looked at him sharply. "Yes. Why, don't you?"

"Yes," Thanet said doubtfully. "Well, yes, of course I do. No one could help feeling sorry for her, in this situation."

"But?"

"But I've just got this niggling feeling . . . perhaps I'm being unfair. Perhaps being an actress means that in a situation like this people will constantly be questioning whether the emotions you display are genuine."

Experience had tempered Lineham's former naivety, the susceptibility to feminine charm which had on at least one occasion seriously impaired his judgement and impeded the progress of a case. And by now he had worked with Thanet long enough to have a healthy respect for his opinion. Whereas once he would have leaped to Gemma Pettifer's defence, now he simply said, "Don't you think she was genuine, then?"

"I'm just not one-hundred-per-cent convinced, that's all."

"Did she say anything specific that makes you doubtful?"

"No, nothing. Though she was evasive at one point, you'll have noticed."

"When she switched what she was going to say? Yes, I did notice that. I wondered why you didn't press the point."

"Things were going smoothly. I didn't want to rock the boat. I was concerned that if I put any pressure on her she might crack."

"Just as well you didn't, in view of the way it suddenly hit her."

"Mm, just as the doctor arrived." Thanet tried to sound neutral and failed. Lineham picked up the implication at once.

"You mean, that sudden breaking-up was deliberate? A performance, put on for our benefit?"

Thanet shook his head. "Let's leave it for the moment, Mike. It's all speculation really, so there's no point in wasting time discussing it." He grinned. "I think Dr Barson thought I'd been giving her the third degree. Anyway, let's see what we have to do now. We'll have to chase up that cocoa mug, check on the paracetamol container in the bathroom . . ."

"We're not just leaving it, then?"

"I don't see how we can, not until we get at least a glimmer of a reason why he did it. I agree, all the circumstantial evidence points to a clear-cut case of suicide — the method he chose, the suicide note, the way he carefully timed it to coincide with the absence of both wife and housekeeper . . . But I'm just not happy about it. If he did kill himself, he must have had a reason, and it's possible that it simply hasn't come to light yet. He might just have found out that he had cancer, for example. If so, anything of that nature will show up in the post mortem. Or he might have been about to go bankrupt, and felt he couldn't face the disgrace . . . I think we'll have to do a bit of discreet checking, treat it as a suspicious death for the moment, just in case. Better to be too careful than kick ourselves later for being slipshod."

"You want me to get the boys in, then?"

"Yes. I'll have a word with Mrs Pettifer. We'll have to take her finger-prints and Mrs Price's, for elimination purposes. Then you'd better get on to his bank. No need to press for details, just find out if his financial situation was healthy or not. And I'll go down to the Health Centre, have a word with his partners, in case something was awry there. One of them might possibly still be there, taking surgery. Let's hope they're not all off on their rounds by now."

"Do you want a search of the house?"

"I'll ask permission. But make it discreet. We really don't want to overplay things at the moment . . . You know, Mike, there is one thing that strikes me as odd. It's only just occurred to me."

"What?"

"Well, Doc Mallard said that he would estimate that Pettifer took the overdose some time between ten and twelve last night, and you know as well as I do that he's hardly ever wrong about something like that. Now, if that is so, why did Pettifer wait four or five hours after his wife left? Why not do it once he was sure she was out of the way?"

"Screwing up sufficient courage?"

"Possibly, I suppose. Perhaps that's why the port was there."

"You mean, he got drunk, first? Or perhaps something happened, between the time she left and the time he did it, to make him decide to."

"If so, it must have been something pretty drastic. From

31

what we've heard of him so far, he doesn't sound the sort of man to commit suicide on impulse without good reason."

The door opened and Dr Barson came into the room. "I'm afraid Mrs Pettifer refuses to settle down until she's seen you again, Inspector," he said tersely.

"Right. I wanted a brief word with her anyway." As they mounted the stairs together Thanet glanced speculatively at the doctor's stony expression. He needed this man's cooperation. "Perhaps I ought to explain, Doctor, that contrary to what you might think, I was consciously careful in what I said to Mrs Pettifer. She was perfectly calm until just a few moments before you arrived. Then it suddenly hit her. You can check with her, if you like."

They had reached the top of the stairs now and Barson stopped. He looked a little shamefaced as he said, "I'm sorry, Inspector. Evidently I've misjudged you. Naturally, when I saw how upset Gemma was . . . I'm very fond of her, of both of them. I've known Arnold — Dr Pettifer — for years. Ever since we were medical students together, as a matter of fact."

Thanet privately breathed a prayer of gratitude that he had attempted to propitiate the man. His knowledge of Pettifer might be invaluable.

"What was he like?"

Barson pursed his lips. "D'you know, I always find that a difficult question to answer, and the better one knows someone, the more difficult it seems to be. One automatically begins to select all the good qualities, as if one were writing a reference. Let me see, now . . . Well, he was an excellent GP — thorough, hardworking, conscientious and a very good diagnostician. He had a rather unfortunate manner though, off-putting. He was very reserved, it was hard to get close to him. Although I've known him so long, I never really felt I understood what made him tick."

"Would you say this business was in character?"

"Good God, no. Arnold was, above all, a sticker. He'd never give up or opt out, however hard the going, certainly not for any reason I could imagine. I'm quite astounded by what's happened."

"You don't happen to know who his doctor was, do you?"

"I was, for what it's worth. I say 'for what it's worth' because, although he was theoretically on my list, in fact he never consulted me in all the years he's been on it, not once. He had excellent health, always, and I imagine he'd dose himself for any minor ailments. So if you're thinking he might have had a terminal illness . . . well, if he did, I certainly knew nothing about it. And *if* he did, of course the post mortem will show it."

"What if he just suspected he had it? People have been known to kill themselves because they were convinced they had cancer, for instance, when they really had nothing seriously wrong with them at all."

Barson shook his head emphatically. "Arnold would never have killed himself on a mere suspicion. No, if ill-health was the reason, it'll emerge soon enough, but frankly I think you're barking up the wrong tree."

"Have you been into his room this morning, to have a look at him?"

"Just briefly, yes. I didn't touch anything, of course." Barson frowned. "Vintage port and drugs. I must admit it's the way out most doctors would choose. By far the most comfortable. I understand there was a note, too."

Thanet showed it to him. Barson groaned. "Oh God — Andrew! I suppose his headmaster will have the unenviable task of breaking the news, poor devil. I'll ask Gemma if she'd like me to ring the school."

Mention of her name reminded them why they were standing here on the landing conversing in whispers and they began to move towards the door of Mrs Pettifer's room.

It was a complete contrast to her husband's monastic little cell. There was a fitted, butter-coloured carpet and the tall windows were hung with floor-length curtains patterned with sprays of wild flowers on a creamy background. The same fabric had been used in the curtains and drapes of the four-poster bed which dominated the room. Tiny, lacy cushions in many shapes and sizes were heaped at one end of the green velvet chaise-longue in the bay window and there was a clutter of silver, cut-glass and expensive-looking jars and bottles on the dressing table. A white satin peignoir trimmed with swans-down had been tossed carelessly across the foot of the lace bedspread. The effect was delicate, light, airy and over-whelmingly feminine. Thanet tried and failed to visualise Pettifer at home in this setting.

Gemma Pettifer was propped up against the lace-trimmed pillows, looking as fragile as a wax doll.

"You wanted to see me?" said Thanet.

"Yes. I've got something to show you. Perhaps it'll convince you." She reached for a large brown envelope on the bedside table. "Yesterday afternoon, my husband brought me a present. He'd picked it up on the way home, he said. I'm sure you'll be able to check that." And she spilled the contents of the envelope out on to the bedspread.

Thanet had no time for more than a glimpse of brightly coloured brochures before Mrs Pettifer selected a piece of paper and handed it to him.

"It was a surprise for me. He knew I'd always wanted to go."

Thanet stared down at the paper. It was a receipt from a travel agency. Yesterday afternoon, only a few hours before he had killed himself, Arnold Pettifer had paid £2,000 for a cruise to the Canaries, with a departure date in three weeks' time.

4

On the way to the Health Centre, Thanet found himself thinking about a man who had become something of a local legend.

Once upon a time (from 1948 to 1973, to be precise,) there lived in Paddock Wood, in Kent, a doctor with a dream. The doctor was DJA Macdonald, the dream to gather together in his village and under one roof all the medical services which the people of his rural area could require. Women would no longer have to spend half a day trailing their children into Tonbridge or Maidstone for dental appointments, old age pensioners would no longer have to expend an alarming proportion of their pensions on bus fares and pregnant women would no longer have to find baby-sitters for their other children or endure the nausea-inducing bus journey into town for their ante-natal care. Doctor Macdonald was determined that his people were going to be the best-cared-for patients in the whole of Kent, and the Woodlands Health Centre in Paddock Wood still thrives — a monument to his vision, patience and determination.

Since then a handful more of these excellent Centres have been established in Kent, but they are, of course, expensive to build and Doctor Macdonalds are few and far between. Sturrenden was fortunate in that its Centre was more or less complete before the economic recession came along to give the kiss of death to many a similar project. Thanet had never visited it before and he looked about with interest as he parked his car and approached the main entrance.

The building was single-storied, flat-roofed and built in the shape of a W, with specialist clinics such as dentistry, chiropody, speech therapy and ante-natal care in one of the long arms and a series of consulting and treatment rooms in the other. In the base of the W were the administrative offices, the reception area and the waiting room, which was cheerful, spacious and furnished with comfortable chairs upholstered in cream, chocolate, orange and black. Everywhere was spotlessly clean.

Thanet approached the Enquiries counter, where two women were engrossed in some of the prodigious quantity of paperwork demanded by the National Health Service. Within a few minutes he was seated in a small, bright office with Mrs Barnet the Administrative Secretary, a slim, trim woman in her mid-forties with neatly-waved greying blonde hair and a general air of reassuring capability. Her hazel eyes rounded as Thanet gently broke the news.

"Dead? Dr *Pet*tifer?" she said, a strangely formal echo of Mrs Pettifer's cry.

Thanet nodded. "And I'm afraid it looks as though he has committed suicide."

She sucked in her breath sharply, as if someone had just hit her hard in the solar plexus. She swallowed. "No," she said. "I don't believe it."

Thanet said nothing, waited.

"It's not possible," she said, after a few moments in which she was clearly trying to assimilate the news. "Not Dr Pettifer."

"Why not?"

"Well, because with some men, yes, you can imagine them doing it, killing themselves if they were desperate, but Dr Pettifer . . . it's just out of character, that's all. He's such a strong person, very . . . powerful, determined. If he's up against something he doesn't sit back and hope it'll go away, or just give up, he fights. And usually wins."

"You're saying, then, that it would be totally out of character for him to kill himself."

"That's right. Totally. And then, well, it was only yesterday he was in — here at the Centre, I mean. Today's his day off, you see, that's why we haven't missed him. Though . . ."

"What?"

"His car. It's still here. And I did wonder . . . I noticed it when I arrived this morning. I thought it must have broken down, that he'd had to leave it here overnight. I was half expecting him to give me a ring about it this morning."

"I'll check. What make is it?"

"A brown Rover. New."

"Right. But you were saying, about yesterday . . ."

"Well, he seemed so cheerful. Unusually so. He wasn't a very forthcoming person." Unconsciously Mrs Barnet had already slipped into the past tense. "He was a very good doctor, everybody respected him, but he could be a bit, well, off-hand I suppose you'd call it, in his manner. Oh, he wasn't rude or anything like that," she added hastily, "I hope I'm not giving the wrong impression. But yesterday, well he was telling me all about this terrific meal he and Mrs Pettifer had had last week. It was their second wedding anniversary, apparently, and they'd been to the Sitting Duck out near Biddenden for a celebration dinner. That's what I mean by unusually cheerful. In the normal way of things he'd never have been so chatty."

"Did he have any health problems, to your knowledge?"

"I don't suppose I'd have known if he did, unless it was something very obvious, but not to my knowledge, no. He always seemed very healthy. Doctors often are. They build up an immunity I suppose, being in constant contact with germs."

"Yes. Though I understand that in fact yesterday Dr Pettifer did think he had a cold coming on."

"Oh, really? Well, he certainly wouldn't have mentioned it to me, if he had. He wasn't one to make a fuss."

"You saw no sign of it, then?"

"No, but then in the early stages of a cold there often are no visible symptoms, are there?"

"No, I suppose not. What about the Health Centre? Were there any problems connected with his practice that might have been worrying him?"

She frowned. "I'm sure there weren't. I'd have known, if there had been. I'm not saying we don't get the odd problem cropping up, it would be a miracle if we didn't in a busy practice like this, but something serious enough for one of the doctors to kill himself . . . no, never."

"How many doctors are in practice here?"

There were, he learnt, three in addition to Pettifer. Dr Pettifer had originally been in practice with his father-in-law by his first marriage. When the old man died Dr Lowrie, now in his late fifties, had come into the practice, followed at intervals by Dr Fir, who was away at present on holiday, and Dr Braintree, who had come in only three years previously and was the baby of the practice. All three were married and only the Braintrees were childless.

The Centre was funded by the Area Health Authority and the medical practice was an independent one, paying rent to and sharing administrative costs with that authority. It was a flourishing practice, having around 11,500 patients on its books — rather a heavy work-load, Thanet learned: it was generally accepted that the standard number of patients per doctor should be around 2,500. Could overwork have been a contributory factor in Pettifer's death? he asked.

Mrs Barnet didn't think so.

"Is there any chance of having a word with either Dr Lowrie or Dr Braintree?"

"Not at the moment, I'm afraid. They're both out on visits. I'll have to contact them of course, to tell them about Dr Pettifer . . . Oh dear, they're so much under pressure at the moment. We were supposed to have had a locum to take over Dr Fir's work while he's on holiday, but unfortunately the man had a car accident the day before he was due to arrive and we weren't able to get a replacement at such short notice. And now, well, goodness knows how we're going to manage." She bit her lip. "That sounds awful, doesn't it, thinking of the Centre when there's poor Mrs Pettifer. . ."

"Life always has to go on," Thanet said gently.

"I suppose so . . . Anyway, let me see." She reached for a desk diary, flicked it open. "Ah yes, I thought so. Dr Lowrie has to be back here at two, to meet someone from the new Family Counselling service they're starting in Sturrenden. When I speak to him I'll tell him you'd like to have a word with him, shall I?"

"That would be kind."

38

"What arrangement shall I make, about your seeing him?"

"Would it be possible for him to get back here a little early, say at a quarter to two? Then I could see him before his meeting."

"I'm sure that'll be all right."

Thanet thanked her and left.

In the car park a mechanic was tinkering with the engine of a brown Rover. Parked alongside was a small blue pick-up with CLOUGH'S FOR CARS on the side. Thanet strolled across.

"Trouble?" he asked, pleasantly.

"Looks like it, don't it?" The mechanic barely glanced up.

"Dr Pettifer's car, isn't it?"

A grunt of assent.

"Serious?"

"Give us a chance, mate. I only just got here, didn't I?"

"Perhaps I'd better introduce myself. Detective Inspector Thanet, Sturrenden CID."

The man's back stiffened. He gave Thanet a wary glance, then straightened up. "Oh?" He was in his thirties, small, wiry and hairy.

"When did you hear that Dr Pettifer's car had broken down?"

"Yesterday afternoon."

"What time?"

"Must've been about half past four, quarter to five. Harry — Mr Clough, that is — come into the workshop and told me."

"What, exactly, did he say?"

"Harry? He said Dr Pettifer'd just rung to say his car wouldn't start."

"And?"

"Well, Harry said he couldn't send someone straight away because the other mechanic was off sick and I was trying to get this job finished for five o'clock, for another customer."

"Was Dr Pettifer put out?"

"Not according to Harry. Harry told him that if he'd like to hang on at the Centre I'd get there as soon as I could, but Dr Pettifer said it didn't really matter. He wasn't on call last

39

night and wouldn't need the car, and he was off duty today and anyway if he needed a car he could always use his wife's.''

"So what arrangement was made?''

"I'd get along as soon as I could this morning and deliver the car back to the house.''

"How did you get the keys?''

"Dr Pettifer said he'd leave them at the desk.''

The receptionist obviously hadn't bothered to mention them to Mrs Barnet, Thanet thought. No doubt there had been other, more urgent matters to attend to.

"Were you surprised that Dr Pettifer didn't want you to see to it right away?''

The man shrugged. "Didn't think about it one way or the other.''

"You'll be delivering the car yourself?''

"Yeah.''

"Well when you do I should just park it and hand the keys to the constable at the door. Mrs Pettifer won't want to be bothered. I don't suppose you've heard, but Dr Pettifer was found dead this morning.''

The man's face sagged and his mouth fell open slightly. "No kidding?''

"I'm afraid not.''

"Heart attack?''

"You'll hear all the details in due course, no doubt. Perhaps you'd let your boss know.''

"Sure.'' The man looked down at the spanner in his hand as if he wondered what it was doing there and then, as Thanet walked to his car, turned slowly to peer once more inside the raised bonnet.

Before driving away Thanet sat for a few minutes, thinking. What now? He wanted to talk to Lineham, but he didn't really have time to go to Pine Lodge and be back by one-forty-five. No, that wasn't strictly true. He did have time, just, but he wanted to be by himself for a while, to think and to assimilate all that he had learned this morning. He made up his mind. He would ring Lineham from a call box and then have a beer and sandwich in the nearest pub. As he drove out the mechanic

40

straightened up and nodded farewell. Thanet raised a hand in response.

He found a phone box on the corner of the next street.

"Mike? Thanet here. Anything new?"

"I rang Pettifer's bank and there doesn't seem to be much point in going down there. The Manager was cagey, of course, but he was definite that Pettifer's financial position was what he called 'very healthy'."

"Have the lads finished yet?"

"Just about. I checked up with the travel agents, by the way. Pettifer did call in to pay for that holiday yesterday afternoon. Just after five, apparently."

"Hmm. So what are you doing now?"

"Still looking around. I'm not sure how thorough you want me to be."

"Thorough. It really does look as though something is beginning to smell."

"Does it?"

Thanet smiled at the eagerness in Lineham's voice. The sergeant's unfailing enthusiasm for his work was one of his most endearing qualities. Thanet had seen so many good men grow blasé and cynical. He hoped it would never happen to Lineham. He told him about the car.

Lineham whistled. "Why bother to get your car repaired if you know you're never going to need it again?"

"Exactly. It isn't as though Mrs Pettifer would need it. She's got a car of her own, apparently, as one might expect. Have you taken a look at Pettifer's desk yet?"

"I didn't think that came under the heading of 'discreet'."

"Good. Leave it, then. I'd like to have a go at it myself. Where's Mrs Pettifer?"

"In bed."

"And Mrs Price?"

"Hasn't stirred out of the kitchen."

"Right. Well, try and find out from her — without making it obvious what you're doing — exactly where Mrs Pettifer stayed last night."

"So that's the way the wind blows, is it?"

"I'm not sure, and that's the truth. Or even if it's blowing at all. If you want to get in touch, I'll be back at the Health Centre at 1.45. I'm seeing one of Pettifer's partners then."

A couple of streets away Thanet found a promising little pub. He went in. There were perhaps half a dozen customers. Thanet ordered a cold beef sandwich and carried his beer across to a corner table. Another day he might have stayed at the bar and chatted. Today he wanted to be alone.

The beer was good, the beef sandwich superb — a great wedge of succulent pink meat between slabs of crusty, home-made bread. Thanet abandoned himself to the pleasure of this rare gastronomic treat and then lit his pipe and sat sipping his beer, staring into space and trying to get his thoughts into some sort of order.

As he had said to Lineham, all the circumstantial evidence seemed to point to suicide — the note, the timing, the method chosen — and yet . . . So far there had not been even a whisper of anything resembling a reason why Pettifer should have killed himself. He had apparently had no financial, health or marital problems, he was respected in his work and his medical practice flourished. Moreover, his wife was pregnant with their first child *and* only yesterday afternoon he had made a booking for an expensive holiday in a fortnight's time. Then there was the business of the car. As Lineham had said, why bother to get your car repaired, if you know you'll never use it again? What was more, each of the four people interviewed so far — wife, housekeeper, secretary and old friend — had violently repudiated the idea of suicide as being out of character, and each of the three women had individually insisted that Pettifer had seemed in especially good spirits yesterday.

No, there was no doubt about it, the whole thing simply didn't hang together. And in view of the man's medical know-ledge it was out of the question that he could have been unaware of the danger of settling down in bed with a lethal sup-ply of alcohol and drugs to hand. Impossible.

Thanet became aware that he was shaking his head and that some of the men at the bar had turned to stare at him. Had he been talking aloud? Embarrassed, he quickly drank off the rest of his beer and rose to leave.

So, he thought as he returned to his car, if suicide looked unlikely and accident were ruled out . . . Unconsciously his shoulders stiffened and his nostrils flared slightly, as if he had just scented danger on the wind.

5

Short and rather plump, with a bald head and gold-rimmed spectacles, Dr Lowrie was the antithesis of his dead partner. The laughter lines around eyes and mouth spoke of a warm and jovial disposition.

"Come in, come in, Inspector." Lowrie advanced, hand outstretched, and settled Thanet in a chair at right-angles to his desk. "This is a terrible thing, terrible. It's ridiculous, I suppose, but I can't help hoping that Mrs Barnet must have got it wrong."

Thanet shook his head. "I'm afraid not."

Lowrie frowned. "How, exactly, did it happen?" Briefly, Thanet gave the details. Lowrie listened in silence, with complete attention, eyes fixed on Thanet's face. Thanet awaited his reaction with interest. If Pettifer had indeed been murdered then Lowrie must be regarded as a potential suspect. And if Lowrie was guilty, this was his cue to present reasons why Pettifer should have killed himself.

"Incredible," Lowrie said, shaking his head in disbelief. "Absolutely and completely incredible."

So Lowrie might be as innocent as he looked.

"I just can't believe it!" Lowrie jumped up, went to stand looking out of the window, hands clasped behind his back. He was silent for a few moments and then he turned. "Look, Inspector, as you can imagine we see a considerable amount of mental illness here." A brief sweep of the hand encompassed the consulting room, the Health Centre itself. "And we become pretty astute at spotting it. Approximately thirty per cent of our patients have anxiety-based or stress-related symptoms. Are you asking me to believe I wouldn't have noticed it in one of my own partners? Now if . . ." he broke off.

"Yes?"

Lowrie shook his head. "Nothing. The point is, I'm certain that if Pettifer had been suffering a degree of strain sufficiently acute for him to kill himself, for God's sake, I would have noticed."

"We often notice least changes in those we know best. Especially if we see them every day."

The doctor shook his head impatiently. "I know that. But I can't accept that it applies here. Dammit, I'm trained to notice that sort of thing. It becomes as automatic as breathing. And I knew Pettifer well. We've been partners for eighteen years. He just wasn't the sort of man to crack under pressure. In fact, he seemed to thrive on it. A challenge was meat and drink to him. If this place had gone up in flames, Pettifer would have been in the thick of it, calmly directing salvage and rescue operations." He shook his head again. "It's no good, I simply can't believe it." He gave a wry smile. "And don't think I'm not aware how often one hears those very words from the friends and relations of suicides. But in this case I do assure you they're justified."

"Are you suggesting that it was an accident, then?"

Lowrie stared at Thanet and then, slowly, returned to his desk and sat down. "My God," he said. "I see what you mean."

"Exactly. You really do think that it is out of the question, that it could have been an accident?"

"Oh absolutely. No doctor in his right mind would go to bed with a supply of pills and a bottle of alcohol on his bedside table."

"Even if he had a cold? Mrs Pettifer said he thought he had one coming on."

"Not for any reason. We're too aware of the dangers of taking an extra pill — or pills — while in a drowsy or semiconscious state. And of course, alcohol compounds the situation. Look, I know the point at issue is that Pettifer wasn't in his right mind, but I absolutely refuse to accept that. Though there's the note of course . . ." Lowrie ran a hand distractedly over his bald pate. "I'm beginning to feel somewhat confused."

45

No more confused than I am, thought Thanet. "Anyway, you see my difficulty. I do ask, of course, that you treat this conversation as confidential. For the moment we are officially treating this as a case of suicide."

"Yes, yes, I see that you must. But . . . Look, Inspector — and of course it goes without saying that this is in confidence — let's not beat about the bush. We're now talking about murder, aren't we?"

"Possibly."

"I really find it difficult to believe that we are having this conversation. To associate Arnold with the idea of suicide is difficult enough, but murder . . ." He gave a little half-laugh. "Before I know where I am you'll be asking for my alibi."

Thanet said nothing, merely raised his eyebrows a fraction.

"Good God, man, you surely can't be thinking . . ." Lowrie's face was a study in outraged disbelief. Then, with a visible effort he pulled himself together. "Well, I suppose that's reasonable enough. After all, I'm the one who's been insisting it couldn't have been suicide. As it happens, I'm lucky. Mrs Barnet and I both attended a meeting in Sturrenden last night. It didn't end until ten — and in case you're thinking I could have slipped out, I'll add that I was in the chair."

"And afterwards?"

"Someone who lives near her offered Mrs Barnet a lift and I went home with a colleague. My wife is away at present, visiting her mother, and I didn't feel like going home early to an empty house."

"And the colleague was . . .?"

"Dr Phillips. Do you know him?"

Thanet's own GP. "Yes . . . 'with', you said . . .?"

"Well, not in the same car, obviously. But I followed his, all the way from the meeting — and stayed there until one in the morning. You can check with him, if you like."

So it looked as though Lowrie really was in the clear. "If it becomes necessary, I will. Though as I said, this is still officially a case of suicide. Meanwhile, perhaps I could enlist your help."

Lowrie sat back, steepled his fingers. "By all means.

46

Anything I can do . . . My two o'clock appointment has been cancelled, so I'm at your disposal."

"Facts first then," said Thanet. "Mrs Barnet has given me a brief outline of the set-up here, so I won't need to bother you with that, but there was one point I wondered about. I gather that your quota of patients in this practice is rather high and that, especially with Dr Fir away at the moment and his locum unable to come at the last minute, the pressure of work has been considerable. Could overwork have been a contributory factor to Dr Pettifer's death, assuming that it was suicide?"

"I don't think so for a moment. Let me explain. Our quotas are high, yes, but different doctors have different methods and those methods determine the amount of time spent with patients. Pettifer was brisk, brief, thorough. He got through his surgeries far more quickly than any of the rest of us. So I really don't think he would have found the high quota a problem."

"You make him sound a bit inhuman."

"Do I? I didn't intend to. I suppose he could appear that way to someone who didn't know him. Certainly he wasn't easy to know. He was pretty reserved, didn't show his feelings much."

"In any case, you wouldn't say that there were any problems with the practice that could have bothered him sufficiently to prey on his mind."

"I'm pretty certain that if there had been I'd have been aware of them."

But there was a shadow at the back of Lowrie's eyes and Thanet recognised the neat evasion, stored it away for future investigation. He didn't want to antagonise Lowrie by pressing him at this point for information he was reluctant to give. There was one matter in which he particularly needed his cooperation.

"I was wondering, for example, if there could have been a patient, or relative of a patient, perhaps, who might have had a grudge against Dr Pettifer? One often hears of cases in which people feel they have been neglected or received the wrong treatment . . ."

"There certainly wasn't anything like that to my knowlege. And if there had been, I should think I'd have known. Such people are anything but quiet and unobtrusive. And surely it would have been impossible for anyone on the fringe of Pettifer's life to stage the circumstances in which he died?"

"Difficult, certainly. Impossible . . . well, I'm not so sure. Given sufficient intelligence and determination . . . I do think it's a possibility we can't afford to ignore. So I was wondering if you might be willing to glance through Dr Pettifer's records and check — I'm sorry, I know that this is a lot to ask, especially as you will now inevitably be under even greater pressure of work . . . I hesitate to offer you anyone to help. I know how important the question of confidentiality is to doctors and in any case the presence of one of my men here might give rise to undesirable speculation."

"Quite. Perhaps I'll ask Mrs Barnet to give me a hand. I can rely absolutely on her discretion . . . Very well, Inspector. But I'm afraid it might take a little time."

"I appreciate that. And thank you. Now, leaving that possibility aside, I must ask you to think again if there could have been any other problem — medical, financial or marital — which might have been preying on his mind."

"I have thought. And no, there wasn't, not to my knowledge. Financially, he was very comfortably off. He didn't depend on the practice for a living. His first wife was a wealthy woman and he inherited most of her estate. Some of it was of course left in trust for their son — adopted son, perhaps I should say."

"Adopted?"

"Yes. He's about fifteen now. Away at school. Nice boy, very. He'll be really cut up about this."

"So the baby which the present Mrs Pettifer is expecting would have been Pettifer's first child."

"Yes. Which makes the idea of suicide even more incomprehensible."

"He was pleased about it?"

"Like a dog with two tails." Lowrie smiled. "Interesting, really, when you think they'd both said in no uncertain terms that they had no intention of having any children."

"Really?"

"Most emphatically. And, frankly, I was a bit surprised how delighted he was about it. He never found it easy to relate to children, didn't even particularly like them, I should say. It was difficult for him to unbend sufficiently to get down to their level . . . But then, I suppose one's own child is different."

"He didn't get on with his adopted son, then? Andrew, isn't it?"

"Yes, Andrew. Oh, don't misunderstand me, he became very fond of the boy. I think he found it difficult when Andy was a baby, but then many men do. But over the years he grew very attached to him, in his own way. Perhaps he realised that the same thing would happen with the new baby. And, as I say, when it's one's own child . . . In any case, I suppose nothing should surprise me in that area any more. I've seen it all. Childless couples who change their mind and have them, couples who don't want them and keep on having them and, worst of all, those who simply can't conceive. Pettifer's first wife, Diana, was one of those. Finally, they decided to adopt. Poor Diana, she had a pretty bad time of it one way and the other. She was only forty when she died."

"Cancer, wasn't it?"

"Yes. Of the stomach." Lowrie grimaced.

"I wonder how the boy feels about the new baby."

"Andy?" Lowrie frowned. "I'm not sure."

"Was he put out when his father married again?"

"He wasn't very happy about it." Lowrie sighed. "It would be less than honest of me if I didn't admit that he and his stepmother didn't get on. He's at a very vulnerable age, of course, and she has had no experience of children, let alone adolescents — who, as you no doubt know, can be the very devil even with the most loving and understanding of parents."

"So I believe." Thanet grinned. "The problems of parenthood never disappear, I'm told. They just change their nature. Er . . . What about Dr Pettifer's relationship with his wife?" He was aware that they were getting on to delicate ground here,

49

wasn't sure how Lowrie would respond. But he needn't have worried.

"He idolised her," Lowrie said promptly. "Absolutely adored her. Let me put it this way. Pettifer may have appeared a cold fish to those who didn't know him, but those who did knew that he had two overriding passions — his wife and his work. And I'd be hard put to it to say which mattered more to him. Certainly he has always been devoted to his work and his second marriage made no difference to his commitment to it, but there's no doubt that ever since he first set eyes on Gemma he's been head over heels in love with her. Extraordinary how a level-headed fellow like him can lose all sense of prudence or commonsense when he goes overboard. He proposed the first week he saw her on stage, you know. It was flowers, gifts, the old stage-door routine every night."

"You think it was an unwise choice, then?"

"Oh no. Not at all." Lowrie was emphatic. "They've been very happy together. I think Gemma found with him exactly what she needed — the security of marriage combined with the freedom to pursue her career."

"He didn't object to her doing so?"

"Not in the least. He was very proud of her reputation as an actress. She is a very fine one, you know."

"Yes. I've seen her. In *Away Day*, a few months ago. But the baby . . . It doesn't sound as though children would fit into her scheme of things."

"Well as I said, he was over the moon about it. She . . . well, I think it took her longer to adjust to the idea. But once she had . . . No, they were both looking forward very much to the child's arrival. As I say, that's one of the reasons why I find the idea of suicide so impossible."

"What about Dr Pettifer's health? Was it good?"

"Disgustingly so. Mind, he took good care of it. He was something of an exercise fanatic. Did his daily dozen every morning, playing squash with Dr Fir twice a week . . . In all the years I've known him, he's never had anything more serious than a common cold. He didn't smoke, drank only occasionally, ate moderately and had perfect sight and hearing — no, there was a brief worry about his eyesight last year, but that came to nothing.''

The telephone rang.

"Excuse me," said Lowrie. Then, "It's for you, Inspector."

It was Lineham. "Sorry to disturb you, sir. We've just had a phone call from Andrew Pettifer's school. He's absconded."

Thanet groaned. "I expect he's heading for home."

"That's what the headmaster thought."

"How long does it take to get here?"

"Depends how he travels. It's only thirty miles by road, so if he hitched a lift he could be here quite soon."

"Is that what they thought he'd do?"

"Yes. Public transport is tricky, apparently. The school's right out in the country."

"I'll get back. I'd more or less finished here anyway. See you shortly."

Thanet told Lowrie what had happened.

"Would you like me to come with you?" offered Lowrie, standing up.

Thanet considered. The boy would no doubt be distressed and it might be a good idea to have medical help at hand. And it would probably help for him to see a familiar face, especially in view of the fact that he didn't get on with his stepmother. There was the housekeeper of course, but perhaps a sympathetic but detached outsider . . . "Thank you," he said. "That's very kind."

"I must get in touch with Dr Braintree," Lowrie said, "to let him know what's happened. But I can easily do that from Pettifer's house. I do think it would be a good idea to be there when Andy arrives."

"Let's hope we'll be in time."

With a shared sense of urgency they hurried to the door.

6

Back at Pine Lodge, Thanet and Dr Lowrie were relieved to find that there was as yet no sign of Andrew. Lowrie at once commandeered the telephone and Lineham beckoned Thanet into the drawing room.

"I hope you don't mind, sir, but I haven't had the body removed yet."

"Why not?"

Lineham looked embarrassed. "The boy, Andrew . . . I didn't know what would be the right thing to do . . . Whether he'd be more upset to see his father dead or to find the body already gone."

"Adoptive father, as a matter of fact. Yes, I see your point." Thanet was surprised. Lineham did not usually demonstrate such sensitivity.

"Oh, Andrew's adopted? I didn't realise."

"Does it make any difference?"

"I don't know. I . . . When my own father was killed, well, for ages I didn't really believe he was dead. Years, even. I never *saw* him dead, you see." Lineham gave a little, awkward laugh. "Stupid, really. I mean, I was only six, much too young to be shown dead bodies anyway but, well, it didn't seem possible that he could be dead, somehow. He'd just said goodbye like any other morning, only that day he never came back. So today I thought . . . idiotic, I suppose. Andrew's practically grown up, isn't he? And if Dr Pettifer was only his adoptive father . . ."

"Only? Don't underestimate the power of a relationship like that, Mike. The very fact that the boy's absconded shows how upset he is. And although fifteen sounds pretty grown up, it's a very vulnerable age. I think you did the right thing." Although he was more than twice that age now, Thanet could still remember the intensity of it, the swings from black despair to dizzy euphoria, the crippling uncertainties which the adolescent has to endure in the search for his final identity. "Anyway, did you manage to find out where Mrs Pettifer stayed last night?"

"The Lombard Hotel, in Lombard Square. I checked."

"Any idea what time she arrived?"

"The receptionist couldn't be sure. The one I spoke to wasn't on duty last night and even if she had been, it's a pretty big hotel and busy, so I don't suppose she'd have remembered. But she did say that judging by the position of Mrs Pettifer's name in the register it would have been early to mid-evening."

"I expect she checked in before meeting her agent for dinner."

"Probably. Anyway, I didn't press it. She did say she could try to find out more if I wished, but I said not to worry at the moment. I didn't want to arouse too much interest at this stage."

"Fine. What about the cocoa mug?"

"Mrs Price found it in the sink, this morning. She automatically washed it up and put it away."

"Pity. Though I don't suppose it matters all that much. But it does corroborate Mrs Pettifer's story. What about the paracetamol container?"

"In the bathroom cabinet, as Mrs Pettifer said. Half full."

Thanet strolled restlessly across to the window. A little wind had sprung up and the branches of the tall shrubs in the garden were swaying and dipping with the sinuous grace of eastern dancers. Fallen leaves stippled the lawn with random patterns of scarlet and gold. "We must remember to ring Clough's garage later on this afternoon, Mike, find out exactly what was wrong with Dr Pettifer's car." Thanet stiffened. "There's a boy turning into the drive. Quickly, tell Dr Lowrie." He stood back and, feeling like an old lady who spies on her neighbours, watched Andrew Pettifer from behind a curtain.

The boy was tall and thin with the lankiness of adolescence. Hands in pockets, shoulders hunched, head down, feet kicking moodily at the gravel, he looked . . . defeated, Thanet thought. The boy paused to glance up at the house and scowled as he noticed for the first time the policeman on duty at the front door. He took his hands out of his pockets and straightened his shoulders before moving forward again.

There was a murmur of voices in the hall and Dr Lowrie put his head around the door. "I'm just going upstairs with Andrew."

Ten minutes later he led the boy into the drawing room, made the introductions.

"Dr Lowrie says my father left a note," Andrew said to Thanet through stiff lips. He was very pale.

Thanet, somewhat belatedly, had slipped the letter into a transparent polythene envelope. "I'm sorry," he said, as Andrew made to take it out, "could you leave it in the cover?"

The boy frowned, shot Thanet a resentful glance before scanning the brief message. Then he read it again. And again. And stilled.

Thanet found that he was holding his breath.

For a long moment the boy remained motionless and then, slowly, raised his head to stare at Thanet.

"My father didn't write this," he said flatly.

Tiny, almost imperceptible movements from Lineham and Dr Lowrie betrayed their tension as Thanet said carefully, "Oh? What makes you say that?"

"This," Andrew's finger stabbed at the plastic. "Whoever wrote this has spelt my name wrong." He put the letter down and feverishly began to empty out his pockets.

The three men waited in silence, too conscious of the significance of the moment to want to smile at the extraordinary collection of objects which mounted up on the low table: grubby handkerchief, notebook, diary, bits of string, a couple of screws, a magnifying glass, pens, pencils, a rubber, half a broken ruler, coins, wallet, golf ball, penknife and a number of tattered envelopes, each scrutinised and discarded. They all knew what he was looking for, of course: a letter from his father.

"Ah . . ." Andrew pounced at last on a crumpled sheet of

paper. "I knew I had it somewhere." He glanced at it, murmured, "Yes", with satisfaction, then laid it on the table to smooth out the creases before handing it to Thanet together with the suicide note. "There you are," he said triumphantly. "He always spelt my name like that. With an E."

Thanet looked. "My dear Andie," the letter began. No possibility of typing error, it was handwritten. He glanced at the note left for Mrs Pettifer, in order to verify what he clearly remembered. "Make it up to Andy for me," Dr Pettifer had written.

"It's a very minute difference," Thanet said, handing both letters to Lineham. Though he was well aware that it could be a significant one.

Andrew was shaking his head vehemently as he stuffed his possessions back into his pockets. "He'd never have spelt my name with a Y," he said. "Never."

"With due respect, Andrew, your father could hardly have been in a normal state of mind at the time."

"I don't care what state of mind he was in. He just wouldn't have spelt it like that. He never, ever has. Anyway, you can check, surely, with the handwriting experts. They'll tell you."

"We will, of course," said Thanet.

"Look," said Andrew, suddenly fierce. "Don't humour me, right? Are you trying to say I don't know what my own father would have written? That's not the only example, you know," he said, pointing at the piece of paper in Thanet's hand, "I've got dozens more. Hundreds. I'll send you the lot if you like and then you'll have to believe me. Because you'll find that never, not in a single one of them, has my father ever spelled my name with a Y on the end. And the interesting thing is, of course, that no one else has seen those letters, no one else would know that, would they? And nobody else would realise, because they sound the same, don't they? They sound just the bloody same . . ." His voice had been rising and now, suddenly, it broke and tears gushed forth, streamed down his face. He dashed them away angrily with the back of one hand, then went to stand looking out of the window, shoulders twitching as he struggled to regain control of himself.

Dr Lowrie took a step towards him and then checked, aware no doubt that any display of sympathy would simply make the battle more difficult.

There was an uncomfortable silence.

Finally, when Thanet judged that the boy was ready, he said, "You do realise the implications of what you're saying, don't you, Andrew?"

Andrew swung around, his eyes hard. "I'm not a complete fool, Inspector. And it seems to me you won't have far to look." His mouth twisted as he glanced up at the ceiling.

"Andy!" Dr Lowrie sounded shocked. "You can't realise what you're saying!" And to Thanet, "He's overwrought, doesn't realise the implications . . ."

"Please, Dr Lowrie!" Andrew broke in. "I'm sorry, I don't want to be rude, but I'm not a child of five, you know. OK, I know I'm not an adult, either, but I do think I'm old enough to have an opinion of my own, and frankly, that's it."

"What on earth is going on?"

They all turned to the door. Gemma Pettifer, in a delicately pretty blue robe with deep ruffles at neck and hem was standing with folds of the soft material clutched just below her breast, emphasising her distended stomach. She looked slightly dazed and flushed with sleep. "I heard shouting . . . Oh, Andy," she said, noticing him for the first time. "My dear . . ." She released her robe and advanced, hands outstretched, to greet him. "I'm so sorry," she said. "So very sorry . . ."

"And so you should be, you cow," shouted Andrew backing away from her, his hard-won self-control flying out of the window. "Keep away from me!"

"*Andy!*" Dr Lowrie and Gemma Pettifer spoke in identical tones of horrified disbelief. Gemma checked in her advance and glanced uncertainly at the doctor, who put a hand protectively on her arm.

"Don't worry, my dear," he said hurriedly. "He's upset, naturally . . ."

"Upset? OF COURSE I'M BLOODY UPSET!" bellowed Andrew. "He was my father, wasn't he? MY FATHER, FOR CHRIST'S SAKE!"

"Your *adoptive* father, actually," said Gemma crisply, each precisely articulated word as deliberately hurtful as a slap on the face.

There was a shocked silence. He's right, Thanet found himself thinking furiously. She really is a cow. And in any case, this has gone on long enough.

"Take Mrs Pettifer back upstairs, please, Sergeant," he said, seizing her elbow with one hand and Lineham's with the other and giving them both a sharp push towards the door.

Mrs Pettifer opened her mouth to protest and then, glancing at the stony faces of the three men, evidently thought better of it. In silence she gathered up the skirt of her robe and swept out of the room, followed by Lineham.

Thanet glanced at Andrew's still, white face and decided to leave Lowrie to comfort the boy as best he could. "I'm going to have a word with Mrs Price," he said. At the door he paused. "Andrew, I wasn't just humouring you, you know. If you're right, I'll get to the bottom of it somehow. That I promise you."

7

"I wish everyone was as well-organised as this," said Thanet.

He and Lineham were going through Dr Pettifer's desk. Accustomed as they were to the chaotic clutter which most people leave behind them, they were impressed by Pettifer's management of his affairs. There were no unpaid bills, no unanswered letters and not a single slip of paper, it seemed, out of place. A row of box files neatly labelled FUEL, INSURANCE, EDUCATION, HOUSEHOLD EXP stood on the ledge at the top of the old roll-top desk.

Thanet reached for the education file. Predictably, this related to Andrew and contained not only correspondence with the school but mementoes of the boy's childhood — hand-made Christmas and birthday cards, drawings and letters in crooked, childish script. Thanet picked up the last bundle of papers in the file: school reports. He slipped off the elastic band, skimmed through them. Andrew was a bright boy, it seemed, hardworking and popular. His mother's death had hit him hard:

. . . Andrew has been subdued and somewhat withdrawn this term and there is no doubt that it is taking him some time to recover from his mother's death. It is therefore not surprising that the standard of his work has slipped, but I am confident that in time he will regain his old sparkle and once more attain the excellent standards which he has achieved in the past.

How long would it take Andrew to regain that "sparkle" this time? Thanet wondered. There was a limit to the number of blows any one person could assimilate without suffering a permanent degree of damage. To be abandoned by not one but two sets of parents was hard indeed. Andrew now had no one of his own left — only a stepmother whom he clearly loathed. Thanet passed the report to Lineham.

Lineham read it, then snorted. "If Pettifer did kill himself, you really would have thought he'd have considered the effect it'd have on Andrew, wouldn't you? He must have been fond of the boy, or he wouldn't have kept all this stuff. Though if you think about it . . ."

"What?"

"Well, isn't it another argument against suicide? Being fond of the boy and realising the effect it would have on him?"

Thanet sighed. "I don't know. People can be overwhelmingly selfish when it comes to personal happiness — or unhappiness, for that matter. How are you getting on with those drawers?"

"Nothing interesting so far. Mostly supplies of stationery, that sort of thing. This one's locked, though," Lineham added, giving a sharp tug.

Thanet thought for a moment. "That bunch of keys upstairs in Dr Pettifer's room, on the chair. Are they still there?"

"Yes."

"Go and fetch them, will you?"

Lineham was back in a minute or so.

"Ah," Thanet said with satisfaction as one of the keys turned sweetly in the lock. "Now then, what have we here? Details of his financial position, by the look of it." Together they pored over the sheaf of papers: bank statements, lists of share-holdings and amounts of money invested, together with dates. Thanet whistled softly as he glanced down the immaculate records. "The bank manager wasn't exaggerating when he said, 'healthy', was he?"

"Beats me why he bothered to work at all, with that lot," said Lineham.

"He was a dedicated doctor, that's why. Lowrie told us that."

"Catch me," said Lineham. "I'd be off to an island in the sun."

"Would you? I wonder. Haven't you come across any personal stuff at all?"

"Not yet, no."

"Funny. Let's take a look at the rest."

But neither of the remaining two drawers yielded anything of interest.

"Nothing personal at all, apart from the stuff about Andrew," said Thanet. "Nothing relating to his first marriage, for example."

"I did come across the marriage certificate in one of the other drawers. But that's all."

"If it wasn't for that, his first wife might never have existed. No letters, no photographs of her — for that matter, no photographs at all, except for that one." This was a large, framed photograph of Gemma Pettifer, a glossy studio portrait. "No family photographs, even . . . Surely everyone accumulates those? Is there anywhere else he could have kept them? A photograph album, perhaps?"

"We certainly haven't come across one. I know you're always interested in that sort of thing and keep my eyes open."

"Tell me, Mike . . . Have you got a desk at home?"

"Not a desk, exactly. A couple of drawers in a side table my mother gave us."

"Tidy?"

Lineham grinned. "Louise is always complaining there's so much stuff in them they won't shut properly. I go through them from time to time, weed things out a bit . . ." He stopped. "I see what you mean," he said slowly.

"Quite. Pettifer may have been tidy-minded, but even the best-organised of men have odds and ends lying about waiting to be filed or dealt with. There's nothing like that here. And together with the fact that there's nothing personal at all . . ."

"He's cleared it all out recently, you mean."

"Looks like it, doesn't it?"

"In which case . . ."

"It's back to suicide again," agreed Thanet.

They contemplated the desk in silence.

"If he did kill himself," Lineham said reluctantly, "then I

suppose it would have been in character for him to have got rid of any personal stuff. I mean, from what we've heard of him, he wasn't the sort of man to relish the idea of someone poking about in his papers after he'd gone."

"I agree." Thanet stood up. "Let's go and have a word with Mrs Price."

The housekeeper's eyes narrowed at Thanet's question. "Now that you mention it, yes, Dr Pettifer did clear out his desk. I remember because he asked me for a plastic sack and later I saw him carry it down the garden and have a bonfire."

"When was this?"

"Let me see, it must be, oh, a good month ago, I should think."

"A month!"

"Easily, yes. Yes, I remember now, I was bottling the Victorias when he came through the kitchen and I always do that in the middle of September."

Five weeks ago, then.

"Where do you burn your rubbish?"

"At the bottom of the garden, behind the laurel hedge."

Little point in looking, after all this time, but Thanet and Lineham went to see for themselves just the same. The sky was overcast, the wind had dropped again and the air was still and heavy with moisture. Fallen leaves from a towering copper beech lay in great crimson swatches upon the dew-heavy grass and dahlias, chrysanthemums and Michaelmas daisies stood out with the brilliance and clarity of gem-stones in the fading light.

The laurel hedge was tall and thick, screening the vegetable garden from the house. A narrow concrete path bisected the neat rows of autumn cauliflowers and brussels sprouts and led to a metal incinerator beside a compost heap.

"Looks as though they've got a gardener," Lineham said, nodding at the weed-free soil.

"Pity. At this time of the year he'd have been burning rubbish regularly a couple of times a week."

They contemplated the incinerator, empty of all but a few charred twigs.

"Five weeks ago!" Lineham said. "Could anybody plan his own suicide as far ahead as that?"

"Perhaps there's no connection." But Thanet couldn't really believe that. No man totally destroys his past if he can visualise a future. Thanet shook his head, hard, as if to try to dissipate his confusion. "Come on," he said. "I've got to have a breathing space, try to sort things out a bit, in my mind." His need to get away was physical too. His nostrils suddenly seemed full of the stench of decay, the autumn garden permeated with a sense of mortality.

"We'll go back to the office and do our reports, like good little boys," he said. "Getting things down on paper might help."

But he doubted it.

8

Before he reached the front door, Thanet could hear the television blaring forth. He frowned. Joan never watched television until after supper, nor did she ever turn the volume up so high. The children must still be up and Joan with Mrs Markham again.

He glanced angrily at the house next door before letting himself in, his morning's resolution to have it out with Joan resurrecting itself and hardening. He was further incensed to find both Bridget and Ben watching a completely unsuitable documentary on violence in Northern Ireland.

"Come on, you two," he said, dropping his coat on a chair and crossing at once to switch off the set. "It's long past your bedtime."

They must have been tired because there were no cries of protest. They simply turned dazed faces towards him and scrambled to their feet, putting up their arms to embrace him.

"Mummy next door?" he said.

They nodded and Ben reached into the pocket of his jeans. "I saved this for you, Daddy."

Thanet smiled and accepted the sticky, unwrapped sweet, liberally coated with fluff. "Thank you, Ben," he said gravely. "Lovely. D'you mind if I save it for after supper?"

Ben shook his head and Thanet placed the sweet ceremoniously on the mantelpiece. Then they all went upstairs, hand in hand.

Ben was in bed and Thanet was kneeling on the bathroom floor drying Bridget when he heard the front door slam. A moment later Joan came upstairs in a rush.

"I'm sorry, darling," she said, stooping to kiss the top of his head, "I just couldn't get away."

"Do you realise," Thanet said, keeping his anger damped down and his voice as conversational as possible for Bridget's sake, "that those were the first words you spoke to me this morning, too?"

Joan compressed her lips. Neither the anger nor the reproach had escaped her. "Ben in bed?"

"Yes."

"I'll just go along and say goodnight, then I'll get supper. It's all prepared, it won't be long."

Thanet realised why when he saw what it was: sausage and chips. Again. Gone were the halcyon days of steak and kidney puddings, delectable desserts. Before she started working full-time Joan had been an excellent cook and the evening meal had been one of the highlights of Thanet's day. Now his anger on the children's behalf was fuelled by the thought that if Joan hadn't spent so much time next door he wouldn't be eating such a dreary meal. It was about time she got her priorities right, he told himself furiously.

"You'll give yourself indigestion if you go on eating as fast as that," Joan said.

The rebuke was the last straw. Thanet looked at his plate, then laid down his knife and fork. "D'you know what the children were doing when I came in this evening?"

"Watching television, I imagine." Joan's tone was defensive.

"Precisely. Watching boys not much older than Sprig hurling petrol bombs at soldiers in the streets of Belfast . . ."

Joan bit her lip. "I didn't realise. I'm sorry."

"I'm sorry, I'm sorry, I'm sorry! That's all you ever seem to say these days!"

"Only because you're always going on at me," Joan retaliated.

"Now wait a minute. You mean, you don't really feel sorry at all? If it weren't for my attitude, you wouldn't? Is that what you're saying?"

"No. Not exactly. Well, I don't know . . . Oh darling, that's not true. I do know what you're complaining about and you're right, I know that too. I know I shouldn't be spending so much

64

time with Mrs Markham, but I just don't seem to be able to get out of it.''

Her capitulation disarmed him. "But why not?" he said, more gently. "I really just don't understand why not.''

"Well, because she's so . . . pathetic. So helpless. I told you, her husband used to do everything for her. Do you realise she's never had to pay a household bill in her life, or keep any kind of budget . . . He used to organise the finances, say what they could or couldn't afford in the way of holiday, clothes, outings . . . She's absolutely lost without him. She just doesn't know how to begin to organise her own life.''

"Then, without wishing to sound hard, isn't it about time she learned?''

"But that's what I'm trying to help her to do!''

"Are you? Are you, really? Come on darling, be honest with yourself.'' Thanet's anger had evaporated now but he knew that it was important, for all their sakes, that he and Joan should settle this issue one way or the other. "Can you truthfully say she's much more independent now than she was a year ago?''

Joan sighed. "I suppose not. But what can I do, Luke? I try, I really do try very hard to get her to do things herself, but she just says, 'Could you do it, dear, you're so much quicker at it than I am.' Or, 'What a pity it takes so long to get to the library. It's such a long walk to the bus stop and then you have to wait around in the cold for so long . . .', and before I know where I am I'm offering to change her books for her on the way home . . .''

"But don't you see? That's just what she's manoeuvring for.''

"Yes I do see, but I seem incapable of reacting in any other way. I get so cross with myself about it.''

Thanet leant across the table to take Joan's hand. "Look, darling, you must see that we can't go on like this indefinitely. I'm not just being selfish, though to be honest I do resent the fact that she seems to be seeing more of you than I am at the moment, but the children need you too, just as much if not more than she does. Look at that business of Sprig's leotard

65

this morning. She was in such a state . . . I hate seeing her go off to school like that.''

"Yes, I know. So do I."

"And then, it's taking too much out of you. You really have enough on your plate, with a full-time job as well as a family to look after and a house to run . . . Try to look at it this way. All the while you're prepared to do things for her, why should she bother? It's much easier and more convenient for her to get you to do them. Don't you see, there's only one way for her to learn how to cope for herself and that's for her to do it. Alone. Otherwise, well, I can see no end to it, can you?''

"I suppose not . . . Yes, you're right, I know that . . . All right, I'll try. I really mean it. I'll just have to be a lot tougher, that's all.'' Joan rose and began to clear the table.

"Leave that. I'll do it, and the washing up. You go and sit down. You look exhausted. Coffee?''

She smiled gratefully. "All right. Thank you darling. Yes, I'd love some.''

Thanet waited until they were both sipping their coffee before saying, "Tell me, as a matter of interest, how you would spell the nickname for Andrew.''

"A-N-D-Y, I suppose. Why?''

"Just wondered. You wouldn't put an I-E on the end, instead of Y?''

"No. I've never heard of it spelt like that. Why?'' she asked again.

"Did you hear about Dr Pettifer?''

"No, what?''

He told her. He always had told her — everything — and since she had started work as a probation officer he had continued to do so, not without trepidation. When Joan had decided that this was the career she wanted, Thanet had tried to dissuade her. The views and attitudes of police and probation officers frequently clash and he had been afraid that this conflict of professional interests would spill over into their private life and they would gradually drift apart. But it had not taken him long to realise that they would be even more likely to do so if he prevented her from doing what she obviously very

66

much wanted to do. So, instead, he had made a conscious effort to maintain between them the mutual trust and confidence which had always been the bedrock of their relationship. He still thought that one day the crunch would come, that they would find themselves on opposite sides of the fence over some fundamental issue, but was satisfied that this way they would be better equipped to deal with it if and when they had to.

Joan listened as she always did, with complete attention, her grey eyes solemn, the lamplight gilding her short, springing, honey-coloured curls.

"So that's why you asked me how I'd spell Andy," she said, when he had finished. "Poor boy, he really does sound most dreadfully upset. And if he can't stand Mrs Pettifer . . . Where is he now?"

"He went to Dr Lowrie's for the night. He'll probably go back to school tomorrow. Lowrie seemed to think it would be better if he didn't have too much time to brood."

"Yes, I can see that. Do you think he could have been mistaken, over the mis-spelling of his name?"

"Well, the note he showed us certainly bore out what he said. He was very overwrought of course, poor kid. And, as I said to him, it was possible his father might have made a mistake, in the circumstances."

"You're having the handwriting checked?"

"Yes. But it'll be a day or two before we get an answer. You know how cautious they are. We mustn't complain — they have to be. But in circumstances like this when we need to have something that'll clinch the matter . . ."

"So what do you think, really? Do you think it was suicide?"

"I don't know." Thanet ran a hand through his hair. "I just don't know." And he didn't. One moment he would veer towards believing that Pettifer had indeed killed himself, the next he would be telling himself that there was too much evidence to the contrary. He said so. "I feel positively schizophrenic about it. The whole thing just doesn't make sense, doesn't hang together. If you look at the set-up of the suicide itself then, yes, it does look as though he did. All three doctors I've spoken to so far — Dr Barson, Doc Mallard and Dr Lowrie — all agree that the method he chose was the way most medical men would opt for, the most comfortable way to go if you know the right dosage of drugs and don't overdo the alcohol . . . Then there's the note, if it's genuine, and the timing, the fact that both his wife and his housekeeper were away overnight — a rather unusual circumstance, I gather . . .''

"Though that could work the other way," Joan suggested. "If it was murder and someone had been waiting for the ideal moment and knew Dr Pettifer'd be alone in the house last night . . .''

"True. But then, there's the fact that he left all his business affairs in such incredibly good order, that he'd cleared his desk of all his personal stuff . . .''

"But five weeks ago, you said. Surely nobody would cold-bloodedly plan his own suicide five weeks ahead and then go on behaving as though he didn't have a care in the world?''

"That's what Lineham said. And I agree, of course. You see what I mean? There's an objection at every turn.''

"Perhaps there's some other reason you just don't know about yet. Perhaps he'd just found out he had terminal cancer . . .''

"If so, it'll show up in the post mortem tomorrow. But by all accounts he certainly wasn't acting like a man who'd just had a death sentence passed on him. On the contrary, everyone seems to agree he was in the best of spirits yesterday — exceptionally so, in fact.''

"He certainly seems to have behaved very oddly for a man who was about to kill himself — paying for that cruise, for instance, only hours before he died.''

"Exactly. Then there's the business of the car. As Lineham said, why bother to get your car repaired if you know you're never going to need it again?''

"What did you say was wrong with it?''

"It's a bit technical," Thanet said dubiously.

Joan grinned. "Try me," she said. "Put it down to my thirst for information.''

68

"Well, it was nothing very serious. Apparently — let's see if I can get it right — over the coil in the new Rover there's a damp-proof cap which is connected to the distributor by a high-tension lead. Engine vibration had loosened the cap and the connection was broken, so the car wouldn't start. It was only a little thing, but one which is not immediately obvious when you lift the bonnet. Clough said that Dr Pettifer knew a little bit about cars and could probably have found the fault himself if he'd been prepared to spend a bit of time looking for it, but I suppose he was in a hurry, knowing that his wife was going to London last night. I expect he wanted to get home before she left."

"Or he might have wanted to catch the travel agents before they closed."

"That's a point, yes, if he'd arranged to call in yesterday afternoon. But, as you say, he wasn't exactly behaving like a man who knew there'd be no tomorrow."

"Luke, are you saying you think there might be some truth in Andrew's accusation of Mrs Pettifer?"

"I just don't know. It was difficult to take it seriously at the time because he was in such a state. I simply thought his grief and anger had to find a focus and she happened to be it. But the way things are going, we certainly can't afford to dismiss the possibility."

"But then, you say she herself is also insisting it couldn't have been suicide. Why should she do that, if she killed him? Surely the last thing she'd want to do is stir up any doubts whatsoever?"

"Unless it's a double bluff — she's aware that there are discrepancies which might make us doubt that it could have been suicide and therefore she's trying to put herself in the clear by insisting it couldn't have been."

"Don't!" said Joan, clutching her head. "I see what you mean. I'm getting as confused as you are."

"And then, what motive could she have? Everyone seems to agree that they were as happy as the day is long."

"Oh come on, darling. It's unlike you to accept that as true, just because everyone says so. You know how deceptive appearances can be. Just think how often you hear people say, 'I'm astounded. I always thought they were the ideal couple', about a marriage that's split up."

"That's true."

"She could have been after his money," Joan suggested. "You say he was very well off."

"But why? She's got everything she wants, surely, materially speaking . . . A lovely home, a housekeeper to run it for her, a car of her own . . ."

"Then perhaps she wanted something else?"

"What, for example?"

"Her freedom?"

"Freedom to do what? Her husband was one hundred per cent behind her in her career. To go to a lover, I suppose you mean."

"Well it's possible, surely? Someone in her position . . . Actors and actresses do seem to change partners fairly frequently, after all."

"I'd thought of it, of course," Thanet said, "but somehow I didn't consider it as a serious possibility. Now, why was that? Perhaps it's because she's pregnant." He grinned sheepishly. "All right, all right, I know. How naive can you get?"

"The sanctity of motherhood," Joan teased.

"Don't rub it in . . . I'll get on to Jennings at West End Central tomorrow, ask him to make a few enquiries at the hotel Mrs Pettifer stayed at."

"Just a minute," Joan said suddenly. "I've just remembered . . . Talking about her being pregnant . . . It rings a bell. Yes, I'm sure there was an article about her in one of the Sunday Colour Supplements. The *Telegraph*, I think."

"Really? I certainly don't remember that. Would we still have it?"

"I'm not sure. I'm trying to think how long ago it was. A few weeks, certainly."

"So the Cubs might not have taken it yet?" Once a month the local Cub Scout group collected newspapers, storing them up to sell at so much a ton for troop funds and charity.

"I'll see if I can find it," said Thanet, heading for the door.

The old newspapers were stored in boxes in the garage.

"It's got a picture of her on the front cover," Joan called after him.

Thanet almost missed it, Gemma looked so different. "She doesn't look a bit like that close to," he said, brandishing the photographs at Joan.

"In what way?"

"Not nearly so glamorous. I hardly recognised her."

Joan laughed. "I bet you'd hardly recognise me if someone spent an hour or two on my make-up and gave me a dress like that to wear."

Gemma was wearing a sumptuous, exotic creation in scarlet and gold brocade.

"I prefer you as you are," said Thanet, kissing the tip of Joan's nose. "Come on, let's see what they have to say about her."

The article was entitled, *THE MOST GIFTED ACTRESS OF OUR TIME*, and in the best journalistic tradition contrived to be both entertaining and informative.

Gemma, it claimed, set herself very high standards and did not spare herself in her efforts to attain them. She took her work very seriously indeed and had always been highly ambitious — which was, the article said, scarcely surprising in view of her background. She had been brought up in a children's home, having been abandoned on a doorstep. ("How *can* people?" murmured Joan.) According to her former Housemother, now retired, Gemma had always had a formidable capacity for hard work and a single-minded determination to succeed. Even while she was still at school it had become obvious that, on stage, she also possessed that rare power to grip and inspire an audience and send people away from a theatre feeling that they have for a brief while lived more intensely, that their experience has been enlarged by the performance they have just witnessed.

Gemma Shade's subsequent career, Thanet read, had more than fulfilled that early promise and her rise to the top had been truly meteoric. Her audiences were regularly moved to wonder and disbelief at the intensity of her portrayal, her

71

ability to become the vessel through which the personality of another takes on a new and vibrant life.

"Ah, this is the bit I was thinking of," said Joan:

Most of us are able to change our minds in private without loss of face. Not so for public figures, and it is to Miss Shade's credit that she has not been afraid, in recent years, to admit to changing hers. She had always said that she would never get married and would never have children. "I'm too self-centred," she used to say gaily, "ever to want to arrange my life around that of another person."

Now married for two years and pregnant, reminded of these words Miss Shade just smiles and say, "Well, perhaps I've grown up a bit since then." And she has, she says, been exceptionally lucky; her doctor husband is completely in favour of her continuing her stage career. And the baby, due in January? "The best New Year present either of us could wish for," she says. "I can't wait to become a mother."

It has been said that maturity improves the quality of an actress's work. If so, Miss Shade's many admirers must contemplate the prospect of her future performances with something approaching awe.

"Interesting woman," commented Joan.

"Yes, well, don't expect me to pronounce on that. My conversation with her was somewhat limited by circumstance."

"What are you going to do, then? Will you go ahead with the inquest?"

"Fortunately, we've got a few days grace before we need to make a final decision on that. Meanwhile, perhaps the post mortem result will help. If not, well, we'll just have to plod on until we're satisfied one way or the other."

"Of course, even if Dr Pettifer didn't kill himself, it doesn't necessarily mean that she did it. There must be a dozen reasons why he could have been murdered."

"Such as?"

"Well . . . two or three, anyway. Doctors are so vulnerable

72

in some ways. He could have mortally offended some psychotic patient . . . or been held to blame for a patient's death by some close relation . . . For that matter, he could even have been having an affair and been killed by a jealous husband. Come on, darling, cheer up. It's early days yet."

"True." Tactfully, he did not say that all these and other possibilities had already crossed his mind. Instead, acknowledging her attempt to console him, he smiled, put up his hand to caress her face.

"What would I do without you?" he said.

9

"Inspector Jennings, West End Central, on the phone for you, sir."

"Hullo, Peter? Luke here."

"About this actress . . ."

"Gemma Shade. Yes."

"I checked with security at the Lombard. I know the chap there, he's an ex-copper. And you were right."

"I was?"

"Yep. Miss Shade had company on Monday night. Sorry we've been so long, but it took a bit of winkling out, apparently. The chambermaid in question was new and had got her room numbers muddled up and was afraid that if she admitted it she'd be in trouble. Anyway, the long and the short of it is, she took Miss Shade early morning tea by mistake and got herself bawled out by lover-boy."

"Ah . . . Did your chap find out who he was?"

"Have a heart. He's not a bloody miracle-worker. Remember, Miss Shade's boyfriend wasn't even there, officially."

"Any description?"

"Youngish and fair-haired, that's all. There was one thing, though . . ."

"Yes?"

"The girl, the chambermaid, said he looked kind of familiar. So I was wondering. Seeing as his lady love's an actress . . ."

"He might be an actor, you mean?"

"Well, it's poss., isn't it?"

"Yes." Thanet thought hard. Jennings could well be right. In which case, it was more than likely that Gemma Pettifer's lover had been in the cast of her last production. And, if she

74

hadn't worked for the last couple of months . . .

"Luke? You still there?"

"Yes. Sorry. Thinking."

"God! You'll be solving cases next!"

"That'll be the day. Look, Peter, if you wanted to find out the gossip about the cast of a play, how would you go about it?"

"Current production?"

"No. Came off a couple of months ago."

"Here in London?"

"In the West End. *Away Day* at the Haymarket, to be precise."

"I'd ask Westwell."

"Who's he?"

"One of our DSs here. Theatre buff."

"Is he there at the moment?"

"Sure. D'you want me to put him on?"

"Please. And Peter, thanks."

"Don't forget you owe me a pint next time I see you."

"I might even make it two."

"The work must be getting to your brain. Hang on."

Thanet grinned. He and Jennings had been friends for years, had helped each other on a number of occasions. He covered the mouth of the receiver while he waited. "She spent the night with a lover," he said to Lineham.

"So I gathered." Lineham made a moue of disgust. "At six months pregnant."

"You don't switch off sex just because you're having a baby, you know," Thanet said with a grin.

"I didn't mean that. I meant . . ."

"Just a moment . . ." Thanet turned back to the phone.

"Inspector Thanet? DS Westwell here."

Thanet explained what he wanted to know.

"*Away Day* . . ." said Westwell thoughtfully. "I missed that, myself."

"So how would you go about finding out if Gemma Shade had an affair with a member of the cast?"

"Well, in the normal way of things I'd give the security

bloke a ring, but unfortunately there's a new chap at the Haymarket. Only been there a month."

"What happened to the last one?"

"He died. Nothing suspicious, a heart attack. So that's out. I should think your next best bet would be the theatre manager, but frankly, I doubt if you'd get him to talk."

"And if that fails?"

"You'd have to go for other members of the cast, I suppose."

"And how would I go about finding them?"

"Sorry, I don't know. But I could find out for you, if you like."

Thanet would have loved to accept this offer, but couldn't bring himself to do so. Asking for help was one thing, making a nuisance of himself another. "Thanks, but it looks as though I'll have to come up to London myself. Tell Inspector Jennings he might get his beer sooner than he thinks. If I can get through the red tape quickly enough, I'll be up this afternoon."

There was a grin in Westwell's voice as he said, "Right, sir."

"Sir," said Lineham doubtfully as Thanet put the phone down.

"Yes? . . . Well, come on man, spit it out." Lineham still occasionally reverted to the diffidence which had once so infuriated Thanet.

"Well, don't you think perhaps you're taking a lot for granted?"

"In assuming first that Mrs Pettifer's lover is an actor and second that he was in her last play with her, you mean?"

Lineham nodded.

"Certainly I am. But as there doesn't seem to be even the slightest whisper of a scandal down here it does seem logical — especially in view of the fact that the chambermaid thought he looked familiar — to assume that he might be an actor. We've got to start somewhere, after all. Can you suggest another way?"

"Tackle Mrs Pettifer."

"I told you, Mike, I don't like the idea. Not yet."

It was now late the following morning and the only

76

interesting snippet of information that had so far come in was that Gemma Pettifer's prints had been found on the drinking glass, tablet container and port bottle on Pettifer's bedside table. Even more interesting was the absence of Pettifer's prints from the first two. Lineham had been all for rushing off to see her at once, but Thanet, more cautious, had held back.

"But surely, now we know she had a motive . . ."

"No." Thanet's tone was final. "It's too early yet. We've got to find out more. And remember, it works both ways. Agreed, this could give her a motive for murder, but it could also give him a reason for suicide."

"You mean, he could have found out . . ."

"He adored that woman, Mike, idolised her. And that's always dangerous. When you discover that your idol has feet of clay . . . Who knows how a man like Pettifer would have reacted?"

"But there's absolutely no indication he did find out."

"True . . . And I must admit, thinking about it, I can't see that it would have been in character for him to opt out like that, give up without a fight . . . It's no good, Mike, it's pointless speculating like this. We've got to have more facts. If only we could have had the PM results today . . ." The post mortem had had to be postponed until next day. Although there were two pathologists in the area, one of them was ill and the other not only hopelessly overworked but booked to spend all afternoon giving evidence at inquests.

"Or if the handwriting experts had come up with something . . ."

"But they haven't. So, tickle them up a bit, will you Mike? Then get someone on to tracking down the history of that bottle of port. I want to know where, when and by whom it was bought. Meanwhile I'll get on to Scotland Yard, see if we can get permission to go and poke about in West End Central."

Thanet was still on the phone when Mallard came in.

"What's up?" he asked, when Thanet had finished. "I heard downstairs that you're working on the Pettifer Case. What case? I thought it was a straightforward suicide."

"It's not as simple as that, I'm afraid, Doc."

77

Quickly, Thanet ran through the mounting list of inexplicable facts. "And then we just heard this morning that Mrs Pettifer was having an affair — that she spent Monday night with her lover."

Mallard grimaced. "Oh, dear. That's another illusion down the drain. I always thought they were a most devoted couple. Anyway, that surely explains the whole thing."

"What do you mean?"

"That he killed himself because he found out. He practically worshipped the ground she walked on, you know."

"Not good enough, Doc," said Thanet, shaking his head. "There's too much to be explained away."

"I agree that Pettifer didn't seem the type to throw in the sponge without a fight . . . Though there is another argument for its having been suicide, you know."

"Oh?"

"One school of thought sees suicide as an act of aggression, an expression of anger, rather than despair."

"That's interesting. I'll have to think about that."

"So, what now?"

"We've got to find out more. That's why I want to go up to . . ."

The phone rang. Thanet picked it up. West End Central, he mouthed at the others. "Yes, DI Thanet here . . ."

Mallard raised his hand in a gesture of farewell and left.

Once again, Thanet explained what he wanted to do in London. Finally, "It's all fixed," he said to Lineham, putting the phone down. "We're to report in at two. There's no reserved parking space in Savile Row, so it'll be easier to go by train." He glanced at the clock: twenty to twelve. "If we hurry we'll just catch the twelve-ten."

"There's plenty of time, surely."

"I want to pick up something from home, on the way."

The detour took a quarter of an hour and Thanet blessed Joan's orderly mind as he went straight to the drawer where she always kept souvenirs of holidays and outings and picked out the theatre programme of *Away Day*. In the train he produced it.

, "You didn't tell me you'd seen *Away Day*."

"I wanted to check something first, in case my memory was playing me tricks. Ah yes . . ." He offered the programme to Lineham. "See what you think."

Lineham flicked quickly through the photographs of the cast. There had been four main characters, two men and two women. "I'd plump for him." Lineham's finger stabbed at the classical features and golden curls of a young actor called Rowan Lee. "He fits the chambermaid's description."

"That's what I thought."

"So that's why you were so set on this trip."

"All right, Mike. Don't sound so aggrieved. I must admit he immediately sprang to mind. But as I said, I wanted to check before saying anything."

"Looks a bit young for her, doesn't he?"

Lee appeared to be in his mid-twenties, a good ten years younger than Gemma Pettifer.

"Perhaps he's older than he looks. You can never tell with these studio portraits. Or it might have been taken some years ago."

"So, are we going to try and see him today?"

"No, I think not. I don't want to risk his contacting Mrs Pettifer. If she's innocent I don't want her unnecessarily upset, and if she's not then when I tackle her I want it to be a complete surprise."

"What exactly are we going to do this afternoon, then?"

"At the moment what I'm really after is confirmation. It's quite possible that we're barking up the wrong tree. So what I want is someone prepared to gossip."

"Deborah Chivers, then."

This was the other woman in the cast.

"If we can get hold of her, yes."

"She could be working this afternoon. It's Wednesday, matinée day."

"I know. She could be anywhere, for that matter. Let's hope she's not off touring the provinces. We'll just have to see."

After the brief courtesy visit to West End Central headquarters in Savile Row they took the tube to Piccadilly Circus and walked down the Haymarket towards the Theatre Royal. They paused for a few moments to admire the classical façade with its six soaring white columns before crossing the road to the main entrance.

"It's supposed to be one of the oldest and classiest theatres in London," Thanet said as they pushed open the swing doors.

The foyer was elegant — milk-white walls with gold mouldings and gilt-framed mirrors, gleaming brass handrails and white leather chairs. The matinée performance must have started, for the place was deserted but for a young man in the box office.

Thanet approached him. "Could I speak to the manager, please?"

"You'll have to go around to the stage door. It's at the back of the theatre, in Suffolk Street. Go out of the main door, turn left and left again."

Suffolk Street was a cul-de-sac of tall white buildings with black wrought-iron balconies at first-floor level. The stage door was at the far end. Lineham edged his way behind Thanet into the tiny space in front of the Enquiries counter while Thanet repeated his request.

"D'you want the theatre manager or the production manager?"

"The theatre manager, I should think."

"I'm afraid he's out, sir." The porter was friendly, middle-aged and balding, with grey hair and grey moustache. He looked very snug in his tiny room, which couldn't have been much more than seven feet square. A real home from home, thought Thanet, noting the square of carpet on the floor, the comfortable tub armchair, the electric kettle. There was even a portable television set.

"Perhaps you could help me, then." Thanet introduced himself. "I suppose you get to know the cast pretty well, while they're playing here?"

"Well, I do and I don't. Depends how long a run it is, how friendly they are and so on."

"But you might have a good idea of, shall we say, what the

relationships between the various members of the cast might be?''

The wary gleam in the man's eye told Thanet that the question had been correctly interpreted. "Oh, I don't know about that, sir. Bit outside my province, that is. I just deal with all the practical stuff, the nuts and bolts, you might say."

Thanet was adept at recognising a lost cause. "Perhaps the production manager could help me, then. Is he in at the moment?"

"That would be Mr Wemsley. Yes, he is. Would you like me to give him a call?"

The young man who came up the stairs behind them in response to Thanet's request looked more like a business executive than Thanet's idea of someone in the theatre world. What did you expect? Thanet asked himself in amusement. Purple suede trousers and shaggy sweater? He introduced himself, taking care to emphasise that his enquiries had no connection with either the current production or the theatre.

Wemsley's anxious frown faded. "Come down to my office." He led the way through the little black metal swing gate and down some uncarpeted stairs. In the office a loudspeaker in the corner was relaying the play on stage.

They all sat down.

"Now then, how exactly can I help you?"

"Well, as I said, we're from Kent CID. We're trying to trace some of the members of the cast of a recent production at this theatre. Of *Away Day*, to be precise."

"Then it's the theatre manager you want," said Wemsley promptly. "And I'm afraid he's out. I'm only here for the duration of this particular production, you see. He's permanent."

"When will he be back?"

"Not for another hour or more. But I've just thought . . . Are you trying to find out who the cast of *Away Day* were, or do you know the names of the people you want to see?"

"Oh, we know who they are." Thanet took the programme from his pocket.

"Then there's no problem. We can look them up in

Spotlight . . . It's a directory of actors and actresses," Wemsley explained to their blank looks. "I've got one here." He reached out for a small stack of books, opened one at random. "You see?" he said, holding it out. "It gives details of professional careers and — this is what you want — agents' names and addresses. Mind you, trying to get a client's address from an agent is harder than trying to get the proverbial blood out of a stone, but as it's the police who're asking you should be all right."

"May I see?"

Ten minutes later they left the theatre with a list of the names, addresses and telephone numbers of the agents of all three other members of the cast of *Away Day*.

"Easier than we thought, eh, Mike?" said Thanet, patting his pocket with satisfaction.

"Bit of luck," Lineham agreed. "Where now?"

"Deborah Chivers' agent first. And as we don't want to waste most of the afternoon fathoming out how to get from A to B by public transport, we'll do it in style." He raised his hand as he spotted an empty cab and they both watched in admiration as the driver manoeuvred his way expertly through the one-way traffic to the kerb.

The spacious foyer of Jacob Solly, Theatrical Agent, was luxuriously furnished with a thick cream carpet and green leather armchairs, most of which were occupied. There was an atmosphere of bored expectancy. Successful clients smiled condescendingly down from the glossy blown-up photographs which adorned the walls. There were a few choice specimens of potted palms and giant ferns which, like the glamorous blonde in the green silk trouser suit behind the reception desk, had clearly been chosen for their sculptural qualities.

Assessing eyes followed Thanet and Lineham across the room.

"Can I help you?" The blonde's smile was as artificial as her eyelashes. She had already dismissed them as being of no interest. Thanet felt a malicious satisfaction at her response to his introduction.

82

"Er . . ." Her eyes darted nervously from telephone to waiting clients to the door marked PRIVATE behind her. It was as if a statue had suddenly become prey to human emotion. She swallowed. "I'm afraid Mr Solly is engaged just now," she said. "But I'll go and see . . . Could you sit down for a moment?"

Interested eyes followed Thanet and Lineham's every movement. Thanet read speculation, resentment, hostility in them. What a life, he thought, staring composedly back. Quickly, he counted. There were fifteen people in the room, of various ages, shapes and sizes. He winked boldly at a woman with a particularly outraged stare and grinned as she hastily began to study her hands. Lineham shifted uncomfortably on the seat beside him.

The blonde emerged briskly from the door marked PRIVATE and approached Thanet. He tried not to recoil too obviously from the overpowering waft of perfume which assailed his nostrils as she bent to murmur, "Mr Solly is free now. This way, please."

Thanet and Lineham looked about them with interest at the room into which they were ushered. By contrast with the foyer this was a cosy masculine cave, with shaggy brown carpet and chestnut-coloured leather armchairs. The brown hessian-covered walls were crammed with theatre posters and more glossy photographs of famous clients. Behind a status-enhancing desk of teak and leather sat a short, plump man in cream suede jacket and silky polo-necked sweater. The shimmer of gold on his fingers was echoed in his smile.

"Come in, come in, Inspector." He rose, extended a soft damp palm to each man in turn.

With difficulty Thanet restrained himself from wiping his hand on the side of his trousers.

Courtesies exchanged, Solly sat back, folded his hands on the solid mound of his belly and said, "Now then. How, exactly, can I help you?"

"We're trying to trace a client of yours," Thanet said. "Deborah Chivers."

"Ah . . ." Solly pursed his moist, full lips and frowned.

83

"Would it be proper to ask in what connection . . . Debbie hasn't been a naughty girl, I hope?" he asked archly.

Thanet hoped his wince didn't show. "No, not at all. We're just hoping that she might be able to give us some information about someone who is involved in a case we're working on."

"Debbie isn't actually . . . uh . . . involved in the case herself?"

"No. Not at all."

Solly sat up with a bounce. "Forgive me, Inspector. I am being remiss in my duty as a host. I won't insult you by offering you alcohol at this hour, but a cup of coffee, perhaps? Or tea?" The gold fillings glinted.

"Thank you, no. I'm afraid our time in London is limited."

"Yes, of course. Well, I see no reason why we shouldn't oblige." He pressed a button. "Make a note of Deborah Chivers' address for the Inspector, will you Marilyn?"

"Do you think there's any likelihood that she might be at home, if we went to see her this afternoon?" Thanet asked.

"Well, she's resting at the moment," Solly said. A flash of gold again. "Our euphemism for 'out of work', as I'm sure you're aware, Inspector. So it's possible. I'll give her a ring if you like, and find out." And swiftly, before Thanet could demur, "Get Debbie on the blower for me, will you Marilyn? Yes, now."

It was pointless to protest. Solly clearly had every intention of warning Deborah Chivers of their impending visit. If he didn't do it now, he'd do it when they'd left, so he might as well be useful to Thanet in the process, perhaps save him a wasted journey.

"Debbie? Solly here, my love. Yes . . . No, afraid not. Not at the moment. I might have something on ice, though. No, I can't say a word just now, in case it doesn't come off. No, you'll just have to be patient, darling. No, something quite different. Now don't be alarmed, but I've got two charming policemen here who want to have a word with you. Yes . . . No, you haven't done anything wrong, love. Just some

84

information they think you might have in connection with some case they're working on. No, no idea. Honestly. The point is, they'd like to come and see you. Right away, I gather. They're only in London for the day. No, truly darling, absolutely no idea. Anyway, I'll tell them you'll be in this afternoon, shall I? Right. Yes, I'll be in touch soon, I hope. Yes. 'Bye for now. And you, sweetie." He put the phone down. "Any time you like," he said to Thanet.

"Thank you."

Marilyn came in, handed a slip of paper to Thanet and swayed out, buttocks visibly caressed by green silk.

' "Uh . . . this way out." Solly ushered them through a door in the far corner of his office.

"Where does she live?" Lineham asked as they emerged on to the street.

Thanet glanced at the piece of paper in his hand. "Maida Vale. It looks as though we'll have to get clearance again. We'd better find a telephone . . . Then," he added recklessly, "we'll take another taxi."

Lineham grinned. "I'd like to see the Super's face when he gets our expenses sheet," he said.

10

The house in front of which the taxi drew up was in a Georgian terrace which had, like so many London streets, suffered the indignity of neglect and was now in the process of becoming fashionable again.

Many of the houses sported newly-pointed brickwork, gleaming white window frames and front doors painted in glossy, sophisticated colours. These, Thanet guessed, were privately owned, testaments to the loving care of their occupants. Number four was clearly rented out and looked like a poor relation, with peeling paint and a general air of neglect. Thanet peered at the row of bells. CHIVERS was the bottom one. He pressed it.

When the door opened Thanet's first impression was of a younger version of Servalan in "Blake's Seven" (one of Bridget's favourite programmes). Deborah Chivers had the same pointed chin, beautiful high wide cheekbones and immaculate cap of glossy black hair cut so short it might almost have been painted on. A deliberate imitation? he wondered. Certainly the effect was dramatic and made even more striking by the girl's clothes: black corduroy-velvet knee-breeches, ribbed tights and a sheer white cotton blouse with a froth of ruffles at neck and wrist. Had she made a special effort on their behalf? Probably not, he decided. Deborah Chivers cared very much how she looked and would habitually make every effort to achieve the effect she wanted.

"Hi," she said. "You the fuzz?"

Thanet was tempted to say, "Sure am, baby," but thought the better of it. He introduced himself formally, showed her his identification.

She was amused. "It *was* a joke," she said. "Come on down."

She turned to lead the way, plunging with the abandon of familiarity into a short, dark stairwell leading to the basement. Thanet and Lineham followed more cautiously. At the bottom she threw open a door.

"*Maison* Chivers," she said. "Make yourself at home." She plumped down cross-legged on to a huge, squashy black floor cushion.

The two policemen instinctively looked around for more conventional forms of seating and found none. Gingerly Thanet lowered himself on to a scarlet cushion. Red for danger, he thought with amusement. If the boys in the office could see me now! From the corner of his eye he noted that Lineham had chosen a yellow perch and with straight face had already taken out notebook and pencil and settled down with an air of calm expectancy. Ten out of ten for self-possession, Thanet thought. Studiously ignoring the mischievous gleam in the girl's eye, he looked about him.

The room was large and was obviously bedroom, sitting room, study, workroom and kitchen, all rolled into one, though attempts had been made to hide the fact. Thanet recognised the type of bed which folds up and pretends to be a bookcase and guessed that the kitchen was hidden away in the far corner behind a wooden screen on which had been pasted dozens of theatre programmes. The brick and plank bookshelves were well stocked, mostly with paperbacks, and there was evidence of industry: under the window was a long worktable covered with drawings and sketches, jars of poster paint and a scattering of pencils and brushes. Pinned up on a large cork board beside the window were more sketches, each with a moustache of multi-coloured wools tacked to it. The girl must be some kind of fashion designer. His eyes swivelled to a clothes rack on castors standing against the wall. Hanging on it were half a dozen women's sweaters which at first he had taken to be the girl's own clothes.

"That's right." The girl was smiling at this lightning scrutiny, aware of his conclusion. "It's my sideline. I sell them to boutiques." She scrambled to her feet, unhooked one of the sweaters and held it against her. "Like it?" It was one of the scenic sweaters currently in fashion.

Thanet did. Very much. "It reminds me of the Dordogne." He and Joan had spent their honeymoon there and had loved it.

She was pleased. "As a matter of fact, it is the Dordogne. Some friends of mine have a cottage there and I spent a few weeks with them, last summer. I'm surprised you recognised it." She stroked the sweater. "I adore doing these. They really are fun. I'll be sorry when the craze is over." She replaced the sweater on the rack and returned to her cushion.

"You do this in between plays?" Thanet said.

Her mouth tugged down at the corners. " 'Fraid so. It's a terrible profession, acting. Too many people chasing too few jobs. Most of us are driven to doing something else, in between. You name it, actors do it, to eat. Unless of course you're up in the stars and then you don't have to worry. I should be so lucky."

"But the last play you were in. That was a good part, surely?"

"*Away Day*? Yes, that was a good one, right enough. But unfortunately it didn't quite catch the public fancy enough to have a long run. So, it was back to the old knitting needles." She grinned. "Is this part of your softening-up technique, Inspector?"

He liked her directness. He smiled back at her. "Yes and no." .

"Why yes and why not?"

"Well, I find that people are always more cooperative, if I can get on good terms with them. But it so happens that *Away Day* is very much what I want to talk to you about."

"OK. So we're on good terms. What about *Away Day*?"

"To be more precise, I want to talk to you about Gemma Shade."

Deborah Chivers had particularly expressive eyes, he thought. They were a clear, pure blue, the colour of southern skies. Now he could have sworn that they darkened by several shades.

"What about Gemma?" she asked warily. "What's she done?"

"Nothing, to my knowledge," said Thanet truthfully. "But we do rather need to know a little more about her life on the stage."

"Why come to me? Why not ask her agent?"

Thanet sighed. There was no point in beating about the bush with this girl. "Because her agent might be biased."

Deborah gave a great shout of laughter and rocked to and fro on her cushion, hugging her knees. "Biased! Oh boy, that really takes the biscuit! Believe me, if you want an *un*biased view of Gemma Shade, I'm the last person you should have come to!"

"Why?" said Thanet softly.

Deborah stopped grinning and sat up. "Because she pinched my man, the old witch. And believe me, Inspector, it hurt. It still does."

"Wouldn't she be, well, a bit old for him? Unless, of course, he's much older than you."

"Just a year, that's all. He's twenty-three. Oh yes, she's too old for him, right enough. But that makes no difference to her, I'm afraid. Gemma Shade likes them young, always has. It's common knowledge in the profession. And she doesn't waste time worrying about whether they're someone else's property, either."

"That would be Rowan Lee you're talking about?"

She winced. "Yes."

"Do you happen to know if she's still seeing him?"

"I don't *know* . . . but yes, I think so. The word is, he's still unavailable, so I guess she hasn't finished with him yet. You'd think she'd have more . . . dignity, now that she looks like the back of a bus."

"The baby, you mean."

"Yes."

"How long ago did this affair begin?"

"Hey, look, why the interest in Gemma's love-life? This isn't going to get Rowan into trouble, is it?"

"I told you, it's Miss Shade we're interested in. So please, how long ago?"

Deborah didn't notice the evasion. The opportunity to talk freely about Gemma was clearly too good to be missed. "Soon after we opened. Say . . . eight or nine months ago."

"What's she like as a person? Leaving aside this predilection she has . . ."

Deborah shrugged. "As I said, I'm not really the best person to ask. But she's a first-rate actress, I'm bound to say that even though I can't stand her. But she's, well, I suppose the best word for it is greedy. She wants everything — fame, fortune, money, adulation, lovers, husband . . ."

"I read somewhere that she'd always said she didn't ever want to get married."

"That was before the Doc turned up. And, as you may or may not know, he is loaded. And his . . . well, wooing is the right word for it, old-fashioned as it may sound — his courtship of Gemma, then, was really something, or so I've been told. That was before I worked with her, of course."

"But if she prefers younger men?"

"For fun, yes. But, let's face it, they're usually broke. So when it came to choosing a husband . . ."

"You really don't like her, do you?"

"No I don't. And I don't mind admitting it. I don't care for people who trample over other people, just use them and throw them on the rubbish heap when they're finished with them . . ."

"So it didn't surprise you that she married Doctor Pettifer?"

"Well, I told you, I didn't know her at the time, though I knew *of* her, of course. But, in retrospect, no, it doesn't. She lost nothing in terms of career, freedom, and gained in terms of security. I know he's older than she is, but that simply means he'll die first and she'll have more stashed away for her old age."

Obviously she hadn't heard about Dr Pettifer's death. Thanet sensed Lineham shift uncomfortably beside him and knew that the sergeant was expecting him now to break the news to her. But it wasn't the right moment. To do so would disrupt the whole tenor of the conversation, bias and distort her response. He couldn't afford to have that happen.

"I must say," Deborah was saying, "I was surprised she didn't have an abortion when she found out she was pregnant."

"Why?"

"Because nothing, nothing whatsoever matters more to that woman than her career. And also because, well, a friend of mine was in the same production as Gemma when the doctor came a-courting, and she says that Gemma told her that one of the reasons why she had decided to accept his proposal was because he didn't expect her to become a breeding machine, was how she put it. In fact, he didn't like children, was positively anti having them and had made quite sure she felt the same before he proposed. 'So I'll be spared that, thank God,' she said. Gemma, I mean. So you see . . .'"

"Yes," Thanet said. "Yes. That is interesting." He shrugged. "Well, they obviously changed their minds."

"And the other thing that always surprised me was that Gemma had married a GP. I mean, boy, is she neurotic about illness!"

"Can't stand blood, you mean? That sort of thing?"

"Oh no. Miles worse than that. If you had a cough or a cold you couldn't go within half a mile of her — in fact, unless it was an actual performance, she'd refuse to go on stage with you. And as for anything infectious, like measles or mumps . . . She just couldn't *bear* anything to do with being ill. D'you know, while we were doing *Away Day* one of the young stage hands had an accident, broke her thigh. We were all very sorry for her because it was her first job in the West End and as you can imagine she was heartbroken about having to drop out. Her family lives up north, so we all took it in turns to go and visit her in hospital, to cheer her up. Except Gemma. She made all sorts of excuses and then, in the end, said straight out that she couldn't bear illness, she couldn't stand hospitals and nothing, but nothing, would induce her to go near one." Deborah grimaced. "So you can see why it surprised me, when I found out she'd married a doctor."

"Perhaps she thought he'd keep her healthy," said Lineham with a grin.

Deborah looked surprised. It was the first time he had spoken and now she gave his youthful good looks an assessing, appreciative stare.

Thanet was amused to see his sergeant flush. Lineham had always been susceptible to a pretty girl, had never been at his best in dealing with them. Thanet and Joan had sometimes wondered how he had ever plucked up sufficient courage to ask Louise, his wife, out in the first place.

"That's a thought," Deborah said. "D'you know, you could just be right. It would tickle her to think she had her own private physician."

Thanet wondered if it was only Gemma who evoked this kind of acid response in the girl. A pity, if not, to be soured, so young. Certainly she'd shown no sign of it until Gemma's name was mentioned. And if she really had been in love with young Lee, it was scarcely surprising that she should feel bitter towards the older woman.

"Well, thank you, Miss Chivers," he said, struggling to rise with dignity from his floor cushion. "You've been most helpful. There's just one other thing . . ."

"Yes?" She came to her feet gracefully, in one supple, fluid movement, smiling and looking up at him expectantly.

He cast a slightly embarrassed glance at Lineham. "Those sweaters you make. Er . . . How much do you charge for them?"

"Thirty pounds," she said promptly. "And that's a fair price. In the shops, individually-designed hand-made ones like this go for double that. And that's not just sales talk, you can check for yourself. I can cut the costs because I haven't the overheads, of course. Why? Do you fancy one?"

"My wife would."

"Come and have a look." She beckoned him across to the rack with a tiny jerk of her head. "What size is she?"

"Er . . . medium. Not fat, not thin . . ."

She laughed. "A typical male answer!" Quickly she flicked through them, extracting three in all. "These should fit, then.

92

Do you like any of them?''

One of them reminded Thanet of the beach where he and Joan had spent many golden afternoons. There were those towering cliffs behind which the sun had sunk each day in a final dazzle of splendour, there were the silken waters of the Dordogne river lapping at the rocks which plunged sheer into the water. On one occasion he and Joan had swum right across to touch them . . . There, too, in the foreground was the wide, pebbly beach overhung by trees. Why, that looked like the very spot where . . .

"That wouldn't be Meyraguet, by any chance?'' he asked. Her eyes lit up. "Yes, it is! D'you know it?''

"Very well indeed.'' That settled it. "My wife would love that one. I'll take it. You won't mind a cheque?''

Rivulets of light rippled across the burnished cap of hair as she shook her head. "Not at all. No tax evasion for me. Believe it or not, Operation Knitting Needles is entirely legit. Blame my Methodist upbringing.'' She folded the sweater carefully into tissue paper and gift-wrapped it.

In the taxi Thanet sank back against the upholstery and glanced at the colourful parcel with delight. He couldn't wait to see Joan's face . . . He turned to Lineham.

"Now then,'' he said briskly. "Tell me what you thought of Miss Chivers.''

11

The children spotted the gaily-wrapped parcel the moment Thanet stepped through the door.

"A present!" they cried. "Who's it for, Daddy? Who's it for?"

Thanet was glad to see that tonight everything seemed normal. Both of them were bathed and in their night-clothes — Joan always allowed them to stay up until six-thirty to wait for their father — and there were savoury smells issuing from the kitchen.

He laid a finger across his lips. "Shh . . . It's for Mummy. Come on."

They followed him in a conspiratorial silence into the kitchen. The radio was on and Joan obviously hadn't heard him arrive home. She was chopping something on the work surface near the cooker, with her back to him.

He tiptoed up behind her, exaggerating his movements for the children's entertainment. Then, lifting his arm above her head, he slowly lowered the parcel to dangle in front of her face. She gave a little cry and the children shrieked with delight.

"What do I get for bringing home the goodies?" he said, smiling.

"It's for me?" Surprise, pleasure, anticipation, appreciation chased each other across Joan's face. "Thank you, darling!" She reached up to kiss him, wiping her hands on her apron, then took the parcel and moved across to the table. Thanet and the children followed her to watch as she began to unwrap it.

"Oh," she breathed, as the sweater emerged from its folds of tissue paper. "Oh, darling, it's beautiful. Really beautiful. Wherever did you find it?"

"In London," Thanet said smugly.

"D'you know," Joan said, holding it up at arm's length to study it. "It reminds me of the Dordogne."

"It is the Dordogne. The girl who made it spent the summer there, last year." He paused. "Does it look familiar?" he asked, smiling.

She considered, head tilted to one side. "Well . . . Meyraguet? Darling, it isn't Meyraguet, is it?"

His face told her she had guessed correctly.

"Meyraguet . . ." she breathed, studying it. When she turned to him again her eyes had the sheen of tears. "What a lovely, lovely present," she said, flinging her arms around him.

He hugged her back, delighted. "Thought you'd like it," he murmured.

"Every time I wear it, it'll remind me . . ."

They exchanged reminiscent smiles. Their honeymoon had been memorable. Joan kissed him again, enthusiastically. The children beamed. Why didn't he do this sort of thing more often, Thanet asked himself.

After supper, though, he noticed that Joan seemed a little subdued.

"What's the matter?" he asked.

She pulled a face. "Louise rang me this morning, asked if I'd meet her at lunchtime."

Thanet groaned. He was fond of Lineham's wife, though she was a little over-powering for his own taste. He could guess what was wrong. "Mother-in-law trouble again?"

"I'm afraid so. Honestly, Luke, I really do wonder what will happen there, in the end. After that business of the wedding, I rather hoped Mike's mother had learned her lesson."

Lineham's wedding had twice been delayed by his mother having mild heart attacks. At the third attempt he had told her that even if she had another attack he would, in fairness to Louise, have to go ahead regardless. She did and he had.

"What happened this time?" Thanet asked.

"Well, apparently they had some friends round to supper last night. Fortunately they knew them well, otherwise . . .

well, anyway, Mike's mother kept on ringing up."

"Did she know they were entertaining?"

"Yes. She rang first at eight, just as they were sitting down to table, saying she didn't feel well, and the soup got cold while they were waiting for Mike to finish the phone call. Then she rang again just as they were all settling down to coffee, after the meal. And then, to cap it all, she rang yet again just after Mike and Louise had got into bed and, I gather, had begun to make love. And that time Mike actually got dressed and went over to see her!"

"You can see why Louise was mad!"

"I should say. But what she finds so frustrating is that Mike won't talk about it, won't even acknowledge that they have a problem."

"I'm not surprised really. Louise can be pretty forceful at times too, you know. I should think he often feels like a worm between two blackbirds."

"I thought you liked Louise!"

"Oh, I do. I do. But I wouldn't want to be married to her."

"She says Mike doesn't even seem to realise how his mother manipulates him, and this makes her furious."

"Poor Mike. But you can understand why he refuses to talk about it, can't you?"

"Why?"

"Well what good would it do? I bet that, by 'talk about it', Louise really means 'get him to see her point of view, put her first'. Nothing else would really satisfy her, now would it?"

"I suppose not." Joan sounded doubtful.

"I'm sure of it. She's not the compromising type. And, looking at it from Mike's point of view, you can understand him feeling that his mother has at least got some claim on him. Louise, after all, has him all the time, but his mother calls on him only occasionally. I can see why Louise gets angry but let's face it, she did know what she was letting herself in for, before she married him. And I don't know whether she'd be any happier if Mike did stop jumping when his mother claims his attention. As I see it, he'd then feel so guilty he'd be as miserable as sin anyway. And she wouldn't like that either, now would she?"

"You do sound unsympathetic, darling, I must say."

"If I do, I'm sorry. But I wouldn't call it unsympathetic, I'd call it realistic. Frankly, I think that neither Mike's mother nor Louise are going to change their spots at this stage. In fact, I can't really see the situation altering until one of them dies."

"Luke!"

"I'm sorry love, but come on, don't you agree with me, underneath?"

Joan bit her lip. "I'm just being an ostrich, really. Yes, I suppose I do. It's just that, well, seeing Louise so miserable . . ."

"It's something she will have to come to terms with, I'm afraid."

"She wondered if you might perhaps have a word with Mike . . .?"

"Me? Not on your life. Mike and I have got a damned good working relationship and I don't want to ruin it. Besides, you must see it really isn't my place to start butting in on his private life without an invitation."

"So you haven't any bright ideas?"

"Just one. If she really feels that the problem is serious — and it does sound as though it's getting that way — then by far the best thing to do is to go to the Marriage Guidance Council."

"Isn't that a bit drastic?"

"Not at all. I should think prevention is better than cure and besides, the only counsellor I've ever met really impressed me. You remember, Mrs Thorpe, in the Julie Holmes case?"

"Yes, I do remember, now you mention it. All right. I'll give Louise a ring tomorrow, see if I can tactfully suggest it."

Marriages, marriages, Thanet thought as he lay awake in bed, later. Who could ever tell what went on behind all those closed front doors? No one but the couples themselves — no, even that was a fallacy. Usually, the two people in a marriage were the last to be able to understand what was happening to them. It took a major upheaval, a crisis, a painful reassessment of self to do that. He remembered his own near-danger point, a couple of years ago, when he and Joan had clashed over her desire to abandon her contented-housewife rôle for a more satisfying job. But they had been lucky. He had been jogged into awareness by the case in which he had been involved at the time and besides, that had been only a temporary dilemma. Lineham and Louise were a different matter; their problem was permanent, rooted in their different character and backgrounds. Any solution they found would be hard-won and painfully achieved. He didn't envy them that.

His mind drifted back to the Pettifer case. Now there was an intriguing marriage. His forehead furrowed as he lay staring up into the darkness, thinking of each partner in turn.

Pettifer, now. A strange man, stern and proud, a man who set high standards not only for himself but, Thanet guessed, for those about him too, reserved in his manner yet capable of a passionate wooing . . . His twin obsessions: his wife and his work. No doubt about how he would have felt had he known that she had been — was still being — unfaithful to him.

If he had known.

Had he?

Thanet considered. There was, so far, not one single scrap of evidence to indicate that he had. They would have to find out, because if he had . . . Well, what if he had? How would he have reacted? He might have cut his wife out of his will, for a start. Thanet made a mental note to check, in the morning. In any case Pettifer must have been desperately hurt, wounded and then angry, yes, overwhelmingly angry. But what would he have *done*? Would he have killed himself?

Thanet thought. He remembered what Doc Mallard had said about suicide — that one school of thought saw it as an act of anger, of aggression rather than despair. Could this have applied in Pettifer's case? Perhaps it would depend on how Pettifer read his wife's character. According to Deborah Chivers, Gemma had no moral scruples whatsoever. True, Deborah was biased, as she herself had freely admitted — but then, Thanet himself had seen how cruel Gemma could be, in that incident with Andrew. But Pettifer, blinded by love, might well have seen her differently. If, then, he had thought her to be a woman of conscience who would be overwhelmed by guilt and remorse and blame herself for her husband's suicide, could he conceivably have decided to revenge himself upon her in this way?

Thanet found himself shaking his head. No. Everything he had so far learnt about Pettifer contradicted the idea. He could imagine Pettifer fighting back — confronting his wife's lover, perhaps, or accusing her outright, or repudiating her even, with an icy coldness which masked his pain. But this . . . No, suicide as the final act of aggression was surely the ultimate gesture of a coward, of a man who felt he couldn't get his own back on life any other way than by voluntarily surrendering it. And Pettifer, by common consensus, had been a fighter, a man who squared up to life and lived it on his own terms.

Conclusion, then: Pettifer had not known of his wife's infidelity.

And this was the only possible reason for suicide that had turned up — yet, Thanet reminded himself. The post-mortem result was still to come.

Then there was Gemma Pettifer — Gemma Shade. The fact that she had two names seemed symbolic of her dual identity: at home in Sturrenden the happily married woman (with a touch of glamour, admittedly, for no one ever quite forgot her public persona), the respectable doctor's wife. And in the theatre world the cat on heat, the older woman with a taste for young men and a reputation for getting what she wanted irrespective of the damage it caused to those who got in her way. "Greedy" was the word Deborah had used, and if so it was understandable, considering the insecurity of Gemma's early life. Deborah had found it astonishing that Gemma should have chosen to marry a country GP, but Thanet felt he could understand it. Medicine was a solid, respectable profession and Pettifer had been able to offer the added advantages of wealth and maturity. Add to that the fact that he had been prepared to allow Gemma complete freedom to pursue her career (and therefore, unknown to him, her lovers) and the proposition must have been irresistible to her.

So, taking the hypothesis that Gemma had killed him, why should she have decided to throw all that security away? Had she become bored with Pettifer? Or, conversely, had she truly fallen in love with Lee? Suppose that, as in the classic murder triangle, she and Lee had wanted not only to be together but to get their hands on Pettifer's considerable wealth — and had conspired together to do so . . . How had they done it, in view of the fact that Pettifer had not taken the overdose for several hours after Gemma left? Obviously, Thanet decided, they must have returned to Sturrenden later on in the evening, after Gemma's dinner with her agent.

He considered the mechanics of the idea. Gemma would have given Pettifer a sufficiently strong drug in the cocoa to send him off into a sound sleep. Then, later, she and Lee would return — by car perhaps. By then Pettifer would be deep in a drugged sleep and it would be a relatively simple matter to administer the overdose . . . But if that was how it had been done, how could Gemma possibly have known that Pettifer would conveniently develop a cold, thereby providing her with the opportunity to slip him the first dose?

For a moment Thanet's mind, poised between sleep and wakefulness, skittered off into a wildly imaginative explanation wherein Gemma somehow managed to get hold of cold germs and administer them to her husband at appropriate intervals before the night of the planned murder . . .

With an effort Thanet dragged his thoughts back into logical channels. Don't be ridiculous, he told himself. It wasn't necessary for Pettifer to have had a cold at all, for Gemma to be able to give him that initial dose. She could originally have planned to give it to him in his tea and then, when he conveniently developed the cold symptoms, decided to use them to her own advantage. For that matter, the whole thing could have been *un*planned, could have been set in motion by that cold of his. Seeing her chance, Gemma could have acted on impulse, grabbed it with both hands.

Though of course, they had only Gemma's word for it that Pettifer had had any cold symptoms at all. For some reason this seemed a significant thought, though Thanet couldn't for the life of him see why. He felt consciousness slipping away as he endeavoured to concentrate on it. It was no good. It would have to wait until morning.

Morning . . . Tomorrow . . . Tomorrow he would have to tackle Gemma, confront her with her adultery . . .

He wasn't looking forward to that.

12

When Thanet arrived at the office next morning he found Lineham engrossed in a report.

"What's that?" Thanet asked.

"Handwriting report."

"Anything interesting?"

"Not really." Lineham handed it over.

Thanet scanned it quickly, read it again more carefully and finally tossed it on to the desk in disgust. "A second opinion! That'll mean another couple of days at least, before we'll know for certain."

"We might not know even then," Lineham pointed out. "There's no guarantee that the second report'll be any more conclusive than the first."

"True." Thanet ran a hand through his hair. "I really was hoping that today we'd have a definite pointer one way or the other. I'm sick of working in a vacuum like this. Is the PM definitely scheduled for today?"

"They're doing it now. They started at eight-thirty so they should be finished soon."

"Good."

"There are three interesting bits of information that have come in, though. First, the bottle of port. According to Mrs Price, Mrs Pettifer gave it to her husband for his birthday. And the wine merchant confirms, we've checked. He remembers because Mrs Pettifer asked his advice in selecting it."

"So it's not surprising her prints are on that, at least."

"The next thing is, I thought it might be useful to know the terms of Dr Pettifer's will — I thought, if he did know his wife was being unfaithful to him, he might well have decided to cut her out."

"And?"

"He made a new will on his marriage. There's money left in trust for Andrew, of course, but all the rest goes to Mrs Pettifer. That will still stands and no changes had been discussed."

"Now that is interesting. What's the third thing?"

"Just before you came in this morning I had a call from PC Sparks."

"Yes, I know him." Sparks was promising material. Thanet had had his eye on him for some time.

"He'd heard that we're taking a bit more than a routine interest in Dr Pettifer's death and the long and the short of it is, he and PC May were on patrol duty in that area the night Pettifer died and around midnight there was a car parked near the entrance to the house next door to Pine Lodge. They noticed it because it was an interesting model, an old Morgan sports car. They didn't think anything of it at the time, assumed it belonged to someone visiting in the area. They just commented briefly in passing and more or less forgot about it."

"Did they get the number?"

"Afraid not."

"Pity. Colour?"

"Dark, that's all."

Thanet reached for his pipe, began to fill it. "Sparks could be right, of course, there could be a perfectly innocent explanation for its being there, but . . ."

"I was thinking, just before you arrived . . . If Mrs Pettifer and her boyfriend were in this together . . ."

"He could have driven her down from London, you mean? Yes, the thought had crossed my mind. We'd better ring Miss Chivers. She'd probably know what sort of car Lee has at the moment, if he's got one."

"I tried, sir. But she's out for the day, apparently."

"I expect the Met could find out for us, without too much difficulty. We'll give them a ring in a minute."

"Anyway, as I say, I was thinking," Lineham said. "Just say she'd been biding her time, waiting for the right moment . . ." Eagerly he presented the scenario which Thanet had worked out in bed the night before. ". . . By midnight Pettifer would have been sufficiently muzzy not to cotton on to what was happening when she roused him to give him the overdose," he finished triumphantly.

Thanet had been lighting his pipe as he listened patiently and now he waited for a moment before he commented, pressing his match box over the bowl to get it drawing properly. Eventually, satisfied, he put the matches back in his pocket and sat back in his chair, waving away the coils of smoke that were obscuring his view of Lineham. "But if she did all that, why be stupid enough to put the whole scheme in jeopardy by taking Lee back to her hotel and spending the night with him? I know they took care not to be seen, but they must have realised the risk was there."

Lineham looked crestfallen. "True."

"And why be so idiotic as to leave her fingerprints all over the glass and so on. *Everyone* knows about fingerprints these days. And why be so vehement in insisting it couldn't have been suicide? Why show us that cruise booking, for instance? Why not just keep mum and hope we'd swallow the idea of suicide — hook, line and sinker?"

"Because she knew we'd be bound to find out he had no reason to kill himself and we'd get suspicious anyway? So she thought she'd put herself in the clear by getting in first?" Lineham pulled a face. "No, it's too feeble, isn't it?"

"It is, rather. But don't think I'm dismissing her entirely. We both know how apparently insuperable objections have a habit of melting away. We just haven't enough information at the moment. Perhaps the PM results will help." Thanet looked at his watch. "Surely they won't be long now . . . While we're waiting, could you give Mrs Pettifer a ring, tell her we'll be out to see her shortly?"

Lineham had only just replaced the receiver when the phone rang. He snatched it up, listened.

"Doc Mallard," he said, handing it to Thanet.

Thanet listened intently for a minute or so and then said, "Yes. Yes, I see. They're positive about that? Right. Oh, just one other point. Was there any sign of a head cold? Yes, a head cold . . . I see. Thanks. 'Bye." He put the phone down. "Doc Mallard was particularly interested, so he went along to watch. It's been confirmed that Pettifer died of an overdose, but of course the stomach contents have yet to be analysed."

"Did he have anything wrong with him?"

"As far as his health was concerned? No, nothing. He was unusually fit and there was no sign of organic disease."

"Nothing creepy, like leukaemia, which might not show up?"

"Well, apparently, if it were sufficiently advanced, leukaemia would show up — in an increase in the size of the spleen. In any case, Doc Mallard was his usual scrupulous self and got them to do an immediate blood test, in case the disease was in its very early stages. And there was nothing . . . I think we'd better play safe, Mike, arrange that the stomach contents are sent to London rather than to County Hall, just in case we have got a murder on our hands. Incidentally, there was one interesting point. There was no sign of a head cold, either."

"How could they tell?"

"There'd be something called hyperaemia — reddening — of the nasal passages. Odd . . . only last night I was thinking, no one else noticed that he had any sign of a cold — I specifically asked."

"But why on earth should Mrs Pettifer say he had a cold if he didn't?"

"I really can't imagine."

"Perhaps he was putting it on, to prevent her going to London."

"But she said he positively insisted she still went."

They stared at each other, baffled.

"It's only a trivial thing of course," Thanet said at last, "but it's like so many other things in this case. It just doesn't make sense. Ah well, perhaps it'll all become clear in the fullness of time. It's pointless to sit about here speculating any longer. Let's go out to see her. We'll just make those phone calls first. You get on to the Met, ask them if they can discreetly find out what sort of car Lee drives — I still don't want him alerted, by the way — and I'll make the arrangements to have the stomach contents sent to London."

On the way to Pine Lodge, Thanet stared moodily out of the window. Yesterday's crisp, bright weather had vanished overnight and the sky was a uniform, leaden grey. A steady drizzle was falling, slicking the pavements and blurring the silhouettes of roof-tops. The faces of passers-by were dour, as if the dreariness of the day had seeped into their souls.

"Why do they think we've got zebra crossings?" muttered Lineham, braking sharply as a pedestrian dashed out from the kerb.

Thanet glanced at the sergeant, his attention caught by some undertone in his voice. Lineham was driving with a frowning concentration, his eyes bleak. Thanet remembered what Joan had said last night. Perhaps he should at least give Lineham the opportunity to talk, if he wanted to.

"Anything wrong, Mike?"

Lineham glanced at him uneasily, shook his head. "I was only thinking about Mrs Pettifer."

Thanet had to accept the statement at its face value. He couldn't press the point. The opening had been there, if Lineham had wished to take it.

"What about her?"

"I really can't make her out."

"No. Ditto. Perhaps it's something to do with what we were saying the other day, that with actors we're constantly wondering if they're putting on a performance or not. And in view of what we've learnt about her since then, it's difficult to believe that she was completely sincere. And yet . . ."

"What?"

"I'm not sure," Thanet said slowly. "It's just that, well, that show of grief . . . There was something odd about it." He thought back, trying to put his finger on the elusive impression. "It's almost," he said at last, "as if she was surprised at herself, at the way she was reacting."

"I don't see what you're getting at."

Thanet grinned. "That's not surprising. I'm not really sure myself. If only we knew whether or not Pettifer knew she'd

106

been unfaithful to him.''

"It does seem to be the only possible reason he could have had, for killing himself.''

"But surely, Mike, if he had known, someone would have noticed? Mrs Price, for instance. She knew him well and she was there, in the house, all the time. Even if Pettifer had put on a brave front at work, to salvage his pride perhaps, surely Mrs Price would have seen some hint of the true state of affairs? But obviously she didn't. If she had, I'd have thought she'd be only too ready to say so. It's obvious she still disapproves of Mrs Pettifer.''

"Perhaps that's why Pettifer felt it necessary to put up a front at home, too.''

"I don't follow you.''

"Well, Pettifer must have been aware that Mrs Price didn't like his wife, disapproved of his second marriage, and I imagine he would have resented her attitude. I should think he would have felt it was none of her business. So, if he found out that she was right and he was wrong, then he would have found it very difficult to lose face by behaving in front of her in such a way as to show her his disillusionment.''

"Possibly. Even so, I can't help feeling it would have shown, in little ways — in a tone of voice, a look, a gesture.''

"Maybe.''

Thanet sighed. "What we really need is the opinion of someone in front of whom the Pettifers wouldn't have been on their guard, someone whose opinion wouldn't have mattered to them, or who could have observed them without their realising it.''

"Next thing we know, you'll be subpoenaing the flies on the wall,'' Lineham said with a grin.

Thanet laughed. "A fly on the wall would be perfect. Incidentally, while I'm talking to Mrs Pettifer, I'd like you to nip up and take a look at her room.''

"Won't she object?''

"I don't see why. After all, she's the one who's insisting he couldn't have killed himself. She can scarcely complain that we're being too thorough. We'll ask permission, of course, but frankly I can't see how she can refuse it. Did you search Andrew's room the other day, by the way?"

"Just a quick look, that's all."

"Go over it again, then."

"You don't think he's involved, do you?"

"Just being careful," Thanet said evasively. "Ah, here we are."

Mrs Price showed them into the drawing room. Gemma Pettifer was lying on the brocade sofa. There was a typescript propped up against the mound of her belly, but she wasn't reading. Thanet had the impression that they were disturbing some profound reverie; the expression on Gemma's face as she looked towards them was uncomprehending, her eyes glazed. She made no attempt to rise.

"Inpsector Thanet, Mrs Pettifer," Mrs Price repeated, raising her voice a little.

Gemma's eyes cleared and now there was recognition in them. "Oh, Inspector, forgive me." Awkwardly she swung her feet to the floor.

"Please," he said quickly, "don't get up. There's no need."

"Do sit down." Her glance included Lineham.

"I wonder . . . my sergeant wasn't able to finish looking around upstairs, the other day," Thanet said. "Do you think . . ."

"In my bedroom, you mean? By all means."

"And in Andrew's room too, if you don't mind."

"Andrew's?" Her eyebrows arched. "Well yes, of course, if it's necessary. Though I don't quite see . . ."

"Just routine," said Thanet. Oh, the usefulness of that blanket expression!

Lineham went out and Thanet sat down, taking his time and deliberately choosing a deep, comfortable armchair. Out of the corner of his eye he saw her relax, the lines of her body settling back into the cushioned depths of the sofa. Briefly, he reviewed in his mind what he had learned about this woman from Deborah Chivers. If the younger woman was to be believed, Gemma was self-centred, careless of other people's feelings, had a penchant for younger men . . . Not a pretty catalogue. Once again, he cursed the cloud of uncertainty which hovered over the manner of Pettifer's death, the resulting ambivalence which he, Thanet, felt towards Gemma Pettifer. Should he treat her as a grieving widow, or as a potential murderess? This wasn't going to be easy.

She was watching him expectantly. "Well?" she said with a faint smile. "What can I do for you, Inspector?"

He decided on strict neutrality. If she thought him unsympathetic, it couldn't be helped.

"The post mortem on your husband was carried out this morning," he began, and saw her flinch. "And it may interest you to know that there was no sign of illness."

"I'm not surprised. I told you, he was very fit, took very good care of his health . . ."

"So there's no possible reason for suicide there."

"But that's what I've been telling you!" she cried impatiently, swinging her feet to the floor and leaning forward intently. "There wasn't any reason, none at all. That's why . . ."

"Mrs Pettifer," Thanet interrupted. "I think I ought to tell you . . . We know about Mr Lee."

"Oh." She was silent for a few moments, folding her hands together and staring down at them. Then she raised her head to flash him a look of defiance. "But that makes no difference. My husband had no idea that Mr Lee and I . . ."

". . . were lovers?" Thanet finished for her. "How can you be sure of that?"

She raised her hands in a helpless gesture. "I just am, that's all."

"But what makes you so certain?"

"Oh come, Inspector. You're married, aren't you? If you'd found out that your wife was being unfaithful, do you mean to say that your attitude towards her would have remained completely unchanged?"

A palpable hit there, Thanet admitted silently. Because of course, it wouldn't have. "What I would or would not do in such circumstances is beside the point, Mrs Pettifer," he said calmly. "The point at issue is what your husband would or

109

would not have done. It is, as I'm sure you will agree, a matter of temperament."

"So?"

"I understand that your husband was rather a reserved man. If he had found out about your . . . affair, might he not simply have said nothing, brooded on it in private and, eventually, unable to live with the knowledge, have killed himself?"

"No!" It was a cry of pain.

Acting? wondered Thanet. If only he could make up his mind.

"Not with me," she was saying. "Not with me. He couldn't have hidden his feelings from me."

Nothing was going to make her budge, he could see that. Even to herself she could not begin to admit the possibility that he might have known of her disloyalty. Perhaps she really had cared for him, after all. And above all, if she had killed him, why not seize on this as the perfect reason for his having committed suicide, thereby putting her in the clear?

"And then there's the baby," she said, unconsciously taking up Thanet's line of thought. "He was so looking forward to the baby coming. Andy's adopted, you know, it would have been Arnold's first child. It took his breath away, when I first told him about it."

"He was surprised?"

"Surprised and delighted." She gave a reminiscent little smile. "He thought, you see, that I didn't want any . . . I'd made a bit of a thing about it, earlier on. Well, I was much younger then . . . Before he asked me to marry him he went to great pains to make sure I knew he wouldn't expect me to produce any children. He knew how much my career meant to me, you see. And he was very proud of me . . ."

"What made you change your mind? About having children, I mean?"

She shrugged. "I didn't actually make a conscious decision. But, underneath, I must have decided I wanted one. They say that if you forget to take the Pill, it shows that subconsciously you're wanting to conceive. So when I did . . . When you suddenly realise that the baby's not an abstract thing, it's actually there inside you, growing bigger with every day that passes . . . And if you've no real justification for killing it, for having an abortion . . . And anyway, I'm established in my profession now. I can pick and choose my parts. Taking time off to have a child isn't going to set me back. And motherhood's an important part of being a woman, isn't it? For all I know, it'll extend my powers as an actress into a whole new dimension.''

Thanet's sympathy — which had, despite his resolution to remain impartial, been growing by the minute — dissolved abruptly. A more self-centred reason for having a child he couldn't imagine.

"Would it surprise you," he said, aware that he was being rude in cutting her off like this, and not caring, "to know that according to the pathologist your husband had no cold symptoms whatsoever?''

And this did astonish her (or was she just acting, dammit?). Her eyes widened and her mouth dropped open slightly. "It certainly does.''

"Why?''

"Well, because he *said* he had a cold coming on. And he wasn't the sort of man to mention it unless he was pretty certain. I mean, usually I had to more or less make him go to bed, if there was anything wrong with him.''

"And that night?''

"That's why I'm surprised at what you say. That night he scarcely needed any persuading at all. He went off to bed like a lamb." She was frowning, looking as baffled as Thanet felt. "It's crazy. If he'd been the sort of man to play up like that in order to stop me going out, I could understand it. But he wasn't. Just the opposite, in fact. As I told you, when I suggested I cancel my engagement, he wouldn't hear of it. Insisted I still went . . .'' Suddenly her face crumpled and she buried it in her hands. "It's all like a nightmare," she said. "I keep thinking I'll wake up and he'll be there . . .''

Thanet could have sworn the emotion was genuine. He waited for a few moments then said, "When your husband came home that night, did he say anything about his car?''

111

He thought her shoulders tensed before she raised her head. "Oh yes," she said, "I meant to mention that to you. It was odd, wasn't it? I didn't even realise his car wasn't in the garage until Clough's left the keys with the policeman at the door."

"You didn't know your husband had left his car at the Centre?"

She shook her head. "He didn't say anything about it, so I assumed he'd driven home as usual. I rang Clough's, after the car was delivered here next morning, and they told me he'd asked them to fix it and bring it back here next day."

"I believe you said you took a taxi to the station?"

"That's right. I always do when I stay in town overnight. I don't like leaving my car in the station car park all night. Otherwise I'd have noticed my husband's car wasn't there when I went into the garage."

"Did he normally mention it, if something went wrong with his car?"

"Yes. Of course, there wasn't much time to talk, that evening. I could see as soon as he arrived home that he was looking under the weather. Though now that you say there was nothing wrong with him . . ." She put up her hands, began to massage her temples with her fingertips. "It's all so confusing . . ."

There was a knock at the door and Lineham came in, carrying a crumpled sheet of paper. "Sorry to interrupt, sir, but I thought you'd like to see this."

Thanet glanced at him sharply. There had been an undercurrent of emotion in Lineham's voice which Thanet couldn't quite identify. He took the proffered sheet of paper and his scalp prickled as he read it. The handwriting was different from that of the suicide note:

My darling, darling Gemma,
    You looked so beautiful last night, I can't get you out of my mind. Lying here on my bed I close my eyes and pretend that you are beside me, that I can touch —

Thanet glanced at Gemma Pettifer, who was watching him expectantly. "Would you excuse us for a moment?"

13

In the hall, he and Lineham conversed in whispers.

"Where did you find this?"

"In Andrew's room. Under one of the pedestals of his desk."

A draft, then, Thanet guessed, scrumpled up and discarded and, unknown to Andrew, kicked out of sight. So, had the final version ever been sent?

"What do you think, sir? Are we going to show it to her?"

Thanet shook his head. "Not just yet."

"But why not? I know she's pregnant and we have to be careful, but why should that always let her off the hook? If she really has seduced him, why should she get away with it?"

"I'm not thinking of her, Mike. Just consider for a moment how Andrew would feel if there isn't any truth in this, if this letter is just part of an adolescent fantasy . . . and we showed it to her."

Lineham's face showed that he had taken the point. "I see what you mean. What are we going to do, then?"

"Nothing for the moment."

Thanet went back into the drawing room. When he said that he and Lineham were leaving now, Gemma Pettifer frowned.

"That piece of paper your sergeant brought in. What was it?"

"I'm afraid I can't tell you that." Thanet was polite, but firm.

"Where did he find it, then? Surely I have a right to know that, at least."

"In Andrew's room."

"*An*drew's room?" The stress on the first syllable said:

113

But what possible interest could there be in anything found in Andrew's room?

"Yes. And now I'm afraid we really must go."

Lineham was waiting in the car.

"Well, Mike, what do you think?" Thanet asked, as he fastened his seat belt. "Fact or fantasy?"

"Thinking it over . . . fantasy."

"Why?"

"Well he is only fifteen . . ."

"Oh come on, Mike, don't be naive. You know as well as I do that these things happen."

"Yes." Lineham paused. "I suppose, if I'm honest, I just don't want it to be true. I felt sorry for Andrew the other day and I don't like the idea of his being in her clutches." He gave a shamefaced grin. "There speaks the detached investigator."

"Full marks for insight, anyway." Thanet was pleased. In his view a readiness to question his own motives and to understand his own reactions were hallmarks of the good detective. "Anyway, as it happens, I'm inclined to agree with you. I may be wrong, of course, but having seen Andrew I just can't visualise him having a torrid affair with his adoptive mother. Fantasising about one, yes . . . though it does explain his attitude to her the other day. Let's go and have a bite to eat, while we think about it."

Lineham waited until they had settled down in a quiet corner of the pub with their beer and pasties before saying, "What did you mean, about the letter explaining Andrew's attitude to Gemma?"

"Well, I think we were all a bit taken aback at that outburst of his, weren't we? But now, well, I can see that if he's had secret hankerings after Gemma he might well feel very guilty about them, angry with himself for having them."

"And he might have directed that anger against her instead?"

"Mmm," said Thanet, his mouth full of pasty. He chewed, swallowed. "He might even imagine that it had something to do with his father's death."

114

"You mean, that his father might have suspected that he and Gemma were having an affair and killed himself because of that?"

"I wouldn't think he'd have been as specific as that. If he had, he'd no doubt have seen how unlikely that was. No, I'd think it would be much more a generalised feeling of guilt, an irrational idea that he might somehow have contributed towards his father's depression. And if he did feel that, then this would account for his vehemence in insisting that it couldn't have been suicide."

"Because if it wasn't, he couldn't have helped bring it about?"

"Exactly."

"You're not suggesting he made up that bit about the spelling of his name?"

"Oh no. He produced evidence to back up what he said, remember. No, he was sincere enough. I'm just saying that we must be careful how much weight we place upon Andrew's opinion in view of what we now know he feels about Gemma."

"Of course, as you said, it could be true, though, couldn't it? They really could be having an affair, couldn't they? After all, we know how much she likes young men . . ."

"According to Deborah Chivers."

"Well yes, according to Deborah Chivers. But Lee's a good ten years younger than Mrs Pettifer, so there is some evidence to support the idea. And as her life has been so much more restricted lately, with the baby coming . . . She could just have thought Andrew would be a convenient stop-gap until she was able to get back to having regular fun and games in London, couldn't she?"

Thanet grinned. "You really don't like her, do you Mike? I thought you were very taken with her at first."

"That was before I got to know more about her." Briefly, Lineham's eyes were shadowed.

Was Lineham also expressing his disillusionment with Louise, Thanet wondered.

"Anyway, I agree with you. It's a possibility we can't

ignore. If they were lovers and Pettifer found out, he could have threatened to throw them both out, refuse to pay for Andrew's education . . ."

"What a prospect!" Lineham said gloomily. "Imagine arresting a fifteen-year-old schoolboy and a pregnant actress twice his age — his adoptive mother at that. The Press would have a field day."

"I don't think we'd better dwell on that one."

"How did Mrs Pettifer react when you told her we knew about her affair with Lee?"

Thanet told him.

"She was really upset at the idea that her husband might have known?"

"Quite independently of the possibility that that might have been why he comitted suicide, yes . . . . Or she seemed to be. That's the trouble. With her I can never make up my mind whether she's genuine or not . . . I really do wish we could find out if he did know."

"I don't see how we can."

"Wait a minute. You know what I was saying about an independent witness . . . I've just remembered. Mrs Barnet, the secretary at the Centre, mentioned some restaurant where Pettifer had taken his wife for an anniversary dinner recently — the Sitting Duck, that was it. Out Biddenden way. Do you know it?"

"I know *of* it. It's a bit beyond my pocket."

"It just occurs to me that if it's a fairly small place the owner might remember them. It might be worth going to see him, ask him how they seemed together."

"Yes."

"You sound doubtful, Mike."

"I'm not sure there'd be much point. After all, it is a public place. If Pettifer was so determined to keep up a front that even his housekeeper didn't know, I can't see that it would help."

"It just might. If Mrs Pettifer is lying and he did know about Lee, they might not have been so concerned to pretend that everything in the garden was lovely in front of a lot of strangers."

"You'd like me to go out there this afternoon, then?"

"I think so. Yes."

"Right." Lineham hesitated and then said, "You know, sir, it's only just occurred to me that for some reason we just aren't bothering to look very hard at anyone but Mrs Pettifer."

"What do you mean?"

"Well, assuming for a moment that it was murder, not suicide, then in the normal way of things, yes, I agree we'd look first at the wife. But, at the same time, we'd be investigating other possibilities — friends, business associates and so on . . . I know Dr Lowrie is checking the files for disturbed patients but apart from that we seem to be concentrating entirely on Mrs Pettifer."

Thanet was staring at him fixedly.

"Sir?" Lineham said uncertainly.

"You're right, Mike," Thanet said softly. "By God, you're right. Now, why is that?" He felt on the verge of recognising an important truth. It was there, hovering just beyond his grasp . . .

"Well," said Lineham, taking him literally. He began to tick the points off on his fingers. "One, there are the fingerprints. Did you ask her to explain them, by the way?"

Thanet was only half listening. "What? No. I'm holding back on that, for the moment."

"Two, we find she's got a lover and therefore a motive. Three, we're beginning to wonder whether we can believe a word she said — there's the business of the cold, for example . . . And that's about it."

They stared at each other blankly.

"You're right, Mike. It just isn't enough for us to be focusing exclusively on her. I can't think how it's happened. I started off with an open mind. When I saw Dr Lowrie, for instance, one of the first things I did was check his alibi. Though I haven't bothered to verify it . . . What the hell's the matter with me? Talk about slipping . . . Thanks Mike. Come on, drink up." Thanet stood up abruptly.

"Where are we going?" Lineham asked, in the car.

"Back to the office first. We're going to do a bit of catching up on lost time, so we'll need two cars. Now let's see . . ." Thanet took out his notebook. "We'll make a list. First, there's Andrew . . ."

"Andrew?"

"Of course. If only for elimination purposes. I don't like the idea, he's upset enough as it is . . . . And I certainly don't think we ought to speak to him directly at this stage — after all, he is at boarding school. It should be easy enough to check his whereabouts on Monday night. Then there's Mrs Price. And the partners — Doctors Lowrie, Braintree and Fir. Fir's away on holiday at the moment, but we'd better verify that. And lastly, there's Lee. That's about it, isn't it?"

"Unless Dr Lowrie has turned anyone up in the files."

"I should have thought he'd have been in touch with us, if he had. Right, we'll split them up between us, leaving Lee out for the moment. I want to wait until we find out whether that Morgan was his or not, first. So you take Andrew and Mrs Price, I'll take the doctors."

"What about the Sitting Duck? Shall I try and fit that in on the way back?"

"Yes." Thanet closed his notebook with a snap. "That's it, then . . . You know, Mike, there's one thing I keep coming back to, over and over again . . ."

"What's that?"

"This business of children. It really puzzles me."

"In what way?"

"Well I think Mrs Pettifer's attitude is understandable, just about. Initially she didn't want them because they would interfere with her career. When she found she was pregnant she'd reached the top of her profession, felt she could afford the time off. Also, she had realised there was a bonus to producing a child — she would enlarge her experience of life with a capital L. But him . . . well you don't make sure your prospective bride doesn't want children unless you're pretty well against having them yourself."

"Unless, as she said, he thought she wouldn't marry him unless he made it clear he didn't want a conventional wife and would be one-hundred-per-cent behind her continuing her career?''

''True. But there was no need to make an issue of it, was there? I mean, if he'd asked her to marry him and she'd refused on the grounds that it could interfere with her career, you could understand him *then* saying, well, I don't expect you to be a coventional wife, there'll be no need to have children and so on . . . But the impression I had — certainly from Deborah Chivers — was that he wanted to make sure Gemma didn't want them *before* he asked her to marry him.''

Lineham was shaking his head. ''I don't agree. I should have thought that, if you didn't like children and didn't want them, it's the very thing you *would* want to check out before you proposed. And remember, Pettifer was no spring chicken either. Apart from his dislike of children he might well have felt he just couldn't face the prospect of nappies, disturbed nights and disruption of routine all over again. People often do feel that, when they're getting on towards middle age.''

''Yes, I agree. But surely it's therefore all the more strange that, when she did tell him she was pregnant, he was over the moon about it.''

''Oh, I don't know. People do change their minds about such things. After all, he was supposed to be devoted to her. He probably didn't want to upset her.''

''Possibly. But I had the impression, from her, that it wasn't something they'd ever discussed, he was just presented with a *fait accompli*. I shouldn't have thought, from what we've heard about him, that he'd have been too pleased about that.''

''Even so, if he doted on her . . .''

''I suppose you're right. That's how it must have been.''

Back at the office there was as yet no word about Lee's car. Lineham set off at once for Merrisham to interview Mrs Price's sister and Thanet settled down to do some checking. First he rang his own doctor, Dr Phillips, who confirmed Lowrie's alibi in every detail. Satisfied, Thanet moved on to Dr Fir. Mrs Barnet at the Centre provided the information that, last Saturday, two days before Dr Pettifer's death, Dr

Fir and his family had left on a 10 a.m. British Airways flight from Heathrow for a three-week stay with his brother-in-law in New Zealand. It proved relatively simple to establish that the Firs had indeed left on their scheduled flight and would have arrived in New Zealand on Monday morning. So unless Fir had abandoned his family half-way and flown back to England . . . Too far-fetched, Thanet decided. Temporarily he shelved Fir as a suspect. Which left Braintree.

Thanet sat back and thought. He was still angry with himself that he had allowed himself to be so . . . blinkered, was the word, in focusing exclusively on Mrs Pettifer. He was glad that Lineham had seen what was happening, but humiliated that he had not been aware of it himself. How had it come about? He felt ruffled, as edgy as a cat that has been stroked the wrong way. He gave a wry grin. It's your ego that's been dented, he told himself. How *had* it come about though, he asked himself again. During that interview with Dr Lowrie he had certainly had an open mind . . . His eyes narrowed. He had just remembered Lowrie's evasiveness when asked if there had been any problems with the practice. It was remiss of him not to have followed that up before now. Perhaps, before seeing Braintree, it might be fruitful to see Lowrie again . . .

A second phone call to Mrs Barnet informed him that it was Dr Lowrie's afternoon off, but that Thanet could find him at the Inn in the Forest until three o'clock. Swimming.

On the way he wondered how Lowrie was getting on with checking Pettifer's files. The way he felt at the moment even a psychopath or two couldn't add much to his confusion.

14

Dr Lowrie was also floundering, though physically not metaphorically.

It was a brave man, thought Thanet, who decided to learn to swim in his late fifties. Most people would be afraid of looking foolish. He sat down in one of the white wrought-iron chairs tastefully arranged in the raised seating area at one end of the pool and waited for Lowrie to finish his lesson.

The Inn in the Forest had once been an undistinguished Victorian country house, its ugliness redeemed only by the beauty of its setting. Surrounded on three sides by dense deciduous woods (which at this time of the year were a kaleidoscope of colour) and on the fourth by a lake, its potential as a money-spinner had quickly been spotted by the one of the major hotel chains. Architects, consultants and environmentalists had been called in and almost before one could say "planning consent" the builders had arrived. Now, one would find it almost impossible to detect the presence of the original building in the shell of concrete, rustic wood and glass which had been constructed around it — and for those who liked canned comfort and a variety of entertainment on tap, it was a holiday paradise. Sailing, swimming, windsurfing, tennis, table-tennis, snooker, a choice of discos and no fewer than four restaurants ranging from the formal to the tastefully sleazy: it offered them all, confident that few prospective customers would spurn all of its attractions.

And although he hated to admit it, Thanet thought, gazing around, they would have been right, for the one redeeming feature in his eyes was the indoor swimming pool. It overlooked the lake, seemed almost, by some trick of perspective, to merge into it. Flanked by tall, curved white concrete wings which supported a high, glass bubble of a roof, it contrived despite its almost aggressive modernity to blend with the lake, the sky, the trees in a way which gave those who swam in it the illusion of being at one with nature. Entrance fees to this pool were high — ten times as much as those for the pool at the new sports centre in Sturrenden — but the setting was so delightful, the water so well-heated and the pool so uncrowded that a swimming session here was truly a delight and local people would bring their children as an occasional special treat. Thanet and his family had been twice, enjoying a picnic afterwards at the lakeside.

Thanet sat back in his chair and allowed himself to sink into a pleasant torpor induced by the warm, steamy atmosphere and the knowledge that there really was nothing to do but wait. Beyond the tall sliding glass doors lightly misted with condensation the colours of the forest trees were blurred, hazy as in an Impressionist painting and as Thanet relaxed the cries of those in the pool blurred too, became distanced as he began to drift towards sleep.

A child's sudden shriek aroused him and he sat up with a start. Dr Lowrie was still in the pool practising the leg movements for the breast stroke, grasping the instructor's long pole to keep afloat. As Thanet watched, the lesson ended and Lowrie waded to the steps and hauled himself out, gasping. Thanet half rose and called his name in a low voice. Lowrie looked up, raised his hand in response and went to retrieve a towel from the far end of the seating area before coming to join Thanet. They greeted each other, Lowrie towelling himself vigorously, his fat little paunch wobbling.

"I'm quite happy to wait while you get dressed," Thanet said.

"No, no. I'll be going in again later, when I've had a breather. I only have time to come once a week, so I have to make the most of it. Marvellous exercise, swimming." Lowrie sat down, towel slung around his shoulders and patted his stomach ruefully. "Though you might not think so, looking at this. Anno Domini, too much good food and too little exercise, I'm afraid. That's why I decided to take up swimming. I only started recently. Marvellous exercise," he repeated. "You use up 480 calories per hour, you know."

Thanet privately thought that he would prefer to deny himself four or five slices of bread a week, the equivalent in calorific value. Lowrie, with the enthusiasm of the newly converted, was still talking about the benefits of his chosen form of exercise: ". . . muscle tone . . . heart rate . . . reduction in weight . . ." punctuated Thanet's consideration of which subject to broach first. There was a lot to talk about.

He decided to begin on neutral ground and, when Lowrie eventually said, "But you haven't come to hear me talk about swimming," responded with, "I was wondering how you were getting on with checking through Dr Pettifer's files."

The jovial lines in Lowrie's face sagged. "I thought that might be why you're here. You're still working on the theory that he might have been murdered, then?"

"At present, yes."

"Are you sure? I mean, is it definite? Have you any conclusive evidence?"

"No. Not as yet. All imponderables, I'm afraid. But we can't afford to let the matter rest, just in case. Too much time would be lost."

"What about the post mortem?"

"Nothing significant. He was a healthy man, as you said. As a matter of interest, did you see him on the afternoon of the day he died?"

"Briefly, yes. Why?"

"Any sign of a cold?"

Lowrie considered. "Not as far as I remember, no."

"And the files?"

"Ah, yes." Lowrie sighed. "Well, I've been working on them every night, right through into the early hours . . ."

"You really should have allowed us to send someone to help you."

"No, I couldn't have done that, not under the circumstances. If we'd been certain it wasn't suicide, perhaps I would have felt justified, but as it was I felt I didn't even want Mrs Barnet to help. Anyway, I've been right through them now. I was going to give you a ring later on this afternoon. I'm afraid

123

there's no one who seems to be even a remote possibility. I told you I didn't think there would be."

"Why not?"

"Two main reasons, I suppose. First, as I said before, if there had been anyone with a strong enough grievance against Pettifer to want to murder him, then I really can't believe that I wouldn't have heard about it. I simply couldn't see him attacking out of the blue. From what I've heard — and I must admit I haven't had any experience of such a situation, thank God — such people usually kick up a terrible stink. Secondly, even if such a person did attempt murder, I can't see him using the drink-and-drugs method. It's too quiet, too . . . comfortable. He'd be wanting not only to release his own feelings of violence, but to make Pettifer suffer in the manner of his death, in payment for the suffering he'd caused. Wouldn't you agree?"

"Yes I do. So I suppose that's that. I apologise for wasting your time."

Lowrie shrugged. "I can see that it had to be done."

Thanet took his pipe from his pocket, held it up. "Do you mind?"

"Go ahead."

Thanet took out his tobacco pouch and began to fill the bowl. The next topic was a delicate one. How best to broach it without making Lowrie clam up, that was the question. He gave the little doctor an assessing glance, caught his eye.

"Come on, Inspector. Out with it. I can see you're wondering how to put what you want to ask me next."

Thanet gave a wry smile. "That was below the belt, Dr Lowrie. I'm the one who's supposed to be reading you, not the other way around."

"Long practice," said Lowrie, with a hint of smugness. "An essential weapon in the GP's armoury. You wouldn't believe how inarticulate some patients can be."

"I'll be frank, then. When I last saw you I asked if there were any problems with the practice which might have preyed on Pettifer's mind. I had the impression you were holding something back."

"I see." Lowrie looked away, through the tall glass doors and across the lake, as if the answer to his dilemma were hidden in the distant trees. "Well," he said at last, "I suppose there's no reason why I shouldn't tell you. If I don't, you won't rest until you find out from someone else . . . The truth is, Pettifer was very autocratic, and this caused certain tensions."

"What sort of tensions?"

"Well take policy decisions, for example. We all have different ideas on how the practice should be run and Pettifer tended to steamroller them. The situation wasn't in the least unusual. You'd find it in many group practices."

"Can you give me an example of the sort of decision you're talking about?"

"Well, take a very simple issue like the number of patients in the practice. As you know, we have around 11,500. Now, in an expanding area like Sturrenden you have a problem. Theoretically the quota of patients per doctor is supposed to be 2,500 — don't ask me why, the powers that be have decided that — so in a practice with four partners that would mean ten thousand patients in toto. So, what happens when you get to eleven thousand? Do you close your list? If not, where do you stop?"

"And what did Dr Pettifer want to do?"

"Go on expanding. Let me explain. We all work in different ways. A man like Pettifer is brisk, thorough, a very good doctor diagnostically, as I said, but not very interested in his patients as people, tending to see them as walking case histories. Therefore he could get through his surgeries pretty briskly and be away on his visits by ten in the morning. Whereas Dr Braintree, for example, the youngest of the partners, is very interested in the psychosomatic origins of his patients' illnesses and therefore tends to spend much longer with them. So in any dispute over increasing our quotas — and believe me, the question is a perennial headache — Pettifer would be for, Braintree against. And Pettifer, of course, would win."

"And you?"

"Would tend toward supporting Braintree. But it would

make no difference. Pettifer had perfected the technique of overruling others with the minimum of fuss. He would listen but refuse to budge. If we became heated, he would become the opposite — ice-cold. It never failed. But I can assure you, Inspector, that none of us ever felt sufficiently strongly about it to want to kill him off to get our own way."

Until now Lowrie had been completely frank, Thanet was sure of it, but suddenly he was convinced that he was lying — or at least skirting around the truth.

"Not about that, perhaps . . . but about something else?"

Lowrie tugged his towel more closely around his shoulders and sighed. "I suppose if I don't tell you, someone else will, and I'd rather you heard it from me and got the facts straight. There has been some trouble between Braintree and Pettifer."

"What kind of trouble?"

Braintree had apparently been precipitated into the classic doctor's nightmare. A prescription of his had been misread, too strong a dosage of a drug had been administered, and a patient had almost died. Despite the fact that the mistake had been as much the dispenser's as the doctor's, Pettifer had been furious, had refused to listen to reason. In his view the whole affair was inexcusable. Doctors' handwriting might be notoriously illegible, but it was criminally irresponsible not to ensure that quantities and strengths of dosage were crystal clear. Braintree, who tended in any case to be over-sensitive and who, to cap it all, was having serious marital problems, had had a minor nervous breakdown as a consequence and had only recently started seeing a low quota of patients again after a gap of nine months.

"So you can imagine, Pettifer hasn't been too popular lately. But I repeat, emphatically, that none of us hated him enough to kill him."

"Not even Braintree?"

"Strangely enough, Braintree least of all. In an odd way he even has reason to be grateful to Pettifer. Braintree's breakdown has brought him and his wife much closer. Perhaps they needed something as dramatic as that to bring them to their senses. They seem much happier together now."

"You haven't once mentioned Dr Fir. How about him? How did he get on with Dr Pettifer?"

"Well enough. If I haven't mentioned him it's because he's a very equable type who gets on well with most people . . . Look, I'm not trying to avoid the issue, but I am getting rather chilly. Have we nearly finished because if not I think I'd better get dressed."

"I'm afraid there are still one or two points I'd like to discuss with you . . . Sorry. You won't get your second dip after all, will you?"

Lowrie stood up. "In that case . . . I won't be long."

He headed for the changing rooms, a short, plump and slightly comic figure in his brief bathing trunks. Thanet watched him go with something approaching affection. He saw so many people in the course of his work and most of them were either nervous, aggressive or devious. Many were outright liars and almost all were on the defensive. It was a pleasure to come across a witness like Dr Lowrie, who was both frank and perceptive as well as cooperative.

Although, he reminded himself as he went across to the hot-drinks dispenser to fetch two cups of coffee, the most dangerous witness of all was the one who could convincingly present himself as credible while having something to conceal . . .

"I thought you could do with a hot drink," he said when Lowrie returned.

"That's very kind of you."

Thanet waited until Lowrie had sipped at his coffee before saying, "Would it surprise you, doctor, to learn that Mrs Pettifer has a lover?"

Lowrie hadn't known, Thanet was sure of it. Astonishment, disbelief, enlightenment flitted in swift succession across the little doctor's chubby features.

"But in that case . . . why all this talk about murder?"

"What do you mean?" Though Thanet knew, of course.

"Well it's obvious, isn't it? I told you before, Inspector, Pettifer worshipped that wife of his. If he'd found out she was being unfaithful to him . . . it's the one reason I could accept for his having committed suicide."

127

"Ah, but did he?" Thanet said softly. "Find out, I mean?"

Lowrie grimaced. "I see what you mean." He was silent for a while, thinking. "No," he said reluctantly at last. "I'd like to say yes, it would simplify matters so much, wouldn't it? But I must admit that, no, I don't think he did. If he had . . . No. He didn't know, I'm sure of it. Which of course leaves us back at square one, doesn't it? Except that . . ." Lowrie's eyes dilated slightly. "Oh," he said. "Oh dear . . . This is beginning to look rather unpleasant, isn't it?"

"Shall we say, it opens up certain avenues of speculation. Which, forgive me, I really don't feel free to discuss with you . . . I wonder, Doctor Lowrie, if you could tell me a little more about Pettifer's attitude to children — or perhaps I should say, to fatherhood?"

"I'm not sure that I can add much to what I said last time."

"I just find it rather surprising that, although he made it clear he didn't want any children, he was apparently delighted when his wife told him she was pregnant."

"I don't think it was so much a matter of his not wanting any as trying to assure her he wouldn't expect her to give up her career to have them. Anyway, I told you, people react in peculiar ways to the prospect of parenthood. When a child is no longer a hypothesis but a reality . . . I suppose it's gut reaction rather than an intellectual response. The idea of being reproduced . . . there's something irresistible about it, to a man who's never had a child of his own."

"What was his attitude to the fact that his first wife couldn't have any?"

"Pretty phlegmatic. To have shown disappointment would, to him, have been disloyalty. Poor Diana, she really went through the mill over it. Had endless tests, a couple of minor operations, you know the sort of thing . . . And yet, strangely enough, I wouldn't have called her the maternal type, either."

"He was fond of her?"

"Fond is a good word. They got on well, had a good relationship, but a man like Pettifer only goes overboard once

128

in a lifetime. That's why it hit him so hard when it happened. I don't think he could ever have visualised feeling as he did about Gemma."

"Why did he marry the first time, then, do you think?"

"It was really almost a business arrangement, I should say. An arranged marriage, though with the consent and cooperation of both parties. Diana was an only child and her father was at that time the senior partner in the practice, and on the verge of retirement. He wanted to see her settled, she wanted a home and a husband and Pettifer . . . well, I suppose he saw the advantages of the match when it was offered him on a plate. And as I said, I think he was genuinely fond of Diana. Fond enough to go along with it when she eventually decided she wanted to adopt." Lowrie gave an indulgent smile. "His mother-in-law, Diana's mother, was a character. When his father-in-law died and she moved away, I really missed her for a time."

"She's still alive?"

"So far as I know. She was much younger than her husband. I have a feeling she went to live with her mother, Diana's grandmother. The old lady must be pretty ancient by now, if she's still with us."

"Where did they go, do you know?"

"Somewhere near Headcorn, I believe. I think I remember hearing something about converting an oast house."

"What was her name?"

"Blaidon. Dr Blaidon, her husband, was the founder member of the practice. At that time it was based in Pine Lodge."

"I had the impression that Dr Pettifer's first wife was a wealthy woman."

"That's right. Her grandfather made a small fortune in the grain business, but her father wasn't interested in carrying it on. He'd always wanted to be a doctor and so Diana's grandfather agreed to set him up in this practice. Dr Blaidon and Pettifer were alike in that having a generous private income didn't stop them from working just as hard as if their living depended on it."

"I wonder how many of us would do that, if we had the

129

choice," Thanet said with a smile, getting to his feet.

"Not I, for one," Lowrie responded. "Oh, I might have once, but now . . . well, it won't be too long before I retire and I must say I'm looking forward to it."

They parted amicably.

The interview with Dr Lowrie had taken rather longer than Thanet had thought it would. He decided to call at the office to see if Lineham was back before trying to get hold of Dr Braintree.

Lineham was on the telephone.

"The adoption agency," he said, when he had finished the call. "I got the address from Dr Pettifer's files. I thought it might be worth checking to see what they thought of the Pettifers as adoptive parents."

"Good idea. And . . .?"

"If Pettifer wasn't too keen, he certainly didn't show it. They were considered an eminently suitable couple."

"Hmm . . . Well, it was worth a phone call, anyway. What else have you found out?"

"It looks as though Andrew's in the clear, you'll be glad to hear. He was playing in an away match in Sussex on Monday afternoon. The coach didn't get back until eight-thirty, then it was supper, baths and bed. He shares a room with two other boys and one of them was sick at about eleven o'clock that night. Andrew fetched the school matron and helped transfer some of the boy's stuff to the sanitorium."

"Good." It was no more than Thanet had expected, but he was still relieved. "What about Mrs Price?"

Lineham grinned broadly. "D'you know what she was up to? Lecturing, if you please!"

"Lecturing?"

"Well, in a manner of speaking. She was giving a talk to the Merrisham Women's Institute on 'Herbs in the Modern Kitchen.' "

"Good for her. I hope they paid her a nice fat fee."

"I don't know about that, but there's no doubt she was there all right. Arrived at the time she said she did, spent the night with her sister, caught the workmen's bus back early the next morning — according to the sister, anyway."

"And you believed her."

"Yes, I did. In any case, the WI meeting didn't break up until ten-fifteen and then Mrs Price's sister asked some friends back to have coffee with them. That took another hour or so. So unless Mrs Price had a magic carpet . . ."

"Did you check up with the friends?"

"One of the women concerned happened to come in while I was talking to Mrs Price's sister. And yes, she confirmed it all — I did it as tactfully as I could. I didn't want to cause a lot of gossip unnecessarily."

"Fair enough. Interesting, though, isn't it? That's why she asked Pettifer for the evening off so far ahead. Three months ago, didn't she say?"

"That's right. I remember."

"He knew as long ago as that," murmured Thanet. Somehow, the thought now seemed significant, though he couldn't see why it should be.

"On the way back I called in at the Sitting Duck,' said Lineham. "It's owned by a chap called Frith. He and his wife wait at table when they're very busy and they both helped serve the Pettifers on the night of the anniversary dinner. They remember the occasion well because Pettifer made such a production of it — a special meal, ordered in advance, all his wife's favourites . . . champagne and roses waiting on the table when they arrived . . ."

"She certainly brought out the romantic in him, didn't she? How did they seem together that evening?"

"All lovey-dovey. Long looks, holding hands, that sort of thing . . ."

The telephone rang. It was the lab. They'd run the tests for paracetamol first, at Thanet's request, with negative results. With the field now wide open for the drug that killed Pettifer, it might be days before they came up with an answer. They did however confirm that Pettifer had taken a milky drink some hours before he died.

"So she was lying about the paracetamol," Lineham said with satisfaction.

"Presumably. Though I don't see why she should have. And I can't really see that it gets us much further."

The telephone rang again. And this time it was important. Lineham could tell by the narrowing of Thanet's eyes, that alert, focusing look. He waited, eagerly.

"Lee does own an old Morgan," Thanet said, putting the phone down. "And it really would be too much of a coincidence if there were two of them in this case. I think we're temporarily entitled to assume that the one parked near Pettifer's house that night was Lee's, don't you? Come on, I think it's time we paid another visit to Mrs Pettifer. She really has got some explaining to do now."

She might be a good actress, he thought as he and Lineham hurried down the stairs, but he didn't see how she was going to talk herself out of this one.

15

It was dark by now and, illumined from within, the stained-glass panels on either side of the front door of Pine Lodge glowed sapphire and emerald, ruby and gold as Lineham brought the car to a halt on the gravelled drive.

It was some minutes before Mrs Price answered the door. She had evidently been upstairs, for they glimpsed a descending blur of movement before she called out nervously, "Who is it?"

"Inspector Thanet, Mrs Price."

Bolts were drawn, a chain rattled and the key turned in the lock before the door swung open. "I'm sorry," she said. "I seem to be a bundle of nerves these days. I am glad you've come, Inspector," she added as the two men stepped past her into the hall. "It's Mrs Pettifer." And her eyes darted sideways and upwards at the stairs.

Thanet noticed that she was wearing her wrap-over flowered apron inside out.

"What's the matter with Mrs Pettifer?" he said.

"I don't know." Mrs Price clasped her hands together and began to massage the back of one hand with the fingers of the other, as if trying to erase her anxiety. "She's been up there for hours, ever since lunch in fact. She said she felt tired, she was going to lie down for a bit. And now, well, she's locked the door and she won't answer."

Thanet and Lineham exchanged a glance, the same thought in both their minds.

"We'll go up and take a look, shall we?" Thanet set off up the stairs without waiting for an answer. Lineham followed and Mrs Price came behind, more slowly.

No light showed beneath Gemma Pettifer's door. Thanet

knocked gently. "Mrs Pettifer," he called in a low voice, trying to betray none of the urgency he felt. "It's Inspector Thanet. I'd like a word, if I may."

No answer.

Thanet called again, a little more loudly, but still there was no sound from within. Finally, "Mrs Pettifer," he said, very distinctly, "you must realise we're getting worried about you. Please, open the door, or I'm afraid we'll have to force it."

Was that a sound? He strained to listen more intently. Then light spilled across the toes of his shoes. He felt taut nerves relax and, glancing over his shoulder at the others, saw his own relief mirrored in their faces.

The sounds within were more distinct now and he waited without urgency, content to be patient. Finally, the door opened.

"Are you all right, Mrs Pettifer?" he said.

A fatuous question. Patently, she wasn't. She looked dazed, drugged — sleeping pills, perhaps? — and her long hair was tangled, matted almost, as if it hadn't been combed for a very long time. Her robe, hastily dragged on, imperfectly concealed her swollen belly and with one hand she clutched it together across her breasts. With the other she supported herself against the door jamb, swaying a little and sagging as if she were on the verge of collapse.

"Perhaps you ought to lie down again," he murmured, acting swiftly. Deftly he stepped around her, began to persuade her back towards the bed, half supporting her. They were almost there when he sensed the beginnings of resistance, a stiffening of her body, and he could almost feel the effort with which she stopped, set her shoulders back and stepped away from his arm.

"It's all right, Inspector, thank you. I . . . it's just that I was still half asleep."

It was an admirable effort, but the flatness of her tone betrayed her. It had been far more than that, he could tell. He studied her face closely, shocked by her bleached pallor, the bruised hollows beneath her eyes and the dullness of the eyes themselves. Delayed shock, he judged. It would be inhuman to

134

question her in this state. She needed a doctor, not a policeman.

She was asking him what he wanted to see her about, seating herself on the chaise-longue near the window.

"It doesn't matter," Thanet said. "It can wait until tomorrow. I can see you're not well. I apologise for disturbing you."

Some of his colleagues, he knew, would find his attitude laughable. The weaker your adversary the better, they would say. And on occasion, with case-hardened villains, he would agree with them. But in a case like this, when even now there was no certainty of murder, only a suspicion of it, the idea of taking advantage of Gemma Pettifer's condition sickened him. He began to move towards the door.

"No, wait!" She lifted her hand imperiously. "I really would rather hear it now," she said. "Otherwise," and she gave a travesty of a smile, "I shall lie awake all night worrying about it."

She might have wanted it to appear a joke, but Thanet could see that she meant it. He hesitated.

"I don't think you're really up to it."

"Nonsense. I'm fine, really. I told you. I was very soundly asleep, that's all, when you knocked. And don't apologise again, it's not necessary. Now please, do sit down, Inspector. It's all right, Mrs Price. Don't look so worried. Give me a few minutes after the Inspector has gone and I'll be down for supper. Something light. A little cold chicken and some salad, I think."

It was a brave attempt and Thanet saluted it by giving in, seating himself on the chair towards which she had waved him. Lineham sat down gingerly on the edge of the bed.

"Now then, Inspector," she said. She folded her hands in her lap and looked at him expectantly.

"Would it surprise you, Mrs Pettifer, to learn that whatever it was that killed your husband, it wasn't paracetamol?"

"Not really. Because I still can't, and won't, believe he committed suicide. In which case I wouldn't expect him to have been given what we normally use."

"But you're still certain that it was paracetamol you

135

gave him earlier in the evening?''

"Oh yes, absolutely. I told you, we never kept anything else in the house — apart from the drugs my husband would carry in his bag, of course. But I would never have dreamt of touching those.''

"Did you actually see your husband take the tablets?''

She frowned, thinking back. "I don't think so . . . No, I remember now, I went back into my room. I was more or less ready to leave by then and I realised I'd forgotten to put out the typescript I wanted to take with me — the play I wanted to discuss with my agent.''

"Could you tell us exactly what you did do, from the time you came upstairs?''

"I'll try. Let me see . . . I got changed while my husband was having a bath. I'd made up earlier, before he got home. When I heard him come out of the bathroom I went downstairs, made the cocoa and took it up to his room. He was in bed by then. I put the mug down on his bedside table and went into the bathroom for the paracetamol. I returned to his room, handed him the tablets, then went back into my room. I took the typescript from the drawer in my bedside table and laid it beside my handbag on the bed. Then I went back into my husband's room, to say goodbye to him.''

"Had he taken the tablets?''

"Well I assumed he had, naturally. After all, he wasn't a child, Inspector. I didn't feel I had to stand over him and watch while he took them.''

"No, I can see that. What was he doing?''

"Sitting up in bed, holding the mug of cocoa.''

"Drinking it?''

"He had both hands clasped around it, as if he was cold. When I came in, he put it down on his bedside table.''

"Was there anything else on the table?''

She passed her hand over her forehead, as if the strain of recalling all these details was beginning to tell on her. "No, I don't think so. No, I'm sure there wasn't.''

"Did he say anything?''

"He said . . . he said . . .'' To Thanet's dismay her face crumpled and her eyes filled with tears. She reached blindly for a box of tissues which stood on a little table beside her.

"Look, I really think we'd better leave this till morning," said Thanet.

She shook her head vehemently. "No. No, it's all right. Really. It's just that . . ." She blew her nose. "It was the last thing he ever said to me, you see, and I didn't know . . . He said, 'Don't kiss me, darling. I don't want you to catch my cold.' " Her lips twisted. "It just seems such a . . . trivial way of ending a life together."

Thanet had heard this many times before. "If only I'd known", people would say. To be deprived of saying goodbye made them feel cheated, as though some premonition should have warned them to invest the occasion with a proper dignity. He sometimes felt that the ideal way to live would be always to treat each day, each encounter with loved ones, as one's last. Only thus could one avoid the endless self-reproach, self-recrimination, with which so many flagellate themselves after a sudden loss. A counsel of perfection, of course, he knew that . . .

"If only I'd insisted on staying . . ." she was saying.

"It's pointless reproaching yourself in that way. Your husband insisted, you said."

"I know. All the same . . . If I'd stayed, he might still be alive now."

"That's really most unlikely. If someone is determined to commit suicide . . ."

"But he didn't!" she flared. "How often do I have to tell you? He couldn't have . . ."

"So you keep on saying. But have you ever given any thoughts to the mechanics of it?"

"What do you mean?"

"Well, we both know that as a doctor he would never have been so stupid as to go to bed with a container of pills and a bottle of alcohol on his bedside table. Agreed?"

She nodded.

"And so, if we rule out both suicide and accident, we are left with only one other alternative."

"Murder," she whispered. "Go on, say it. I've said it over

137

and over again in my mind and now I've just got to say it aloud. Murder, murder, murd . . ." She was shaking and her mouth was out of control. She pressed the back of one hand against her lips and stared at Thanet, her eyes huge and pleading, begging for understanding.

"Mrs Pettifer," said Thanet. "I really must insist that we continue this conversation tomorrow morning. After a good night's rest . . ."

"But don't you see, I won't get a good night's rest if we stop now! Look, I'm sorry . . . It was just such a relief to get it out at last . . . Just give me a few moments and I'll be all right . . ." She put her head back and took several deep, rhythmic breaths. Then she ran her hand through her hair, faced him gravely. "You see," she said. "I'm fine now."

Thanet did see. He saw that Gemma Pettifer was able to discipline her physical reactions to a quite remarkable degree, somehow to divorce mind and body so that her outward behaviour gave no indication of her true feelings. It was, he supposed, an essential element of the actor's craft. He had heard of actors who could be in a towering rage behind the scenes and could simply switch that anger off, could walk on stage and take part in the sweetest of love scenes without betraying even a hint of the true state of their emotions. So, how much could he believe of what Gemma allowed him to see? And yet . . . he studied her near-haggard appearance, the drained pallor of her skin . . . She had not known that she was going to have an audience tonight. Was he being unjust to her? Or — and he could not dismiss the possibility — was this the face of guilt?

She was waiting, watching him intently. "You were saying that we are left with only one other alternative, Inspector."

Mentally, he shrugged his shoulders. If this was what she wanted . . .

"Murder, as you so rightly said, Mrs Pettifer. But if someone did kill your husband, how did he manage to do it? There was no sign of a forced entry, so how did he get in? And how did he administer the overdose?"

"Well . . ." She fell silent, her eyes abstracted. "I suppose," she said at last, "if it was some patient of my husband's, someone with a grudge against him . . . One does hear of such things, after all. Someone who felt that he had been badly treated, or who had lost a relation — a wife, or even a child — and felt that my husband had been neglectful or had prescribed the wrong course of treatment . . ."

Or a junior doctor who felt he'd been given a raw deal, thought Thanet. "Do you know of any such person?"

"No. But then, I wouldn't have. My husband never discussed his work with me." She shivered and drew her robe more closely about her.

Thanet remembered her revulsion towards any kind of sickness.

"Go on," he said.

"Well, my husband was a very conscientious man. Even if he hadn't been feeling well himself, if a patient had come knocking at the door Arnold might well have gone down to see what was the matter."

"Would he have let him in?"

"Oh, I should think so. In any case, he would hardly have stayed talking on the doorstep in his dressing gown, would he?"

"And then?"

"Well, if the man had appeared distressed, Arnold could have offered him a drink . . ." She grimaced. "No, to be honest, I can't see Arnold offering a patient a drink . . . Well, then, could this visitor have knocked my husband out, carried him upstairs and then have dissolved the tablets, got him to drink the solution while he was still dazed, before he came around properly?"

"But your husband wasn't knocked out. There was no sign of a blow to the head or indeed of any other sign of violence."

"Then it must have been someone he knew socially, someone to whom Arnold would have offered a drink. Then the drug could have been slipped into Arnold's glass . . ." Her eyes flew open wide.

"What is it?"

"I've just thought. How stupid of me not to have seen it

139

before, how incredibly stupid . . ."

"What?"

"Desmond Braintree! There was all that performance about an illegible prescription!" Breathlessly she related once more the facts given to Thanet by Dr Lowrie. "Don't you see?" she finished.

Had she had Braintree in mind right from the beginning of this conversation? Thanet wondered. Had he been watching once more a carefully calculated performance?

"Mrs Pettifer," he said, avoiding a direct answer, "let me just get this clear. You are suggesting that your husband's death was murder, carefully arranged to look like suicide."

"Yes," she said impatiently. "Of course I am, yes. And . . ."

"Please, just a moment. Now, if that is so, perhaps you could help me to understand one or two points which are puzzling me."

"By all means, if I can."

Thanet gave her an assessing look. Was she fit to be challenged? He could scarcely stop now. He seemed to have manoeuvred himself into a position where he had no choice but to go on. And after all, he told himself, she had several times been given the opportunity to call a halt, if she so wished.

"First, then," he said, ticking off his fingers, "you tell us that your husband had a cold. But he didn't. Two, you tell us that you gave him paracetamol, but we know that he didn't take any. Three . . ."

He paused. Gemma Pettifer was sitting quite still on the very edge of the chaise-longue, leaning forward and staring at him as if mesmerised.

"Three. You say that when you left your husband in bed that night there was nothing on his bedside table. But *your* fingerprints as well as his were on the bottle of port which we found on that table after his death and what is more your fingerprints and *yours alone* were found on both the empty glass and on the container which had held the tablets that killed him . . . Mike, quick!"

Gemma Pettifer's eyes had rolled up, her body had begun to sag, to slide. Both men leapt forward.

They just managed to catch her before she hit the floor.

16

"She's guilty, isn't she?" said Lineham. "I mean, the way she reacted . . ."

"I don't know," Thanet snapped. "And that's the truth."

They were driving back to the office. When Gemma Pettifer had collapsed they had carried her across to her bed and summoned first Mrs Price, then Dr Barson, who had come at once. Thanet was still smarting from the memory of Barson's comments when he had seen his patient's condition.

"I should have trusted my own judgement," Thanet growled, "and not gone on when she insisted. I could see she was . . ."

Lineham wasn't listening. "It's obvious she was just trying to put us off the scent by pointing us in the direction of Dr Braintree. We surely don't need much more before we . . ."

"Mike."

". . . charge her. We still haven't questioned her . . ."

"Mike!"

". . . about the car, of course. But if she was here that night . . ."

"MIKE!"

Lineham cast an astonished glance at Thanet, who very rarely raised his voice. "Yes?"

"Just ease your foot off that accelerator, will you? You're making me nervous. And stop letting your imagination run away with you."

"Imagination! Those things you mentioned to her weren't imagination, were they? Nor was her reaction . . ."

"Maybe not. But neither are they conclusive enough to make me want to charge her. Just because she's a liar, it doesn't necessarily mean that she's a murderer."

"I can see that. But the fingerprints . . ."

"Their significance could be demolished by any good defence counsel. The container could well have been used before, handled by her on some previous occasion. Ditto the glass."

"But the fact that his prints weren't on either of them . . .!"

"I agree, that's difficult to explain away. Nevertheless, it's not enough for a conviction and you know it."

"Then there's the note. If Pettifer didn't write it, she'd have had a better opportunity to practise copying his handwriting than anyone."

"Yes, *if*. We still don't know it wasn't genuine. Anyway, you know how easy it is to come unstuck over circumstantial evidence. We need more than that, much more, before she could be charged."

"But there is more! There's motive . . ."

Grudgingly Thanet conceded that he had to agree to that.

"And opportunity, too. Now that we know Lee's car was seen in the vicinity that night."

"We don't *know*," Thanet objected. "We're just assuming."

"Well, yes, I realise that, but you said yourself that it would be too much of a coincidence if there were two vintage Morgans in this case."

"I'm well aware what I said," snapped Thanet.

Lineham knew when to let something drop. He allowed several minutes to pass before he said diffidently, "As a matter of interest, sir, why didn't you bring the matter of the car up first? I mean, that was why we went to see her, after all."

"Honestly, Mike, I sometimes wonder if you're human! You could see for yourself the state she was in . . ."

"If it was genuine. Well," he said, to Thanet's furious look, "you did say yourself that it was difficult to tell if she was acting or not."

"All right, Mike. Look, I'm sorry. There's no reason why you should be getting the sharp edge of my tongue, just because I'm feeling guilty about her passing out like that. But it was a genuine collapse. Dr Barson was pretty unequivocal about that, wasn't he?"

They exchanged rueful grins.

"Look," Thanet said, "I concede all the points you're making. Dammit, I know that practically everything new we learn seems to point to her, and yet . . . The truth is, Mike, there's something about this case that makes me very uneasy."

"Uneasy?"

"Yes. It's all wrong, somehow. Not just the things which don't add up. It feels wrong. And I just can't see why. What is more, I simply don't understand why, if she did kill him and set it up to look like suicide, she should be handing us the theory on a plate, putting the noose around her own neck, so to speak."

Lineham had no answer to that. They had arrived back now, and they climbed the stairs to the office in silence.

Thanet checked quickly to see if anything interesting had come in, but nothing had. He plumped down into his chair with a sigh. His back gave a protesting twinge. This was an infallible signal that it was time he went home. Ever since he had injured it a few years ago it had played up when he was tired. He eased himself into a more comfortable position and glanced at his watch: half past seven and the day's reports still to do.

"Better get on with it, I suppose," he said.

Lineham nodded, pulled his typewriter towards him and began to peck at it, two-fingered.

But Thanet remained quite still, gazing into space. Gemma Pettifer bothered him. His feeling of guilt had ebbed and he was angry with himself for having over-reacted. After all, he told himself irritably, if she were guilty, he simply could not allow diffidence to put a straitjacket on him. Sooner or later she would have to be tackled and that was that. But next time he would consult Dr Barson first, insist that Barson accompany him, if possible. He made a mental note to ring Barson first thing in the morning.

Meanwhile, there was another possible approach to the problem.

"Fancy a trip to London tomorrow, Mike?"

Lineham raised an abstracted face. "Sir?"

Thanet explained. It was time to tackle Gemma's lover, Rowan Lee. Also, the night porter at the Lombard should be questioned, to see if he had noticed the pair return to the hotel in the early hours of Tuesday morning. Lineham would have to go to London alone. If Barson agreed, Thanet wanted to see Gemma Pettifer again in the morning. Afterwards, he would interview Dr Braintree and then, if he could trace her . . . Here he grew vague, despite Lineham's evident curiosity.

Thanet returned to his musing. Gemma Pettifer. She really was an enigma. If only he could make up his mind whether her distress was genuine . . . Thinking back, he was becoming more and more convinced that it was. In anyone else he would unhesitatingly have diagnosed delayed shock, perhaps even the first stages of a plunge into clinical depression. And if that were true . . . well, he didn't understand it. By all accounts she was hard, self-seeking, had married her husband for security rather than love. He would have expected a show of grief, yes, but this . . .

With a sigh, he settled down to his reports.

17

Thanet rang Dr Barson at a quarter to nine next morning, as early as he felt he decently could. Barson was testy. It was his morning off surgery but he had a number of visits to make. And he wasn't happy about Gemma Pettifer being questioned until he had seen her again. She was one of the first people on his list this morning.

"In that case," said Thanet eagerly, "suppose I meet you there, wait until you've seen her. If you think she's fit, I'll talk to her, if not, I'll leave it for today. But frankly, I really do need to see her if it's at all possible. If you like, you could stay with her while I talk to her, and if you think it's too much for her, I'll stop." He couldn't, he felt, be much more cooperative or considerate than that.

Barson grudgingly agreed, muttering that he had better things to do with his time but that, if it was that urgent . . .

It was, Thanet assured him, and the matter was settled; they would meet at Pine Lodge in half an hour.

When Thanet turned in between the white-painted pillars, Barson's car was already parked in the drive. The doctor had been with Mrs Pettifer for a quarter of an hour or so, Mrs Price said.

"How is she this morning?"

Mrs Price grimaced. "Quiet. Wouldn't eat any breakfast."

It was interesting, Thanet thought as he waited in the drawing room for Barson to come down and give his verdict, that Mrs Price was showing this degree of concern. Initially he had been certain that she didn't like Gemma, was covertly hostile to her. Perhaps Gemma's rapidly advancing pregnancy was arousing Mrs Price's protective instincts. But Thanet suspected that it was more than that. If, at some point over the last few days, Mrs Price had had a belated change of heart towards her late employer's wife, it could only be because she believed her to be genuinely grief-stricken by Pettifer's death. And if Gemma had convinced a hostile Mrs Price of her sincerity . . .

Barson entered the room. "I should think you could see her briefly now, if you must." Barson was both grudging and disapproving. "She insists she wants to see you anyway."

"How is she this morning?" Thanet asked, for the second time.

"I suppose one could say, as well as might be expected," Barson said sardonically. "After all, she has just had a severe shock in her husband's death, and she is pregnant, we must remember that. We don't want to put the child at risk too."

"Believe it or not, doctor, I agree, wholeheartedly. Which is why I rang you this morning. You may think me inhuman, but I am only doing my job, after all. I'm sure that your work too has distasteful aspects, that you sometimes have to do things that you really would prefer to avoid but can't . . ."

Barson looked a little shamefaced. "You're right, and I'm sorry, Inspector. I know I must have come over hot and strong last night. But you in turn must appreciate that my first concern has to be for my patient."

"I do," Thanet said. "Naturally. And now, having reached some measure of agreement, perhaps we could go up. And I meant it when I said stop me if you think she's not up to it. She wants to see me, you said . . .?"

Gemma was still in bed, leaning back against the piled-up pillows as if exhausted. Her hair had been brushed back and tied loosely at the nape of her neck, accentuating the pallor of her skin and that taut, stretched look about the eyes which Thanet didn't like one little bit. Privately, he thought she looked worse than last night and was glad that Barson was there. Even now he hesitated. He really did not want a miscarriage on his conscience. But the decision was quickly taken out of his hands. As soon as she saw him, urgency flared in Gemma's eyes, dispelling that frightening blankness.

"Inspector," she said. "I'm so glad you came. There's something I must tell you. Please . . ." and she indicated the chair beside the bed.

147

Thanet sat down and then watched with amused admiration as she skilfully persuaded Dr Barson that his presence was unnecessary but that she would be grateful if he could wait downstairs for a little while longer in case she needed him. Thanet reminded himself not to underestimate her in the coming interview.

When Barson had reluctantly left the room she said, "I really am glad you came, Inspector. It's been worrying me . . . You see, I haven't been quite frank with you."

So, confession time, thought Thanet, wondering what was coming. He settled down to listen.

She was frowning, her fingers plucking nervously at the bedspread. "You remember I told you that, when I realised my husband wasn't well that night, I suggested that I cancel my trip to London, but that he insisted I still go?"

She waited for Thanet's nod before continuing.

"Well I wasn't very happy about it, as you can imagine, especially as Mrs Price was away for the night, but I had been so looking forward to discussing this new part with my agent — I hardly ever seem to go out, these days — so I said that I would compromise, come straight home after dinner instead of spending the night in town as I'd intended. But he said no, there was no need, a cold was nothing to fuss about and he'd be perfectly all right. Then he suggested that, if it would make me any happier, I could give him a ring about ten o'clock, before he settled down for the night. It wouldn't disturb him, he said, he had no intention of going to sleep during the evening in case he then wouldn't be able to sleep through the night."

"Well, it seemed a good idea, so that's what I did. I had dinner, got back to the hotel about ten with . . . with Mr Lee. We . . . we didn't want to be seen going up to my room together, so he went into the bar for a drink and followed me up ten minutes later. Meanwhile I rang Arnold . . ."

Her fingers had increased their nervous activity and now she plucked at a thread which had worked loose. "He sounded very strange . . ."

"Strange?"

148

"Well, urgent. In a state. Most uncharacteristic, I assure you. Arnold was the last man in the world to flap about anything."

"What did he say, exactly?"

"He said, 'Gemma, for God's sake get down here as fast as you can.' "

"Go on."

"I asked him what was the matter, but he wouldn't tell me, said he'd give me the details when I got here. Then he said, 'You will come, won't you?' So I promised I'd leave immediately and he rang off."

"Was he speaking clearly?"

She frowned. "What do you . . . Oh, you mean, was he already drugged, by then? No, he sounded perfectly coherent."

"So what did you do?" Thanet knew, of course, but he wanted to hear the story from Gemma herself.

"Well, I was frightened, naturally. It was so unlike Arnold to be alarmist. I really thought it must be something serious. But it was too late to catch the ten-twenty from Victoria and I knew the next train wasn't until twelve-fifteen. If I waited for that, I wouldn't get home until after two — and if it was that urgent . . . So I asked Rowan if he would drive me down." She grimaced. "I know it doesn't sound very good, getting my lover to answer my husband's SOS, but I really couldn't think what else to do. I could have taken a taxi, I suppose, but Rowan was there, on the spot, and his car was parked near by and it seemed the obvious solution. He wasn't very pleased, of course, but he agreed and we left at once."

"You checked out of the hotel?"

"I didn't bother. I didn't want to be held up. They know me there, I always use the same hotel when I stay in town, so I knew it wouldn't matter about the bill, I could always settle up later. So I just stuffed my nightdress and my toilet stuff into my shoulder bag and left. That's all I ever bother to take when I'm only away for one night. Anyway, we got to Sturrenden about a quarter to twelve. Rowan's car practically came out of the Ark, so it took longer than I'd hoped. I was on tenterhooks

149

all the way, and when I got here and found that Arnold was out, I was furious, I can tell you."

Thanet was astounded. "Out?"

"Well, that's what I thought at the time. Now, of course, looking back . . ." She bit her lip. "He must already have been . . ." Tears filled her eyes and she dashed them away impatiently. "If only I'd *known* . . ."

Thanet waited for a few moments until she had regained her composure and then said, "Look, if you want to stop there for the moment . . ."

"No! I'd rather finish, get it over with. You can't imagine how I've dreaded telling you."

Thanet could. And if her story was true . . . Suspend judgement, he told himself. Let's hear the rest of it. "If you're sure, then . . ."

"I am."

"Well then, let's go back a little. When you arrived, what did you do, exactly?"

"Well, when we got here the house was in darkness and I was surprised. I suppose I'd expected lights to be blazing everywhere, a sort of signal of a state of emergency. So I was a bit nonplussed. Rowan said he'd hang around for a little while until he was sure everything was all right, and we arranged a signal, switching the bedroom light on and off twice, if I didn't need him. He was to wait a quarter of an hour . . . Anyway, when I got to the front door I found I couldn't get in. It was locked and bolted on the inside. I tried throwing gravel up at our bedroom window, but nothing happened. So then I went around to the back. I knew I wouldn't be able to get in that way because I didn't have a key, but I did think that there might possibly be a window open or something . . . not that I particularly wanted to go crawling through windows in the middle of the night like this," and she indicated the mound of her belly beneath the bedclothes, "but I wasn't thinking very coherently . . . And then I saw that Arnold's car had gone from the garage. And, as I said, I was *furious*."

"Furious?"

"Well, I immediately thought that he'd gone out on a night

150

call. At that point, you see, I had no idea that he hadn't come home in the car that afternoon as usual, that he'd left it at the Centre. So I assumed that he'd done what he always did when he had to go out at night, left the front door locked and bolted and let himself out the back way — it's much closer to the garage."

"But he wasn't on duty that night."

"No, I know. But if there'd been some emergency, if the doctor on duty had already been called out and someone urgently needed treatment. . . . It's happened before. My husband was a very conscientious doctor, Inspector. He wouldn't have allowed the fact that he was theoretically off duty to stop him answering a call — or the fact that he was feeling under the weather himself, either. So, as I say, I was livid. To think that he'd dragged me all the way down from London worrying myself sick and then had the nerve to go out knowing I wouldn't even be able to get into the house . . ."

"But didn't you wonder why he should have done such a thing? I mean, by all accounts your husband was most solicitous for your welfare . . ."

"Of course I wondered! I went back and told Rowan what had happened and we . . . well, we decided there was only one conclusion we could draw . . ." She broke off, lips trembling.

Thanet could see what was coming but he said nothing, simply waited.

She glanced at him uneasily and then said, "We thought that Arnold must somehow have found out about us and that he'd arranged the whole thing on purpose, to punish me."

"You mean, he knew before you left, and stage-managed the whole performance — the cold, the phone call . . .?"

"Oh, no. Absolutely not. I'd swear to that. When I left him that evening, everything was as usual between us, I'm certain of it. No, we assumed that somehow he'd found out during the course of the evening."

"How?"

"I've no idea. A phone call from a so-called well-meaning 'friend', I suppose . . . anything . . . Anyway, that's what we thought. So, as you can imagine, I was dreading getting home

151

next morning. I knew he'd be in, it was his morning off. And then, when I found out what had really happened . . . I was *there*, don't you see, at the crucial time. If I'd somehow got in, found him then, it might not have been too late to save him . . ." She buried her face in her hands, began to weep.

"I'll call Dr Barson."

"Just a moment . . ." She lifted a streaming face, put out a hand to restrain him.

Thanet waited while she took a tissue from a box on the bedside table, mopped at her eyes and blew her nose.

"I know you don't think much of me," she said at last in a low voice. "And I don't blame you." Her nose wrinkled in self-disgust. "The ungrateful, unfaithful wife . . . I've played the part so many times on stage it didn't seem wrong, some-how, to play it in real life. I don't know whether you can believe it, but I'll tell you this." She lifted her head with something like pride. "My husband loved me very much, but I never deceived him in *that* way — never pretended to love him in return. He said he didn't mind, he was prepared to wait, that he'd be such a perfect husband that I'd be bound to grow to love him in the end. He made a joke of it. The irony is . . ." and her com-posure began to slip again, "that it was true. I had grown to love him . . . but I never realised, until it was too late."

18

Predictably, Barson was furious to find Gemma in tears.

"I thought you promised not to upset her," he muttered angrily.

"She insisted . . ."

"Then you should have over-ruled her," Barson snapped.

Gemma lifted a drowned face. "Please don't blame Inspector Thanet, Charles," she said. "He wanted to stop, several times, but I just wouldn't let him. Anyway," she said, pausing to blow her nose, "it may not look like it at the moment but it's an enormous relief to have got all that off my chest. I'll be much better now, you'll see."

If Barson was curious he did not show it, simply said a dismissive goodbye to Thanet, who obediently left the room.

Downstairs, Thanet hesitated. There was something he would like to ask Barson. He decided to wait.

Barson came down about ten minutes later. "I thought you'd gone," he said curtly.

"No. There's something I wanted to . . ."

"You're not seeing her again today and that's that. I refuse to risk it. There's a limit to what someone in her condition can take."

"No, no. It's you I wanted to see."

Barson's anger had carried them through the hall and across the drive. Now he paused in the act of getting into his car. "Me?"

"Yes. It occurred to me . . . You told me you'd known Dr Pettifer a long time. That you were medical students together."

"That's right."

"I wonder if you could tell me . . . Would you say that he

153

was a vindictive man?"

The question took Barson by surprise. Slowly he straightened up and stood with one hand on the car door, the other on the roof. "Vindictive . . .?"

Thanet waited.

"I wouldn't have said so," Barson said slowly. "But then, we've always been on good terms even if we haven't been what I'd call close friends."

"I know. That's why I was wondering about your student days. You must have seen quite a lot of each other then . . ."

"There was one incident," Barson said slowly, with that look of surprise which Thanet had often seen on the face of a witness recalling an incident long buried in the past. "I'd forgotten all about it. There was a character called Taylor, who was a bit of a practical joker — well, I suppose there usually is, in any fair-sized group of students. Arnold of course was totally lacking in any sense of humour. He was very serious-minded, dedicated to his work even then . . . Look, I'm not sure that I want to go on talking about this."

"Dr Barson," Thanet said softly, "you are an intelligent man. I find myself wondering why you have never questioned the necessity of our repeated visits to Mrs Pettifer."

Barson's eyes slid away from Thanet's. Then he lifted his hands in a little gesture of defeat. "All right, I'll confess. I rang Dr Lowrie, to commiserate, that first day. You'd just been to see him and he was still rather shaken. He told me that you weren't satisfied, that there might even be a possibility of its having been murder. He told me in confidence and I have spoken about it to no one, I assure you."

"I see. In that case you must surely understand that I really do have to try to find out all I can about Dr Pettifer. I don't ask questions just to satisfy idle curiosity, I promise you."

Barson studied Thanet's face for a moment before saying, "I believe you."

"In that case, could you go on with what you were telling me just now?"

Barson sighed. "I suppose so. It just smacks of disloyalty, that's all. Though why it should feel worse to speak ill of the dead than of the living I can't imagine."

"Perhaps it's because they can't strike back."

Barson gave a rueful smile. "You're probably right. So . . . where was I?"

"You were saying how serious-minded Pettifer was."

"That's right. Well, he was. So I suppose it was inevitable that sooner or later he should have become Taylor's target."

"What happened?"

"Well, it was a bit much really. One day Taylor slipped a diuretic into Pettifer's coffee."

"What's a diuretic?"

"Makes you want to pass water all the time. Anyway, Taylor stupidly mistimed the thing. Instead of giving Pettifer the stuff at a time when Pettifer would at least have the opportunity to go and pee when he wanted to, he gave it to him when there was to be an important lecture later on that morning. God, I can't think how the incident could have slipped my mind. It was hideously embarrassing . . . Fortunately Pettifer was sitting near the back, but he didn't make it to the door. You can imagine how he felt . . ."

"I can imagine how anyone would have felt, in circumstances like that." But Pettifer especially, Thanet thought. Stern, proud, this would have been precisely the sort of humiliation he was least equipped to bear. "So, what happened?"

"For a long time, nothing. Everyone knew who was responsible, of course, but nothing overt was said, either to or by Pettifer. We felt sorry for him, felt Taylor'd gone a bit far and the whole thing had turned sour. Pettifer had never been on particularly friendly terms with Taylor and now he more or less ignored him. And he made no move to retaliate until the following June."

"What did he do?"

"It was simple but lethal. Devilishly clever, too. We were taking our finals, you see, and on the first day Pettifer slipped lactulose into Taylor's breakfast cornflakes. It was easy enough to do, the plates of cereal were all set out and we used to take it in turns to distribute a trayful. And lactulose is near

155

enough tasteless and colourless . . . It's an aperient," he explained to Thanet's blank look, "produces the same effect as a diuretic, but on the bowels instead of the bladder."

"Diarrhoea . . ."

"Galloping diarrhoea in this case."

"God, what a revenge! What happened to Taylor?"

"He managed to scrape through his exams, just. But he had been one of the most promising students of the year . . ."

So, Thanet thought, watching Barson drive away, here was a side of Pettifer's character hitherto unsuspected. He wanted to think over the interview with Gemma Pettifer, but he didn't want to sit here in the car in full view of her windows. He drove out of Brompton Lane and parked around the corner.

This was a pleasant residential street with wide pavements punctuated by ornamental cherry trees. The leaden skies of yesterday had disappeared overnight, blown away by the frisky wind which was plucking at the dying leaves, tossing them in the air and then cradling them as they floated to the ground. At the far end of the road an old man was moving methodically along the pavement, brushing the leaves first into long crimson ribbons snaking along the gutters, then into piles which he finally shovelled into a metal container on wheels.

Thanet watched him absentmindedly, his thoughts far away. He still couldn't make up his mind about Gemma Pettifer. She was convincing, yes, but then she had spent many years perfecting the art of being so. Suppose that she was lying, that the whole thing was a very clever scheme to kill her husband and deflect attention from herself by playing the unfaithful wife who realises too late the depth of her devotion to her husband . . . Suppose that the stories of the cold, the paracetamol, the promised phone call, Pettifer's cry for help were an ingenious tissue of lies devised to explain away her presence on the spot at the crucial time . . .

Or . . . Thanet's pulse beat faster as a completely new idea came into his head. Suppose that Gemma's story was true, that the deception was not hers but Pettifer's. Suppose that, contrary to her belief, he had indeed found out about her lover, had stage-managed the performance of illness and phone call,

156

but that, contrary to appearances, Pettifer had intended the suicide to be an *attempt only*. Suppose that Gemma had been meant to arrive in time, rush him to hospital and, filled with guilt, be for ever afterwards a loving, faithful wife? Such a plan would neatly have served the dual purpose of revealing to Gemma the depth of his despair and bringing her smartly to heel. And it would explain so much — why Pettifer had arranged to have his car repaired, for example, why he had obviously envisaged a future in which he and Gemma would be able to enjoy a luxury cruise together. Or perhaps the cruise had been intended to prick Gemma's conscience — even to underline the generosity of the love she was rejecting . . .

So, what had gone wrong?

She hadn't been able to get into the house.

And there was the rock upon which this ingenious theory foundered. Surely, if Pettifer's life had depended on it, he wouldn't have made the mistake of bolting the door against his only hope of rescue?

For that matter, why had he bolted the door at all, if he was expecting her home?

Perhaps he had counted on the fact that Gemma, disturbed by his appeal, would be determined to get into the house somehow. But she hadn't because, when she had gone around to try the back door, she had seen . . .

Thanet jerked bolt upright in his seat. That was it! *She had seen that the car was missing.* And that had made her angry, had made her feel that she had been dragged down from London in the middle of the night on false pretences. She had gone back to London, leaving Pettifer to die, his plan ruined by the simple fact that he had forgotten the significance that missing car would have for her.

"You all right, Guv?"

The street sweeper was knocking on the car window, his face creased with concern.

Thanet wound down the window. "Oh yes, fine, thanks. I was just thinking."

The man grinned. "You want to be careful. All them faces you was making . . . If that's what thinking does for you . . ."

Thanet grinned back. "You've got a bit of a job on there, haven't you?" he said, nodding at the leaf-strewn pavements, the metal container. "I thought they had special lorries to do that these days."

"They have. In theory, like. But one of them's broke down, so they gives me a ring . . . I'm retired, see. 'Want your old job back for a coupla days, Ern?' they says. 'Why not?' says I. 'Earn a bit of extra towards Christmas.' And it makes a change, working again."

It was so easy for plans to go awry, Thanet thought as he drove away. Something unexpected turned up and that was that.

But, leaving aside the possibility that Pettifer's plan had misfired, there was to Thanet's mind one serious objection to this new theory of his: he couldn't really see Pettifer as a man who would resort to suicide as emotional blackmail. The explanation might be neat, logical, feasible even, but was it psychologically sound?

Thanet burned to discuss it all with Lineham, but Lineham was in London, unavailable until late afternoon. Thanet decided that meanwhile he would stick to his original plans for the day. He stopped at a phone box, asked Bentley to try and trace Mrs Blaidon, Pettifer's mother-in-law by his first marriage, and to arrange if possible for Thanet to go and see her this afternoon. Then he drove to the Medical Centre. Braintree was next on the list.

The receptionist was apologetic. "I'm afraid you've just missed him."

"Do you happen to know where he'll be going first?"

"I'm sorry. I know the names of all the people doctor'll be visiting, of course, but I've no idea in what order. He arranged that to suit himself."

"Have you any bright ideas how I can contact him?"

"Good morning, Inspector." It was Lowrie, on his way out. "How's it going?"

"I was hoping to have a word with Dr Braintree this morning, but I've just missed him, apparently."

"Inspector?" Mrs Barnet had come out of her little office,

158

had obviously heard this brief exchange. "Did you say you wanted to see Dr Braintree? Only I was talking to him just before he left, and he said that he had to call in at home before starting his visits. If you hurry, you might catch him there."

"Thank you." Hurriedly, Thanet scrawled down the address.

As he turned to leave, Lowrie said sharply, "Just one point, Inspector." Taking Thanet by the arm he drew him aside, spoke softly. "Braintree . . . I know you've got to do your job, but go easy on him, will you? As I told you, he's had a rough time lately, one way and the other. He shouldn't really be back at work yet, but with so much to do . . . And now, of course, with Fir on holiday and Pettifer gone . . . I've managed to persuade a colleague of mine who's retired to help out until Fir comes back, but if Braintree were to crack up again we'd really be in the soup."

"Don't worry, I'll be careful," Thanet said.

Braintree lived in a peaceful little cul-de-sac of new neo-Georgian houses in one of the better suburbs of Sturrenden. Thanet rang the bell beside a purple front door which looked like an advertisement for high-gloss paint, winced at the musical chimes and waited, studying the house. Being new, it was to be expected that it should be in good condition, but it positively sparkled with the effort and energy that had been lavished on it. The windows shone, the small square panes were row upon row of little mirrors, and the paintwork was gleaming, spotless.

The woman who opened the door was equally trim in a neat cotton shirtwaister and frilly apron. Her face was scrubbed and shiny, her hair cut in an uncompromising bob.

"Yes?" she said, with a smile which did not reach her eyes.

Thanet explained.

"You'd better come in," she said, with a quick, darting glance to left and right, up and down the road.

The hall was close-carpeted and, just inside the front door, on a little rubber mat obviously placed there for the purpose, stood a pair of man's shoes. Mrs Braintree herself was wearing slippers and to his astonishment Thanet caught a brief,

159

assessing glance at his own inoffensive suede Hush Puppies. He waited incredulously for her to ask him to remove them.

But she didn't. She pushed open a door on their right and said, "If you wait in here, I'll fetch him."

The room was expensively furnished and totally devoid of character — magnolia emulsion paint on the walls, mushroom velvet curtains and three-piece suite. There was a sheepskin rug in front of the imitation-log gas fire, an island of luxury on the broad expanse of highly-polished parquet floor, but Thanet couldn't imagine that Mrs Braintree would ever contemplate using it for anything as untidy as making love. There was a television set, but no stereo system, no radio, no books, nor any magazines or newspapers to lend the room a human face. It was as bleak and impersonal as a room setting in a furnishing store.

Thanet began to feel sorry for Braintree. How could the spirit flourish in an atmosphere as sterile as this? I bet she was a nurse before she married him, he thought, and if she was I'm glad she never had to look after me. Yes, he thought as she came back into the room with her husband, she would have lacked that inner warmth which somehow survives despite the relentless drudgery and constant proximity to human suffering. Mrs Braintree wouldn't ever have had to hold back from becoming emotionally involved. Her patients to her would have been flesh, bones, blood, not people.

"You wanted to see me, Inspector?"

"Just briefly, if you can spare the time. It's about Dr Pettifer, of course." Thanet studied with interest the youngest of the partners in Pettifer's practice.

Dr Braintree was in his early thirties. Tall, thin and slightly hunched, with black hair which flopped over his forehead, he looked like a dejected crow.

"Do sit down."

"Thank you." Thanet glanced meaningfully at Mrs Braintree, hoping that she would take the hint and go, but she either didn't notice or chose to ignore it, plumping herself squarely down beside her husband on the settee.

Thanet seated himself opposite them.

"This won't take too long I hope, Inspector. I have a number of visits to make before lunch." Braintree caught Thanet's involuntary glance at his slippers and looked uncomfortable.

"I hope not too, doctor. I'm making routine enquiries and naturally I'm asking the same questions of everyone connected with Dr Pettifer. First of all, could you tell me if you thought him to be unusually depressed at the time of his death."

"No, not at all."

"Or if you know of any possible reason for his suicide?"

"No, none."

"But he must have had one, mustn't he?" cut in Mrs Braintree. "Or he wouldn't have done it. Stands to reason."

Thanet ignored the interruption, preoccupied with how to put the next question. Remembering Dr Lowrie's plea he decided on an oblique approach.

"How did you and he get on together?"

But his delicacy was wasted.

"You've been listening to gossip!" burst out Mrs Braintree. "You have, haven't you? And it's not true, is it Des? You shouldn't believe all you hear, Inspector. There's a lot of people about always willing to shoot down other people's reputations."

"I can assure you that I don't believe all I hear, Mrs Braintree. But I do have to listen, and check. Which is what I am doing now."

"But why? How could it matter whether him and Des got on or not? Which they did, anyway, but . . ."

"You must see that Dr Pettifer's state of mind at the time of his death is highly relevant . . ."

"So that's it! You're looking for a scapegoat. And you've decided my husband's it. That is it, isn't it!" Her face was pink, her eyes bulged and she seemed unaccountably to have grown bigger as she sat there.

Braintree, by contrast, seemed to have shrunk.

"Betty,' he said, in a feeble attempt at admonition.

"But that *is* what he's trying to do, can't you see?" she said, turning to him. "And you're not going to get away with it," she flung at Thanet.

"Mrs Braintree!" he said. "I'm not trying to get away with anything. I just want to . . ."

"My husband's done nothing to be ashamed of and . . ."

"Please. Would you mind . . ."

"I'm not going to sit here and . . ."

"Mrs Braintree! WILL YOU BE QUIET!"

There was a second's astounded silence and then she shot up, like a jack-in-the box. "I'm not going to sit here and be insulted in my own home. Des, it's time you were getting on with your rounds."

"Doctor Braintree," Thanet said in a quiet, deadly tone, "is going to stay where he is until he has answered the questions I wish to put to him. Alternatively," he went on, raising his voice as she opened her mouth to protest, "he can accompany me to the police station where we should be able to talk IN PEACE."

She stared at him for a moment longer and then, turning on her heel, flounced out of the room. Thanet could have sworn he heard the ghostly rustle of starched skirts. He expected her to slam the door and was interested to see that she carefully left it a little ajar.

"I'm sorry, Inspector." Braintree made a hopeless gesture. "My wife means well. She just tends to get a little worked up, that's all. Since my . . . illness, she has tended to be somewhat overprotective."

"Perfectly understandable." Thanet thought briefly and with gratitude of Joan's loving and equable temperament. "And I expect she's rather upset about Dr Pettifer's death. Everyone is, naturally."

"Quite. And of course, with Dr Fir still away, the work load is a bit much at present. So if we could be fairly brief . . ."

Thanet lowered his voice. "I'll be honest with you, doctor, and ask you to . . ." He remembered the door. He rose, shut it and returned to his chair before continuing. Braintree had got the message, he could see. ". . . to keep what I say in strictest confidence. You'll have gathered we're not very happy about this business. There seems to have been no reason whatsoever for Dr Pettifer to commit suicide — which means, of course,

162

that we really have to satisfy ourselves that there was nothing . . . well . . . sinister about his death.''

Braintree had turned the colour of grubby linen. He glanced at the door, edged forward on his seat. "You mean, he might have been *murdered*?" His voice was no more than a horrified whisper.

Thanet found that he, too, was sitting on the edge of his chair. We must look like a pair of conspirators, he thought. "It's no more than the remotest of possibilities," he said, wishing that this were true. "But you must see that, all the while it's on the cards, we can't sit around doing nothing."

"Of course. So, how can I help, Inspector?" His tone was fearful.

Thanet could see that Lowrie was right. He would have to be careful. Briefly, resentment flared in him. He was sick and tired of handling people with kid gloves. This was, potentially at least, a murder enquiry, he reminded himself, and if Braintree couldn't be asked a simple, straightforward question, then he wasn't fit to be back at work.

"If you could just tell me where you were on Monday evening?"

"Oh, my God!" Braintree buried his face in his hands. "I just can't *think*," he moaned. He raked his hair with his fingers.

Thanet waited.

"Monday evening . . .?" Braintree said, speaking through clenched teeth.

"Dr Lowrie was at a meeting with Mrs Barnet," prompted Thanet. "Perhaps you were on call?"

Braintree's face was suddenly luminous with relief. "I remember now! Betty and I were at the Tennis Club end-of-season dinner dance, at the Wayfarers."

"You weren't on call, then?"

"No, Lowrie was. If we're on duty and we have to go out, we just leave phone numbers so that we can quickly be contacted. Originally, I was supposed to be on duty on Monday, but I swopped with Lowrie, because of the dinner dance — I don't like drinking alcohol if I'm on call," he explained.

163

Lowrie was only attending a meeting and Mrs Lowrie is away at the moment, he was quite happy to exchange."

"I see." Quickly, Thanet took the details. Braintree had taken evening surgery. The last patient had not left until six-thirty. Braintree had had a scramble to get home, change and be ready by seven; then the two other couples in their party had arrived for a drink before they all left for the dinner dance, which had ended at 1 am.

It could all easily be checked, verified by people who could have no possible reason for lying, Thanet thought as he took names and addresses. He was therefore inclined to believe it. He thanked Braintree and managed to get away without a further encounter with Mrs Braintree, whom he glimpsed hovering in the kitchen doorway as he hurried through the hall. No doubt she would pounce upon her husband the moment the front door closed.

So that promising avenue had turned out to be a dead end, Thanet thought as he climbed into his car. And he was back to the old dilemma: suicide, or murder?

The pendulum began to tick away in his brain again as he headed back towards the centre of town.

It was, it wasn't. It was, it wasn't.

And — she did, she didn't. She did, she didn't.

19

Wondering if he was wasting his time, Thanet set off after lunch to keep the appointment which Bentley had managed to arrange with Mrs Blaidon. It was a glorious autumn afternoon and before long he began to feel as though he had been let out on holiday. He hadn't been in what he thought of as "proper country" for some time and now he wound down the car window to breathe in great draughts of sweet, clean air. All about him the rich landscape of Kent slumbered in the mellow warmth, satisfied that once again it had yielded up its abundance and could now lie dormant, replenishing itself with the strength necessary to bring forth next year's harvest.

At one point Thanet stopped the car and pulled into the side of the road, drawn by the beauty of the view. Leaning on a five-barred gate he gazed with profound satisfaction at the multi-coloured patchwork spread out before him. Fields of stubble, scorched black by the ritual purification of post-harvest fires, and meadows dotted with grazing sheep and cattle intermingled with orchards and woodlands in a satisfying natural harmony made breathtaking by the glowing colours of the autumn foliage. Along the hedgerows ripening blackberries hung in clusters and the glowing berries of hawthorn and wild rose were festooned with the fluffy white trails of the wild clematis, so aptly called Old Man's Beard.

Thanet plucked a handful of blackberries and ate them, their sun-ripened warmth seeming to encapsulate for him the essence of the richness about him. He had lived in Kent all his life and, although he never thought of himself as a country-man, knew that if he were ever to be uprooted from all this something in him would wither and die.

The village of Borden was tucked away at the heart of a

complex, twisting network of narrow country lanes. Thanet twice lost his way and it was with relief that he at last found it and stopped to ask for directions from an old man leaning on the tiny wicket gate of his front garden and puffing peacefully at his pipe.

The man considered Thanet's question, then removed his pipe in a leisurely manner. "Catchpenny Oast?" he repeated. "That'll be Mrs Blaidon's place."

"That's right."

"You goes up there about half a mile," the old man said, pointing with the stem of his pipe, "then just past the King's Arms you turns left, and a bit further on you'll see her sticking up above the yew hedge."

Presumably he was referring to the Oast house and not to its owner, thought Thanet with an inward smile as he thanked him. The tall, conical roofs of the oast houses, topped with their white cowls, are one of the most distinctive features of the Kentish landscape. Now that relatively few of them still perform their original function of drying the famous Kentish hops, many have been converted into delightful homes.

The yew hedge surrounding Mrs Blaidon's garden was tall and thick, immaculately clipped. Thanet parked his car at the side of the road and approached the white five-barred gate. As he unlatched it a large black-and-white cat sitting on one of the gateposts jumped down and stalked off sedately around the corner of the house, disappearing from view with a contemptuous flick of the tail.

Catchpenny Oast was a most attractive conversion. Efforts had clearly been made to retain as far as possible the original features of the building and to ensure that any new materials were carefully matched with the old. Thanet approved of the casement windows with the traditional small square panes and the heavy old wrought-iron fittings on the bleached, weathered wood of the massive front door.

Before he could knock, however, the cat reappeared and without a glance at Thanet returned to its perch on the gatepost.

"Ah, there you are. Thought you'd got lost." A woman had

166

appeared at the corner of the house and now advanced towards him, peeling off her gardening gloves and stuffing them into the capacious pockets of her canvas apron. She put out her hand. "Inspector Thanet, I presume."

Dismissing the fanciful notion that the cat had informed her of his arrival Thanet shook hands, studying her with interest. Not exactly a face to launch a thousand ships, he thought, but certainly one to catch and hold the interest; long and narrow, with slightly protruding teeth and unusually penetrating brown eyes. Her greying brown hair was caught up in an undisciplined bun.

She led him around the side of the house, removing her apron as she went. Underneath she was wearing a baggy tweed skirt, a woollen blouse and a shapeless brown cardigan held together at the front with a big safety pin.

"We're outside," she said. "Lovely day, brought Mother out."

At the back of the house, tucked into the angle between the roundel and the rest of the house, was a little paved terrace furnished with comfortable cane chairs and a bamboo table. In the most sheltered corner, so swathed in shawls and rugs as to be almost invisible, sat an old, old lady. Two rheumy eyes gazed vacantly out across the garden. Beside her, curled up on the trailing corner of one of the rugs, slept a tabby cat and a third cat, ginger this time, raised its head lazily to survey Thanet from the cushioned comfort of one of the chairs.

Mrs Blaidon dropped her apron on to the table and crossed to bend over her mother.

"We've got a visitor, Mother," she said loudly.

Slowly the old lady's eyes focused on her daughter's face.

"A visitor!" Mrs Blaidon repeated, even more loudly, pointing with vigorous stabs of her finger at Thanet.

The eyes swivelled slowly to Thanet and then, in mild bewilderment, back to Mrs Blaidon, who patted her mother's lap reassuringly before straightening up.

"Deaf as a post," she explained unnecessarily, mouth tucked down ruefully at the corners. "And stubborn, with it. Won't wear a hearing aid for love nor money. Sit down," she added abruptly.

167

He did so, wondering if her curiously staccato mode of speech had come about through years of living with someone who was deaf.

Mrs Blaidon scooped up the ginger cat and sat down on the chair it had occupied, settling it absentmindedly on her lap. It was such an habitual gesture that Thanet wondered if she was even aware that it was there.

"Right," she said, eyes bright with interest. "I'm bursting with curiosity. About Arnold, is it?"

"You've heard about his death, then?"

'Andy rang up. Hadn't heard from him since Christmas. In a state. Won't be hypocritical, pretend I'm sorry Arnold's dead."

"You didn't like him?"

She pulled a face. "Cold fish. Did you know him?"

"Only by sight."

"If you had, you'd know what I mean. Ghastly man. Andy right, then?"

No point in beating about the bush with this one, Thanet thought. Polite formalities would be brushed aside like so many flies. Straight to the point in as few words as possible would be the approach that Mrs Blaidon would appreciate.

"Well?" she said impatiently. "Was he murdered or wasn't he?"

"We don't know yet."

"Taking your time, aren't you?"

"Complications," Thanet said, equally terse. He was disconcerted to see a gleam of amusement in her eye.

"Don't huff."

Thanet opened his mouth to deny the allegation, realised that he would be wasting his time. Instead, he grinned. "It doesn't sound as though you'd be surprised if he had been."

"Not really."

"Why?"

"Told you. Awful man. Never understood why Diana married him. No, not true. Desperate for a husband. Simple as that."

"He was the sort of man who made enemies?"

She frowned. "Bit strong, that. Not the sort to make friends, that's all. No warmth in him. Good doctor, though. Loved his work, grant you that. Nothing else, though."

"Not even your daughter?"

She gave a bark of laughter. "Loved her money, more likely."

"And Andrew?"

Her expression softened. "Fond of him in the end. But never should have adopted, not cut out to be parents, those two."

"You mean, your daughter wasn't keen on children either? Then why on earth . . .?"

"Fifteen years ago things were different. If you didn't have children . . . Pariahs, almost. More enlightened nowadays. Diana felt some kind of freak. Damned unfair, the woman always blamed. She really resented that, I can tell you. Adopted in self-defence, really."

Thanet stared at her, wondering if he had heard aright. Could he have misinterpreted that peculiar shorthand speech of hers?

"What do you mean, that it's unfair that the woman should always be blamed?"

"Not her fault they couldn't have children. His."

His fault. So *Pettifer had been sterile*. And if that were so . . .

As his entire thinking about the case began to somersault Thanet pulled himself up short. This was so important he couldn't risk misinterpretation, dared not accept as fact something which might be only a biased guess.

"Who told you that?"

"Diana, of course."

"She could have been trying to put the blame on him because she couldn't face the fact that the fault was hers."

Mrs Blaidon waved her hand dismissively. "Psychological clap-trap."

"But I understood that she even had an operation . . ."

"Blocked tubes. Soon put right. That's when she found out. Until then, Arnold never had any tests. But when her tubes were cleared and still no patter of tiny feet . . . Saw the written

169

report from the hospital myself. Sperm count non-existent, it said. Nothing you can do about that. But look here, aren't we straying a bit? What the devil has Arnold's sperm count got to do with his death?''

Didn't you know that his second wife is having a baby? Thanet wanted to say. But he didn't. She would find out soon enough and put two and two together. As soon as he decently could he brought the conversation to a close and left.

Pettifer had been sterile.

Therefore he must have known that Gemma had a lover right from the very first moment she told him that she was pregnant, several months ago. And if that was so . . .

Thanet felt that he was on the very brink of a completely new understanding of the case. It was as though he was looking at it through a kaleidoscope. The pattern he had seen until a few minutes ago had suddenly fragmented and now all the pieces were whirling around in meaningless gyrations. Perhaps in a little while they would begin to float down, to settle and he would see the true picture beginning to take shape.

Meanwhile . . . The questions came thick and fast.

Why, for months, had Pettifer played the role of delighted expectant father, knowing that the child could not be his?

If he had loved Gemma as passionately as everyone seemed to think, how had he managed to conceal so effectively the jealousy he must have felt?

And, above all, why? Why had he never, by word or implication, indicated that he knew of her infidelity?

Thanet felt convinced that if he could only find the answer to this last question, the case would be solved.

20

"Where the hell have you been?"

For the last hour Thanet had been pacing about his office like a caged bear, burning with impatience for Lineham's return.

Lineham looked taken aback by this greeting, as well he might.

"In London, sir . . ."

"I know you've been in London, man. But what took you so long?"

"Well I had a bit of bother tracking down Mr Lee. First of all I . . ."

"All right, all right." Thanet waved away the explanations, then sat down heavily behind his desk. He was being unreasonable and he knew it. "Hell, I'm sorry Mike. I'm sure you haven't been wasting your time. It's just that there have been developments in the Pettifer case and I didn't want to go home until I'd discussed them with you."

"Oh? What?" Lineham said eagerly.

"All in good time. Tell me what you found out in London."

Lineham had gone first to the hotel. The manager had checked his records and had confirmed that, yes, Gemma had made one long-distance phone call at around ten o'clock that night. He had given Lineham the night-porter's address and the poor man had duly been roused from his well-earned slumbers and had confirmed that although he hadn't seen Gemma and Lee leave the hotel just after ten, he had seen them return at around 1.30 am. He had not questioned Lee's presence as he had seen him with Gemma on a number of previous occasions and assumed he had every right to be there.

It had then taken Lineham some time to track down Lee,

whom he had finally run to earth at the rehearsals of a fringe theatre group in Putney.

"And a pretty weird lot they were, too," he said, eyes rounding reminiscently. "Do you know . . ."

"Lee, Mike. What about Lee?"

Lineham's top lip curled up contemptuously. "Male-model type. The sort you see on knitting patterns. Appeals to women, I suppose. Good-looking, skin-tight trousers, shirt unbuttoned to the waist, gold medallion nestling in the hair on his chest, that sort of thing."

Thanet grinned. "Not your idea of masculine charm, eh, Mike?"

Lineham ignored Thanet's teasing. "He was still hopping mad with Mrs Pettifer."

"What about?"

"Her getting him to drive over a hundred miles at night to answer a dud SOS from her husband. I gather the atmosphere on the way back to London was distinctly frosty. In fact, I have a feeling that that affair won't be going on much longer."

"Gave you that impression, did he?"

Lineham looked disgusted. "It was the way he talked about her . . . 'You know what older women are,' wink, wink. 'They can teach you a thing or two but after that, well you've got to admit that their charms are somewhat faded.' Yuk!"

"Delightful. Anyway, I gather he confirmed her story."

"Oh yes, down to the last detail."

"What do you think, Mike, now you've seen him? Do you think he and Mrs Pettifer did the foul deed together?"

"Not on your life! Honestly, sir, I don't think that one would put his neck on the chopping block for anyone. What a nice girl like Deborah Chivers can see in him really beats me."

"You're sure?"

"As sure as I can be."

"Even taking into account the fact that he's an actor too? And, whatever you think of him as a person, a good one?"

"Believe me, I'd be only too delighted to be giving a different answer. But no, I think his involvement begins and ends with his driving her down to Sturrenden and back that night."

172

"Hmm. Only, as I said, things have changed a bit since this morning. The last of our other suspects, Braintree, is now out of the running — I checked while I was waiting for you to get back and, believe me, his alibi's cast-iron. And I learnt one very interesting fact from Pettifer's mother-in-law by his first marriage." Thanet stopped, took out his pipe and began to fill it.

"Yes?"

Mischievously, Thanet prolonged the suspense for a moment or two longer, waited until his pipe was drawing properly before dropping his bombshell.

"*Sterile?*" Lineham's face was a study. "But that means . . ."

"Yes?"

"Well, that the baby isn't his, for a start. And that he must have known it wasn't right from the beginning. Which means . . ." Lineham paused, taking in the implications.

". . . that our pillar of respectability and integrity has been lying in his teeth for months. Living a lie, in fact. And damned convincingly, too. He certainly had us fooled," Thanet added, with a degree of bitterness.

"And his wife, too?"

"Ah, now that's what I'd really like to know. Did he tell her he knew, or not?"

"He couldn't have, surely, sir. I can't believe that if he had they would have been able to hide the fact that their relationship had changed from Mrs Price, for example, who was living in the same house with them all the time."

"And why should they bother to keep up a pretence like that, anyway? I mean, I can imagine Pettifer not wanting other people to know he'd been made a fool of — can't you? — carrying on as though nothing had happened because he couldn't bear to lose face. But why should she?"

"Perhaps he threatened to divorce her if she didn't."

Thanet shook his head. "It's no good, Mike, it just doesn't ring true. If there was collusion between them, then she really put her heart and soul into it, didn't she? Think of the anniversary dinner. Why should she bother to put on an act like that in front of a lot of complete strangers? No, the more I think about it, the more inclined I am to believe he didn't tell her."

"But why should he have, for that matter? I mean . . ."

The phone rang. "It's for you," Thanet said, passing it to Lineham.

"Yes? Oh, hullo, Mother. Look, is this important? It really isn't very conven — . . . Oh. Oh, I see. Well, I don't know. Louise'll be expecting me. Yes. Yes, I do see. Yes. Well, I suppose I could. All right, I'll call in on my way home. I'm not sure." He glanced at his watch. "I can't be certain." There was irritation in his voice now. "I really can't be sure . . . Say an hour, then. I'm sorry, mother, you know how it is, I just can't be more definite than that. No, I'm not cross. Yes. Yes. See you later, then. 'Bye." He shot an apologetic glance at Thanet. "My mother," he said unnecessarily as he put the phone down. "A minor crisis. Do you think . . . Would you mind if I just made a quick call to Louise, sir?"

"Go ahead."

Lineham lifted the receiver, began to dial, stopped. Gently, he put the phone down again. "I'll leave it for the moment," he said sheepishly.

Obviously Lineham was hoping that if he was late getting home Louise would simply assume that he had been delayed at work. That way, a clash over his mother's demands could be avoided. Thanet opened his mouth, clamped it shut again. Lineham's private life was not his concern unless or until Mike brought himself to ask outright for Thanet's advice or opinion, as he had on occasion in the past. But it was hard to stand by and watch this gradual widening of the rift between Mike and Louise. Thanet was fond of them both. Now, he found himself hoping that he wouldn't later on kick himself for not having spoken out in time.

"Of course," said Lineham, "there's always the possibility that he didn't tell her because he just hoped the problem would go away."

Thanet wondered if Lineham realised just how accurately this suggestion mirrored his attitude to his own domestic problems. He shook his head. "I just can't believe that, Mike. From what we've learnt of him, that just wouldn't be in

174

character. Everyone agrees he was the sort of man who tackled problems head on. And he was such a proud man . . ."

"Perhaps he didn't tell her because he didn't want her to know he was sterile."

"I thought of that, but that's no answer either. There was no need for her to know, was there? After all, he could have learnt about the affair in a number of ways, couldn't he?"

"True. Though I suppose that if he didn't want her to know he was sterile, then when she first told him about the baby he'd have had to pretend to be pleased, wouldn't he?"

"Not necessarily. After all, he'd made it clear he didn't particularly want children. I shouldn't have thought she'd have been in the least bit surprised if he hadn't been very happy about it to begin with, especially as he hadn't been consulted. Even so, everyone agrees he was — or appeared — delighted about it in the following months. And that I simply cannot swallow. Pettifer being pleased that his wife was carrying another man's child . . . So we come back to the same question, don't we? Why the elaborate charade?"

"You don't think we're trying to make it too complicated, sir? After all, it could simply be that he loved her so much he was prepared to have her on any terms. Then he might have found, as time went on and the affair didn't come to an end, that he just couldn't face the prospect of going on like that indefinitely, and decided to kill himself."

"Or perhaps Doc Mallard was right. You remember what he said, about suicide sometimes being an expression of anger rather than of despair?"

"You mean, he did it to punish her?"

"No, that doesn't feel right either, does it? Though it could have been like that, I suppose. Hell, Mike, we're just not getting anywhere, are we? I think it's time we called it a day."

He was sick and tired of going around in circles, he thought as he drove home. His earlier elation had vanished and he felt no nearer now to solving the thing than he had when they first started working on it. His head felt thick, his temples throbbed and he told himself that the best thing now would be to put the case right out of his mind for the evening. He had learnt from past experience that this could be a most fruitful exercise. Superficially at least he had a respite while underneath his subconscious continued to work away at the problem.

As it happened, circumstances conspired to help him carry out this decision, though not in a manner he would have chosen. When he arrived home he found Joan in the sitting room with Ben, wrapped in a blanket, on her lap.

Concern twisted Thanet's stomach. "What's the matter?" he said. He glanced at the clock. Half past eight. Ben should have been asleep over an hour ago.

"Ben can't get to sleep," Joan said, smoothing the child's hair gently back on his forehead. "He's got pains in his tum, haven't you, darling? And a temperature." Her eyes met Thanet's, dark with anxiety, and he knew at once what she was thinking.

Appendicitis?

Apparently not. The doctor had been, diagnosed nothing more serious than a chill in the stomach. "He said Ben'll be better by morning. And we'll have to watch what he eats for a few days."

"I'll take over now," said Thanet. "I'll have supper later. We'll pop you into bed shall we, Ben, where you'll be more comfortable — and then I'll read you a story, shall I?"

Ben nodded, his eyes overbright, cheeks flushed.

Thanet carried him upstairs and settled down to entertain him, consumed with anxiety. He read three *Paddington* stories, played one game of ludo and then, at Ben's request, "tried" to solve some of the puzzles in Ben's comic with him. Ben was growing sleepy now but he was clearly determined not to relinquish the unusual pleasure of having his father's exclusive attention. Eventually Thanet said, "Just one more then, Ben, and that's it."

But the concession proved unnecessary. Ben's eyes were closing and in a few minutes he was asleep. Thanet gently tucked him in and switched off the light, leaving the bedroom door ajar so that they would be able to hear if he called out in the night.

"Asleep?" Joan asked.

"At last." Thanet sat down with a sigh of relief.

176

"I'll get your supper."

While Thanet was eating they discussed Ben's indisposition for a little while and then Joan said, "I've got something to tell you. And I'm warning you, you won't like it."

Thanet looked at her warily. "Oh?" And then, as she still hesitated. "Go on, then."

"You won't bite my head off?" But she was smiling.

"Don't I always?" He smiled back. "All the same, you can't expect me to give hostages to fortune. Tell me what it is."

"Mrs Markham wants me to drive her down to Bexhill on Sunday. Her son has asked her down for a couple of weeks."

"Then why can't he come and fetch her?" Thanet exploded. "He's got a car, hasn't he? Why should you go flogging all the way down to Bexhill? Joan, you did promise . . ."

"I know, I know, but . . ."

"And what about the children? I know it's supposed to be my weekend off, but the way things are going it doesn't look as if I'm going to get it, so I won't be here to babysit." Not to mention the fact that if, by any remote chance, he was free on Sunday, he didn't see why he and the children should be deprived of Joan's company . . .

"Mary said she'd have them. Or they could come with me, of course. For the ride."

"But why can't her son fetch her?"

"He's away on a course this weekend."

"Then why can't she go next weekend? Or travel by public transport? Thousands of people do."

Joan shook her head stubbornly. "There are reasons why it has to be this weekend. If they leave it, her grandson will be home — he's been away in the States for a year — then they won't have the room to put her up."

"Then why couldn't they have invited her before? I'm sorry, darling, I don't want to be unreasonable, but . . ."

Joan laid two fingers gently against his lips. "Just listen for a moment, will you darling? I know I've been manoeuvred into it again, and frankly, I'm rather cross about it. You're right, I can see that now, she really is expert at it and I've made up my mind that this is the last time I allow myself to be manipulated like this." She took her fingers away, then said complacently, "In fact, you'll be pleased to hear I've already told her so — not in quite those terms, of course. I tried to break it gently, but I made it clear that when she comes back from her holiday I won't be able to continue popping in night and morning and running all her errands for her, as I have been doing. She wasn't very pleased, of course, but I stuck to my guns . . . So there you are. This is my last grand gesture. Truly."

Thanet raised both hands in mock surrender. "All right, all right, I give in." He reached out for her. "It'll be good to have you back," he murmured into her hair.

She pulled a little away from him to look into his face. "The trouble with you," she said, "is that you'd really like me to channel all my energies in your direction." Her kiss softened the impact of this undeniable truth.

"Especially a certain kind of energy," he agreed with a grin, tugging her to her feet. "An early night, don't you think?"

Much later, lying back relaxed and content, Thanet felt curiously wide awake. Usually, after making love, it was he who drifted quickly into sleep and Joan who tended to lie awake, but tonight it was the other way around. Her soft, deep breathing told him that she was already sound asleep and he turned on to his right side, in his favourite sleeping position, and determined to follow her example as quickly as possible.

Half an hour later he was telling himself that he really ought to have known that this was the one way to ensure that he stayed wide awake.

Turning on to his back he folded his arms behind his head and resigned himself to a long bout of insomnia. It was the Pettifer case, of course. Usually he slept like a log, but in each major enquiry there came a point where a sleepless night or two seemed inevitable.

What was so frustrating about this one, of course, was that after four days work they still weren't even sure whether it had been suicide or murder. Each new bit of evidence that

178

came along seemed to point to Gemma Pettifer's guilt, and yet . . . For some reason he was still unconvinced.

Why?

Deliberately now he made himself go back once more to the beginning and gradually trace the logical progression of the case against her. This got him nowhere, so he started again, this time trying to pinpoint those elusive moments when he had felt himself close to understanding the truth of what had happened.

It made no difference. At the end of it he was still as undecided as ever. He peered at the bedside clock, groaned inwardly. Half past two. He would feel like a limp rag in the morning. Yet again he composed himself for sleep, forcing his mind into other channels. He thought of Lineham and his mother, of Louise, of Joan and Mrs Markham, of Ben . . .

He stiffened. Had Ben cried out? Carefully, so as not to wake Joan, Thanet got out of bed, threw on his dressing gown and, shivering a little, went to check. Ben wanted to go to the lavatory. Thanet carried him to the bathroom and back and tucked him into bed with a smile, hiding his anxiety. Ben's forehead was still hot.

"Still got a pain in your tum?"

Ben shook his head. "Can we play another game, Daddy?" he said.

At half past two in the morning? Thanet opened his mouth to refuse, then closed it again. Why not? he thought. He wasn't in the least sleepy and if it would settle Ben down again . . .

"Please?"

"All right then." Thanet sat down on the bed, cuddled Ben to his side. "What shall we play?"

Ben selected "Spot the Ten Deliberate Mistakes". They took it in turns. By the eighth mistake Ben's eyelids were drooping, by the tenth he had dozed off. Thanet sat very still for a while, wanting to be certain that Ben was sound asleep before risking any movement. Idly, he studied the puzzle picture, looking for the tenth deliberate mistake. Ah yes, there it was . . .

Suddenly it was as though a window blind had snapped up in his mind, allowing enlightenment to come flooding in. His brain began to race, to check and cross-check, to test the bizarre explanation of Pettifer's death which had so unexpectedly presented itself to him.

Was it possible?

With absent-minded gentleness he made sure that Ben was comfortable and returned to his own bed, snuggling up gratefully to the warmth radiating from Joan as she slept.

Was it?

Certainly it explained away so much — everything, in fact, that had so puzzled them. But there was one major snag. His mind twisted and turned, seeking a way around it.

But it was still there when he at last fell asleep.

21

While he shaved next morning Thanet reviewed his solution and found that he still felt the same way about it. It was correct, he was convinced of it, he felt its essential rightness deep down inside him . . . And yet, there was that one great stumbling block — no, not just a stumbling block but an insurmountable wall of illogicality which would have to be scaled before he could truly be satisfied. He couldn't wait to discuss the whole thing with Lineham.

But he had to curb his impatience. When he arrived at the office he found Lineham already at work. Thanet took in the mounded litter of reports on Lineham's desk, the sergeant's bleary eyes and day-old stubble and said, "What the hell have you been playing at, Mike? You look as though you haven't been to bed all night."

"Well, as a matter of fact . . ."

". . . you haven't. Well for God's sake go and get yourself freshened up. We'll leave explanations until you're looking a bit less like the morning after the night before. And get a move on. We have to talk."

Lineham's red-rimmed eyes travelled slowly over Thanet's face and then he groaned, said, "I knew it", and put his head in his hands.

"What's the matter?" Thanet said, beginning now to be concerned. "Are you ill or something?" He devoutly hoped the "or something" was not a serious rift with Louise. If Lineham had been here all night . . .

"No. It's not that. It's just . . . Oh, never mind." Lineham began to close files and shuffle them into neat stacks.

"What do you mean? You can't act as though the world's come to an end and then say, 'never mind'."

181

Lineham sat back in his chair and looked at Thanet. "Well, just tell me this, sir . . . That look on your face . . . You've cracked it, haven't you?"

"The Pettifer case, you mean? I think so, yes, but . . ."

The look of despair on Lineham's face was so exaggerated as to have been comic, Thanet felt, had it not so patently been genuine. "What is the matter, Mike?" he said, gently.

"It's just that . . . Oh, you'll just think I'm a fool. Or presumptuous. One or the other, for sure."

"How do you know, until you've tried me?"

Something in Thanet's voice must have given Lineham reassurance because he studied the older man's face for a moment and then said, "Well, there's no reason why I shouldn't, I suppose. It's just that, for once," he burst out, "just for once, I'd hoped I'd get there first." He shrugged. "I've spent the whole night working through the files. I've so often seen you do it, when you feel we're getting close to a solution, and I thought . . . Oh, I'm a damned fool, that's all."

"Go and freshen up, Mike, then come back and we'll talk about it. But just get this into your head, will you? At your age, *I* would have felt — in fact, I often did feel — precisely as you are feeling now. Now go. And get yourself some breakfast while you're about it. No one can work efficiently on an empty stomach and I need your help."

Lineham went. While he was gone, Thanet turned the situation over in his mind. It was true that at Mike's age he had frequently felt as Mike did now — but with a difference. Thanet wasn't certain but he sensed in the sergeant some deeper need this time to have solved the case first, a compensatory need perhaps. But to compensate for what? A sense of failure in some area of his life? Of course — his relationship with Louise. That must be it. The trouble between them must be even more serious than Thanet had thought. Or had he just been choosing to ignore what he didn't want to see? He remembered the conversation with Joan the other day, how she had urged him to speak to Lineham, and he frowned. Had he been shirking his responsibilities simply because they were

182

unpalatable? No, dammit, he had given Lineham enough openings to talk, if the sergeant chose to do so. Besides, if Lineham's marriage really was on the rocks then he needed expert help, not the well-intentioned fumblings of the amateur Thanet felt himself to be. But Lineham's work . . . well, that was a different matter. Lineham's state of mind in that area was fairly and squarely Thanet's responsibility and he would have to think of some way in which the sergeant could receive that boost to his morale which he so clearly needed.

By the time Lineham returned, looking relatively fresh and alert, Thanet thought he saw how this could be done.

"Now, then, Mike," he said, "sit down and let's see if we can get this straight. It's true that I think I can now see exactly what happened in the Pettifer case — though there is one big snag I'm hoping you'll be able to help me with — so there's no point in pretending you're going to get there first. But I don't see why it still shouldn't be perfectly possible for you to work it out for yourself if you want to."

"What do you mean?" There was a wary gleam of anticipation in Lineham's eyes, as if he'd like to believe Thanet but couldn't quite bring himself to do so.

"Put it this way. Why not look on this case as a learning exercise. Then, if you do manage to work it out for yourself, next time you'll find it that much easier. Practice and experience really do count, you know."

"I don't see how I could. I've been thinking all night," Lineham gestured at the files, "and I've got precisely nowhere."

"Look Mike," said Thanet, leaning sideways to take his pipe from his pocket, "a good detective not only has to be intelligent, persevering and prepared to do endless boring, routine work, he also needs one other quality." Thanet took his pipe apart, blew through the stem and, satisfied, reassembled it. "Some people call it intuition and talk about it as if it were magic. Some consider it unreliable — and, admittedly, the dictionary definition of intuition is 'immediate apprehension by the mind without reasoning'. I don't quite see it like that. I see it, rather, as the ability to make connections which are there but are not immediately apparent. Subterranean connections, I suppose you could call them."

"I don't follow you." Lineham was sitting back in his chair, arms folded, listening intently. Clearly the therapy was working and Thanet tried not to feel too smug.

"Well, say a man has a motor-bike accident. The *apparent* cause of the accident is that someone stepped off the kerb without looking and caused the driver to swerve, skid and crash. But the *real* reason was that, the night before, the man who stepped off the kerb had had a row with his girlfriend and he was thinking so hard about that that he wasn't looking where he was going. The connection between this girl and the man on the motor-bike is not immediately apparent, but it's there all right. Life's made up of subterranean connections like that and part of our job is to try to work out what they are. Now when you apply this to the Pettifer case . . ."

"Yes?" Lineham was engrossed now, eager.

Thanet took out his pouch and began to fill his pipe, pressing the tobacco carefully down in the bowl with his forefinger as he talked. "Well, when I was thinking about it last night I began in the usual way, looking back and reassessing, the sort of thing we do all the time. Now this case was unusual in that, whereas we normally know from the start whether a murder has been committed or not, this time we were not sure. So I took that as my starting point."

"You mean, you began by looking at the reasons why we suspected that it might not have been suicide."

"Yes. Now, you go on from there."

Lineham's eyes narrowed in concentration. "Well, first of all, there was general agreement that Pettifer had no reason to kill himself. His housekeeper, his wife, his secretary, his partner, all said the same thing, that he had no financial worries, he was in good health and he had no marital problems either." Lineham's eyes darkened and Thanet said quickly, "That's right. That's important. No one around him at any time suspected that there was anything wrong between them. Of course, we soon found out that Mrs Pettifer had a lover; but we still believed her husband had been unaware of this until, quite by chance, we discovered from his previous mother-in-law that Pettifer was sterile and must therefore have known about his wife's infidelity for months, right from the time she first told him she was pregnant.''

"Not by chance, sir." Lineham was looking discouraged again. "I'd never have thought of going to see her. Why *did* you?"

"A general uneasiness, I suppose, revolving around the question of children. Things just didn't add up. The inconsistencies in Pettifer's attitude were too great. He apparently took pains to make sure his second wife wouldn't want children before he even asked her to marry him, yet everyone agreed he was over the moon when she became pregnant. Then Dr Lowrie told me that Pettifer didn't really like children — that, although Pettifer became fond of his adopted son, initially he had agreed to the adoption chiefly to please his first wife. Anyway, let's leave that for the moment, go back to the reasons why we suspected it might not have been suicide.''

Lineham considered. "Well I suppose the first specific indication was that holiday booking. You don't pay a couple of thousand quid for a holiday just a few hours before you intend to kill yourself.''

Thanet was lighting up now and he waited until the match had burned down to the end before extinguishing it with a quick flick of the wrist and saying, "Quite. Go on.''

"Then there was the car. Why bother to arrange for your car to be repaired if you know you'll never need it again? And the next thing was the note." Lineham was getting into his stride now. "The mis-spelling of Andrew's nickname, I mean. That really did seem suspicious, because if Pettifer had always spelt it one way he was hardly likely to alter it, even under stress — and of course that rather peculiar spelling was the sort of thing that no one but Andrew would know about unless they had actually seen Pettifer's letters to Andrew. And then we found out about the fingerprints. Why should Mrs Pettifer's prints be on not only the port bottle but the tablet container and glass too, when according to her she hadn't handled any of them? Later we found she'd given Pettifer the port for his birthday, but that didn't explain the other prints away. Even more interesting, of course, was the fact that, although Pettifer's prints were also on the bottle, they weren't on either container or glass . . .''

"Exactly. So by this point we had moved on from a general suspicion of murder to having a specific suspect."

"Mrs Pettifer. Yes." Lineham was frowning in concentration. "Then came the discovery that she had a lover, which meant that she also had a possible motive for wanting her husband out of the way."

"Go on."

"Well, next we got the PM results, which showed that Pettifer had been in perfect health, so that our last hope of finding a possible reason for suicide was gone . . .''

". . . unless, of course, he had killed himself through grief because he had found out that his wife had a lover."

"Yes, but at the time we still didn't think he had found out. There was absolutely nothing in his behaviour to indicate that he had. On the contrary, everyone agreed that he was in the best of spirits . . .'' Lineham stopped, his forehead creased. "Though it really is beyond me to understand why he should have chosen to carry on all those months as though nothing had happened . . .''

Thanet waited. Would Lineham at last see the crucial significance of this aspect of Pettifer's behaviour?

Apparently not. Lineham shook his head sharply, as if to clear it of confusion. "I just can't see . . .''

"Leave it for the moment. You will, shortly, if I'm not mistaken. Get back to the post mortem."

"Yes, well the other interesting thing about that was that there were no signs of the cold which Mrs Pettifer claimed was the reason why her husband had gone to bed early and she'd had to dose him with paracetamol. And, when we asked around, we discovered that no one else had noticed any cold symptoms. For that matter, we later heard that there were no traces of paracetamol in his stomach . . .''

"In short, her story was riddled with discrepancies."

"Exactly. And then," Lineham went on eagerly, "to cap it all, we discover that the night Pettifer died Mrs Pettifer got her lover to drive her down to Pine Lodge from London in the middle of the night. She claims she did this in response to her husband's request during a phone call which she says he *asked* her to make, and also says that when she did get here she couldn't get into the house and drove straight back to London in a huff. Lee confirms that they drove back almost at once, but he didn't go up to the house with her and the point is that she was there at Pine Lodge alone for ten minutes or so round about the time Pettifer took the overdose. So, not only did she have motive, she could well also have had opportunity. *But* . . ." Lineham paused.

"Yes, this is where it becomes interesting, isn't it? But . . ."

"But," Lineham went on slowly, picking his words now as he thought aloud, "so much of what she said or did seemed incomprehensible. Why, if she had killed him and arranged it to look like suicide, did she keep insisting it couldn't have been? Why produce the holiday booking, to back up what she was saying — why not just keep quiet about it? Why say he had a cold if he hadn't? Or claim to have given him paracetamol if she didn't? Why, above all, if she did murder him, didn't she give herself a decent alibi, rather than go off to spend the night in a London hotel with her lover. And why *volunteer* the information that she and Lee had made that suspicious dash down to Sturrenden in the middle of the night when she had no idea that we were already on to it? There's the possibility of course that she was trying to deflect suspicion by appearing to be ultra-helpful, a bewildered innocent, so to speak, but that still didn't explain why her story was riddled with discrepancies. Unless . . ." he said hesitantly.

Lineham was almost there. Thanet found that he was holding his breath. He was aware, too, of an uncomfortable emotion which was rather difficult to identify. What was it? he asked himself while he waited. Chagrin, perhaps, that by simple logic Lineham was apparently about to arrive at the solution which Thanet had thought attainable only by his own more intuitive approach?

"Unless she said and did all those things in good faith," Lineham concluded.

He sounded bewildered, disorientated, as though he had scaled what he thought was the mountain peak only to find further heights stretching away ahead of him.

"Go on. Go on, dammit. Don't stop. Follow it through."

"But how, sir? I just don't see where all this is leading."

"You will. You will. Just go on. If she said and did all those things in good faith . . ."

"Then," said Lineham slowly, "I suppose someone must have convinced her that they were true."

"Who?" said Thanet softly.

"It could only have been . . ." Lineham stopped. "No, it couldn't have been."

"Who? Dammit, say it, man."

"*Pettifer?*" Lineham's face was a study in bewilderment.

Thanet gave a slow, satisfied nod. "Pettifer."

"But that's crazy!" Lineham burst out.

"Is it? Just think about it, Mike. Why, for instance, should he say he had a cold, if he hadn't?"

"To make her feel sorry for him? So that she wouldn't go to London? No, it couldn't have been that. She said he insisted she went. And, if we're working on the premise that she's been acting in good faith, telling the truth all along . . . It's no good. I just can't see why the hell he should lie about a thing like that."

"Oh, come on, Mike. Don't give in!" Thanet puffed over-vigorously at his pipe in his urgency and a shower of sparks cascaded over his lap. He jumped up, flapping his hand at them. "And stop grinning, will you?"

"Shall I dial 999?"

"Just keep your mind on the job," growled Thanet, sitting down again. If he heard another joke about the Fire Service . . . He had never lived down the day when he had unwittingly set his wastepaper basket alight with an imperfectly extinguished match, just before leaving the office. It had been several years before the burnt carpet had finally been renewed amidst much grumbling from above about waste of tax-payers money, rank carelessness and the dangers and undesirability

188

of smoking (the Chief himself being a non-smoker, of course).

"Come on, now. Why should he have deliberately misled her?" Thanet persisted.

Lineham gritted his teeth in frustration, thumped his fist on his desk. "It's no good. I just can't see it."

"All right, calm down. Let's try another tack. Go back to what you were saying a moment ago, that he must have known about his wife's unfaithfulness for months, right from the moment he first learnt she was pregnant, but that he apparently did nothing about it. Thinking about him, about the sort of man he was, how would you have expected him to react when she told him?"

Lineham considered. "I was thinking about this, last night. I'd guess he would have been very upset, of course, but he wouldn't have shown it at the time . . . Partly because he was a very controlled sort of person and partly because he couldn't have let her know that her news had immediately told him that she was being unfaithful to him, without giving his secret away."

"That he was sterile. Yes. So, to cover up his real feelings, he pretends to be pleased. Then what?"

"I'm not sure. When he'd had time to think about it, I imagine he'd have been very angry. I certainly don't think he could have dismissed it from his mind. We know from what Dr Barson told you that he was the type to bear a grudge and if he was feeling thoroughly disillusioned . . . I think he'd have wanted to punish her."

"Yes, but how?"

"Well, there was no point in confronting her with it. She might simply have left him to go to her lover. And even if she didn't, things would never have been the same between them again. Anyway, that wouldn't exactly have been punishing her, would it? And we know he didn't disinherit her."

"Which in itself is interesting, isn't it?"

"So what was the point of killing himself! It just leaves her free to go to Lee as a rich woman."

"Slow down, Mike. You're in too much of a hurry. Try to think yourself back into his mind. He wants to punish her. And the problem is, how? Now, look at that thought in the light of what he actually did. What *did* he do?"

"Well . . . nothing, so far as I can see."

"I don't think that's quite true. Think back to what everyone said about him, about their marriage."

"That everything in the garden seemed to be rosy, you mean?"

"Too rosy?"

Lineham's eyes narrowed. "You mean, that it was deliberate policy, on his part, to give that impression?"

"Think of the day he died. They all agreed that he was in unusually high spirits, didn't they?"

"You mean, that was all a sham? A calculated attempt to mislead them?"

"Them, yes. And, perhaps . . . us?"

"*Us*? But . . ."

"So think, Mike. What have we got now? A desire for revenge, on his wife. A deliberate effort to mislead everyone who knew him and, as a consequence, anyone who might investigate his death. So that everyone would say that he had no possible reason for suicide . . ."

Thanet stopped. Lineham's eyes had gone blank, his mouth had dropped open. He looked, quite literally, stunned.

"You see?" Thanet said, on a long exhalation of satisfaction.

Lineham's lips moved, but no sound emerged. Finally, "*He set her up* . . ." he croaked. "That's what you mean, isn't it?" He was silent for a moment or two then he burst out, "But that really is crazy! Absolutely stark staring bonkers! Sorry, sir, but you can't seriously expect me to believe that in order to punish his wife he decided to kill himself so as to get her convicted of murdering him! Talk about cutting off his nose to spite his face!"

"But why not? Don't you see, it's the perfect solution. In one fell swoop he gets his revenge on his wife *and* makes sure she won't be free to go to her lover or to inherit."

"Perfect solution! Aren't you forgetting one small detail, that he has to kill himself off in the process?"

190

"Ah yes. Well, that's the snag I mentioned to you earlier."

"Snag!" Lineham took a deep breath and with a visible attempt at self-control and reasonableness went on, "Look sir, I don't want to be rude or . . . insubordinate, and I know you've come up with some pretty weird ideas before and you've been proved right, but . . ."

"This time, you think I've gone over the top, right? Don't worry, Mike, I can sympathise with how you feel. And I must admit, I felt exactly the same myself, when I first worked it out — congratulations, by the way. You did it, didn't you?"

"Did what?"

"Worked it out. Yourself."

"Did I, sir?"

"Well, I admit I had to give you a little nudge now and then, but . . ."

"No, I didn't mean that. I mean, I'm just not convinced we've reached the right conclusion, that's all. Look, sir, Dr Pettifer was an intelligent man. If he really was as vindictive as you seem to think he was, why not work out a way of taking his revenge that would not only leave him alive and kicking but would give him the pleasure of *seeing* his wife suffer. This way he wouldn't even have the satisfaction of knowing if his plan had worked."

"Perhaps he was past caring. Anyway, crazy as it may sound, I'm convinced that that's the way it was." Thanet tapped out his pipe and crossed restlessly to the window. "The trouble is, Mike, there's a piece of the puzzle missing. Somewhere there's a piece of information which would explain everything, something that would make us say, 'Ah, yes, so *that*'s why he did it.' "

The telephone rang. Lineham picked it up, listened, glanced sharply at Thanet. "I'll tell him," he said, a grin spreading slowly across his face. "I expect he'll come out right away." He replaced the receiver.

"Well?"

Lineham continued to grin.

"Mike, if you don't take that silly smirk off your face and tell me . . . Who was that, anyway?"

"If you'd answered the phone and I'd asked that question, I think you'd have said it was Fate, sir."

"Mike . . ." Thanet felt like grinding his teeth.

"It was Mrs Pettifer. Urgent, she said."

"Did she tell you what it was about?"

"She didn't want to discuss it on the telephone. But apparently she had a letter this morning. Which, she says, will explain everything."

We must look like two Cheshire cats, thought Thanet, as he said, "What are we waiting for? Let's go."

22

"I gather she didn't say who it was from," Thanet said.

Lineham shook his head. He was driving fast, but with concentration. "Said she'd rather not say, until she sees us."

"I wonder . . ." Thanet knew that there was really no point in speculating, but couldn't help himself.

"Her husband?" suggested Lineham, with a mischievous glance at Thanet.

"One of those 'Voice from the Grave' things, you mean? A bit melodramatic, don't you think? Besides, he'd hardly have written two letters, surely? If he'd had anything to say, he'd have said it in the suicide note."

"Except that suicide notes are always made public. Perhaps he didn't want anyone but his wife to read this one."

"Possible, I suppose. How did she sound? Mrs Pettifer?"

"Relieved, I should say."

"Relieved . . ." mused Thanet. "Anyway," he said as they turned into Brompton Lane, "we'll soon find out now."

Mrs Price answered the door promptly. There was an earthenware jug of chrysanthemums and copper-beech leaves on the oak blanket-chest this morning, their glowing colours reflected in the highly polished surface. "Mrs Pettifer will be down in just a moment." She led them into the drawing room.

"How is she today?" Thanet asked.

Mrs Price gave a slight shrug. "Seems a bit better. More cheerful. I think she had some good news in the post this morning. Didn't touch her breakfast, though."

Footsteps could be heard on the stairs and a moment later Gemma Pettifer entered the room. Traces of yesterday's despair still lingered in the dark smudges beneath her eyes, but the beaten, defeated air had quite vanished away. This morning she had taken trouble with her make-up and her hair was newly washed, floating about her shoulders in a gleaming curtain. She was wearing another filmy Indian cotton dress, this time in a pale, limpid green which emphasised the colour of her eyes. For the first time Thanet recognised that illusion of beauty which she always succeeded in creating upon the stage. This was the Gemma with whom Pettifer had fallen in love. She was carrying an envelope and a heavy book.

"Good morning, Inspector," she said. "Good morning, Sergeant. Do sit down. Mrs Price, what I have to say concerns Dr Pettifer's death and you have been with him so long . . . do stay, if you wish." She sat down in one of the wing chairs beside the fireplace.

Thanet chose the matching armchair on the other side of the hearth. Mrs Price sat down stiffly on the small upright chair in front of the little writing desk and Lineham perched on the edge of the settee. He took out his notebook.

"This came this morning." Gemma handed the envelope to Thanet.

Anticipation fizzed through his veins as he took it, extracted the single sheet of paper. He glanced at the signature. Benedict Randall? Thanet had never heard of him. Quickly, he skimmed the brief note.

Dear Mrs Pettifer,

I did not return from holiday until yesterday and have only just learned of your husband's death. He was a fine doctor and a friend of many years standing and it is a tragedy that he was unable to come to terms with what was happening to him. Inevitably, I cannot help feeling a measure of guilt in not having recognised the depth and degree of his distress.

If there is, at any time, any way in which I may be of service to you, please do not hesitate to call on me.

My most sincere condolences,
Benedict Randall

Thanet's mind raced as he read. Whatever could the man be

194

referring to? There could be only one possible explanation. But in that case, why hadn't . . .?

"He assumes, as you see, that I would know what he was talking about," Gemma said. Like Lineham and Mrs Price, she had been watching Thanet eagerly.

"And what *was* he talking about? May I?" Thanet waited for her nod before handing the letter to Lineham.

"Well, I'd no idea, of course, so I rang him up. We'd met briefly, once or twice. He's a consultant neurologist at Sturrenden General. He's very well known in his field, has a practice in Harley Street."

"What did he say?"

"That my husband was suffering from disseminated sclerosis — multiple sclerosis, it's often called."

Mrs Price drew in her breath sharply, with a slight hissing sound.

"Yes," Gemma said, glancing at her. "You'd well be able to understand what that would mean to him, Mrs Price." She turned back to Thanet. "Apparently my husband asked Mr Randall never to mention this diagnosis to anyone, not even to me if by any chance we should meet. Mr Randall assumed that Arnold wanted to tell me in his own good time and also assumed that Arnold's death had released him from that promise. He was pretty shattered to find that I still didn't know anything about it." She shook her head. "My husband couldn't have borne it, Inspector. He was so proud, so fiercely independent . . . the prospect would have been truly intolerable to him." She shivered and, so fleetingly that Thanet could almost have thought that he had imagined it, there was a flicker of repulsion in her eyes. Thanet remembered what Deborah Chivers had told him of Gemma's loathing of illness.

"I've heard of it of course," Thanet said, "but I know very little about it."

"Mr Randall explained it to me. And I've just been looking it up in a medical dictionary." She opened the book on her lap at a marked place and handed it to Thanet.

" '*A disease in which nerve linings around scattered small areas of the brain and spinal cord are attacked by some unknown agent,*' " Thanet read aloud. " '*In severe cases tissue may be destroyed and nerves cease to function.*' "

"By an unknown agent," Lineham said. "That's pretty terrifying."

"I know." Gemma's eyes were dark with imagined horror. "Mr Randall said that the cause of it is not known. It doesn't run in families — thank God," and she folded her arms protectively across her body. "And it's not contagious. It's a disease, apparently, of temperate climates, like ours, and my husband was rather older than people normally are when it first attacks. It says in there," and she nodded at the dictionary, "that the typical victim is a young adult."

"What are the symptoms?" Lineham was staring at Gemma with a kind of fascinated dread.

" '*Weakness, pins and needles,*' " Thanet read aloud, " '*double vision or impaired eyesight, difficulty in walking or in intricate movements such as threading a needle.*' Apparently they last a few days, then they may disappear. But they will recur after widely varying intervals of weeks, months, even years. The pattern is of a series of attacks with these periods of recovery in between. It says here that this is why the disease is frequently not diagnosed in its early stages. Presumably the symptoms disappear, the victim shrugs it off and forgets about it until the next time."

"That's right," Gemma said. "Mr Randall said that this can happen a number of times over a period of years before the patient finally does something about it."

"So your husband suspected that he might have fallen victim to it and consulted Mr Randall."

"That's right. Being a doctor, of course, he was able to refer himself direct to a consultant. People normally have to go through their GPs. And also, he naturally became suspicious far earlier than most people would have."

"Which is why his condition had not yet become obvious and none of the people about him suspected the truth."

"Exactly."

"I remember Dr Lowrie mentioning to me that your husband thought at one time that he might have to have

196

reading glasses, but that it turned out to be unnecessary. That may well have been one of the earlier attacks."

"That's what Mr Randall said. Apparently my husband had his eyes tested, but by then the symptoms had vanished and his eyesight appeared perfect. Then there was the time he pulled a muscle in his leg. Apparently it's very common for people to trip over nothing . . ."

"I remember that," Mrs Price intervened. "Oh, sorry, Mrs Pettifer, I didn't mean to interrupt."

"That's all right, Mrs Price. Do go on."

"I saw it happen, that's all. I was looking out of the kitchen window. Dr Pettifer was walking down the garden path and he stumbled, tripped and fell over suddenly, just like that. I ran out, but he was already getting up again. But I couldn't understand it at all. There was just nothing he could have tripped over, I looked."

"And how long ago was that, did you say?" asked Thanet.

"About eighteen months ago."

"Just a few months after we were married," Gemma said. "So you see . . ." She shivered and there, once again, was that flicker of repulsion.

Oh yes, Thanet saw all right. Here then at last was a believable reason for Pettifer to have committed suicide, Pettifer the "exercise fanatic" as Lowrie had called him . . . To endure not only increasing immobility, paralysis and dependence but the disgust of the wife he adored . . . Tragedy indeed. Learning of her unfaithfulness must have been the last straw.

"But the post mortem," Lineham was saying, and Thanet looked at him with approval. It was a point he had been about to raise himself. "Why didn't anything show up in the post mortem?"

"I asked Mr Randall about that," Gemma said. "Apparently it wouldn't show up in a routine post mortem, especially in the early stages of the disease. Even a really good pathologist could miss it. Are you all right, Mrs Price?"

The housekeeper had taken out a handkerchief and was wiping her eyes. Now she shook her head, her face crumpled with grief. "I can't believe it," she said. "To think that the

197

doctor . . ." She shook her head again, stood up blindly. "If you'd excuse me," she said.

Gemma crossed to put an arm around the housekeeper's shoulders as she blundered to the door. "Why don't you go and lie down for a while? Take the day off, if you like. I can manage perfectly well, I'm sure."

Mrs Price blew her nose, straightened her shoulders. "I'm better off doing things," she said. "But thank you."

It looked as though the two women were beginning to come to terms with each other at last, Thanet thought, watching them.

When the housekeeper had left the room, Gemma came back and stood in front of the fireplace, facing Thanet. "So there we are, Inspector. I must say that, although I feel very sad on my husband's behalf," and her eyes glistened with unshed tears which she blinked away, "it's a great relief to me to know that there was a reason . . ."

Thanet was aware that Lineham had made a tiny, restless movement.

". . . and so glad, for the baby's sake, that the mystery has been cleared up." She laid a protective hand on the mound of her stomach. "It'll be bad enough as it is, knowing that his father committed suicide, but never to have known why . . ."

Thanet stood up. "Yes. There is just one last question I'd like to ask you, though. Whose suggestion was it that you go to London that night — as opposed to any other night, I mean. Yours or your husband's?"

She considered, head on one side. "His, I think. Yes, it was. I'd been reading a script, considering a part and, as I think I told you before, I simply couldn't make up my mind whether to take it or not, and Arnold said, why didn't I go up to see my agent, discuss it with him."

"When was this?"

"Oh, let me see . . . Some time early last week."

"And which of you suggested you go on Monday?"

"Arnold did. I remember because I knew that Mrs Price was going to be away for the night and I suggested I go some other time instead. Arnold said no, that it would give him a chance to get on with something he'd been planning for some time. It was he who suggested I stay the night in London. He said it would be less tiring for me . . ." Her face was beginning to disintegrate. "I'd forgotten that. I suppose he wanted us both out of the house. He probably didn't want to risk one of us finding him before . . . before . . ." She shook her head as the tears brimmed over and began to roll down her cheeks.

Lineham was looking at Thanet with outraged expectancy. Clearly he was waiting for Thanet to disillusion her.

"What I can't bear," she said, "is the thought that he changed his mind at the last minute, that he called me for help and I . . . just went away, left him to die. If only I'd forced my way in, somehow . . ."

"I shouldn't dwell too much on that if I were you. Knowing your husband, what sort of a life do you think it would have been for him, as time went on?"

She compressed her lips, shook her head. "I suppose you're right," she said doubtfully.

Thanet stood up. "Anyway, it does seem as though the mystery is explained at last. I shouldn't think we'll need to trouble you again."

She blew her nose, made an effort to smile, followed them out into the hall. "You know . . ." she said.

With the front door half open Thanet and Lineham paused, turned politely.

"Those cruise tickets," she said. "I'm beginning to think of them as Arnold's last message to me. I think he was saying, Go on living. And enjoy it."

The briefest of glances at Lineham's face was enough. With a hasty goodbye to Gemma Pettifer, Thanet hustled him out to the car. He propelled the sergeant into the passenger seat. Safer, this time, if he took the wheel himself.

"Go on living and enjoy it, indeed!" Lineham exploded as they fastened their seat belts. "Incredible, isn't it? Really incredible!"

"What is, exactly?" Lineham needed to get it off his chest.

"And all that stuff about the baby. Who is she trying to fool?"

"Herself, perhaps?" Thanet said softly. "Or perhaps she really does believe it. After all, Mike, you must remember that as far as she's concerned, her husband could well be the father. She has no idea he was sterile, we can be sure of that."

"But it's all wrong!"

"What is?"

"To let her go on thinking . . . all those things she is thinking. That he killed himself solely because of his illness, for a start. That he didn't know she was being unfaithful to him . . . That he thought the baby was his . . . And all that rubbish about the cruise being a gift for the future and him wanting her to be happy, when we know that he tried to set her up on a murder charge, for God's sake!"

"You're convinced now, then?"

"Oh yes. No doubt about it. You were right — as usual," he added with a wry grin. "But surely, sir, you're not just going to leave it like that?"

"You mean, you think it's my duty to explain all this to her?"

"Well, yes."

"Why?"

"Well . . ."

"To punish her for her sins, is that it?"

Lineham had the grace to look abashed.

"No, Mike. My brief is finished and that's that. Our job was to get at the truth of the matter and that we've done. And besides, she may not realise it at the moment, but she's going to pay all right, in her own way."

"What do you mean?"

"Wait until we get back to the office and I'll tell you. Though that demonstration you gave earlier shows that you're perfectly capable of working it out for yourself."

Lineham did not reply and a glance at his face told Thanet that the challenge had been taken up, the sergeant's righteous indignation diverted.

Thanet swerved to avoid a cyclist who had suddenly wobbled out in front of the car. They were approaching the centre of the town now and the mid-morning traffic was building up.

He settled down to concentrate on his driving.

23

With the Pettifer case closed, Thanet felt free to take Sunday off. Any residual paperwork could be done on Monday. But Joan had promised to drive Mrs Markham to Bexhill . . .

"Why don't I drive you down?" he suggested. "It's a glorious day. We could take a picnic, to the beach."

"Lovely idea, darling." Joan hugged him. "I'll wear my new sweater, to celebrate."

"Smashing, Dad!" (Ben)

"A whole day off, Daddy!" (Bridget)

"Yes, poppet. A whole day." Thanet suppressed a twinge of guilt that this should seem so unusual an occurrence.

The sun shone, the roads were empty, they were all in a holiday mood and the journey was soon over. They delivered Mrs Markham into the arms of her suitably appreciative daughter-in-law, then went down to the beach. They hadn't been here before and were delighted to find that it was sandy.

"I'm glad I packed the buckets and spades," murmured Joan as they settled down.

Bridget and Ben immediately began to discuss and sketch out on the sand ambitious plans for a moated castle complete with drawbridge. Joan and Thanet watched them for a while and then agreed to take it in turns to keep an eye on them while the other relaxed.

Thanet loved the sun and a day as warm as this so late in the year was a bonus indeed. He lay revelling in its mellow warmth, conscious of it soaking into his skin, his flesh, his very bones, it seemed. The plaintive mewing of the gulls, the rhythmic sigh of the sea and the distant cries of children playing receded into a distant music that soothed the spirit. Wonderful to relax like this, he thought. Wonderful not to have to think about work. Glad the Pettifer case is finished . . .

His own voice echoed in his mind. "*You see, Mike, a good detective also needs one other quality: intuition.*" Well, Mike had shown him just how essential intuition was.

"What's the matter?" Joan said.

"Nothing. Why?"

"You groaned."

"Did I?"

"Well, sort of. A little groan."

Thanet rolled over, sat up. "I was just thinking what a conceited, condescending, patronising idiot I am."

"Wow! Is that all?"

"That's all."

They grinned at each other.

"And what, exactly, put that ego-boosting thought into your head?"

"I was thinking about Mike." And he told her about Lineham's bitter disappointment that he hadn't beaten Thanet to it, of his own sense of Lineham's need to achieve at that particular moment, of his stratagem to help him do it.

"And did it work?"

"Yes. Only too well."

"So, what are you worrying about?"

"The way I lectured him first. Pontificated. Babbled on about intuition, subterranean connections . . ."

"Subterranean connections?"

Thanet explained. ". . . It makes my toes curl to think about it."

"But why? You did get there before him, after all."

"I know, but . . . It was the *way* Mike did it. Oh, I know I had to push him a little, to keep him going. If he has a fault in this respect, it's to give up too soon. But he did get there. And by logic."

"So?"

"Well, it shook me. There I was, thinking I had something special, the policeman's nose, some people call it . . ."

"Well, it is something special. Maybe Mike was able to get there by logic, deduction, whatever you like to call it, this

202

time — but another time it might simply not work."

"That's true, I suppose."

"Anyway, if you didn't get there by logic, how did you get there?"

Thanet had of course told Joan about the outcome of the case, but until now there had been no opportunity to talk at leisure.

Thanet considered. "Well, I suppose the turning point for me was the discovery that Pettifer was sterile."

"Why was that so important?"

"Because it destroyed his credibility. It showed that he'd been acting out a lie to everyone, including his wife, in pretending that there was nothing wrong with their marriage. It made me question everything I had until then accepted. I simply couldn't believe, from what I'd heard about him, that he could just have shrugged his shoulders and ignored his wife's infidelity. And yet he obviously *wanted* everyone to believe he was unaware of it. So I had to ask myself, why?"

"Why do you say you don't feel he could have accepted it? Some men can."

Thanet shook his head. "Not Pettifer. He was a proud man. Reserved, and devious, too. And vindictive. There's a story Dr Barson told me about him . . ." Thanet related it to Joan.

She wrinkled her nose. "Nasty."

"Quite. It shows that Pettifer wasn't the type to forgive and forget. And especially where his wife was concerned. Everyone agreed, he idolised her. He would have been shattered. And he'd have wanted revenge, I was convinced of it. Of course, when we finally heard about the multiple sclerosis everything became clear at last."

"Poor man. It's a terrible, terrible disease."

"I know. And for someone like Pettifer . . . He must have been in despair. As his wife said, it would have been truly intolerable for him to know that as time went on he would become increasingly dependent, immobile . . . To have envisaged progressive paralysis, years spent in a wheelchair as an invalid . . . And of course, he would have been aware of her revulsion from any kind of sickness. I should imagine that, even before she told him she was pregnant and he learned she'd been unfaithful to him, he must already have contemplated the possibility of suicide at some future date, when the symptoms became more pronounced.''

"He'd have been angry, too," said Joan. "People often are, with a disease like that. They think, naturally, 'Why me?' ''

"I agree. And then she told him about the baby. Now, looking back, I'd guess that it was at that point that his anger switched direction and focused on her.''

"D'you remember that book I read a year or two ago?" Joan said suddenly. "By that American woman? The one about women as murderers.''

"Vaguely. I meant to read it, didn't I, and never got around to it.''

"That's right. I told you at the time you'd have found it interesting. Anyway, the author said that her thinking on the subject had been shaped by the realisation that murder could be a psychological alternative to suicide. She said that, especially in Victorian times, trapped in desperately unhappy marriages by force of circumstance — no money, no chance of supporting themselves by taking a job, no divorce — they often had only two choices, murder or suicide.''

"I'm not sure what you're saying. That Pettifer was in that position?''

"To some extent, yes. His hands were tied in so many ways, weren't they? He couldn't make his illness go away, he couldn't try to forget his wife had been unfaithful because the baby would always be there as a reminder . . .''

"That's true. And of course, we must remember that at the time she didn't know he was sterile — she still doesn't, for that matter — and she would naturally have expected him to think that he was the father of the child. So he had no freedom of choice there, either: he couldn't say he wasn't without letting her know of his sterility, so he dared not show her what the news really meant to him. I should think he was so afraid of giving his secret away that he covered up his confusion by reacting the opposite way and pretending to be pleased. And then, when he thought about it, he saw how he could use that initial reaction to his own advantage. He saw how he could put an end to his own intolerable situation *and* punish her at the same time. He would kill himself and somehow make sure that she would be blamed for his death. It must have appeared the perfect solution. This way she wouldn't be free to go to her lover or enjoy the wealth she would inherit . . ."

Joan shuddered. "Really, it makes me shiver to think about it. To be so cold-blooded . . ."

Thanet squeezed her hand. "I know . . . Anyway, I'd guess he took his time working out the details of his plan. The most important thing was to make sure that no one would believe he had any reason to commit suicide. This is why it was so vital to convince everyone that he was unaware of his wife's infidelity. I don't suppose it entered his head for a moment that we'd find out that he was sterile. He couldn't have realised that his first wife had told her mother, and even if he had I don't suppose he would have thought we might find out that way. He hadn't seen his mother-in-law for years, they didn't get on, and she must have seemed so remote from his present existence that I don't suppose she even came into his calculations. And he made sure — or so he thought — that we wouldn't find out about his illness, by asking Mr Randall, the neurologist, not to mention it to anyone, even Mrs Pettifer."

"There was a risk there, though, surely. He must have realised that Mr Randall might consider himself absolved from the promise by Dr Pettifer's death."

"True. But it was a risk he had to take. He could hardly go to the length of asking the man to consider his promise binding even after death, without making him suspicious that suicide was on the cards. And in that case Mr Randall might have considered himself justified in breaking that promise and approaching Mrs Pettifer."

"True."

"He had to take some risks, after all. The best he could do was try to foresee as many loopholes as possible, and stop them up. He dared not change his will as insurance against his wife inheriting if his plan went wrong, for example, because that would have told us that he knew about her affair."

"So this was why right up to the end he went on behaving as though he expected to have a future — why he arranged to have his car repaired, for example."

"Yes. And booked that cruise. All designed to make us think it couldn't have been suicide."

"And went on pretending to be delighted about the baby," Joan said with a sigh.

"Exactly. Meanwhile, he made his personal preparations for his death, put his affairs in order and cleared his desk. He was the sort of man who would hate the thought of anyone going through his private correspondence, even after he was dead. That desk of his, together with the method he chose to kill himself, were the only things which made me think he might have killed himself after all. He'd kept the clearance to a minimum, but there was such a vast, obvious absence of personal paraphernalia."

"Yes, I meant to ask you about the method he chose. You said that all the doctors you spoke to agreed that it was the one they would opt for. If he wanted to make sure you thought it was murder, why didn't he choose something less . . . oh, dear, what's the right word? Comfortable?"

"I know. That stumped me too. Then I thought, well, yes, he desperately wanted his plan to succeed, but all the other methods would have seemed either so difficult to set up or so messy or painful that in the end he thought, what the hell, you only die once, I'll go out gracefully."

"Yes, I can see that. I suppose that's how it must have been. Just a minute . . ." Joan scrambled to her feet. The castle was taking shape. Bridget was creating the building itself, Ben digging out the moat. Now they were both claiming the right to construct the most interesting part, the drawbridge with its tunnel beneath. Thanet looked on indulgently as Joan arbitrated. God, what a lucky man he was! He sent up a silent prayer of gratitude as he waited for her to return.

"All settled?"

"More or less. Anyway, what were you saying?"

"Well, having firmly established in everyone's minds the picture of a man with everything to live for, he moved on to

206

planning the details of the suicide/apparent-murder. What he had to do was lay a careful trail for the police to follow so that they would be sufficiently suspicious to feel they had to dig a little."

"Which is what happened."

"Yes. The first bit of planted 'evidence' was of course the note, with its mis-spelling of Andrew's nickname."

"Ah yes, I remember you asking about that right at the beginning."

"I suppose that, knowing Andrew, Pettifer counted on his demanding to see the note and spotting the mistake, as indeed he did."

"That was another risk, surely? What if Andrew had never seen it?"

"Then other things would have made us suspicious anyway. This was just an additional pointer that it hadn't been suicide. For all we know there may yet be other 'clues' we haven't yet discovered. Interestingly enough, though, it was this very bit of 'evidence' — which was supposed to, and did make us suspect that it might have been murder — that in the end put me on to the fact that it had been suicide after all. Together with something else that had absolutely nothing to do with the case. That was where my famous 'intuition' came in."

"What do you mean? No, tell me later, when you've finished explaining what Pettifer planned to do."

"Well, as I said, he wanted first to make us suspect that it was murder and then point us specifically in the direction of his wife. And this was where things began to get complicated. He wanted to ensure that she would appear to have not only motive but means and opportunity as well. In addition, he wanted to discredit her, underline her apparent guilt by making her appear an out-and-out liar."

"A tall order."

"Very. But then, he was a clever man, and, as I said, there was no hurry. Time was on his side. The very nature of his particular disease meant that there was no risk of it being spotted in a routine post mortem in its early stages.

"Anyway, I would think that his decision as to when to stage his 'murder' was made as far back as August, when Mrs Price received an invitation to speak at a Women's Institute meeting in Merrisham last Monday, and asked him if she could spend the night at her sister's. That gave him three clear months in which to work things out. It wouldn't surprise me if, during that time, he employed a private detective to follow Gemma, find out where and when she was meeting her lover. He wanted somehow to manipulate her into spending the night of the 'murder' in London, so that he would have the house to himself. He must have hoped that she would grab the opportunity for a night with Lee so that as soon as we became suspicious of her and checked her alibi we would discover her infidelity.''

"And therefore her motive."

"Exactly. In the event, Fate was on his side. Gemma was asked to consider a part in a new play and couldn't make up her mind whether to take it. Pettifer persuaded her into a trip to London on Monday night to discuss the matter with her agent. Meanwhile he had been elaborating his plan. I think, you know, that he probably enjoyed doing that, in a macabre kind of way. It wasn't enough for him that she should simply have appeared to commit the 'murder' before leaving for London. He wanted to enmesh her in a whole web of deceit so that everything she said or did would serve only to incriminate her further.''

"You make him sound really diabolical."

"He just wanted to hit back, I think, for what had happened to him. At life, at her . . . at her especially. The higher the pedestal, the more shattering the fall. Anyway, his plan was very neat, very simple, really. He would pretend illness, nothing so serious that it would keep her at home, but sufficient to give her a conscience about going out and make her fall in with his suggestion that she give him a ring around ten o'clock to check that he was all right. Then, when she rang him, he would make a panic-stricken request for her to return home at once. Knowing how uncharacteristic of him such behaviour was, she was sure to do as he asked . . .''

"He must have thought she cared about him to that degree, then."

"I suppose so, yes. But he wasn't taking any chances. He got her to promise to leave immediately, before he rang off. The next problem . . ."

"Just a minute. I'm sorry, perhaps I'm being a bit dim, but I don't quite see the point of all that. You say he had to get her down to Sturrenden late at night, presumably so that you — the police — would then find out that she was on the spot at the time the overdose was administered."

"That's right. He wanted us to think that she had slipped him just enough sodium amytal — that was the drug he used, by the way, we heard yesterday — in the cocoa she gave him before she left, for him to go off into a really sound sleep so that when she returned later to finish him off he would still be sufficiently drugged not to realise what was happening. I bet that if Mrs Price hadn't washed the mug we'd have found traces of sodium amytal in it."

"But how would you know she had been there later that night? I mean, if those two men on patrol hadn't noticed Lee's rather unusual sports car or if Gemma hadn't been spending the night with Lee and had come in a taxi . . . it was taking a chance, surely?"

"Perhaps Dr Pettifer had more faith in the police than you have, my love," Thanet said with a grin. "No, sooner or later it would have come out, via the hotel perhaps. Anyway, as I was saying, the next problem was to make sure not only that when she got here she couldn't get in, but that she wouldn't attempt to break in, either. And this he managed by leaving his car at the Centre, without her knowledge. It was supposed to have broken down, but it wouldn't surprise me in the least if he immobilised it on purpose. He knew enough about cars to be able to do it, to make sure the fault was one which could have come about accidentally, so that the mechanic wouldn't be suspicious. Then, before he took the overdose, he bolted and barred the front door so that she wouldn't be able to get in that way and banked on the fact that, when she went around to the back and saw his car wasn't there, she'd assume he'd gone out on a night call."

"Another risk."

"Yes, but it worked. You have to hand it to him. The risks were all calculated, based on his understanding of her character, and most of them paid off. She did react to much of what he planned exactly as he intended she should. And he made sure that there were other little touches of circumstantial evidence to incriminate her. At some time during those three months he must have set aside the drinking glass and the tablet container with her prints on them, made sure they were protected from dust so that the fingerprints would appear fresh . . ."

"So, what went wrong? Why didn't it work, in the end?"

"Chiefly, I think, because his understanding of her didn't go deep enough. He misread the depth of her feeling for him. He thought that because she had a lover, she didn't care about him, her husband. Being the sort of man he was, he wouldn't have been able to understand that her lovers were for her really no more than a diversion, a physical appetite perhaps, or a sop to her ego. Playthings, really, I suppose. For him a sexual relationship meant commitment and he couldn't have begun to understand that she could be committed to her husband while enjoying an affair with someone else."

"You really think she did feel deeply for him, then?"

"Yes, I do. Mind, I don't think even she was aware just how deeply until he was dead. I think that it was this realisation that hit her so hard, coming too late, as it did. Anyway, the result was that, whereas I suppose he expected her to deny, bluster, appear more and more guilty as each new bit of incriminating information came along, in fact she reacted in precisely the opposite manner. She insisted from the start that it couldn't have been suicide and, if it had been murder, seemed hell-bent on incriminating herself. She would have had to be the most inefficient murderer in the annals of crime to have made such a mess of her story. It was as full of holes as a colander, and the discrepancies were so pointless, so incomprehensible. No, I don't think either of them had any idea how much she cared for him."

"Sad, wasn't it — that he died not knowing, I mean." Joan was silent for a while, thinking; idly picking up handful after handful of sand and watching it trickle away through her fingers.

"So," she said at last, "how did you cotton on, in the end? It was to do with the mis-spelling of Andrew's name in the suicide note, you said?"

"Yes. Well, it wasn't just that. All week . . ."

"Just a minute," Joan said suddenly. "Sorry to interrupt, darling, but what about the other note, the one you found in Andrew's bedroom? Did you find out any more about it?"

"No. I'm still convinced that there was nothing between him and Gemma. But the trouble was that I couldn't be certain without either tackling Andrew himself or Gemma — and I didn't want to do that and risk embarrassing the boy if the whole thing was no more than a fantasy. I felt that to know we knew how he felt about Gemma would just have caused him unnecessary distress, and he had enough to cope with as it was."

"I agree. Poor boy. He must feel completely lost, now. What will happen to him, do you know?"

"It's been arranged that he'll live with his grandmother — well, adoptive grandmother, really. Mrs Blaidon." Thanet gave a reminiscent smile. "You'd have liked her. And she seemed fond of Andrew."

"I should think that's far and away the best arrangement in the circumstances. Anyway, do go on with what you were saying."

"Where was I? Oh, yes, explaining how I finally came to see what had been going on. Well, as I said, although it was the mis-spelling of Andrew's name in that first note which eventually put me on the right track, there was much more to it than that. All week the clues came along so neatly — Gemma's guilt seemed too obvious, the explanations too pat. And all along I felt uncomfortable, uneasy. I knew something was wrong, but I couldn't put my finger on it. I felt as though I was being nudged further and further along a road I didn't want to follow . . . as if someone was pulling the strings and there I was, dancing against my will. Like a puppet."

Joan grimaced. "A puppet for a corpse. What a macabre notion."

"A delightfully graphic way of describing it, darling. But yes, that was it, exactly. Though, as I say, I didn't realise it for some time. I just had this feeling of resentment which people get when they're being manipulated into something against their will."

"I know what you mean. Like me and Mrs Markham."

"Well, as a matter of fact, I think Mrs Markham had a lot to do with my understanding, in the end, what was happening."

"What do you mean?"

"Well, the night I finally worked it out, we'd had that discussion about driving her down here today, do you remember? Though I must admit," Thanet added, gazing around at the sunlight sparkling on the water, the near-deserted beach and Bridget and Ben rushing to and from the water's edge with buckets of water for the moat, "it wasn't such a bad idea after all. The point is, she'd been in my mind all week — Mrs Markham, I mean — the way she had you dancing attendance on her. To be honest, I think now, looking back, that one of the reasons why I became increasingly angry with you for allowing her to manipulate you like that was because subconsciously I was aware that precisely the same thing was happening to me, and I didn't like it one little bit. I think I was taking out my anger and frustration at my own situation on you. Anyway, to get back to how I came to work it out, if you remember I'd just learnt that afternoon that Pettifer had been sterile and as I said this discovery had turned my previous thinking about the case upside down. The final thing which made it all click was, believe it or not, a game I was playing with Ben."

"With Ben?"

"Yes. In the early hours of the morning, when you were snoring your head off."

"I wasn't!"

"All right, calm down, I was teasing. Anyway, I forgot to tell you, but Ben woke up in the night wanting to go to the lavatory. When I put him back to bed he said he wanted to play another game — little monkey, wasn't he, trying to wring the last ounce of concession out of being unwell. But he was still very hot and I thought he'd get off to sleep again more quickly if I agreed. We played 'Spot the Deliberate Mistake'.''

"Yes, he's very good at that, isn't he?"

"I know. Well, he was asleep before we'd finished but I decided I'd wait a few more minutes to make sure he'd gone off properly. I dared not move in case I disturbed him so I just sat there, staring down at this puzzle with all this stuff about the Pettifer case and Mrs Markham floating around in my mind — and suddenly, simultaneously it seemed, I thought, *Deliberate Mistake* and *My God, that's what's been happening to me* — meaning the manipulation, of course. And that was it. The whole thing just fell together. Suddenly I saw it all — the deliberate mis-spelling of the name, the reason why Pettifer had gone on pretending ignorance of his wife's infidelity, the way he'd planned his revenge — everything, that is, but the reason why he had chosen to die. For that, I had to wait until next morning. But even before I heard about his illness I was convinced I'd hit on the truth, however incredible it might seem.'' Thanet laughed. ''You should have seen Mike's face when he finally worked it out for himself. He thought I'd finally flipped.''

"You say 'worked it out for himself', but did he really?"

"Well, as I said, I did have to give him a gentle push from time to time, when he stopped. But he got there, in the end. That's why . . .''

"All right, I know. That's why you felt such a fool, etcetera, etcetera. But the fact is, darling, I doubt if he would have, without your help."

"But . . .''

"No, listen. You yourself gave the reason why. Even when he'd reached the correct conclusion, he couldn't believe that it was true. I think that it's because he can't yet think beyond the likely that he has never yet solved a major case before you. He's got some kind of internal barrier in his brain which prevents him from going down paths which subconsciously he can see are going to lead to unacceptable conclusions. Whereas you tend to let your mind run free . . . Why are you staring at me like that?''

A slow smile spread across Thanet's face. "You know, you could well be right."

"Well don't sound so surprised! I'm not a complete moron, you know. How condescending can you get!"

Thanet mimed contrition.

"Why are you making funny faces, Daddy?" It was Bridget, watching him with interest.

"Mummy made a joke," Thanet said, with a teasing glance at Joan.

"Come and see our castle." Bridget tugged at his hand.

Reluctantly Thanet rose, helped Joan up. Dutifully they admired the children's creation.

"Make me a sand-car now, Daddy," Ben said. "Big enough for me to sit in?"

"Me too, Daddy, me too," Bridget chimed in.

"Sounds a long job," said Thanet. "Mummy and I have been sitting down so long we want to stretch our legs. A little walk, first, then we'll make your cars."

Bridget and Ben raced away, wheeling and curving across the wide, empty expanse of sand. Thanet and Joan followed more sedately, holding hands.

"You know, I feel sorry for Mrs Pettifer," Joan said at last. "For you the case is over now, finished, but for her . . . well, I don't suppose it ever will be."

"That's one of the depressing things about serious crimes, the long-term effect they have on the innocent people connected with them."

"You'd call her innocent?"

Thanet shrugged. "Innocent or not, she's going to have to pay in her own way, I think."

"What do you mean?"

"Well, Mike and I couldn't agree on this. He thought she ought to have been told — about the baby, about what her husband tried to do to her."

"But why?"

"I think he thought that she was getting off too lightly, that she ought to be brought to a realisation of her responsibility in the matter."

"But you disagreed."

"Yes. For one thing, it's outside my brief. I see myself as an instrument of justice, not a dispenser of it. And then, as I said, I think she will pay in the end. For one thing I think she was genuinely shaken to find out how much she cared for her husband and she's going to have to come to terms with her regrets that her attitude to him wasn't different while he was still alive, as well as the sense of loss I think she's genuinely feeling. And, although at the moment she's relieved to find that there was a genuine reason for his suicide and feels absolved of any personal guilt, sooner or later she's going to see it rather differently. She's going to realise that what must really have tipped the balance for him was that, knowing how she felt about sickness, he simply couldn't face the prospect of eventually becoming an object of repulsion to her. And I'd guess that at that point she's bound to begin to feel a measure of guilt. Perhaps she'll go on feeling it for the rest of her life. I don't know. Maybe I'm wrong. Maybe I'm overestimating the strength of her feeling for him, her degree of sensitivity, the power of her conscience. But I don't think so."

Bridget and Ben were racing back towards them.

"Can we go back now, Daddy? Can we make the cars?"

"Race you!" he challenged.

They all set off at a run, Thanet and Joan deliberately holding back, allowing the children a sense of victory.

Thanet picked up a spade. "I can't do both at once, though, can I? Perhaps . . .?" He raised his eyebrows at Joan, who had flopped down upon the sand, puffing.

She pulled a face. "And I thought I was going to have a lazy day."

But he could see that she didn't really mind.

"Come on then," she said, getting to her feet. "Daddy's biggest, so he can help Ben, who's smallest. And you and I will work together, Sprig."

Enough of the dead, thought Thanet. Life is for the living.

Sand went scudding in all directions as they set to work with a will.

DEAD BY MORNING

Dorothy Simpson

On a snowy, February morning, Leo Martindale is found dead in a ditch outside the gates of his ancestral home – apparently a hit and run victim.

After an absence – and a silence – of twenty-five years, he had just returned to Kent to claim his vast inheritance. Is his death an accident? Or is it, as Inspector Thanet of Sturrenden CID begins to suspect, murder?

As his investigation proceeds, Thanet finds a profusion of suspects – all glad to see the last of Leo Martindale, and more importantly, all with opportunity to kill him. In a fog of conflicting suspicions, Inspector Thanet struggles to solve one of his toughest cases . . .

'Well-rounded characters, a satisfying mind-teaser, the best of British'
The Observer

'A thoroughly traditional detective story'
Today

CRIME

SUSPICIOUS DEATH

Dorothy Simpson

ACCIDENT, SUICIDE ... OR MURDER?

The woman in the blue sequined cocktail dress was dragged from her watery grave beneath a bridge. A highly suspicious death – and Inspector Thanet is called in to investigate.

The more he learns about the late Marcia Salden, mistress of Telford Green Manor, the less likely a candidate she seemed for suicide. A successful self-made woman with a thriving business, she had everything she wanted, including the mansion she had coveted since childhood. She also had a knack for stirring up trouble ...

As Inspector Thanet attempts to unravel the complex sequence of events surrounding her death, he discovers that if Mrs Salden hadn't managed to get herself murdered, it wasn't for want of trying ...

'As good a Dorothy Simpson as we have seen for some time'
TLS

'Tantalising ...'
She

CRIME

LAST SEEN ALIVE

Dorothy Simpson

It was all of twenty years since Alicia Parnell last saw Sturrenden. While she was still a schoolgirl a jilted boyfriend had killed himself, and her parents had tactfully moved away from that corner of Kent. Nevertheless the old crowd were delighted to welcome her when she turned up out of the blue one day. Just why she'd come back, though, no one could guess.

But within hours Alicia was found strangled in her room at the Black Swan. And for Inspector Thanet – who had known all of them since his youth – there were special problems. Could he have lived most of his life alongside someone who harboured a grudge so strong that only Alicia's death could settle the matter? Or would his investigations turn up fresh scandals, a murky undercurrent to life in that placid old market town of which even he had been blissfully – and tragically – ignorant?

'A seamless crime story that offers a startling and believable surprise ending'
Publishers Weekly

'Well organised . . . a cunningly contrived plot'
TLS

CRIME

DOOMED TO DIE

Dorothy Simpson

Perdita Master always sought solitude. Now her wish has
been granted – permanently and brutally. Her body is
found in the home of a prominent local barrister – a
chilling confirmation of her childhood fear that she was
doomed to die young.

But why? As Inspector Thanet and Sergeant Lineham
begin their investigations, it becomes apparent that the
clue to the murder lies in the beautiful artist's past. Had
she always been deeply unhappy, even before her stormy
marriage to the difficult, jealous Giles? And what was the
root of the turbulent emotions that she could only express
through her art? Whatever the reason behind Perdita's
untimely death, Inspector Thanet soon realizes that he
will have to read the desperate mind of the victim, as well
as that of the murderer, to find the answer ...

'The deception is brought off with conjurer's bravura'
Matthew Coady, *Guardian*

'A first-class detective story with well-rounded characters
and emotional problems which hold your interest'
Annabel

'A subtle tale, dealing with people's dilemmas and
emotions. Simpson fans will be well-satisfied'
Yorkshire Post

CRIME

Other bestselling Warner titles available by mail:

☐	The Night She Died	Dorothy Simpson	£3.99
☐	Six Feet Under	Dorothy Simpson	£5.99
☐	Puppet For a Corpse	Dorothy Simpson	£4.99
☐	Last Seen Alive	Dorothy Simpson	£5.99
☐	Suspicious Death	Dorothy Simpson	£5.99
☐	Dead by Morning	Dorothy Simpson	£5.99
☐	Doomed to Die	Dorothy Simpson	£5.99
☐	Wake the Dead	Dorothy Simpson	£5.99
☐	No Laughing Matter	Dorothy Simpson	£5.99
☐	Second Inspector Thanet Omnibus	Dorothy Simpson	£9.99
☐	Third Inspector Thanet Omnibus	Dorothy Simpson	£9.99

The prices shown above are correct at time of going to press. However, the publishers reserve the right to increase prices on covers from those previously advertised without prior notice.

WARNER BOOKS

WARNER BOOKS
P.O. Box 121, Kettering, Northants NN14 4ZQ
Tel: 01832 737525, Fax: 01832 733076
Email: aspenhouse@FSBDial.co.uk

POST AND PACKING:
Payments can be made as follows: cheque, postal order (payable to Warner Books) or by credit cards. Do not send cash or currency.

All U.K. Orders　　　**FREE OF CHARGE**
E.E.C. & Overseas　　25% of order value

Name (Block Letters) _____

Address_____

_____

Post/zip code:_____

☐ Please keep me in touch with future Warner publications

☐ I enclose my remittance £_____

☐ I wish to pay by Visa/Access/Mastercard/Eurocard

Card Expiry Date

_____